Rocket Robinson

and the Secret of the Saint

for my family

Please direct all inquiries to:

BoilerRoom Studios
2149 W. Giddings Ave.
Chicago, IL 60625

www.rocketrobinson.com

ISBN: 978-0-9893655-2-9

Library of Congress Control Number: 2016946135

Printed in the United States of America

Rocket Robinson
and the Secret of the Saint

Sean O'Neill

BOILERROOM
STUDIOS

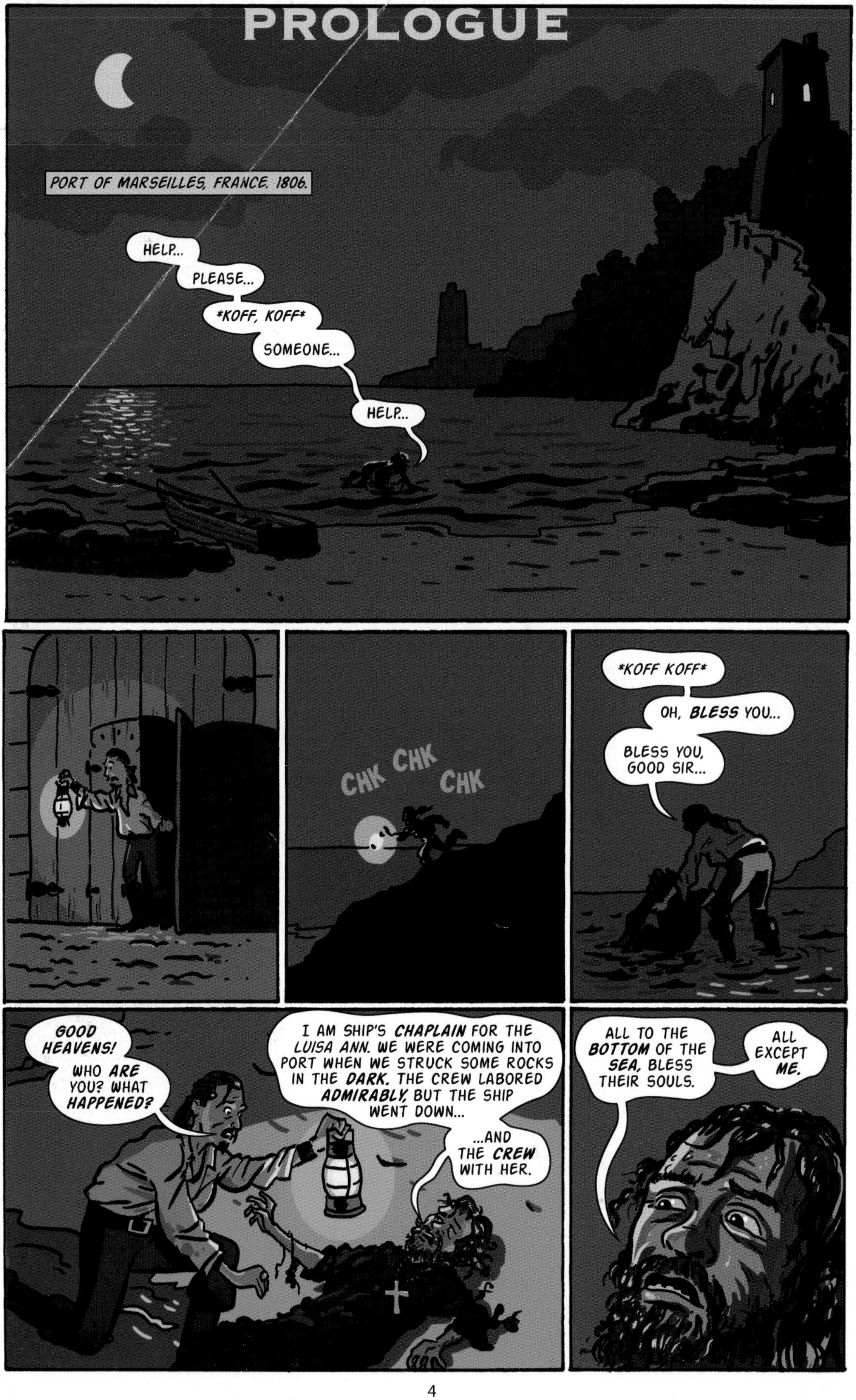
PROLOGUE
PORT OF MARSEILLES, FRANCE. 1806.
HELP...
PLEASE...
KOFF, KOFF
SOMEONE...
HELP...
CHK CHK CHK
KOFF KOFF
OH, BLESS YOU...
BLESS YOU, GOOD SIR...
GOOD HEAVENS!
WHO ARE YOU? WHAT HAPPENED?
I AM SHIP'S CHAPLAIN FOR THE LUISA ANN. WE WERE COMING INTO PORT WHEN WE STRUCK SOME ROCKS IN THE DARK. THE CREW LABORED ADMIRABLY, BUT THE SHIP WENT DOWN...
...AND THE CREW WITH HER.
ALL TO THE BOTTOM OF THE SEA, BLESS THEIR SOULS.
ALL EXCEPT ME.

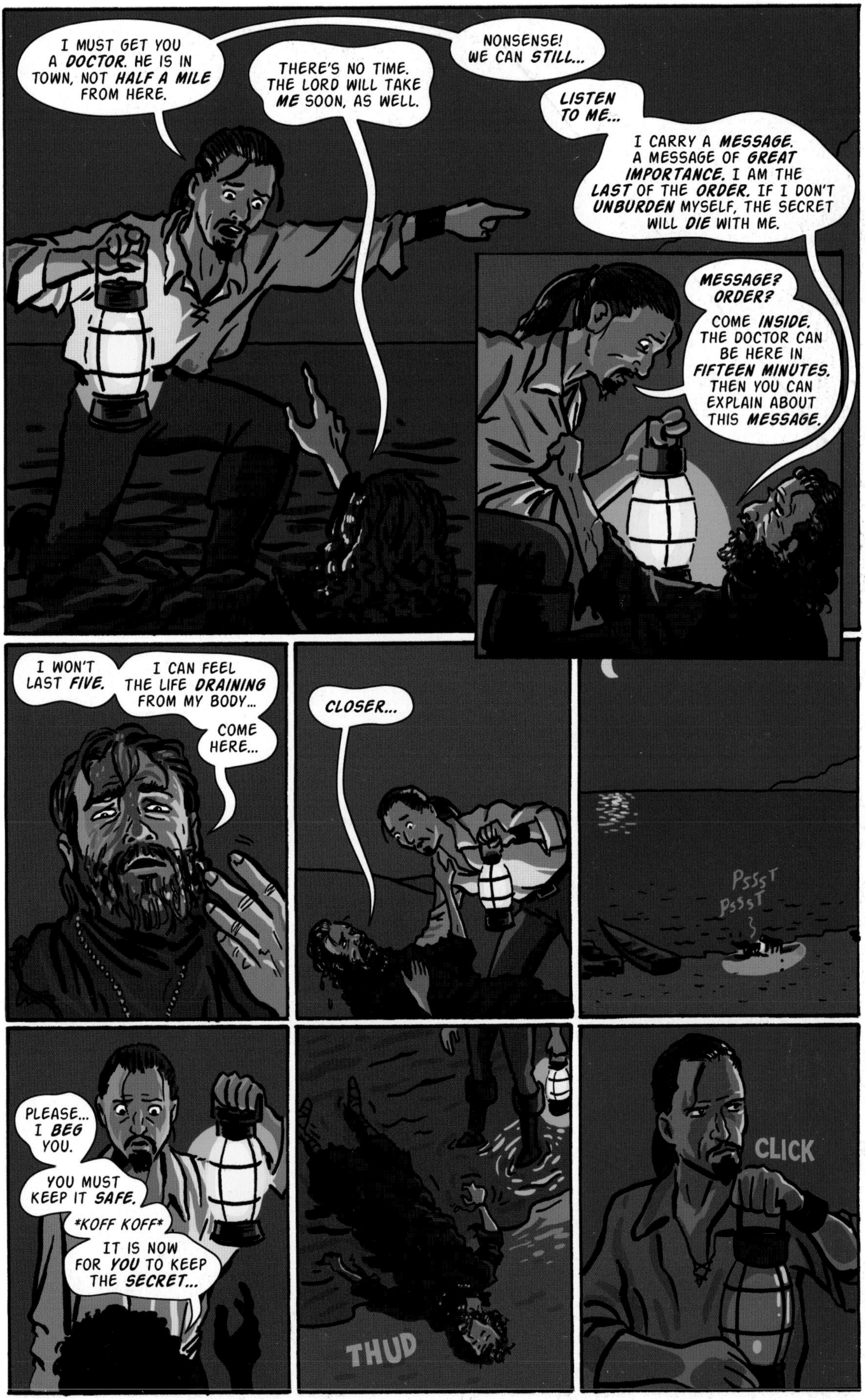
I MUST GET YOU A DOCTOR. HE IS IN TOWN, NOT HALF A MILE FROM HERE.
THERE'S NO TIME. THE LORD WILL TAKE ME SOON, AS WELL.
NONSENSE! WE CAN STILL...
LISTEN TO ME...
I CARRY A MESSAGE. A MESSAGE OF GREAT IMPORTANCE. I AM THE LAST OF THE ORDER. IF I DON'T UNBURDEN MYSELF, THE SECRET WILL DIE WITH ME.
MESSAGE? ORDER?
COME INSIDE. THE DOCTOR CAN BE HERE IN FIFTEEN MINUTES. THEN YOU CAN EXPLAIN ABOUT THIS MESSAGE.
I WON'T LAST FIVE.
I CAN FEEL THE LIFE DRAINING FROM MY BODY...
COME HERE...
CLOSER...
PSSST
PSSST
PLEASE... I BEG YOU.
YOU MUST KEEP IT SAFE.
KOFF KOFF
IT IS NOW FOR YOU TO KEEP THE SECRET...
THUD
CLICK

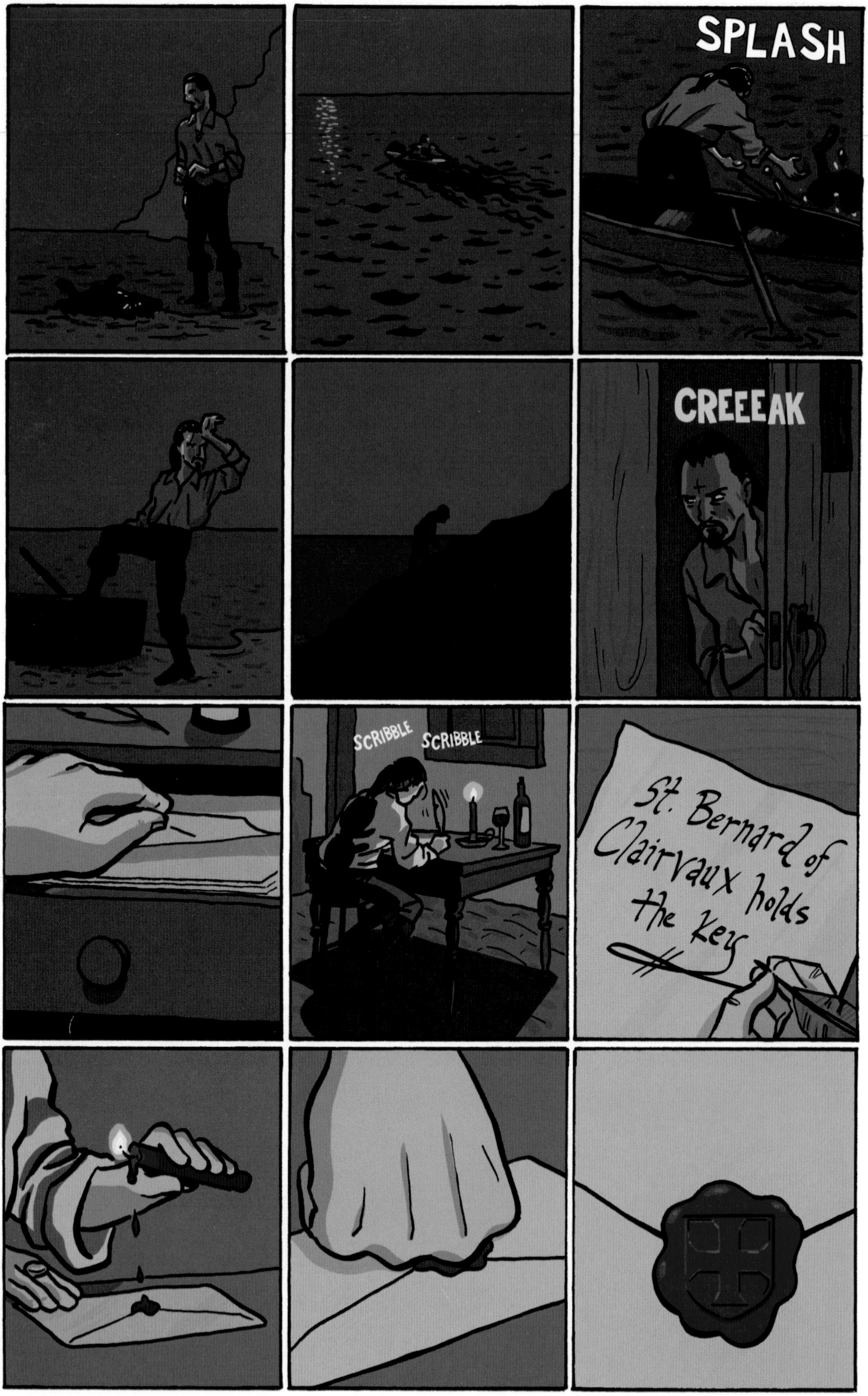
SPLASH
CREEEAK
SCRIBBLE
SCRIBBLE
St. Bernard of Clairvaux holds the key

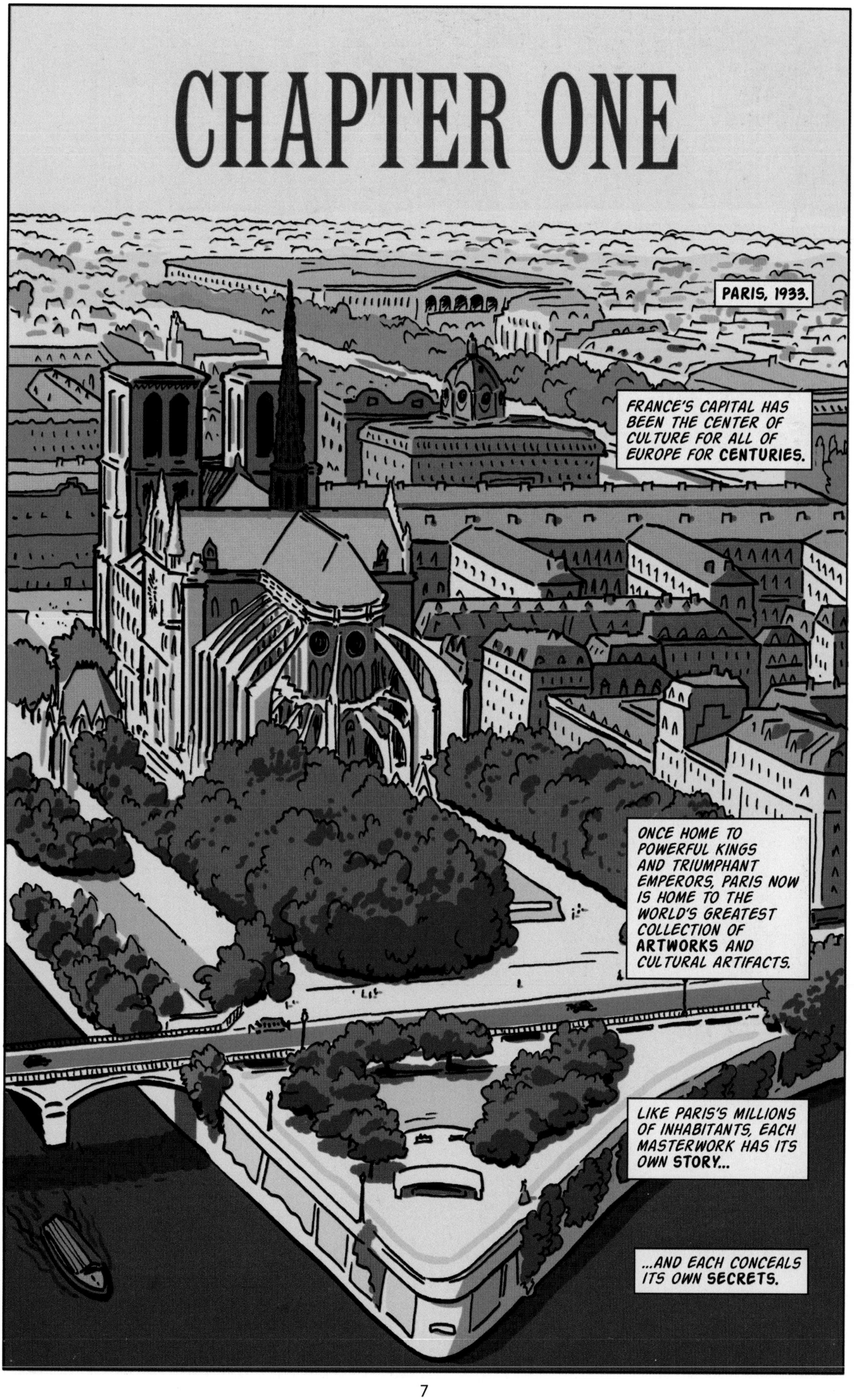
CHAPTER ONE
PARIS, 1933.
FRANCE'S CAPITAL HAS BEEN THE CENTER OF CULTURE FOR ALL OF EUROPE FOR **CENTURIES.**
ONCE HOME TO POWERFUL KINGS AND TRIUMPHANT EMPERORS, PARIS NOW IS HOME TO THE WORLD'S GREATEST COLLECTION OF **ARTWORKS** AND CULTURAL ARTIFACTS.
LIKE PARIS'S MILLIONS OF INHABITANTS, EACH MASTERWORK HAS ITS OWN **STORY...**
...AND EACH CONCEALS ITS OWN **SECRETS.**

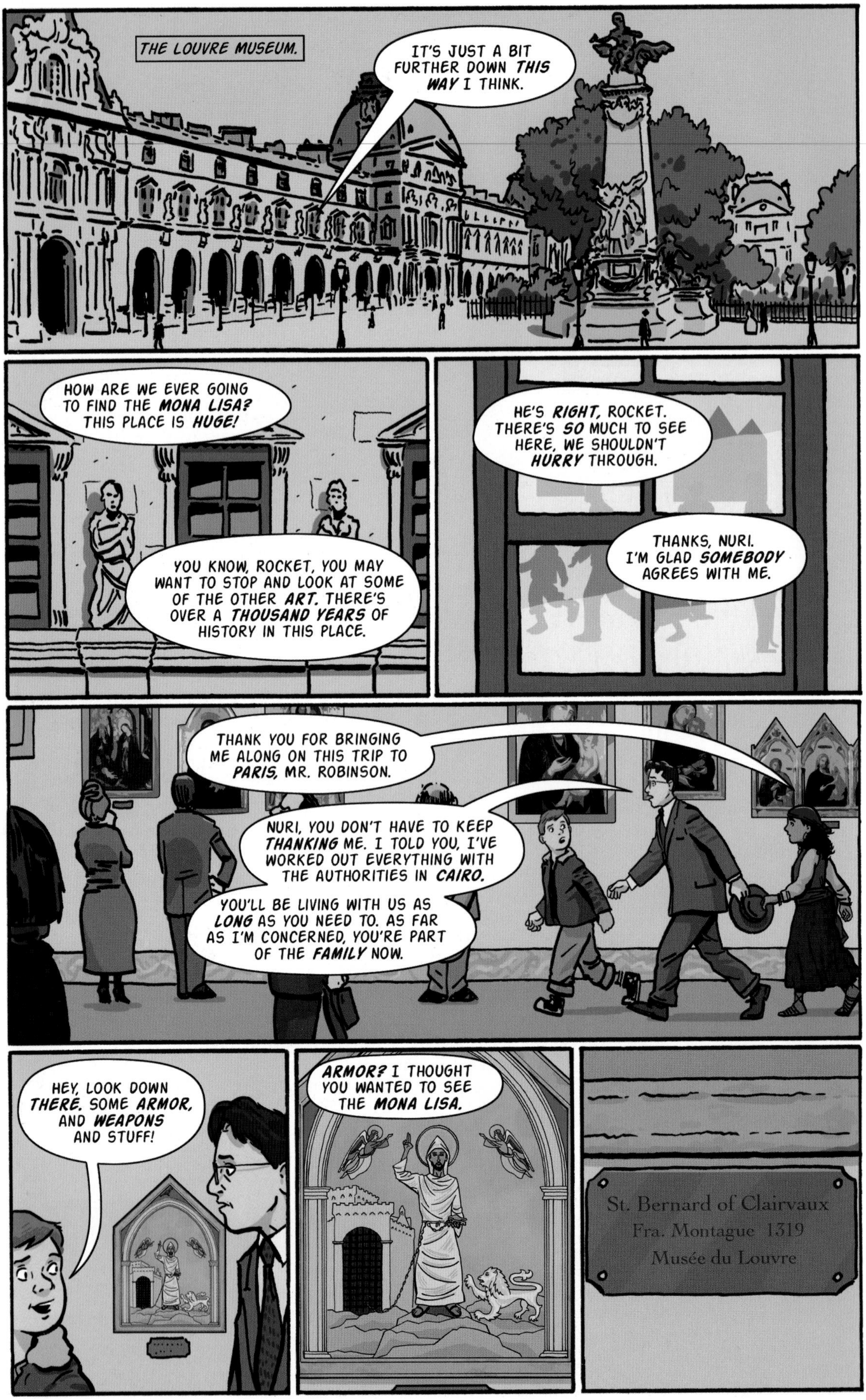
THE LOUVRE MUSEUM.
IT'S JUST A BIT FURTHER DOWN THIS WAY I THINK.
HOW ARE WE EVER GOING TO FIND THE MONA LISA? THIS PLACE IS HUGE!
YOU KNOW, ROCKET, YOU MAY WANT TO STOP AND LOOK AT SOME OF THE OTHER ART. THERE'S OVER A THOUSAND YEARS OF HISTORY IN THIS PLACE.
HE'S RIGHT, ROCKET. THERE'S SO MUCH TO SEE HERE, WE SHOULDN'T HURRY THROUGH.
THANKS, NURI. I'M GLAD SOMEBODY AGREES WITH ME.
THANK YOU FOR BRINGING ME ALONG ON THIS TRIP TO PARIS, MR. ROBINSON.
NURI, YOU DON'T HAVE TO KEEP THANKING ME. I TOLD YOU, I'VE WORKED OUT EVERYTHING WITH THE AUTHORITIES IN CAIRO.
YOU'LL BE LIVING WITH US AS LONG AS YOU NEED TO. AS FAR AS I'M CONCERNED, YOU'RE PART OF THE FAMILY NOW.
HEY, LOOK DOWN THERE. SOME ARMOR, AND WEAPONS AND STUFF!
ARMOR? I THOUGHT YOU WANTED TO SEE THE MONA LISA.
St. Bernard of Clairvaux
Fra. Montague 1319
Musée du Louvre

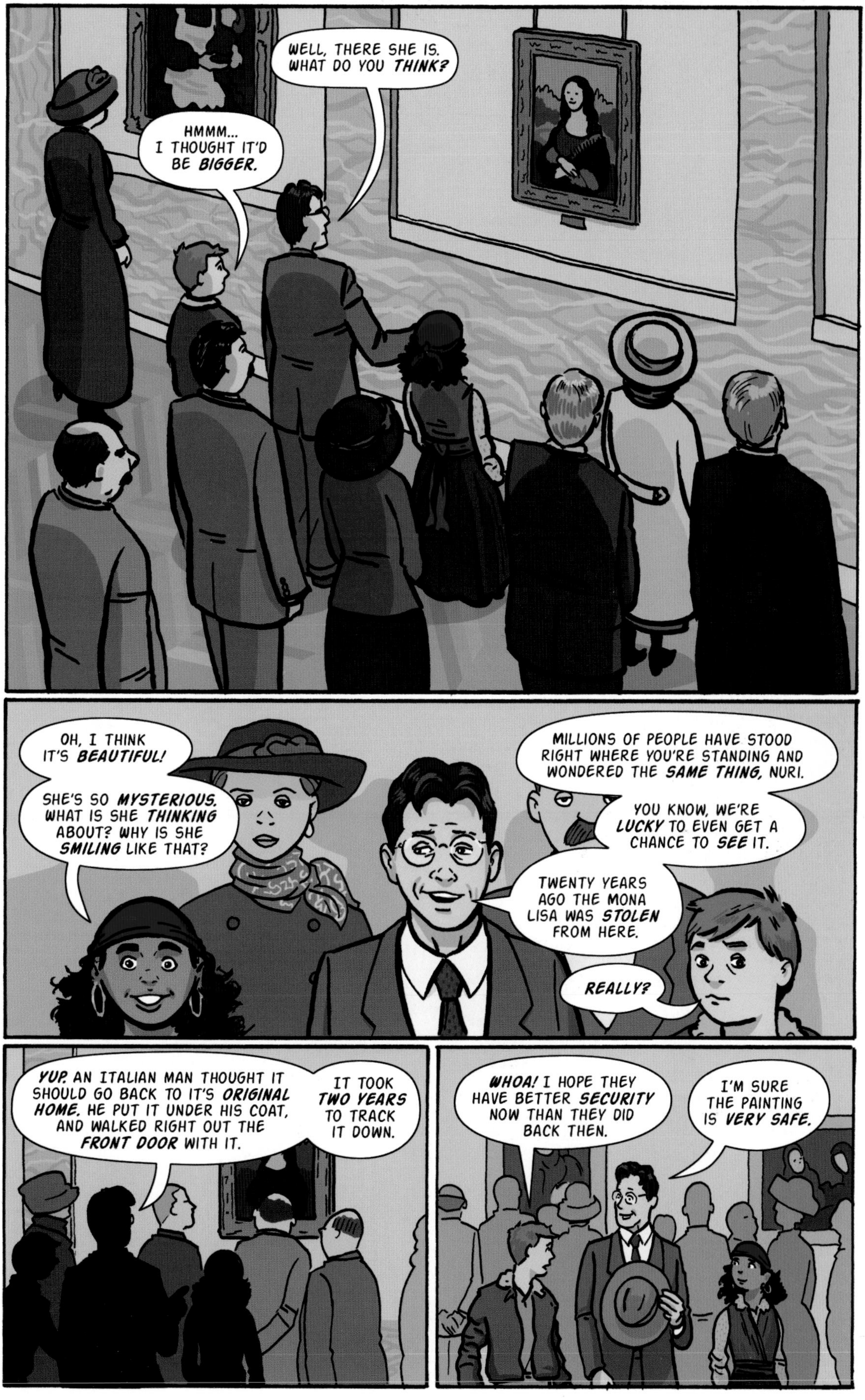
WELL, THERE SHE IS. WHAT DO YOU THINK?
HMMM... I THOUGHT IT'D BE BIGGER.
OH, I THINK IT'S BEAUTIFUL!
SHE'S SO MYSTERIOUS. WHAT IS SHE THINKING ABOUT? WHY IS SHE SMILING LIKE THAT?
MILLIONS OF PEOPLE HAVE STOOD RIGHT WHERE YOU'RE STANDING AND WONDERED THE SAME THING, NURI.
YOU KNOW, WE'RE LUCKY TO EVEN GET A CHANCE TO SEE IT.
TWENTY YEARS AGO THE MONA LISA WAS STOLEN FROM HERE.
REALLY?
YUP. AN ITALIAN MAN THOUGHT IT SHOULD GO BACK TO IT'S ORIGINAL HOME. HE PUT IT UNDER HIS COAT, AND WALKED RIGHT OUT THE FRONT DOOR WITH IT.
IT TOOK TWO YEARS TO TRACK IT DOWN.
WHOA! I HOPE THEY HAVE BETTER SECURITY NOW THAN THEY DID BACK THEN.
I'M SURE THE PAINTING IS VERY SAFE.

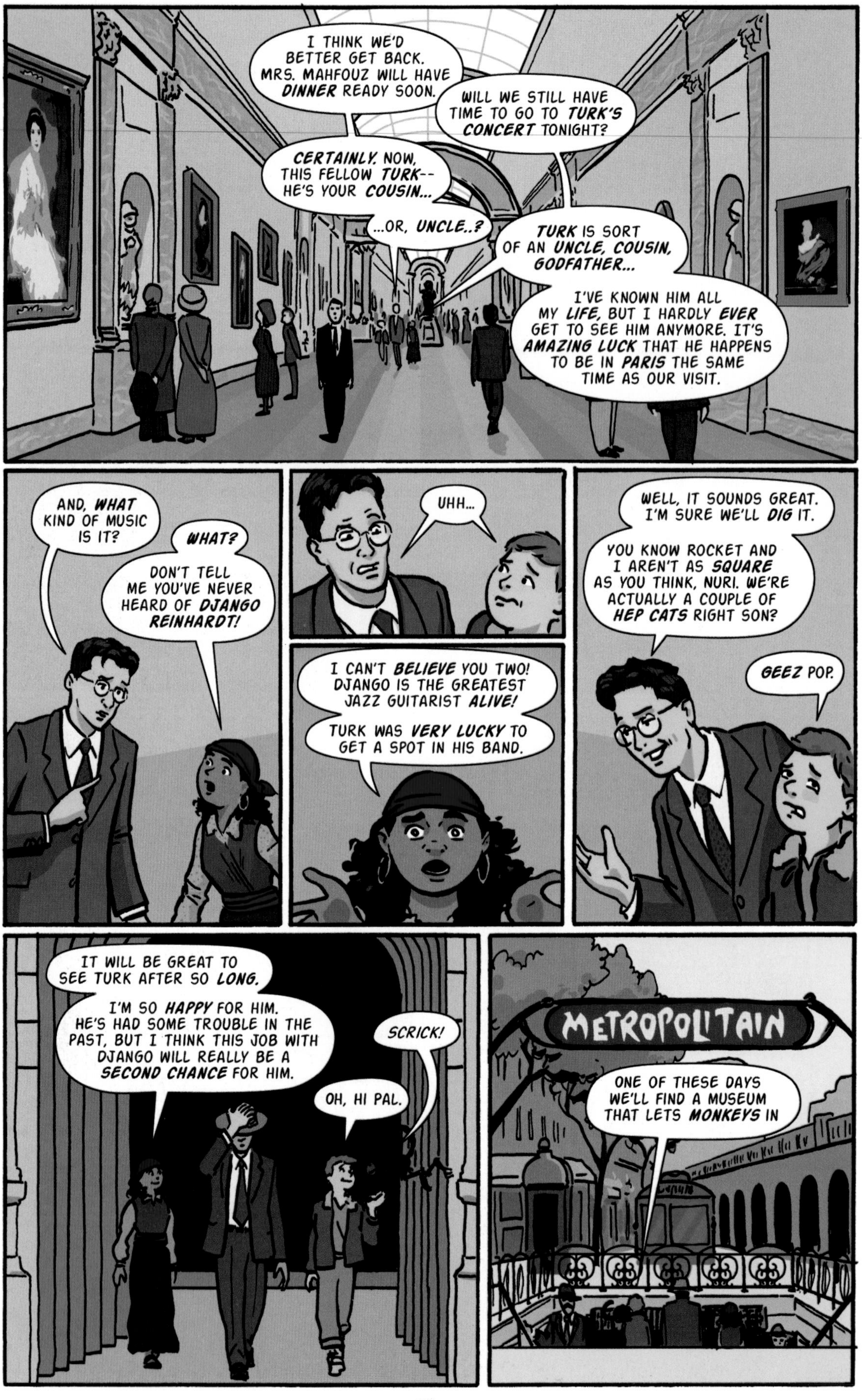
I THINK WE'D BETTER GET BACK. MRS. MAHFOUZ WILL HAVE DINNER READY SOON.
WILL WE STILL HAVE TIME TO GO TO TURK'S CONCERT TONIGHT?
CERTAINLY. NOW, THIS FELLOW TURK-- HE'S YOUR COUSIN...
...OR, UNCLE..?
TURK IS SORT OF AN UNCLE, COUSIN, GODFATHER...
I'VE KNOWN HIM ALL MY LIFE, BUT I HARDLY EVER GET TO SEE HIM ANYMORE. IT'S AMAZING LUCK THAT HE HAPPENS TO BE IN PARIS THE SAME TIME AS OUR VISIT.
AND, WHAT KIND OF MUSIC IS IT?
WHAT?
DON'T TELL ME YOU'VE NEVER HEARD OF DJANGO REINHARDT!
UHH...
I CAN'T BELIEVE YOU TWO! DJANGO IS THE GREATEST JAZZ GUITARIST ALIVE!
TURK WAS VERY LUCKY TO GET A SPOT IN HIS BAND.
WELL, IT SOUNDS GREAT. I'M SURE WE'LL DIG IT.
YOU KNOW ROCKET AND I AREN'T AS SQUARE AS YOU THINK, NURI. WE'RE ACTUALLY A COUPLE OF HEP CATS RIGHT SON?
GEEZ POP.
IT WILL BE GREAT TO SEE TURK AFTER SO LONG.
I'M SO HAPPY FOR HIM. HE'S HAD SOME TROUBLE IN THE PAST, BUT I THINK THIS JOB WITH DJANGO WILL REALLY BE A SECOND CHANCE FOR HIM.
SCRICK!
OH, HI PAL.
METROPOLITAIN
ONE OF THESE DAYS WE'LL FIND A MUSEUM THAT LETS MONKEYS IN

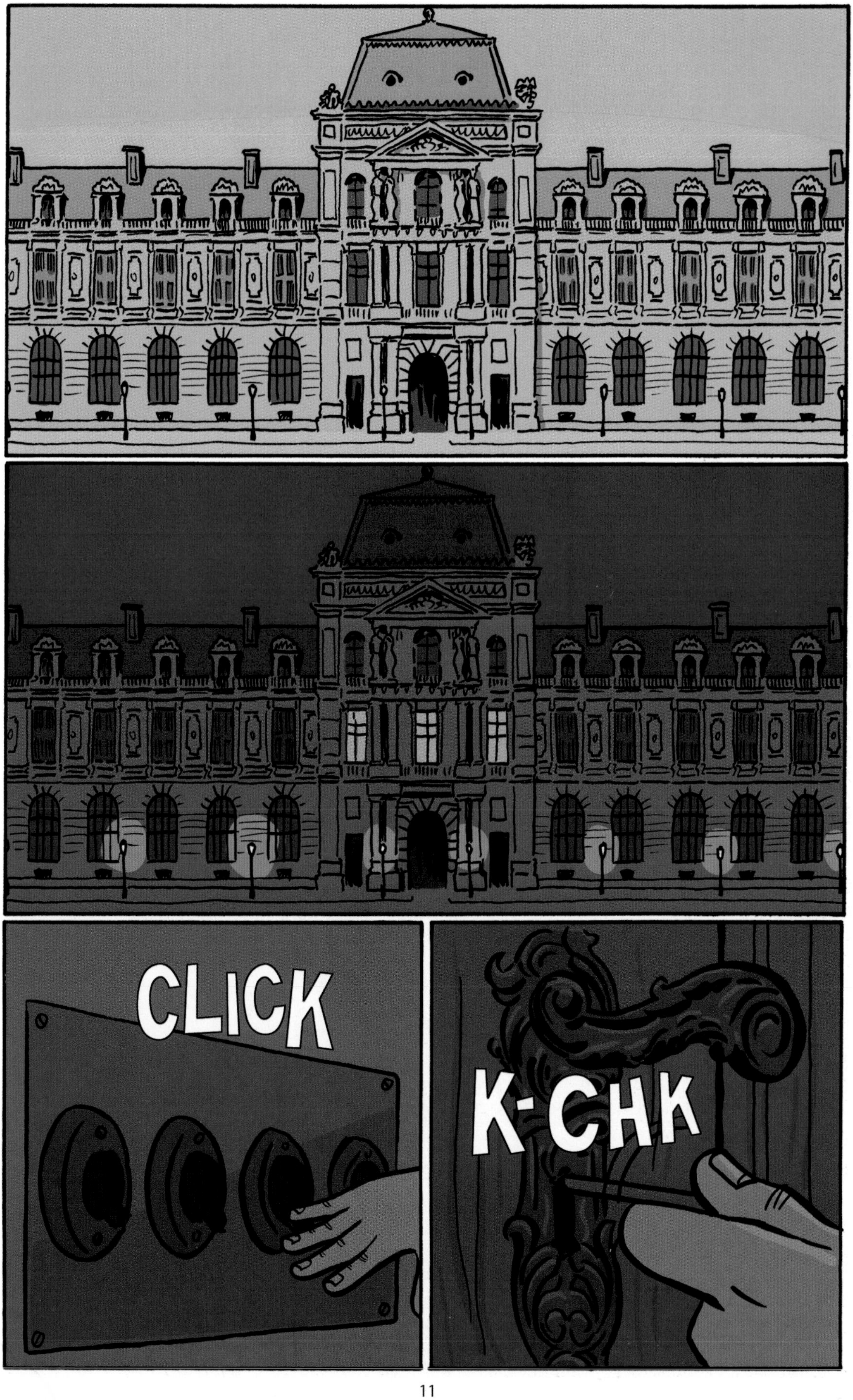
CLICK
K-CHK

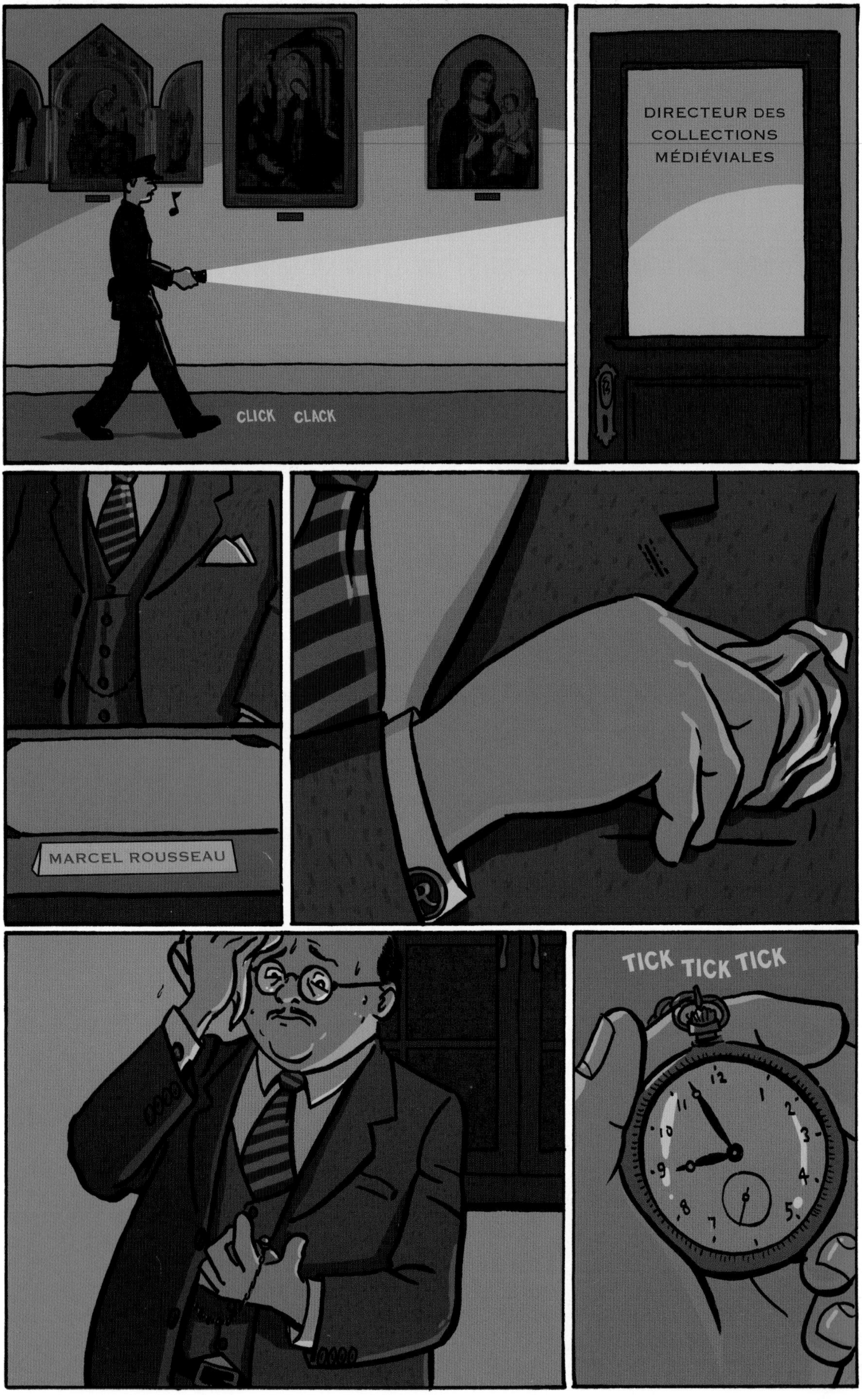
CLICK CLACK
DIRECTEUR DES
COLLECTIONS
MÉDIÉVIALES
MARCEL ROUSSEAU
TICK TICK TICK

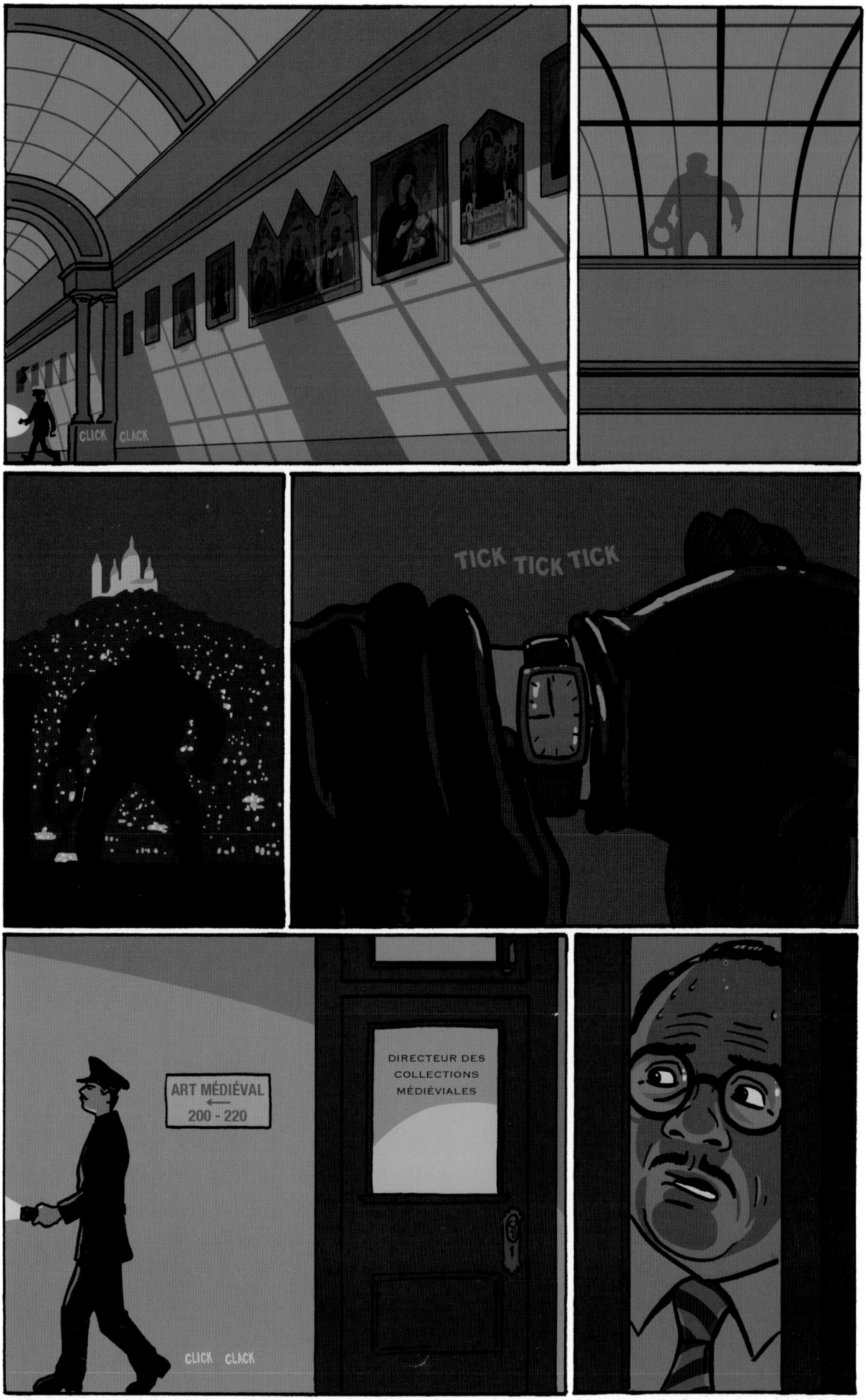
CLICK
CLACK
TICK
TICK TICK
ART MÉDIÉVAL
200 - 220
DIRECTEUR DES
COLLECTIONS
MÉDIÉVIALES
CLICK
CLACK

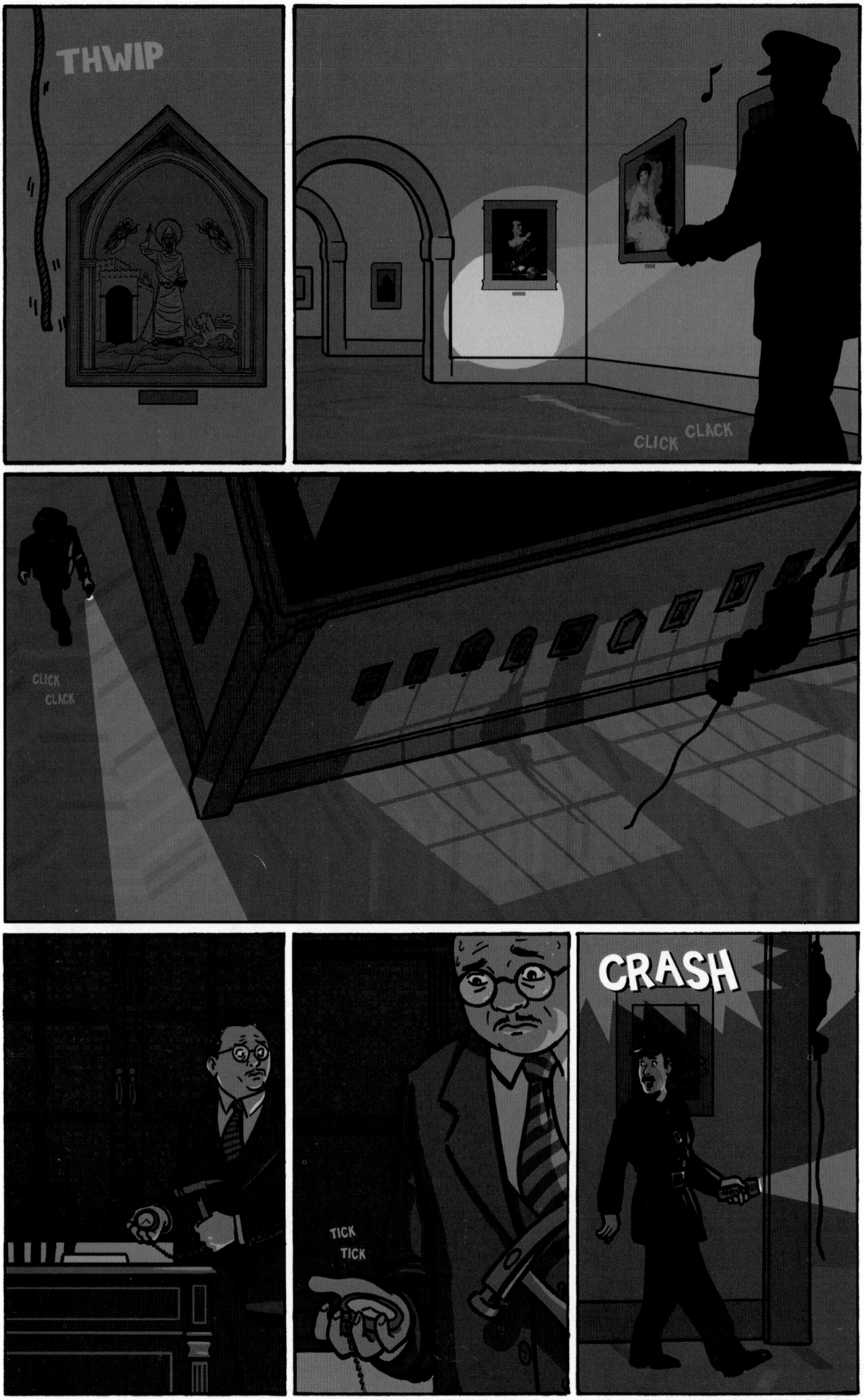
THWIP
CLICK
CLACK
CLICK
CLACK
TICK
TICK
CRASH

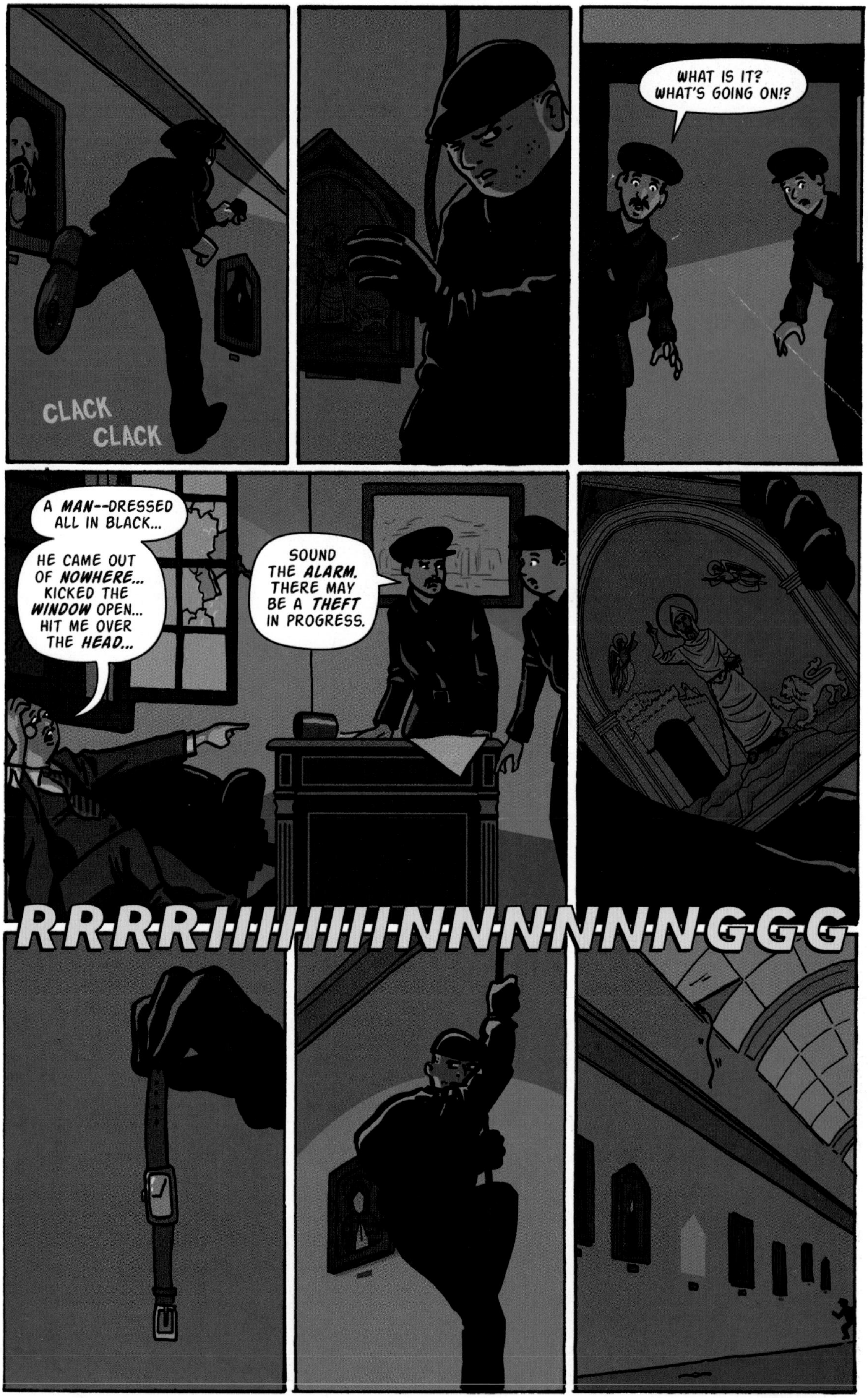
CLACK
CLACK
WHAT IS IT? WHAT'S GOING ON!?
A MAN--DRESSED ALL IN BLACK...
HE CAME OUT OF NOWHERE... KICKED THE WINDOW OPEN... HIT ME OVER THE HEAD...
SOUND THE ALARM. THERE MAY BE A THEFT IN PROGRESS.
RRRRIIIIIIIIINNNNNNNGGG

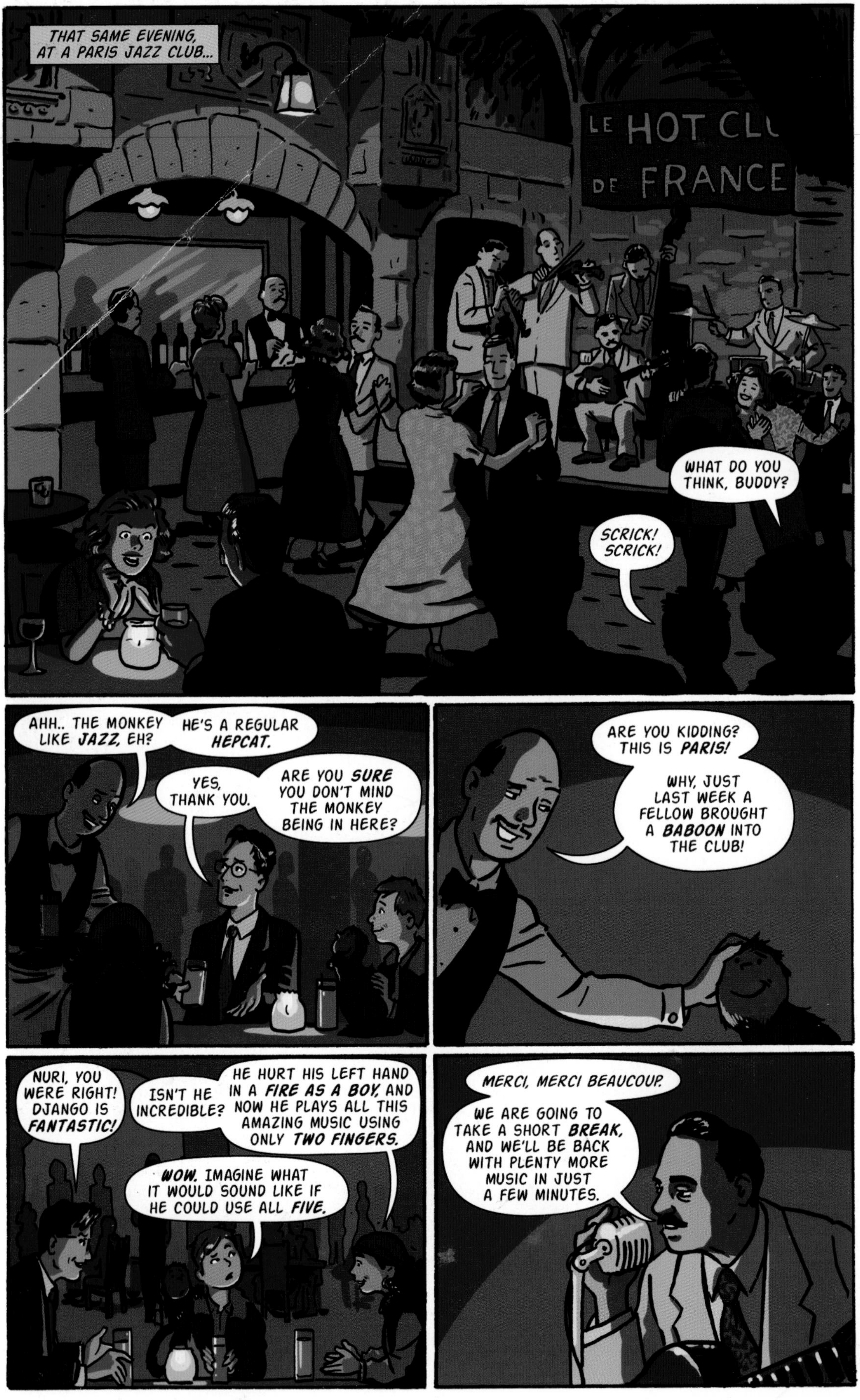
THAT SAME EVENING, AT A PARIS JAZZ CLUB...
LE HOT CLU
DE FRANCE
WHAT DO YOU THINK, BUDDY?
SCRICK! SCRICK!
AHH.. THE MONKEY LIKE JAZZ, EH?
HE'S A REGULAR HEPCAT.
YES, THANK YOU.
ARE YOU SURE YOU DON'T MIND THE MONKEY BEING IN HERE?
ARE YOU KIDDING? THIS IS PARIS!
WHY, JUST LAST WEEK A FELLOW BROUGHT A BABOON INTO THE CLUB!
NURI, YOU WERE RIGHT! DJANGO IS FANTASTIC!
ISN'T HE INCREDIBLE?
HE HURT HIS LEFT HAND IN A FIRE AS A BOY, AND NOW HE PLAYS ALL THIS AMAZING MUSIC USING ONLY TWO FINGERS.
WOW. IMAGINE WHAT IT WOULD SOUND LIKE IF HE COULD USE ALL FIVE.
MERCI, MERCI BEAUCOUP.
WE ARE GOING TO TAKE A SHORT BREAK, AND WE'LL BE BACK WITH PLENTY MORE MUSIC IN JUST A FEW MINUTES.

UNCLE TURK!!

AH.. MON CHERI, NURI!

LOOK AT HOW *BIG* YOU'VE GOTTEN! LAST TIME I SAW YOU, YOU WERE JUST A *BABY!*

NOT REALLY A *BABY!* I WAS *NINE* YEARS OLD!

HMM.. I GUESS WHEN YOU GET AS *OLD* AS ME, TIME SEEMS TO PASS MORE *QUICKLY.*

IT IS *SO* GOOD TO SEE YOU. WHAT BRINGS YOU TO PARIS?

I'M HERE WITH MY FRIEND, *ROCKET.* WE MET IN CAIRO, AND HE AND HIS FATHER HAVE GIVEN ME A PLACE TO LIVE FOR A WHILE...

...FOR AS LONG AS SHE *LIKES.*

HI TURK. *RONALD ROBINSON.* I'M ROCKET'S FATHER.

AND WHO IS *THIS* LITTLE FELLOW?

THIS IS *SCREECH.*

ROCKET AND SCREECH, EH? SOUNDS LIKE THE NAME OF A NEW *JAZZ COMBO.*

TOO BAD I'M NOT A *MUSICIAN.*

I SURE DID LIKE THE *MUSIC,* THOUGH. YOU GUYS WERE *GREAT.*

AH... YES. DJANGO IS A *GENIUS.*

A *BRILLIANT* MUSICIAN AND A VERY GENEROUS *MAN.*

I AM *VERY GRATEFUL* TO HIM FOR GIVING ME A *SECOND CHANCE.*

SECOND CHANCE..?

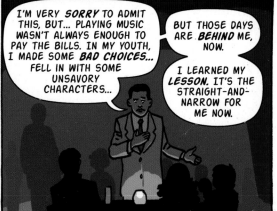

I'M VERY *SORRY* TO ADMIT THIS, BUT... PLAYING MUSIC WASN'T ALWAYS ENOUGH TO PAY THE BILLS. IN MY YOUTH, I MADE SOME *BAD CHOICES...* FELL IN WITH SOME UNSAVORY CHARACTERS...

BUT THOSE DAYS ARE *BEHIND* ME, NOW.

I LEARNED MY *LESSON.* IT'S THE STRAIGHT-AND-NARROW FOR ME NOW.

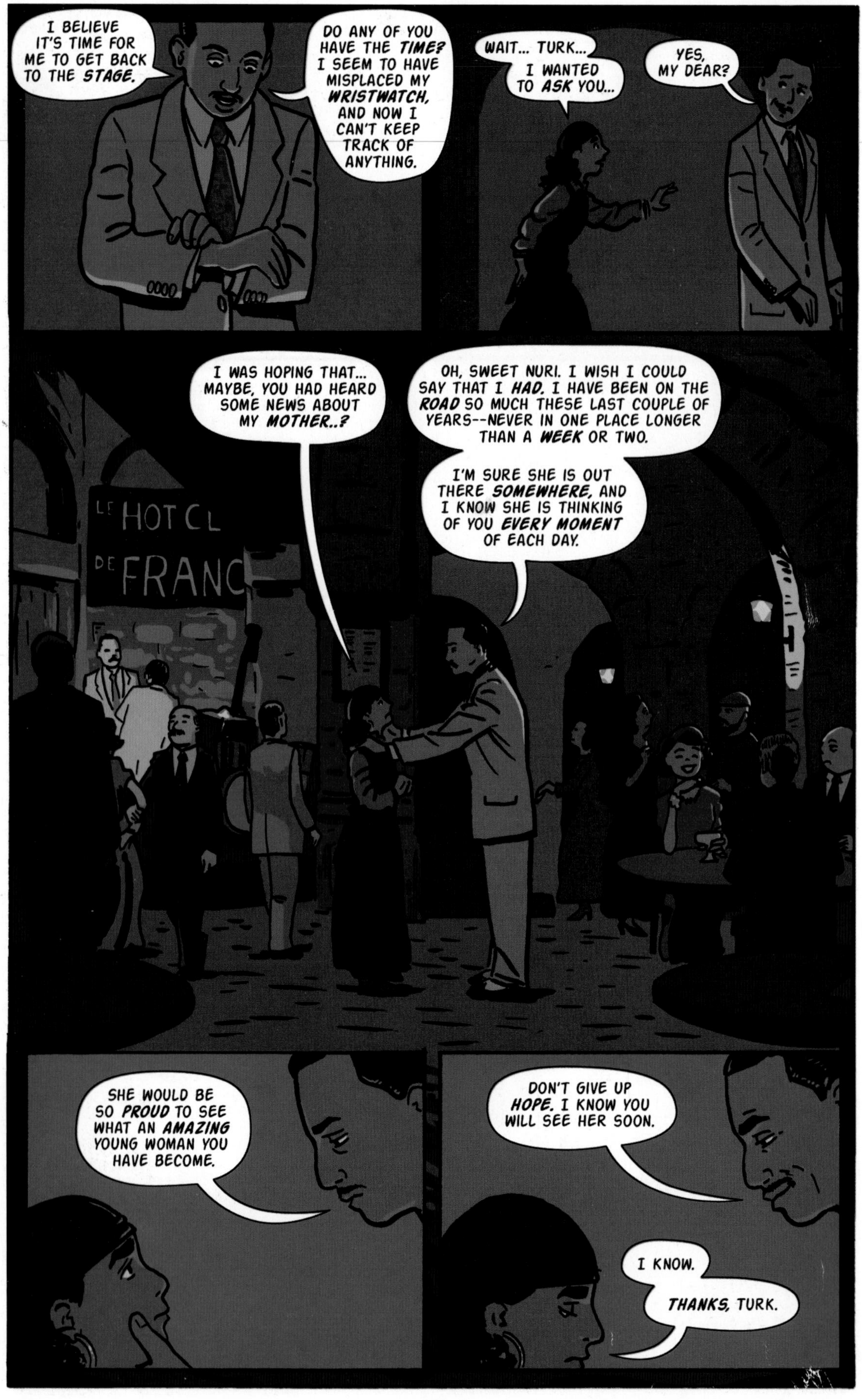
I BELIEVE IT'S TIME FOR ME TO GET BACK TO THE *STAGE.*
DO ANY OF YOU HAVE THE *TIME?* I SEEM TO HAVE MISPLACED MY *WRISTWATCH,* AND NOW I CAN'T KEEP TRACK OF ANYTHING.
WAIT... TURK...
I WANTED TO *ASK* YOU...
YES, MY DEAR?
I WAS HOPING THAT... MAYBE, YOU HAD HEARD SOME NEWS ABOUT MY *MOTHER..?*
OH, SWEET NURI. I WISH I COULD SAY THAT I *HAD.* I HAVE BEEN ON THE *ROAD* SO MUCH THESE LAST COUPLE OF YEARS--NEVER IN ONE PLACE LONGER THAN A *WEEK* OR TWO.
I'M SURE SHE IS OUT THERE *SOMEWHERE,* AND I KNOW SHE IS THINKING OF YOU *EVERY MOMENT* OF EACH DAY.
SHE WOULD BE SO *PROUD* TO SEE WHAT AN *AMAZING* YOUNG WOMAN YOU HAVE BECOME.
DON'T GIVE UP *HOPE.* I KNOW YOU WILL SEE HER SOON.
I KNOW.
THANKS, TURK.

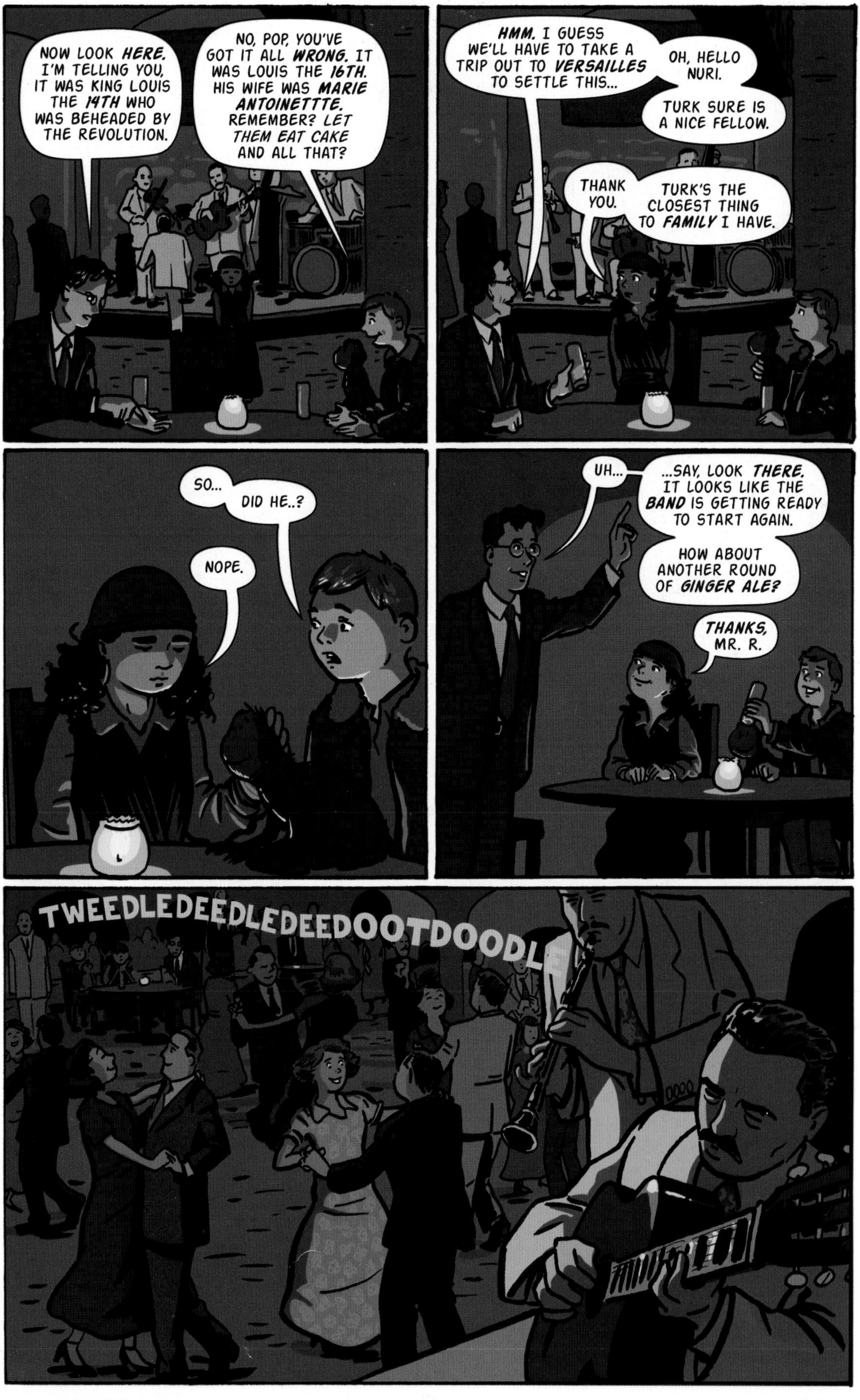
NOW LOOK HERE. I'M TELLING YOU, IT WAS KING LOUIS THE 14TH WHO WAS BEHEADED BY THE REVOLUTION.
NO, POP, YOU'VE GOT IT ALL WRONG. IT WAS LOUIS THE 16TH. HIS WIFE WAS MARIE ANTOINETTTE. REMEMBER? LET THEM EAT CAKE AND ALL THAT?
HMM. I GUESS WE'LL HAVE TO TAKE A TRIP OUT TO VERSAILLES TO SETTLE THIS...
OH, HELLO NURI.
TURK SURE IS A NICE FELLOW.
THANK YOU.
TURK'S THE CLOSEST THING TO FAMILY I HAVE.
SO...
DID HE..?
NOPE.
UH...
...SAY, LOOK THERE. IT LOOKS LIKE THE BAND IS GETTING READY TO START AGAIN.
HOW ABOUT ANOTHER ROUND OF GINGER ALE?
THANKS, MR. R.
TWEEDLEDEEDLEDEEDOOTDOODLE

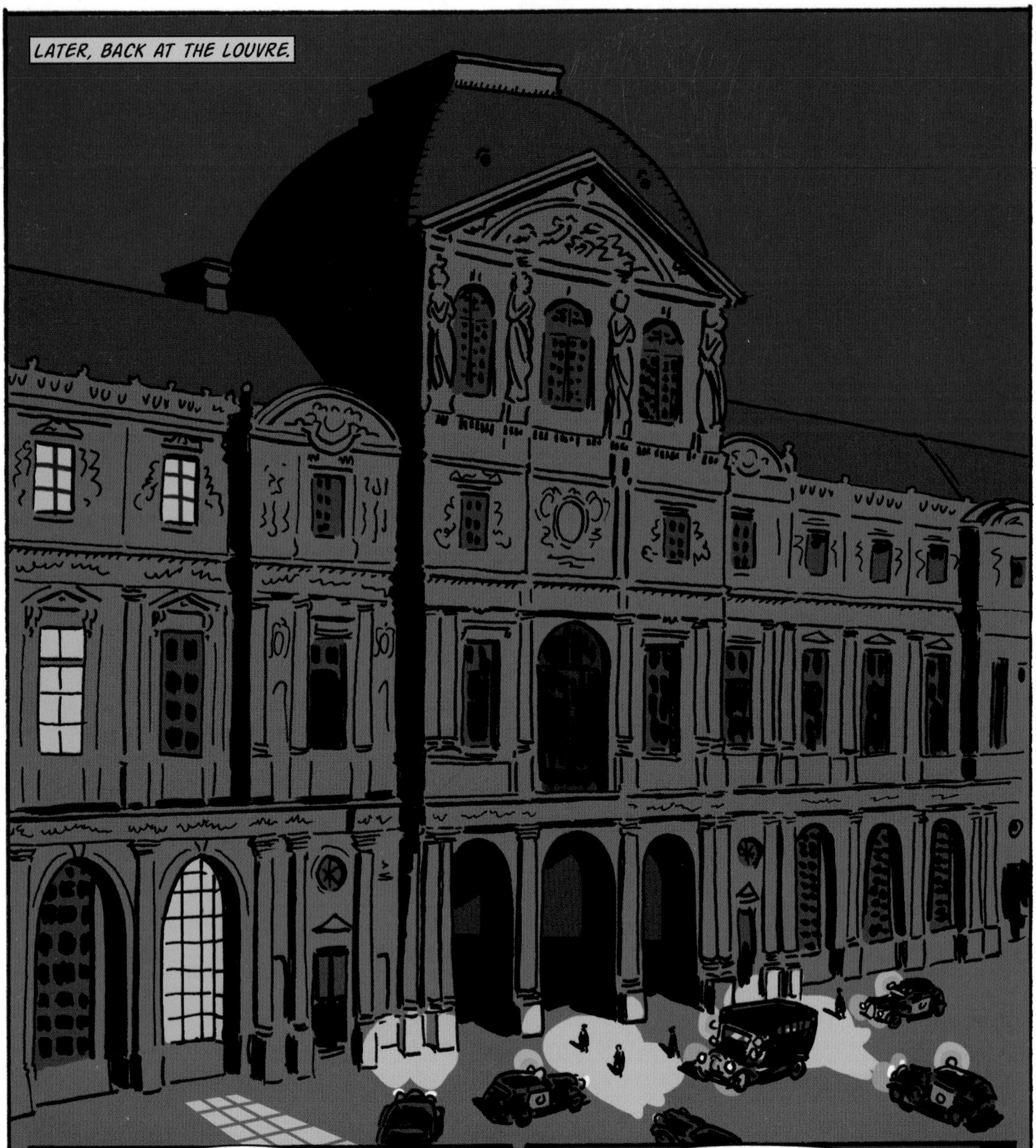
LATER, BACK AT THE LOUVRE.

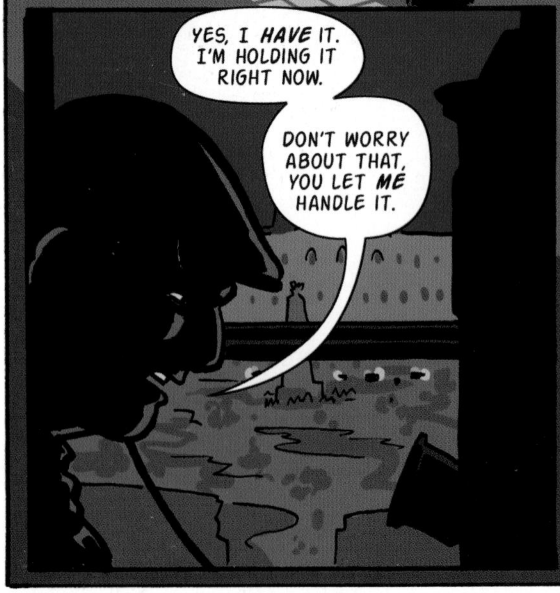
YES, I HAVE IT. I'M HOLDING IT RIGHT NOW.
DON'T WORRY ABOUT THAT, YOU LET ME HANDLE IT.

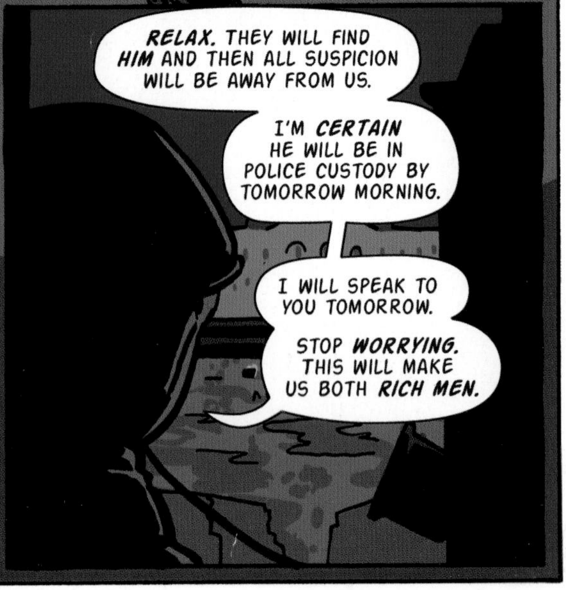
RELAX. THEY WILL FIND HIM AND THEN ALL SUSPICION WILL BE AWAY FROM US.
I'M CERTAIN HE WILL BE IN POLICE CUSTODY BY TOMORROW MORNING.
I WILL SPEAK TO YOU TOMORROW.
STOP WORRYING. THIS WILL MAKE US BOTH RICH MEN.

CHAPTER TWO

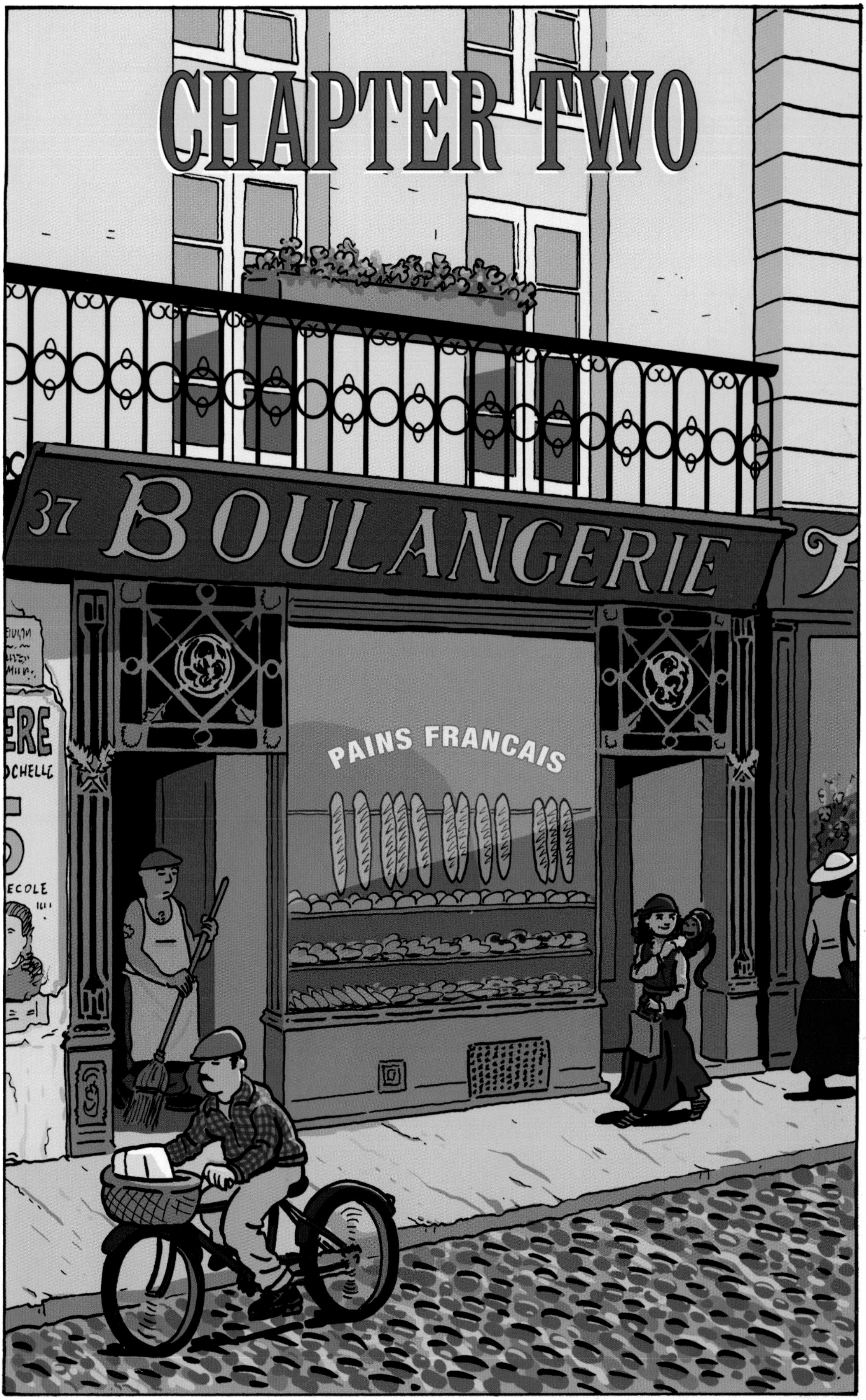
37 BOULANGERIE
PAINS FRANCAIS

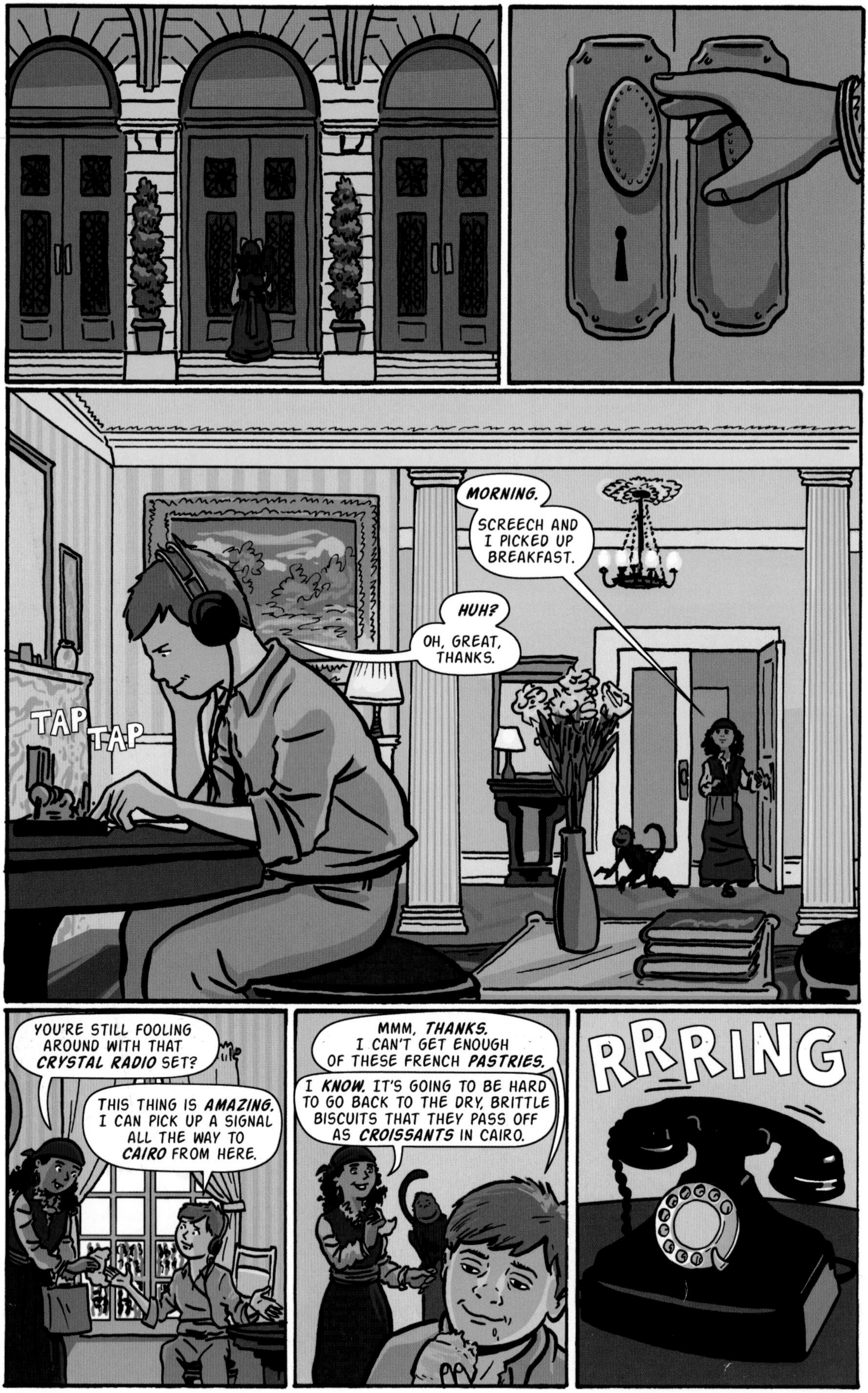
MORNING.
SCREECH AND I PICKED UP BREAKFAST.
HUH?
OH, GREAT, THANKS.
TAP TAP
YOU'RE STILL FOOLING AROUND WITH THAT CRYSTAL RADIO SET?
THIS THING IS AMAZING. I CAN PICK UP A SIGNAL ALL THE WAY TO CAIRO FROM HERE.
MMM, THANKS. I CAN'T GET ENOUGH OF THESE FRENCH PASTRIES.
I KNOW. IT'S GOING TO BE HARD TO GO BACK TO THE DRY, BRITTLE BISCUITS THAT THEY PASS OFF AS CROISSANTS IN CAIRO.
RRRING

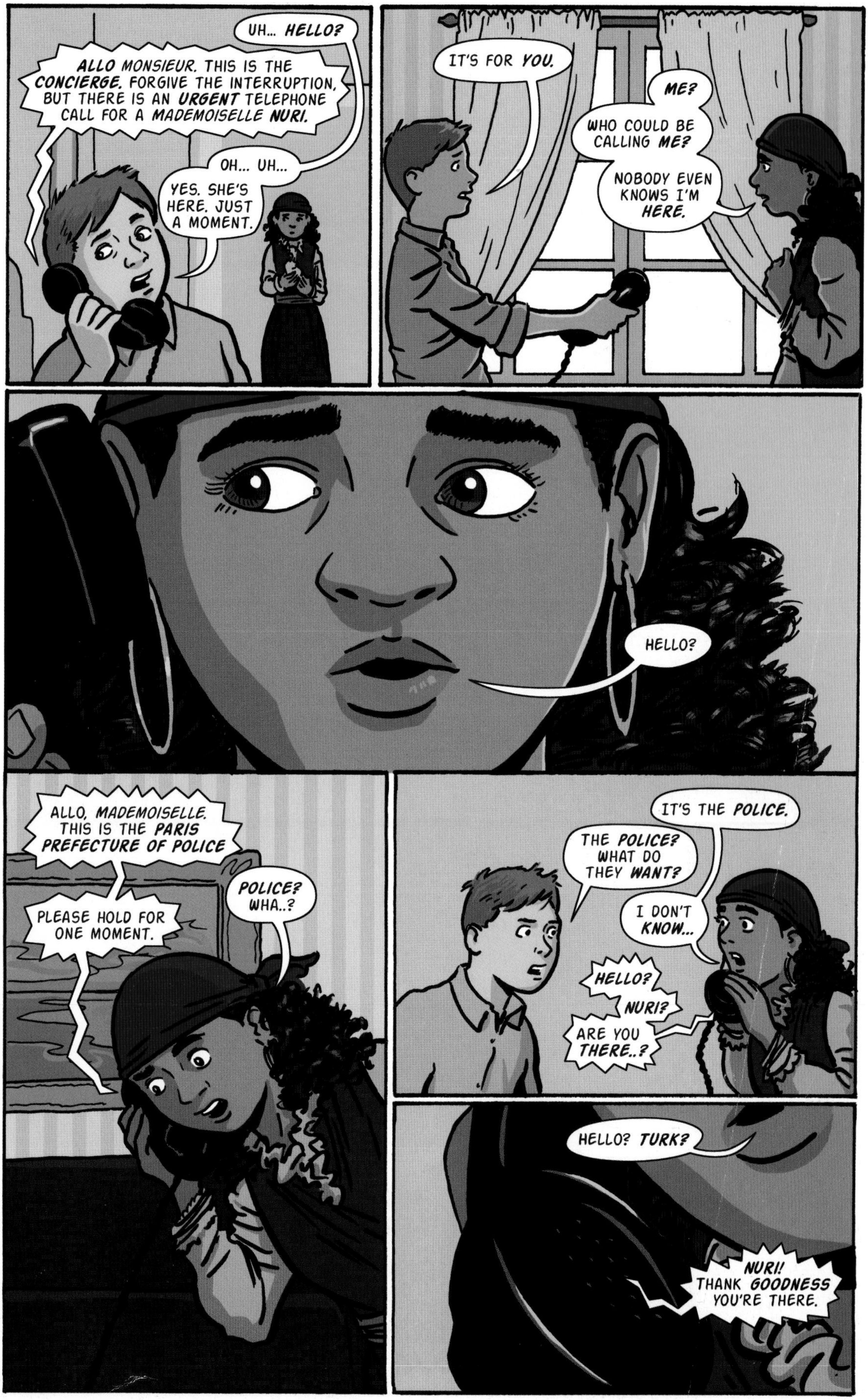
UH... HELLO?
ALLO MONSIEUR. THIS IS THE CONCIERGE. FORGIVE THE INTERRUPTION, BUT THERE IS AN URGENT TELEPHONE CALL FOR A MADEMOISELLE NURI.
OH... UH...
YES. SHE'S HERE. JUST A MOMENT.
IT'S FOR YOU.
ME?
WHO COULD BE CALLING ME?
NOBODY EVEN KNOWS I'M HERE.
HELLO?
ALLO, MADEMOISELLE. THIS IS THE PARIS PREFECTURE OF POLICE
PLEASE HOLD FOR ONE MOMENT.
POLICE? WHA..?
IT'S THE POLICE.
THE POLICE? WHAT DO THEY WANT?
I DON'T KNOW...
HELLO?
NURI?
ARE YOU THERE..?
HELLO? TURK?
NURI! THANK GOODNESS YOU'RE THERE.

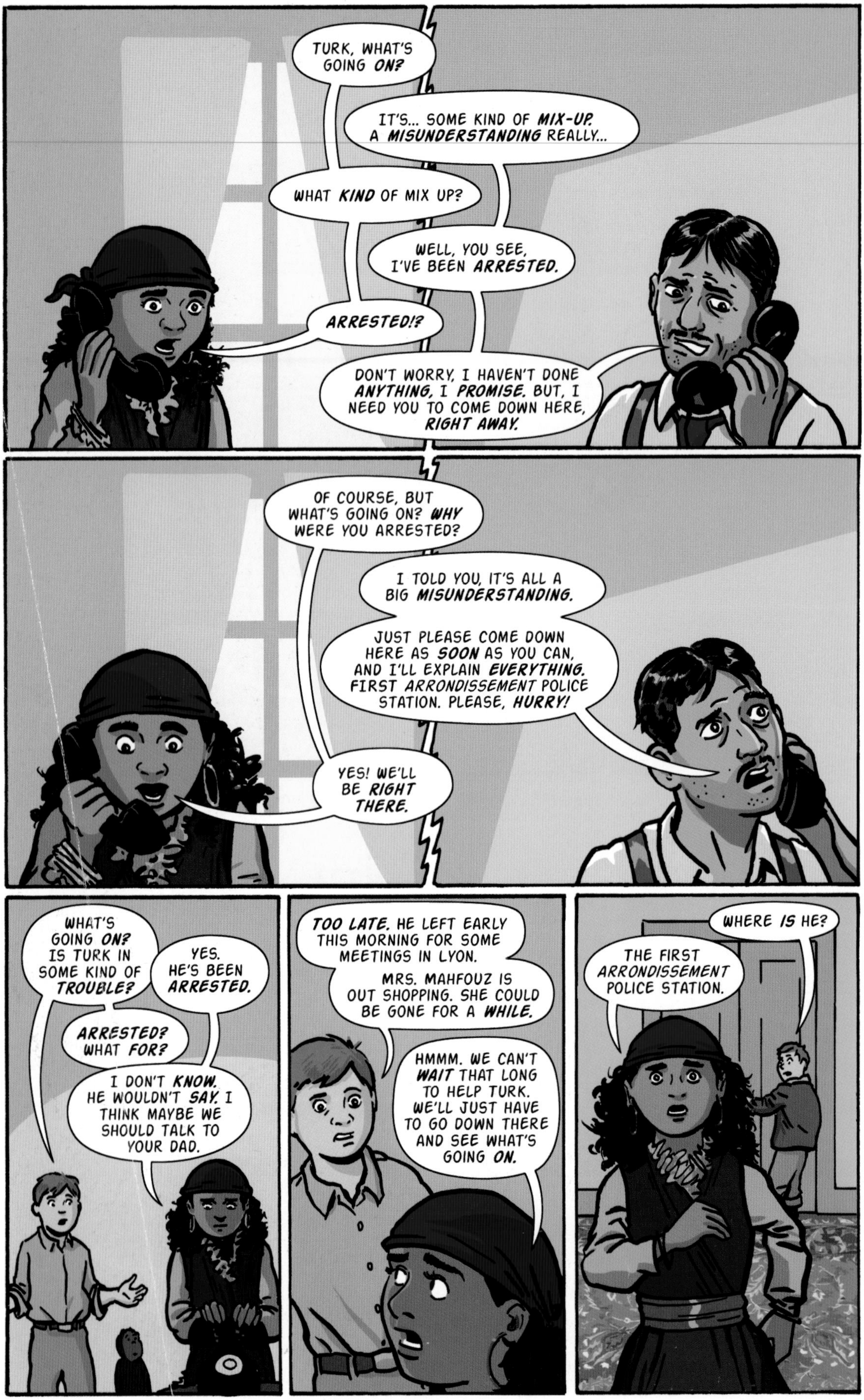
TURK, WHAT'S GOING ON?
IT'S... SOME KIND OF MIX-UP. A MISUNDERSTANDING REALLY...
WHAT KIND OF MIX UP?
WELL, YOU SEE, I'VE BEEN ARRESTED.
ARRESTED!?
DON'T WORRY, I HAVEN'T DONE ANYTHING, I PROMISE. BUT, I NEED YOU TO COME DOWN HERE, RIGHT AWAY.
OF COURSE, BUT WHAT'S GOING ON? WHY WERE YOU ARRESTED?
I TOLD YOU, IT'S ALL A BIG MISUNDERSTANDING.
JUST PLEASE COME DOWN HERE AS SOON AS YOU CAN, AND I'LL EXPLAIN EVERYTHING. FIRST ARRONDISSEMENT POLICE STATION. PLEASE, HURRY!
YES! WE'LL BE RIGHT THERE.
WHAT'S GOING ON? IS TURK IN SOME KIND OF TROUBLE?
YES. HE'S BEEN ARRESTED.
ARRESTED? WHAT FOR?
I DON'T KNOW. HE WOULDN'T SAY. I THINK MAYBE WE SHOULD TALK TO YOUR DAD.
TOO LATE. HE LEFT EARLY THIS MORNING FOR SOME MEETINGS IN LYON.
MRS. MAHFOUZ IS OUT SHOPPING. SHE COULD BE GONE FOR A WHILE.
HMMM. WE CAN'T WAIT THAT LONG TO HELP TURK. WE'LL JUST HAVE TO GO DOWN THERE AND SEE WHAT'S GOING ON.
WHERE IS HE?
THE FIRST ARRONDISSEMENT POLICE STATION.

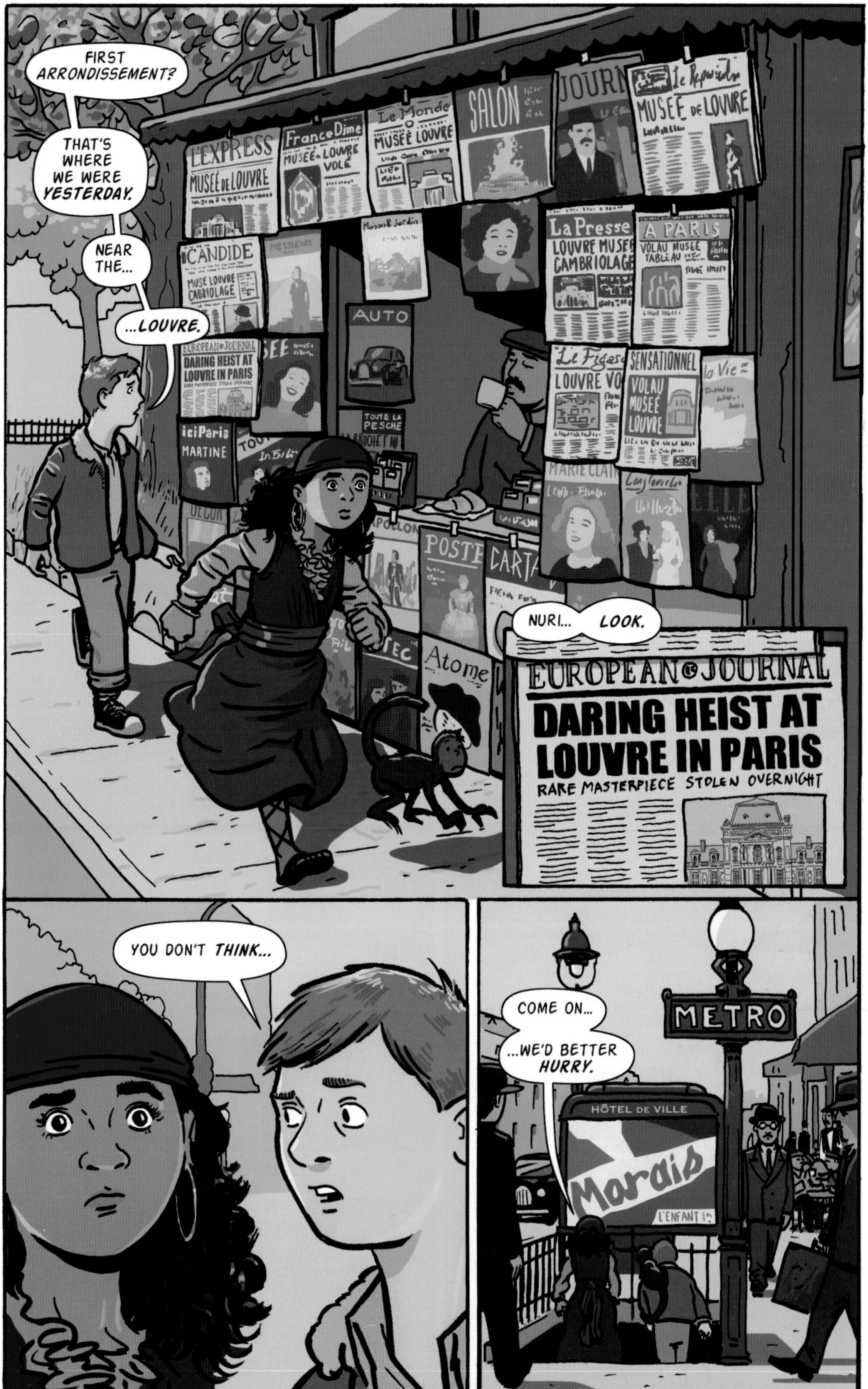
FIRST ARRONDISSEMENT?
THAT'S WHERE WE WERE YESTERDAY.
NEAR THE...
...LOUVRE.
NURI... LOOK.
EUROPEAN JOURNAL
DARING HEIST AT LOUVRE IN PARIS
RARE MASTERPIECE STOLEN OVERNIGHT
YOU DON'T THINK...
COME ON...
...WE'D BETTER HURRY.
METRO
HÔTEL DE VILLE

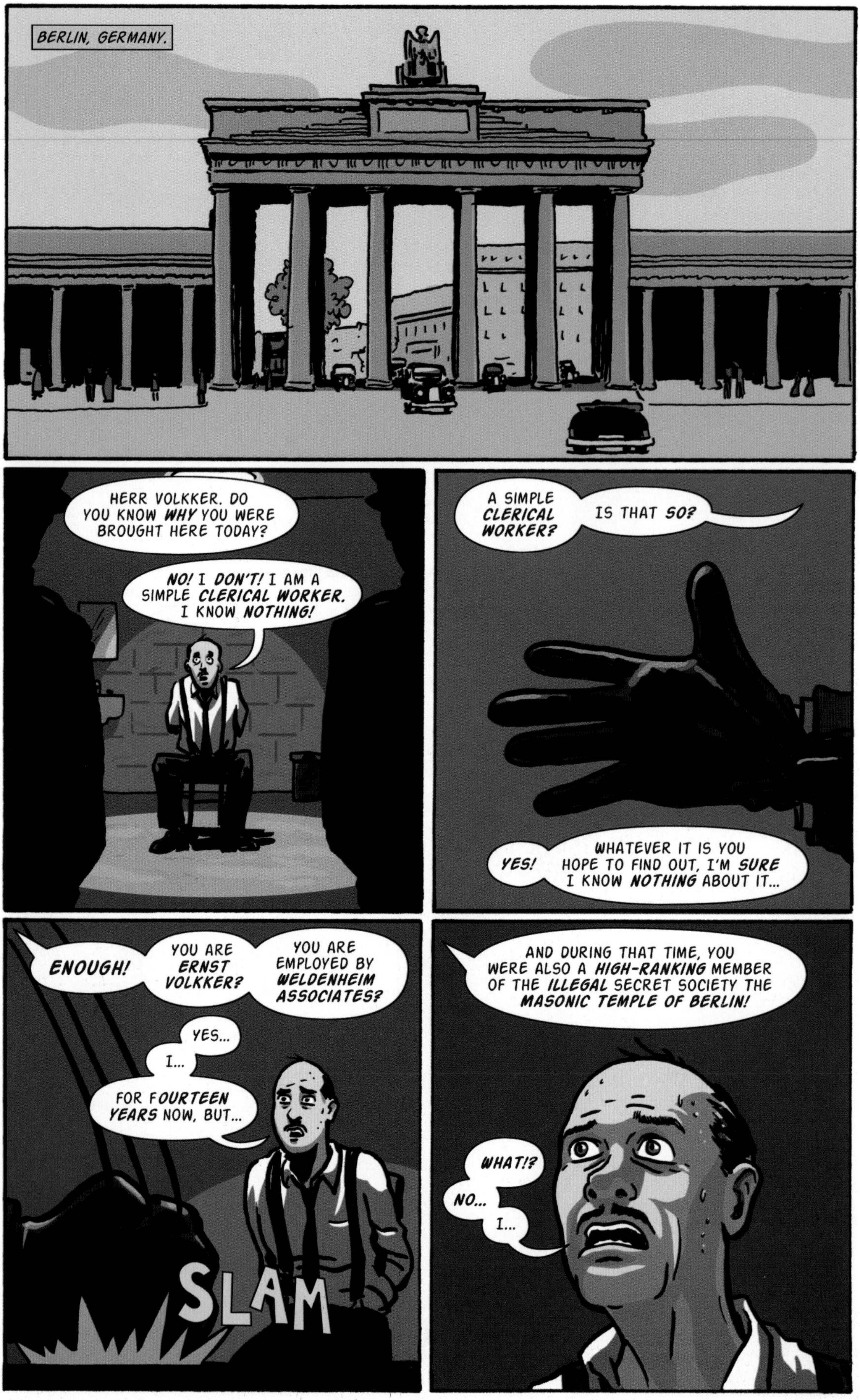
BERLIN, GERMANY.
HERR VOLKKER. DO YOU KNOW WHY YOU WERE BROUGHT HERE TODAY?
NO! I DON'T! I AM A SIMPLE CLERICAL WORKER. I KNOW NOTHING!
A SIMPLE CLERICAL WORKER?
IS THAT SO?
YES!
WHATEVER IT IS YOU HOPE TO FIND OUT, I'M SURE I KNOW NOTHING ABOUT IT...
ENOUGH!
YOU ARE ERNST VOLKKER?
YOU ARE EMPLOYED BY WELDENHEIM ASSOCIATES?
YES...
I...
FOR FOURTEEN YEARS NOW, BUT...
SLAM
AND DURING THAT TIME, YOU WERE ALSO A HIGH-RANKING MEMBER OF THE ILLEGAL SECRET SOCIETY THE MASONIC TEMPLE OF BERLIN!
WHAT!?
NO...
I...

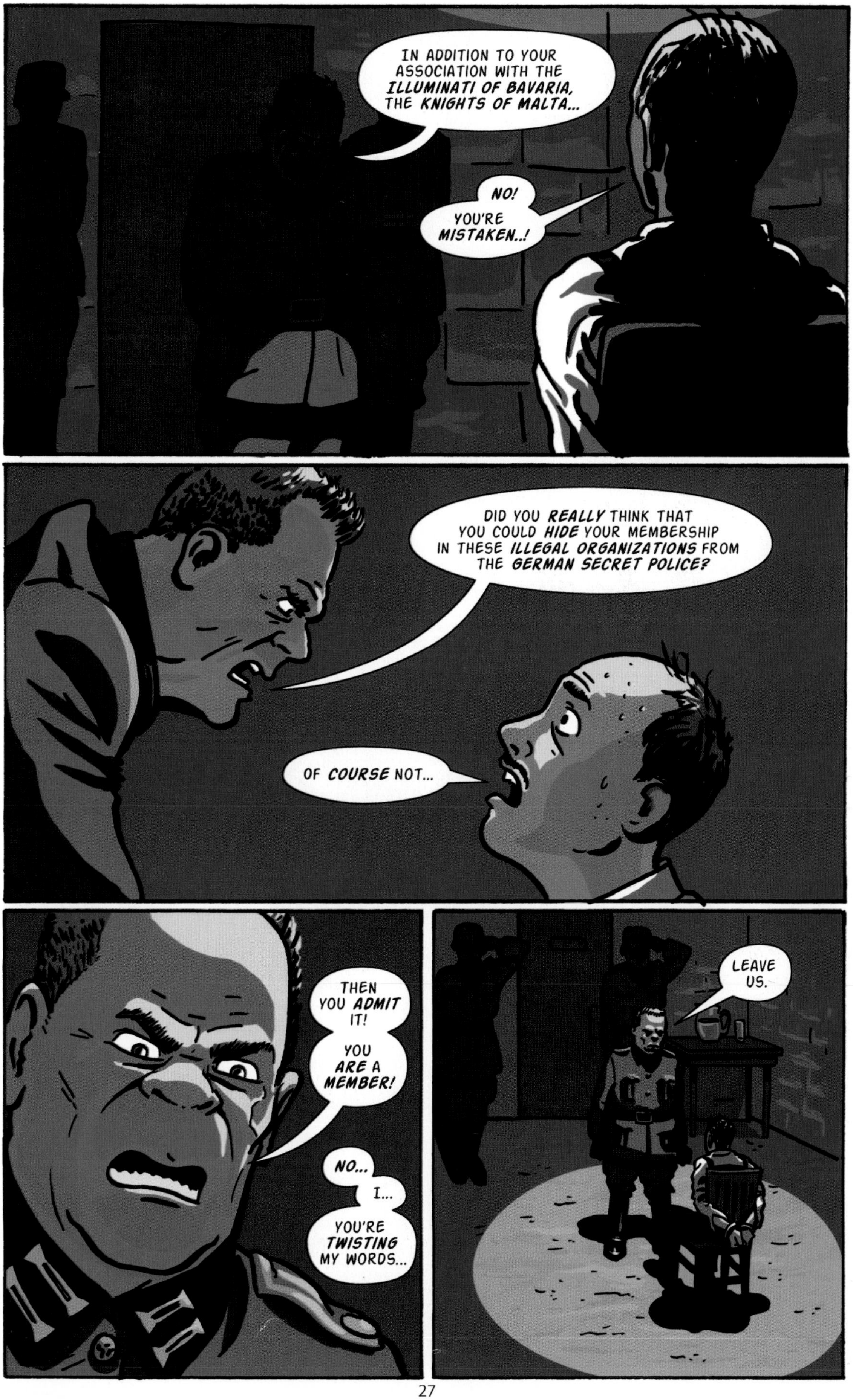
IN ADDITION TO YOUR ASSOCIATION WITH THE ILLUMINATI OF BAVARIA, THE KNIGHTS OF MALTA...
NO! YOU'RE MISTAKEN..!
DID YOU REALLY THINK THAT YOU COULD HIDE YOUR MEMBERSHIP IN THESE ILLEGAL ORGANIZATIONS FROM THE GERMAN SECRET POLICE?
OF COURSE NOT...
THEN YOU ADMIT IT!
YOU ARE A MEMBER!
NO...
I...
YOU'RE TWISTING MY WORDS...
LEAVE US.

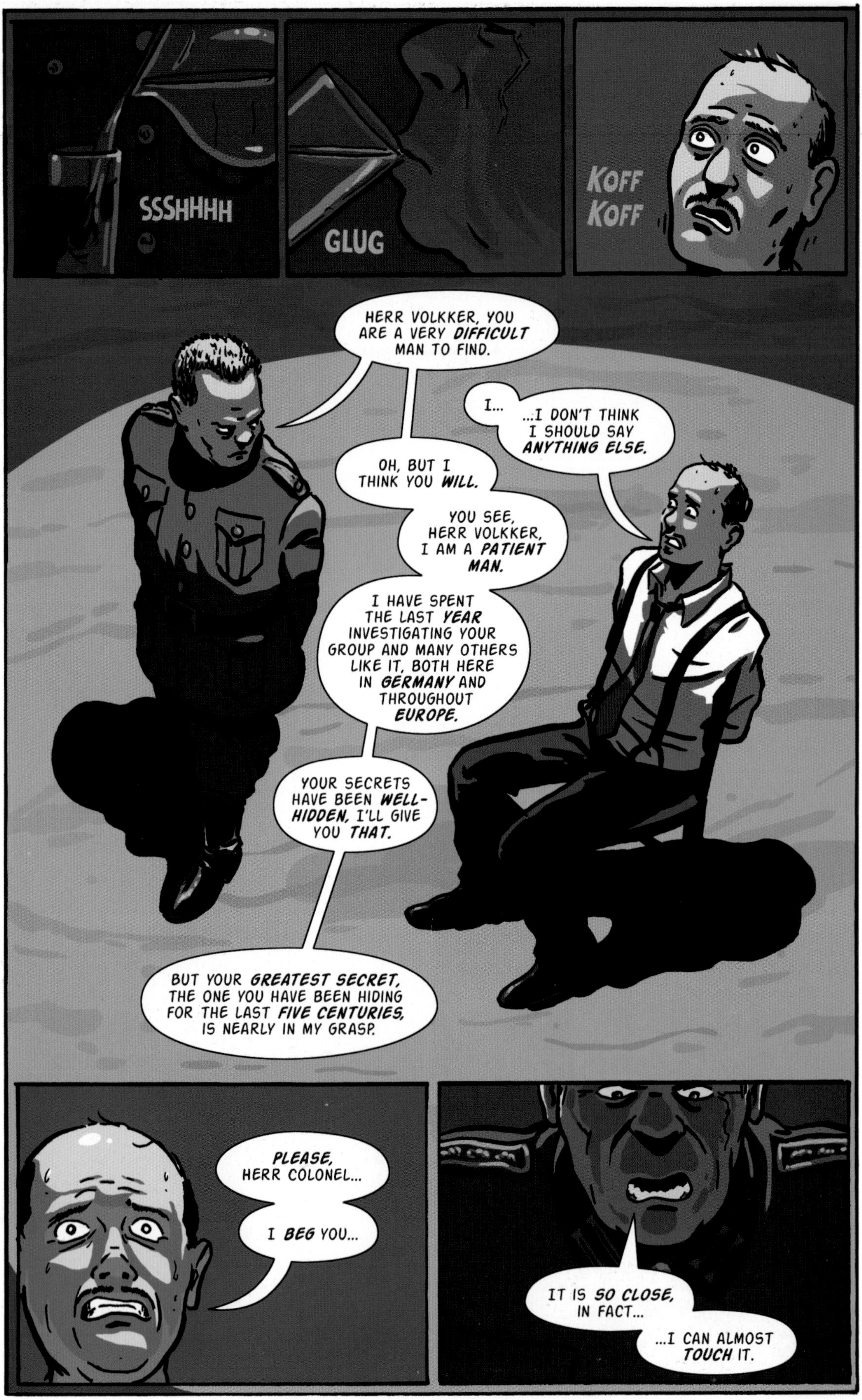
SSSHHHH
GLUG
KOFF KOFF
HERR VOLKKER, YOU ARE A VERY DIFFICULT MAN TO FIND.
I...
...I DON'T THINK I SHOULD SAY ANYTHING ELSE.
OH, BUT I THINK YOU WILL.
YOU SEE, HERR VOLKKER, I AM A PATIENT MAN.
I HAVE SPENT THE LAST YEAR INVESTIGATING YOUR GROUP AND MANY OTHERS LIKE IT, BOTH HERE IN GERMANY AND THROUGHOUT EUROPE.
YOUR SECRETS HAVE BEEN WELL-HIDDEN, I'LL GIVE YOU THAT.
BUT YOUR GREATEST SECRET, THE ONE YOU HAVE BEEN HIDING FOR THE LAST FIVE CENTURIES, IS NEARLY IN MY GRASP.
PLEASE, HERR COLONEL...
I BEG YOU...
IT IS SO CLOSE, IN FACT...
...I CAN ALMOST TOUCH IT.

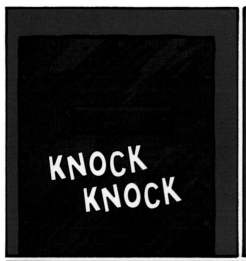

KNOCK
KNOCK

FORGIVE ME SIR, BUT THE OTHER OFFICERS HAVE GATHERED AND THEY AWAIT YOUR ARRIVAL UPSTAIRS.

AH. SAVED BY THE BELL, EH HERR VOLKKER? WELL, NOT TO WORRY. WE WILL CONTINUE OUR CONVERSATION VERY SOON.

IN THE MEANTIME, I LEAVE YOU IN THE VERY CAPABLE HANDS OF LIEUTENANT SCHNELLER HERE.

FIND OUT WHAT HE KNOWS.

IT IS OF THE UTMOST IMPORTANCE.

DO YOU UNDERSTAND?

LEAVE IT TO ME, COLONEL.

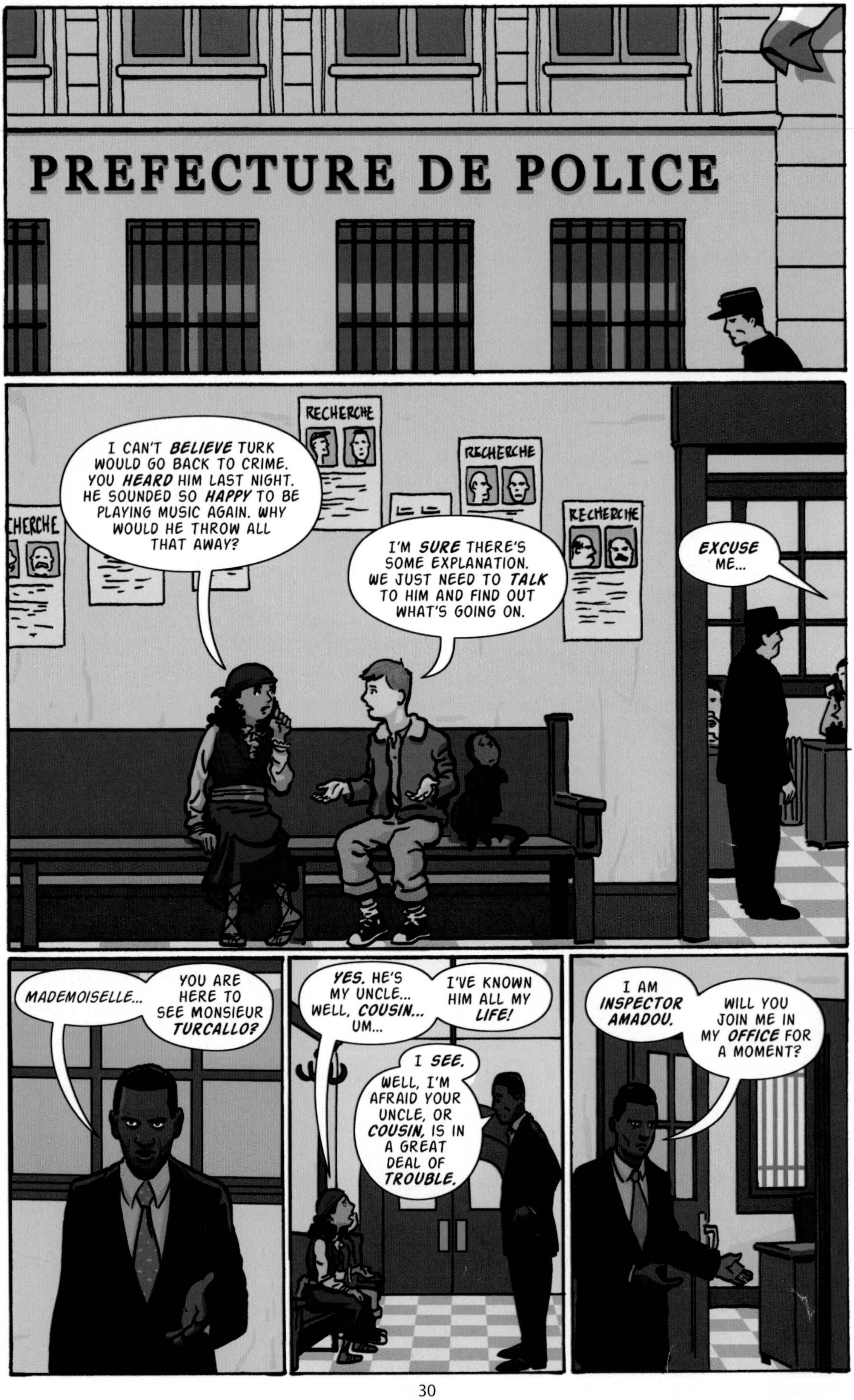
PREFECTURE DE POLICE
RECHERCHE
RECHERCHE
RECHERCHE
I CAN'T BELIEVE TURK WOULD GO BACK TO CRIME. YOU HEARD HIM LAST NIGHT. HE SOUNDED SO HAPPY TO BE PLAYING MUSIC AGAIN. WHY WOULD HE THROW ALL THAT AWAY?
I'M SURE THERE'S SOME EXPLANATION. WE JUST NEED TO TALK TO HIM AND FIND OUT WHAT'S GOING ON.
EXCUSE ME...
MADEMOISELLE...
YOU ARE HERE TO SEE MONSIEUR TURCALLO?
YES. HE'S MY UNCLE... WELL, COUSIN... UM...
I'VE KNOWN HIM ALL MY LIFE!
I SEE.
WELL, I'M AFRAID YOUR UNCLE, OR COUSIN, IS IN A GREAT DEAL OF TROUBLE.
I AM INSPECTOR AMADOU.
WILL YOU JOIN ME IN MY OFFICE FOR A MOMENT?

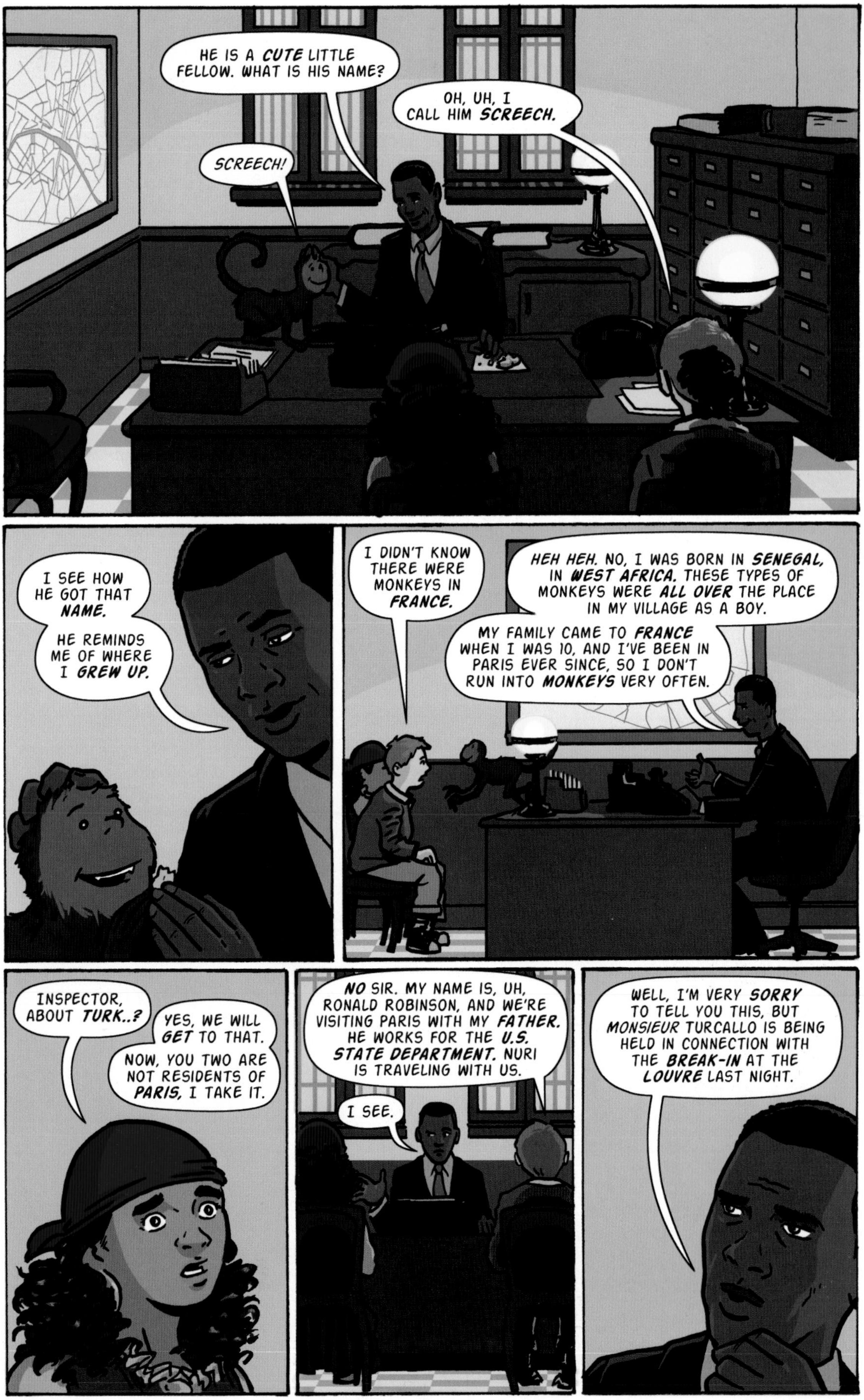
HE IS A CUTE LITTLE FELLOW. WHAT IS HIS NAME?
SCREECH!
OH, UH, I CALL HIM SCREECH.
I SEE HOW HE GOT THAT NAME.
HE REMINDS ME OF WHERE I GREW UP.
I DIDN'T KNOW THERE WERE MONKEYS IN FRANCE.
HEH HEH. NO, I WAS BORN IN SENEGAL, IN WEST AFRICA. THESE TYPES OF MONKEYS WERE ALL OVER THE PLACE IN MY VILLAGE AS A BOY.
MY FAMILY CAME TO FRANCE WHEN I WAS 10, AND I'VE BEEN IN PARIS EVER SINCE, SO I DON'T RUN INTO MONKEYS VERY OFTEN.
INSPECTOR, ABOUT TURK..?
YES, WE WILL GET TO THAT.
NOW, YOU TWO ARE NOT RESIDENTS OF PARIS, I TAKE IT.
NO SIR. MY NAME IS, UH, RONALD ROBINSON, AND WE'RE VISITING PARIS WITH MY FATHER. HE WORKS FOR THE U.S. STATE DEPARTMENT. NURI IS TRAVELING WITH US.
I SEE.
WELL, I'M VERY SORRY TO TELL YOU THIS, BUT MONSIEUR TURCALLO IS BEING HELD IN CONNECTION WITH THE BREAK-IN AT THE LOUVRE LAST NIGHT.

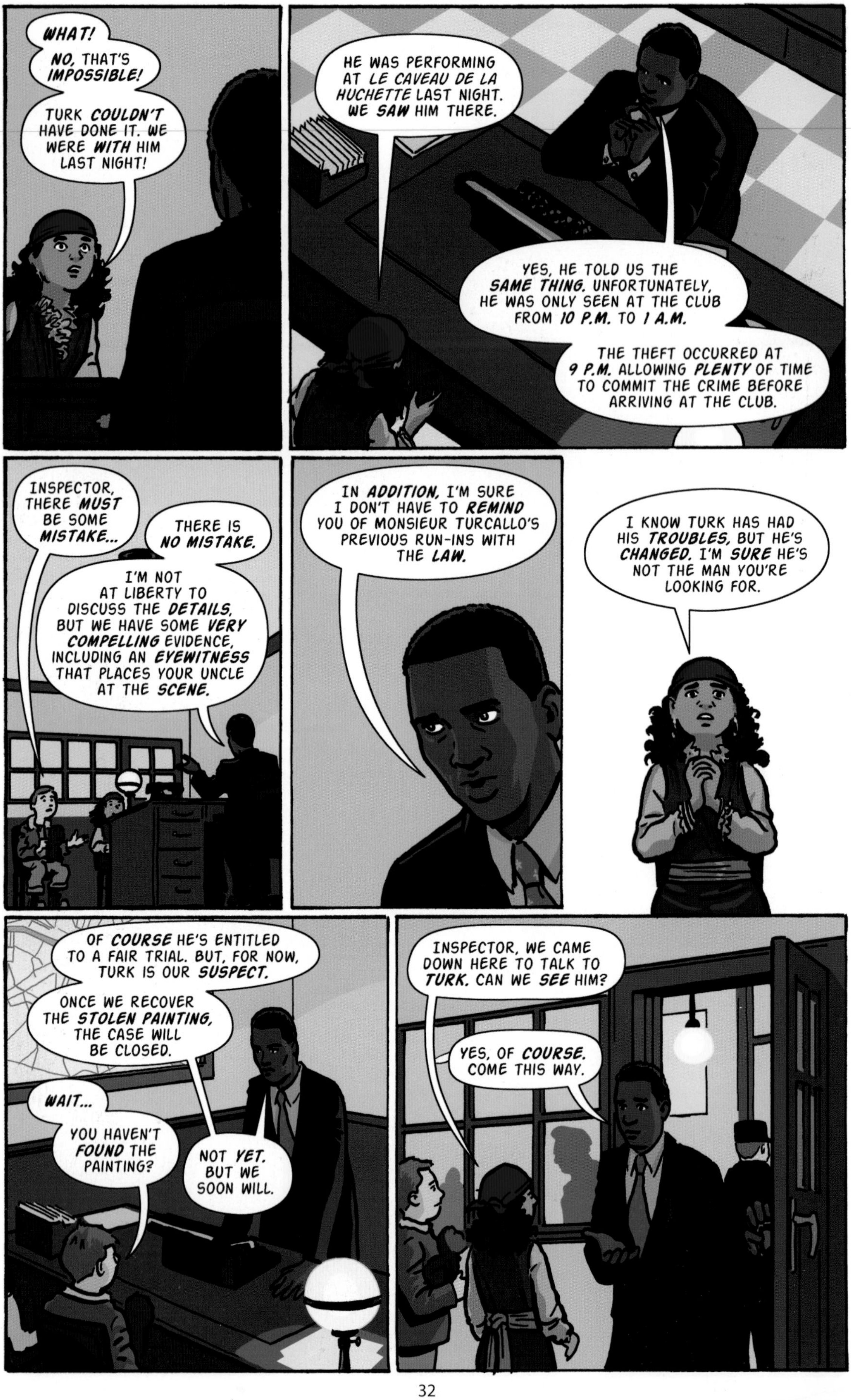
WHAT!
NO, THAT'S IMPOSSIBLE!
TURK COULDN'T HAVE DONE IT. WE WERE WITH HIM LAST NIGHT!
HE WAS PERFORMING AT LE CAVEAU DE LA HUCHETTE LAST NIGHT. WE SAW HIM THERE.
YES, HE TOLD US THE SAME THING. UNFORTUNATELY, HE WAS ONLY SEEN AT THE CLUB FROM 10 P.M. TO 1 A.M.
THE THEFT OCCURRED AT 9 P.M. ALLOWING PLENTY OF TIME TO COMMIT THE CRIME BEFORE ARRIVING AT THE CLUB.
INSPECTOR, THERE MUST BE SOME MISTAKE...
THERE IS NO MISTAKE.
I'M NOT AT LIBERTY TO DISCUSS THE DETAILS, BUT WE HAVE SOME VERY COMPELLING EVIDENCE, INCLUDING AN EYEWITNESS THAT PLACES YOUR UNCLE AT THE SCENE.
IN ADDITION, I'M SURE I DON'T HAVE TO REMIND YOU OF MONSIEUR TURCALLO'S PREVIOUS RUN-INS WITH THE LAW.
I KNOW TURK HAS HAD HIS TROUBLES, BUT HE'S CHANGED. I'M SURE HE'S NOT THE MAN YOU'RE LOOKING FOR.
OF COURSE HE'S ENTITLED TO A FAIR TRIAL. BUT, FOR NOW, TURK IS OUR SUSPECT.
ONCE WE RECOVER THE STOLEN PAINTING, THE CASE WILL BE CLOSED.
WAIT...
YOU HAVEN'T FOUND THE PAINTING?
NOT YET. BUT WE SOON WILL.
INSPECTOR, WE CAME DOWN HERE TO TALK TO TURK. CAN WE SEE HIM?
YES, OF COURSE. COME THIS WAY.

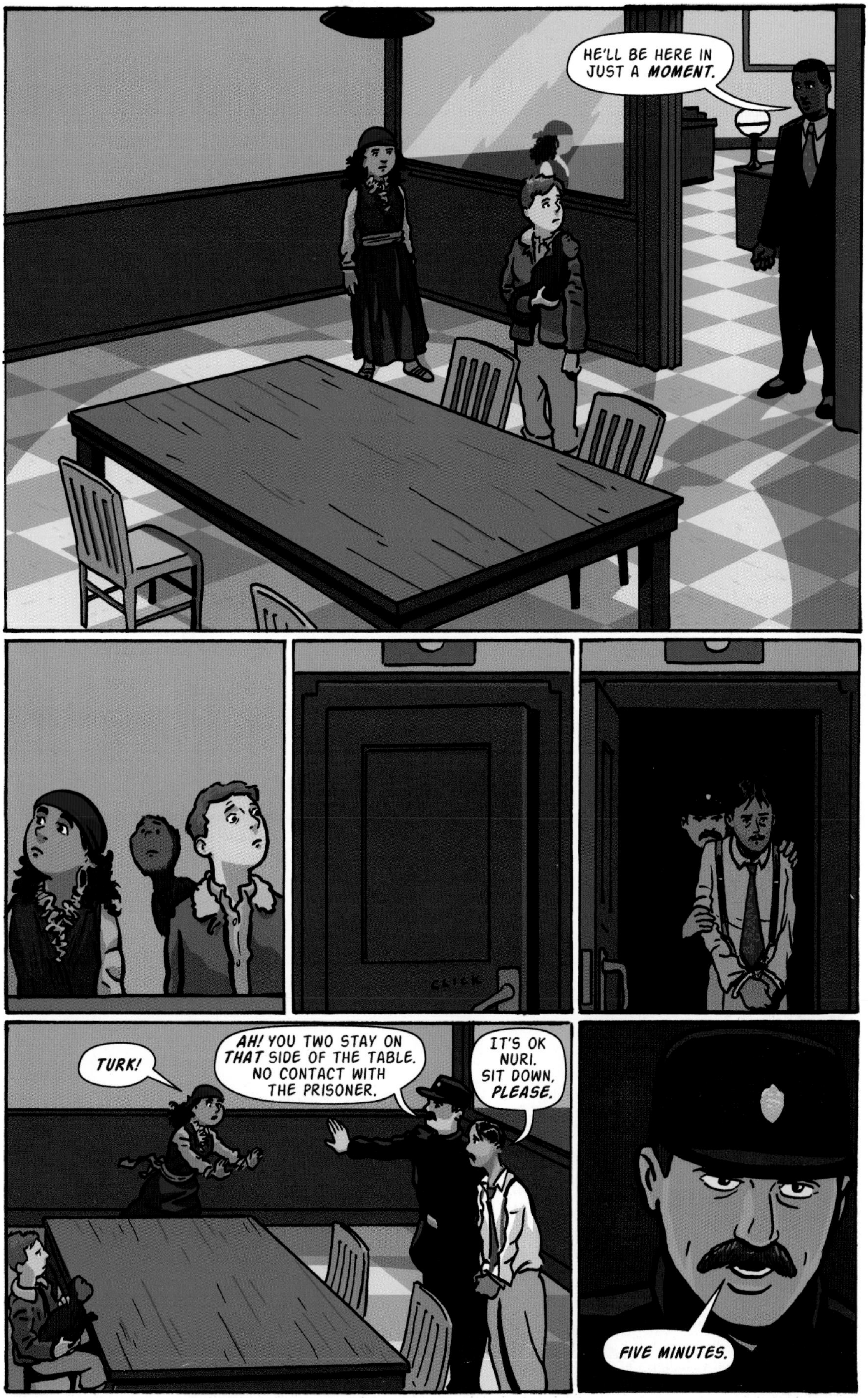
HE'LL BE HERE IN JUST A *MOMENT.*
CLICK
TURK!
AH! YOU TWO STAY ON *THAT* SIDE OF THE TABLE. NO CONTACT WITH THE PRISONER.
IT'S OK NURI. SIT DOWN, *PLEASE.*
FIVE MINUTES.

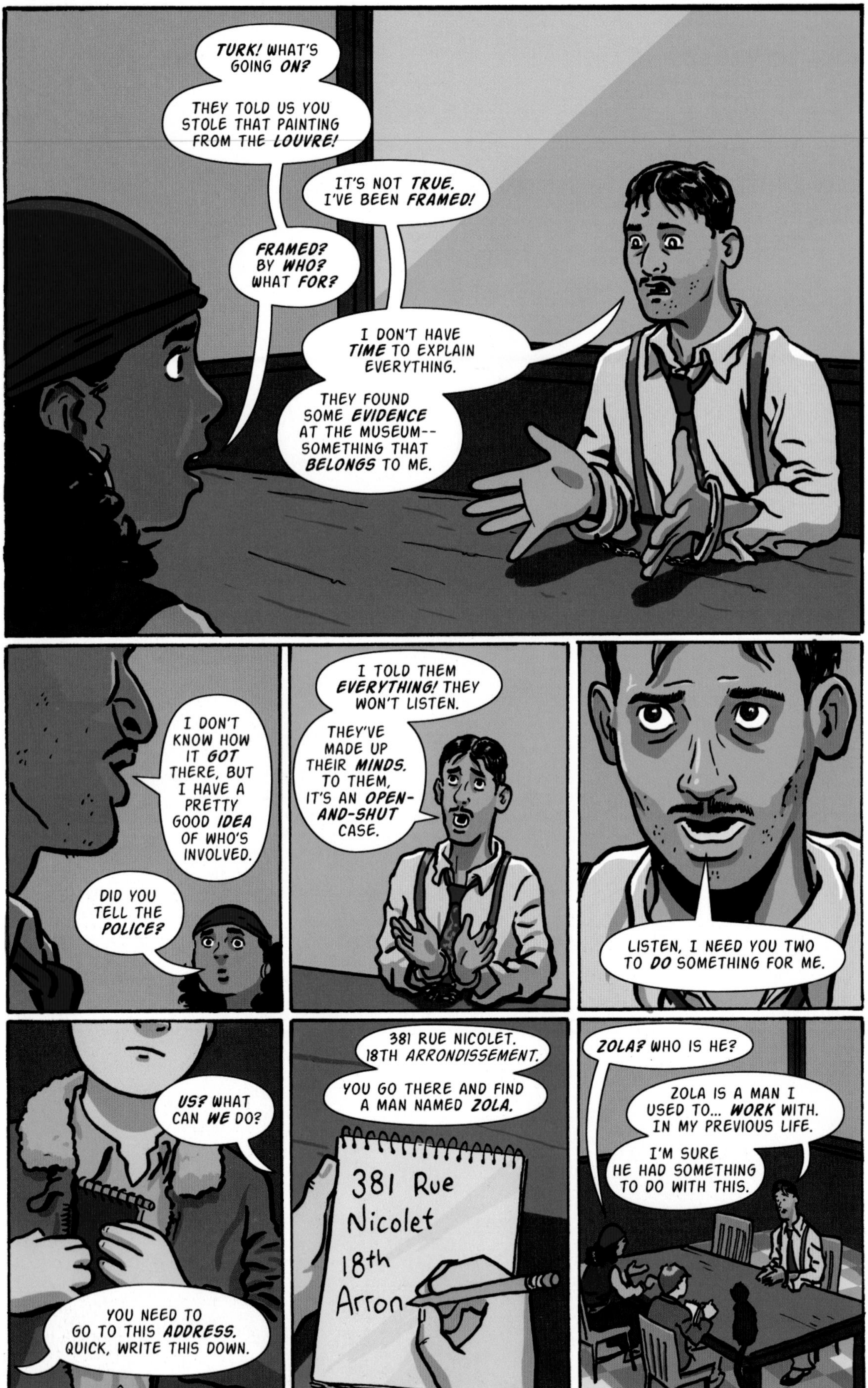
TURK! WHAT'S GOING ON?
THEY TOLD US YOU STOLE THAT PAINTING FROM THE LOUVRE!
IT'S NOT TRUE. I'VE BEEN FRAMED!
FRAMED? BY WHO? WHAT FOR?
I DON'T HAVE TIME TO EXPLAIN EVERYTHING.
THEY FOUND SOME EVIDENCE AT THE MUSEUM-- SOMETHING THAT BELONGS TO ME.
I DON'T KNOW HOW IT GOT THERE, BUT I HAVE A PRETTY GOOD IDEA OF WHO'S INVOLVED.
DID YOU TELL THE POLICE?
I TOLD THEM EVERYTHING! THEY WON'T LISTEN.
THEY'VE MADE UP THEIR MINDS. TO THEM, IT'S AN OPEN-AND-SHUT CASE.
LISTEN, I NEED YOU TWO TO DO SOMETHING FOR ME.
US? WHAT CAN WE DO?
YOU NEED TO GO TO THIS ADDRESS. QUICK, WRITE THIS DOWN.
381 RUE NICOLET. 18TH ARRONDISSEMENT.
YOU GO THERE AND FIND A MAN NAMED ZOLA.
381 Rue Nicolet 18th Arron
ZOLA? WHO IS HE?
ZOLA IS A MAN I USED TO... WORK WITH. IN MY PREVIOUS LIFE.
I'M SURE HE HAD SOMETHING TO DO WITH THIS.

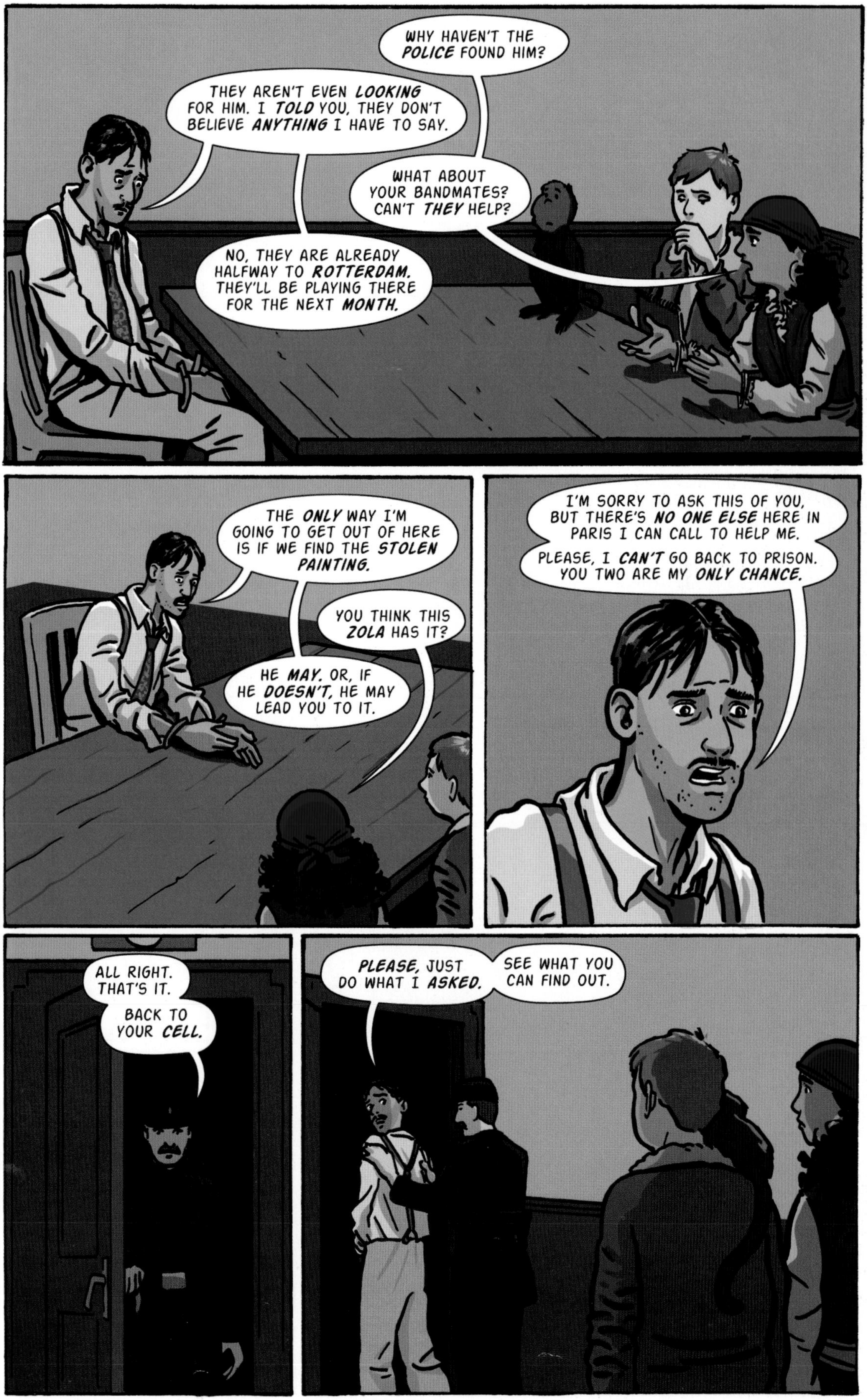

THEY AREN'T EVEN LOOKING FOR HIM. I TOLD YOU, THEY DON'T BELIEVE ANYTHING I HAVE TO SAY.
WHY HAVEN'T THE POLICE FOUND HIM?
WHAT ABOUT YOUR BANDMATES? CAN'T THEY HELP?
NO, THEY ARE ALREADY HALFWAY TO ROTTERDAM. THEY'LL BE PLAYING THERE FOR THE NEXT MONTH.
THE ONLY WAY I'M GOING TO GET OUT OF HERE IS IF WE FIND THE STOLEN PAINTING.
YOU THINK THIS ZOLA HAS IT?
HE MAY. OR, IF HE DOESN'T, HE MAY LEAD YOU TO IT.
I'M SORRY TO ASK THIS OF YOU, BUT THERE'S NO ONE ELSE HERE IN PARIS I CAN CALL TO HELP ME.
PLEASE, I CAN'T GO BACK TO PRISON. YOU TWO ARE MY ONLY CHANCE.
ALL RIGHT. THAT'S IT.
BACK TO YOUR CELL.
PLEASE, JUST DO WHAT I ASKED.
SEE WHAT YOU CAN FIND OUT.

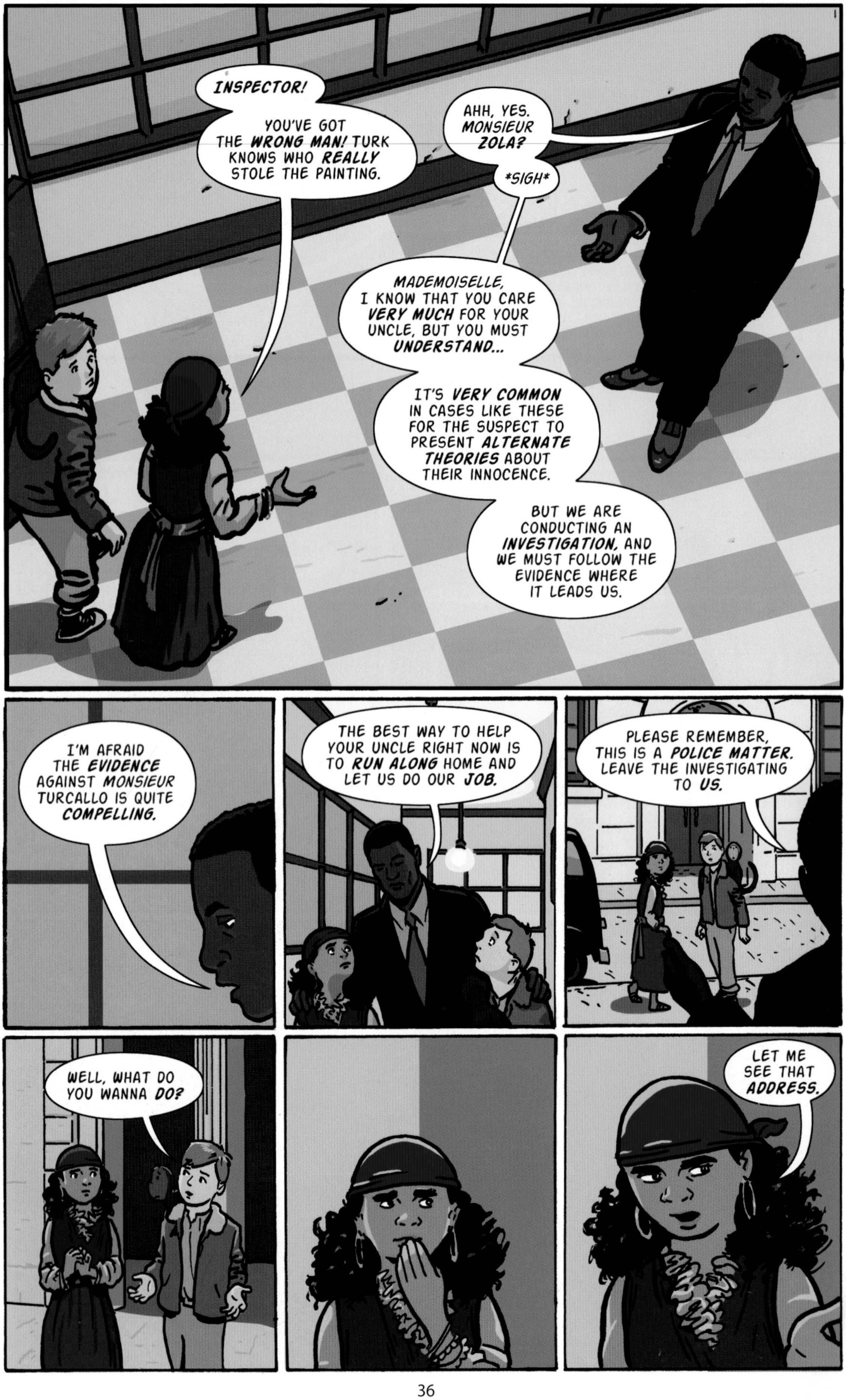
INSPECTOR!
YOU'VE GOT THE WRONG MAN! TURK KNOWS WHO REALLY STOLE THE PAINTING.
AHH, YES. MONSIEUR ZOLA?
SIGH
MADEMOISELLE, I KNOW THAT YOU CARE VERY MUCH FOR YOUR UNCLE, BUT YOU MUST UNDERSTAND...
IT'S VERY COMMON IN CASES LIKE THESE FOR THE SUSPECT TO PRESENT ALTERNATE THEORIES ABOUT THEIR INNOCENCE.
BUT WE ARE CONDUCTING AN INVESTIGATION, AND WE MUST FOLLOW THE EVIDENCE WHERE IT LEADS US.
I'M AFRAID THE EVIDENCE AGAINST MONSIEUR TURCALLO IS QUITE COMPELLING.
THE BEST WAY TO HELP YOUR UNCLE RIGHT NOW IS TO RUN ALONG HOME AND LET US DO OUR JOB.
PLEASE REMEMBER, THIS IS A POLICE MATTER. LEAVE THE INVESTIGATING TO US.
WELL, WHAT DO YOU WANNA DO?
LET ME SEE THAT ADDRESS.

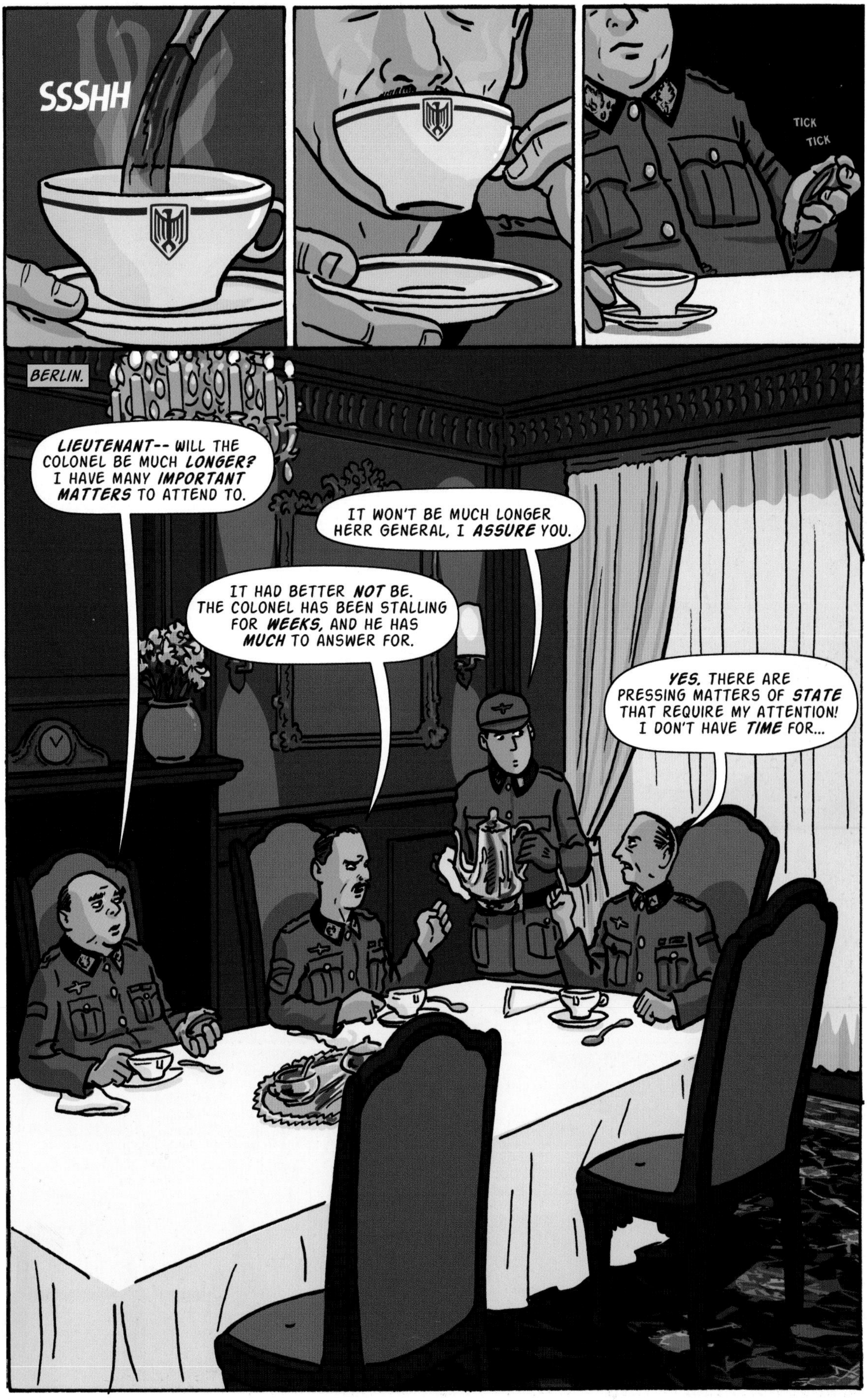
SSSHH
TICK
TICK
BERLIN.
LIEUTENANT-- WILL THE COLONEL BE MUCH LONGER? I HAVE MANY IMPORTANT MATTERS TO ATTEND TO.
IT WON'T BE MUCH LONGER HERR GENERAL, I ASSURE YOU.
IT HAD BETTER NOT BE. THE COLONEL HAS BEEN STALLING FOR WEEKS, AND HE HAS MUCH TO ANSWER FOR.
YES. THERE ARE PRESSING MATTERS OF STATE THAT REQUIRE MY ATTENTION! I DON'T HAVE TIME FOR...

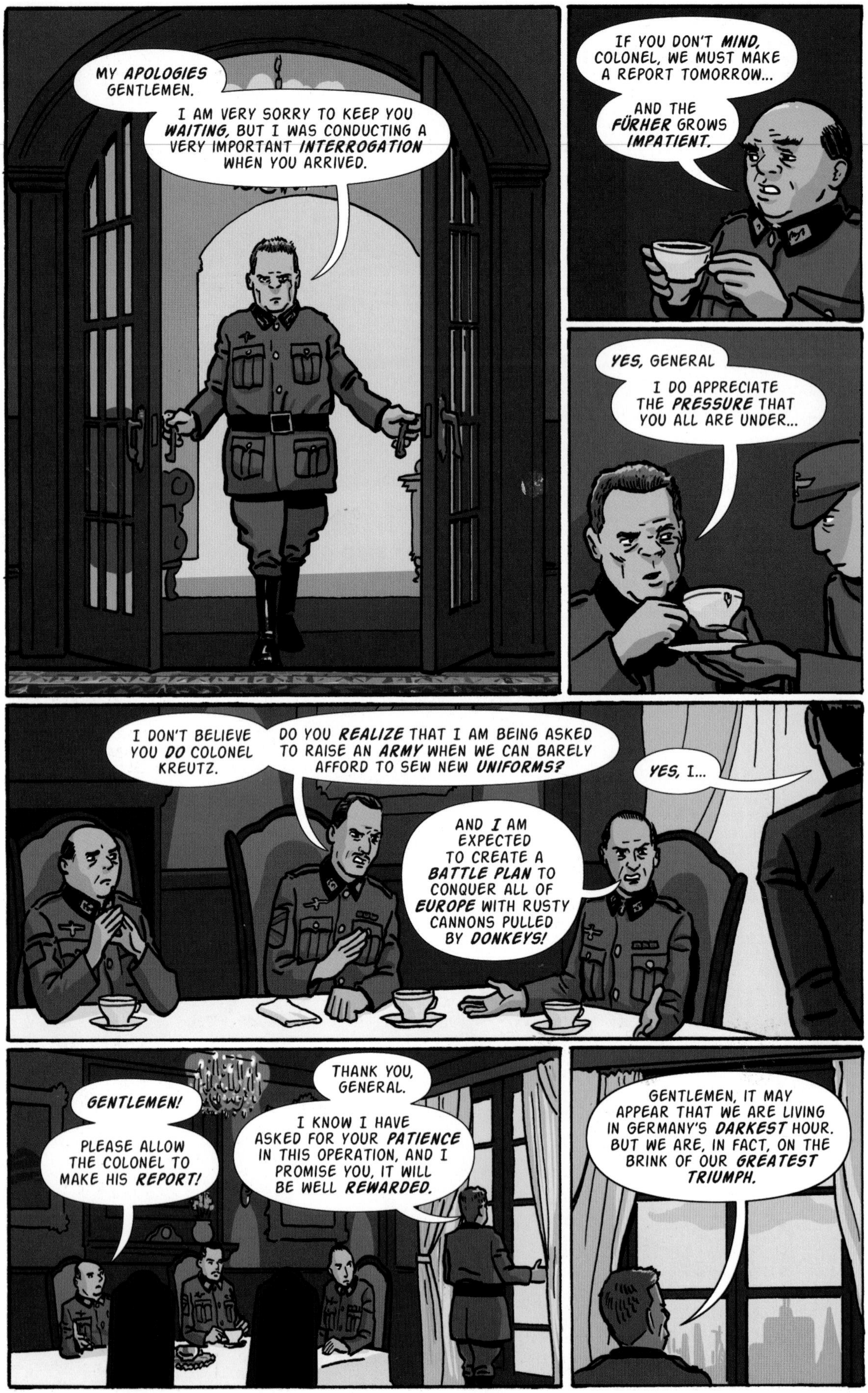
MY APOLOGIES GENTLEMEN.
I AM VERY SORRY TO KEEP YOU WAITING, BUT I WAS CONDUCTING A VERY IMPORTANT INTERROGATION WHEN YOU ARRIVED.
IF YOU DON'T MIND, COLONEL, WE MUST MAKE A REPORT TOMORROW...
AND THE FÜRHER GROWS IMPATIENT.
YES, GENERAL
I DO APPRECIATE THE PRESSURE THAT YOU ALL ARE UNDER...
I DON'T BELIEVE YOU DO COLONEL KREUTZ.
DO YOU REALIZE THAT I AM BEING ASKED TO RAISE AN ARMY WHEN WE CAN BARELY AFFORD TO SEW NEW UNIFORMS?
AND I AM EXPECTED TO CREATE A BATTLE PLAN TO CONQUER ALL OF EUROPE WITH RUSTY CANNONS PULLED BY DONKEYS!
YES, I...
GENTLEMEN!
PLEASE ALLOW THE COLONEL TO MAKE HIS REPORT!
THANK YOU, GENERAL.
I KNOW I HAVE ASKED FOR YOUR PATIENCE IN THIS OPERATION, AND I PROMISE YOU, IT WILL BE WELL REWARDED.
GENTLEMEN, IT MAY APPEAR THAT WE ARE LIVING IN GERMANY'S DARKEST HOUR. BUT WE ARE, IN FACT, ON THE BRINK OF OUR GREATEST TRIUMPH.

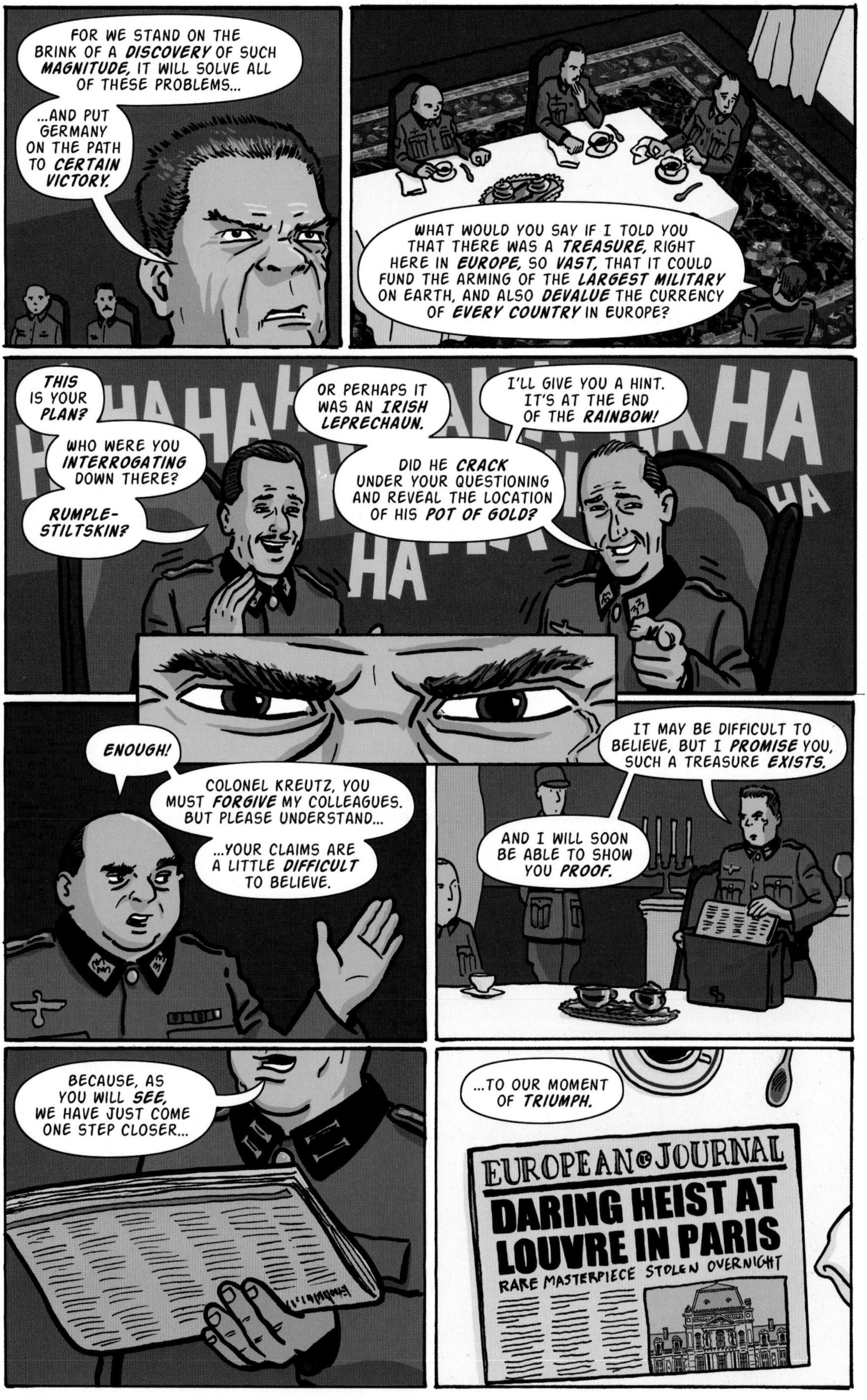
FOR WE STAND ON THE BRINK OF A DISCOVERY OF SUCH MAGNITUDE, IT WILL SOLVE ALL OF THESE PROBLEMS...
...AND PUT GERMANY ON THE PATH TO CERTAIN VICTORY.
WHAT WOULD YOU SAY IF I TOLD YOU THAT THERE WAS A TREASURE, RIGHT HERE IN EUROPE, SO VAST, THAT IT COULD FUND THE ARMING OF THE LARGEST MILITARY ON EARTH, AND ALSO DEVALUE THE CURRENCY OF EVERY COUNTRY IN EUROPE?
HAHAHAHAHA
THIS IS YOUR PLAN?
WHO WERE YOU INTERROGATING DOWN THERE?
RUMPLE-STILTSKIN?
OR PERHAPS IT WAS AN IRISH LEPRECHAUN.
DID HE CRACK UNDER YOUR QUESTIONING AND REVEAL THE LOCATION OF HIS POT OF GOLD?
I'LL GIVE YOU A HINT. IT'S AT THE END OF THE RAINBOW!
HA
HA
ENOUGH!
COLONEL KREUTZ, YOU MUST FORGIVE MY COLLEAGUES. BUT PLEASE UNDERSTAND...
...YOUR CLAIMS ARE A LITTLE DIFFICULT TO BELIEVE.
IT MAY BE DIFFICULT TO BELIEVE, BUT I PROMISE YOU, SUCH A TREASURE EXISTS.
AND I WILL SOON BE ABLE TO SHOW YOU PROOF.
BECAUSE, AS YOU WILL SEE, WE HAVE JUST COME ONE STEP CLOSER...
...TO OUR MOMENT OF TRIUMPH.
EUROPEAN JOURNAL
DARING HEIST AT LOUVRE IN PARIS
RARE MASTERPIECE STOLEN OVERNIGHT

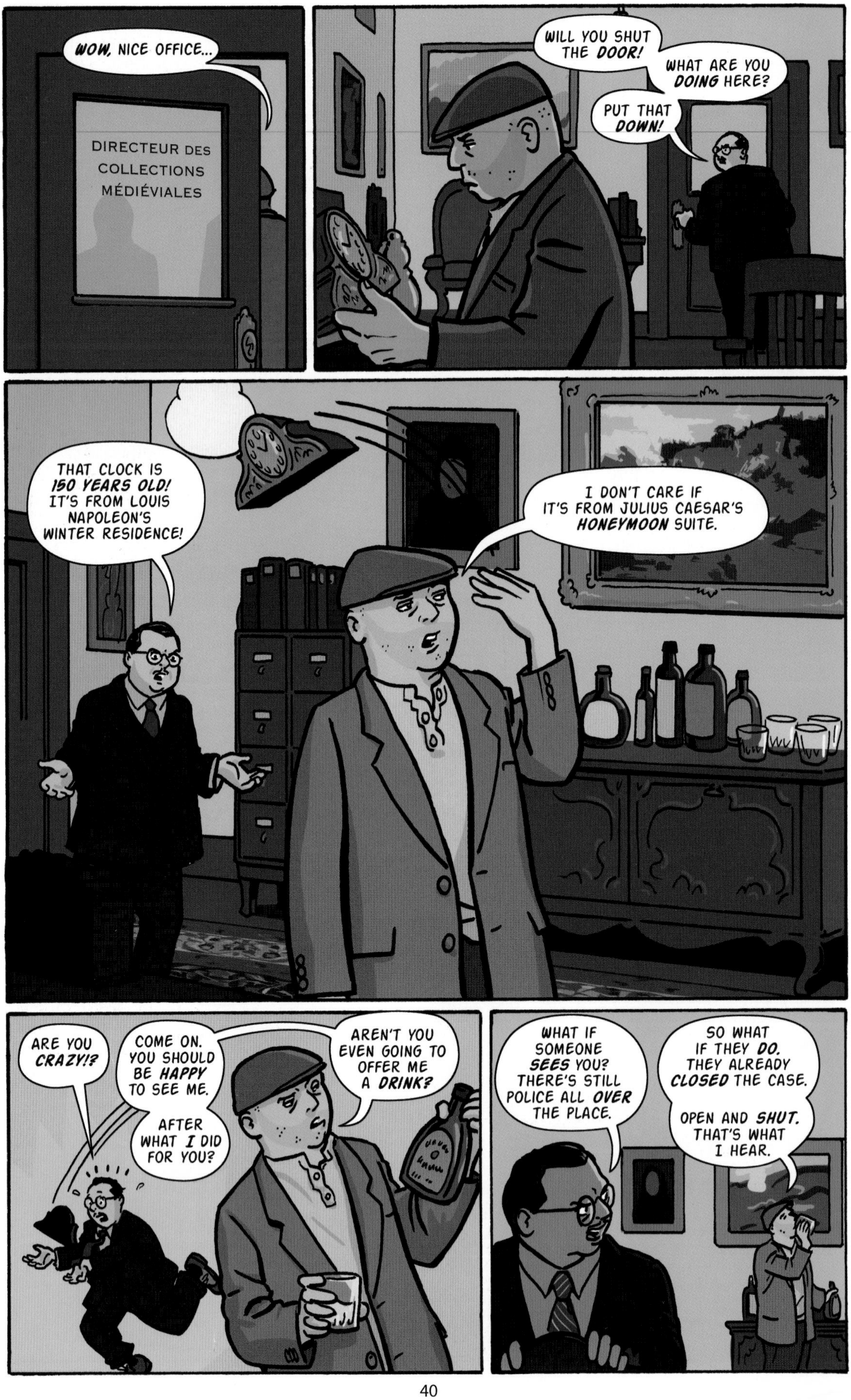

WOW, NICE OFFICE...
DIRECTEUR DES COLLECTIONS MÉDIÉVIALES
WILL YOU SHUT THE DOOR!
WHAT ARE YOU DOING HERE?
PUT THAT DOWN!
THAT CLOCK IS 150 YEARS OLD! IT'S FROM LOUIS NAPOLEON'S WINTER RESIDENCE!
I DON'T CARE IF IT'S FROM JULIUS CAESAR'S HONEYMOON SUITE.
ARE YOU CRAZY!?
COME ON. YOU SHOULD BE HAPPY TO SEE ME.
AFTER WHAT I DID FOR YOU?
AREN'T YOU EVEN GOING TO OFFER ME A DRINK?
WHAT IF SOMEONE SEES YOU? THERE'S STILL POLICE ALL OVER THE PLACE.
SO WHAT IF THEY DO. THEY ALREADY CLOSED THE CASE.
OPEN AND SHUT. THAT'S WHAT I HEAR.

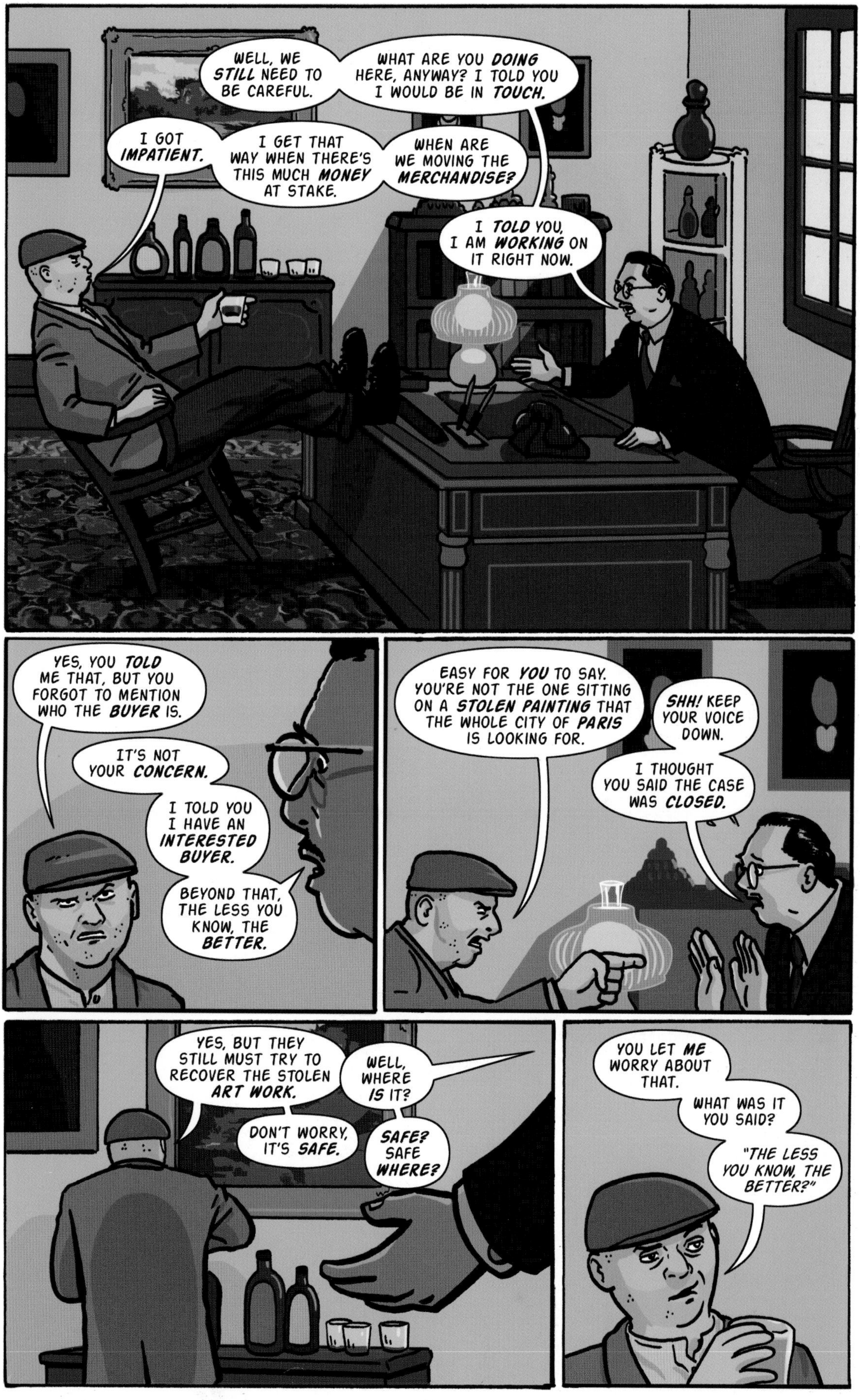

WELL, WE STILL NEED TO BE CAREFUL.
WHAT ARE YOU DOING HERE, ANYWAY? I TOLD YOU I WOULD BE IN TOUCH.
I GOT IMPATIENT.
I GET THAT WAY WHEN THERE'S THIS MUCH MONEY AT STAKE.
WHEN ARE WE MOVING THE MERCHANDISE?
I TOLD YOU, I AM WORKING ON IT RIGHT NOW.
YES, YOU TOLD ME THAT, BUT YOU FORGOT TO MENTION WHO THE BUYER IS.
IT'S NOT YOUR CONCERN.
I TOLD YOU I HAVE AN INTERESTED BUYER.
BEYOND THAT, THE LESS YOU KNOW, THE BETTER.
EASY FOR YOU TO SAY. YOU'RE NOT THE ONE SITTING ON A STOLEN PAINTING THAT THE WHOLE CITY OF PARIS IS LOOKING FOR.
SHH! KEEP YOUR VOICE DOWN.
I THOUGHT YOU SAID THE CASE WAS CLOSED.
YES, BUT THEY STILL MUST TRY TO RECOVER THE STOLEN ART WORK.
DON'T WORRY, IT'S SAFE.
WELL, WHERE IS IT?
SAFE? SAFE WHERE?
YOU LET ME WORRY ABOUT THAT.
WHAT WAS IT YOU SAID?
"THE LESS YOU KNOW, THE BETTER?"

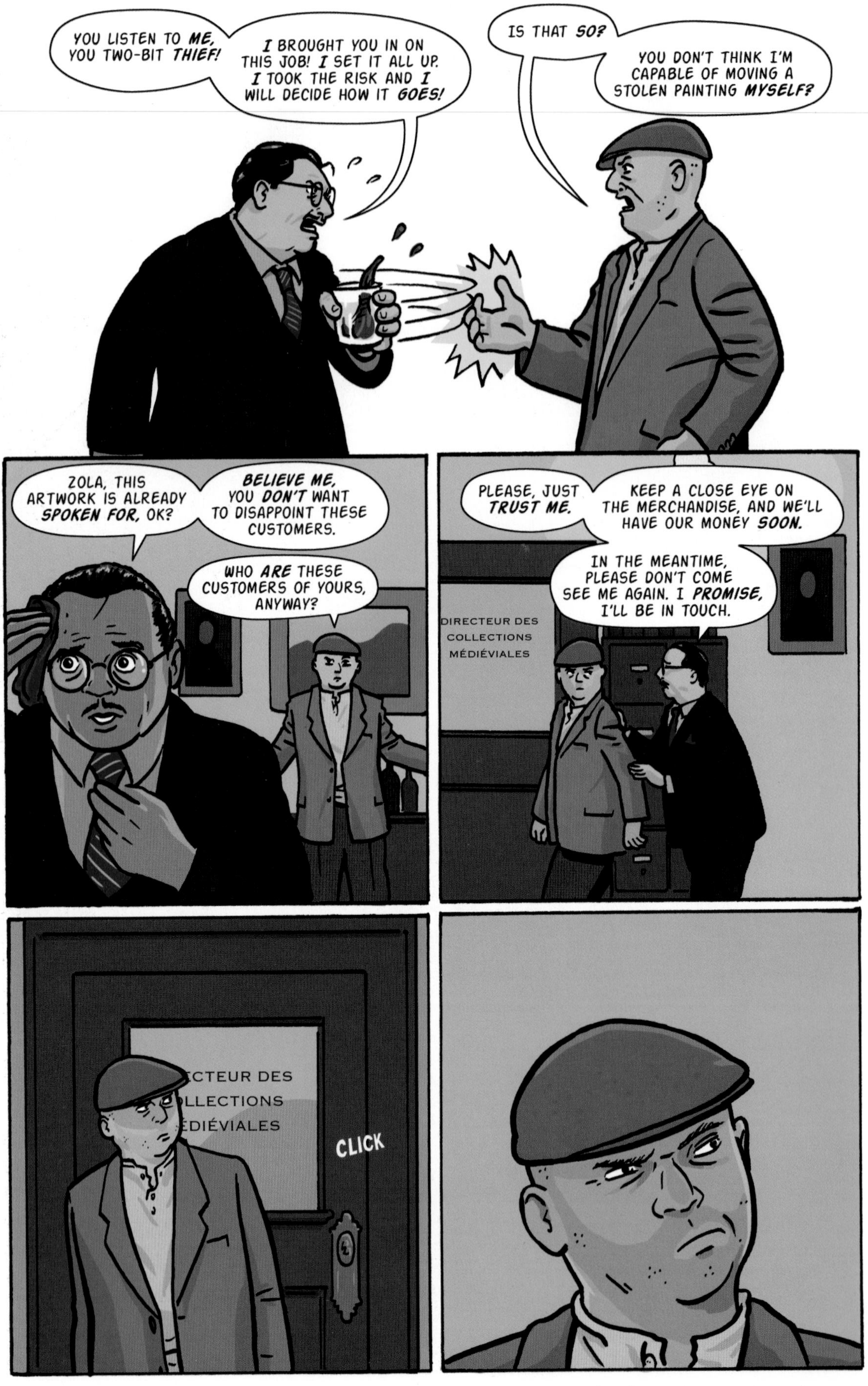
YOU LISTEN TO ME, YOU TWO-BIT THIEF!
I BROUGHT YOU IN ON THIS JOB! I SET IT ALL UP. I TOOK THE RISK AND I WILL DECIDE HOW IT GOES!
IS THAT SO?
YOU DON'T THINK I'M CAPABLE OF MOVING A STOLEN PAINTING MYSELF?
ZOLA, THIS ARTWORK IS ALREADY SPOKEN FOR, OK?
BELIEVE ME, YOU DON'T WANT TO DISAPPOINT THESE CUSTOMERS.
WHO ARE THESE CUSTOMERS OF YOURS, ANYWAY?
PLEASE, JUST TRUST ME.
KEEP A CLOSE EYE ON THE MERCHANDISE, AND WE'LL HAVE OUR MONEY SOON.
IN THE MEANTIME, PLEASE DON'T COME SEE ME AGAIN. I PROMISE, I'LL BE IN TOUCH.
DIRECTEUR DES COLLECTIONS MÉDIÉVIALES
CLICK

CHAPTER THREE

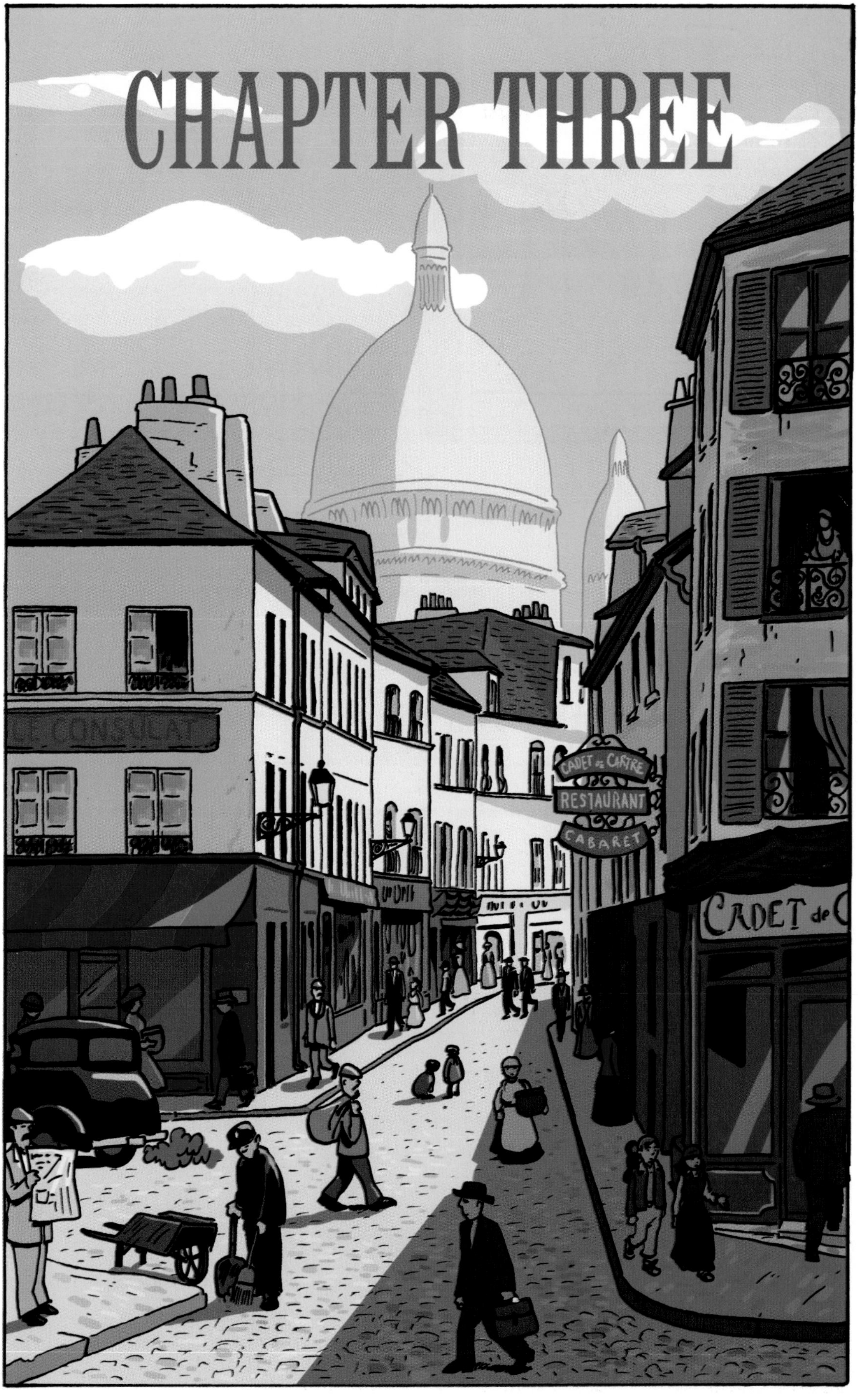
LE CONSULAT
CADET de CARTRE
RESTAURANT
CABARET
CADET de C

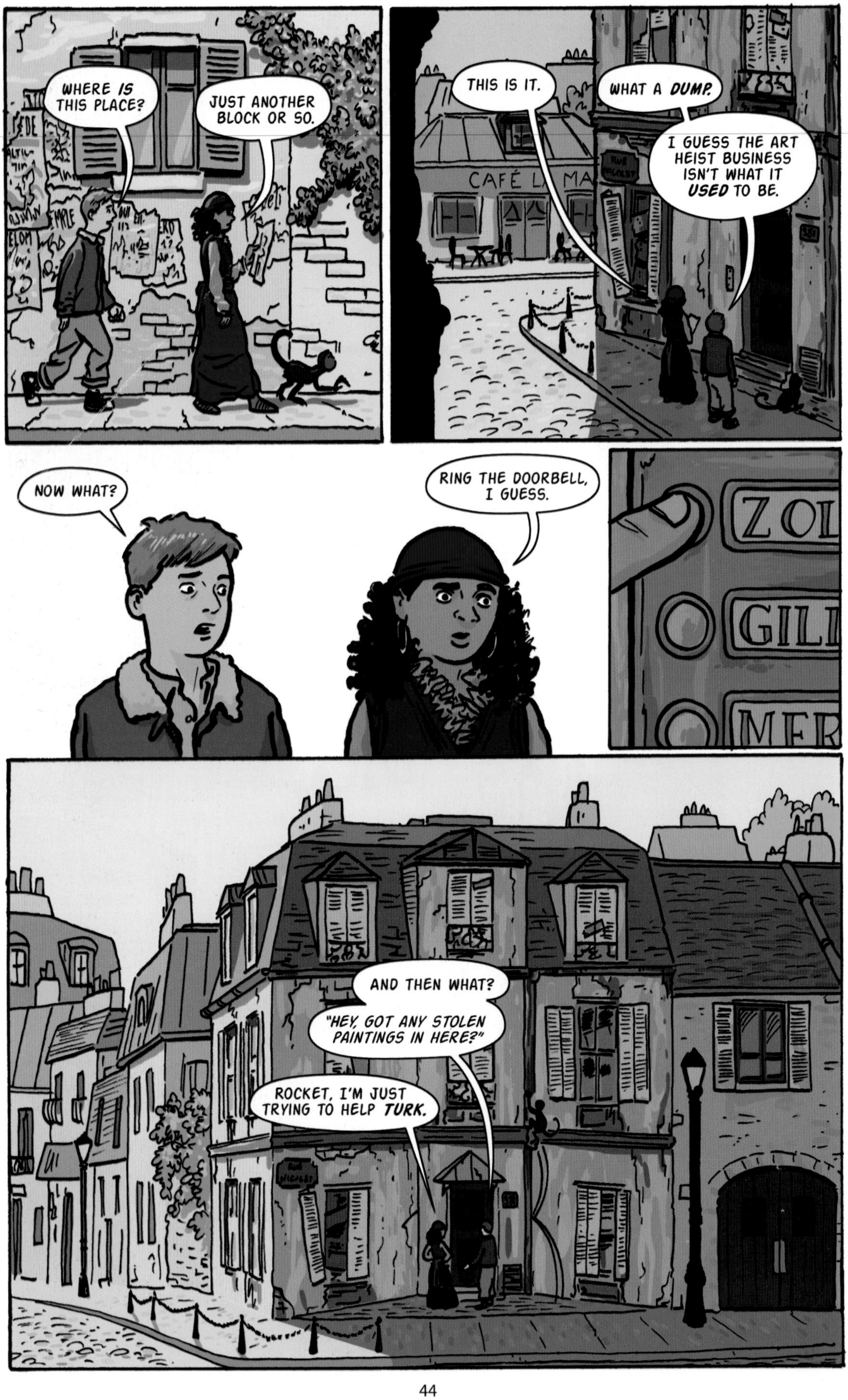
WHERE IS THIS PLACE?
JUST ANOTHER BLOCK OR SO.
THIS IS IT.
WHAT A DUMP.
I GUESS THE ART HEIST BUSINESS ISN'T WHAT IT USED TO BE.
CAFÉ LA MA
NOW WHAT?
RING THE DOORBELL, I GUESS.
ZOL
GIL
MER
AND THEN WHAT?
"HEY, GOT ANY STOLEN PAINTINGS IN HERE?"
ROCKET, I'M JUST TRYING TO HELP TURK.

I KNOW, I KNOW.

IT'S JUST OCCURRING TO ME THAT MAYBE WE SHOULD HAVE *PLANNED IN ADVANCE* A LITTLE.

PLANNED IN *ADVANCE?*

LIKE WHEN WE TOOK A RAFT DOWN THE *CURSED RIVER* IN CAIRO? *THAT* KIND OF PLANNED IN ADVANCE?

THAT WAS *DIFFERENT.* WE DIDN'T HAVE TIME TO MAKE A PLAN...

WE DON'T HAVE TIME *NOW,* EITHER. TURK IS *COUNTING* ON US!

IT DOESN'T MAKE ANY DIFFERENCE.

I DON'T THINK ANYBODY'S *HOME.*

ALL RIGHT. SO LET'S GO TO THAT CAFÉ OVER THERE, HAVE A COUPLE OF *CROISSANTS* AND MAKE A *PLAN...*

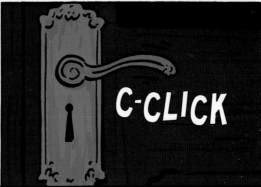

C-CLICK

SQUEEEAAK

SCRICK!

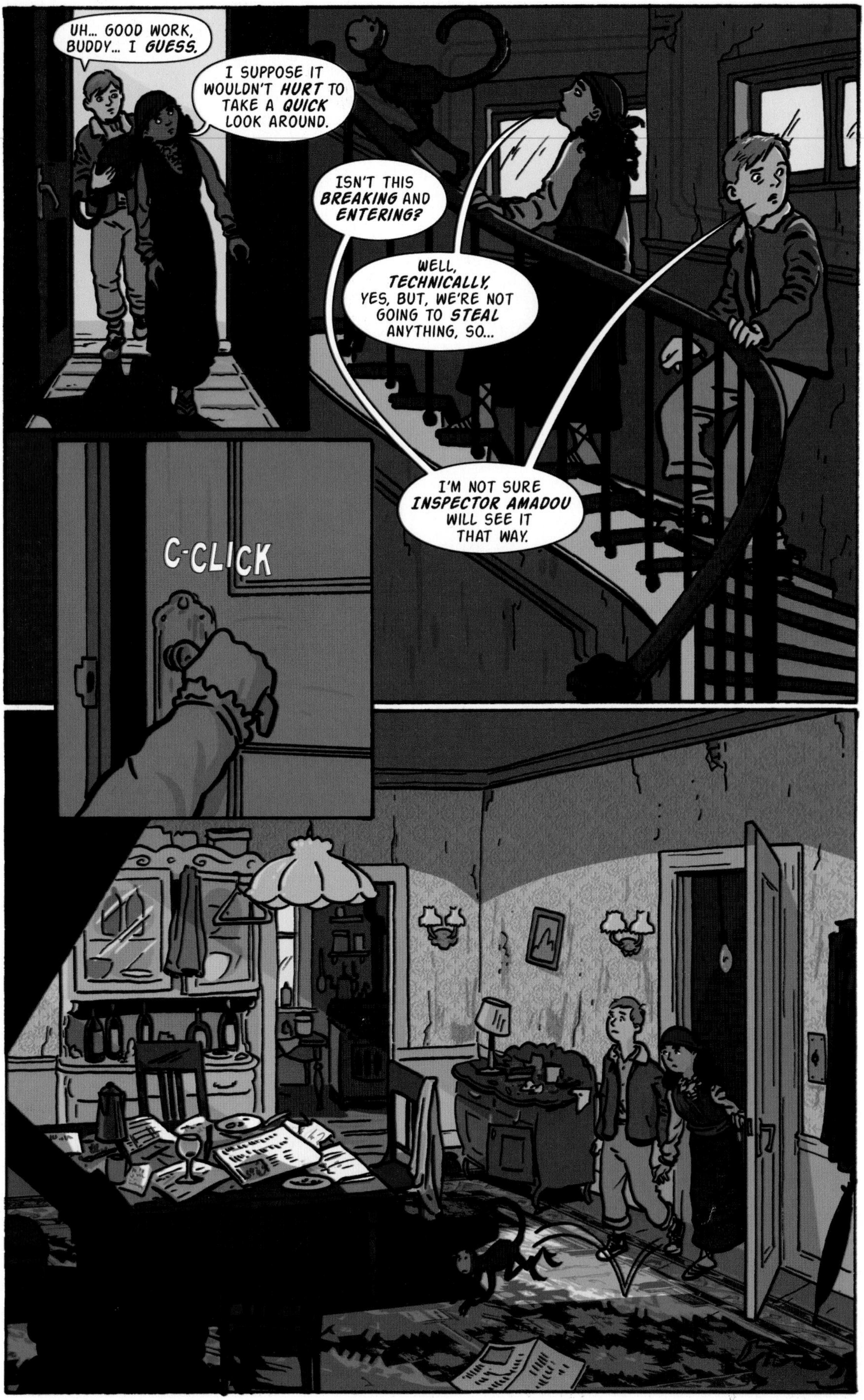
UH... GOOD WORK, BUDDY... I GUESS.
I SUPPOSE IT WOULDN'T HURT TO TAKE A QUICK LOOK AROUND.
ISN'T THIS BREAKING AND ENTERING?
WELL, TECHNICALLY, YES, BUT, WE'RE NOT GOING TO STEAL ANYTHING, SO...
I'M NOT SURE INSPECTOR AMADOU WILL SEE IT THAT WAY.
C-CLICK

UGGHH.

WHOEVER THIS GUY IS, HE'S NOT REALLY INTO *HOUSEKEEPING.*

IF HE *DIDN'T* DO THE ROBBERY, HE CERTAINLY IS *INTERESTED* IN IT...

Le Monde

LE VOL D'ART À LOUVRE

LA POLICE RECHERCHE CHEF D'OEUVLE DESPAPU

Le Figaro

LOUVRE RECHERC...

HUH?

NURI, LOOK AT *THIS.*

PAR PARIS (LYON)

ARR TOURS

3E CLASSE MAI 17 10:30

10:30 TRAIN TO *TOURS.*

MAY 17. THAT'S *TOMORROW.*

SCREECH! SCREECH!

WHAT *IS* IT BUDDY?

SCRICK! SCRICK!

UH OH. YOU THINK THAT'S *HIM?*

SCREECH SURE SEEMS TO *THINK* SO, AND I TEND TO *AGREE* WITH HIM.

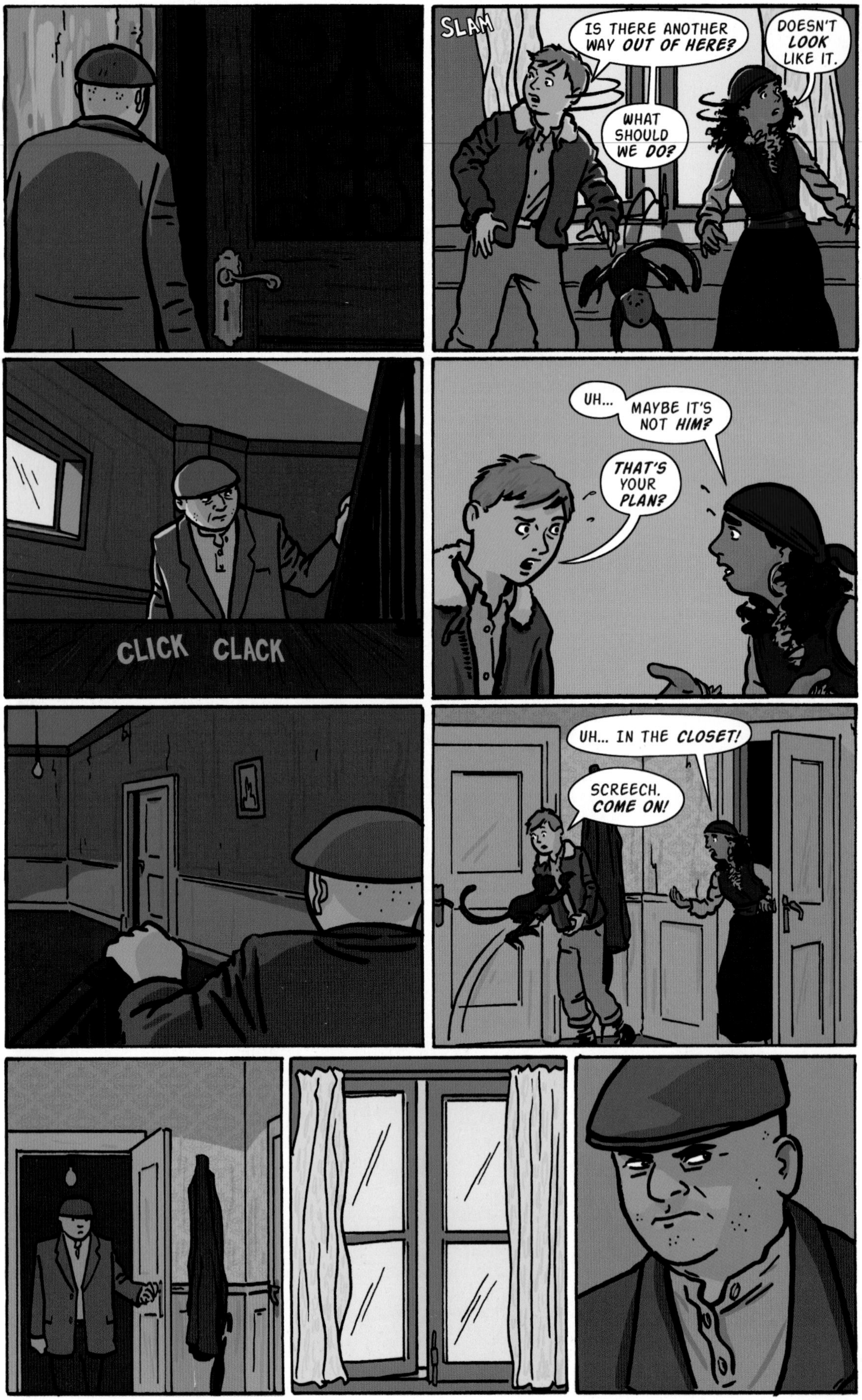
SLAM
IS THERE ANOTHER WAY OUT OF HERE?
WHAT SHOULD WE DO?
DOESN'T LOOK LIKE IT.
CLICK CLACK
UH...
MAYBE IT'S NOT HIM?
THAT'S YOUR PLAN?
UH... IN THE CLOSET!
SCREECH. COME ON!

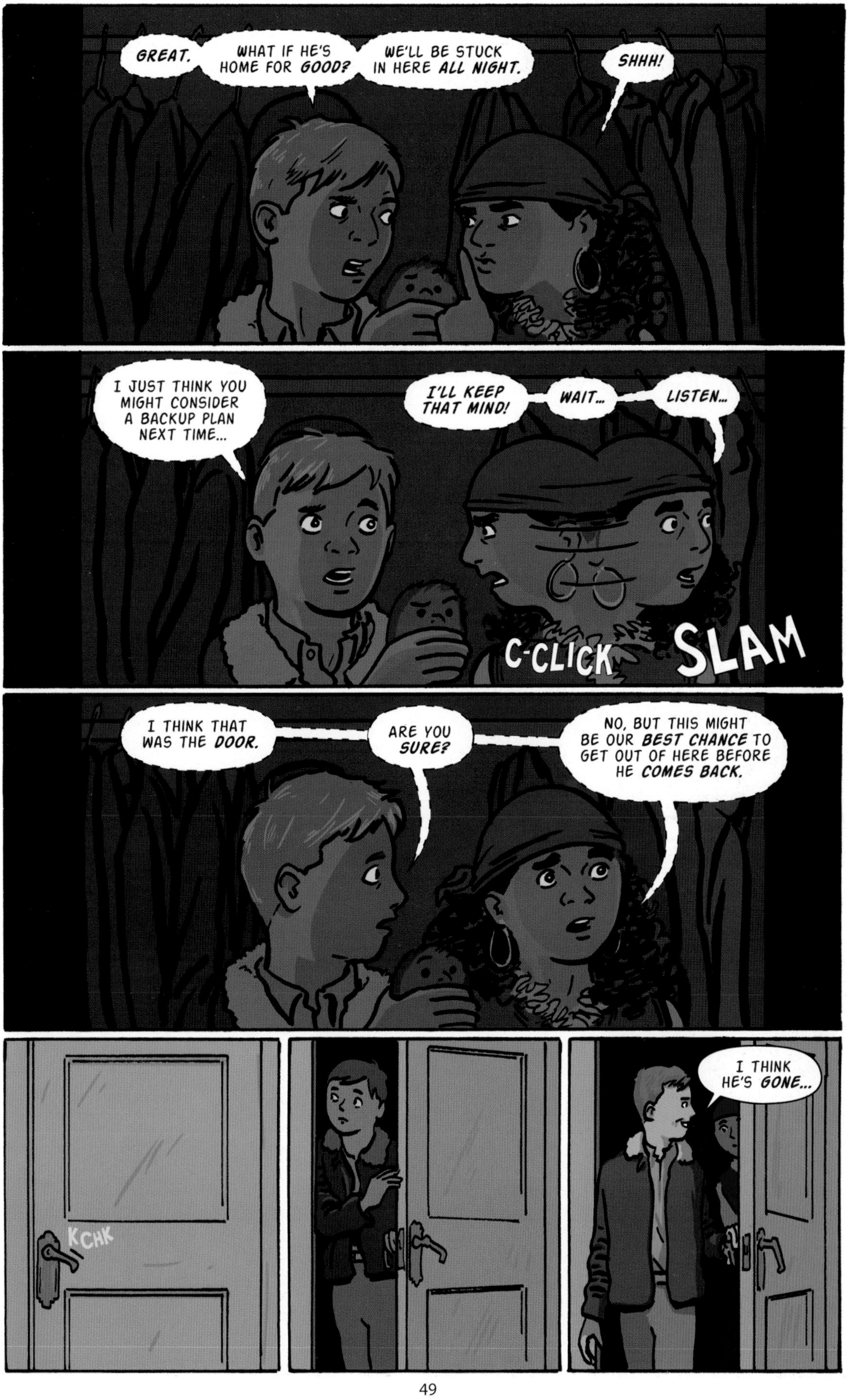
GREAT.
WHAT IF HE'S HOME FOR GOOD?
WE'LL BE STUCK IN HERE ALL NIGHT.
SHHH!
I JUST THINK YOU MIGHT CONSIDER A BACKUP PLAN NEXT TIME...
I'LL KEEP THAT MIND!
WAIT...
LISTEN...
C-CLICK
SLAM
I THINK THAT WAS THE DOOR.
ARE YOU SURE?
NO, BUT THIS MIGHT BE OUR BEST CHANCE TO GET OUT OF HERE BEFORE HE COMES BACK.
KCHK
I THINK HE'S GONE...

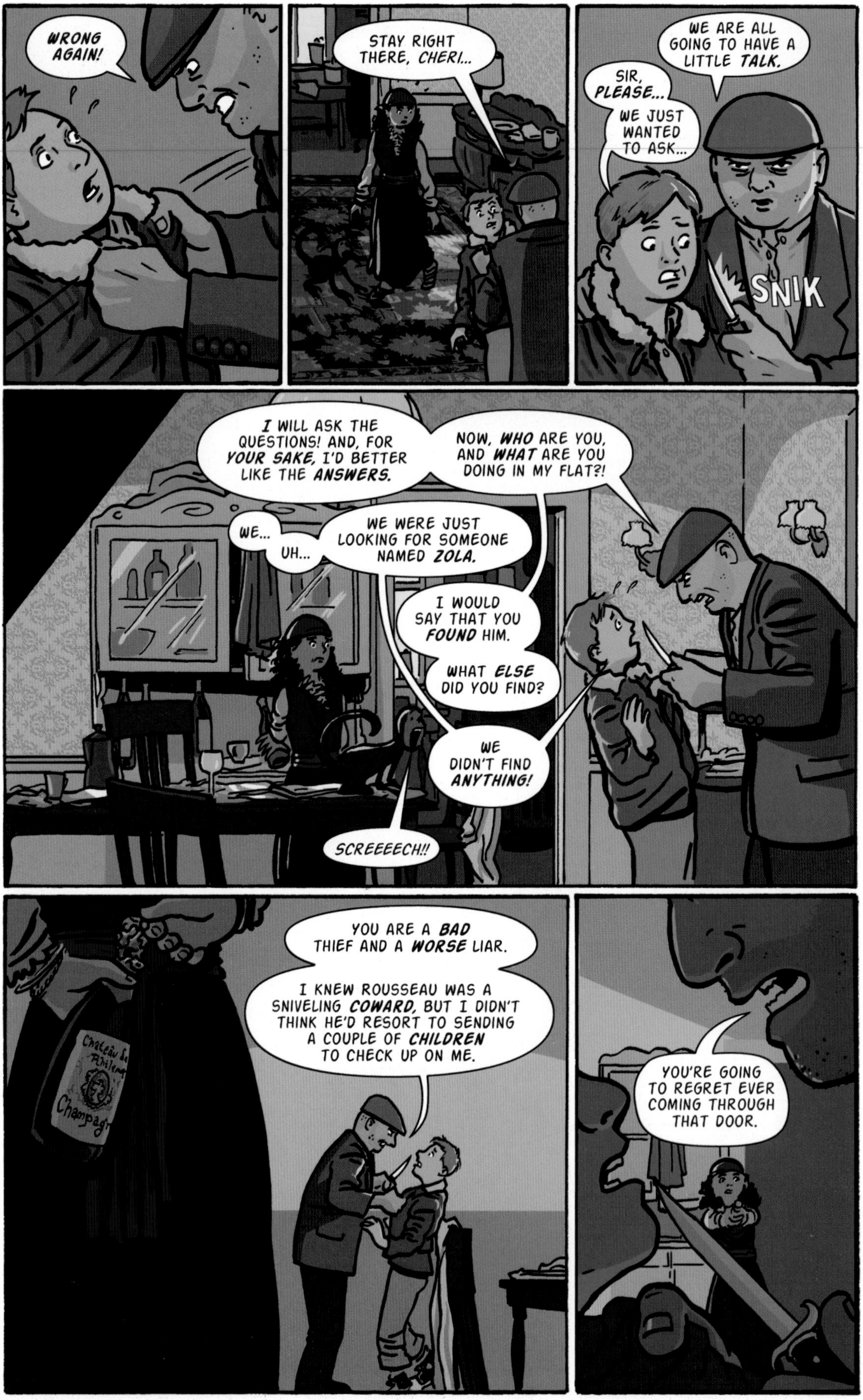
WRONG AGAIN!
STAY RIGHT THERE, CHERI...
SIR, PLEASE...
WE ARE ALL GOING TO HAVE A LITTLE TALK.
WE JUST WANTED TO ASK...
SNIK
I WILL ASK THE QUESTIONS! AND, FOR YOUR SAKE, I'D BETTER LIKE THE ANSWERS.
NOW, WHO ARE YOU, AND WHAT ARE YOU DOING IN MY FLAT?!
WE...
UH...
WE WERE JUST LOOKING FOR SOMEONE NAMED ZOLA.
I WOULD SAY THAT YOU FOUND HIM.
WHAT ELSE DID YOU FIND?
WE DIDN'T FIND ANYTHING!
SCREEEECH!!
YOU ARE A BAD THIEF AND A WORSE LIAR.
I KNEW ROUSSEAU WAS A SNIVELING COWARD, BUT I DIDN'T THINK HE'D RESORT TO SENDING A COUPLE OF CHILDREN TO CHECK UP ON ME.
YOU'RE GOING TO REGRET EVER COMING THROUGH THAT DOOR.

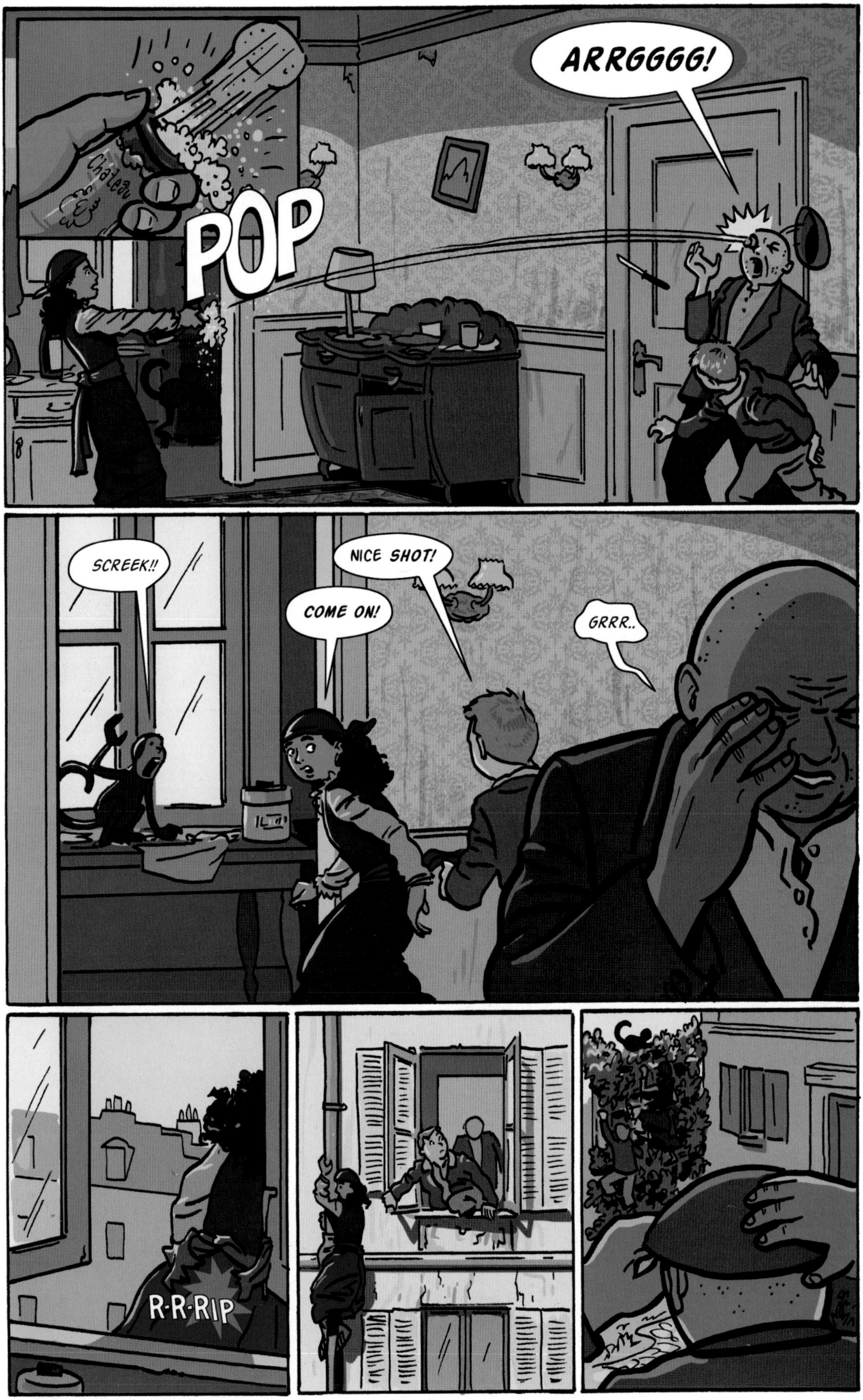
POP
ARRGGGG!
SCREEK!!
NICE SHOT!
COME ON!
GRRR..
R-R-RIP

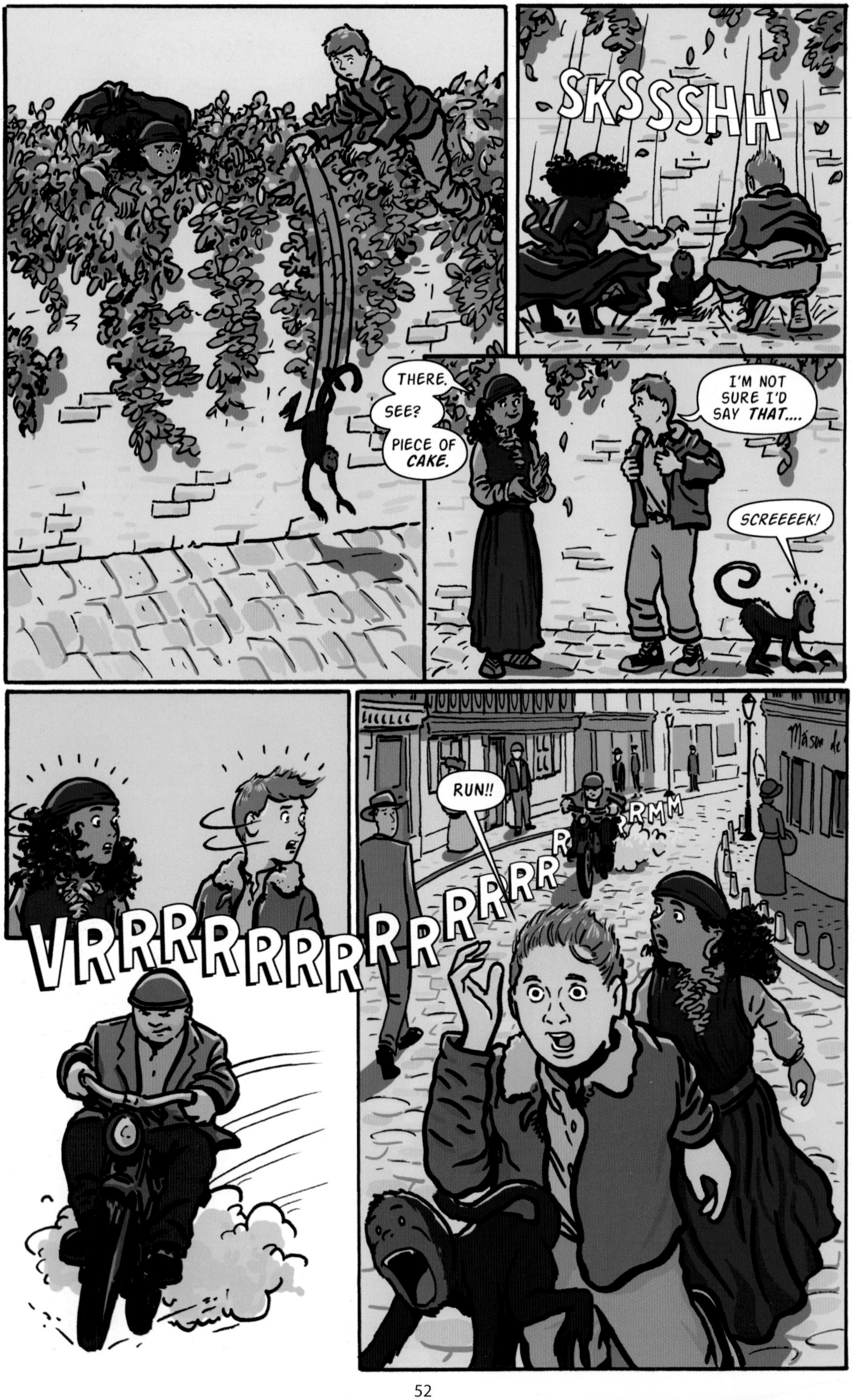
SKSSSHH
THERE.
SEE?
PIECE OF CAKE.
I'M NOT SURE I'D SAY THAT....
SCREEEEK!
VRRRRRRRRRRRRRRRMM
RUN!!

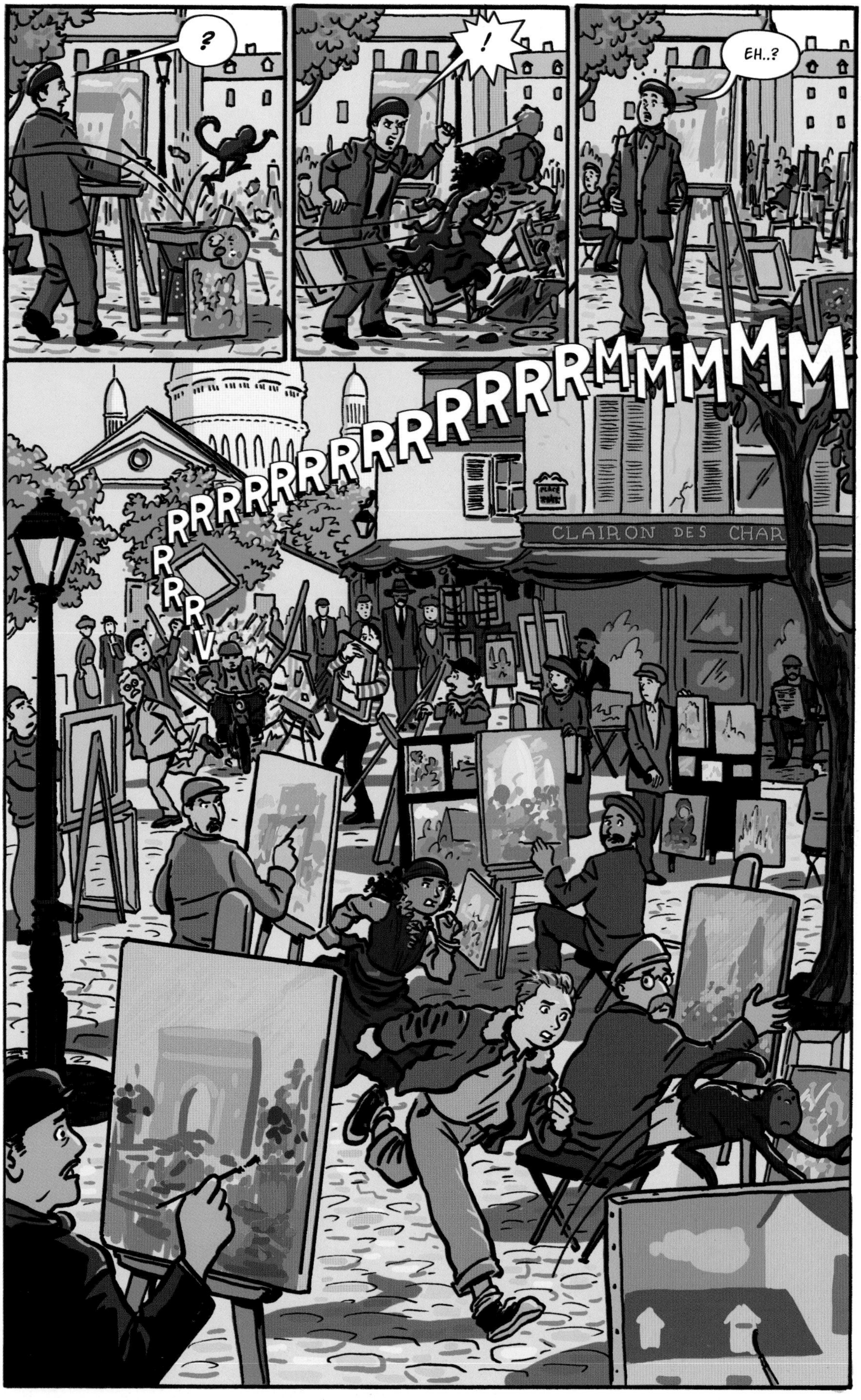
?
!
EH..?
VRRRRRRRRRRRRRRRRMMMMM
CLAIRON DES CHAR

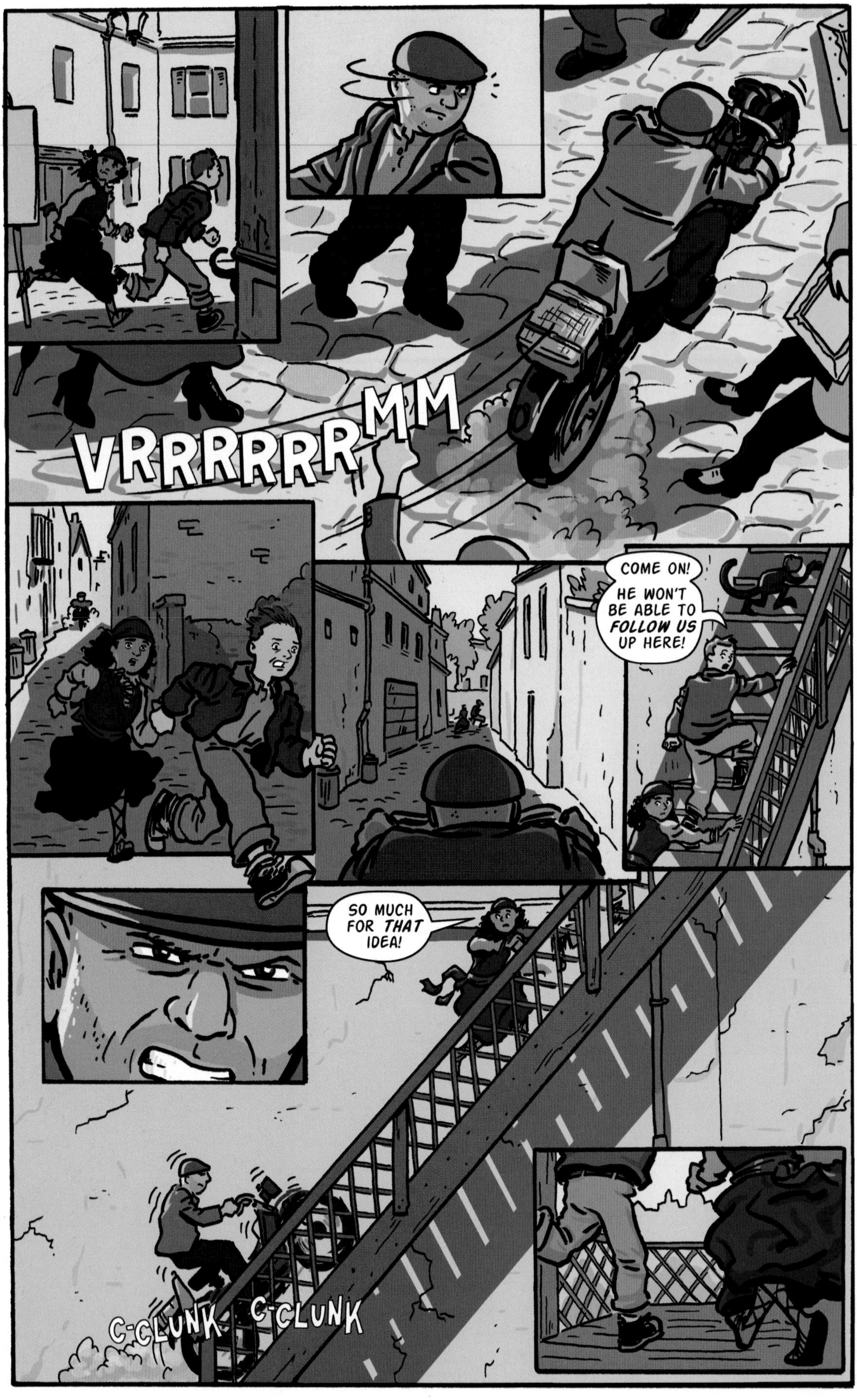
VRRRRRRMM
COME ON! HE WON'T BE ABLE TO FOLLOW US UP HERE!
SO MUCH FOR THAT IDEA!
C-CLUNK C-CLUNK

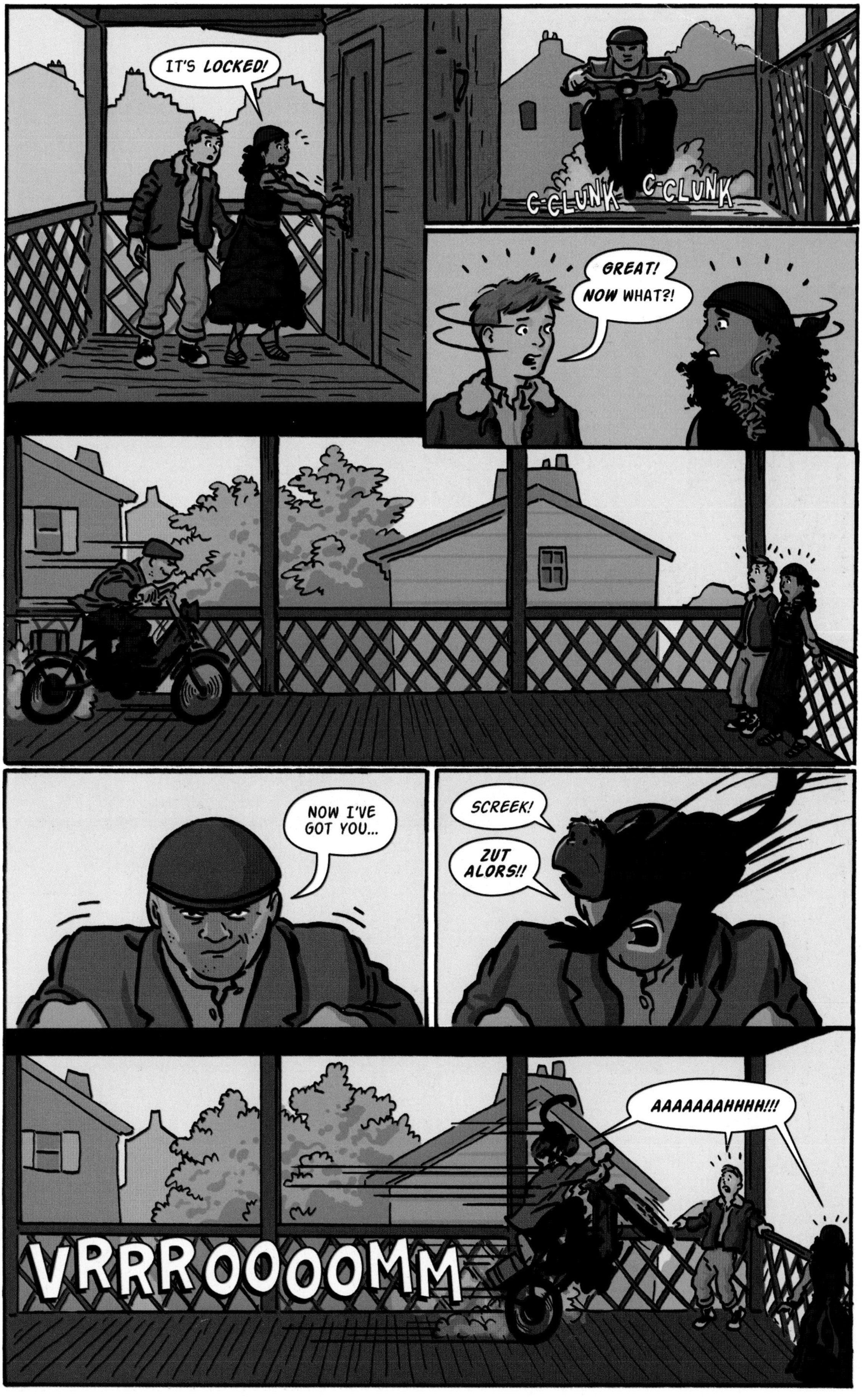
IT'S LOCKED!
C-CLUNK C-CLUNK
GREAT! NOW WHAT?!
NOW I'VE GOT YOU...
SCREEK!
ZUT ALORS!!
AAAAAAAHHHH!!!
VRRROOOOMM

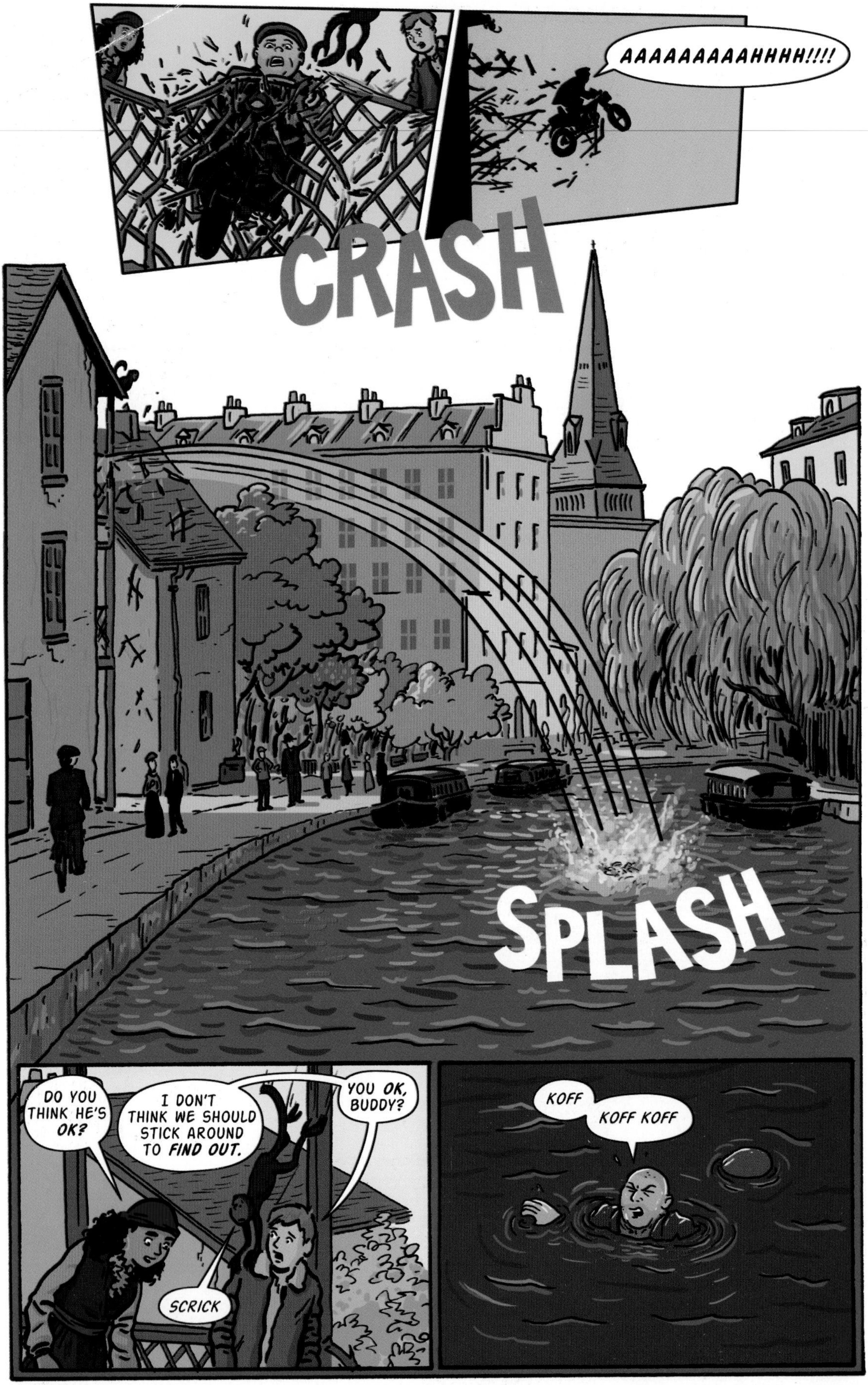
AAAAAAAAAAHHHH!!!!
CRASH
SPLASH
DO YOU THINK HE'S OK?
I DON'T THINK WE SHOULD STICK AROUND TO FIND OUT.
YOU OK, BUDDY?
SCRICK
KOFF
KOFF KOFF

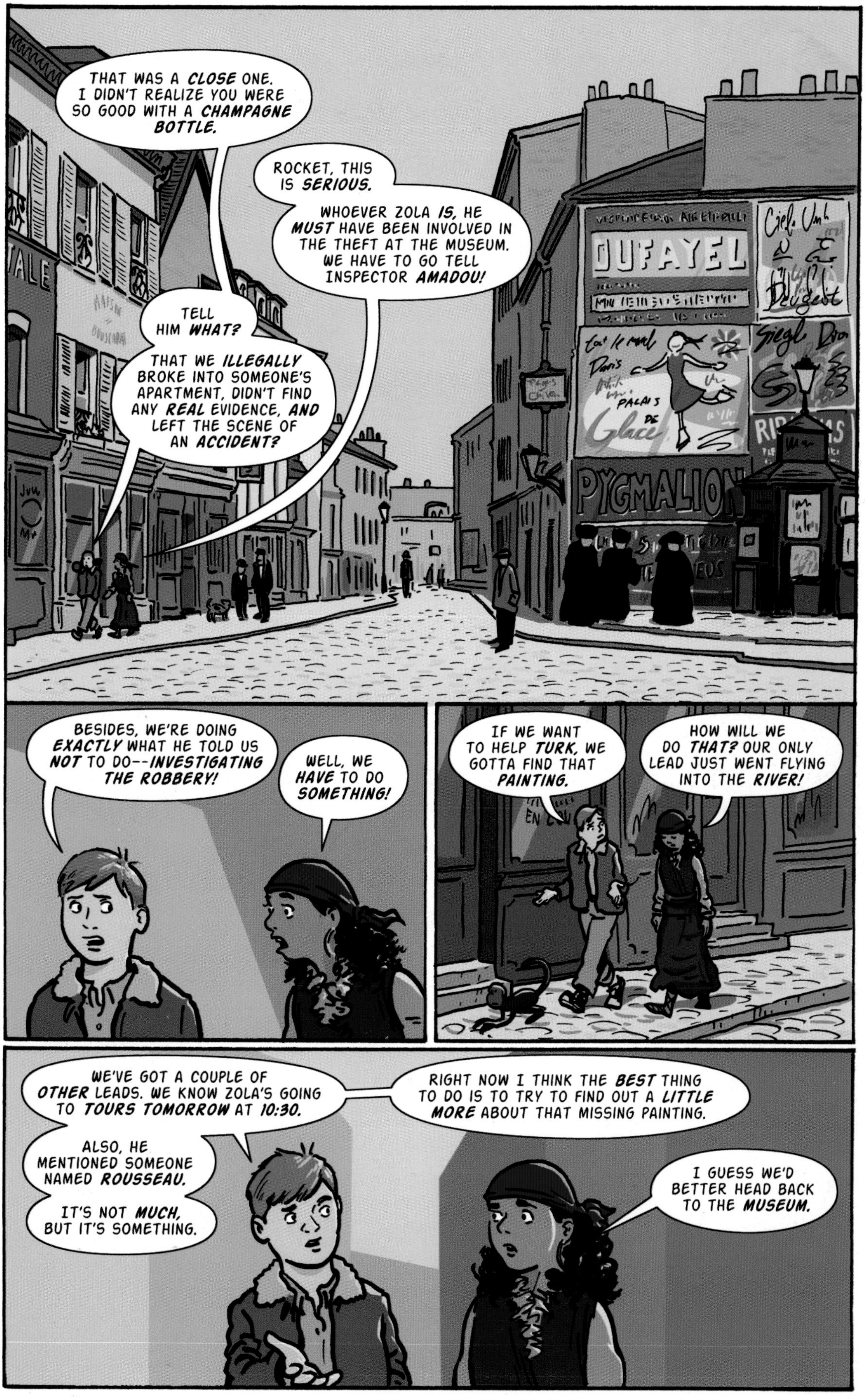
THAT WAS A CLOSE ONE. I DIDN'T REALIZE YOU WERE SO GOOD WITH A CHAMPAGNE BOTTLE.
ROCKET, THIS IS SERIOUS.
WHOEVER ZOLA IS, HE MUST HAVE BEEN INVOLVED IN THE THEFT AT THE MUSEUM. WE HAVE TO GO TELL INSPECTOR AMADOU!
TELL HIM WHAT?
THAT WE ILLEGALLY BROKE INTO SOMEONE'S APARTMENT, DIDN'T FIND ANY REAL EVIDENCE, AND LEFT THE SCENE OF AN ACCIDENT?
DUFAYEL
PYGMALION
BESIDES, WE'RE DOING EXACTLY WHAT HE TOLD US NOT TO DO--INVESTIGATING THE ROBBERY!
WELL, WE HAVE TO DO SOMETHING!
IF WE WANT TO HELP TURK, WE GOTTA FIND THAT PAINTING.
HOW WILL WE DO THAT? OUR ONLY LEAD JUST WENT FLYING INTO THE RIVER!
WE'VE GOT A COUPLE OF OTHER LEADS. WE KNOW ZOLA'S GOING TO TOURS TOMORROW AT 10:30.
ALSO, HE MENTIONED SOMEONE NAMED ROUSSEAU.
IT'S NOT MUCH, BUT IT'S SOMETHING.
RIGHT NOW I THINK THE BEST THING TO DO IS TO TRY TO FIND OUT A LITTLE MORE ABOUT THAT MISSING PAINTING.
I GUESS WE'D BETTER HEAD BACK TO THE MUSEUM.

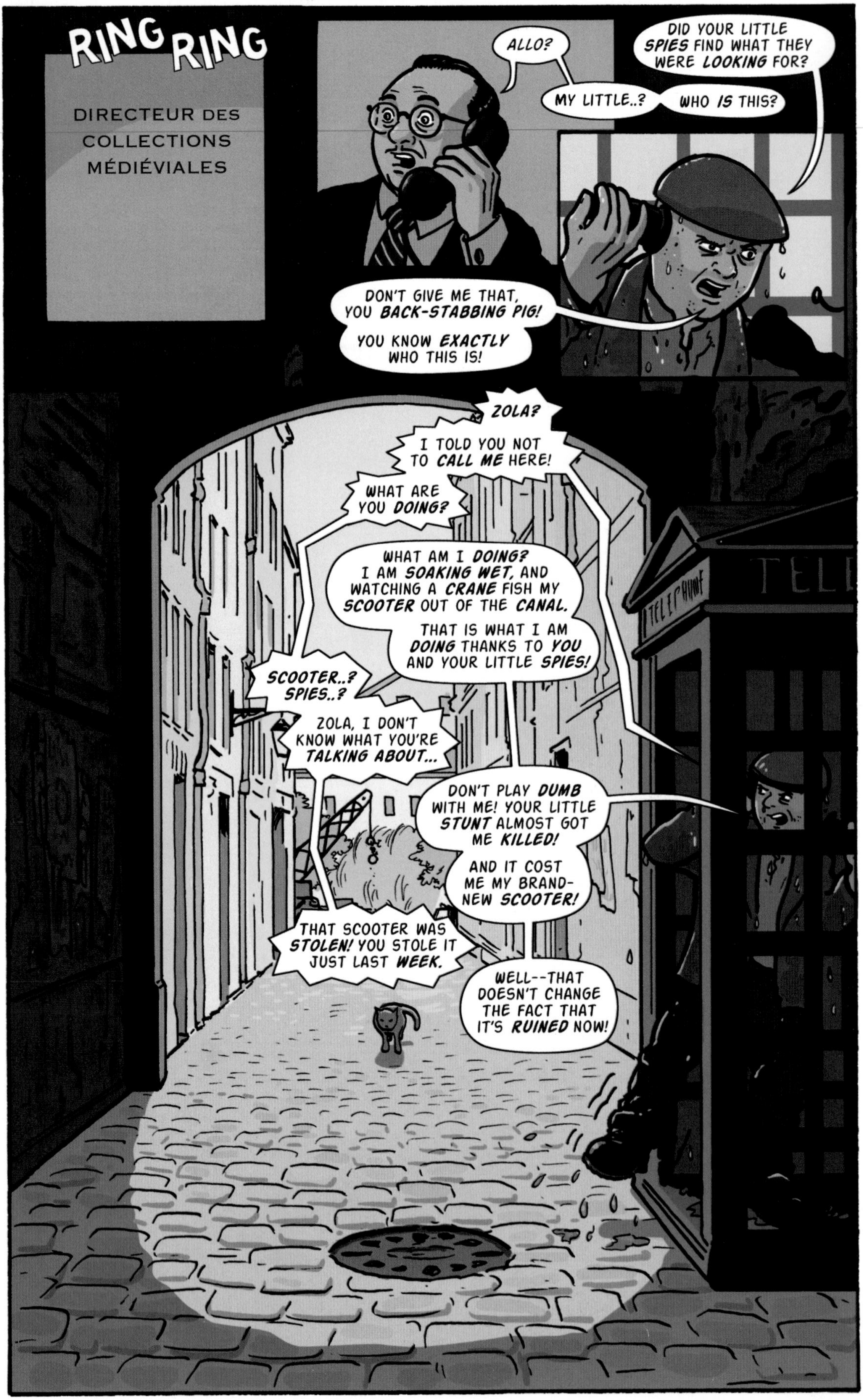
RING RING
DIRECTEUR DES COLLECTIONS MÉDIÉVIALES
ALLO?
DID YOUR LITTLE SPIES FIND WHAT THEY WERE LOOKING FOR?
MY LITTLE..?
WHO IS THIS?
DON'T GIVE ME THAT, YOU BACK-STABBING PIG!
YOU KNOW EXACTLY WHO THIS IS!
ZOLA?
I TOLD YOU NOT TO CALL ME HERE!
WHAT ARE YOU DOING?
WHAT AM I DOING? I AM SOAKING WET, AND WATCHING A CRANE FISH MY SCOOTER OUT OF THE CANAL.
THAT IS WHAT I AM DOING THANKS TO YOU AND YOUR LITTLE SPIES!
SCOOTER..? SPIES..?
ZOLA, I DON'T KNOW WHAT YOU'RE TALKING ABOUT...
DON'T PLAY DUMB WITH ME! YOUR LITTLE STUNT ALMOST GOT ME KILLED!
AND IT COST ME MY BRAND-NEW SCOOTER!
THAT SCOOTER WAS STOLEN! YOU STOLE IT JUST LAST WEEK.
WELL--THAT DOESN'T CHANGE THE FACT THAT IT'S RUINED NOW!

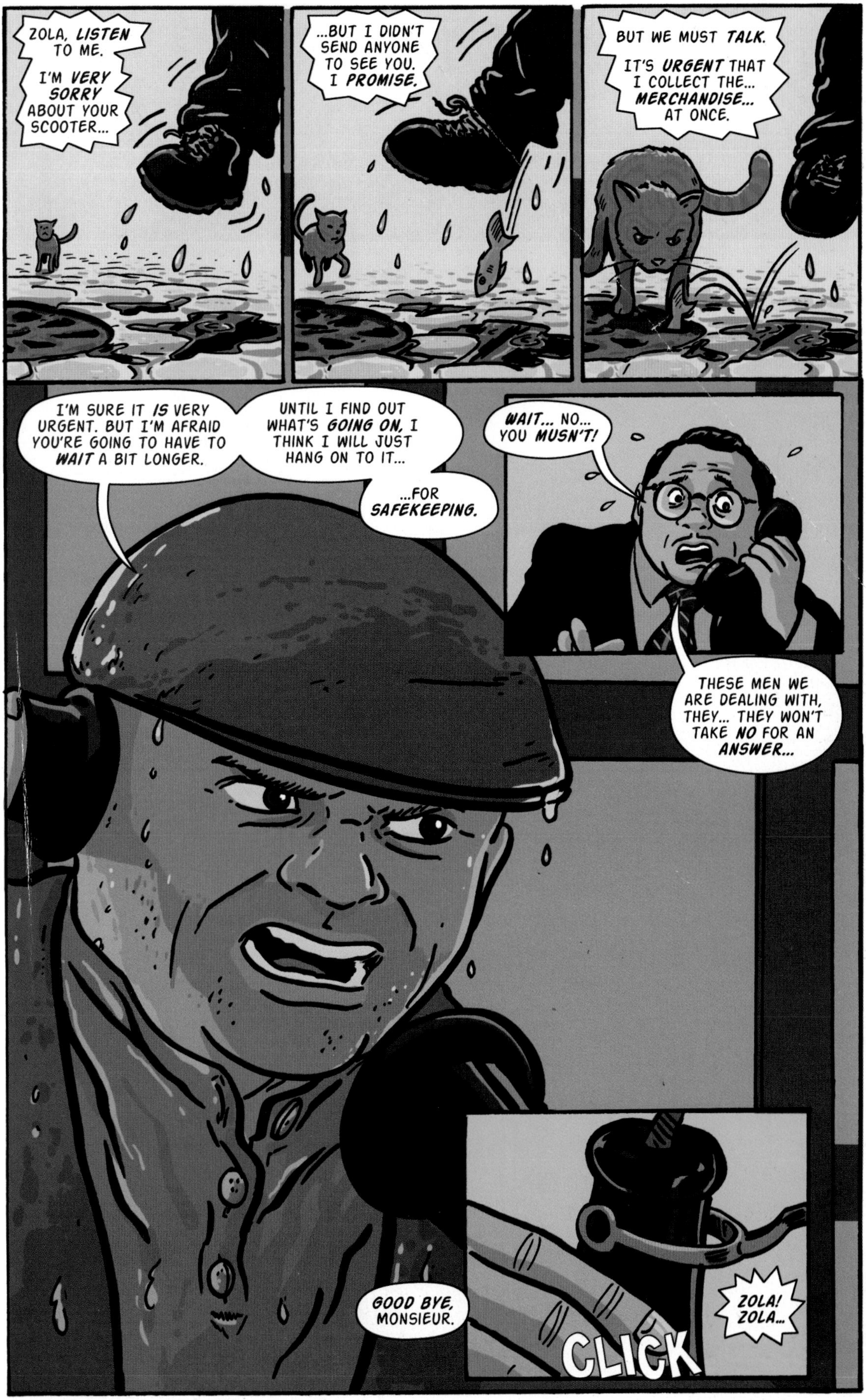
ZOLA, LISTEN TO ME.
I'M VERY SORRY ABOUT YOUR SCOOTER...
...BUT I DIDN'T SEND ANYONE TO SEE YOU. I PROMISE.
BUT WE MUST TALK.
IT'S URGENT THAT I COLLECT THE... MERCHANDISE... AT ONCE.
I'M SURE IT IS VERY URGENT. BUT I'M AFRAID YOU'RE GOING TO HAVE TO WAIT A BIT LONGER.
UNTIL I FIND OUT WHAT'S GOING ON, I THINK I WILL JUST HANG ON TO IT...
...FOR SAFEKEEPING.
WAIT... NO... YOU MUSN'T!
THESE MEN WE ARE DEALING WITH, THEY... THEY WON'T TAKE NO FOR AN ANSWER...
GOOD BYE, MONSIEUR.
ZOLA! ZOLA...
CLICK

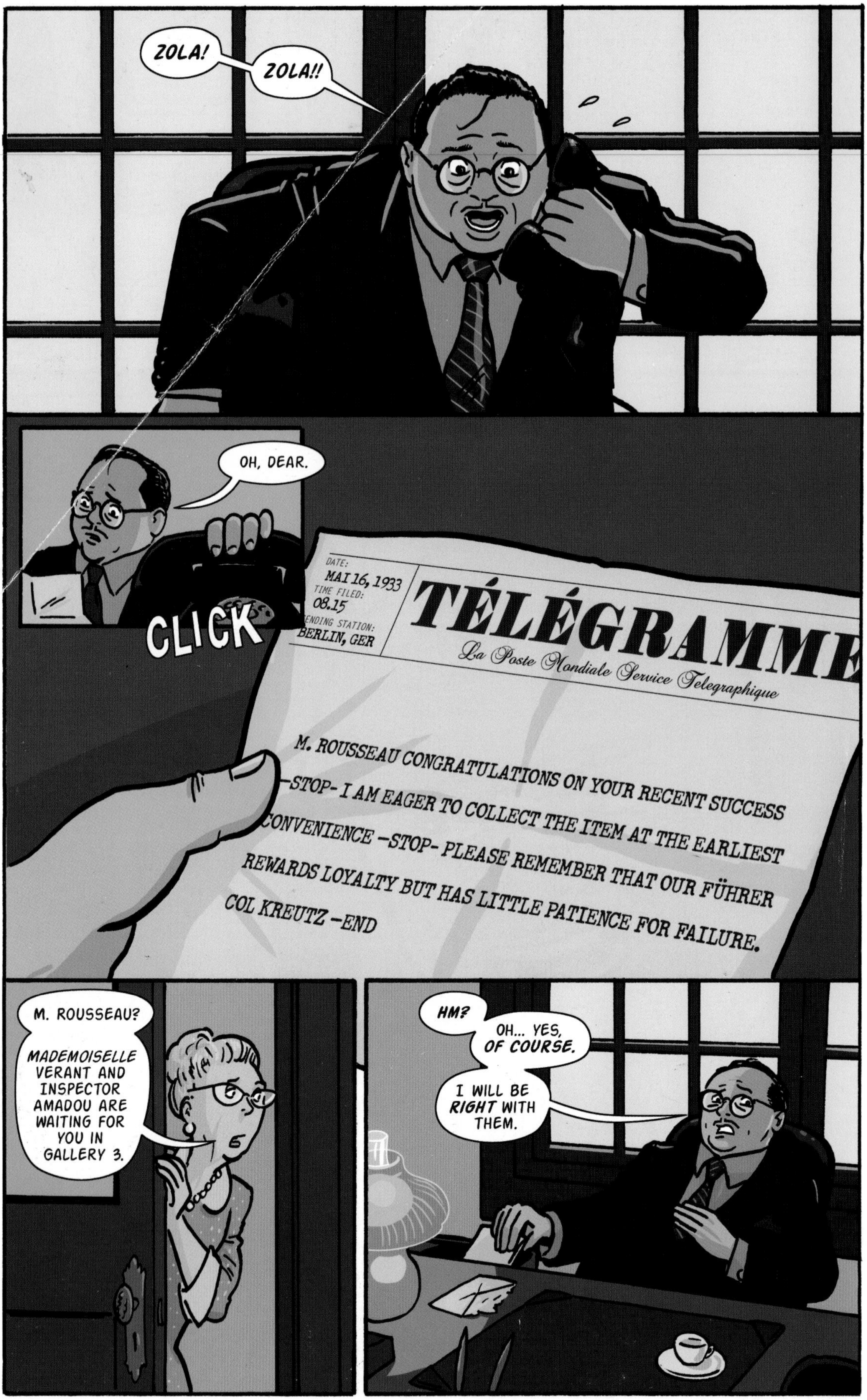
ZOLA!
ZOLA!!
OH, DEAR.
CLICK
DATE: MAI 16, 1933
TIME FILED: 08.15
SENDING STATION: BERLIN, GER
TÉLÉGRAMME
La Poste Mondiale Service Telegraphique
M. ROUSSEAU CONGRATULATIONS ON YOUR RECENT SUCCESS -STOP- I AM EAGER TO COLLECT THE ITEM AT THE EARLIEST CONVENIENCE -STOP- PLEASE REMEMBER THAT OUR FÜHRER REWARDS LOYALTY BUT HAS LITTLE PATIENCE FOR FAILURE. COL KREUTZ -END
M. ROUSSEAU?
MADEMOISELLE VERANT AND INSPECTOR AMADOU ARE WAITING FOR YOU IN GALLERY 3.
HM?
OH... YES, OF COURSE.
I WILL BE RIGHT WITH THEM.

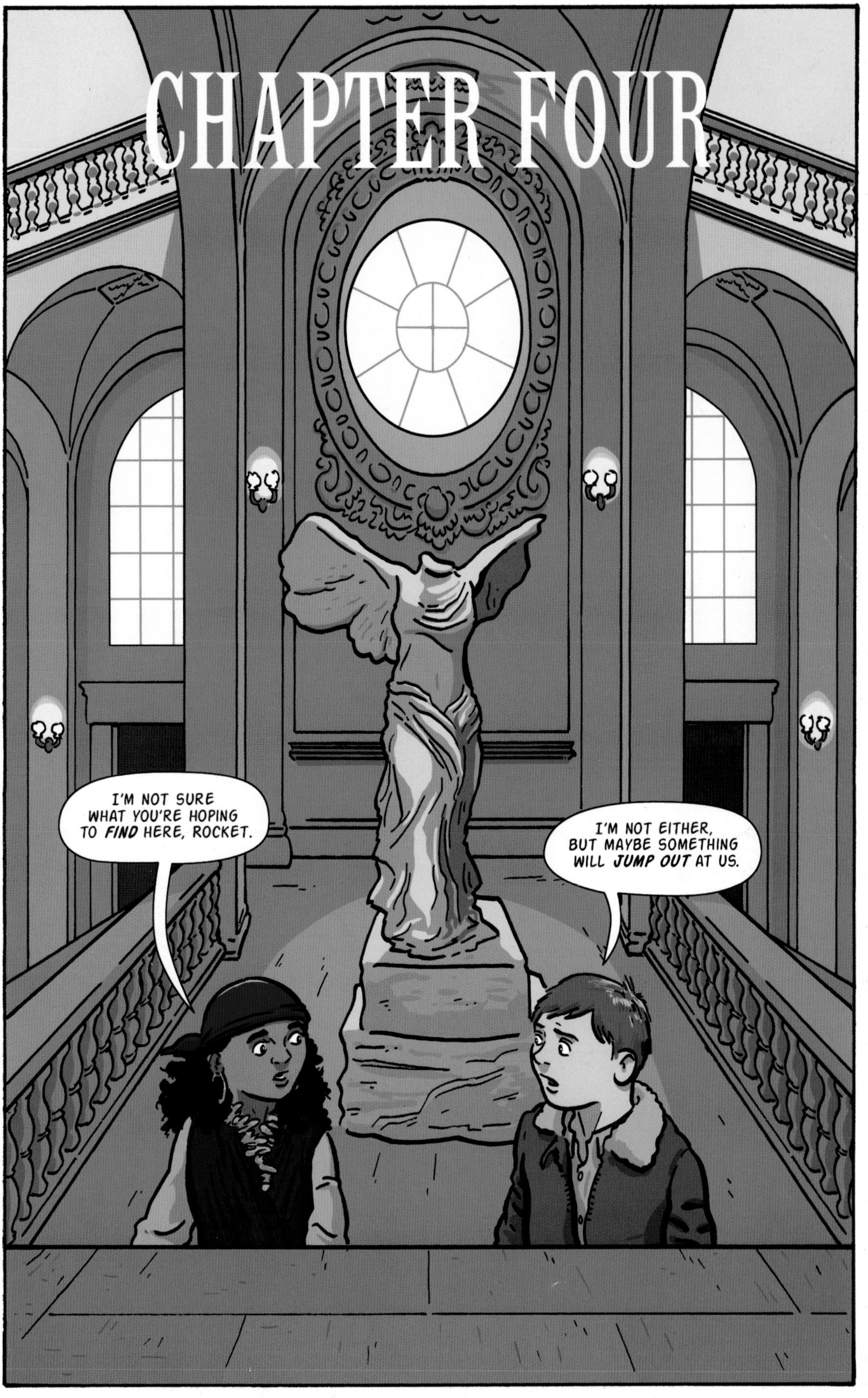
CHAPTER FOUR
I'M NOT SURE WHAT YOU'RE HOPING TO FIND HERE, ROCKET.
I'M NOT EITHER, BUT MAYBE SOMETHING WILL JUMP OUT AT US.

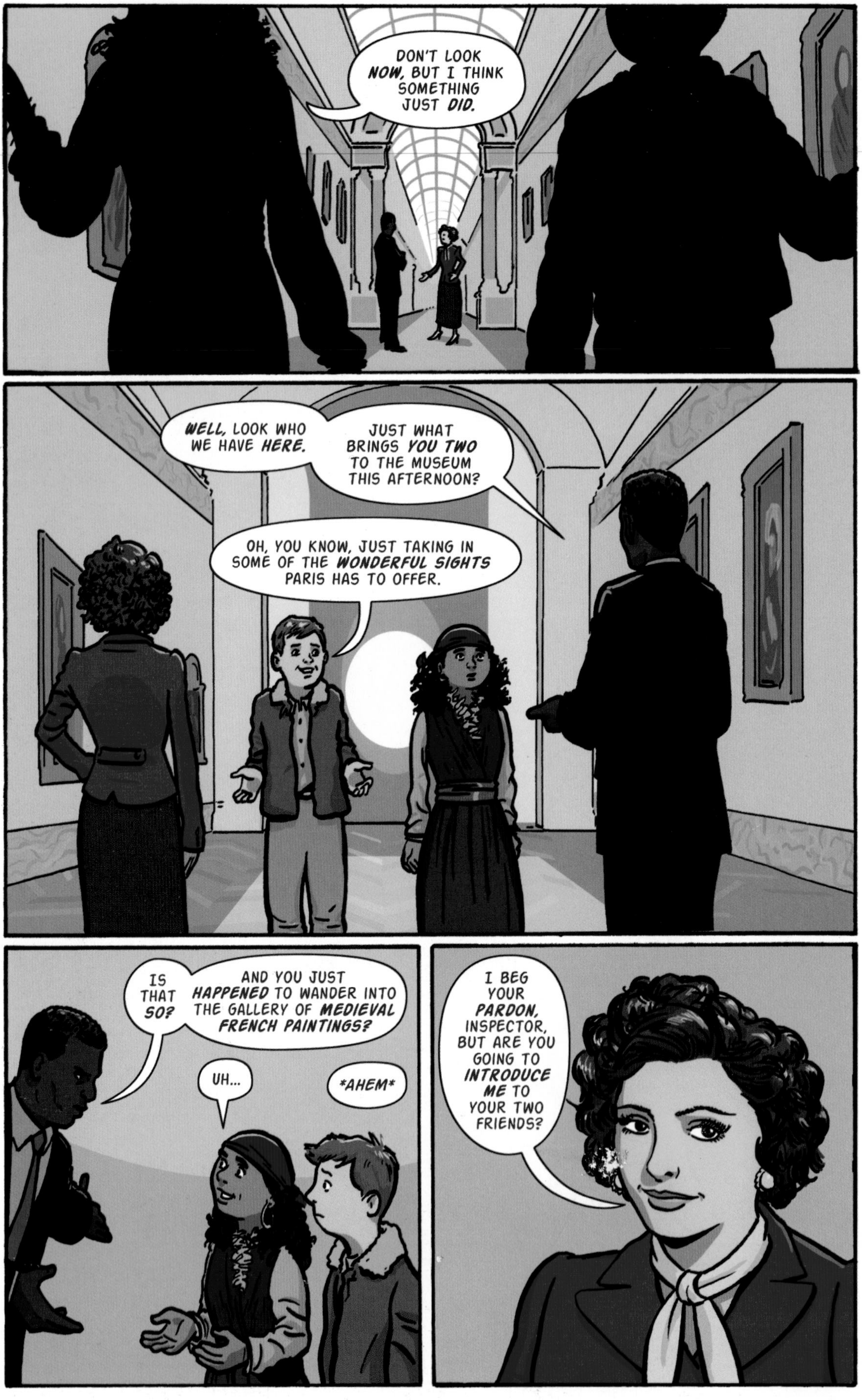
DON'T LOOK NOW, BUT I THINK SOMETHING JUST DID.
WELL, LOOK WHO WE HAVE HERE.
JUST WHAT BRINGS YOU TWO TO THE MUSEUM THIS AFTERNOON?
OH, YOU KNOW, JUST TAKING IN SOME OF THE WONDERFUL SIGHTS PARIS HAS TO OFFER.
IS THAT SO?
AND YOU JUST HAPPENED TO WANDER INTO THE GALLERY OF MEDIEVAL FRENCH PAINTINGS?
UH...
AHEM
I BEG YOUR PARDON, INSPECTOR, BUT ARE YOU GOING TO INTRODUCE ME TO YOUR TWO FRIENDS?

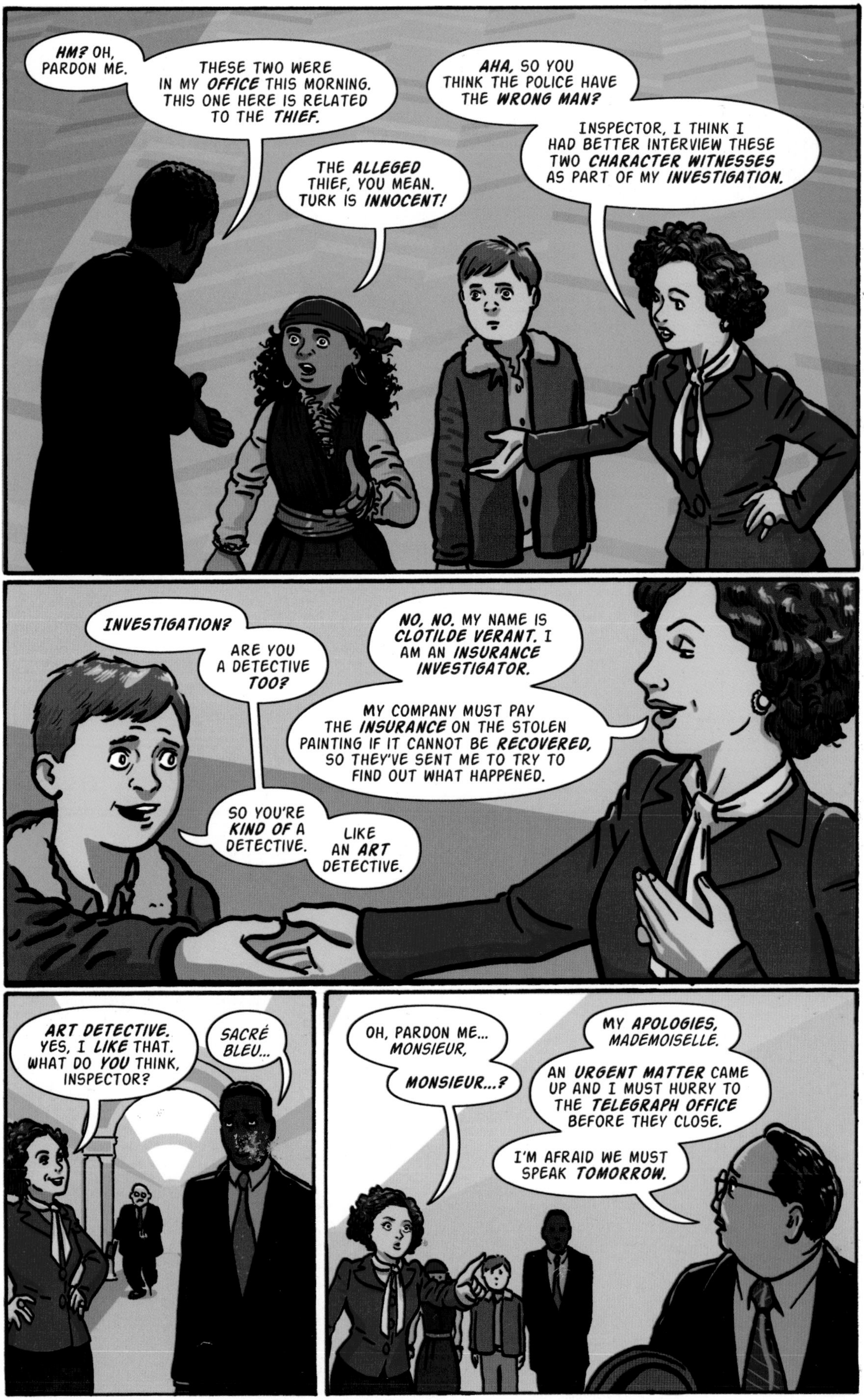
HM? OH, PARDON ME.
THESE TWO WERE IN MY OFFICE THIS MORNING. THIS ONE HERE IS RELATED TO THE THIEF.
THE ALLEGED THIEF, YOU MEAN. TURK IS INNOCENT!
AHA, SO YOU THINK THE POLICE HAVE THE WRONG MAN?
INSPECTOR, I THINK I HAD BETTER INTERVIEW THESE TWO CHARACTER WITNESSES AS PART OF MY INVESTIGATION.
INVESTIGATION?
ARE YOU A DETECTIVE TOO?
NO, NO. MY NAME IS CLOTILDE VERANT. I AM AN INSURANCE INVESTIGATOR.
MY COMPANY MUST PAY THE INSURANCE ON THE STOLEN PAINTING IF IT CANNOT BE RECOVERED, SO THEY'VE SENT ME TO TRY TO FIND OUT WHAT HAPPENED.
SO YOU'RE KIND OF A DETECTIVE.
LIKE AN ART DETECTIVE.
ART DETECTIVE. YES, I LIKE THAT. WHAT DO YOU THINK, INSPECTOR?
SACRÉ BLEU...
OH, PARDON ME... MONSIEUR,
MONSIEUR...?
MY APOLOGIES, MADEMOISELLE.
AN URGENT MATTER CAME UP AND I MUST HURRY TO THE TELEGRAPH OFFICE BEFORE THEY CLOSE.
I'M AFRAID WE MUST SPEAK TOMORROW.

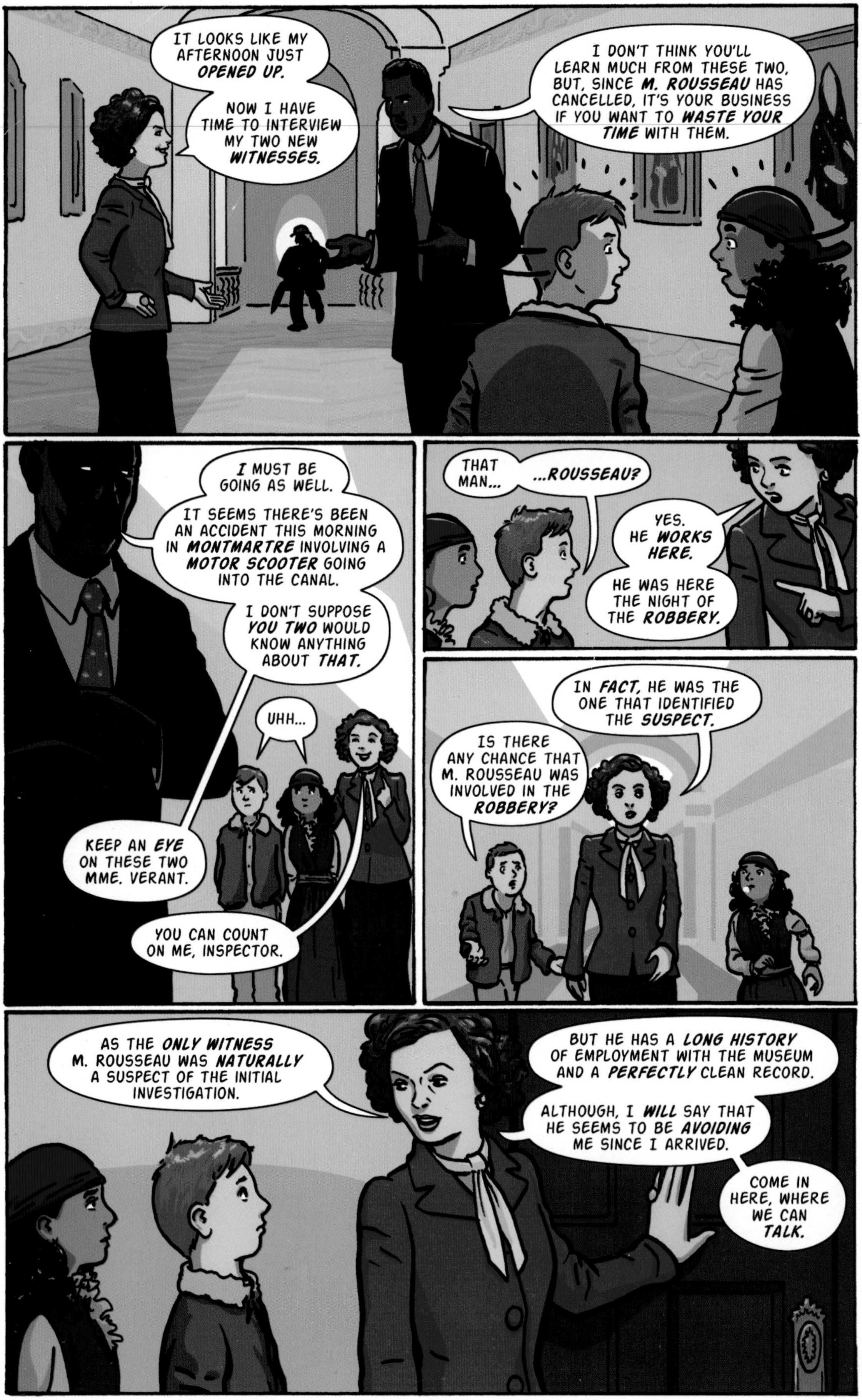
IT LOOKS LIKE MY AFTERNOON JUST OPENED UP.
NOW I HAVE TIME TO INTERVIEW MY TWO NEW WITNESSES.
I DON'T THINK YOU'LL LEARN MUCH FROM THESE TWO, BUT, SINCE M. ROUSSEAU HAS CANCELLED, IT'S YOUR BUSINESS IF YOU WANT TO WASTE YOUR TIME WITH THEM.
I MUST BE GOING AS WELL.
IT SEEMS THERE'S BEEN AN ACCIDENT THIS MORNING IN MONTMARTRE INVOLVING A MOTOR SCOOTER GOING INTO THE CANAL.
I DON'T SUPPOSE YOU TWO WOULD KNOW ANYTHING ABOUT THAT.
UHH...
KEEP AN EYE ON THESE TWO MME. VERANT.
YOU CAN COUNT ON ME, INSPECTOR.
THAT MAN...
...ROUSSEAU?
YES. HE WORKS HERE.
HE WAS HERE THE NIGHT OF THE ROBBERY.
IN FACT, HE WAS THE ONE THAT IDENTIFIED THE SUSPECT.
IS THERE ANY CHANCE THAT M. ROUSSEAU WAS INVOLVED IN THE ROBBERY?
AS THE ONLY WITNESS M. ROUSSEAU WAS NATURALLY A SUSPECT OF THE INITIAL INVESTIGATION.
BUT HE HAS A LONG HISTORY OF EMPLOYMENT WITH THE MUSEUM AND A PERFECTLY CLEAN RECORD.
ALTHOUGH, I WILL SAY THAT HE SEEMS TO BE AVOIDING ME SINCE I ARRIVED.
COME IN HERE, WHERE WE CAN TALK.

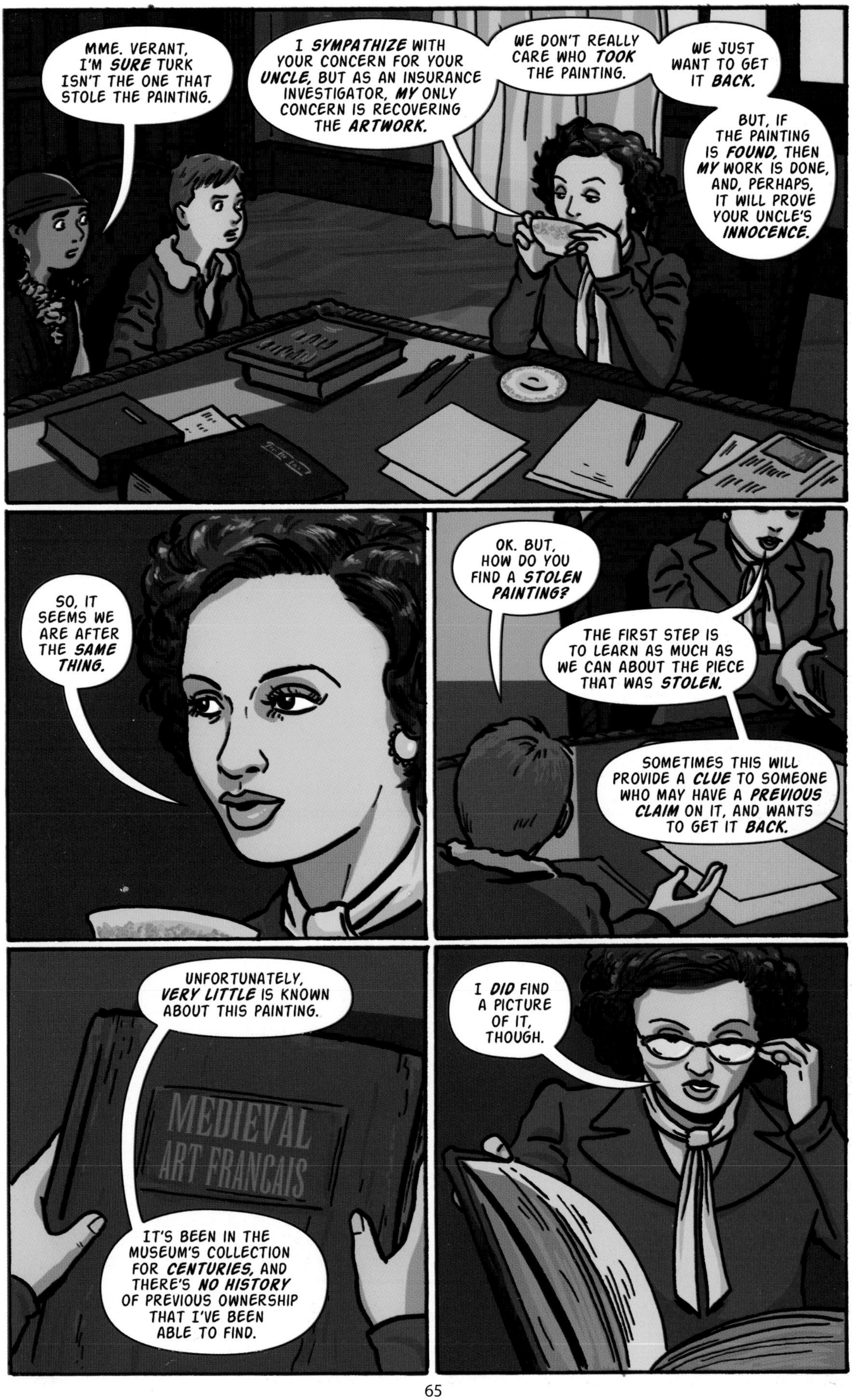
MME. VERANT, I'M SURE TURK ISN'T THE ONE THAT STOLE THE PAINTING.
I SYMPATHIZE WITH YOUR CONCERN FOR YOUR UNCLE, BUT AS AN INSURANCE INVESTIGATOR, MY ONLY CONCERN IS RECOVERING THE ARTWORK.
WE DON'T REALLY CARE WHO TOOK THE PAINTING.
WE JUST WANT TO GET IT BACK.
BUT, IF THE PAINTING IS FOUND, THEN MY WORK IS DONE, AND, PERHAPS, IT WILL PROVE YOUR UNCLE'S INNOCENCE.
SO, IT SEEMS WE ARE AFTER THE SAME THING.
OK. BUT, HOW DO YOU FIND A STOLEN PAINTING?
THE FIRST STEP IS TO LEARN AS MUCH AS WE CAN ABOUT THE PIECE THAT WAS STOLEN.
SOMETIMES THIS WILL PROVIDE A CLUE TO SOMEONE WHO MAY HAVE A PREVIOUS CLAIM ON IT, AND WANTS TO GET IT BACK.
UNFORTUNATELY, VERY LITTLE IS KNOWN ABOUT THIS PAINTING.
MEDIEVAL ART FRANCAIS
IT'S BEEN IN THE MUSEUM'S COLLECTION FOR CENTURIES, AND THERE'S NO HISTORY OF PREVIOUS OWNERSHIP THAT I'VE BEEN ABLE TO FIND.
I DID FIND A PICTURE OF IT, THOUGH.

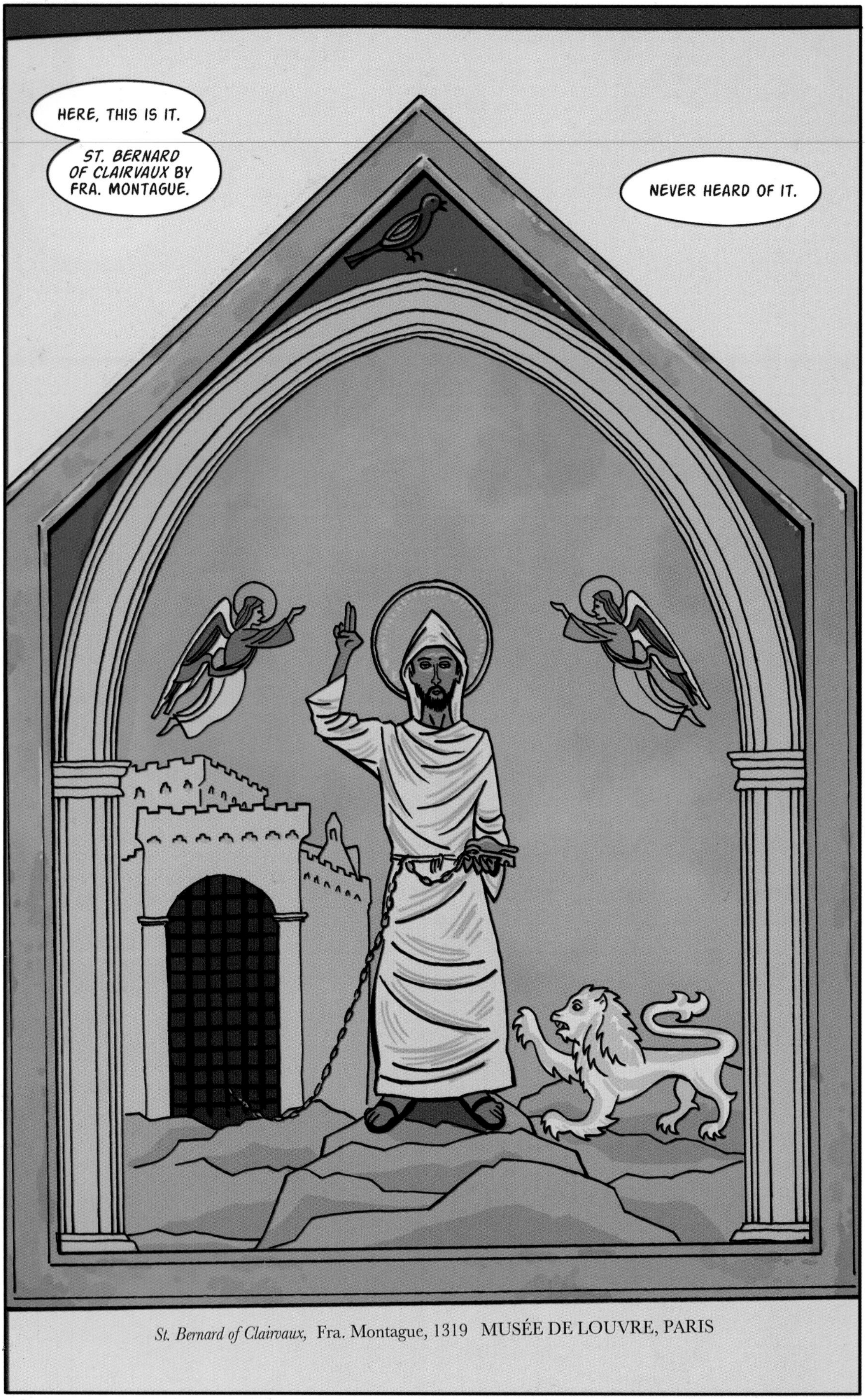
HERE, THIS IS IT.
ST. BERNARD OF CLAIRVAUX BY FRA. MONTAGUE.
NEVER HEARD OF IT.

St. Bernard of Clairvaux, Fra. Montague, 1319 MUSÉE DE LOUVRE, PARIS

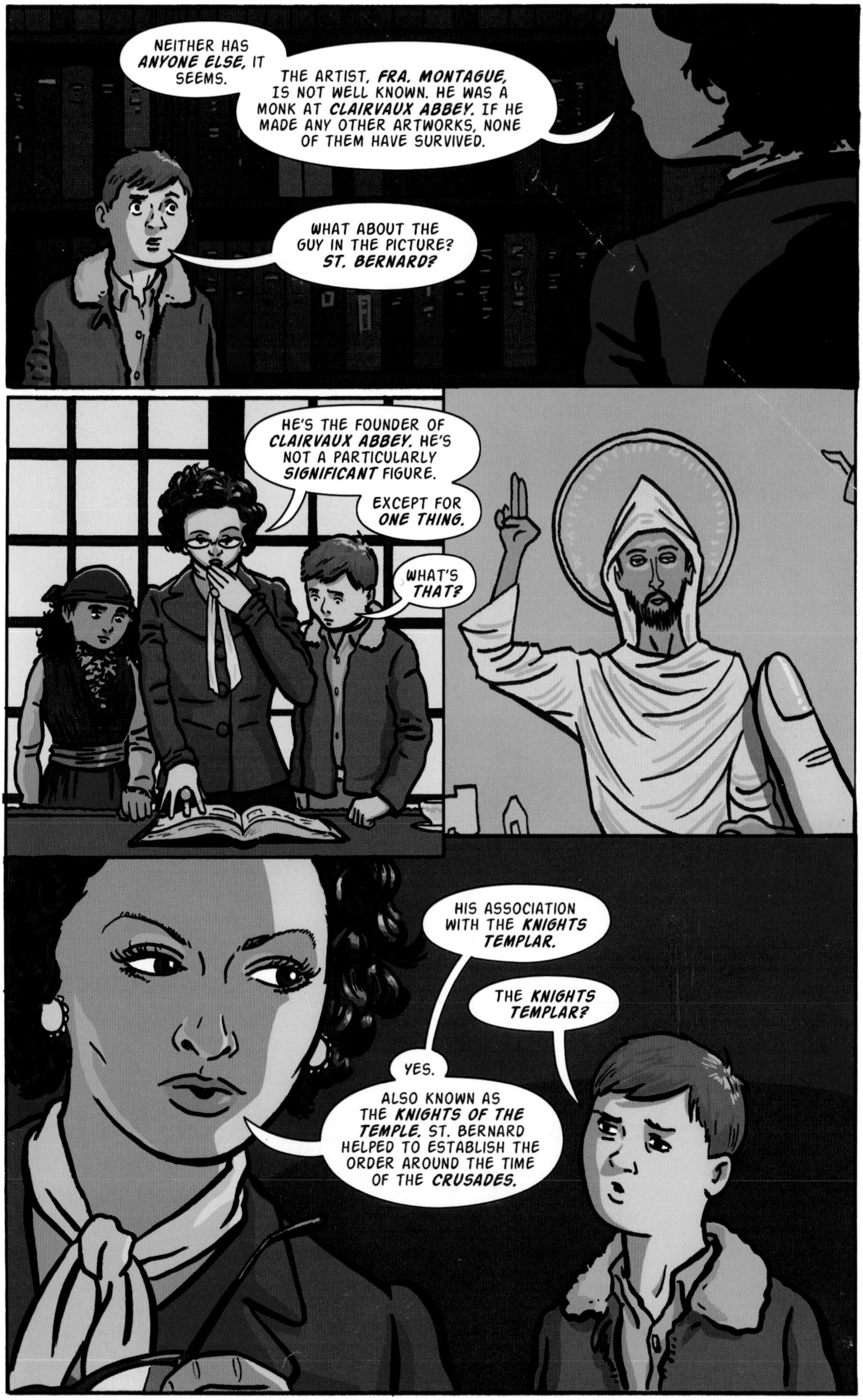

NEITHER HAS ANYONE ELSE, IT SEEMS.
THE ARTIST, FRA. MONTAGUE, IS NOT WELL KNOWN. HE WAS A MONK AT CLAIRVAUX ABBEY. IF HE MADE ANY OTHER ARTWORKS, NONE OF THEM HAVE SURVIVED.
WHAT ABOUT THE GUY IN THE PICTURE? ST. BERNARD?
HE'S THE FOUNDER OF CLAIRVAUX ABBEY. HE'S NOT A PARTICULARLY SIGNIFICANT FIGURE.
EXCEPT FOR ONE THING.
WHAT'S THAT?
HIS ASSOCIATION WITH THE KNIGHTS TEMPLAR.
THE KNIGHTS TEMPLAR?
YES.
ALSO KNOWN AS THE KNIGHTS OF THE TEMPLE. ST. BERNARD HELPED TO ESTABLISH THE ORDER AROUND THE TIME OF THE CRUSADES.

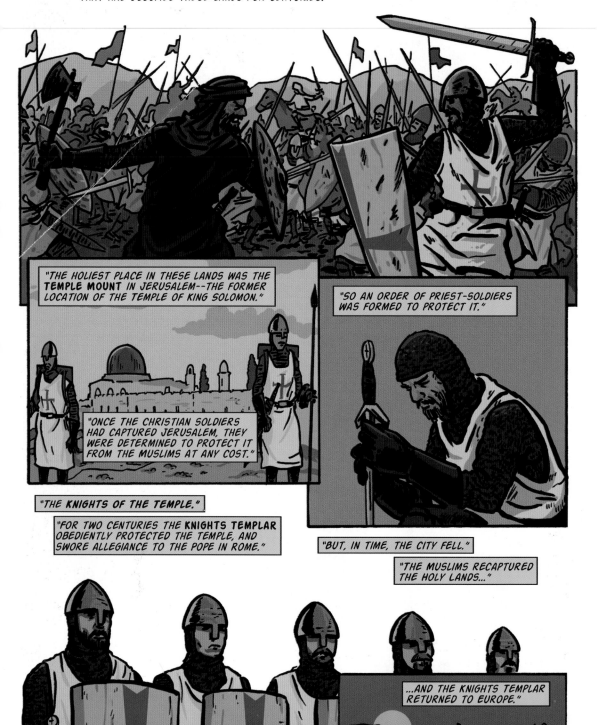

"THE CRUSADES, AS YOU REMEMBER, WERE A SERIES OF WARS FOUGHT BY EUROPEAN CHRISTIANS TO TAKE BACK THE HOLY LANDS OF THE BIBLE FROM THE MUSLIMS THAT HAD OCCUPIED THESE LANDS FOR CENTURIES."

"THE HOLIEST PLACE IN THESE LANDS WAS THE **TEMPLE MOUNT** IN JERUSALEM--THE FORMER LOCATION OF THE TEMPLE OF KING SOLOMON."

"ONCE THE CHRISTIAN SOLDIERS HAD CAPTURED JERUSALEM, THEY WERE DETERMINED TO PROTECT IT FROM THE MUSLIMS AT ANY COST."

"SO AN ORDER OF PRIEST-SOLDIERS WAS FORMED TO PROTECT IT."

"THE **KNIGHTS OF THE TEMPLE.**"

"FOR TWO CENTURIES THE **KNIGHTS TEMPLAR** OBEDIENTLY PROTECTED THE TEMPLE, AND SWORE ALLEGIANCE TO THE POPE IN ROME."

"BUT, IN TIME, THE CITY FELL."

"THE MUSLIMS RECAPTURED THE HOLY LANDS..."

"...AND THE KNIGHTS TEMPLAR RETURNED TO EUROPE."

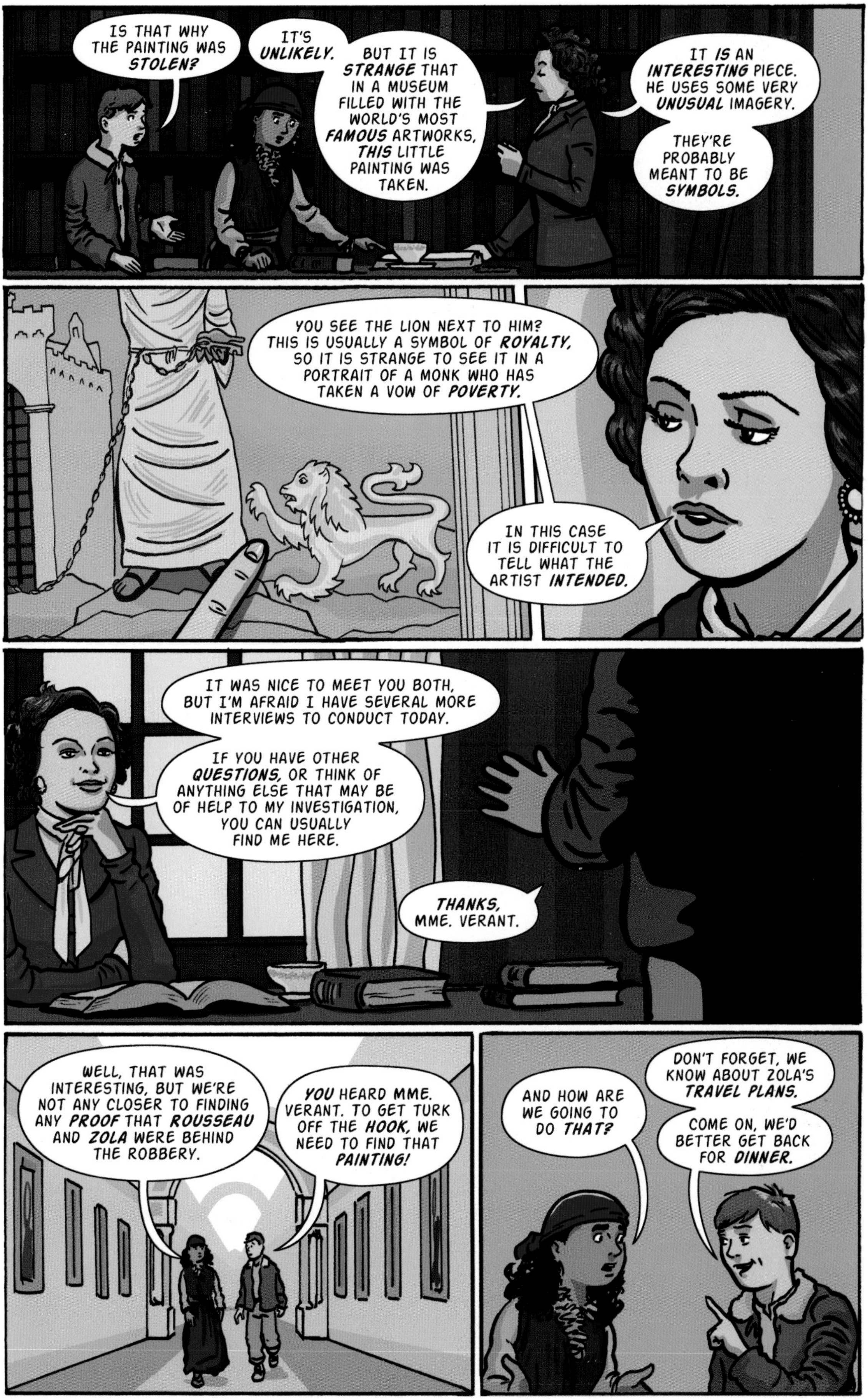
IS THAT WHY THE PAINTING WAS **STOLEN?**
IT'S **UNLIKELY.**
BUT IT IS **STRANGE** THAT IN A MUSEUM FILLED WITH THE WORLD'S MOST **FAMOUS** ARTWORKS, **THIS** LITTLE PAINTING WAS TAKEN.
IT **IS** AN **INTERESTING** PIECE. HE USES SOME VERY **UNUSUAL** IMAGERY.
THEY'RE PROBABLY MEANT TO BE **SYMBOLS.**
YOU SEE THE LION NEXT TO HIM? THIS IS USUALLY A SYMBOL OF **ROYALTY,** SO IT IS STRANGE TO SEE IT IN A PORTRAIT OF A MONK WHO HAS TAKEN A VOW OF **POVERTY.**
IN THIS CASE IT IS DIFFICULT TO TELL WHAT THE ARTIST **INTENDED.**
IT WAS NICE TO MEET YOU BOTH, BUT I'M AFRAID I HAVE SEVERAL MORE INTERVIEWS TO CONDUCT TODAY.
IF YOU HAVE OTHER **QUESTIONS,** OR THINK OF ANYTHING ELSE THAT MAY BE OF HELP TO MY INVESTIGATION, YOU CAN USUALLY FIND ME HERE.
THANKS, MME. VERANT.
WELL, THAT WAS INTERESTING, BUT WE'RE NOT ANY CLOSER TO FINDING ANY **PROOF** THAT **ROUSSEAU** AND **ZOLA** WERE BEHIND THE ROBBERY.
YOU HEARD MME. VERANT. TO GET TURK OFF THE **HOOK,** WE NEED TO FIND THAT **PAINTING!**
AND HOW ARE WE GOING TO DO **THAT?**
DON'T FORGET, WE KNOW ABOUT ZOLA'S **TRAVEL PLANS.**
COME ON, WE'D BETTER GET BACK FOR **DINNER.**

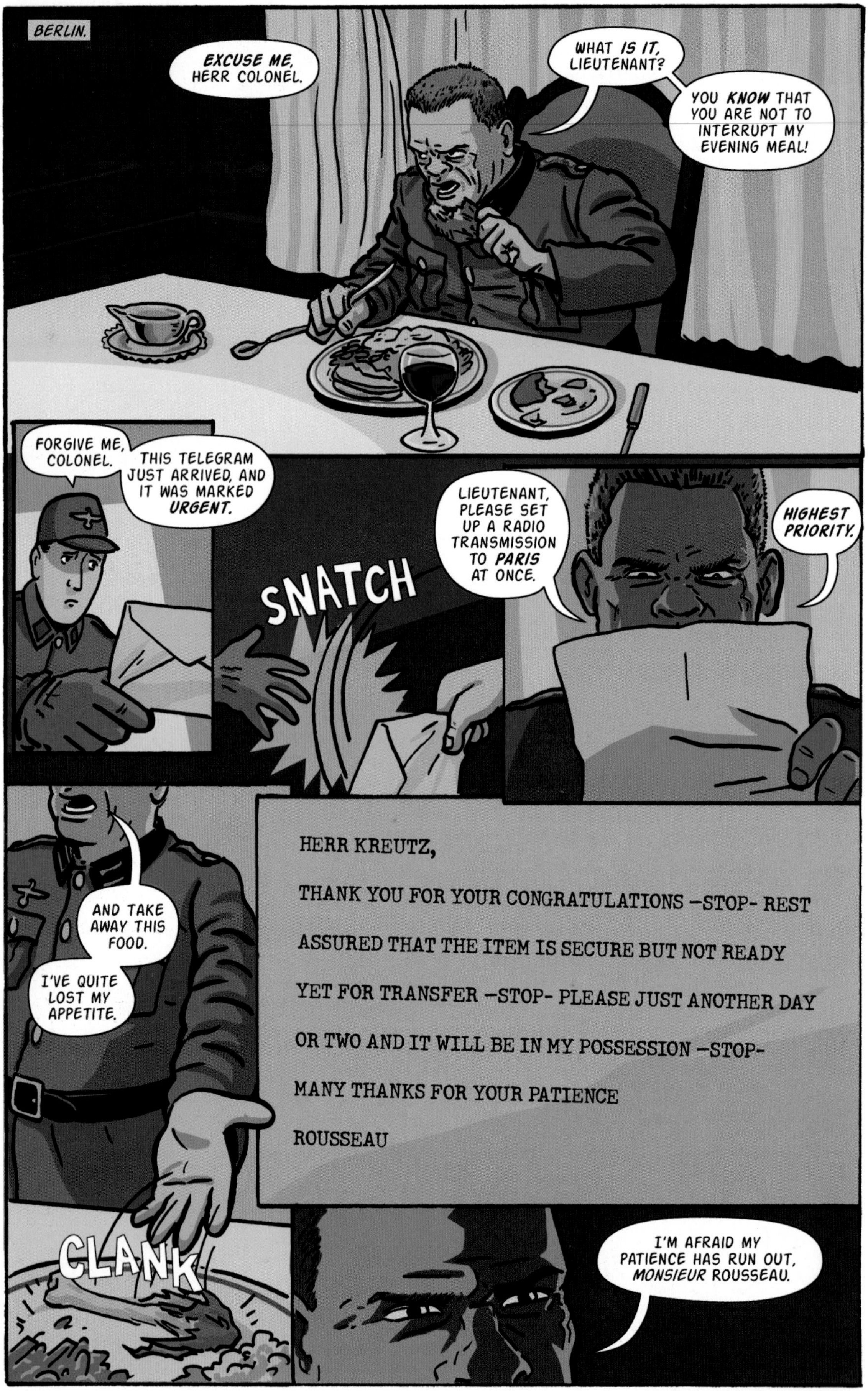
BERLIN.
EXCUSE ME, HERR COLONEL.
WHAT IS IT, LIEUTENANT?
YOU KNOW THAT YOU ARE NOT TO INTERRUPT MY EVENING MEAL!
FORGIVE ME, COLONEL.
THIS TELEGRAM JUST ARRIVED, AND IT WAS MARKED URGENT.
SNATCH
LIEUTENANT, PLEASE SET UP A RADIO TRANSMISSION TO PARIS AT ONCE.
HIGHEST PRIORITY.
AND TAKE AWAY THIS FOOD.
I'VE QUITE LOST MY APPETITE.
HERR KREUTZ,
THANK YOU FOR YOUR CONGRATULATIONS –STOP– REST ASSURED THAT THE ITEM IS SECURE BUT NOT READY YET FOR TRANSFER –STOP– PLEASE JUST ANOTHER DAY OR TWO AND IT WILL BE IN MY POSSESSION –STOP–
MANY THANKS FOR YOUR PATIENCE
ROUSSEAU
CLANK
I'M AFRAID MY PATIENCE HAS RUN OUT, MONSIEUR ROUSSEAU.

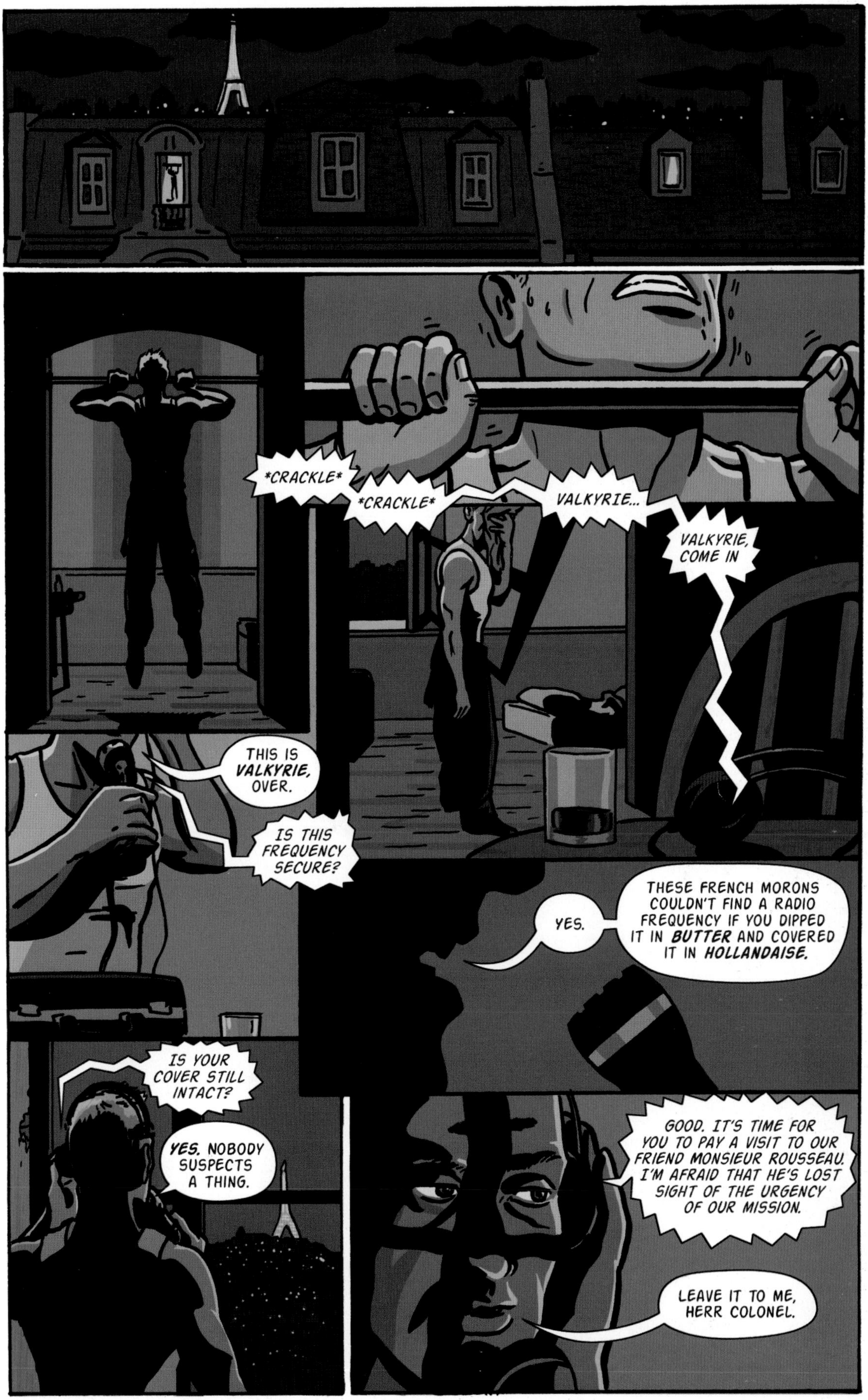
CRACKLE
CRACKLE
VALKYRIE...
VALKYRIE, COME IN
THIS IS VALKYRIE, OVER.
IS THIS FREQUENCY SECURE?
YES.
THESE FRENCH MORONS COULDN'T FIND A RADIO FREQUENCY IF YOU DIPPED IT IN BUTTER AND COVERED IT IN HOLLANDAISE.
IS YOUR COVER STILL INTACT?
YES. NOBODY SUSPECTS A THING.
GOOD. IT'S TIME FOR YOU TO PAY A VISIT TO OUR FRIEND MONSIEUR ROUSSEAU. I'M AFRAID THAT HE'S LOST SIGHT OF THE URGENCY OF OUR MISSION.
LEAVE IT TO ME, HERR COLONEL.

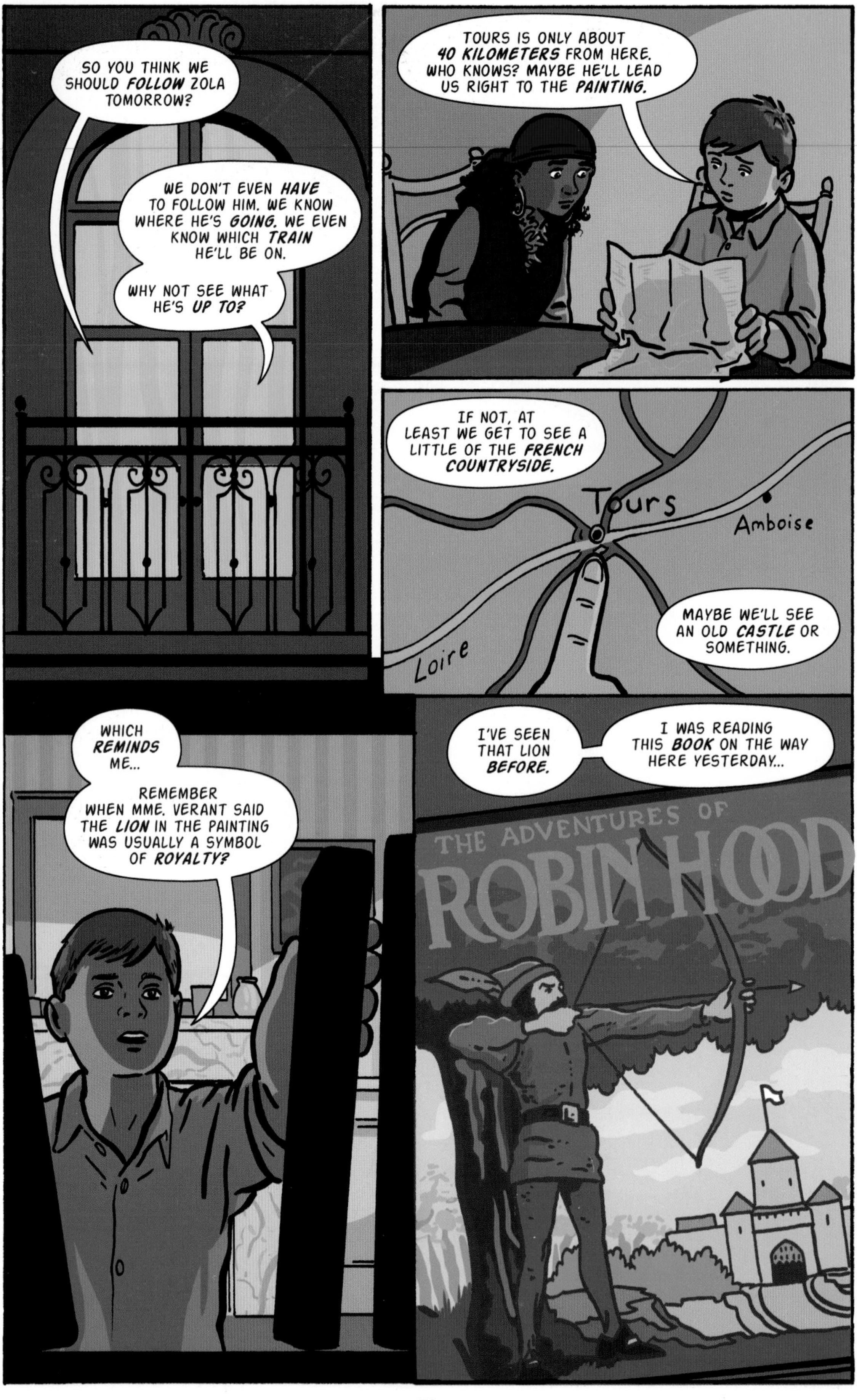
SO YOU THINK WE SHOULD FOLLOW ZOLA TOMORROW?
WE DON'T EVEN HAVE TO FOLLOW HIM. WE KNOW WHERE HE'S GOING. WE EVEN KNOW WHICH TRAIN HE'LL BE ON.
WHY NOT SEE WHAT HE'S UP TO?
TOURS IS ONLY ABOUT 40 KILOMETERS FROM HERE. WHO KNOWS? MAYBE HE'LL LEAD US RIGHT TO THE PAINTING.
IF NOT, AT LEAST WE GET TO SEE A LITTLE OF THE FRENCH COUNTRYSIDE.
Tours
Amboise
Loire
MAYBE WE'LL SEE AN OLD CASTLE OR SOMETHING.
WHICH REMINDS ME...
REMEMBER WHEN MME. VERANT SAID THE LION IN THE PAINTING WAS USUALLY A SYMBOL OF ROYALTY?
I'VE SEEN THAT LION BEFORE.
I WAS READING THIS BOOK ON THE WAY HERE YESTERDAY...
THE ADVENTURES OF
ROBIN HOOD

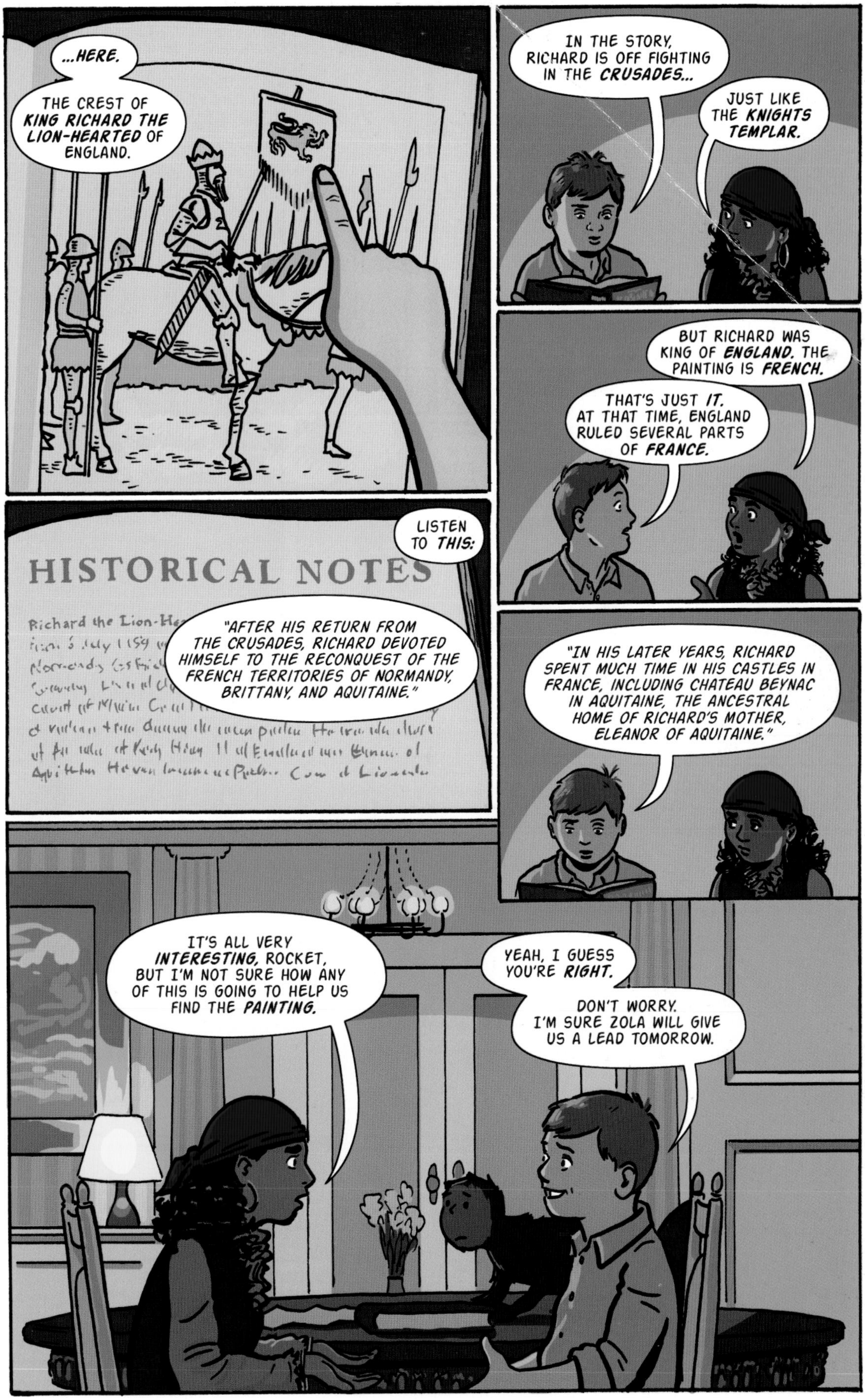
...HERE.
THE CREST OF KING RICHARD THE LION-HEARTED OF ENGLAND.
IN THE STORY, RICHARD IS OFF FIGHTING IN THE CRUSADES...
JUST LIKE THE KNIGHTS TEMPLAR.
BUT RICHARD WAS KING OF ENGLAND. THE PAINTING IS FRENCH.
THAT'S JUST IT. AT THAT TIME, ENGLAND RULED SEVERAL PARTS OF FRANCE.
LISTEN TO THIS:
HISTORICAL NOTES
"AFTER HIS RETURN FROM THE CRUSADES, RICHARD DEVOTED HIMSELF TO THE RECONQUEST OF THE FRENCH TERRITORIES OF NORMANDY, BRITTANY, AND AQUITAINE."
"IN HIS LATER YEARS, RICHARD SPENT MUCH TIME IN HIS CASTLES IN FRANCE, INCLUDING CHATEAU BEYNAC IN AQUITAINE, THE ANCESTRAL HOME OF RICHARD'S MOTHER, ELEANOR OF AQUITAINE."
IT'S ALL VERY INTERESTING, ROCKET, BUT I'M NOT SURE HOW ANY OF THIS IS GOING TO HELP US FIND THE PAINTING.
YEAH, I GUESS YOU'RE RIGHT.
DON'T WORRY. I'M SURE ZOLA WILL GIVE US A LEAD TOMORROW.

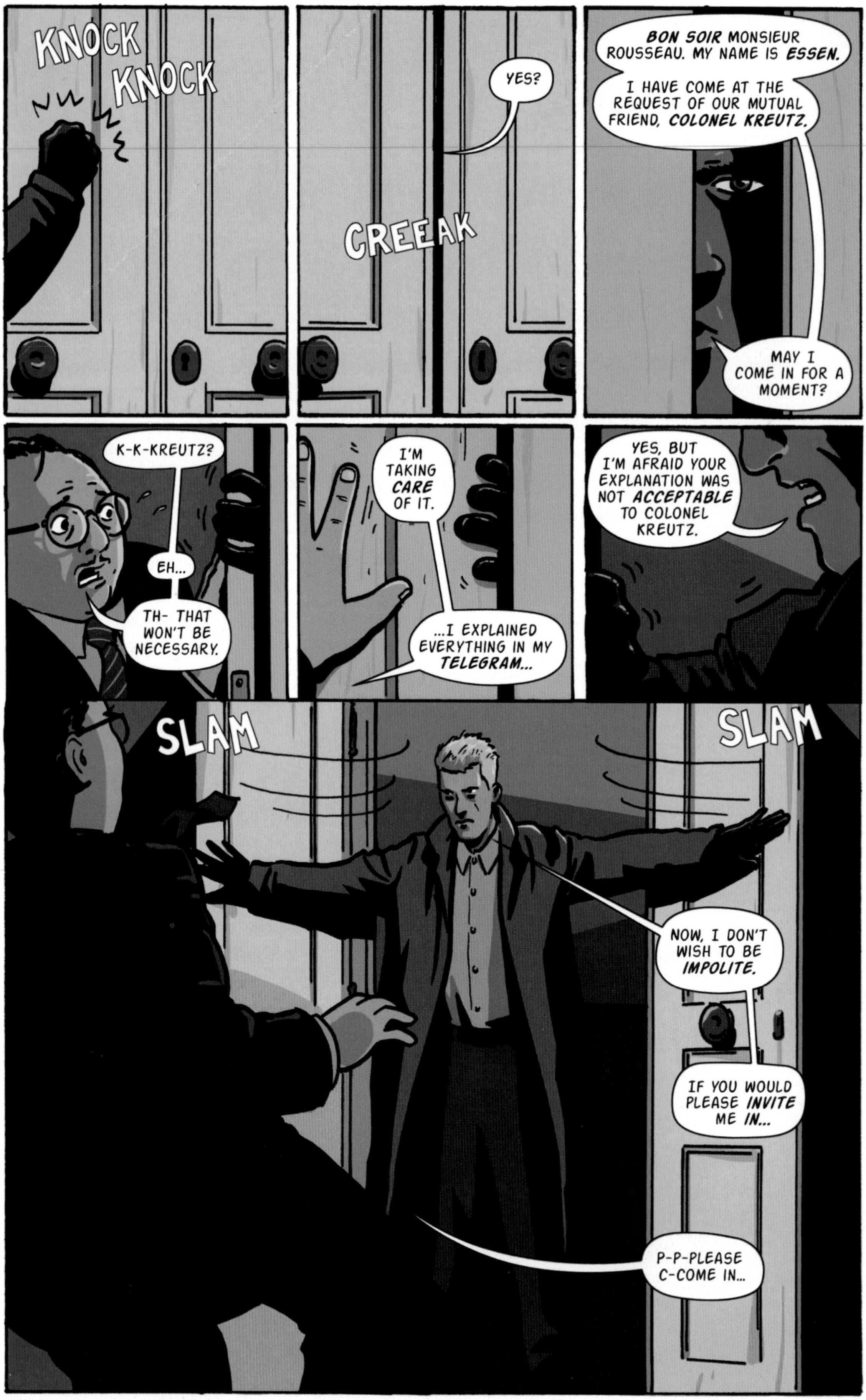
KNOCK
KNOCK
YES?
CREEAK
BON SOIR MONSIEUR ROUSSEAU. MY NAME IS ESSEN.
I HAVE COME AT THE REQUEST OF OUR MUTUAL FRIEND, COLONEL KREUTZ.
MAY I COME IN FOR A MOMENT?
K-K-KREUTZ?
EH...
TH- THAT WON'T BE NECESSARY.
I'M TAKING CARE OF IT.
...I EXPLAINED EVERYTHING IN MY TELEGRAM...
YES, BUT I'M AFRAID YOUR EXPLANATION WAS NOT ACCEPTABLE TO COLONEL KREUTZ.
SLAM
SLAM
NOW, I DON'T WISH TO BE IMPOLITE.
IF YOU WOULD PLEASE INVITE ME IN...
P-P-PLEASE C-COME IN...

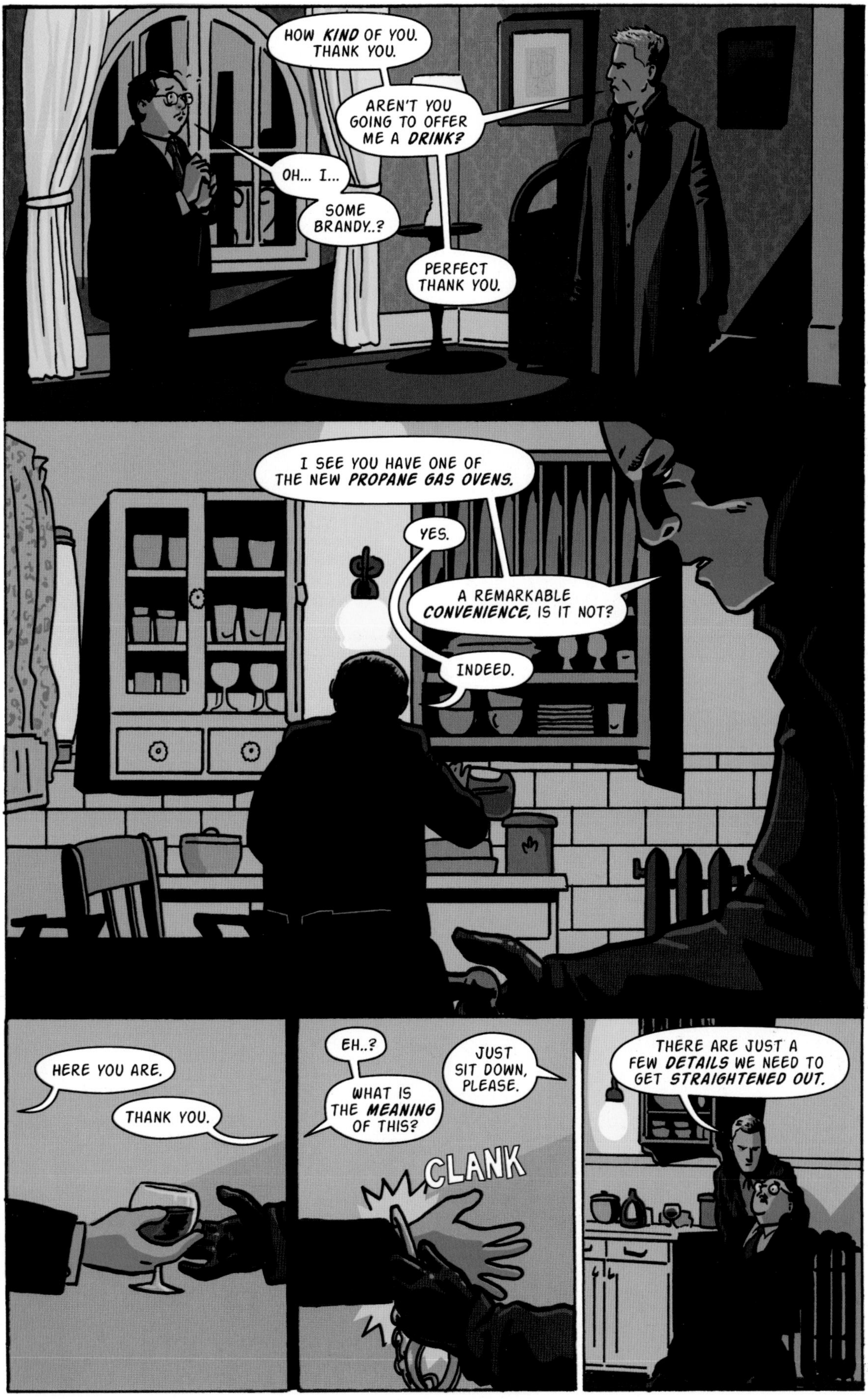
HOW KIND OF YOU. THANK YOU.
AREN'T YOU GOING TO OFFER ME A DRINK?
OH... I...
SOME BRANDY..?
PERFECT THANK YOU.
I SEE YOU HAVE ONE OF THE NEW PROPANE GAS OVENS.
YES.
A REMARKABLE CONVENIENCE, IS IT NOT?
INDEED.
HERE YOU ARE.
THANK YOU.
EH..?
WHAT IS THE MEANING OF THIS?
JUST SIT DOWN, PLEASE.
CLANK
THERE ARE JUST A FEW DETAILS WE NEED TO GET STRAIGHTENED OUT.

I TOLD KREUTZ IN MY CABLE!

THE ITEM... IS... SAFE!

HE WILL HAVE IT... SOON! I PROMISE!

HE WILL INDEED HAVE IT SOON.

I AM CERTAIN OF THAT.

YOU KNOW, M. ROUSSEAU, YOU MUST BE CAREFUL WITH THESE PROPANE STOVES.

THE GAS IS QUITE FLAMMABLE.

WHAT ARE YOU DOING?

SSSSS
CLICK

IF YOU FAIL TO LIGHT THE FLAME PROPERLY, GAS CAN LEAK INTO THE ROOM, CREATING A VERY DANGEROUS SITUATION.

IT DOESN'T TAKE MUCH TO IGNITE THE GAS. EVEN JUST A SIMPLE...

...SPARK WILL DO IT.

ARE YOU MAD?!?

CHK

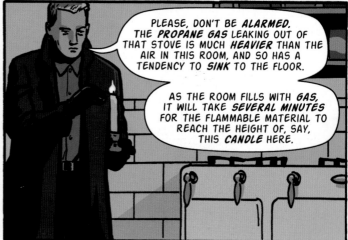

PLEASE, DON'T BE ALARMED. THE PROPANE GAS LEAKING OUT OF THAT STOVE IS MUCH HEAVIER THAN THE AIR IN THIS ROOM, AND SO HAS A TENDENCY TO SINK TO THE FLOOR.

AS THE ROOM FILLS WITH GAS, IT WILL TAKE SEVERAL MINUTES FOR THE FLAMMABLE MATERIAL TO REACH THE HEIGHT OF, SAY, THIS CANDLE HERE.

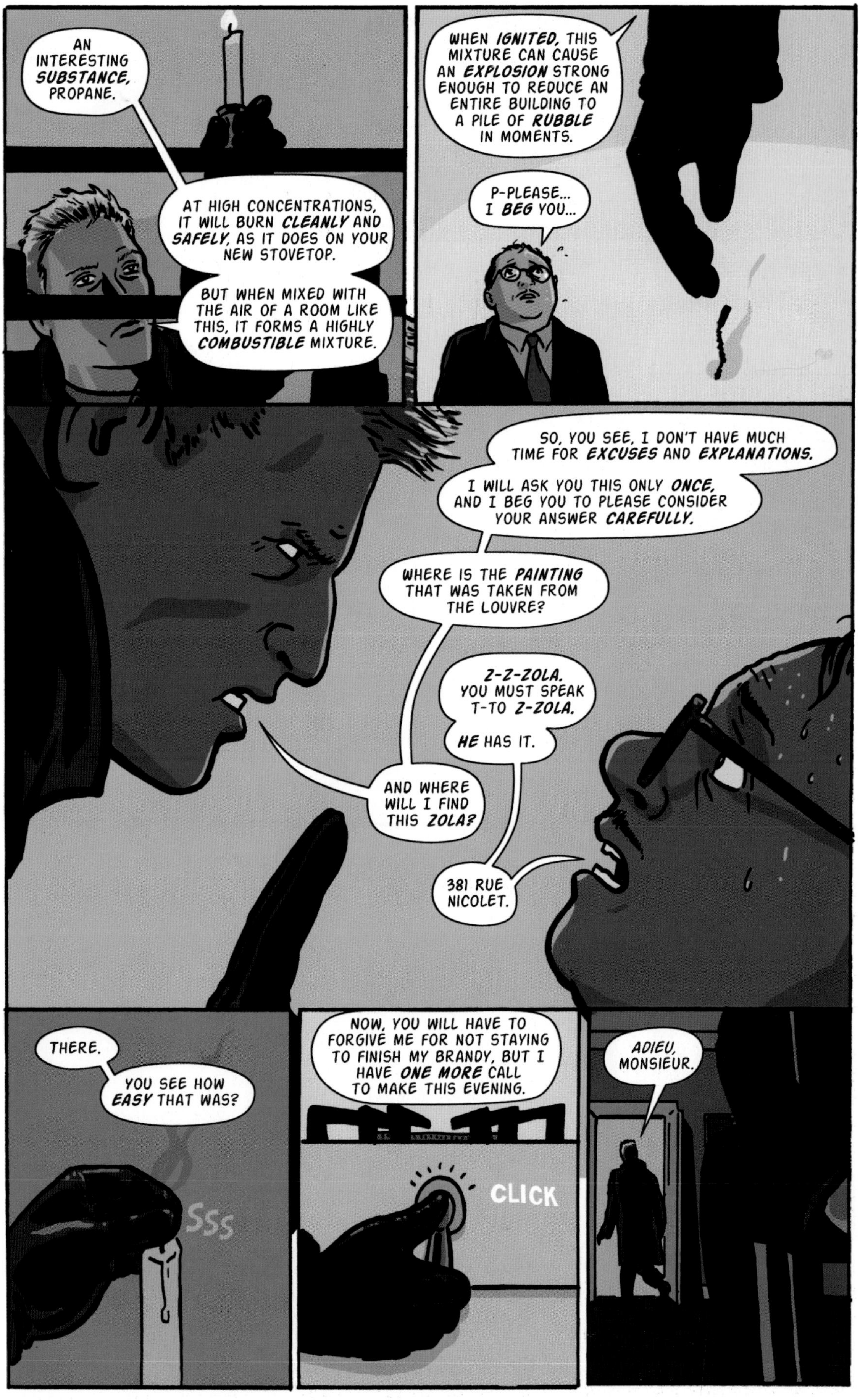
AN INTERESTING SUBSTANCE, PROPANE.
AT HIGH CONCENTRATIONS, IT WILL BURN CLEANLY AND SAFELY, AS IT DOES ON YOUR NEW STOVETOP.
BUT WHEN MIXED WITH THE AIR OF A ROOM LIKE THIS, IT FORMS A HIGHLY COMBUSTIBLE MIXTURE.
WHEN IGNITED, THIS MIXTURE CAN CAUSE AN EXPLOSION STRONG ENOUGH TO REDUCE AN ENTIRE BUILDING TO A PILE OF RUBBLE IN MOMENTS.
P-PLEASE... I BEG YOU...
SO, YOU SEE, I DON'T HAVE MUCH TIME FOR EXCUSES AND EXPLANATIONS.
I WILL ASK YOU THIS ONLY ONCE, AND I BEG YOU TO PLEASE CONSIDER YOUR ANSWER CAREFULLY.
WHERE IS THE PAINTING THAT WAS TAKEN FROM THE LOUVRE?
Z-Z-ZOLA. YOU MUST SPEAK T-TO Z-ZOLA.
HE HAS IT.
AND WHERE WILL I FIND THIS ZOLA?
381 RUE NICOLET.
THERE.
YOU SEE HOW EASY THAT WAS?
SSS
NOW, YOU WILL HAVE TO FORGIVE ME FOR NOT STAYING TO FINISH MY BRANDY, BUT I HAVE ONE MORE CALL TO MAKE THIS EVENING.
CLICK
ADIEU, MONSIEUR.

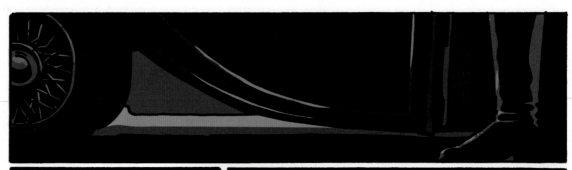

THIS WAY, GENERAL

I STILL DON'T UNDERSTAND WHY ALL OF THIS *CLOAK AND DAGGER* BUSINESS IS NECESSARY.

PLEASE ACCEPT MY *SINCEREST* APOLOGIES GENERAL, BUT COLONEL KREUTZ IS VERY...

...CAREFUL, SHALL WE SAY.

KNOCK KNOCK

SSSHHK

GENERAL.

WELCOME.

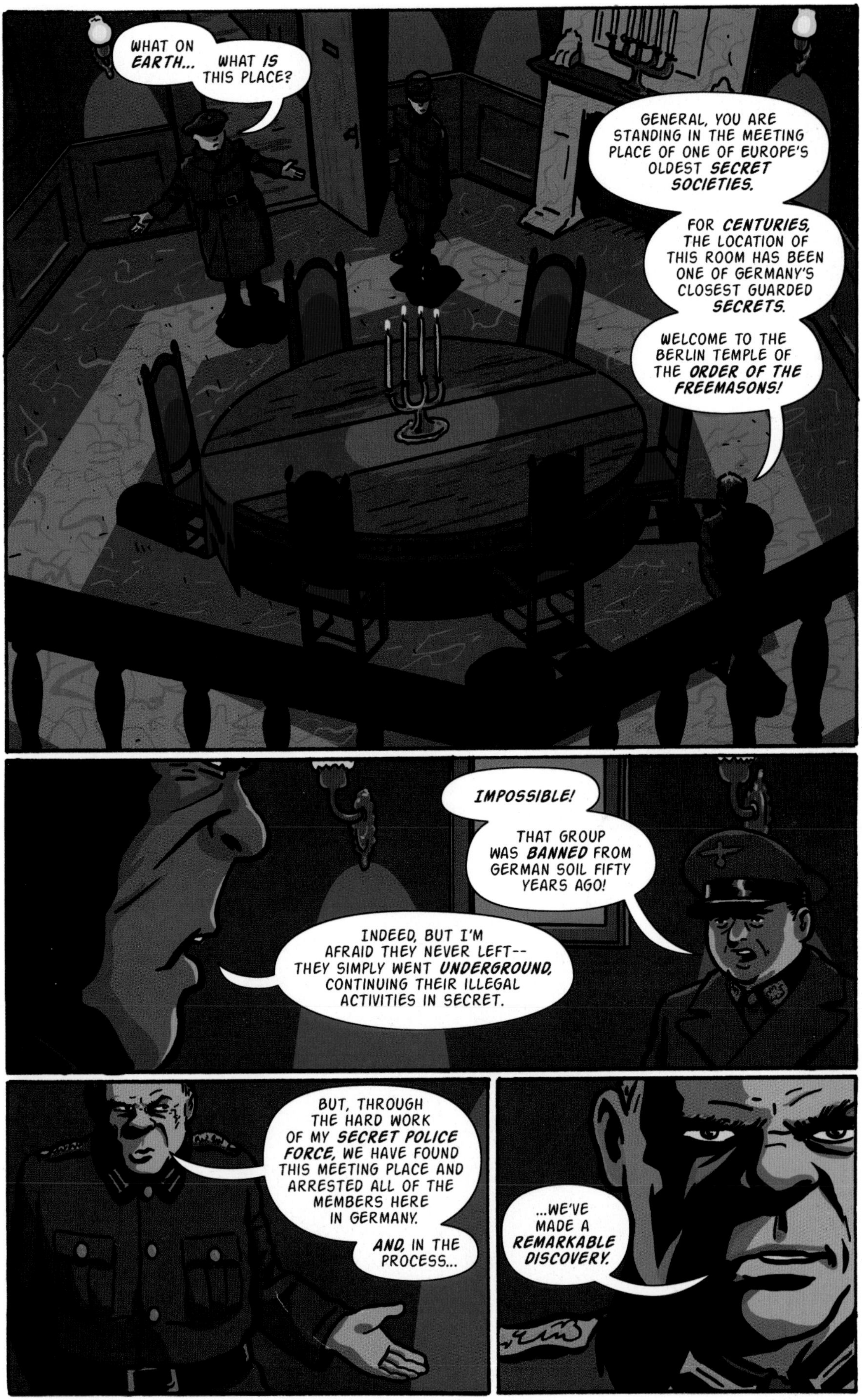
WHAT ON EARTH... WHAT IS THIS PLACE?
GENERAL, YOU ARE STANDING IN THE MEETING PLACE OF ONE OF EUROPE'S OLDEST SECRET SOCIETIES.
FOR CENTURIES, THE LOCATION OF THIS ROOM HAS BEEN ONE OF GERMANY'S CLOSEST GUARDED SECRETS.
WELCOME TO THE BERLIN TEMPLE OF THE ORDER OF THE FREEMASONS!
IMPOSSIBLE!
THAT GROUP WAS BANNED FROM GERMAN SOIL FIFTY YEARS AGO!
INDEED, BUT I'M AFRAID THEY NEVER LEFT-- THEY SIMPLY WENT UNDERGROUND, CONTINUING THEIR ILLEGAL ACTIVITIES IN SECRET.
BUT, THROUGH THE HARD WORK OF MY SECRET POLICE FORCE, WE HAVE FOUND THIS MEETING PLACE AND ARRESTED ALL OF THE MEMBERS HERE IN GERMANY.
AND, IN THE PROCESS...
...WE'VE MADE A REMARKABLE DISCOVERY.

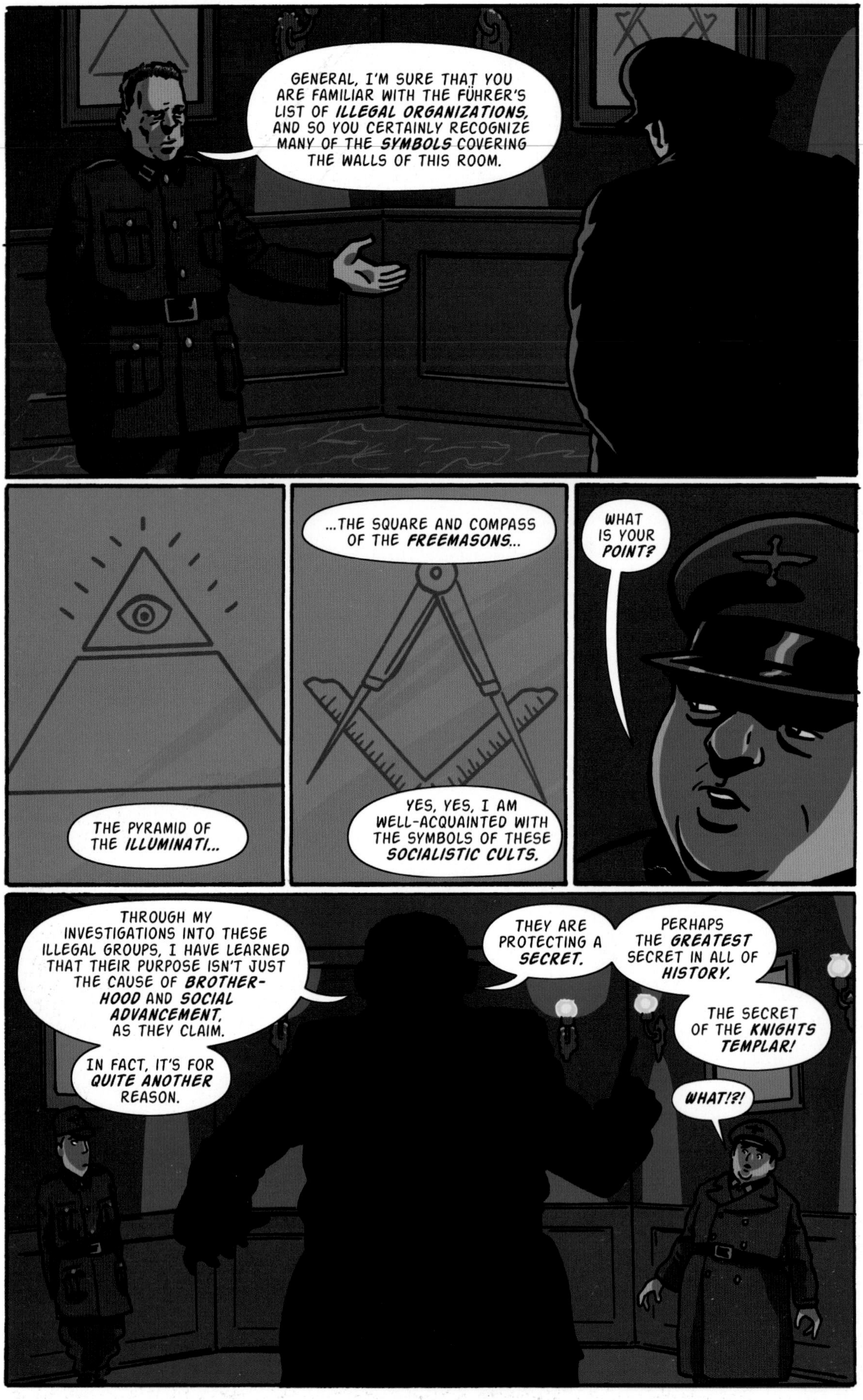
GENERAL, I'M SURE THAT YOU ARE FAMILIAR WITH THE FÜHRER'S LIST OF ILLEGAL ORGANIZATIONS, AND SO YOU CERTAINLY RECOGNIZE MANY OF THE SYMBOLS COVERING THE WALLS OF THIS ROOM.
THE PYRAMID OF THE ILLUMINATI...
...THE SQUARE AND COMPASS OF THE FREEMASONS...
YES, YES, I AM WELL-ACQUAINTED WITH THE SYMBOLS OF THESE SOCIALISTIC CULTS.
WHAT IS YOUR POINT?
THROUGH MY INVESTIGATIONS INTO THESE ILLEGAL GROUPS, I HAVE LEARNED THAT THEIR PURPOSE ISN'T JUST THE CAUSE OF BROTHERHOOD AND SOCIAL ADVANCEMENT, AS THEY CLAIM.
IN FACT, IT'S FOR QUITE ANOTHER REASON.
THEY ARE PROTECTING A SECRET.
PERHAPS THE GREATEST SECRET IN ALL OF HISTORY.
THE SECRET OF THE KNIGHTS TEMPLAR!
WHAT!?!

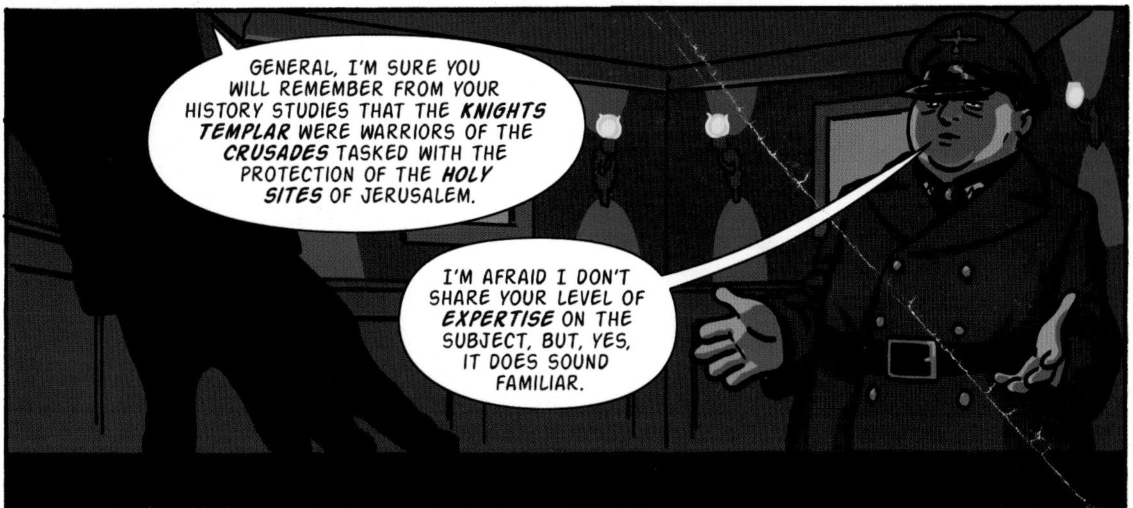
GENERAL, I'M SURE YOU WILL REMEMBER FROM YOUR HISTORY STUDIES THAT THE KNIGHTS TEMPLAR WERE WARRIORS OF THE CRUSADES TASKED WITH THE PROTECTION OF THE HOLY SITES OF JERUSALEM.
I'M AFRAID I DON'T SHARE YOUR LEVEL OF EXPERTISE ON THE SUBJECT, BUT, YES, IT DOES SOUND FAMILIAR.

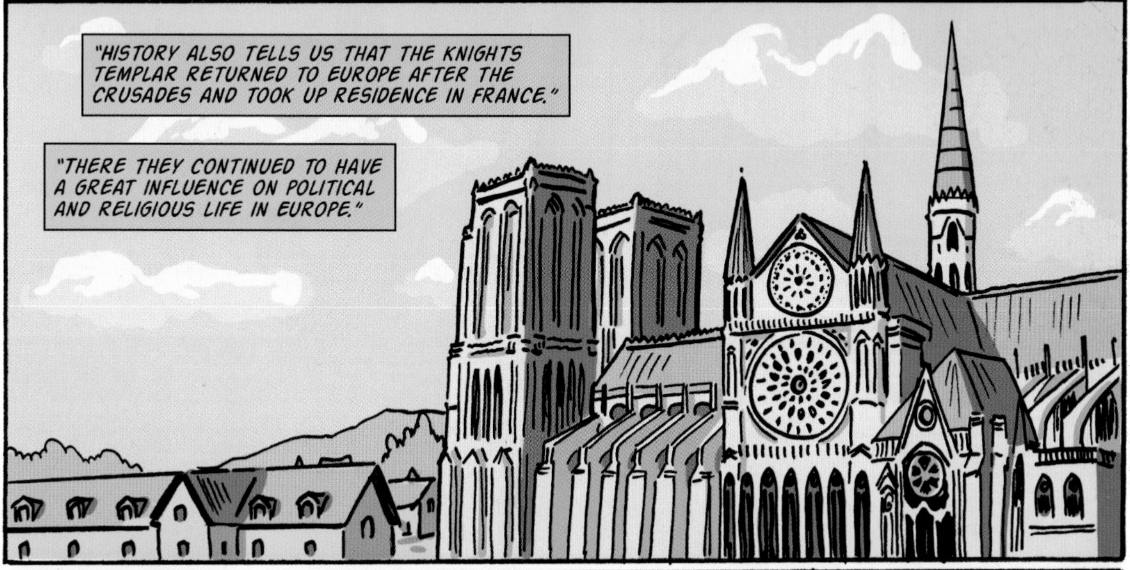
"HISTORY ALSO TELLS US THAT THE KNIGHTS TEMPLAR RETURNED TO EUROPE AFTER THE CRUSADES AND TOOK UP RESIDENCE IN FRANCE."
"THERE THEY CONTINUED TO HAVE A GREAT INFLUENCE ON POLITICAL AND RELIGIOUS LIFE IN EUROPE."

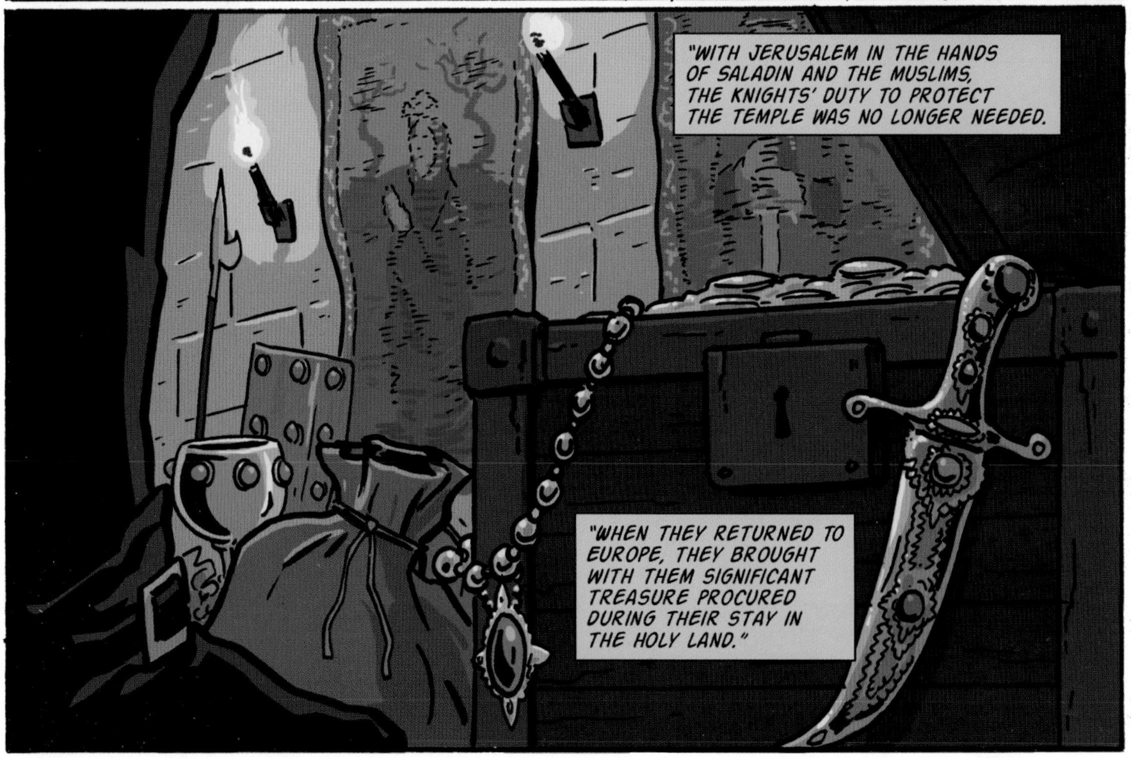
"WITH JERUSALEM IN THE HANDS OF SALADIN AND THE MUSLIMS, THE KNIGHTS' DUTY TO PROTECT THE TEMPLE WAS NO LONGER NEEDED.
"WHEN THEY RETURNED TO EUROPE, THEY BROUGHT WITH THEM SIGNIFICANT TREASURE PROCURED DURING THEIR STAY IN THE HOLY LAND."

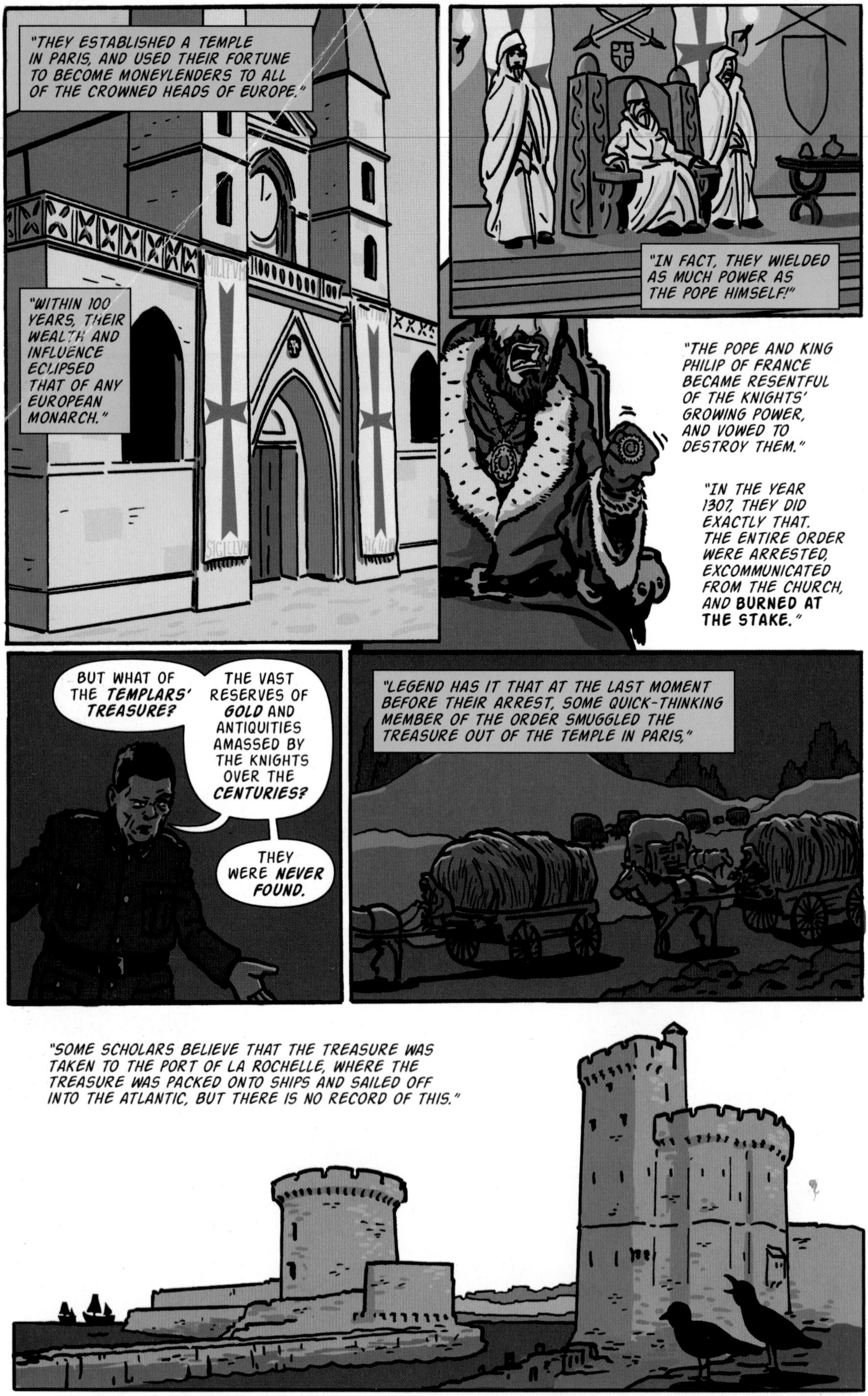
"THEY ESTABLISHED A TEMPLE IN PARIS, AND USED THEIR FORTUNE TO BECOME MONEYLENDERS TO ALL OF THE CROWNED HEADS OF EUROPE."
MILITVM
SIGILLVM
"WITHIN 100 YEARS, THEIR WEALTH AND INFLUENCE ECLIPSED THAT OF ANY EUROPEAN MONARCH."
"IN FACT, THEY WIELDED AS MUCH POWER AS THE POPE HIMSELF!"
"THE POPE AND KING PHILIP OF FRANCE BECAME RESENTFUL OF THE KNIGHTS' GROWING POWER, AND VOWED TO DESTROY THEM."
"IN THE YEAR 1307, THEY DID EXACTLY THAT. THE ENTIRE ORDER WERE ARRESTED, EXCOMMUNICATED FROM THE CHURCH, AND **BURNED AT THE STAKE.**"
BUT WHAT OF THE ***TEMPLARS' TREASURE?***
THE VAST RESERVES OF ***GOLD*** AND ANTIQUITIES AMASSED BY THE KNIGHTS OVER THE ***CENTURIES?***
THEY WERE ***NEVER FOUND.***
"LEGEND HAS IT THAT AT THE LAST MOMENT BEFORE THEIR ARREST, SOME QUICK-THINKING MEMBER OF THE ORDER SMUGGLED THE TREASURE OUT OF THE TEMPLE IN PARIS,"
"SOME SCHOLARS BELIEVE THAT THE TREASURE WAS TAKEN TO THE PORT OF LA ROCHELLE, WHERE THE TREASURE WAS PACKED ONTO SHIPS AND SAILED OFF INTO THE ATLANTIC, BUT THERE IS NO RECORD OF THIS."

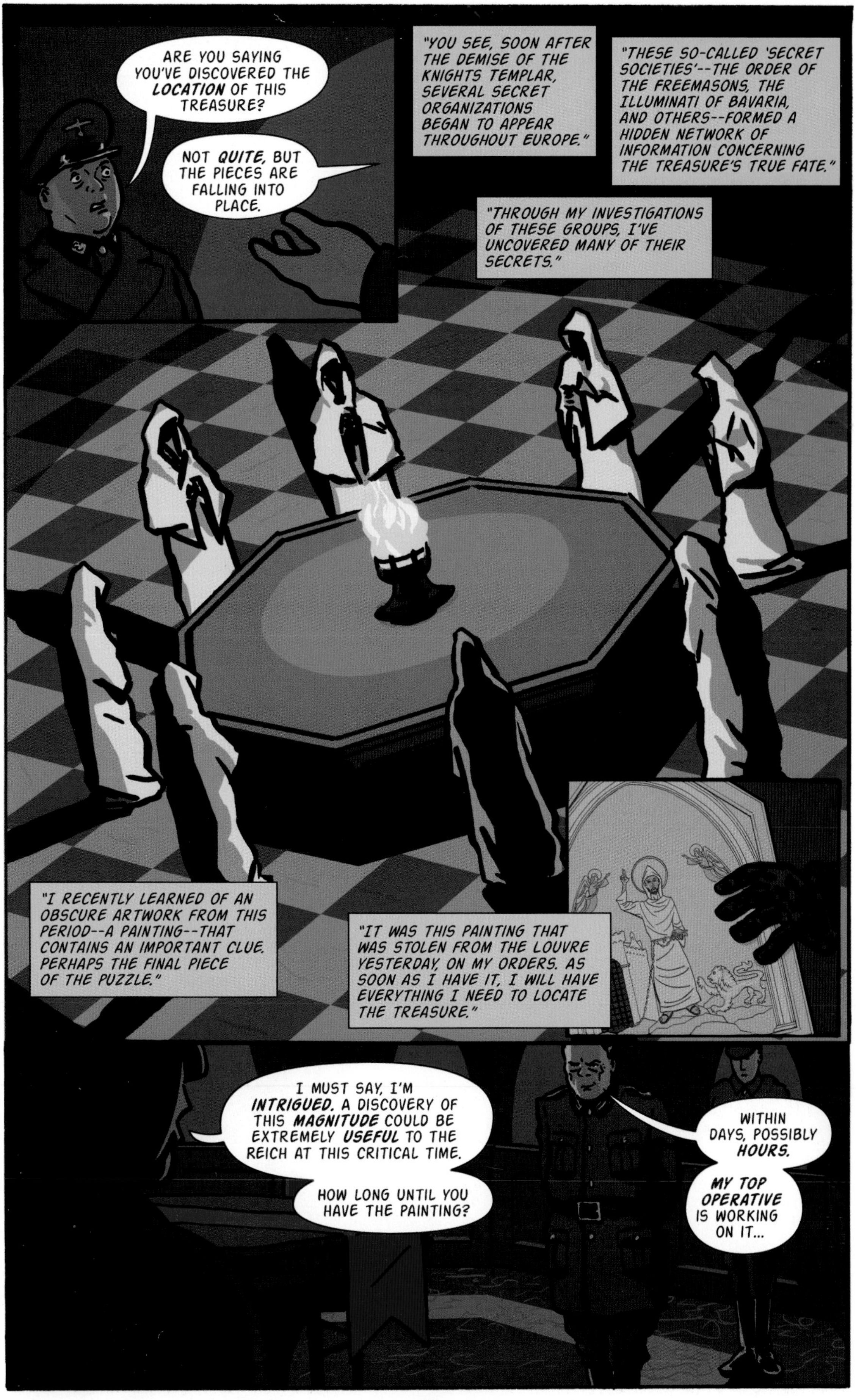

ARE YOU SAYING YOU'VE DISCOVERED THE **LOCATION** OF THIS TREASURE?
NOT **QUITE**, BUT THE PIECES ARE FALLING INTO PLACE.
"YOU SEE, SOON AFTER THE DEMISE OF THE KNIGHTS TEMPLAR, SEVERAL SECRET ORGANIZATIONS BEGAN TO APPEAR THROUGHOUT EUROPE."
"THESE SO-CALLED 'SECRET SOCIETIES'--THE ORDER OF THE FREEMASONS, THE ILLUMINATI OF BAVARIA, AND OTHERS--FORMED A HIDDEN NETWORK OF INFORMATION CONCERNING THE TREASURE'S TRUE FATE."
"THROUGH MY INVESTIGATIONS OF THESE GROUPS, I'VE UNCOVERED MANY OF THEIR SECRETS."
"I RECENTLY LEARNED OF AN OBSCURE ARTWORK FROM THIS PERIOD--A PAINTING--THAT CONTAINS AN IMPORTANT CLUE. PERHAPS THE FINAL PIECE OF THE PUZZLE."
"IT WAS THIS PAINTING THAT WAS STOLEN FROM THE LOUVRE YESTERDAY, ON MY ORDERS. AS SOON AS I HAVE IT, I WILL HAVE EVERYTHING I NEED TO LOCATE THE TREASURE."
I MUST SAY, I'M **INTRIGUED.** A DISCOVERY OF THIS **MAGNITUDE** COULD BE EXTREMELY **USEFUL** TO THE REICH AT THIS CRITICAL TIME.
HOW LONG UNTIL YOU HAVE THE PAINTING?
WITHIN DAYS, POSSIBLY **HOURS.**
MY TOP OPERATIVE IS WORKING ON IT...

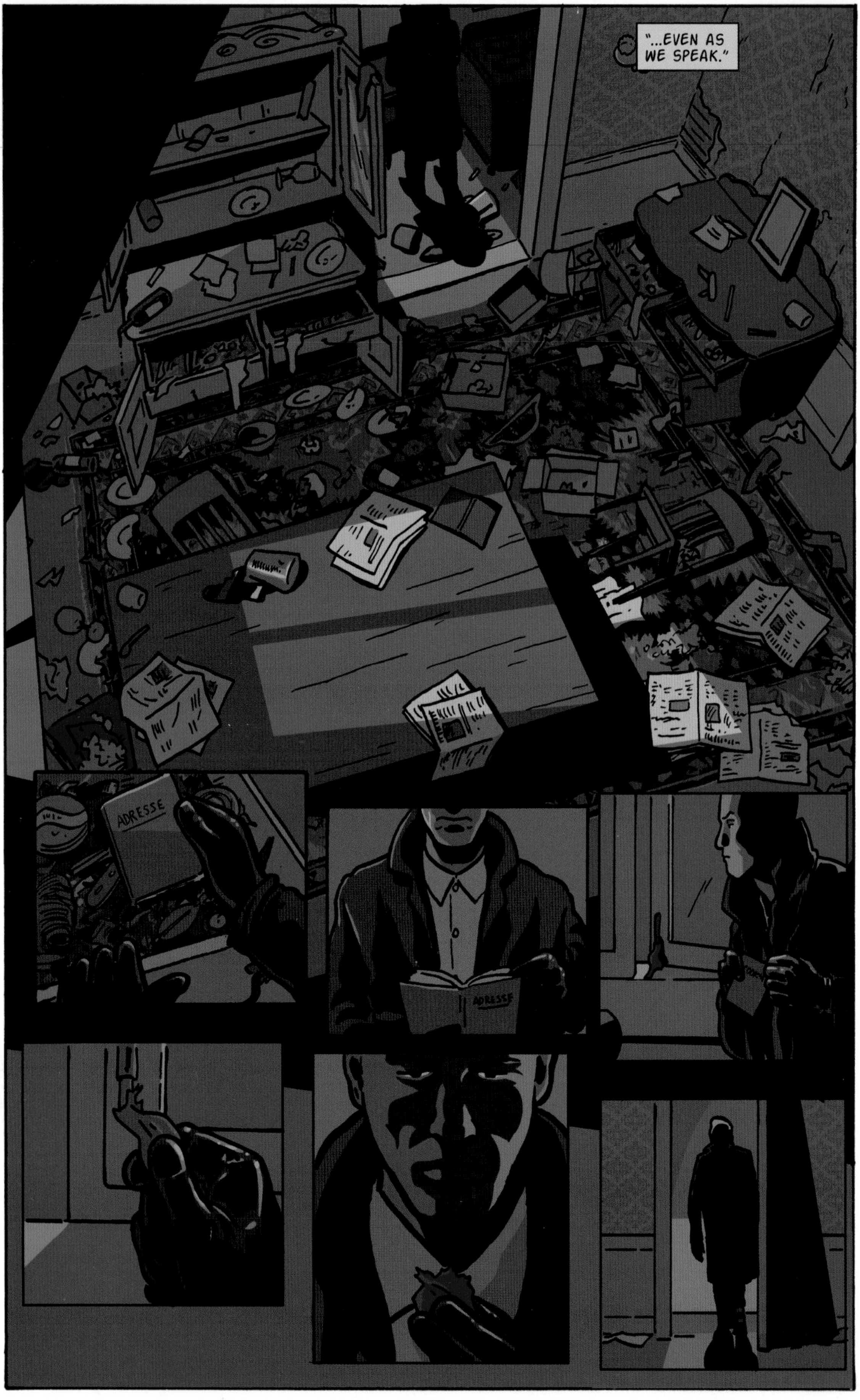
"...EVEN AS WE SPEAK."
ADRESSE
ADRESSE

CHAPTER FIVE

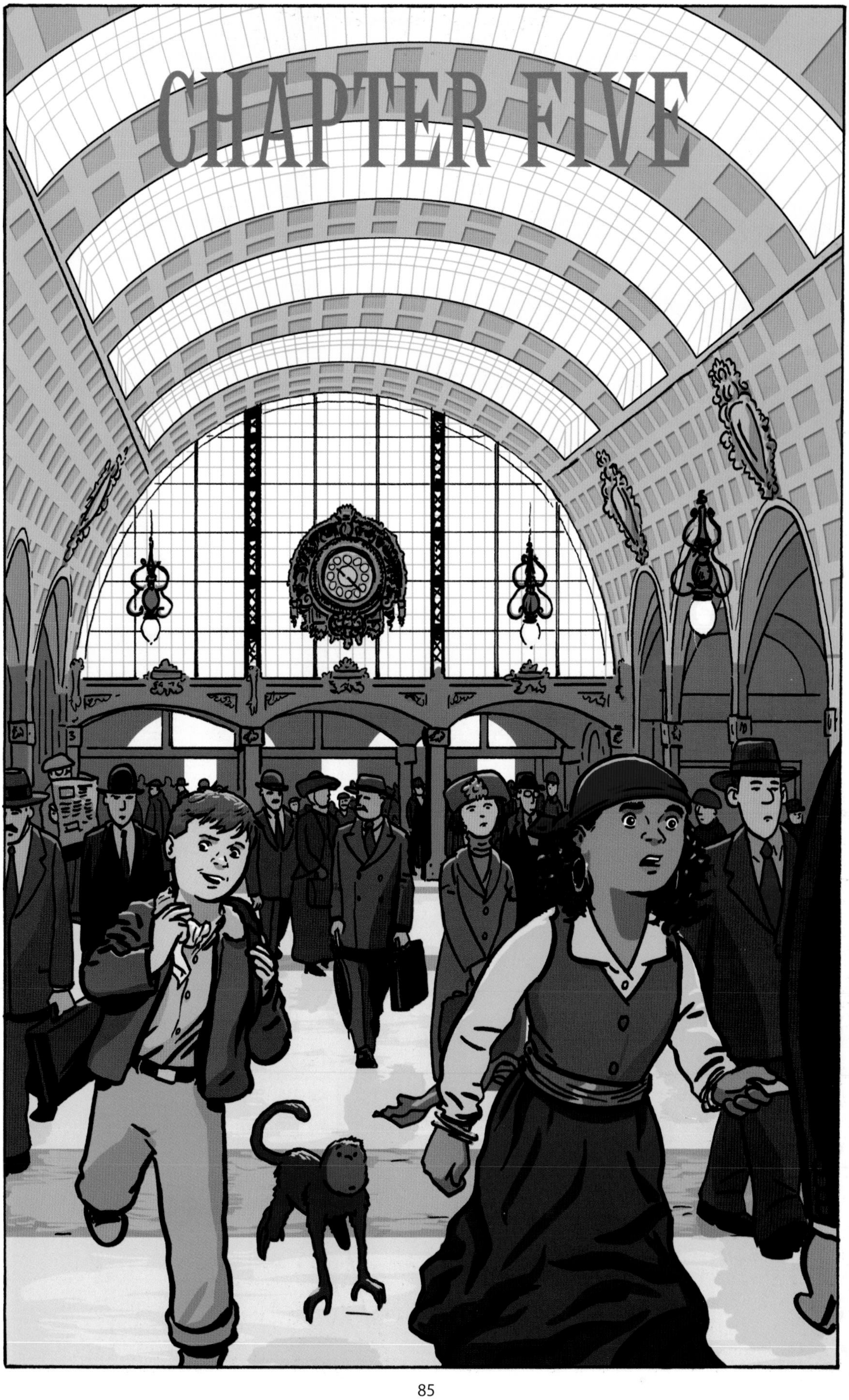

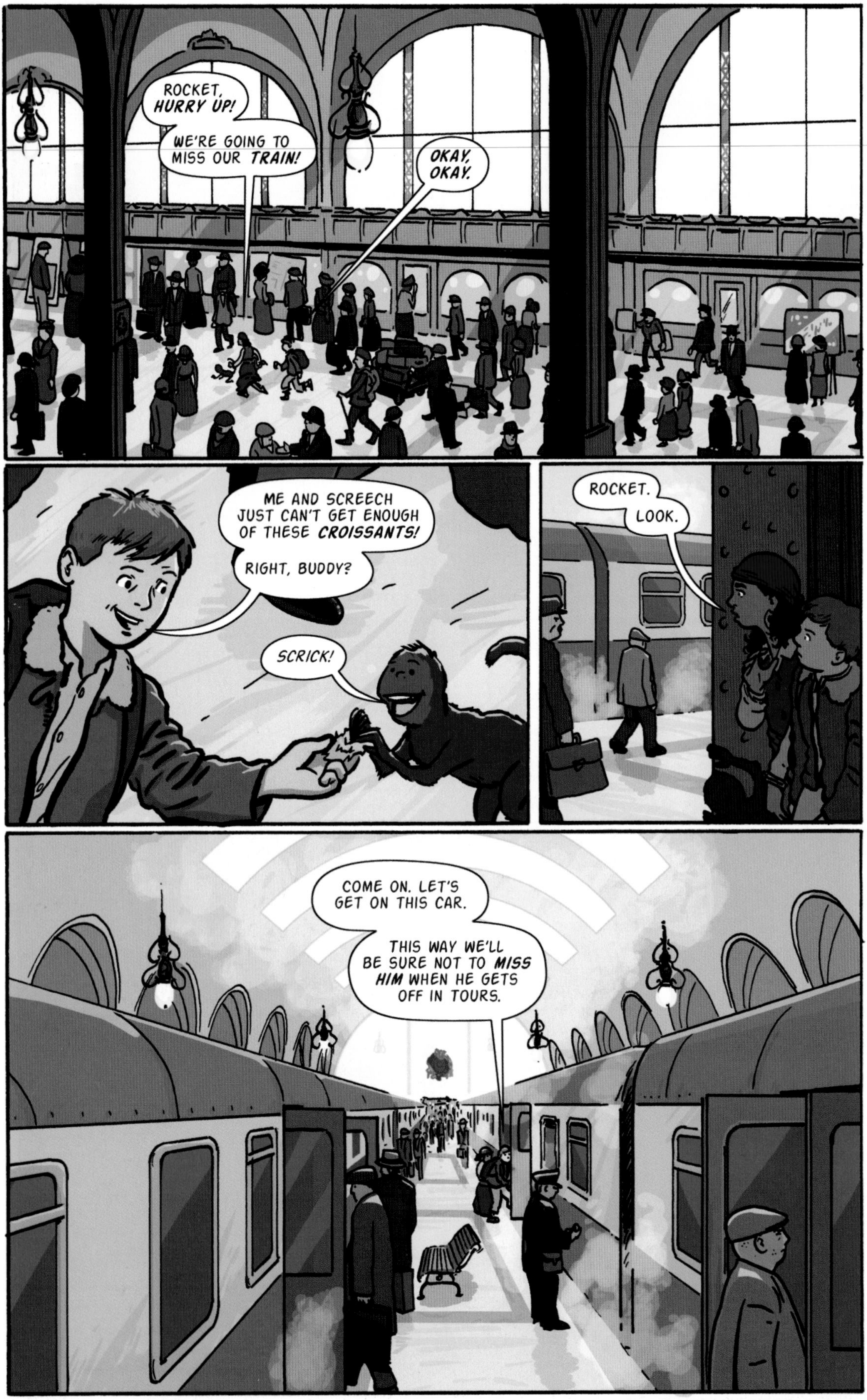
ROCKET, HURRY UP!
WE'RE GOING TO MISS OUR TRAIN!
OKAY, OKAY.
ME AND SCREECH JUST CAN'T GET ENOUGH OF THESE CROISSANTS!
RIGHT, BUDDY?
SCRICK!
ROCKET.
LOOK.
COME ON. LET'S GET ON THIS CAR.
THIS WAY WE'LL BE SURE NOT TO MISS HIM WHEN HE GETS OFF IN TOURS.

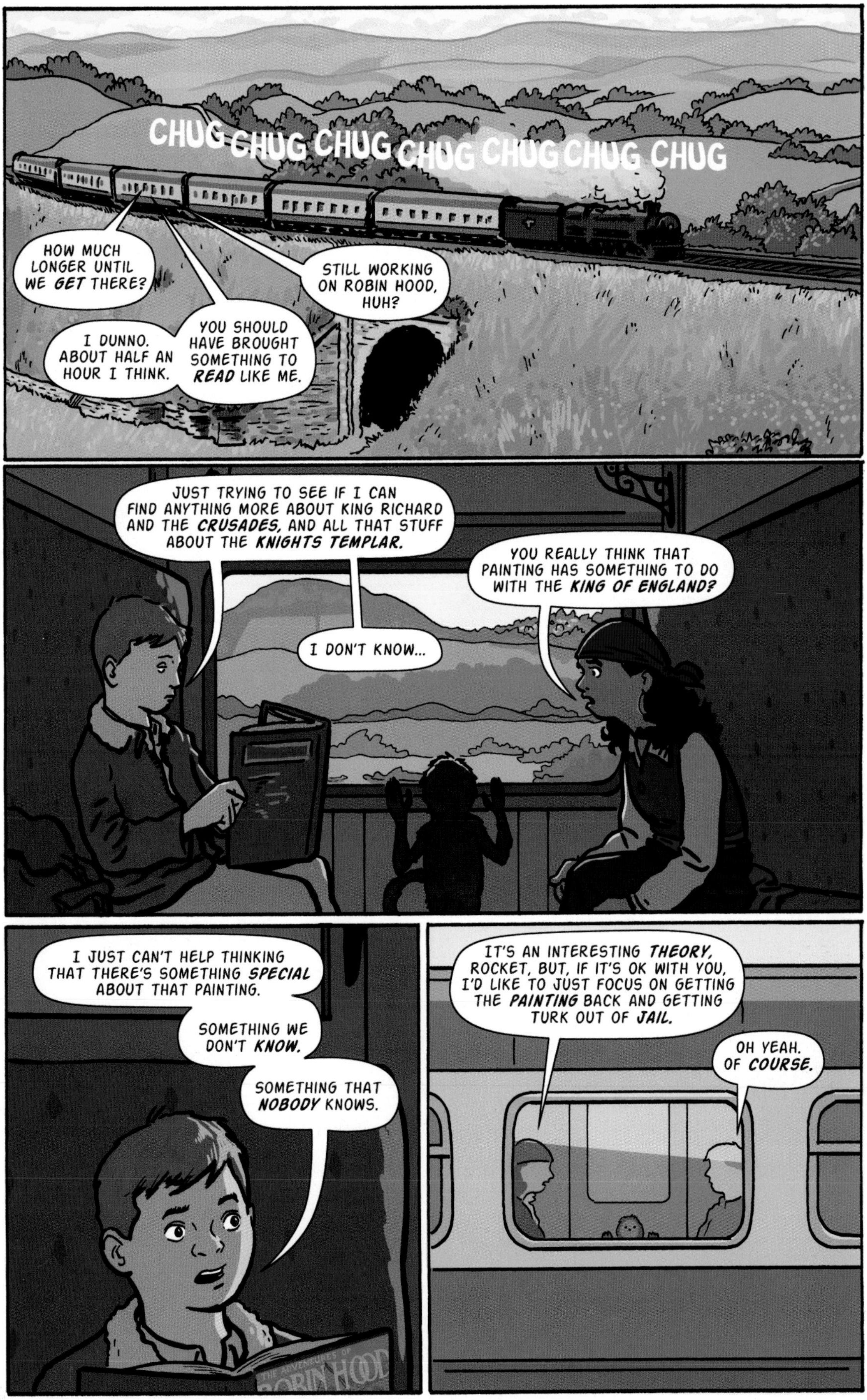
CHUG CHUG CHUG CHUG CHUG CHUG CHUG
HOW MUCH LONGER UNTIL WE GET THERE?
STILL WORKING ON ROBIN HOOD, HUH?
I DUNNO. ABOUT HALF AN HOUR I THINK.
YOU SHOULD HAVE BROUGHT SOMETHING TO READ LIKE ME.
JUST TRYING TO SEE IF I CAN FIND ANYTHING MORE ABOUT KING RICHARD AND THE CRUSADES, AND ALL THAT STUFF ABOUT THE KNIGHTS TEMPLAR.
YOU REALLY THINK THAT PAINTING HAS SOMETHING TO DO WITH THE KING OF ENGLAND?
I DON'T KNOW...
I JUST CAN'T HELP THINKING THAT THERE'S SOMETHING SPECIAL ABOUT THAT PAINTING.
SOMETHING WE DON'T KNOW.
SOMETHING THAT NOBODY KNOWS.
THE ADVENTURES OF ROBIN HOOD
IT'S AN INTERESTING THEORY, ROCKET, BUT, IF IT'S OK WITH YOU, I'D LIKE TO JUST FOCUS ON GETTING THE PAINTING BACK AND GETTING TURK OUT OF JAIL.
OH YEAH. OF COURSE.

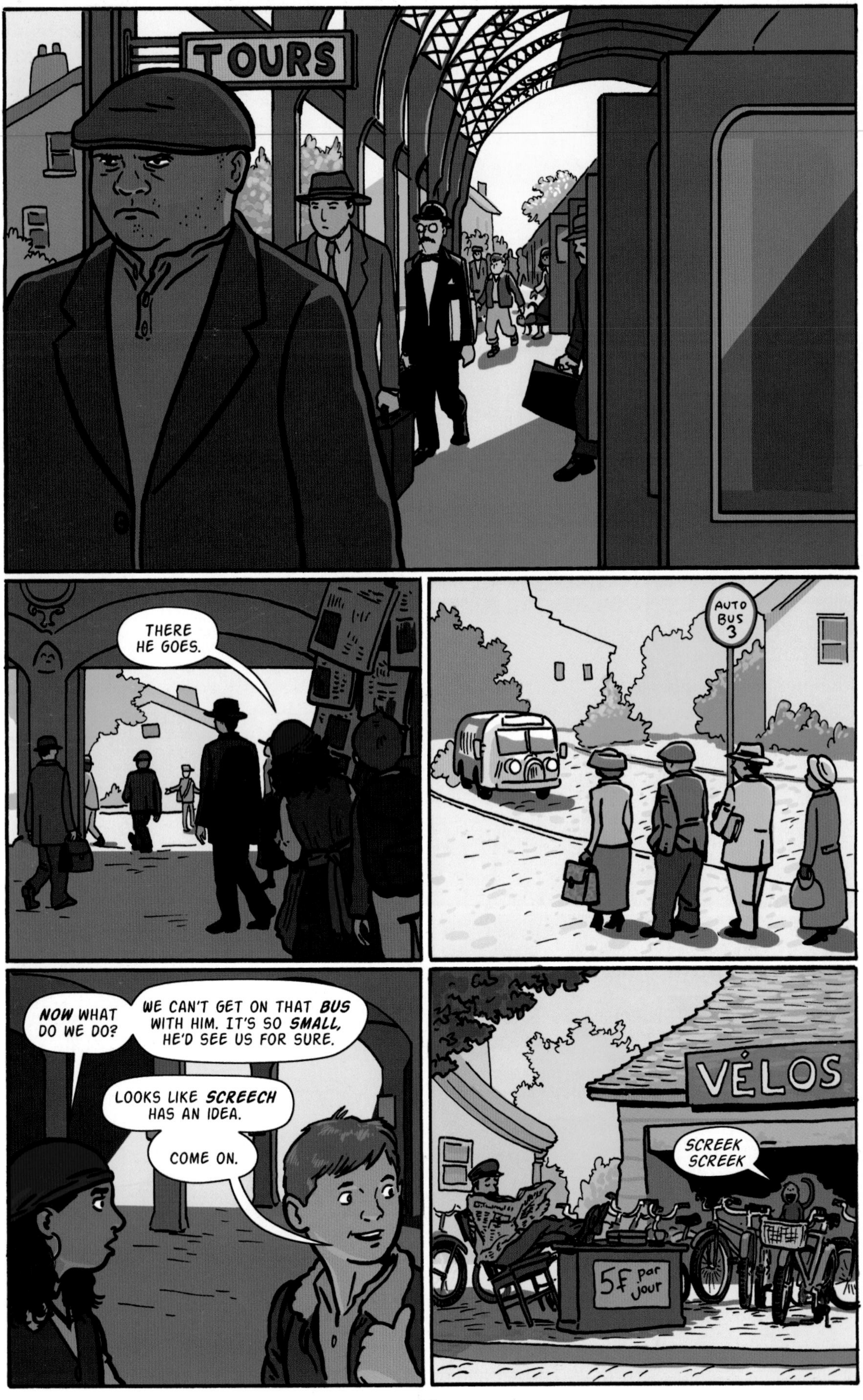
TOURS
THERE HE GOES.
AUTO BUS 3
NOW WHAT DO WE DO?
WE CAN'T GET ON THAT BUS WITH HIM. IT'S SO SMALL, HE'D SEE US FOR SURE.
LOOKS LIKE SCREECH HAS AN IDEA.
COME ON.
VÉLOS
SCREEK SCREEK
5F par jour

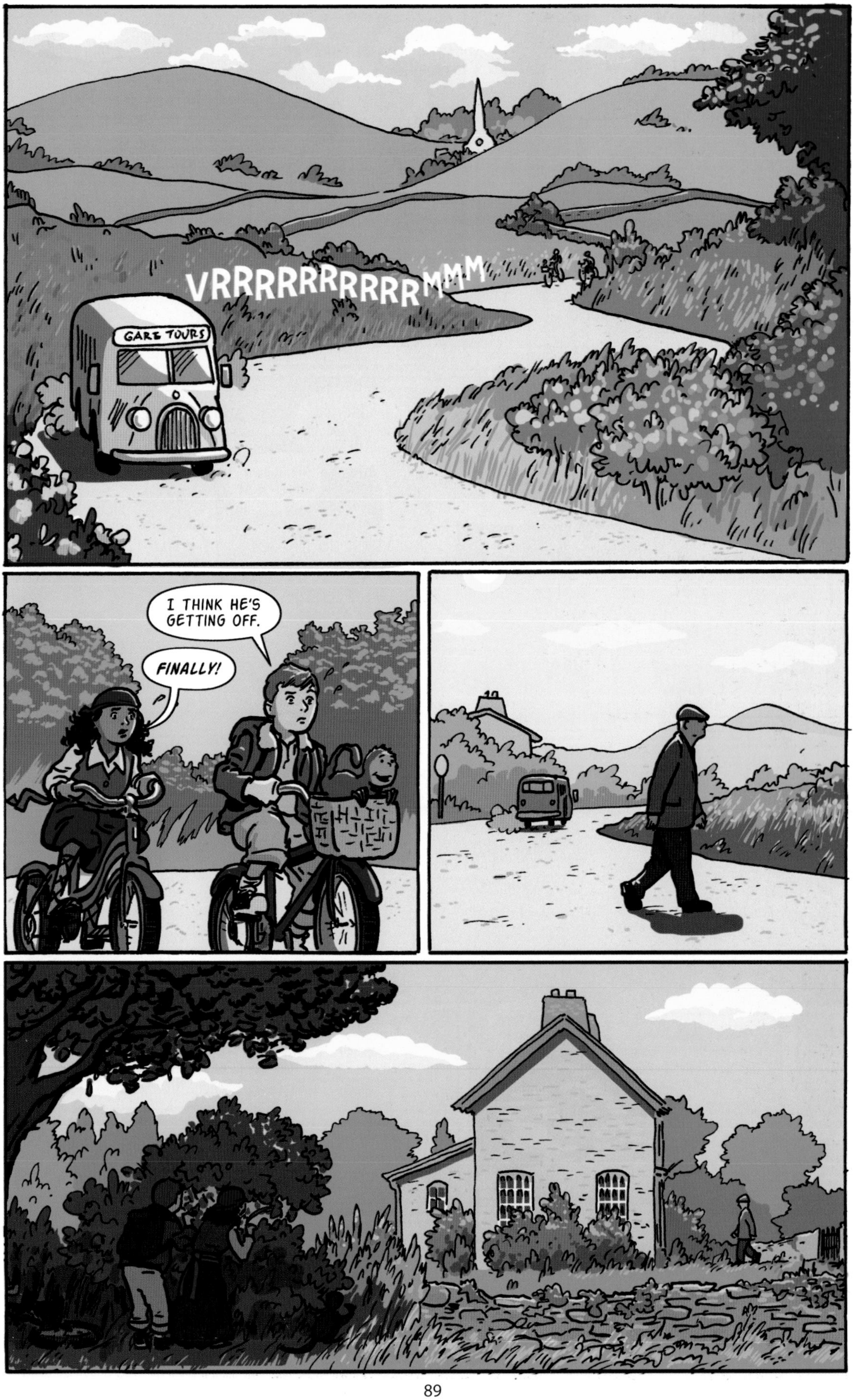
GARE TOURS
VRRRRRRRRRRRMMM
I THINK HE'S GETTING OFF.
FINALLY!

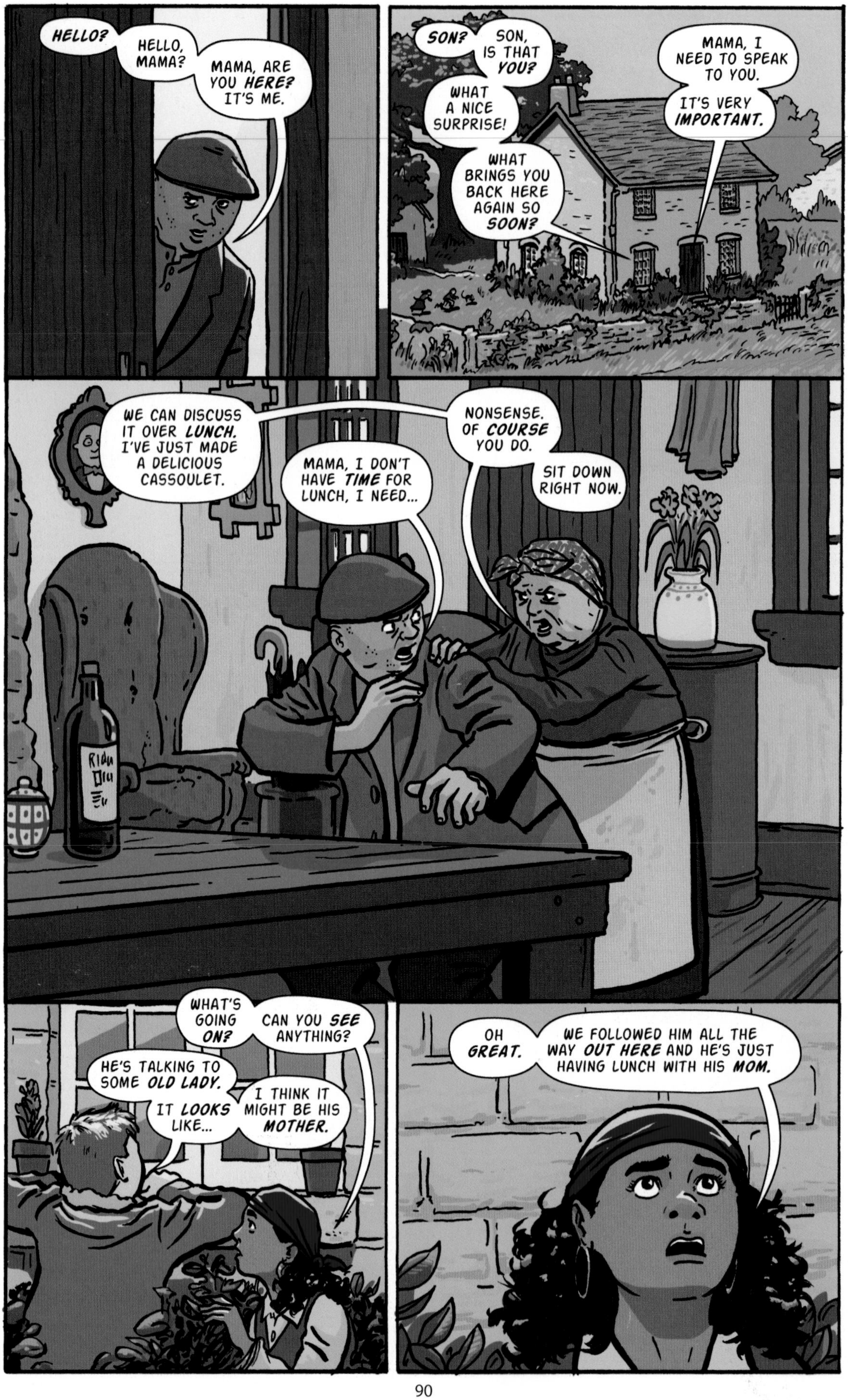
HELLO?
HELLO, MAMA?
MAMA, ARE YOU *HERE?* IT'S ME.
SON?
SON, IS THAT *YOU?*
WHAT A NICE SURPRISE!
WHAT BRINGS YOU BACK HERE AGAIN SO *SOON?*
MAMA, I NEED TO SPEAK TO YOU.
IT'S VERY *IMPORTANT.*
WE CAN DISCUSS IT OVER *LUNCH.* I'VE JUST MADE A DELICIOUS CASSOULET.
MAMA, I DON'T HAVE *TIME* FOR LUNCH, I NEED...
NONSENSE. OF *COURSE* YOU DO.
SIT DOWN RIGHT NOW.
WHAT'S GOING *ON?*
CAN YOU *SEE* ANYTHING?
HE'S TALKING TO SOME *OLD LADY.*
IT *LOOKS* LIKE...
I THINK IT MIGHT BE HIS *MOTHER.*
OH *GREAT.*
WE FOLLOWED HIM ALL THE WAY *OUT HERE* AND HE'S JUST HAVING LUNCH WITH HIS *MOM.*

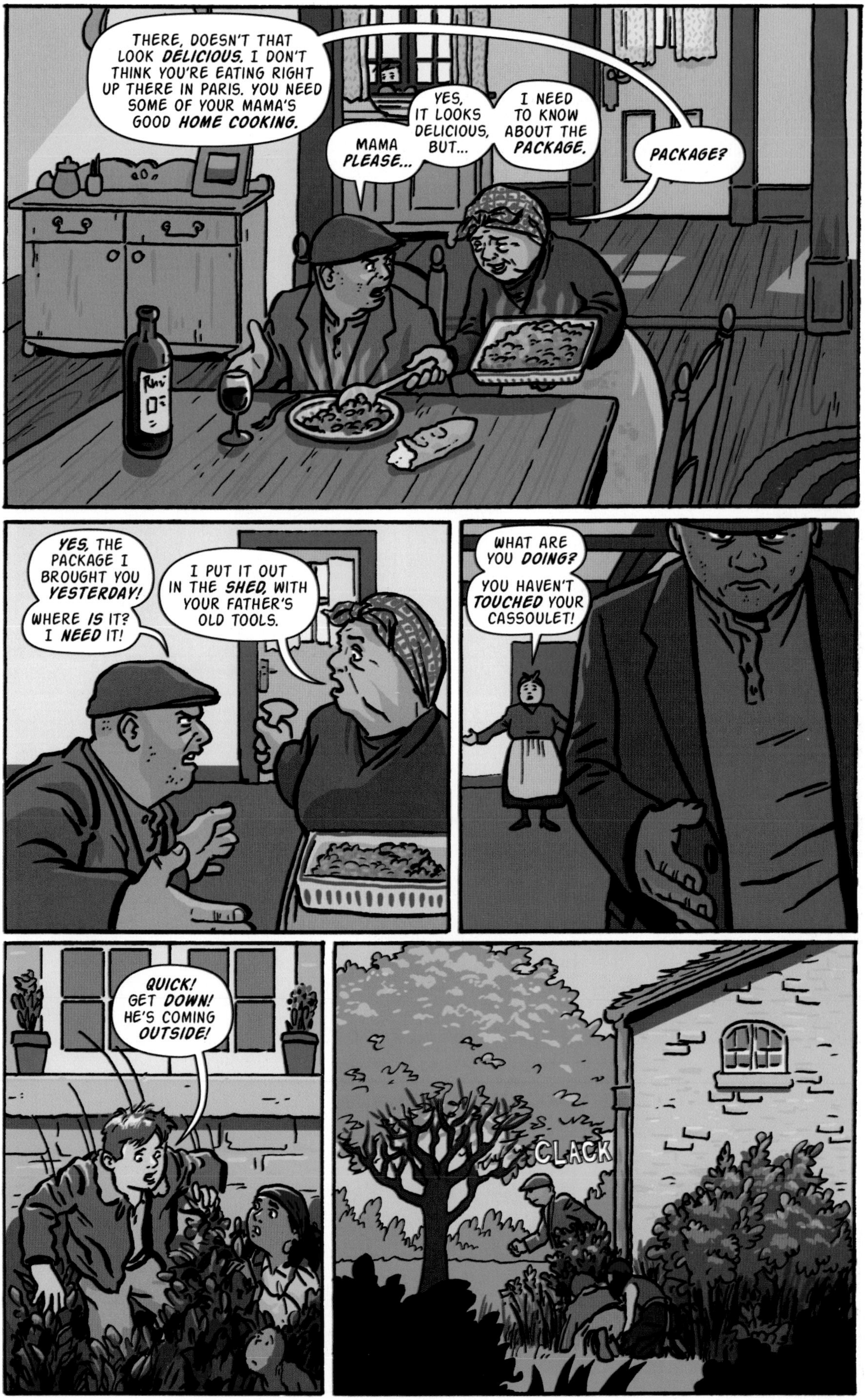
THERE, DOESN'T THAT LOOK DELICIOUS. I DON'T THINK YOU'RE EATING RIGHT UP THERE IN PARIS. YOU NEED SOME OF YOUR MAMA'S GOOD HOME COOKING.
MAMA PLEASE...
YES, IT LOOKS DELICIOUS, BUT...
I NEED TO KNOW ABOUT THE PACKAGE.
PACKAGE?
YES, THE PACKAGE I BROUGHT YOU YESTERDAY!
WHERE IS IT? I NEED IT!
I PUT IT OUT IN THE SHED, WITH YOUR FATHER'S OLD TOOLS.
WHAT ARE YOU DOING?
YOU HAVEN'T TOUCHED YOUR CASSOULET!
QUICK! GET DOWN! HE'S COMING OUTSIDE!
CLACK

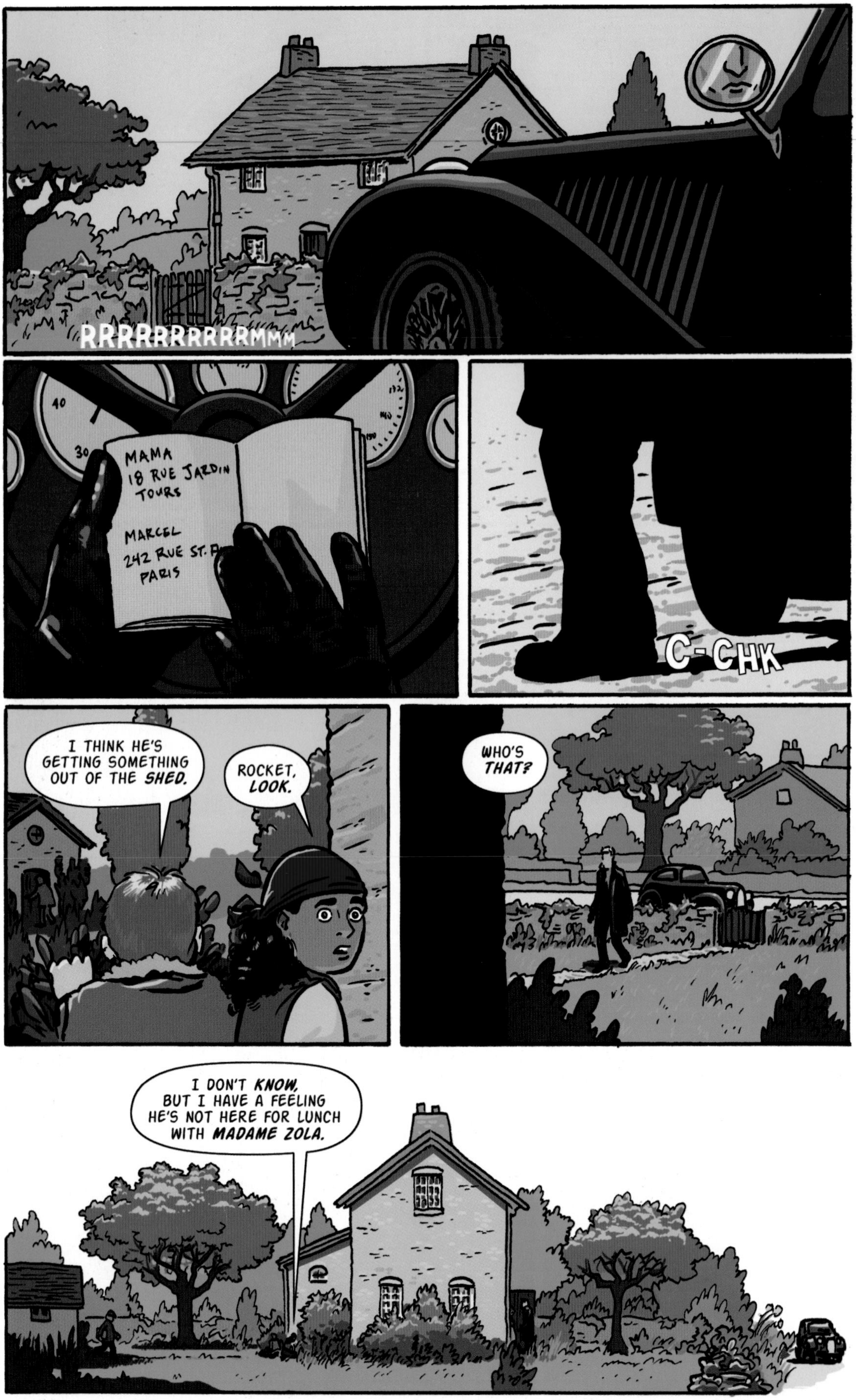
RRRRRRRRRRRMMM
MAMA
18 RUE JARDIN
TOURS
MARCEL
242 RUE ST. P
PARIS
C-CHK
I THINK HE'S GETTING SOMETHING OUT OF THE SHED.
ROCKET, LOOK.
WHO'S THAT?
I DON'T KNOW, BUT I HAVE A FEELING HE'S NOT HERE FOR LUNCH WITH MADAME ZOLA.

PLEASE, COME IN. WOULD YOU LIKE SOMETHING TO *EAT?*

NO THANK YOU, MADAME. THIS WON'T TAKE VERY LONG.

I NEED TO ASK YOU SOMETHING ABOUT YOUR *SON...*

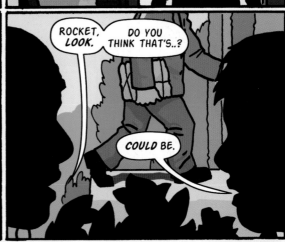

WELL, IN THAT CASE, YOU CAN ASK HIM *YOURSELF.*

HE'S RIGHT IN THE *BACK GARDEN.*

ROCKET, *LOOK.*

DO YOU THINK THAT'S..?

COULD BE.

MAMA!

I TOLD YOU TO BE *CAREFUL* WITH THIS!

IT WAS UNDER A *PILE* OF...

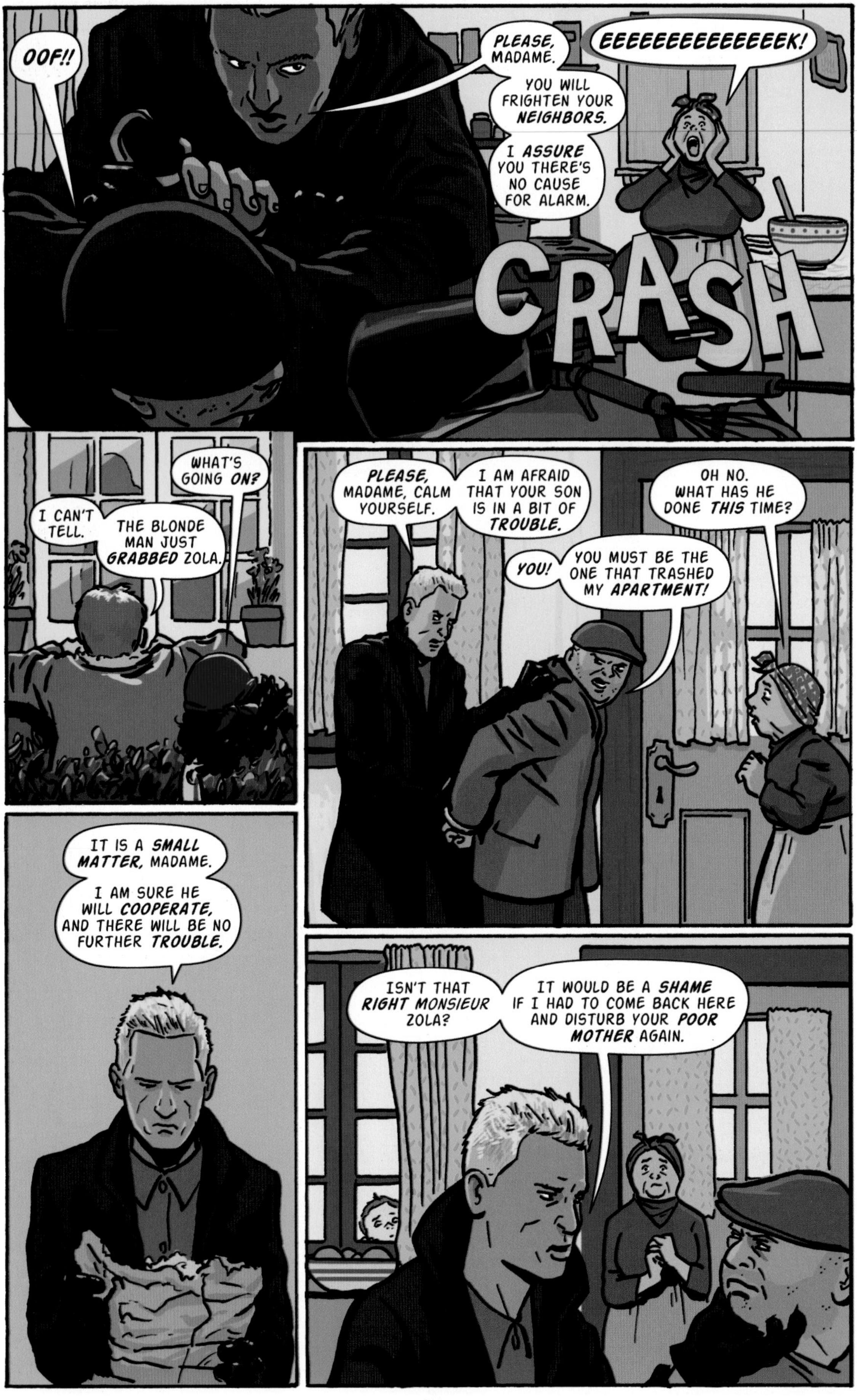
OOF!!
EEEEEEEEEEEEEEK!
PLEASE, MADAME.
YOU WILL FRIGHTEN YOUR NEIGHBORS.
I ASSURE YOU THERE'S NO CAUSE FOR ALARM.
CRASH
WHAT'S GOING ON?
I CAN'T TELL.
THE BLONDE MAN JUST GRABBED ZOLA.
PLEASE, MADAME, CALM YOURSELF.
I AM AFRAID THAT YOUR SON IS IN A BIT OF TROUBLE.
OH NO. WHAT HAS HE DONE THIS TIME?
YOU!
YOU MUST BE THE ONE THAT TRASHED MY APARTMENT!
IT IS A SMALL MATTER, MADAME.
I AM SURE HE WILL COOPERATE, AND THERE WILL BE NO FURTHER TROUBLE.
ISN'T THAT RIGHT MONSIEUR ZOLA?
IT WOULD BE A SHAME IF I HAD TO COME BACK HERE AND DISTURB YOUR POOR MOTHER AGAIN.

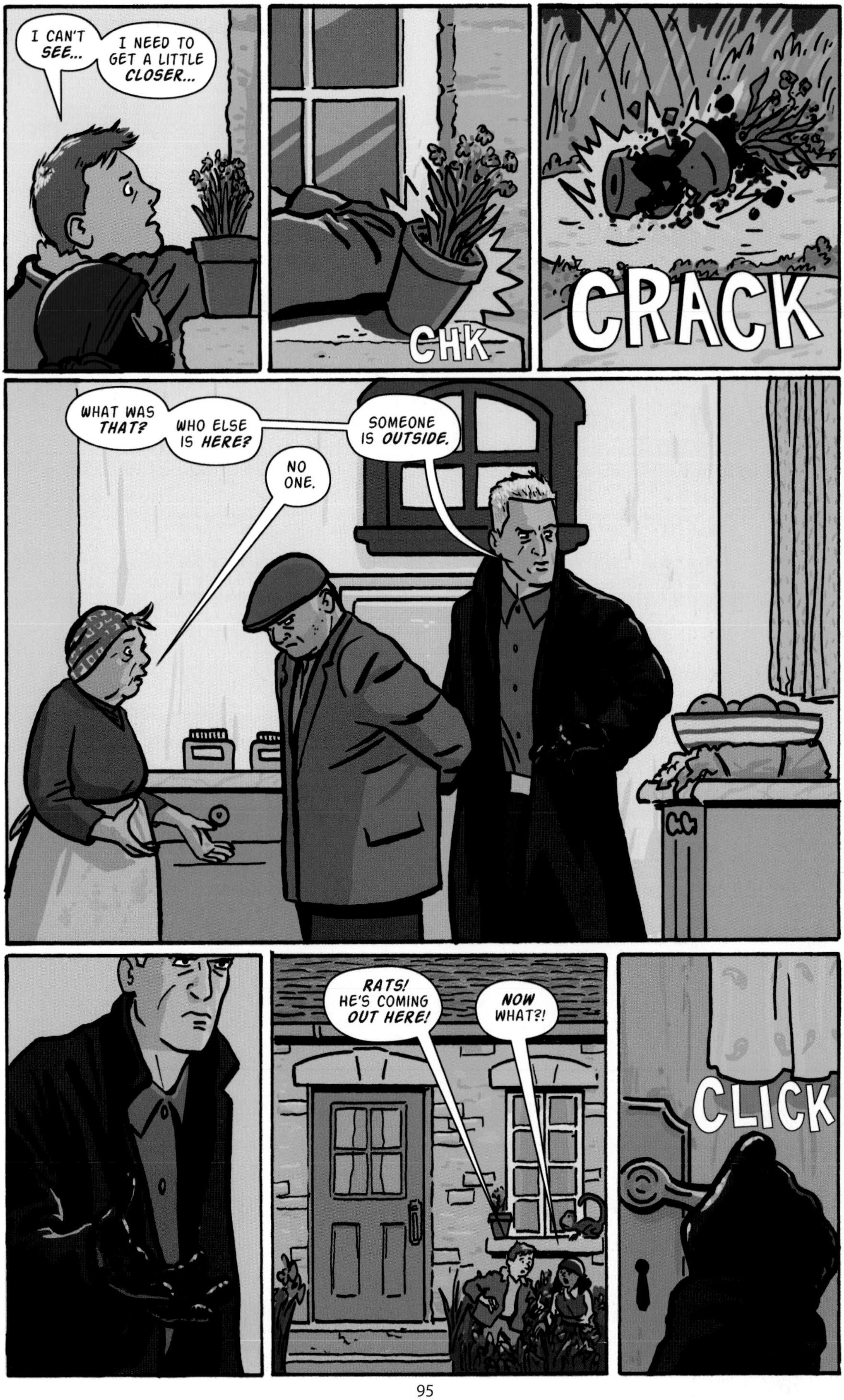
I CAN'T SEE...
I NEED TO GET A LITTLE CLOSER...
CHK
CRACK
WHAT WAS THAT?
WHO ELSE IS HERE?
NO ONE.
SOMEONE IS OUTSIDE.
RATS! HE'S COMING OUT HERE!
NOW WHAT?!
CLICK

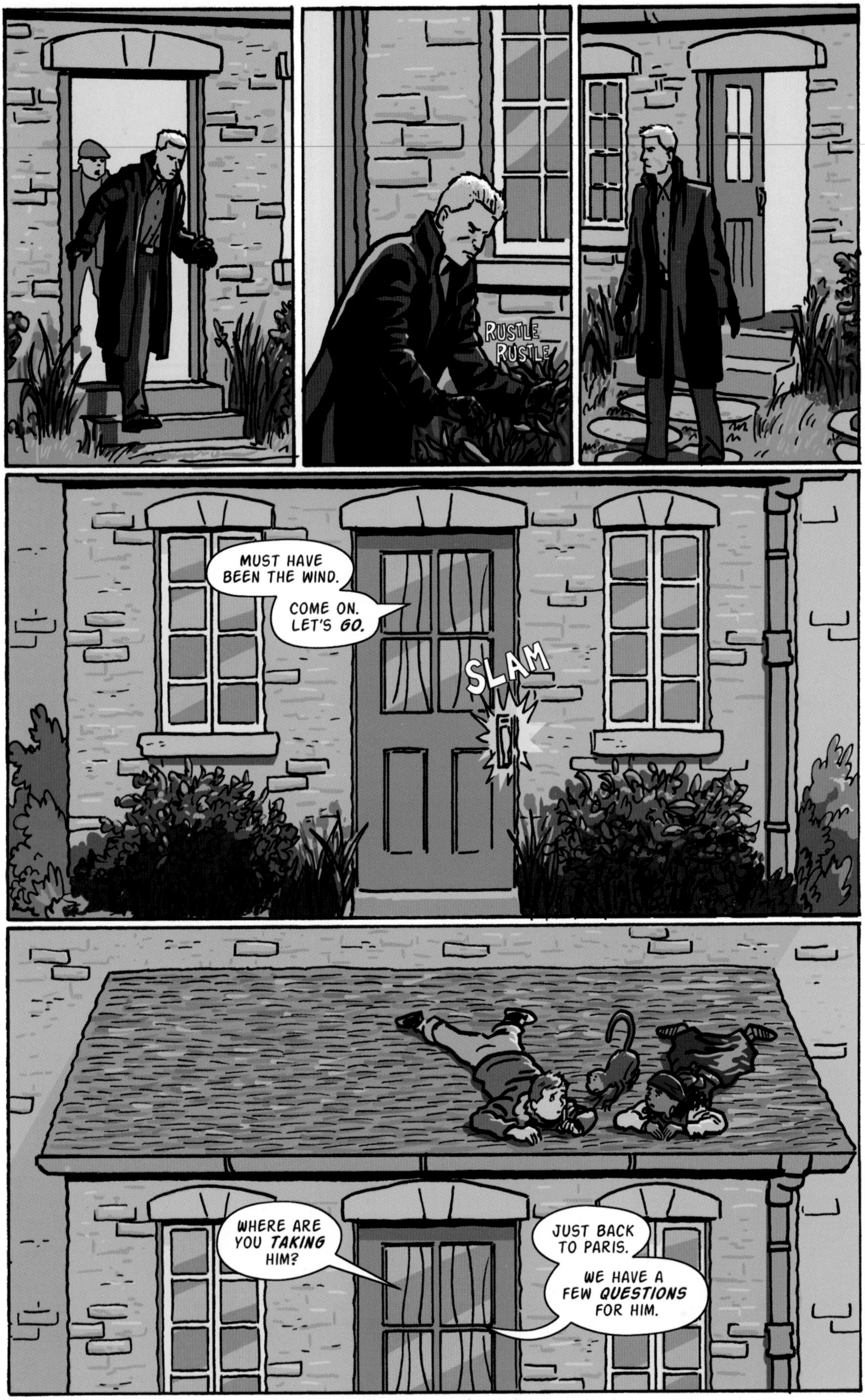
RUSTLE
RUSTLE
MUST HAVE BEEN THE WIND.
COME ON. LET'S GO.
SLAM
WHERE ARE YOU TAKING HIM?
JUST BACK TO PARIS.
WE HAVE A FEW QUESTIONS FOR HIM.

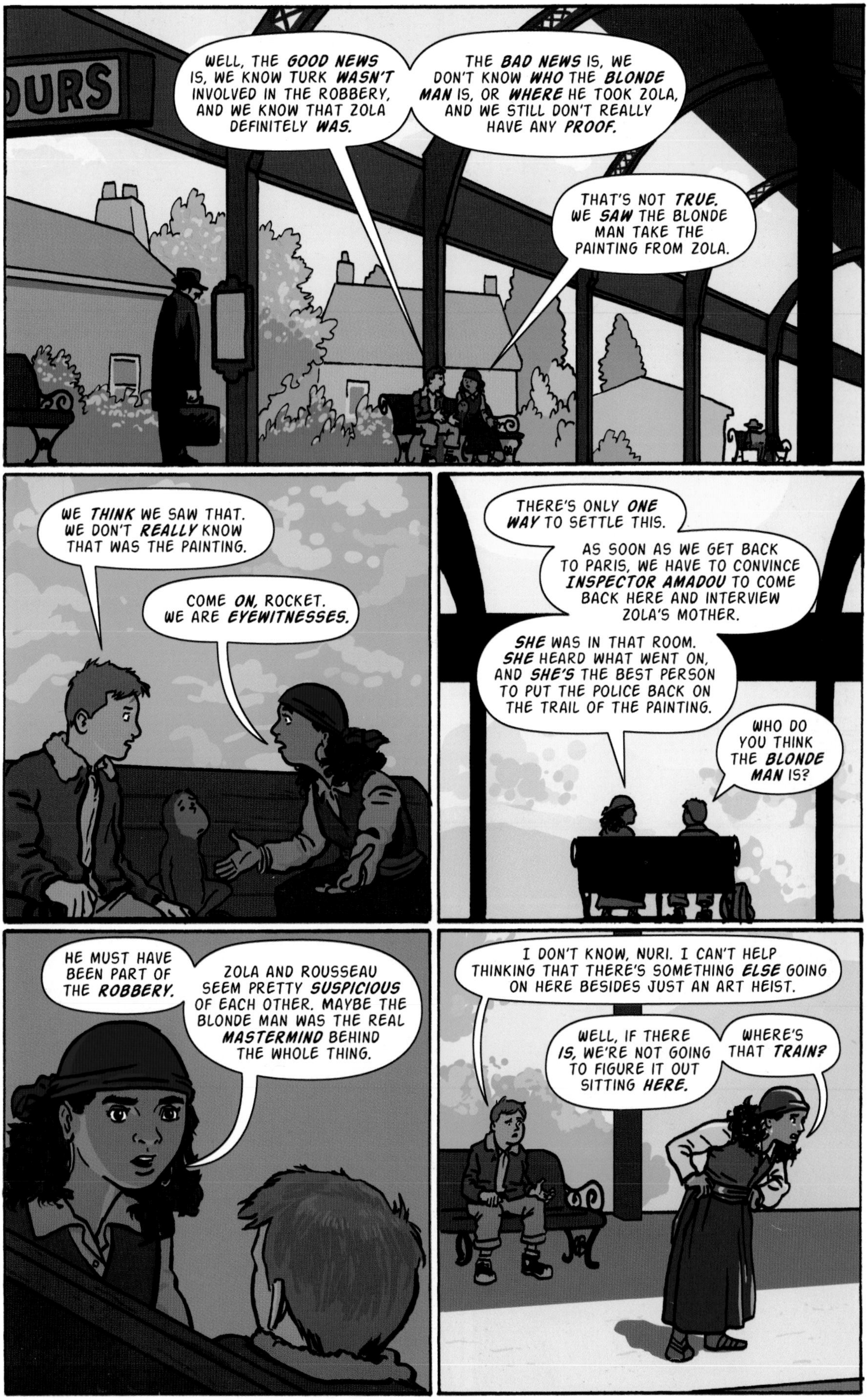
DURS
WELL, THE GOOD NEWS IS, WE KNOW TURK WASN'T INVOLVED IN THE ROBBERY, AND WE KNOW THAT ZOLA DEFINITELY WAS.
THE BAD NEWS IS, WE DON'T KNOW WHO THE BLONDE MAN IS, OR WHERE HE TOOK ZOLA, AND WE STILL DON'T REALLY HAVE ANY PROOF.
THAT'S NOT TRUE. WE SAW THE BLONDE MAN TAKE THE PAINTING FROM ZOLA.
WE THINK WE SAW THAT. WE DON'T REALLY KNOW THAT WAS THE PAINTING.
COME ON, ROCKET. WE ARE EYEWITNESSES.
THERE'S ONLY ONE WAY TO SETTLE THIS.
AS SOON AS WE GET BACK TO PARIS, WE HAVE TO CONVINCE INSPECTOR AMADOU TO COME BACK HERE AND INTERVIEW ZOLA'S MOTHER.
SHE WAS IN THAT ROOM. SHE HEARD WHAT WENT ON, AND SHE'S THE BEST PERSON TO PUT THE POLICE BACK ON THE TRAIL OF THE PAINTING.
WHO DO YOU THINK THE BLONDE MAN IS?
HE MUST HAVE BEEN PART OF THE ROBBERY.
ZOLA AND ROUSSEAU SEEM PRETTY SUSPICIOUS OF EACH OTHER. MAYBE THE BLONDE MAN WAS THE REAL MASTERMIND BEHIND THE WHOLE THING.
I DON'T KNOW, NURI. I CAN'T HELP THINKING THAT THERE'S SOMETHING ELSE GOING ON HERE BESIDES JUST AN ART HEIST.
WELL, IF THERE IS, WE'RE NOT GOING TO FIGURE IT OUT SITTING HERE.
WHERE'S THAT TRAIN?

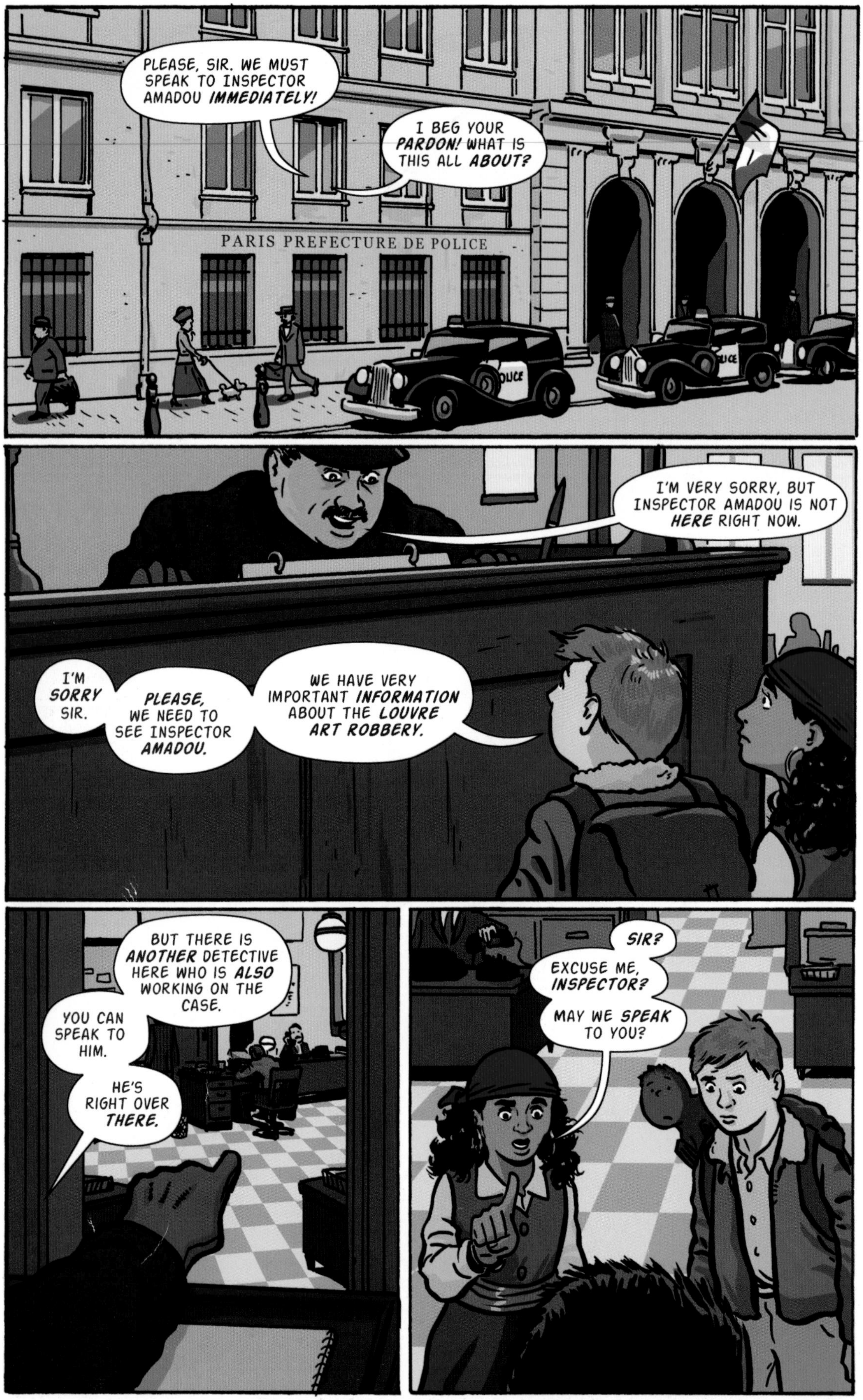
PLEASE, SIR. WE MUST SPEAK TO INSPECTOR AMADOU *IMMEDIATELY!*
I BEG YOUR *PARDON!* WHAT IS THIS ALL *ABOUT?*
PARIS PREFECTURE DE POLICE
I'M VERY SORRY, BUT INSPECTOR AMADOU IS NOT *HERE* RIGHT NOW.
I'M *SORRY* SIR.
PLEASE, WE NEED TO SEE INSPECTOR *AMADOU.*
WE HAVE VERY IMPORTANT *INFORMATION* ABOUT THE *LOUVRE ART ROBBERY.*
BUT THERE IS *ANOTHER* DETECTIVE HERE WHO IS *ALSO* WORKING ON THE CASE.
YOU CAN SPEAK TO HIM.
HE'S RIGHT OVER *THERE.*
SIR?
EXCUSE ME, *INSPECTOR?*
MAY WE *SPEAK* TO YOU?

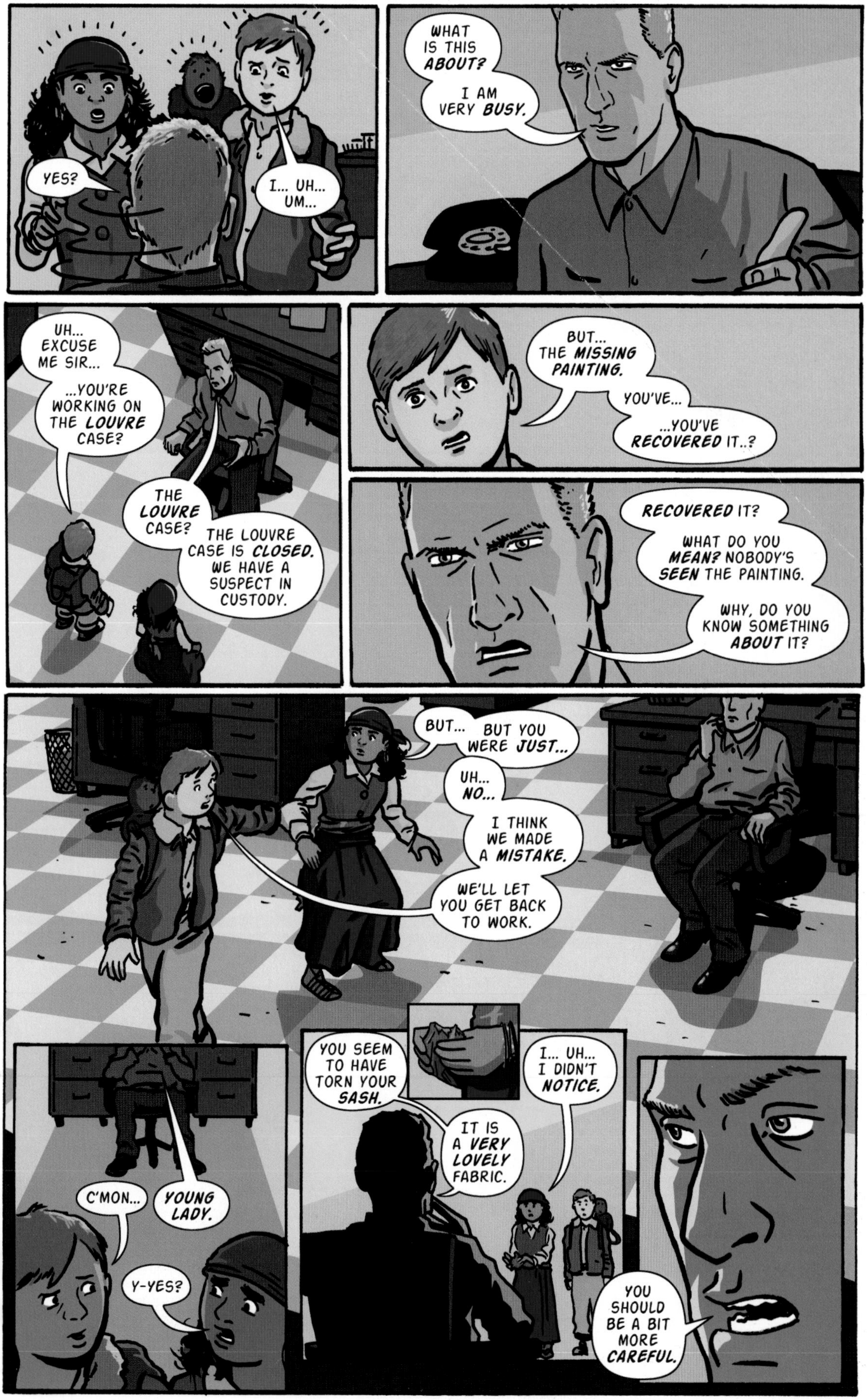
YES?
I... UH... UM...
WHAT IS THIS ABOUT?
I AM VERY BUSY.
UH... EXCUSE ME SIR...
...YOU'RE WORKING ON THE LOUVRE CASE?
THE LOUVRE CASE?
THE LOUVRE CASE IS CLOSED. WE HAVE A SUSPECT IN CUSTODY.
BUT... THE MISSING PAINTING.
YOU'VE...
...YOU'VE RECOVERED IT..?
RECOVERED IT?
WHAT DO YOU MEAN? NOBODY'S SEEN THE PAINTING.
WHY, DO YOU KNOW SOMETHING ABOUT IT?
BUT...
BUT YOU WERE JUST...
UH... NO...
I THINK WE MADE A MISTAKE.
WE'LL LET YOU GET BACK TO WORK.
C'MON...
YOUNG LADY.
Y-YES?
YOU SEEM TO HAVE TORN YOUR SASH.
IT IS A VERY LOVELY FABRIC.
I... UH... I DIDN'T NOTICE.
YOU SHOULD BE A BIT MORE CAREFUL.

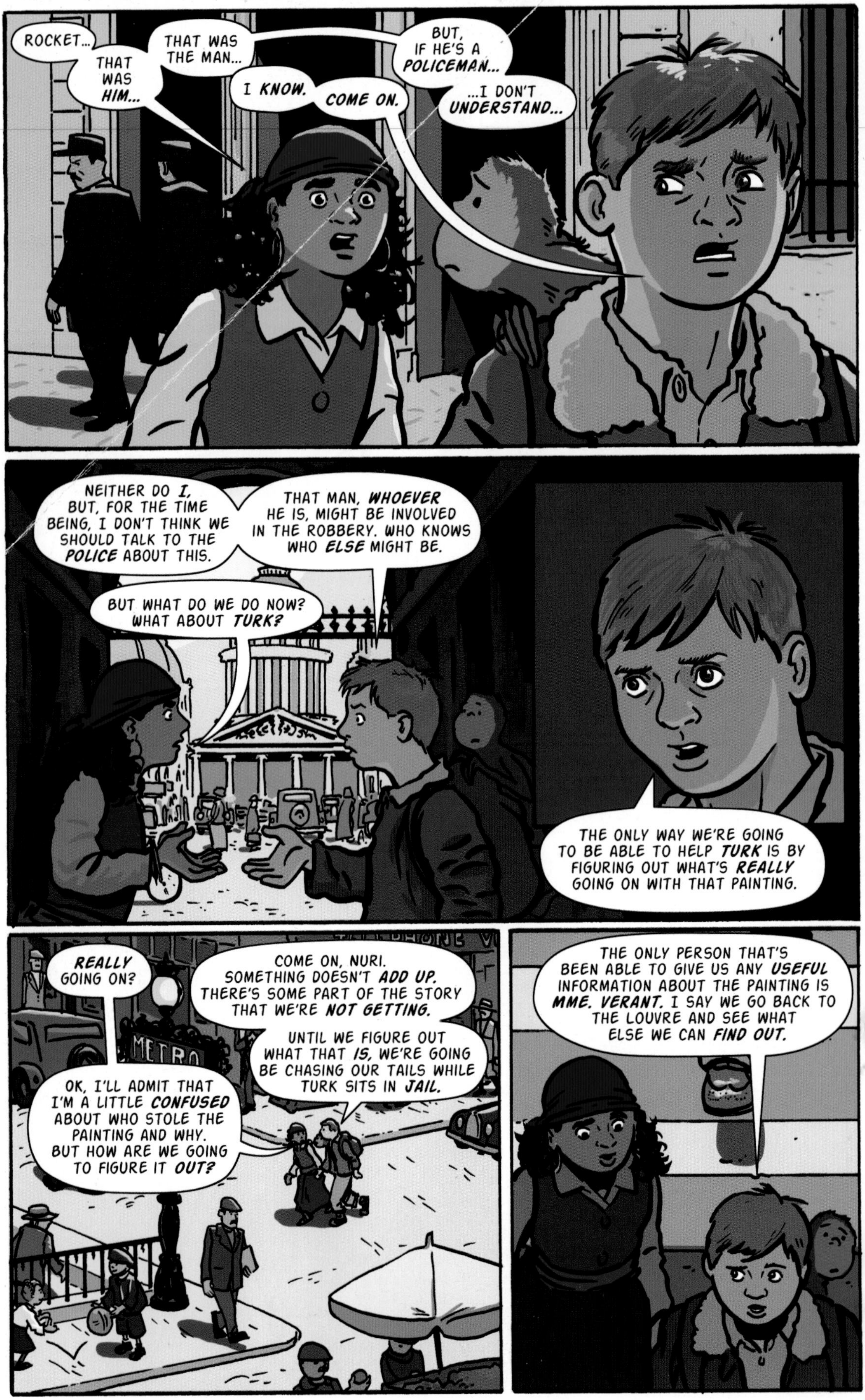
ROCKET...
THAT WAS HIM...
THAT WAS THE MAN...
I KNOW.
COME ON.
BUT, IF HE'S A POLICEMAN...
...I DON'T UNDERSTAND...
NEITHER DO I, BUT, FOR THE TIME BEING, I DON'T THINK WE SHOULD TALK TO THE POLICE ABOUT THIS.
THAT MAN, WHOEVER HE IS, MIGHT BE INVOLVED IN THE ROBBERY. WHO KNOWS WHO ELSE MIGHT BE.
BUT WHAT DO WE DO NOW? WHAT ABOUT TURK?
THE ONLY WAY WE'RE GOING TO BE ABLE TO HELP TURK IS BY FIGURING OUT WHAT'S REALLY GOING ON WITH THAT PAINTING.
REALLY GOING ON?
COME ON, NURI. SOMETHING DOESN'T ADD UP. THERE'S SOME PART OF THE STORY THAT WE'RE NOT GETTING.
METRO
OK, I'LL ADMIT THAT I'M A LITTLE CONFUSED ABOUT WHO STOLE THE PAINTING AND WHY. BUT HOW ARE WE GOING TO FIGURE IT OUT?
UNTIL WE FIGURE OUT WHAT THAT IS, WE'RE GOING BE CHASING OUR TAILS WHILE TURK SITS IN JAIL.
THE ONLY PERSON THAT'S BEEN ABLE TO GIVE US ANY USEFUL INFORMATION ABOUT THE PAINTING IS MME. VERANT. I SAY WE GO BACK TO THE LOUVRE AND SEE WHAT ELSE WE CAN FIND OUT.

WELL, LOOK WHO IT *IS*.

JUST COULDN'T STAY AWAY FROM THE EXCITING WORLD OF *MEDIEVAL ART*, HM?

HI MME. VERANT. SORRY TO BOTHER YOU BUT, WE HAVE A FEW MORE *QUESTIONS*.

IT'S NO *BOTHER*.

AFTER A DAY IN THIS MUSTY OLD LIBRARY, IT'S NICE TO TALK TO SOME *ACTUAL PEOPLE*.

WHAT'S ON YOUR MIND?

THIS MIGHT SOUND *STRANGE*, BUT, I THINK THERE MIGHT BE *MORE* TO THIS PAINTING THAN WE THOUGHT.

ACTUALLY, I THINK YOU MIGHT BE *RIGHT* ABOUT THAT.

REALLY?

I'VE BEEN RESEARCHING DOWN HERE EVER SINCE THE *THEFT*, AND I'VE BEEN ABLE TO UNCOVER A *LITTLE MORE* ABOUT THE PAINTING'S HISTORY.

REMEMBER WHEN I SAID THAT WE USUALLY TRY TO FIND OUT IF ANYONE HAD A *PREVIOUS CLAIM* ON A MISSING ARTWORK?

CLANDESTIN

IT TURNS OUT THAT AN OLD FRENCH FAMILY BY THE NAME OF *ST. GERMAIN* HAS SOME INTEREST IN THE PAINTING. A FELLOW WHO CALLS HIMSELF THE *COMTE DE ST. GERMAIN* HAS MADE SEVERAL INQUIRIES ABOUT IT OVER THE YEARS.

HE LIVES HERE IN *PARIS*, AND HE'S QUITE A COLLECTOR OF ALL THINGS RELATED TO THE *KNIGHTS TEMPLAR*.

...ent. Ceux qui ont et ceux qui ma frappaient à la porte de M. Myriel chercher l'aumône que le...
déposer...

LE MINISTÈRE FRANCAIS DE L'ART   000

Demande d'infor

LE MINISTÈRE FRANCAIS DE L'ART   00042

Demande d'inform

09.11.1927   M. St. Germain, Esq.

St. Bernard of Clairvaux by Fra. Montague

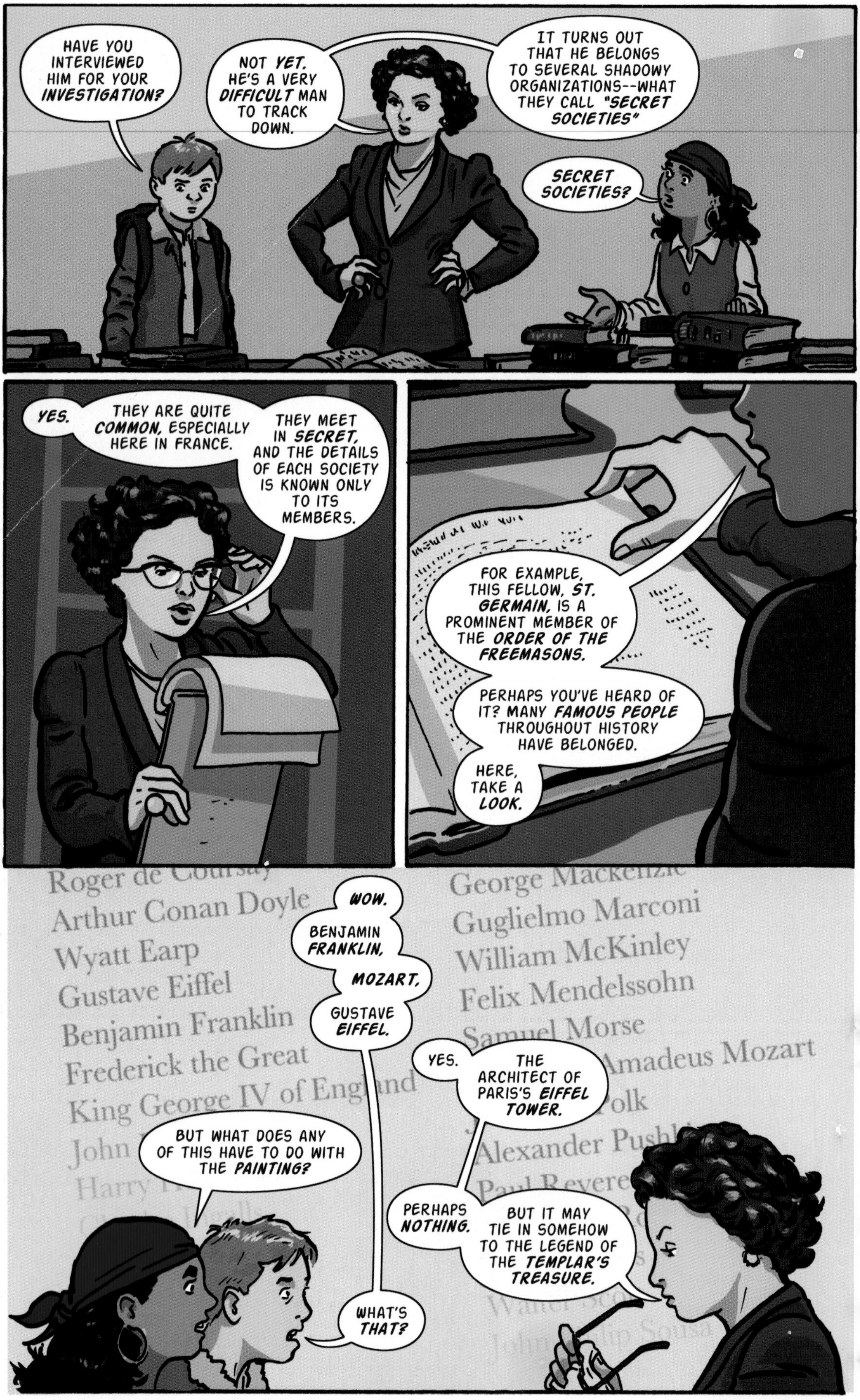
HAVE YOU INTERVIEWED HIM FOR YOUR INVESTIGATION?
NOT YET. HE'S A VERY DIFFICULT MAN TO TRACK DOWN.
IT TURNS OUT THAT HE BELONGS TO SEVERAL SHADOWY ORGANIZATIONS--WHAT THEY CALL "SECRET SOCIETIES"
SECRET SOCIETIES?
YES.
THEY ARE QUITE COMMON, ESPECIALLY HERE IN FRANCE.
THEY MEET IN SECRET, AND THE DETAILS OF EACH SOCIETY IS KNOWN ONLY TO ITS MEMBERS.
FOR EXAMPLE, THIS FELLOW, ST. GERMAIN, IS A PROMINENT MEMBER OF THE ORDER OF THE FREEMASONS.
PERHAPS YOU'VE HEARD OF IT? MANY FAMOUS PEOPLE THROUGHOUT HISTORY HAVE BELONGED.
HERE, TAKE A LOOK.
Arthur Conan Doyle
Wyatt Earp
Gustave Eiffel
Benjamin Franklin
Frederick the Great
Guglielmo Marconi
William McKinley
Felix Mendelssohn
WOW.
BENJAMIN FRANKLIN,
MOZART,
GUSTAVE EIFFEL.
YES.
THE ARCHITECT OF PARIS'S EIFFEL TOWER.
BUT WHAT DOES ANY OF THIS HAVE TO DO WITH THE PAINTING?
PERHAPS NOTHING.
BUT IT MAY TIE IN SOMEHOW TO THE LEGEND OF THE TEMPLAR'S TREASURE.
WHAT'S THAT?

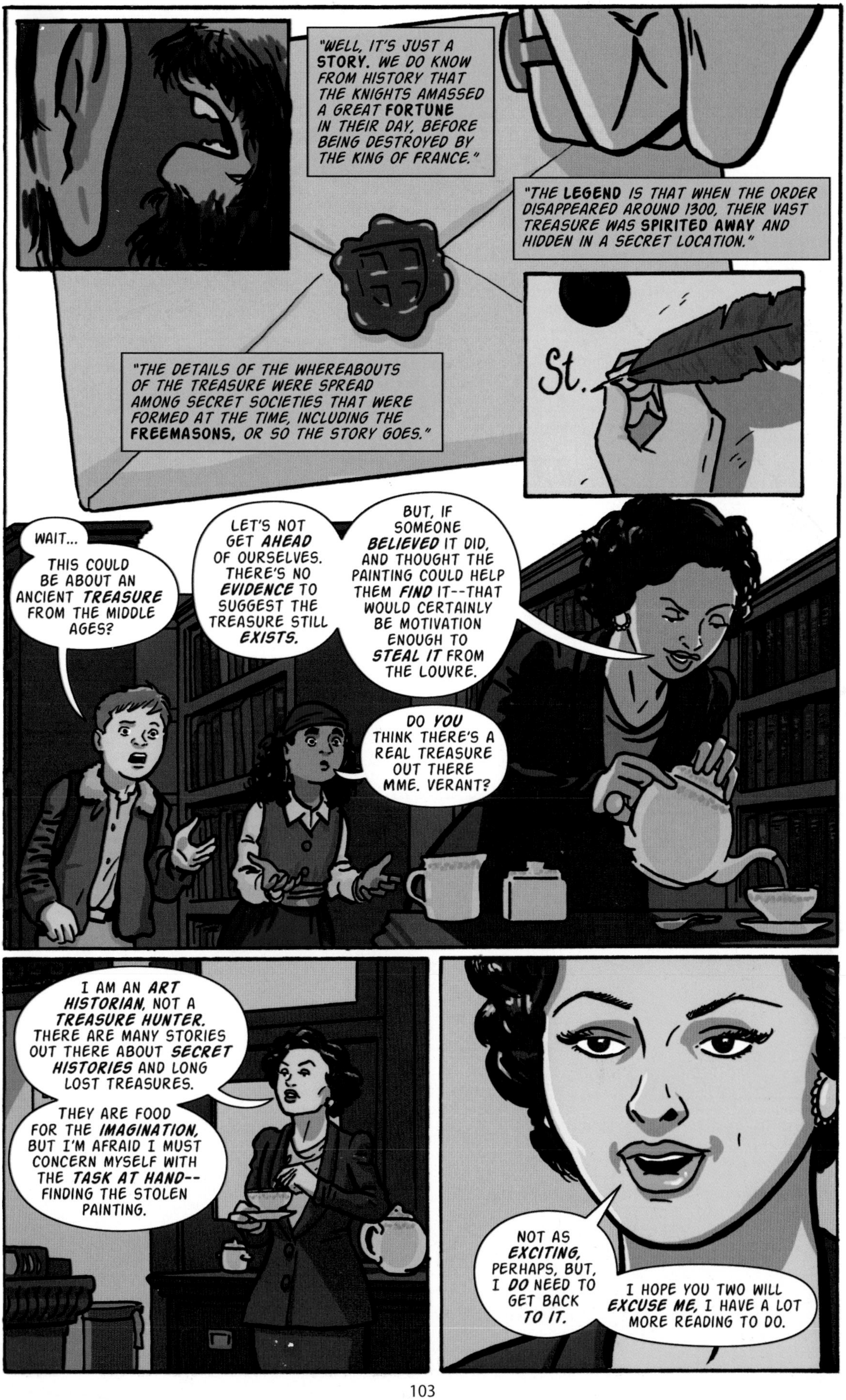
"WELL, IT'S JUST A STORY. WE DO KNOW FROM HISTORY THAT THE KNIGHTS AMASSED A GREAT FORTUNE IN THEIR DAY, BEFORE BEING DESTROYED BY THE KING OF FRANCE."
"THE LEGEND IS THAT WHEN THE ORDER DISAPPEARED AROUND 1300, THEIR VAST TREASURE WAS SPIRITED AWAY AND HIDDEN IN A SECRET LOCATION."
"THE DETAILS OF THE WHEREABOUTS OF THE TREASURE WERE SPREAD AMONG SECRET SOCIETIES THAT WERE FORMED AT THE TIME, INCLUDING THE FREEMASONS, OR SO THE STORY GOES."
St.
WAIT...
THIS COULD BE ABOUT AN ANCIENT TREASURE FROM THE MIDDLE AGES?
LET'S NOT GET AHEAD OF OURSELVES. THERE'S NO EVIDENCE TO SUGGEST THE TREASURE STILL EXISTS.
BUT, IF SOMEONE BELIEVED IT DID, AND THOUGHT THE PAINTING COULD HELP THEM FIND IT--THAT WOULD CERTAINLY BE MOTIVATION ENOUGH TO STEAL IT FROM THE LOUVRE.
DO YOU THINK THERE'S A REAL TREASURE OUT THERE MME. VERANT?
I AM AN ART HISTORIAN, NOT A TREASURE HUNTER. THERE ARE MANY STORIES OUT THERE ABOUT SECRET HISTORIES AND LONG LOST TREASURES.
THEY ARE FOOD FOR THE IMAGINATION, BUT I'M AFRAID I MUST CONCERN MYSELF WITH THE TASK AT HAND-- FINDING THE STOLEN PAINTING.
NOT AS EXCITING, PERHAPS, BUT, I DO NEED TO GET BACK TO IT.
I HOPE YOU TWO WILL EXCUSE ME, I HAVE A LOT MORE READING TO DO.

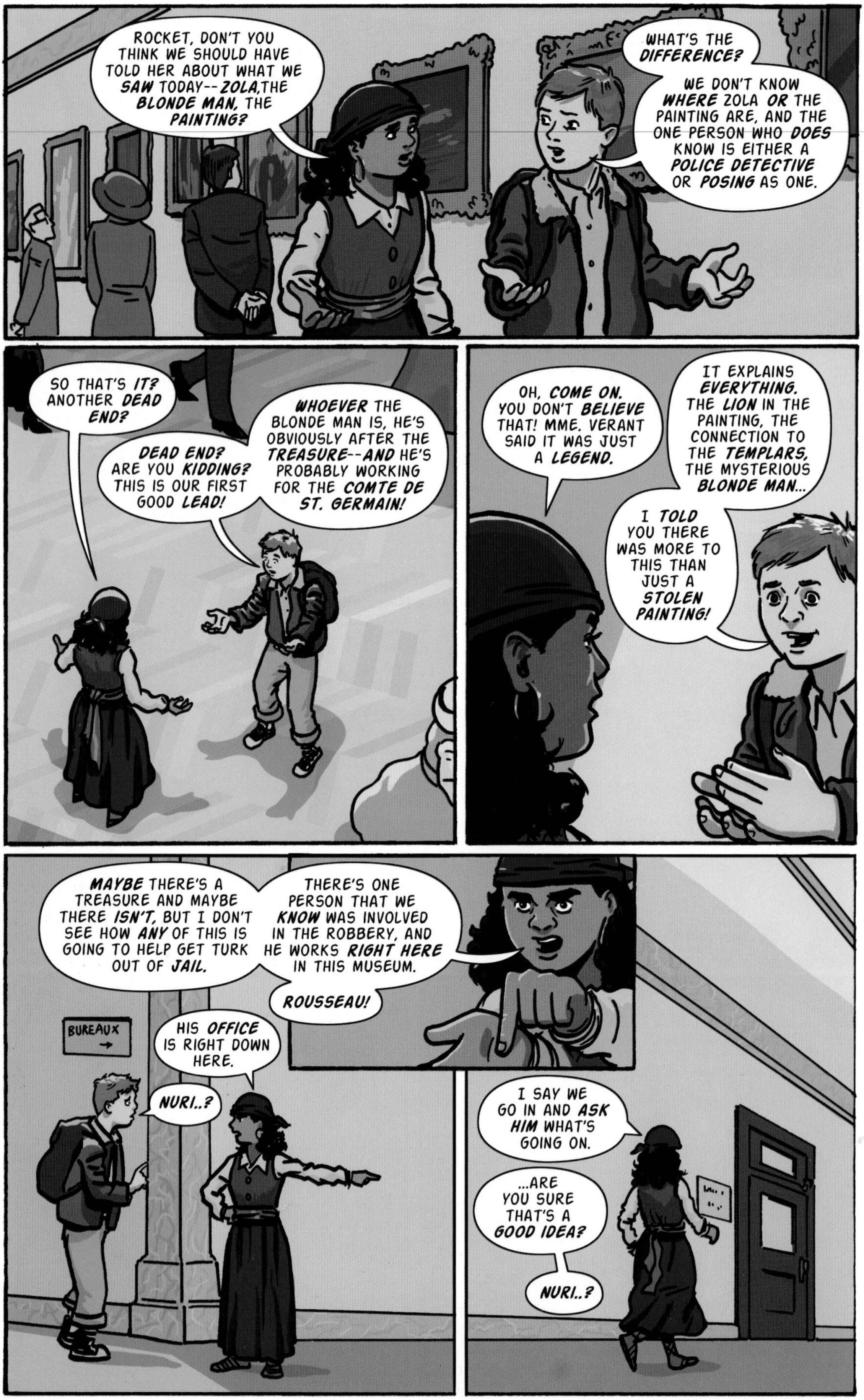
ROCKET, DON'T YOU THINK WE SHOULD HAVE TOLD HER ABOUT WHAT WE SAW TODAY--ZOLA, THE BLONDE MAN, THE PAINTING?
WHAT'S THE DIFFERENCE?
WE DON'T KNOW WHERE ZOLA OR THE PAINTING ARE, AND THE ONE PERSON WHO DOES KNOW IS EITHER A POLICE DETECTIVE OR POSING AS ONE.
SO THAT'S IT? ANOTHER DEAD END?
DEAD END? ARE YOU KIDDING? THIS IS OUR FIRST GOOD LEAD!
WHOEVER THE BLONDE MAN IS, HE'S OBVIOUSLY AFTER THE TREASURE--AND HE'S PROBABLY WORKING FOR THE COMTE DE ST. GERMAIN!
OH, COME ON. YOU DON'T BELIEVE THAT! MME. VERANT SAID IT WAS JUST A LEGEND.
IT EXPLAINS EVERYTHING. THE LION IN THE PAINTING, THE CONNECTION TO THE TEMPLARS, THE MYSTERIOUS BLONDE MAN...
I TOLD YOU THERE WAS MORE TO THIS THAN JUST A STOLEN PAINTING!
MAYBE THERE'S A TREASURE AND MAYBE THERE ISN'T, BUT I DON'T SEE HOW ANY OF THIS IS GOING TO HELP GET TURK OUT OF JAIL.
THERE'S ONE PERSON THAT WE KNOW WAS INVOLVED IN THE ROBBERY, AND HE WORKS RIGHT HERE IN THIS MUSEUM.
ROUSSEAU!
BUREAUX →
HIS OFFICE IS RIGHT DOWN HERE.
NURI..?
I SAY WE GO IN AND ASK HIM WHAT'S GOING ON.
...ARE YOU SURE THAT'S A GOOD IDEA?
NURI..?

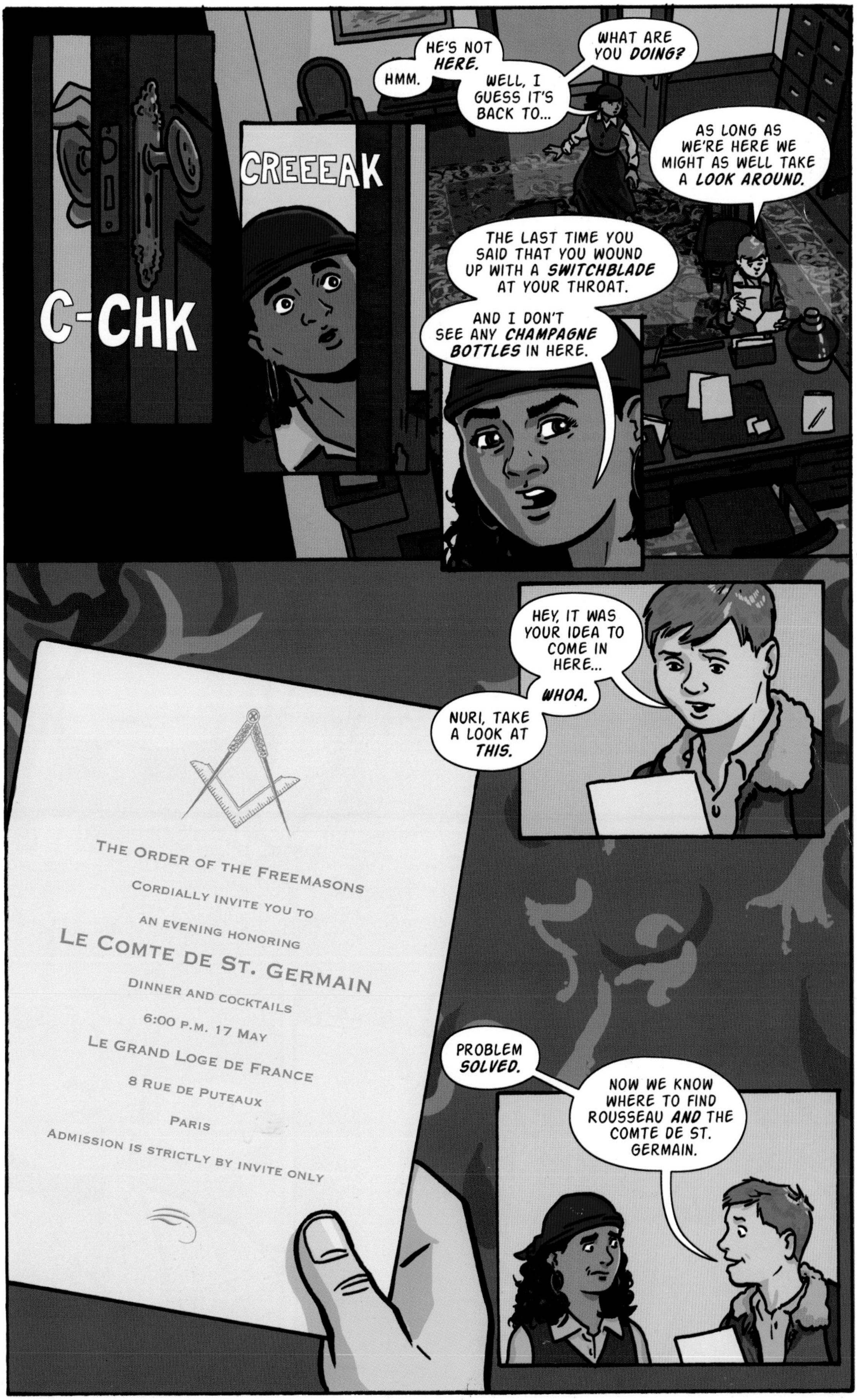
C-CHK
CREEEAK
HMM.
HE'S NOT HERE.
WELL, I GUESS IT'S BACK TO...
WHAT ARE YOU DOING?
AS LONG AS WE'RE HERE WE MIGHT AS WELL TAKE A LOOK AROUND.
THE LAST TIME YOU SAID THAT YOU WOUND UP WITH A SWITCHBLADE AT YOUR THROAT.
AND I DON'T SEE ANY CHAMPAGNE BOTTLES IN HERE.
HEY, IT WAS YOUR IDEA TO COME IN HERE...
WHOA.
NURI, TAKE A LOOK AT THIS.
THE ORDER OF THE FREEMASONS
CORDIALLY INVITE YOU TO
AN EVENING HONORING
LE COMTE DE ST. GERMAIN
DINNER AND COCKTAILS
6:00 P.M. 17 MAY
LE GRAND LOGE DE FRANCE
8 RUE DE PUTEAUX
PARIS
ADMISSION IS STRICTLY BY INVITE ONLY
PROBLEM SOLVED.
NOW WE KNOW WHERE TO FIND ROUSSEAU AND THE COMTE DE ST. GERMAIN.

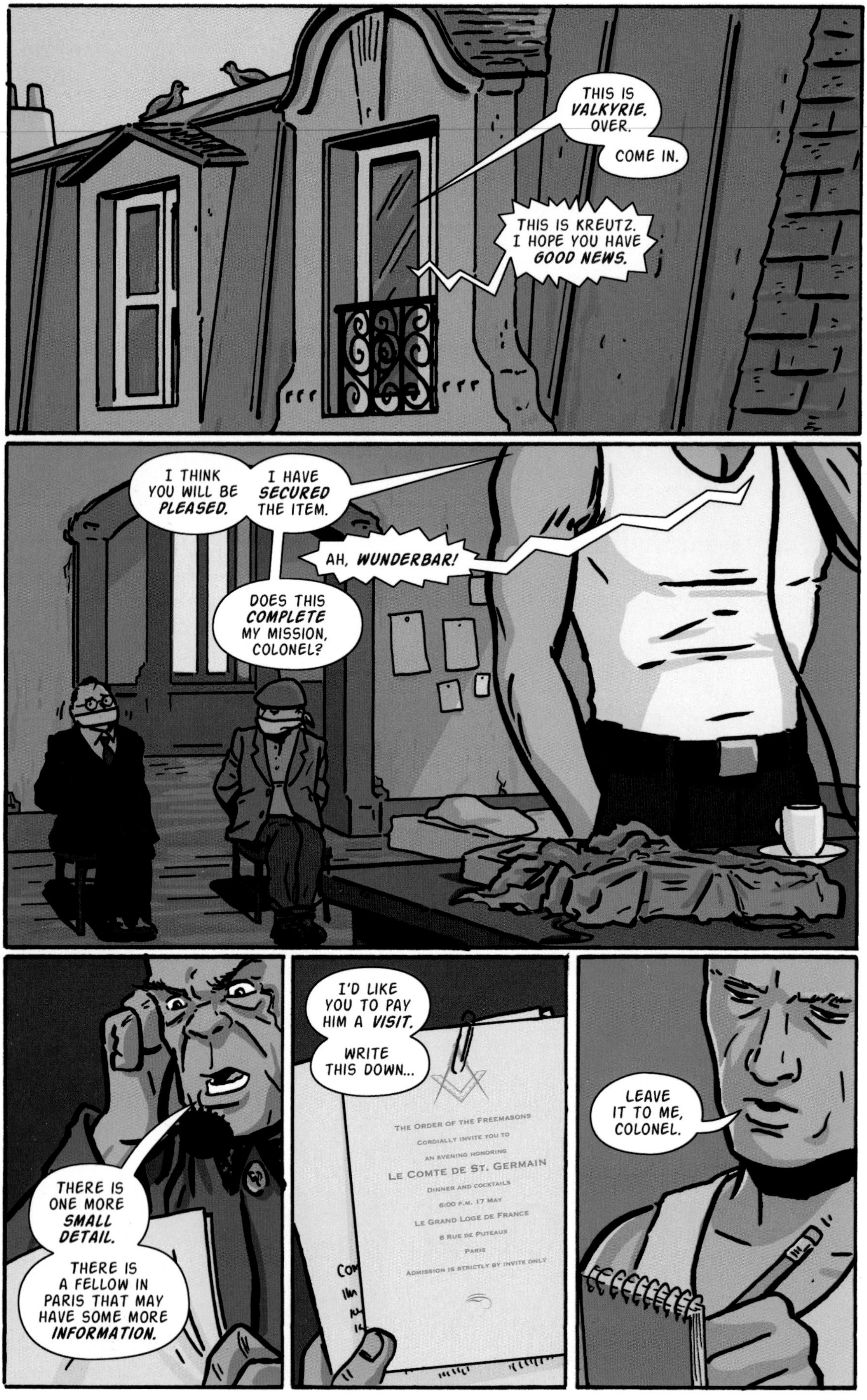

THIS IS VALKYRIE. OVER.
COME IN.
THIS IS KREUTZ. I HOPE YOU HAVE GOOD NEWS.
I THINK YOU WILL BE PLEASED.
I HAVE SECURED THE ITEM.
AH, WUNDERBAR!
DOES THIS COMPLETE MY MISSION, COLONEL?
THERE IS ONE MORE SMALL DETAIL.
THERE IS A FELLOW IN PARIS THAT MAY HAVE SOME MORE INFORMATION.
I'D LIKE YOU TO PAY HIM A VISIT.
WRITE THIS DOWN...
The Order of the Freemasons
Cordially invite you to
an evening honoring
Le Comte de St. Germain
Dinner and cocktails
6:00 p.m. 17 May
Le Grand Loge de France
8 Rue de Puteaux
Paris
Admission is strictly by invite only
LEAVE IT TO ME, COLONEL.

CHAPTER SIX

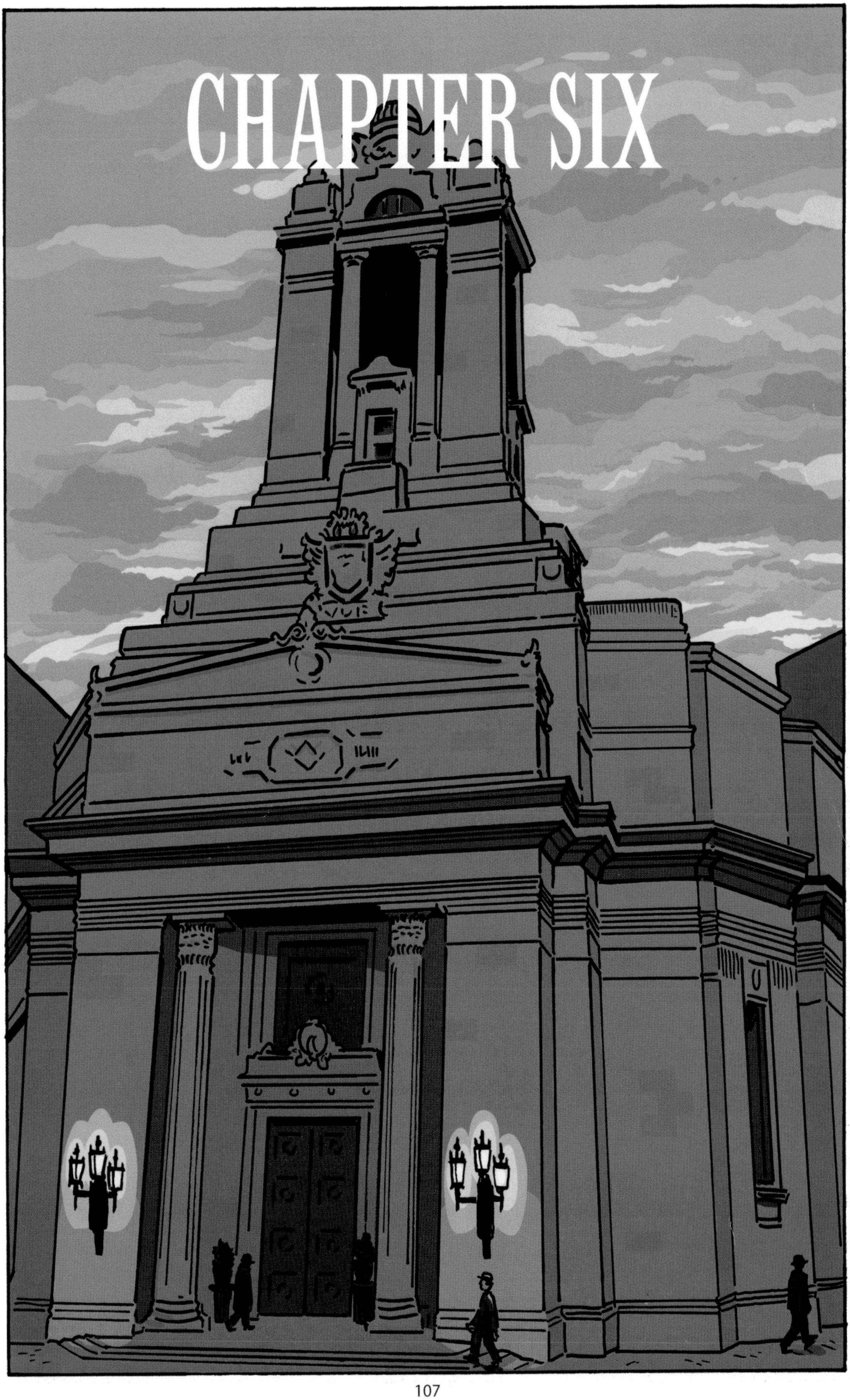

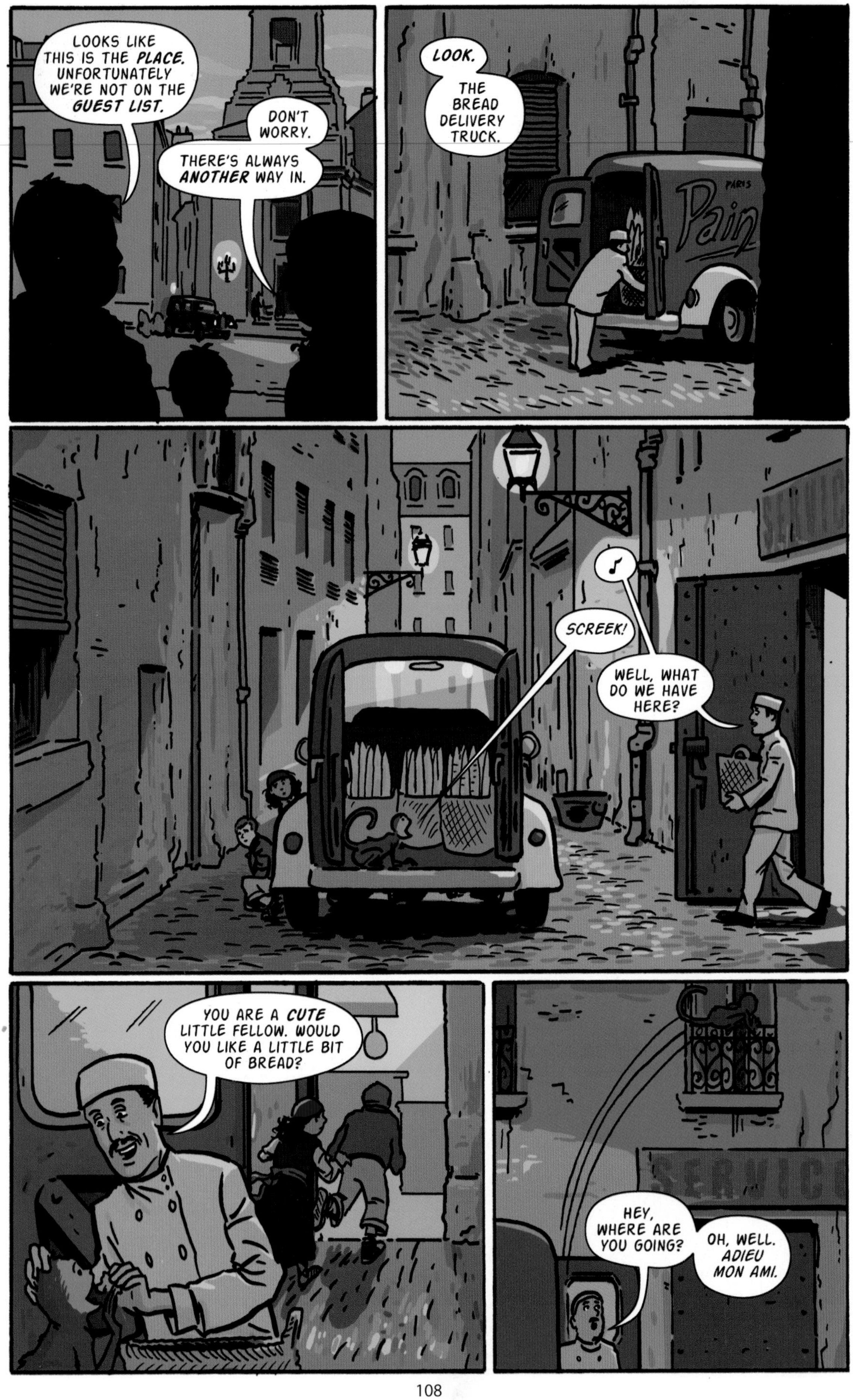
LOOKS LIKE THIS IS THE PLACE. UNFORTUNATELY WE'RE NOT ON THE GUEST LIST.
DON'T WORRY.
THERE'S ALWAYS ANOTHER WAY IN.
LOOK.
THE BREAD DELIVERY TRUCK.
PARIS
Pain
♪
SCREEK!
WELL, WHAT DO WE HAVE HERE?
YOU ARE A CUTE LITTLE FELLOW. WOULD YOU LIKE A LITTLE BIT OF BREAD?
HEY, WHERE ARE YOU GOING?
OH, WELL. ADIEU MON AMI.

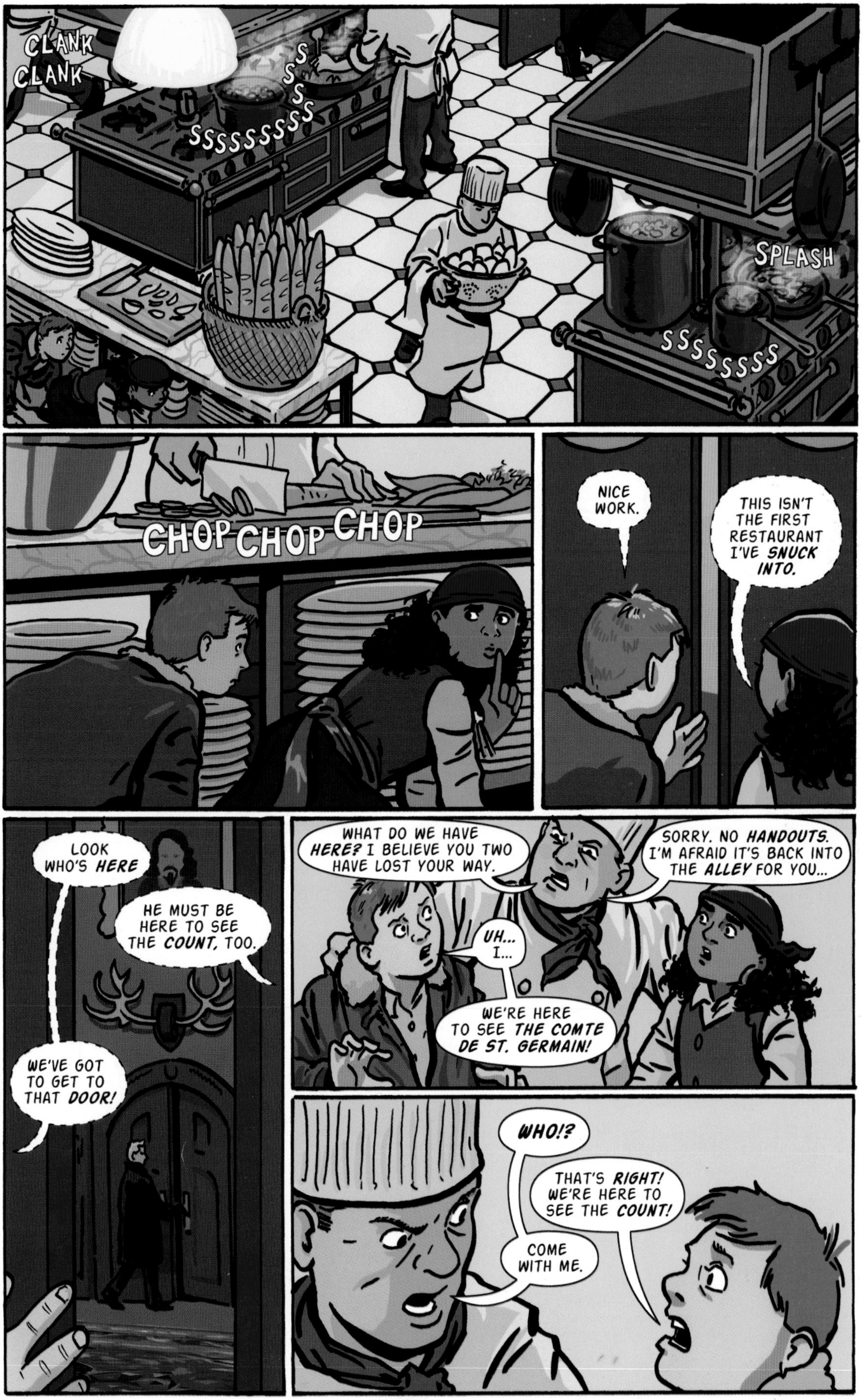
CLANK
CLANK
SSSSSSSSSSSSS
SPLASH
SSSSSSSSS
CHOP CHOP CHOP
NICE WORK.
THIS ISN'T THE FIRST RESTAURANT I'VE SNUCK INTO.
LOOK WHO'S HERE
HE MUST BE HERE TO SEE THE COUNT, TOO.
WE'VE GOT TO GET TO THAT DOOR!
WHAT DO WE HAVE HERE? I BELIEVE YOU TWO HAVE LOST YOUR WAY.
SORRY. NO HANDOUTS. I'M AFRAID IT'S BACK INTO THE ALLEY FOR YOU...
UH... I...
WE'RE HERE TO SEE THE COMTE DE ST. GERMAIN!
WHO!?
THAT'S RIGHT! WE'RE HERE TO SEE THE COUNT!
COME WITH ME.

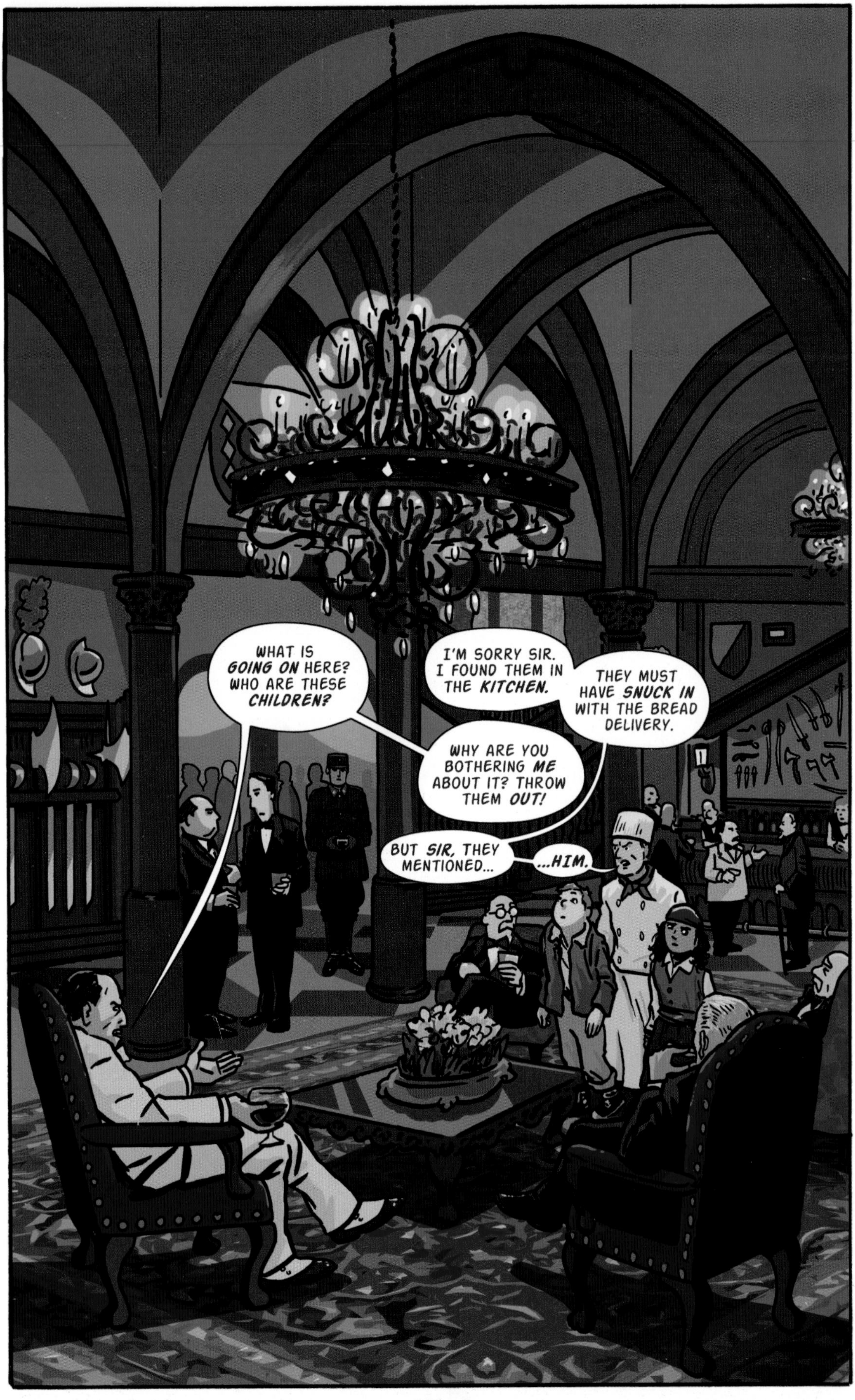
WHAT IS GOING ON HERE? WHO ARE THESE CHILDREN?
I'M SORRY SIR. I FOUND THEM IN THE KITCHEN.
THEY MUST HAVE SNUCK IN WITH THE BREAD DELIVERY.
WHY ARE YOU BOTHERING ME ABOUT IT? THROW THEM OUT!
BUT SIR, THEY MENTIONED...
...HIM.

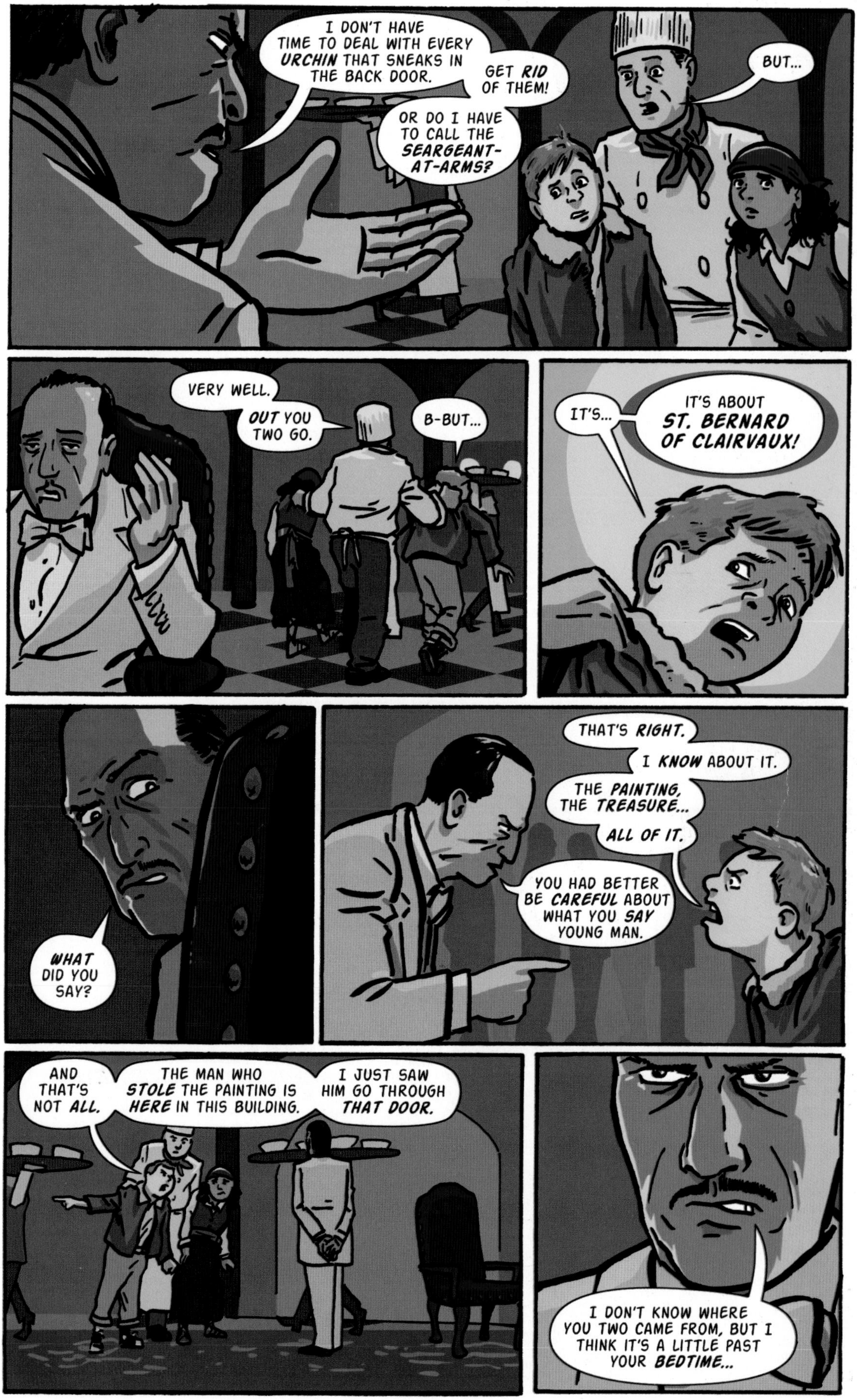
I DON'T HAVE TIME TO DEAL WITH EVERY URCHIN THAT SNEAKS IN THE BACK DOOR.
GET RID OF THEM!
OR DO I HAVE TO CALL THE SEARGEANT-AT-ARMS?
BUT...
VERY WELL.
OUT YOU TWO GO.
B-BUT...
IT'S...
IT'S ABOUT ST. BERNARD OF CLAIRVAUX!
WHAT DID YOU SAY?
THAT'S RIGHT.
I KNOW ABOUT IT.
THE PAINTING, THE TREASURE...
ALL OF IT.
YOU HAD BETTER BE CAREFUL ABOUT WHAT YOU SAY YOUNG MAN.
AND THAT'S NOT ALL.
THE MAN WHO STOLE THE PAINTING IS HERE IN THIS BUILDING.
I JUST SAW HIM GO THROUGH THAT DOOR.
I DON'T KNOW WHERE YOU TWO CAME FROM, BUT I THINK IT'S A LITTLE PAST YOUR BEDTIME...

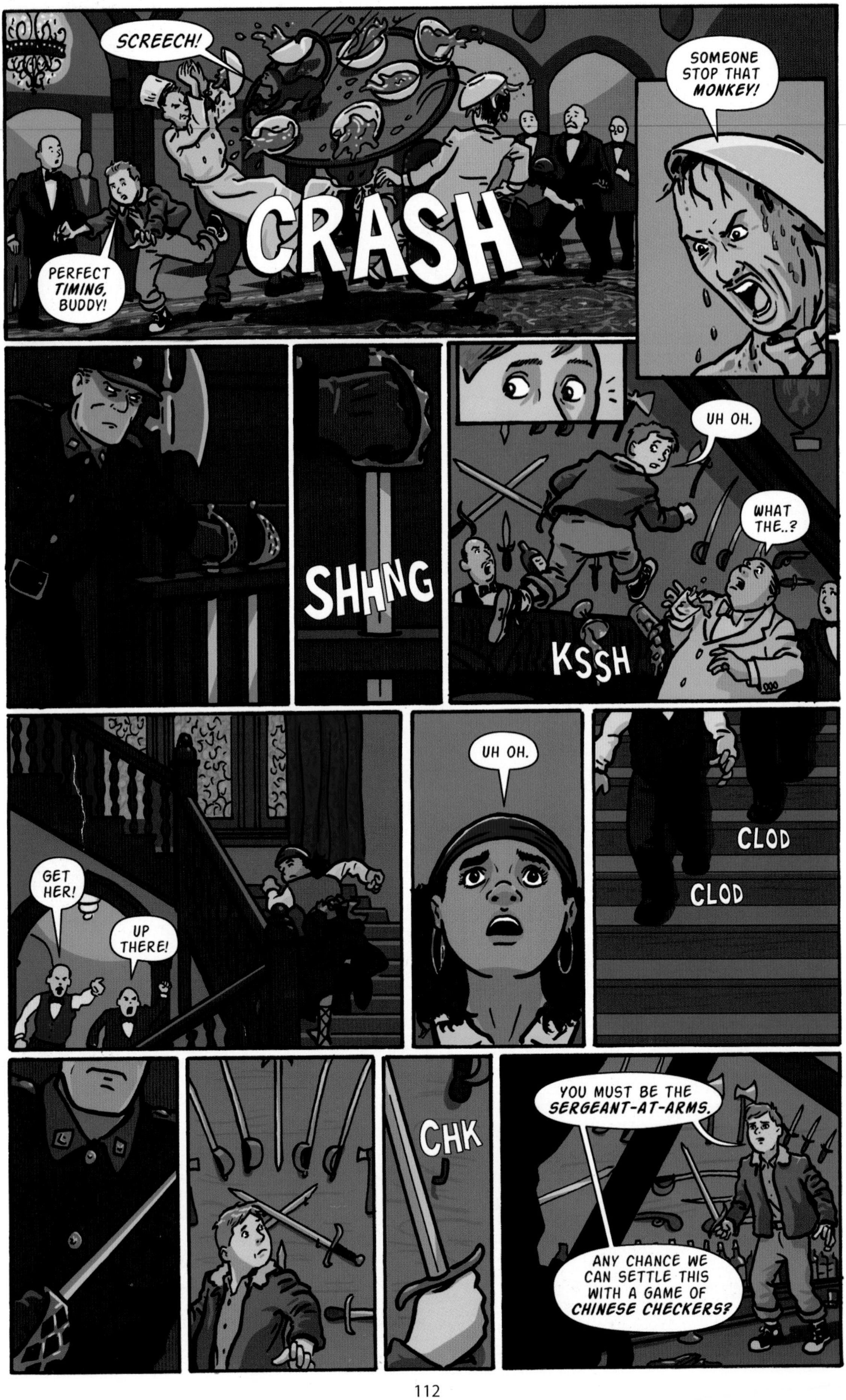
SCREECH!
SOMEONE STOP THAT MONKEY!
CRASH
PERFECT TIMING, BUDDY!
SHHNG
UH OH.
WHAT THE..?
KSSH
GET HER!
UP THERE!
UH OH.
CLOD
CLOD
CHK
YOU MUST BE THE SERGEANT-AT-ARMS.
ANY CHANCE WE CAN SETTLE THIS WITH A GAME OF CHINESE CHECKERS?

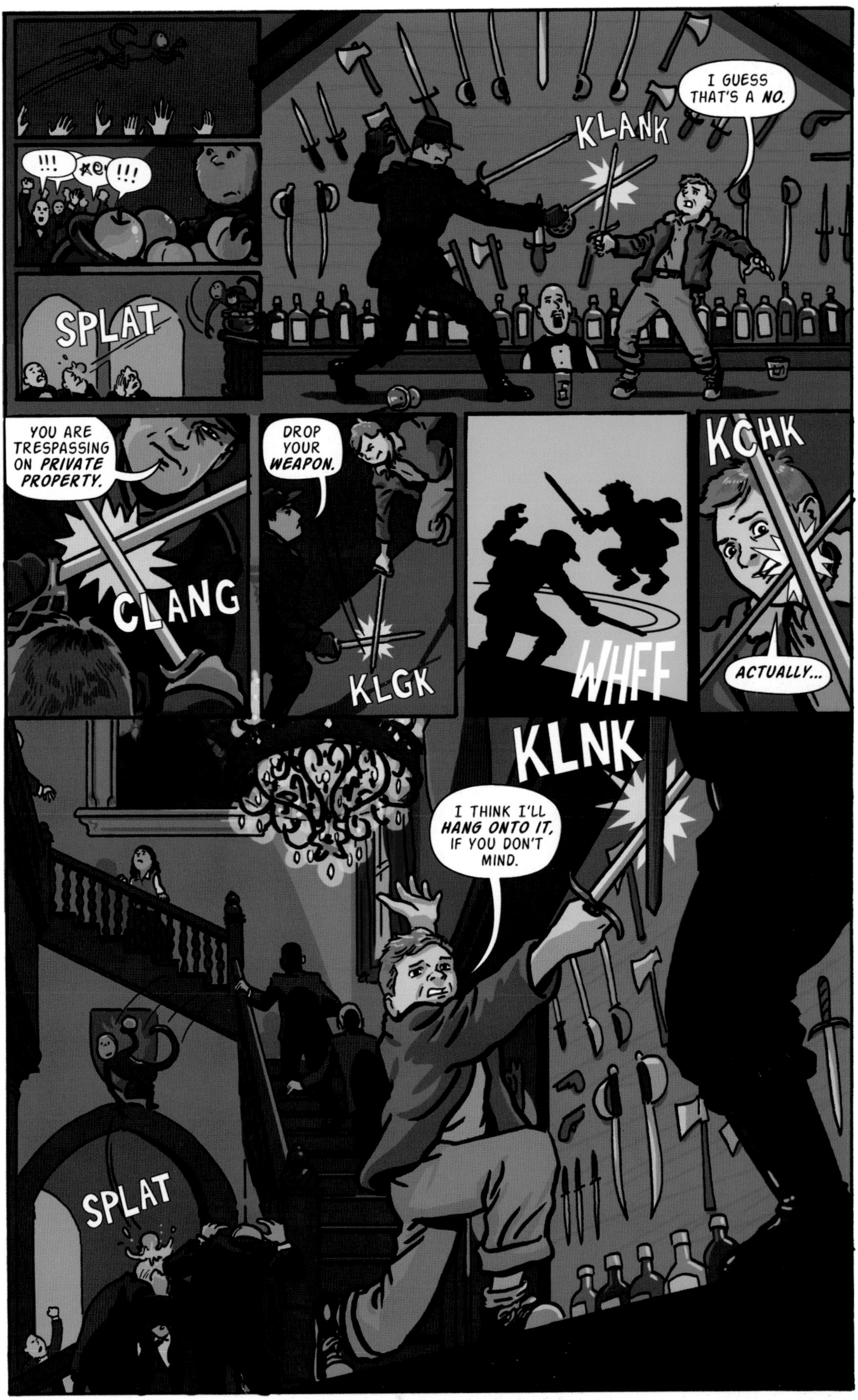
!!!
✗@
!!!
SPLAT
KLANK
I GUESS THAT'S A NO.
YOU ARE TRESPASSING ON PRIVATE PROPERTY.
CLANG
DROP YOUR WEAPON.
KLGK
WHFF
KCHK
ACTUALLY...
KLNK
I THINK I'LL HANG ONTO IT, IF YOU DON'T MIND.
SPLAT

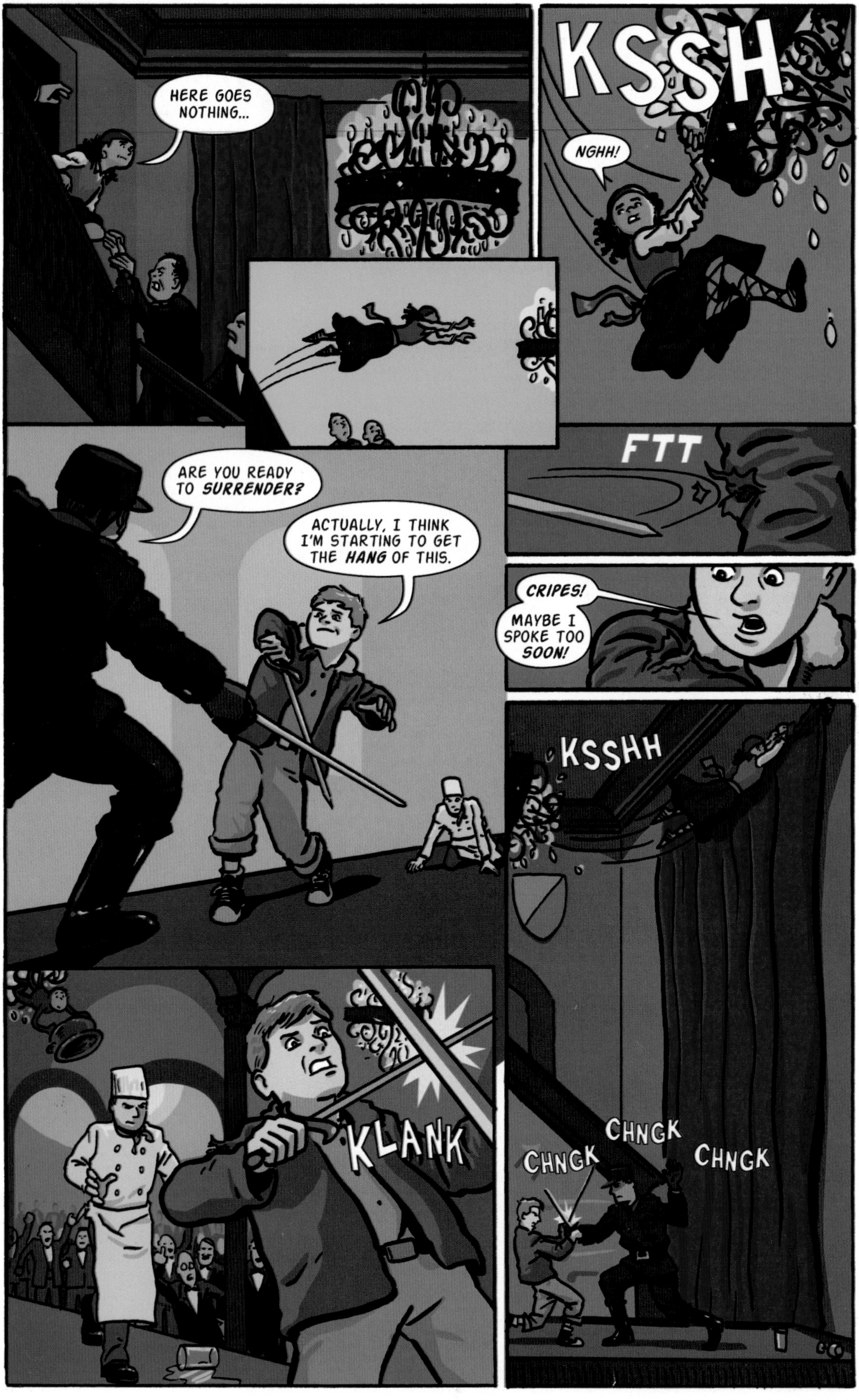
HERE GOES NOTHING...
KSSH
NGHH!
ARE YOU READY TO SURRENDER?
ACTUALLY, I THINK I'M STARTING TO GET THE HANG OF THIS.
FTT
CRIPES!
MAYBE I SPOKE TOO SOON!
KSSHH
KLANK
CHNGK
CHNGK
CHNGK

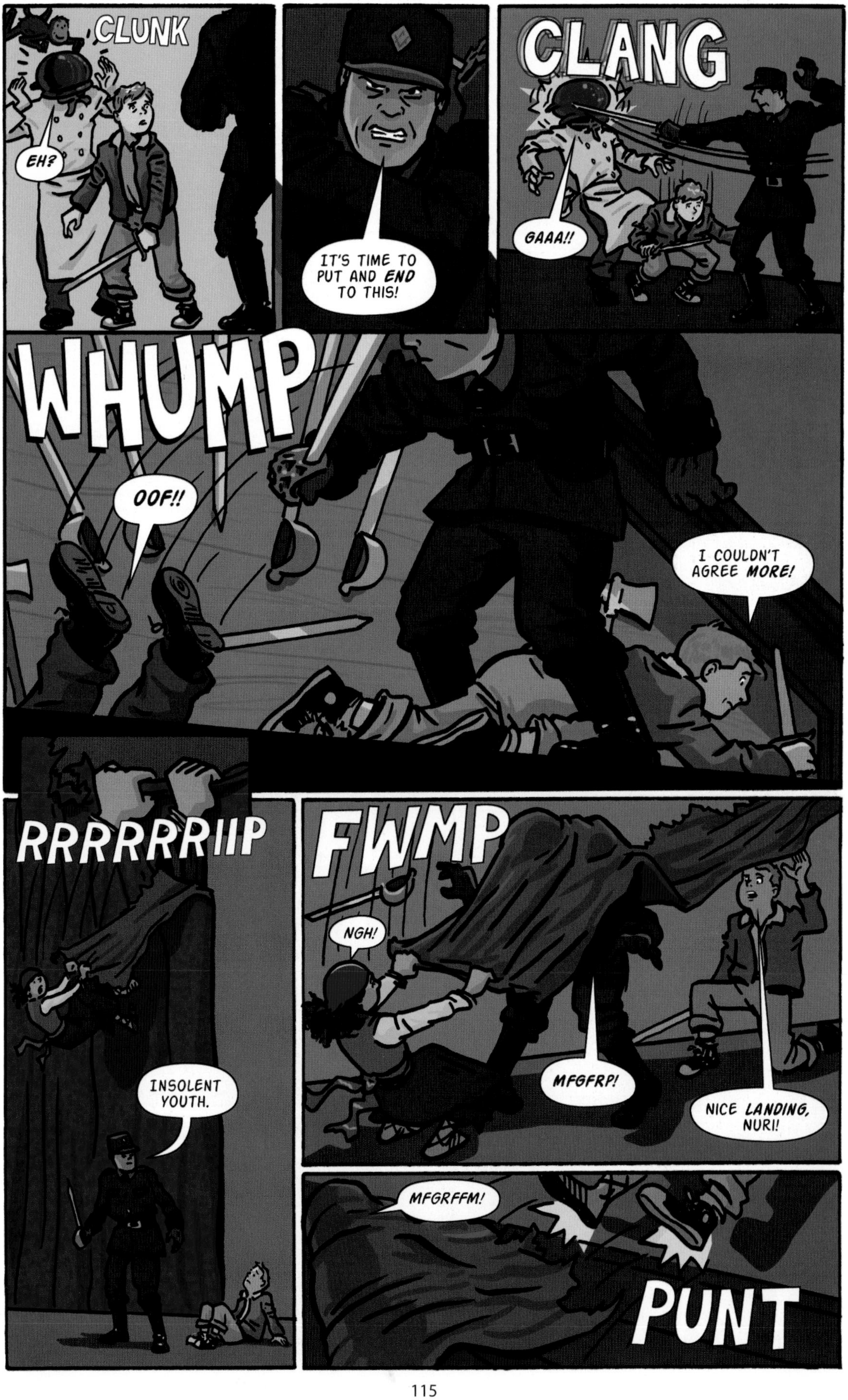
CLUNK
EH?
IT'S TIME TO PUT AND END TO THIS!
CLANG
GAAA!!
WHUMP
OOF!!
I COULDN'T AGREE MORE!
RRRRRRIIP
INSOLENT YOUTH.
FWMP
NGH!
MFGFRP!
NICE LANDING, NURI!
MFGRFFM!
PUNT

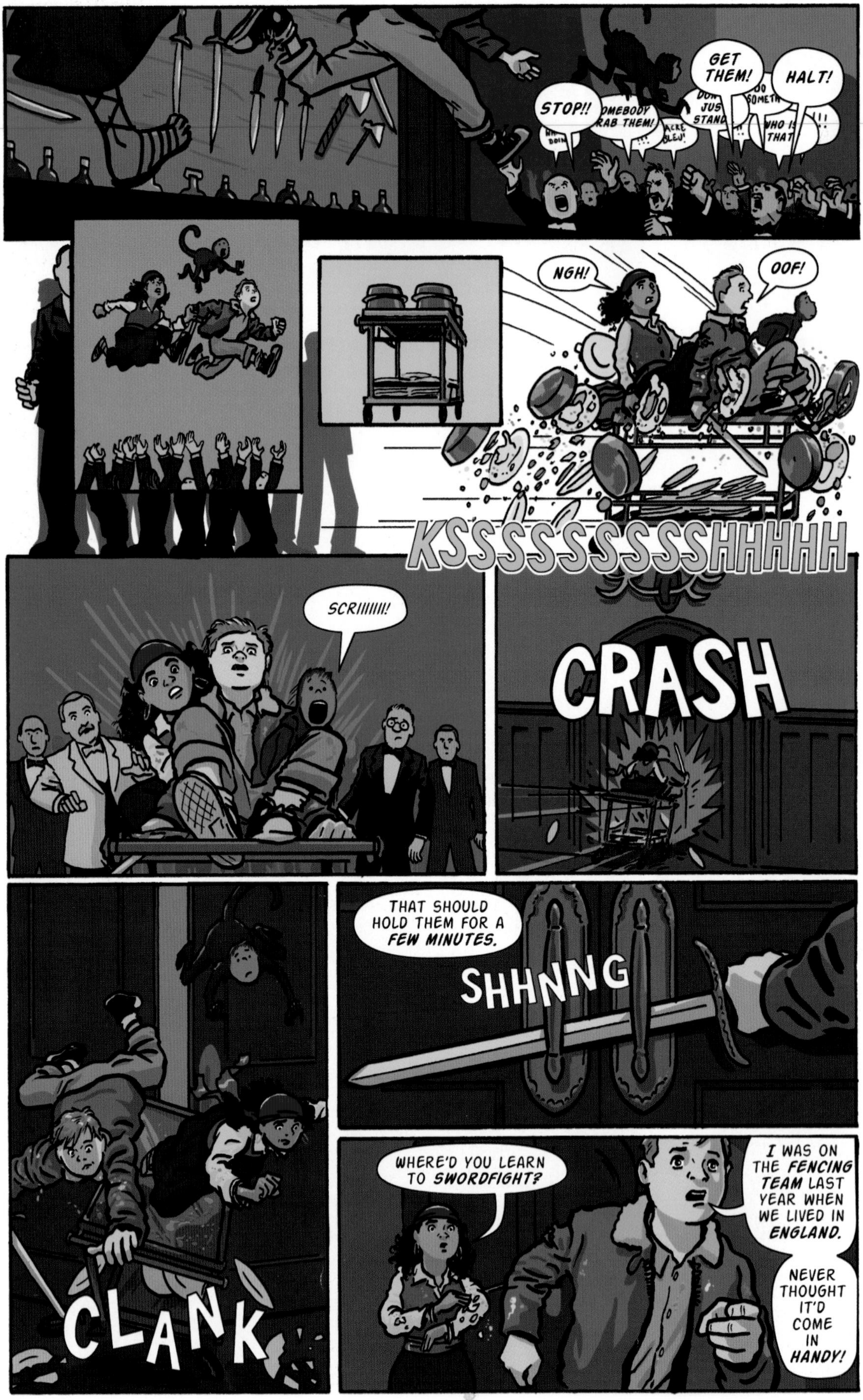

STOP!!
GET THEM!
HALT!
NGH!
OOF!
KSSSSSSSSSHHHHH
SCRIIIIIII!
CRASH
CLANK
THAT SHOULD HOLD THEM FOR A *FEW MINUTES.*
SHHNNG
WHERE'D YOU LEARN TO *SWORDFIGHT?*
I WAS ON THE *FENCING TEAM* LAST YEAR WHEN WE LIVED IN *ENGLAND.*
NEVER THOUGHT IT'D COME IN *HANDY!*

BAM BAM

WILL SOMEONE *PLEASE* GET THAT *DOOR* OPEN!?!

NOW WHAT?

THIS IS WHERE THE *BLONDE MAN* WENT.

BMM BMM

THE *COUNT* MUST BE SOMEWHERE BACK HERE.

MAYBE IN HERE.

Creeeak

HELLO?

COMTE DE ST. GERMAIN?

I DON'T THINK HE CAN *HEAR* YOU, ROCKET.

HE LOOKS...

I THINK HE'S *DEAD*.

THE *BLONDE MAN* MUST HAVE KILLED HIM.

BUT *WHY?*

I DON'T KNOW, BUT I DON'T THINK WE SHOULD *STICK AROUND* TO FIND OUT.

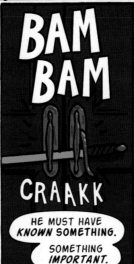

BAM BAM

CRAAKK

HE MUST HAVE *KNOWN* SOMETHING.

SOMETHING *IMPORTANT*.

NURI, LOOK AT HIS *HAND*.

I DON'T *WANT* TO, ROCKET. IT'S *CREEPY*.

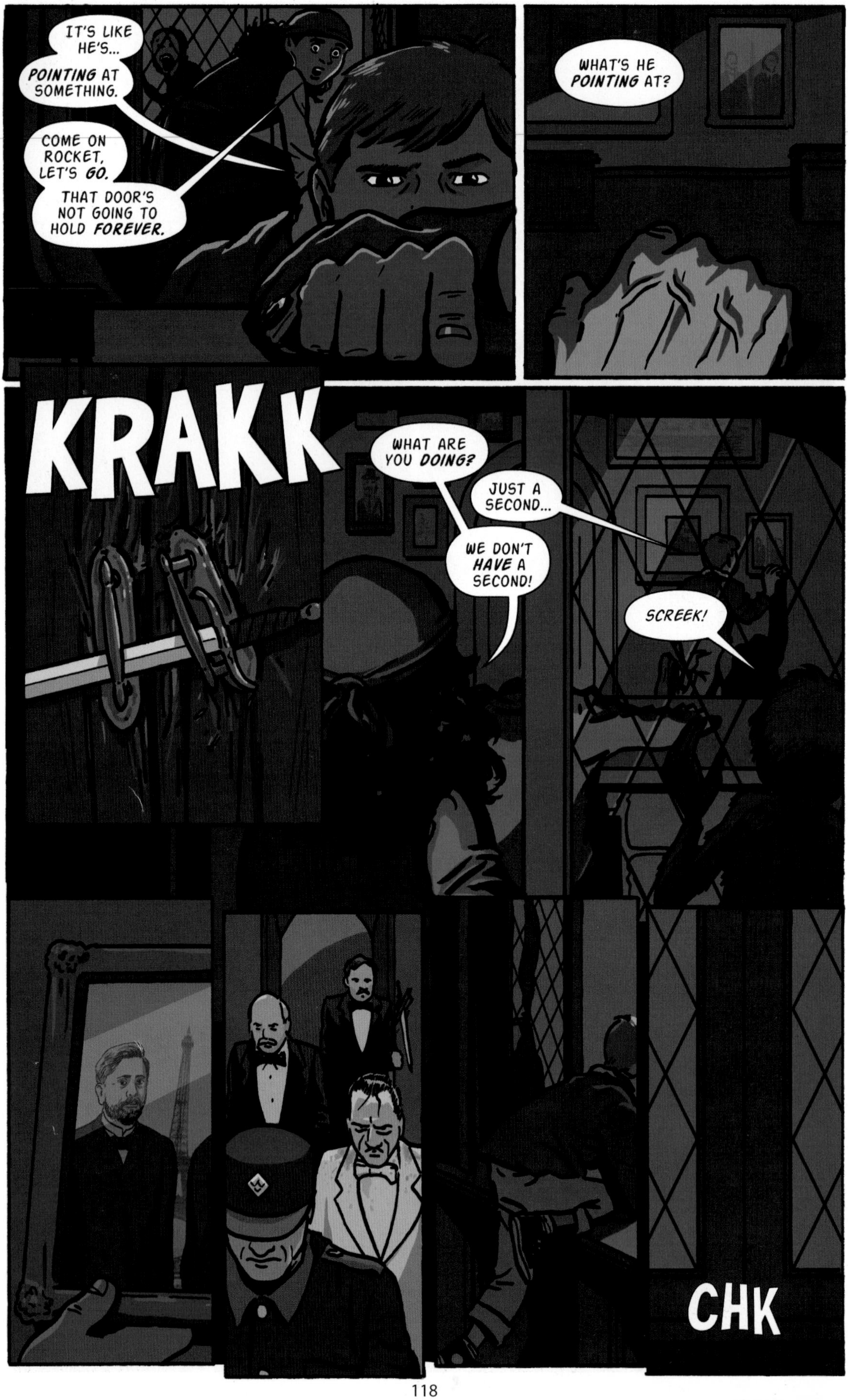
IT'S LIKE HE'S... POINTING AT SOMETHING.
COME ON ROCKET, LET'S GO.
THAT DOOR'S NOT GOING TO HOLD FOREVER.
WHAT'S HE POINTING AT?
KRAKK
WHAT ARE YOU DOING?
JUST A SECOND...
WE DON'T HAVE A SECOND!
SCREEK!
CHK

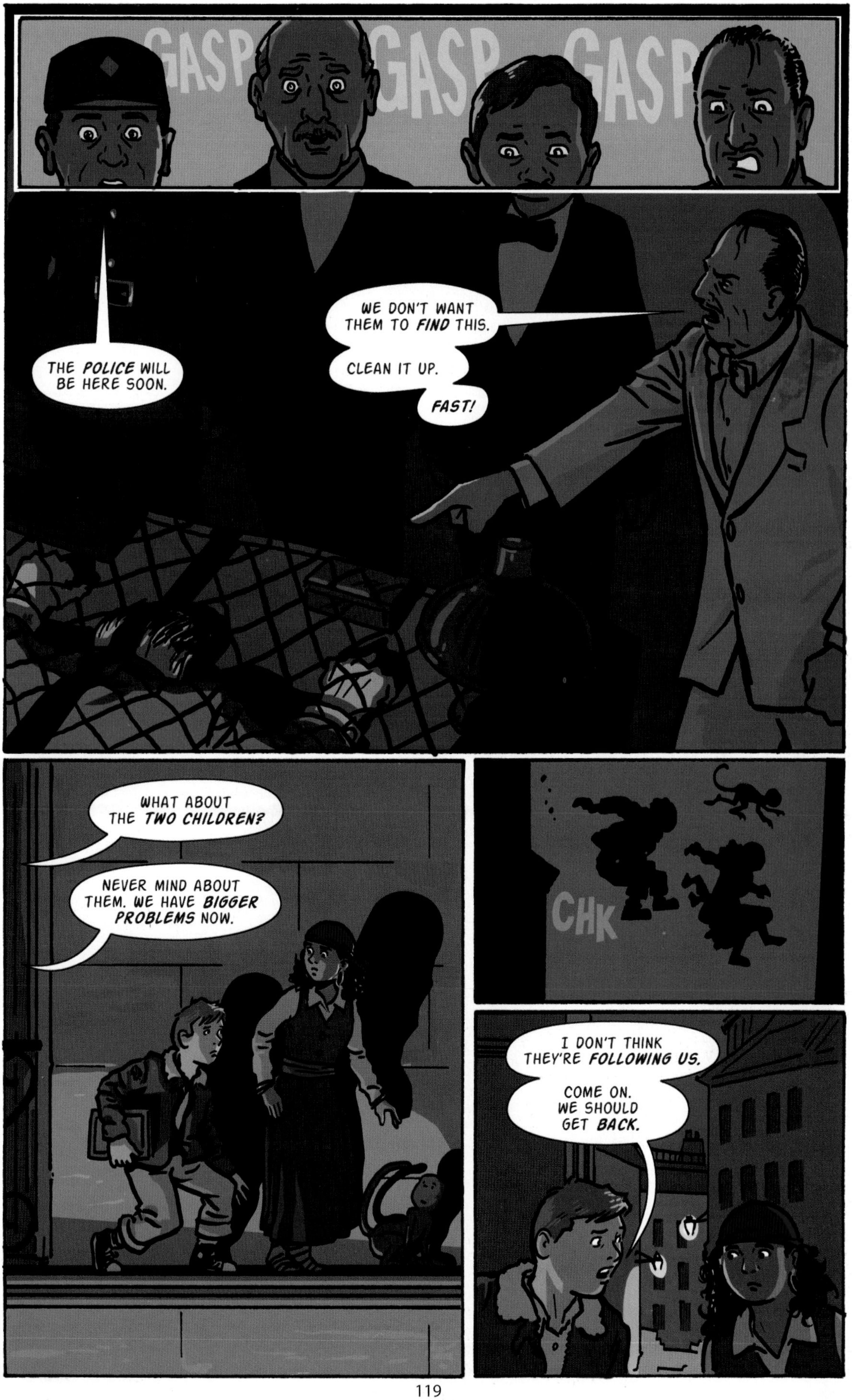
GASP GASP GASP
THE POLICE WILL BE HERE SOON.
WE DON'T WANT THEM TO FIND THIS.
CLEAN IT UP.
FAST!
WHAT ABOUT THE TWO CHILDREN?
NEVER MIND ABOUT THEM. WE HAVE BIGGER PROBLEMS NOW.
CHK
I DON'T THINK THEY'RE FOLLOWING US.
COME ON. WE SHOULD GET BACK.

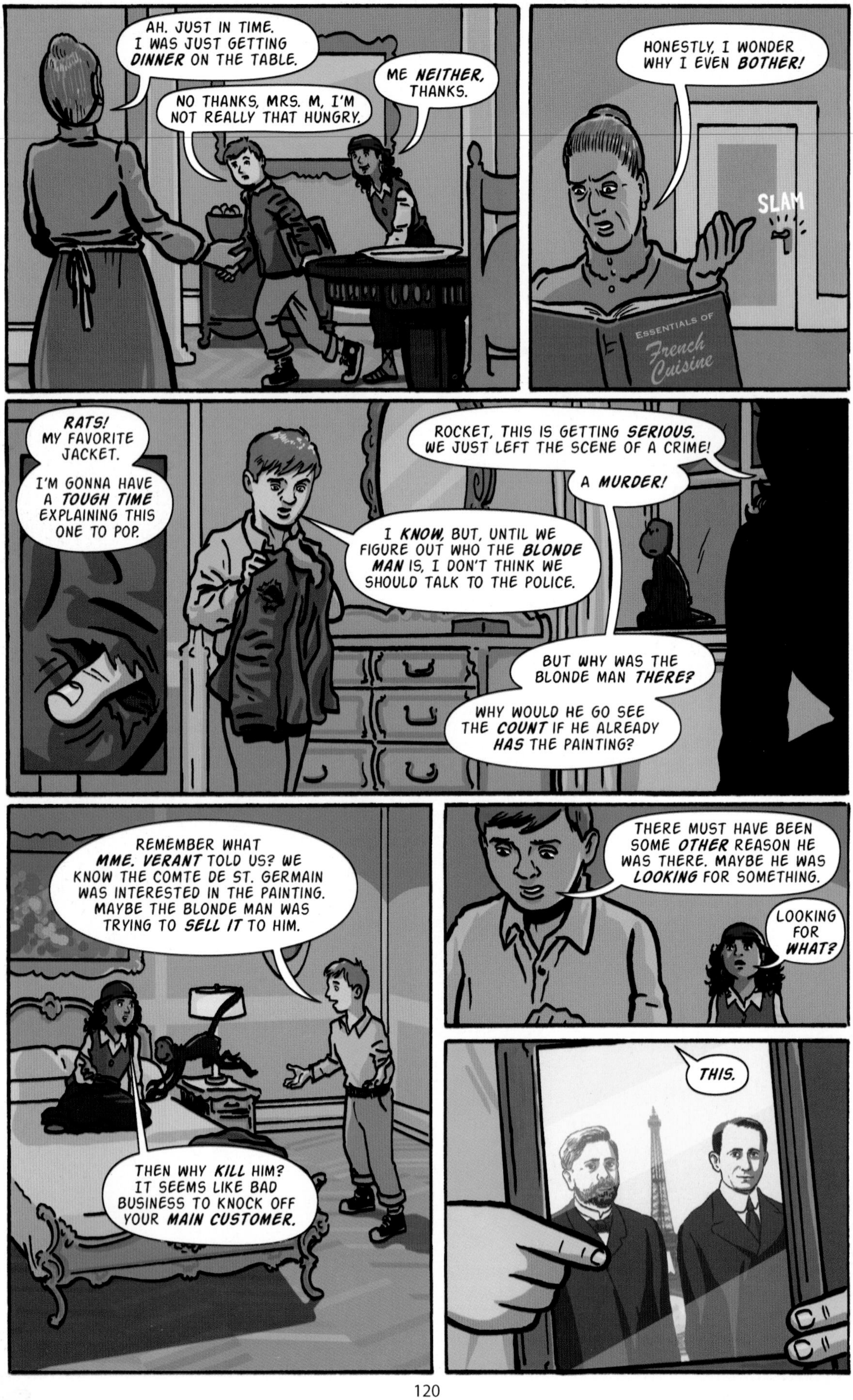
AH. JUST IN TIME. I WAS JUST GETTING DINNER ON THE TABLE.
NO THANKS, MRS. M, I'M NOT REALLY THAT HUNGRY.
ME NEITHER, THANKS.
HONESTLY, I WONDER WHY I EVEN BOTHER!
SLAM
ESSENTIALS OF French Cuisine
RATS! MY FAVORITE JACKET.
I'M GONNA HAVE A TOUGH TIME EXPLAINING THIS ONE TO POP.
ROCKET, THIS IS GETTING SERIOUS. WE JUST LEFT THE SCENE OF A CRIME!
A MURDER!
I KNOW, BUT, UNTIL WE FIGURE OUT WHO THE BLONDE MAN IS, I DON'T THINK WE SHOULD TALK TO THE POLICE.
BUT WHY WAS THE BLONDE MAN THERE?
WHY WOULD HE GO SEE THE COUNT IF HE ALREADY HAS THE PAINTING?
REMEMBER WHAT MME. VERANT TOLD US? WE KNOW THE COMTE DE ST. GERMAIN WAS INTERESTED IN THE PAINTING. MAYBE THE BLONDE MAN WAS TRYING TO SELL IT TO HIM.
THEN WHY KILL HIM? IT SEEMS LIKE BAD BUSINESS TO KNOCK OFF YOUR MAIN CUSTOMER.
THERE MUST HAVE BEEN SOME OTHER REASON HE WAS THERE. MAYBE HE WAS LOOKING FOR SOMETHING.
LOOKING FOR WHAT?
THIS.

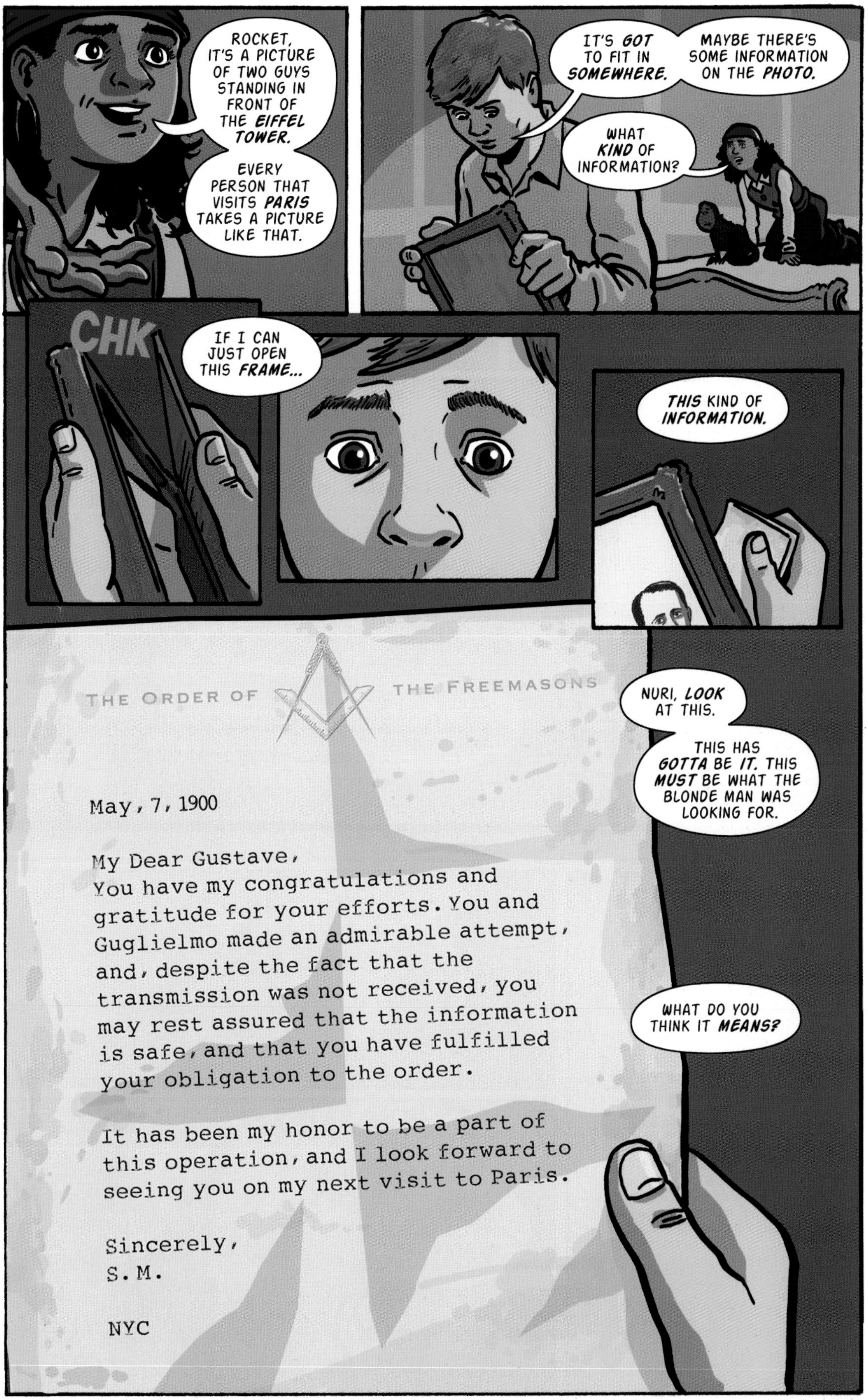

ROCKET, IT'S A PICTURE OF TWO GUYS STANDING IN FRONT OF THE *EIFFEL TOWER.*
EVERY PERSON THAT VISITS *PARIS* TAKES A PICTURE LIKE THAT.
IT'S *GOT* TO FIT IN *SOMEWHERE.*
MAYBE THERE'S SOME INFORMATION ON THE *PHOTO.*
WHAT *KIND* OF INFORMATION?
CHK
IF I CAN JUST OPEN THIS *FRAME...*
THIS KIND OF *INFORMATION.*
THE ORDER OF THE FREEMASONS
May, 7, 1900
My Dear Gustave,
You have my congratulations and gratitude for your efforts. You and Guglielmo made an admirable attempt, and, despite the fact that the transmission was not received, you may rest assured that the information is safe, and that you have fulfilled your obligation to the order.
It has been my honor to be a part of this operation, and I look forward to seeing you on my next visit to Paris.
Sincerely,
S. M.
NYC
NURI, *LOOK* AT THIS.
THIS HAS *GOTTA* BE *IT.* THIS *MUST* BE WHAT THE BLONDE MAN WAS LOOKING FOR.
WHAT DO YOU THINK IT *MEANS?*

GUSTAVE...

WAIT, REMEMBER THE LIST OF FAMOUS *FREEMASONS*?

GUSTAVE EIFFEL! DESIGNER OF THE *EIFFEL TOWER!*

WHO'S THIS OTHER GUY, *GUGLIELMO*? AND WHAT'S THIS ABOUT A *TRANSMISSION*?

GUGLIELMO...

...MARCONI! IT'S *GOTTA* BE!

WHO?

GUGLIELMO *MARCONI* WAS AN ITALIAN INVENTOR WHO MADE THE FIRST *WIRELESS RADIO TRANSMITTER.*

THIS LETTER CAME FROM *NEW YORK.* THEY MUST HAVE BEEN TRYING TO MAKE A *TRANSATLANTIC RADIO TRANSMISSION!*

AND WHAT BETTER PLACE TO TRANSMIT FROM THAN THE *TALLEST STRUCTURE* IN *EUROPE?*

BUT WHAT DOES THIS HAVE TO DO WITH THE *PAINTING?*

OBVIOUSLY, THE PAINTING IS A *CLUE* TO THE LOCATION OF THE *TREASURE.*

AND YOU'RE SAYING THAT LETTER IS *ALSO* A CLUE?

PROBABLY *NOT,* BUT I BET WHATEVER WAS IN THAT WIRELESS MESSAGE *WAS.*

May, 7, 1900

My Dear Gustave,
You have my congratulati...
gratitude for your effor...
Guglielmo made an admir...
and, despite the fact th...
...ansmission was not re...

HOW ARE WE EVER GOING TO FIND *THAT?*

WELL, WE KNOW WHO *SENT IT...*

...AND *WHERE* IT WAS SENT *FROM.*

I THINK IT'S TIME WE PAID A *VISIT* TO PARIS'S *NUMBER ONE ATTRACTION.*

PARIS GUIDEBOOK

guide to

CHAPTER SEVEN

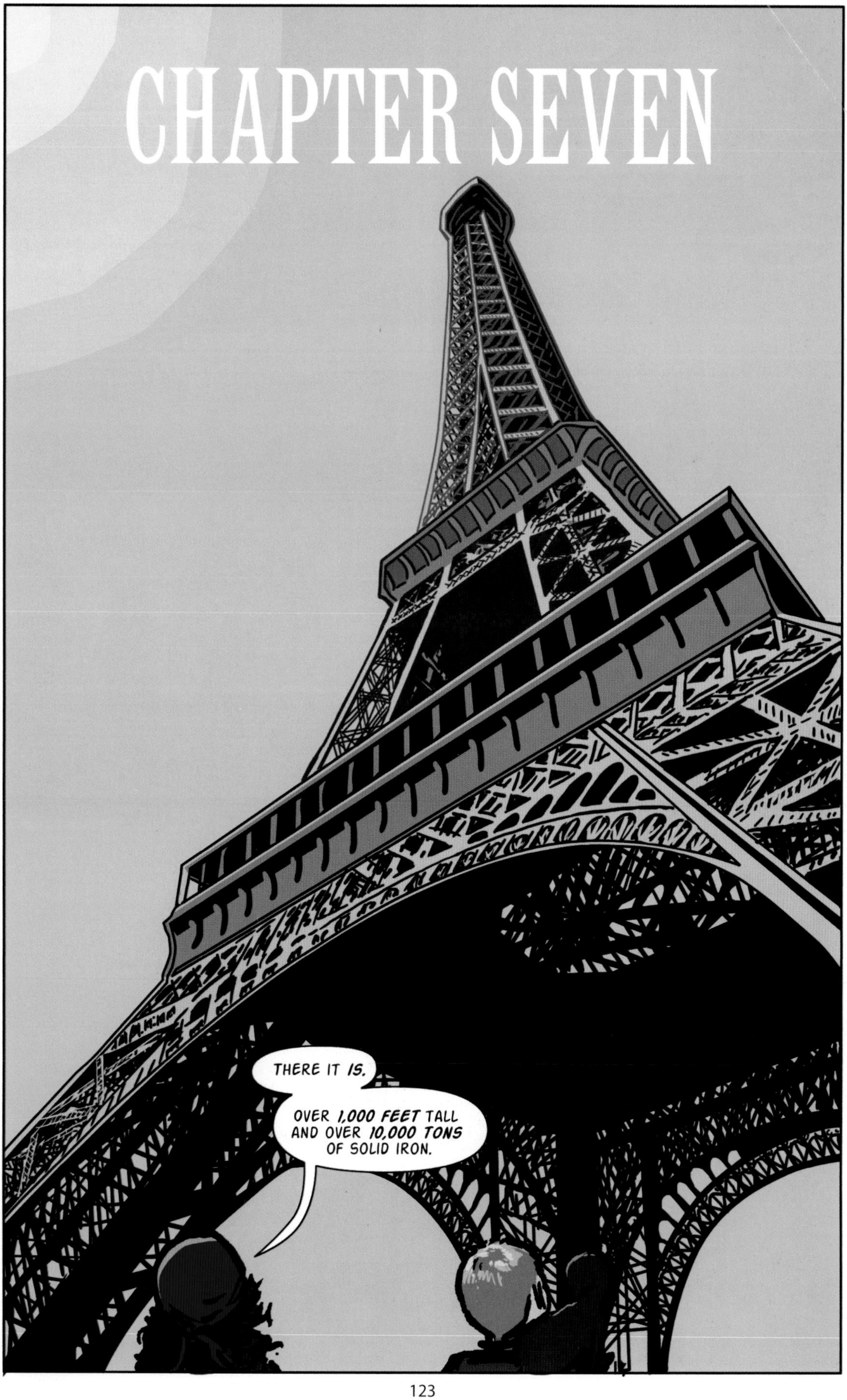
THERE IT *IS.*
OVER *1,000 FEET* TALL AND OVER *10,000 TONS* OF SOLID IRON.

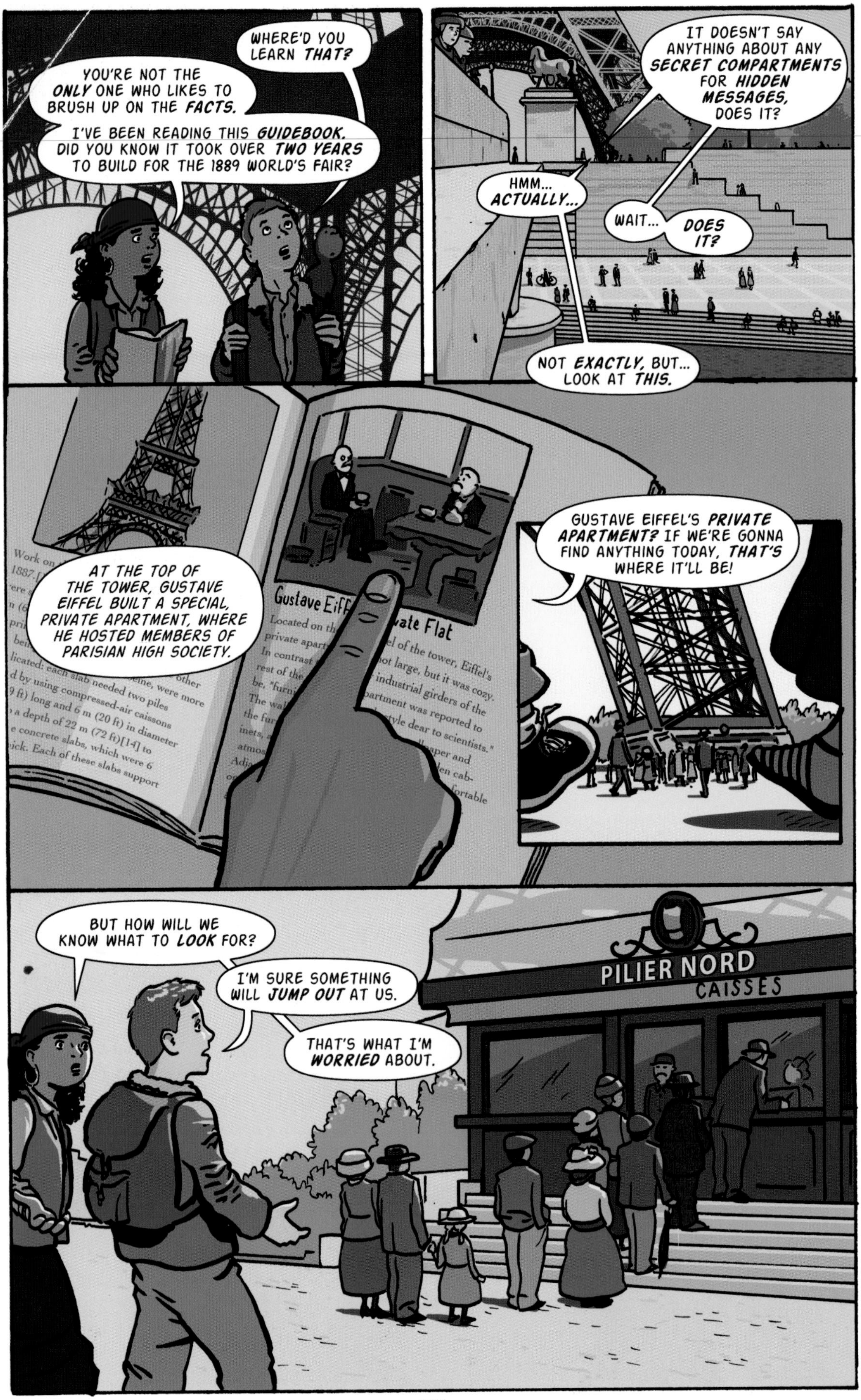

YOU'RE NOT THE ONLY ONE WHO LIKES TO BRUSH UP ON THE FACTS.
WHERE'D YOU LEARN THAT?
I'VE BEEN READING THIS GUIDEBOOK. DID YOU KNOW IT TOOK OVER TWO YEARS TO BUILD FOR THE 1889 WORLD'S FAIR?
IT DOESN'T SAY ANYTHING ABOUT ANY SECRET COMPARTMENTS FOR HIDDEN MESSAGES, DOES IT?
HMM... ACTUALLY...
WAIT...
DOES IT?
NOT EXACTLY, BUT... LOOK AT THIS.
AT THE TOP OF THE TOWER, GUSTAVE EIFFEL BUILT A SPECIAL, PRIVATE APARTMENT, WHERE HE HOSTED MEMBERS OF PARISIAN HIGH SOCIETY.
GUSTAVE EIFFEL'S PRIVATE APARTMENT? IF WE'RE GONNA FIND ANYTHING TODAY, THAT'S WHERE IT'LL BE!
BUT HOW WILL WE KNOW WHAT TO LOOK FOR?
I'M SURE SOMETHING WILL JUMP OUT AT US.
THAT'S WHAT I'M WORRIED ABOUT.
PILIER NORD
CAISSES

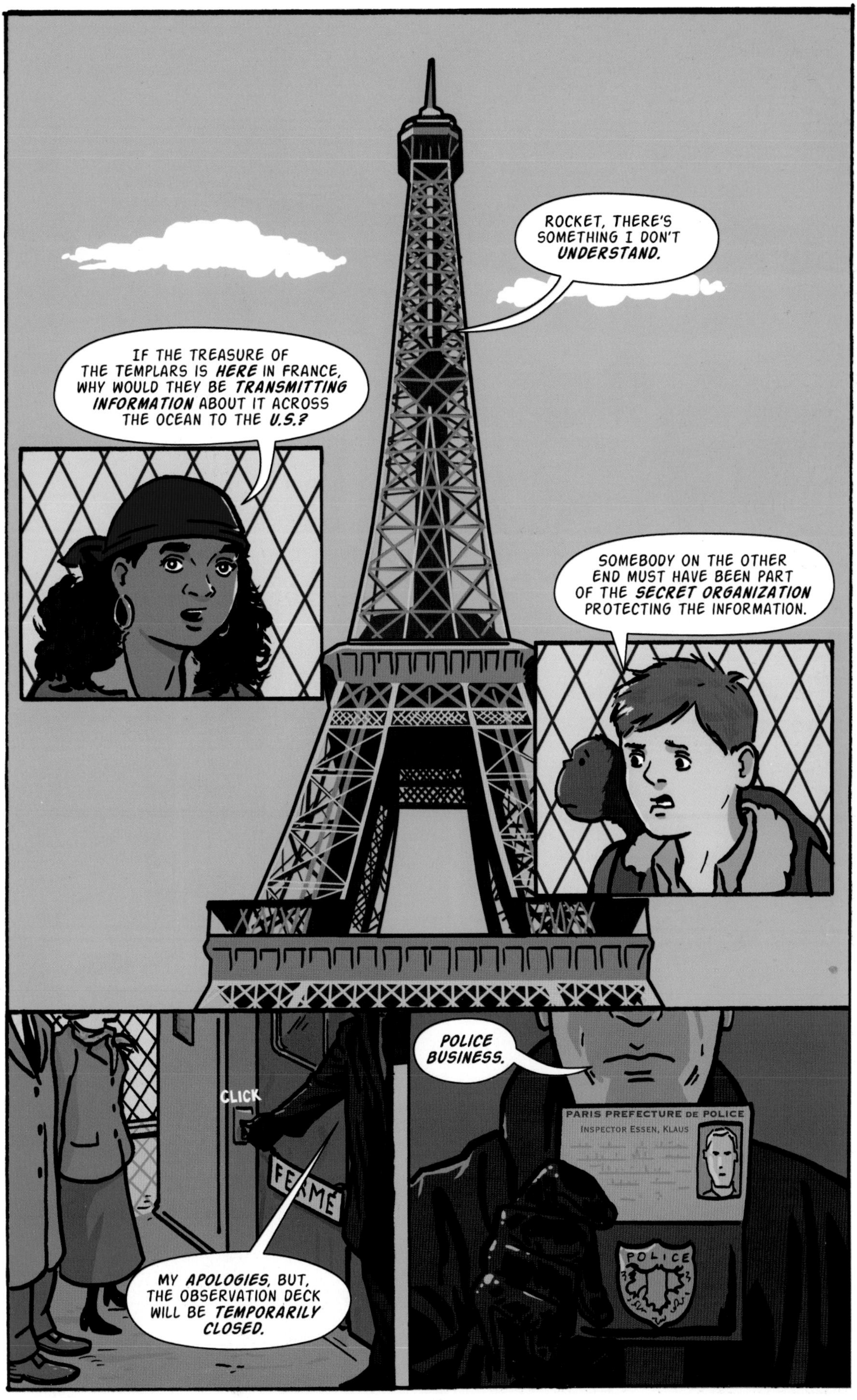
ROCKET, THERE'S SOMETHING I DON'T UNDERSTAND.
IF THE TREASURE OF THE TEMPLARS IS HERE IN FRANCE, WHY WOULD THEY BE TRANSMITTING INFORMATION ABOUT IT ACROSS THE OCEAN TO THE U.S.?
SOMEBODY ON THE OTHER END MUST HAVE BEEN PART OF THE SECRET ORGANIZATION PROTECTING THE INFORMATION.
CLICK
FERMÉ
MY APOLOGIES, BUT, THE OBSERVATION DECK WILL BE TEMPORARILY CLOSED.
POLICE BUSINESS.
PARIS PREFECTURE DE POLICE
INSPECTOR ESSEN, KLAUS
POLICE

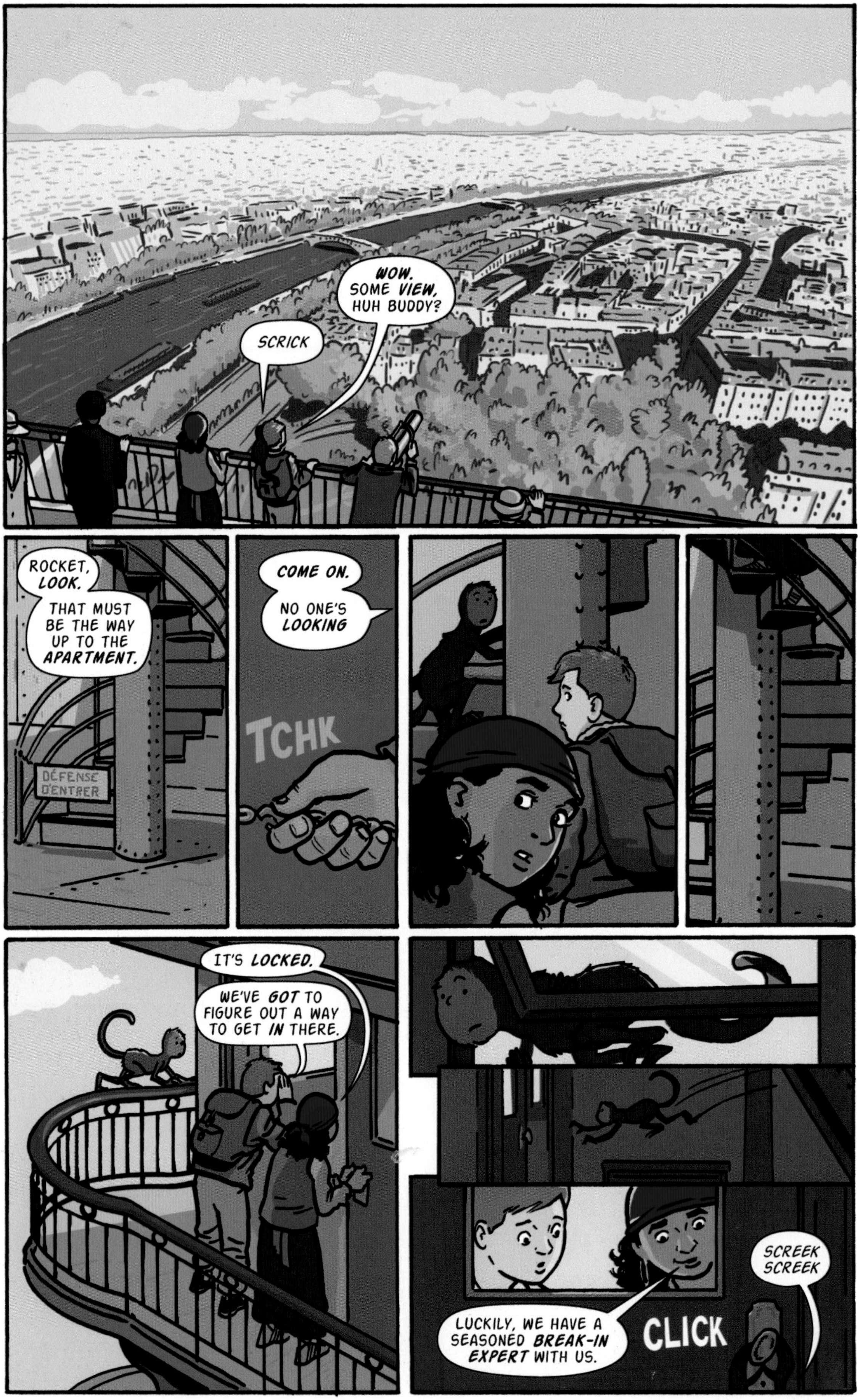
WOW. SOME VIEW, HUH BUDDY?
SCRICK
ROCKET, LOOK.
THAT MUST BE THE WAY UP TO THE APARTMENT.
DÉFENSE D'ENTRER
COME ON.
NO ONE'S LOOKING
TCHK
IT'S LOCKED.
WE'VE GOT TO FIGURE OUT A WAY TO GET IN THERE.
SCREEK SCREEK
CLICK
LUCKILY, WE HAVE A SEASONED BREAK-IN EXPERT WITH US.

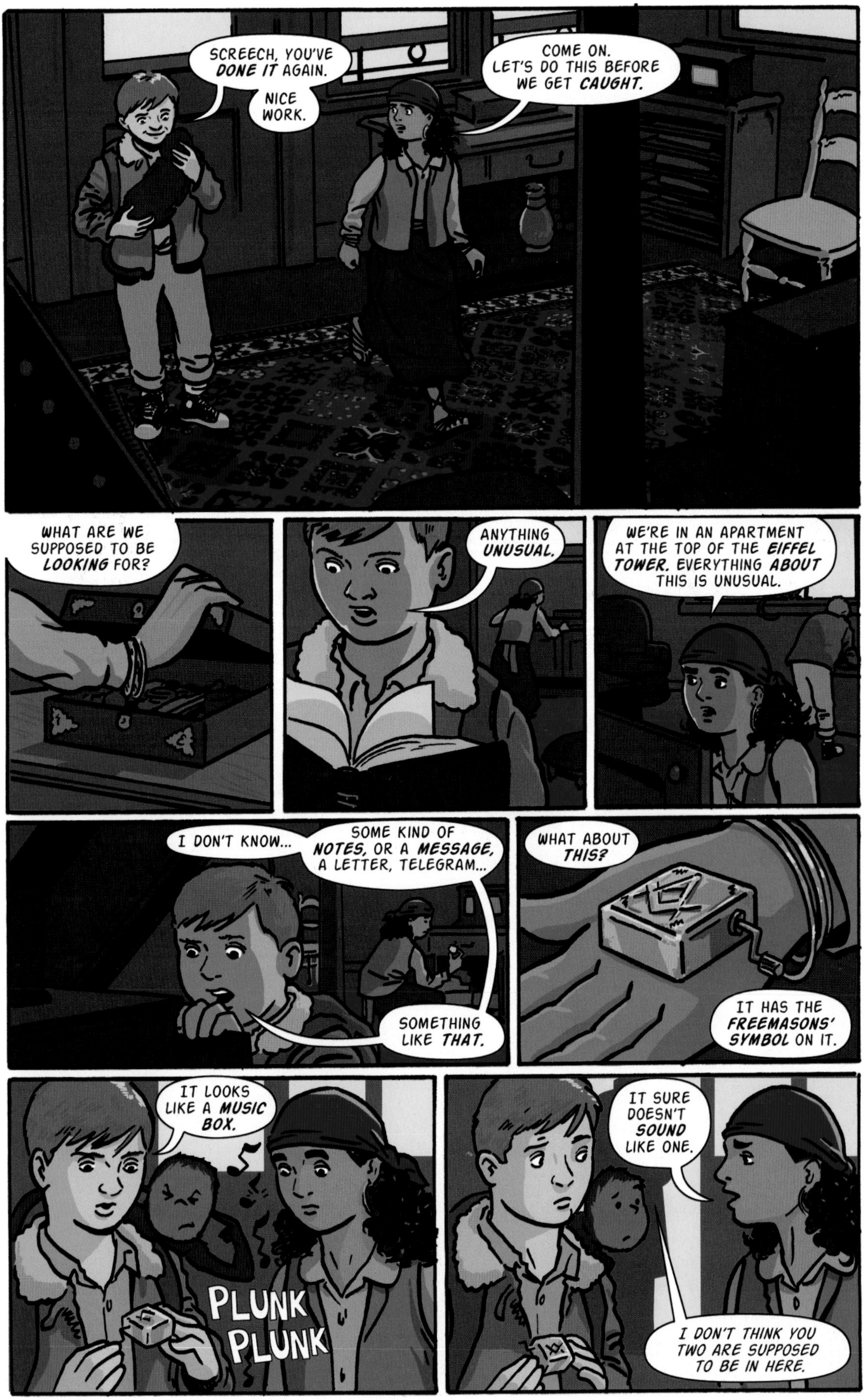
SCREECH, YOU'VE DONE IT AGAIN.
NICE WORK.
COME ON. LET'S DO THIS BEFORE WE GET CAUGHT.
WHAT ARE WE SUPPOSED TO BE LOOKING FOR?
ANYTHING UNUSUAL.
WE'RE IN AN APARTMENT AT THE TOP OF THE EIFFEL TOWER. EVERYTHING ABOUT THIS IS UNUSUAL.
I DON'T KNOW...
SOME KIND OF NOTES, OR A MESSAGE, A LETTER, TELEGRAM...
SOMETHING LIKE THAT.
WHAT ABOUT THIS?
IT HAS THE FREEMASONS' SYMBOL ON IT.
IT LOOKS LIKE A MUSIC BOX.
PLUNK PLUNK
IT SURE DOESN'T SOUND LIKE ONE.
I DON'T THINK YOU TWO ARE SUPPOSED TO BE IN HERE.

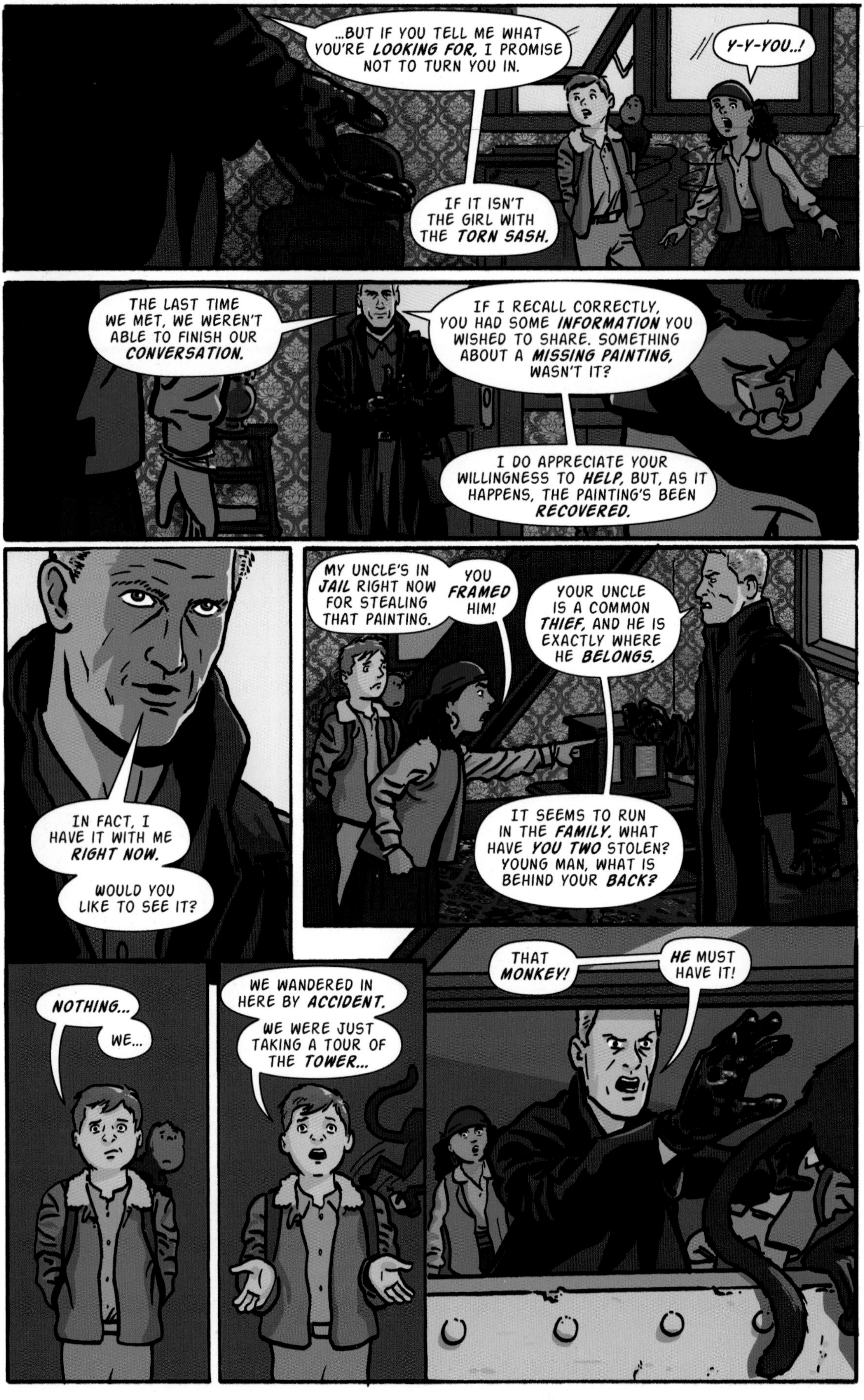
...BUT IF YOU TELL ME WHAT YOU'RE LOOKING FOR, I PROMISE NOT TO TURN YOU IN.
Y-Y-YOU..!
IF IT ISN'T THE GIRL WITH THE TORN SASH.
THE LAST TIME WE MET, WE WEREN'T ABLE TO FINISH OUR CONVERSATION.
IF I RECALL CORRECTLY, YOU HAD SOME INFORMATION YOU WISHED TO SHARE. SOMETHING ABOUT A MISSING PAINTING, WASN'T IT?
I DO APPRECIATE YOUR WILLINGNESS TO HELP, BUT, AS IT HAPPENS, THE PAINTING'S BEEN RECOVERED.
IN FACT, I HAVE IT WITH ME RIGHT NOW.
WOULD YOU LIKE TO SEE IT?
MY UNCLE'S IN JAIL RIGHT NOW FOR STEALING THAT PAINTING.
YOU FRAMED HIM!
YOUR UNCLE IS A COMMON THIEF, AND HE IS EXACTLY WHERE HE BELONGS.
IT SEEMS TO RUN IN THE FAMILY. WHAT HAVE YOU TWO STOLEN? YOUNG MAN, WHAT IS BEHIND YOUR BACK?
NOTHING...
WE...
WE WANDERED IN HERE BY ACCIDENT.
WE WERE JUST TAKING A TOUR OF THE TOWER...
THAT MONKEY!
HE MUST HAVE IT!

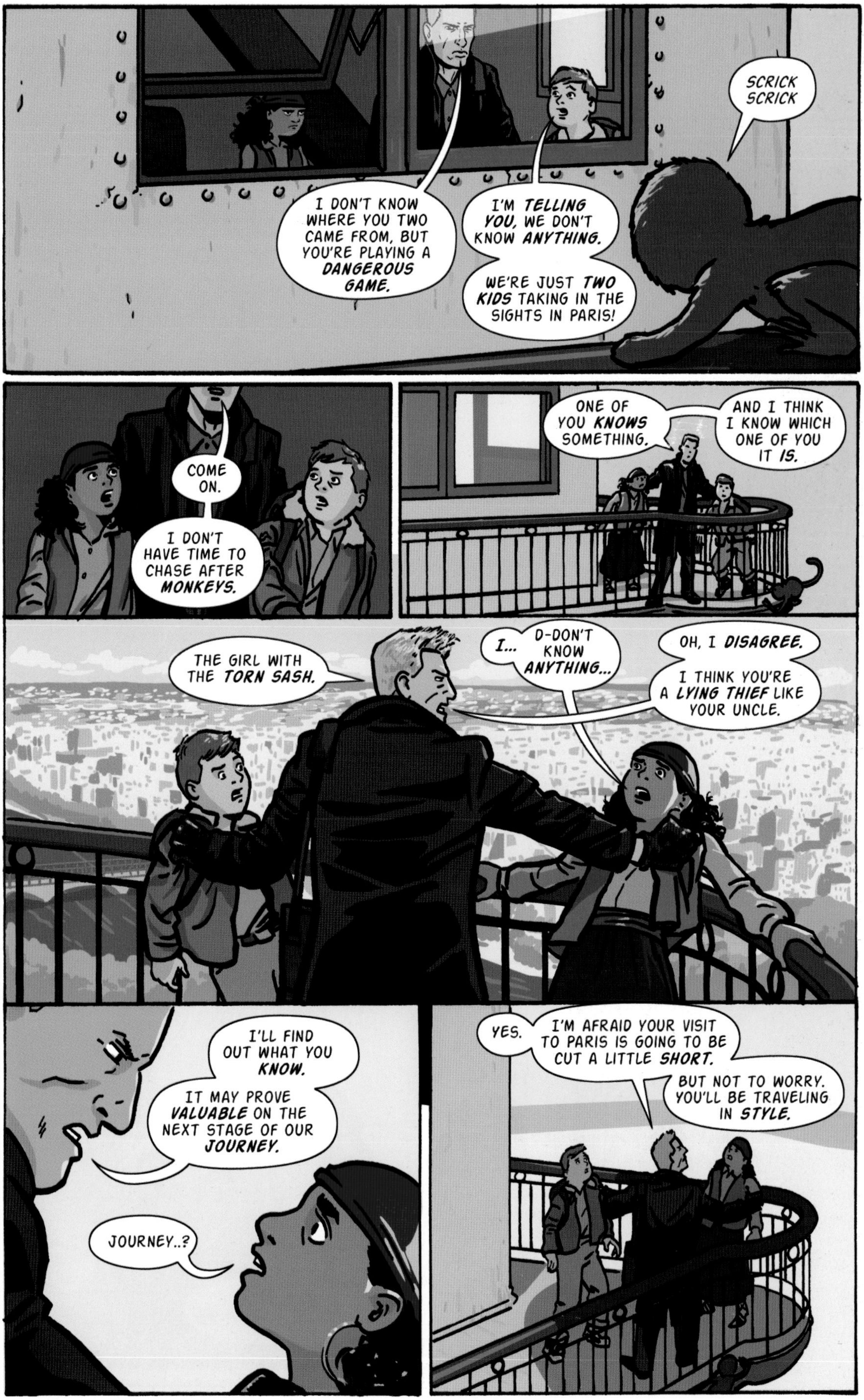
I DON'T KNOW WHERE YOU TWO CAME FROM, BUT YOU'RE PLAYING A DANGEROUS GAME.
I'M TELLING YOU, WE DON'T KNOW ANYTHING.
WE'RE JUST TWO KIDS TAKING IN THE SIGHTS IN PARIS!
SCRICK SCRICK
COME ON.
I DON'T HAVE TIME TO CHASE AFTER MONKEYS.
ONE OF YOU KNOWS SOMETHING.
AND I THINK I KNOW WHICH ONE OF YOU IT IS.
THE GIRL WITH THE TORN SASH.
I... D-DON'T KNOW ANYTHING...
OH, I DISAGREE.
I THINK YOU'RE A LYING THIEF LIKE YOUR UNCLE.
I'LL FIND OUT WHAT YOU KNOW.
IT MAY PROVE VALUABLE ON THE NEXT STAGE OF OUR JOURNEY.
JOURNEY..?
YES.
I'M AFRAID YOUR VISIT TO PARIS IS GOING TO BE CUT A LITTLE SHORT.
BUT NOT TO WORRY. YOU'LL BE TRAVELING IN STYLE.

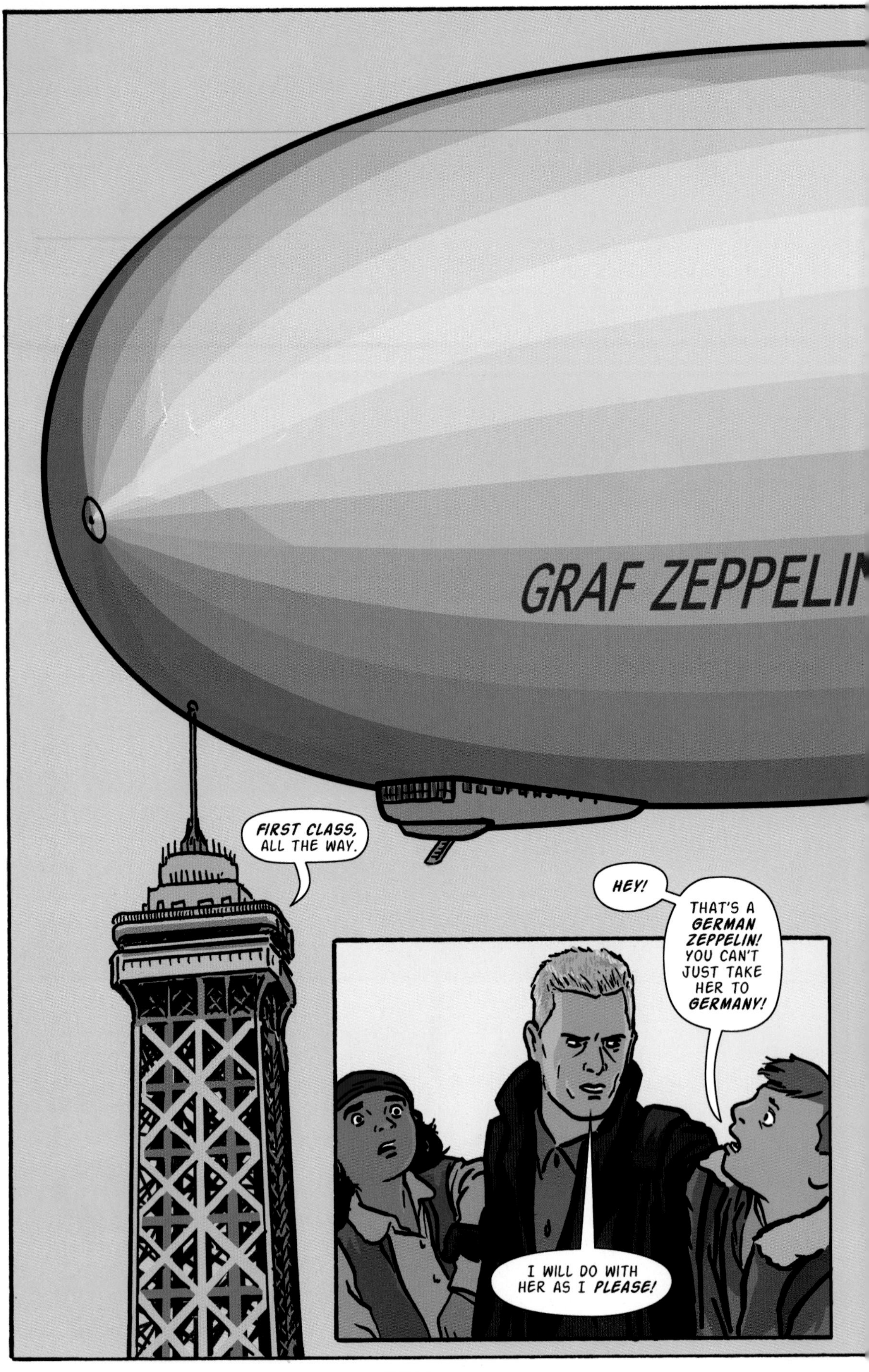

GRAF ZEPPELIN
FIRST CLASS, ALL THE WAY.
HEY!
THAT'S A GERMAN ZEPPELIN! YOU CAN'T JUST TAKE HER TO GERMANY!
I WILL DO WITH HER AS I PLEASE!

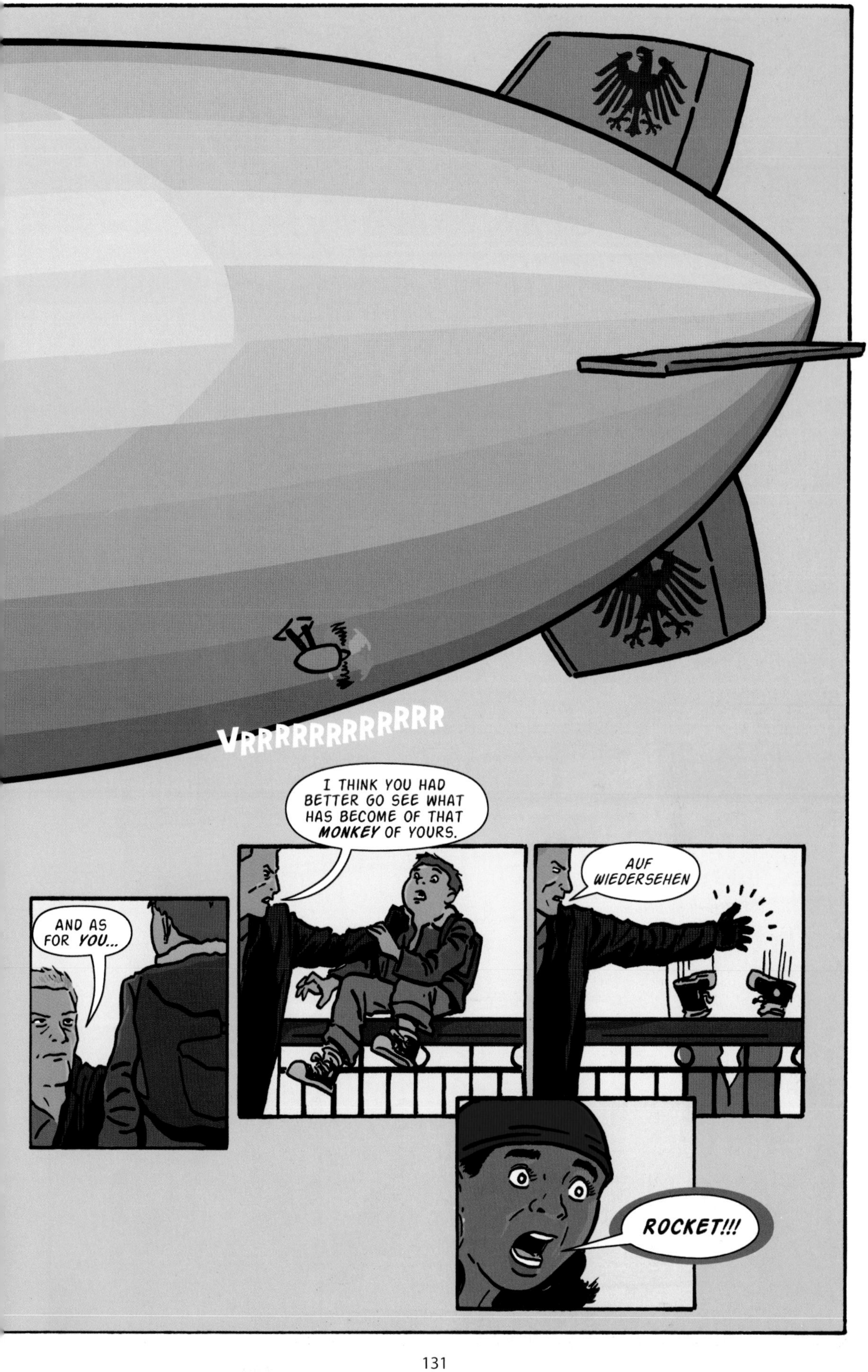
VRRRRRRRRRRR
AND AS FOR YOU...
I THINK YOU HAD BETTER GO SEE WHAT HAS BECOME OF THAT MONKEY OF YOURS.
AUF WIEDERSEHEN
ROCKET!!!

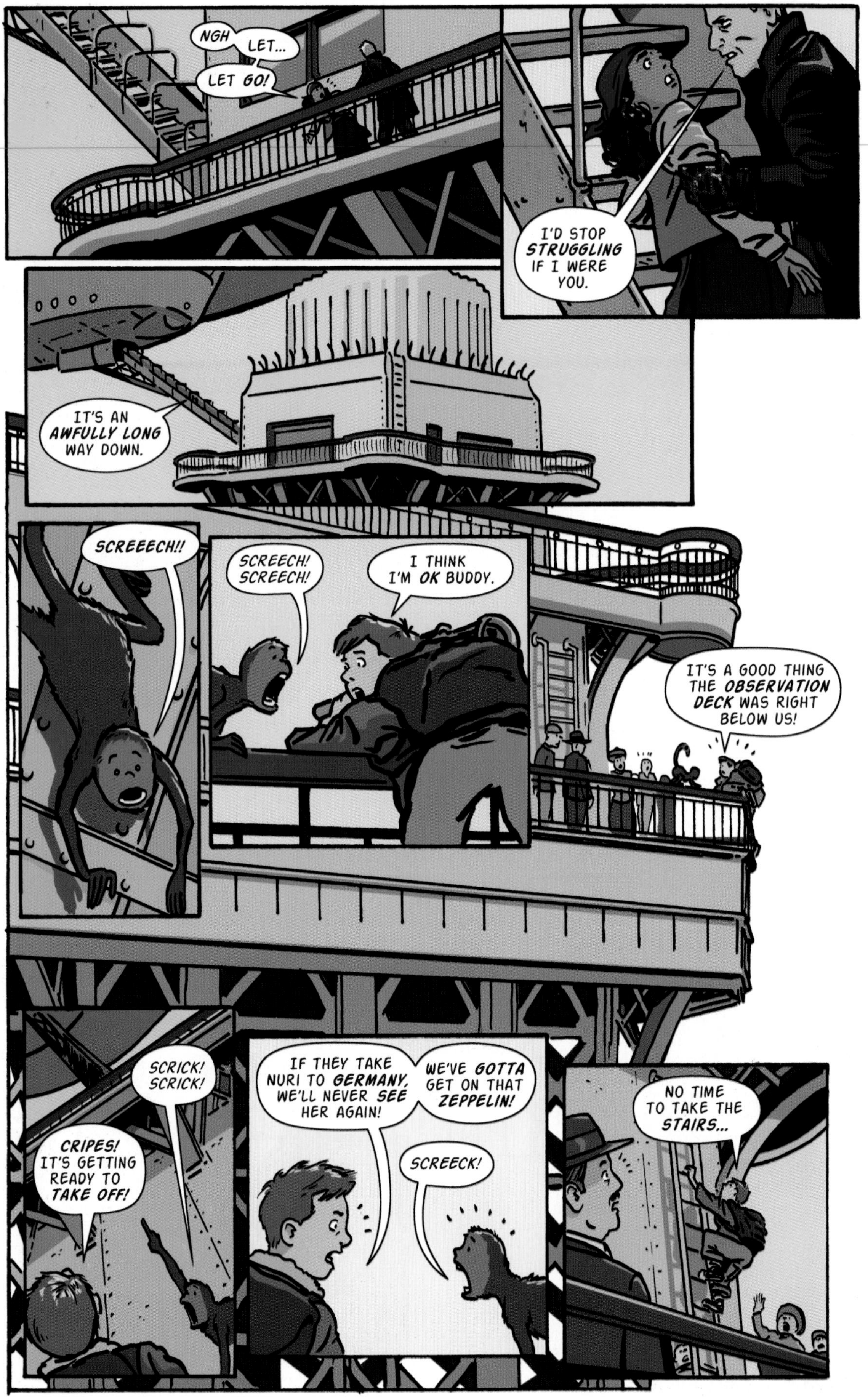
NGH
LET...
LET GO!
I'D STOP STRUGGLING IF I WERE YOU.
IT'S AN AWFULLY LONG WAY DOWN.
SCREEECH!!
SCREECH! SCREECH!
I THINK I'M OK BUDDY.
IT'S A GOOD THING THE OBSERVATION DECK WAS RIGHT BELOW US!
SCRICK! SCRICK!
CRIPES! IT'S GETTING READY TO TAKE OFF!
IF THEY TAKE NURI TO GERMANY, WE'LL NEVER SEE HER AGAIN!
WE'VE GOTTA GET ON THAT ZEPPELIN!
SCREECK!
NO TIME TO TAKE THE STAIRS...

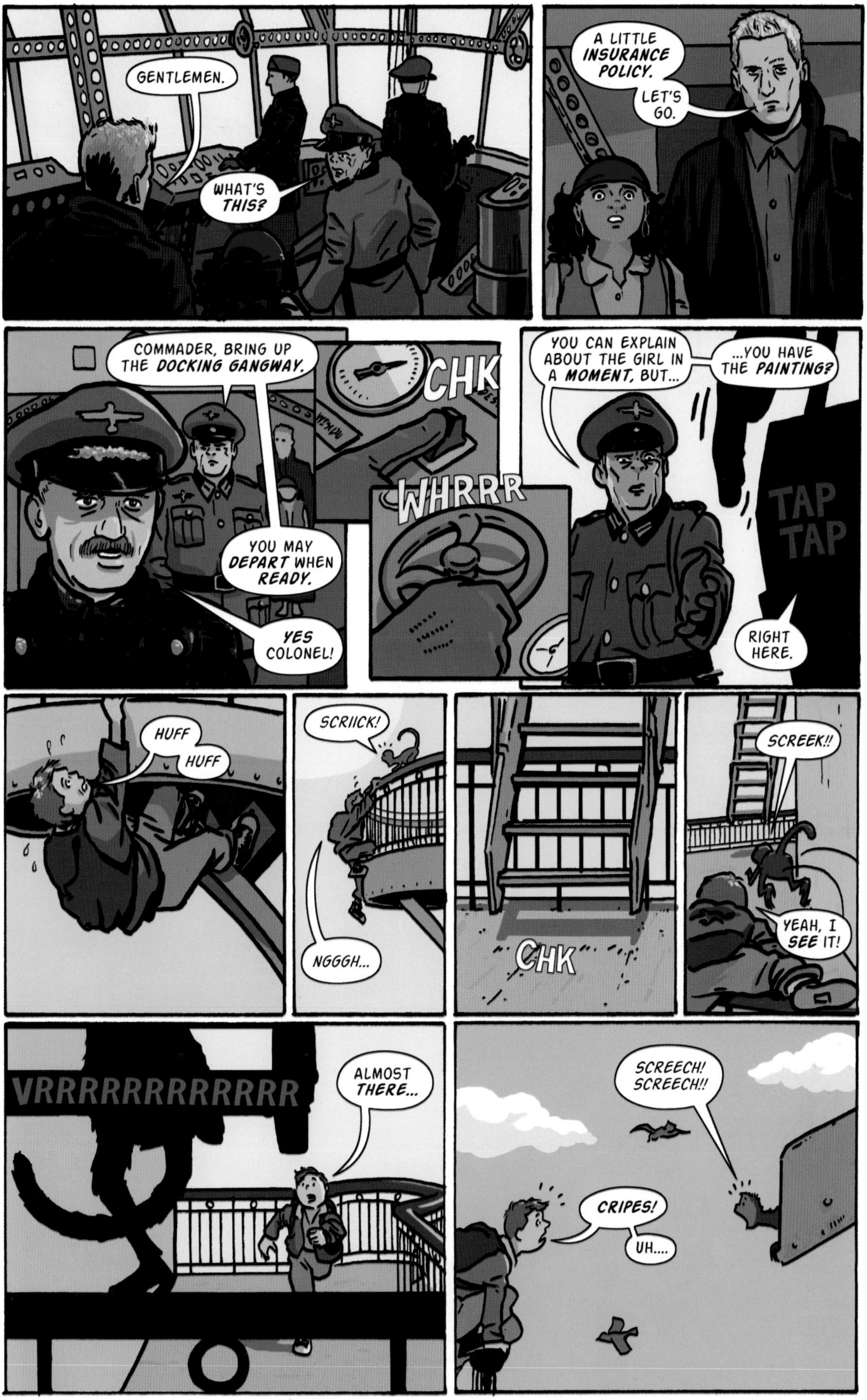
GENTLEMEN.
WHAT'S THIS?
A LITTLE INSURANCE POLICY.
LET'S GO.
COMMADER, BRING UP THE DOCKING GANGWAY.
YOU MAY DEPART WHEN READY.
YES COLONEL!
CHK
WHRRR
YOU CAN EXPLAIN ABOUT THE GIRL IN A MOMENT, BUT...
...YOU HAVE THE PAINTING?
TAP TAP
RIGHT HERE.
HUFF
HUFF
SCRIICK!
NGGGH...
CHK
SCREEK!!
YEAH, I SEE IT!
VRRRRRRRRRRRR
ALMOST THERE...
SCREECH! SCREECH!!
CRIPES!
UH....

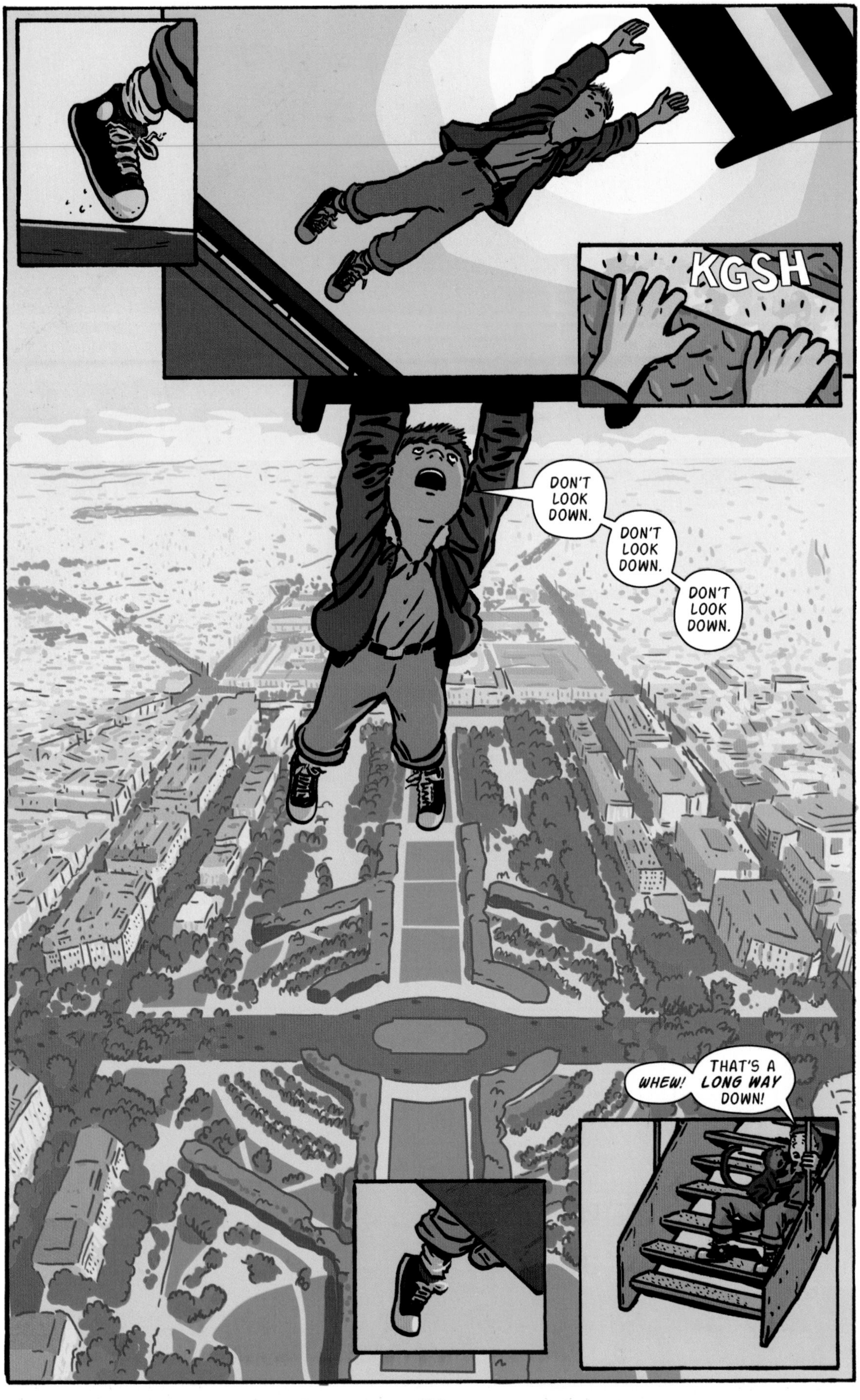
KGSH
DON'T LOOK DOWN.
DON'T LOOK DOWN.
DON'T LOOK DOWN.
WHEW!
THAT'S A LONG WAY DOWN!

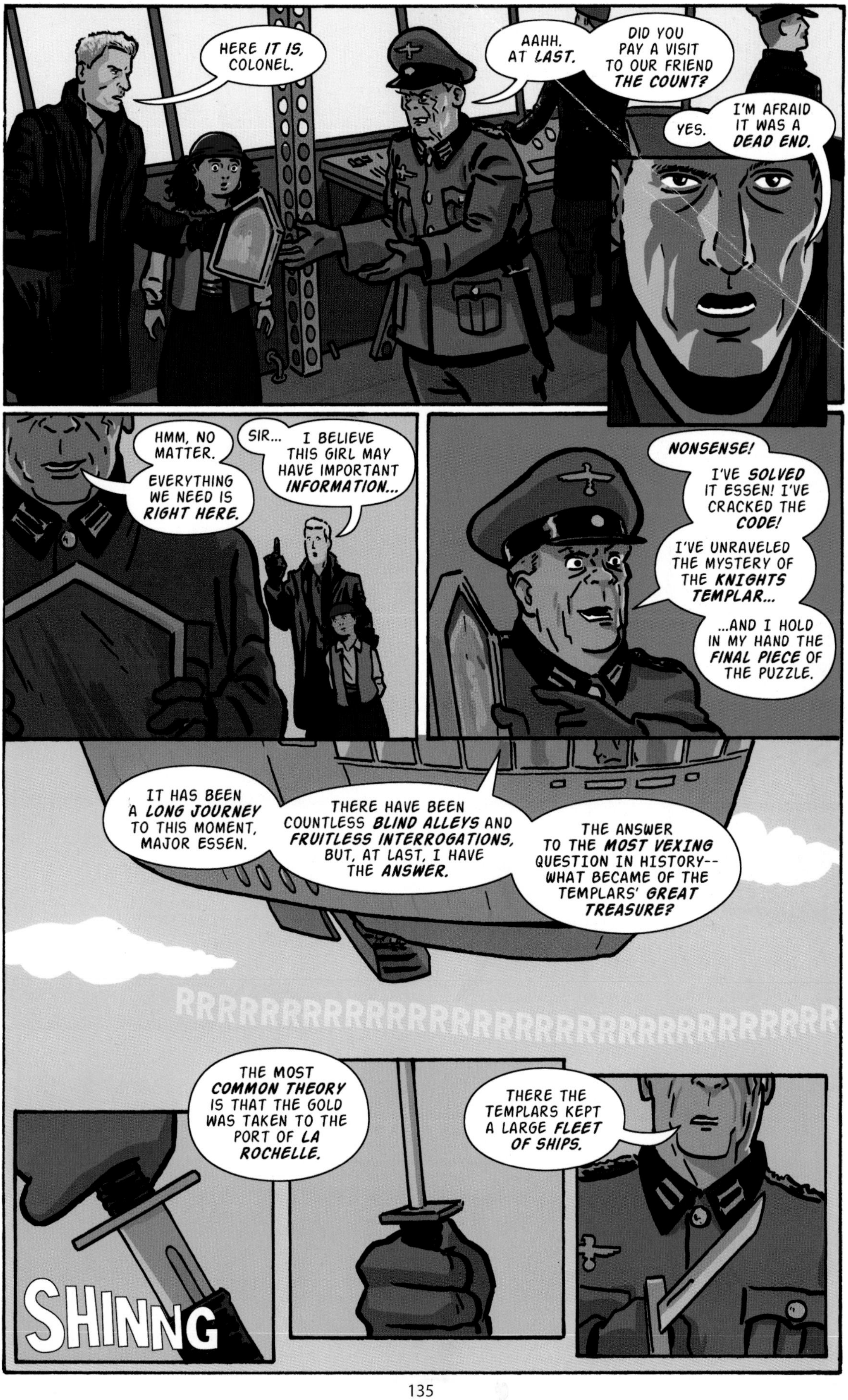
HERE IT IS, COLONEL.
AAHH. AT LAST.
DID YOU PAY A VISIT TO OUR FRIEND THE COUNT?
YES.
I'M AFRAID IT WAS A DEAD END.
HMM, NO MATTER.
EVERYTHING WE NEED IS RIGHT HERE.
SIR... I BELIEVE THIS GIRL MAY HAVE IMPORTANT INFORMATION...
NONSENSE!
I'VE SOLVED IT ESSEN! I'VE CRACKED THE CODE!
I'VE UNRAVELED THE MYSTERY OF THE KNIGHTS TEMPLAR...
...AND I HOLD IN MY HAND THE FINAL PIECE OF THE PUZZLE.
IT HAS BEEN A LONG JOURNEY TO THIS MOMENT, MAJOR ESSEN.
THERE HAVE BEEN COUNTLESS BLIND ALLEYS AND FRUITLESS INTERROGATIONS, BUT, AT LAST, I HAVE THE ANSWER.
THE ANSWER TO THE MOST VEXING QUESTION IN HISTORY-- WHAT BECAME OF THE TEMPLARS' GREAT TREASURE?
RRRRRRRRRRRRRRRRRRRRRRRRRRRRRR
THE MOST COMMON THEORY IS THAT THE GOLD WAS TAKEN TO THE PORT OF LA ROCHELLE.
THERE THE TEMPLARS KEPT A LARGE FLEET OF SHIPS.
SHINNG

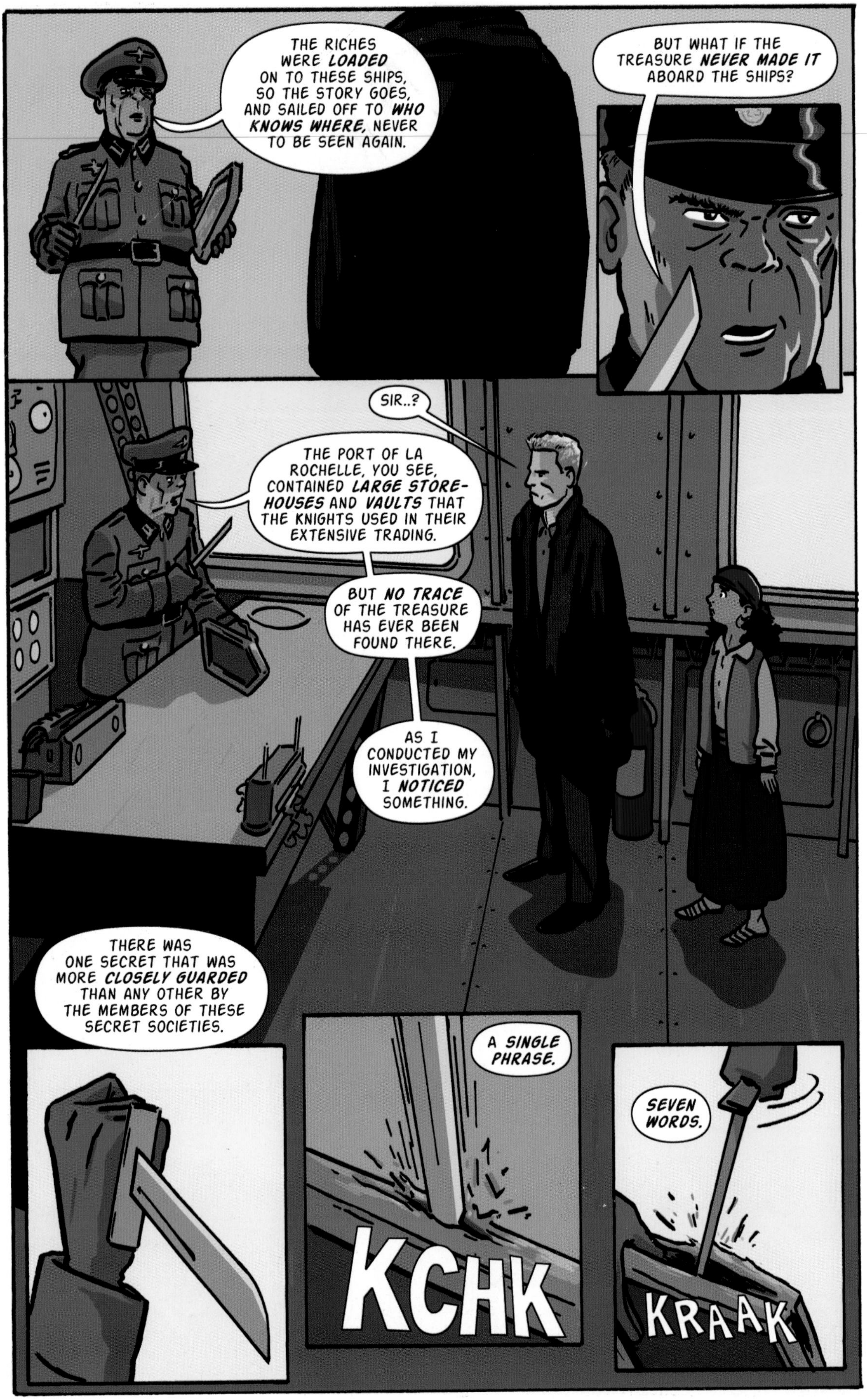
THE RICHES WERE LOADED ON TO THESE SHIPS, SO THE STORY GOES, AND SAILED OFF TO WHO KNOWS WHERE, NEVER TO BE SEEN AGAIN.
BUT WHAT IF THE TREASURE NEVER MADE IT ABOARD THE SHIPS?
SIR..?
THE PORT OF LA ROCHELLE, YOU SEE, CONTAINED LARGE STORE-HOUSES AND VAULTS THAT THE KNIGHTS USED IN THEIR EXTENSIVE TRADING.
BUT NO TRACE OF THE TREASURE HAS EVER BEEN FOUND THERE.
AS I CONDUCTED MY INVESTIGATION, I NOTICED SOMETHING.
THERE WAS ONE SECRET THAT WAS MORE CLOSELY GUARDED THAN ANY OTHER BY THE MEMBERS OF THESE SECRET SOCIETIES.
A SINGLE PHRASE.
KCHK
SEVEN WORDS.
KRAAK

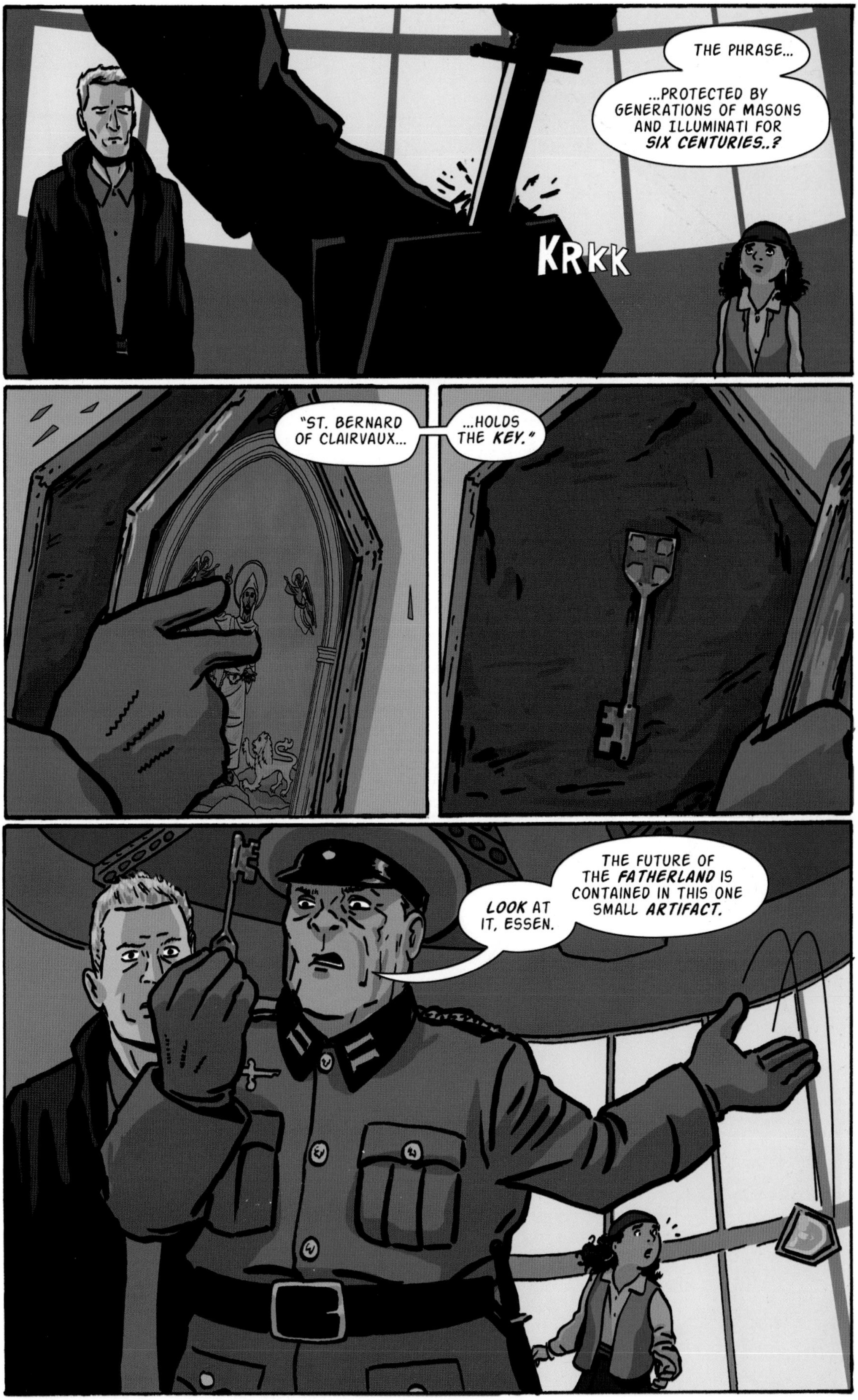
THE PHRASE...
...PROTECTED BY GENERATIONS OF MASONS AND ILLUMINATI FOR SIX CENTURIES..?
KRKK
"ST. BERNARD OF CLAIRVAUX...
...HOLDS THE KEY."
LOOK AT IT, ESSEN.
THE FUTURE OF THE FATHERLAND IS CONTAINED IN THIS ONE SMALL ARTIFACT.

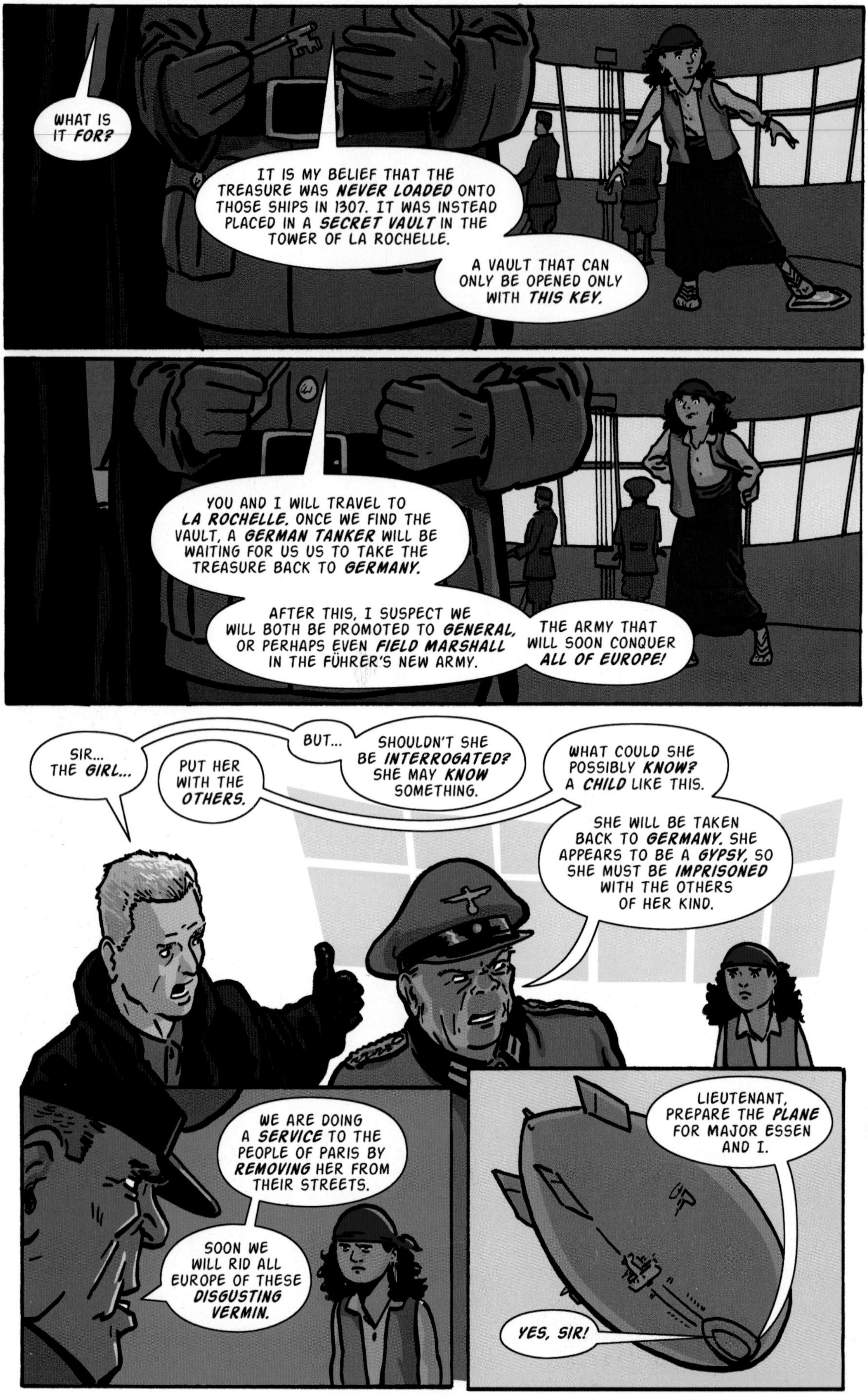

WHAT IS IT FOR?
IT IS MY BELIEF THAT THE TREASURE WAS NEVER LOADED ONTO THOSE SHIPS IN 1307. IT WAS INSTEAD PLACED IN A SECRET VAULT IN THE TOWER OF LA ROCHELLE.
A VAULT THAT CAN ONLY BE OPENED ONLY WITH THIS KEY.
YOU AND I WILL TRAVEL TO LA ROCHELLE. ONCE WE FIND THE VAULT, A GERMAN TANKER WILL BE WAITING FOR US US TO TAKE THE TREASURE BACK TO GERMANY.
AFTER THIS, I SUSPECT WE WILL BOTH BE PROMOTED TO GENERAL, OR PERHAPS EVEN FIELD MARSHALL IN THE FÜHRER'S NEW ARMY.
THE ARMY THAT WILL SOON CONQUER ALL OF EUROPE!
SIR... THE GIRL...
PUT HER WITH THE OTHERS.
BUT...
SHOULDN'T SHE BE INTERROGATED? SHE MAY KNOW SOMETHING.
WHAT COULD SHE POSSIBLY KNOW? A CHILD LIKE THIS.
SHE WILL BE TAKEN BACK TO GERMANY. SHE APPEARS TO BE A GYPSY, SO SHE MUST BE IMPRISONED WITH THE OTHERS OF HER KIND.
WE ARE DOING A SERVICE TO THE PEOPLE OF PARIS BY REMOVING HER FROM THEIR STREETS.
SOON WE WILL RID ALL EUROPE OF THESE DISGUSTING VERMIN.
LIEUTENANT, PREPARE THE PLANE FOR MAJOR ESSEN AND I.
YES, SIR!

CHAPTER EIGHT

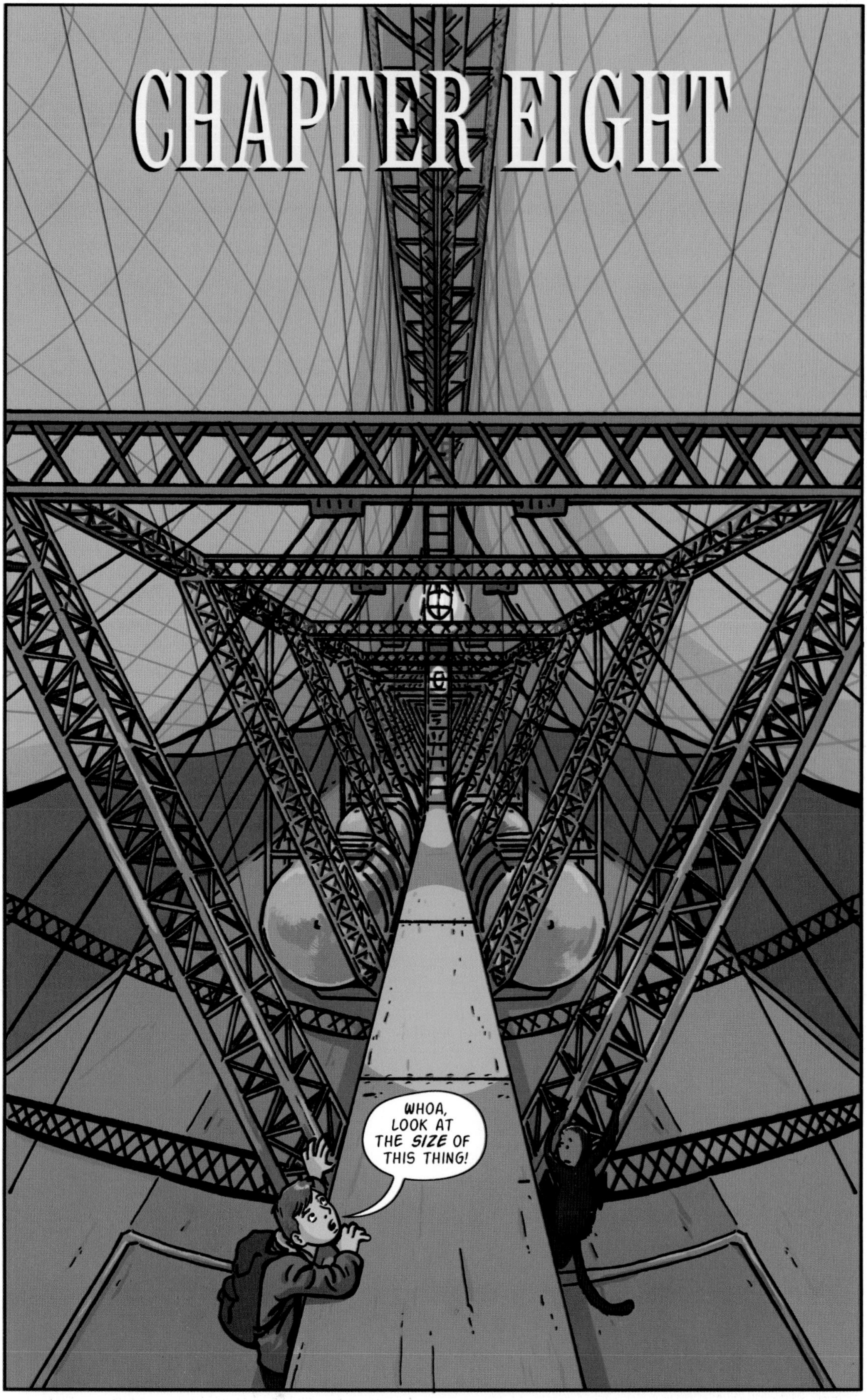
WHOA, LOOK AT THE *SIZE* OF THIS THING!

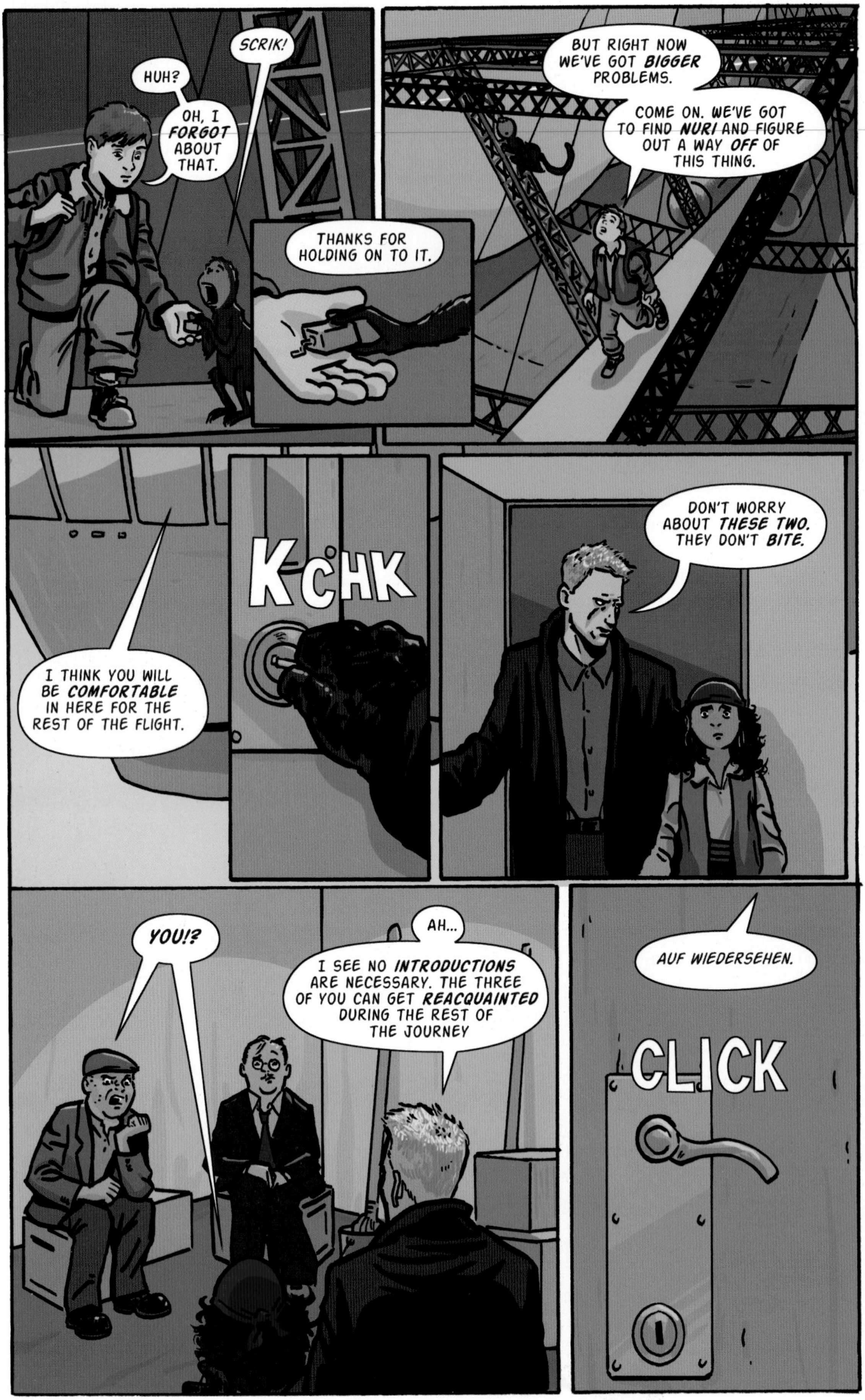
HUH?
OH, I FORGOT ABOUT THAT.
SCRIK!
THANKS FOR HOLDING ON TO IT.
BUT RIGHT NOW WE'VE GOT BIGGER PROBLEMS.
COME ON. WE'VE GOT TO FIND NURI AND FIGURE OUT A WAY OFF OF THIS THING.
I THINK YOU WILL BE COMFORTABLE IN HERE FOR THE REST OF THE FLIGHT.
KCHK
DON'T WORRY ABOUT THESE TWO. THEY DON'T BITE.
YOU!?
AH...
I SEE NO INTRODUCTIONS ARE NECESSARY. THE THREE OF YOU CAN GET REACQUAINTED DURING THE REST OF THE JOURNEY
AUF WIEDERSEHEN.
CLICK

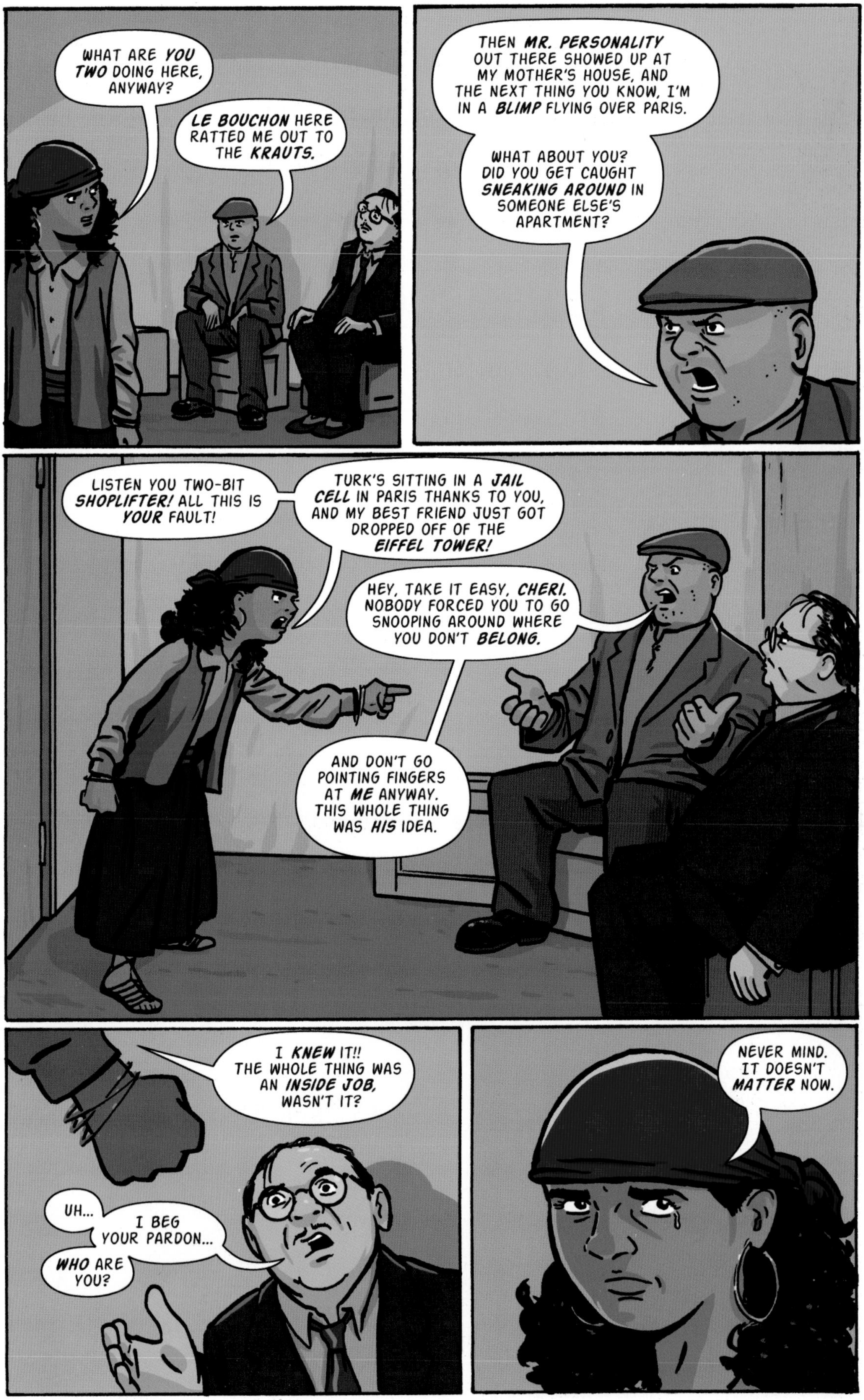
WHAT ARE YOU TWO DOING HERE, ANYWAY?
LE BOUCHON HERE RATTED ME OUT TO THE KRAUTS.
THEN MR. PERSONALITY OUT THERE SHOWED UP AT MY MOTHER'S HOUSE, AND THE NEXT THING YOU KNOW, I'M IN A BLIMP FLYING OVER PARIS.
WHAT ABOUT YOU? DID YOU GET CAUGHT SNEAKING AROUND IN SOMEONE ELSE'S APARTMENT?
LISTEN YOU TWO-BIT SHOPLIFTER! ALL THIS IS YOUR FAULT!
TURK'S SITTING IN A JAIL CELL IN PARIS THANKS TO YOU, AND MY BEST FRIEND JUST GOT DROPPED OFF OF THE EIFFEL TOWER!
HEY, TAKE IT EASY, CHERI. NOBODY FORCED YOU TO GO SNOOPING AROUND WHERE YOU DON'T BELONG.
AND DON'T GO POINTING FINGERS AT ME ANYWAY. THIS WHOLE THING WAS HIS IDEA.
I KNEW IT!! THE WHOLE THING WAS AN INSIDE JOB, WASN'T IT?
UH...
I BEG YOUR PARDON...
WHO ARE YOU?
NEVER MIND. IT DOESN'T MATTER NOW.

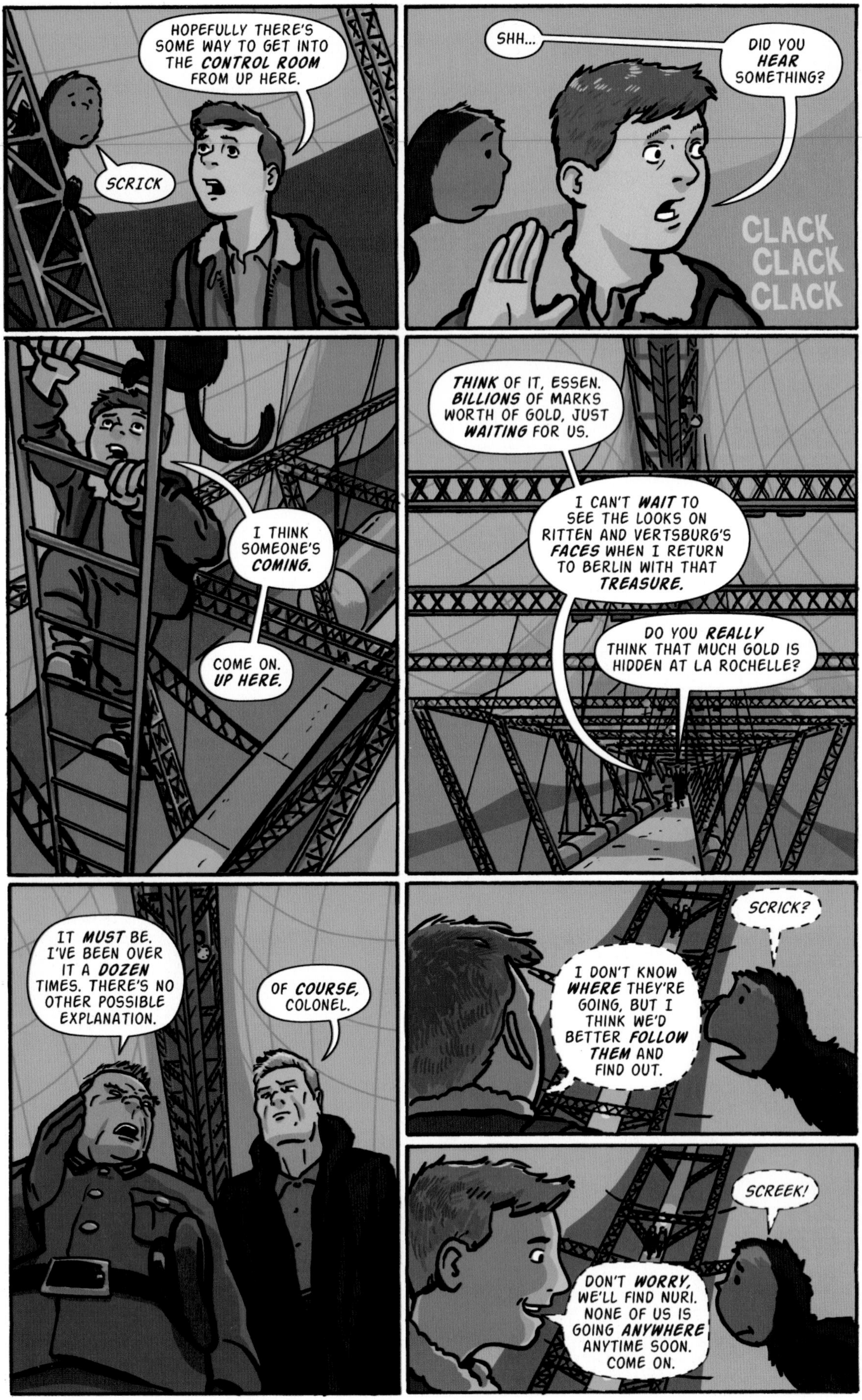

HOPEFULLY THERE'S SOME WAY TO GET INTO THE CONTROL ROOM FROM UP HERE.
SCRICK
SHH...
DID YOU HEAR SOMETHING?
CLACK CLACK CLACK
I THINK SOMEONE'S COMING.
COME ON. UP HERE.
THINK OF IT, ESSEN. BILLIONS OF MARKS WORTH OF GOLD, JUST WAITING FOR US.
I CAN'T WAIT TO SEE THE LOOKS ON RITTEN AND VERTSBURG'S FACES WHEN I RETURN TO BERLIN WITH THAT TREASURE.
DO YOU REALLY THINK THAT MUCH GOLD IS HIDDEN AT LA ROCHELLE?
IT MUST BE. I'VE BEEN OVER IT A DOZEN TIMES. THERE'S NO OTHER POSSIBLE EXPLANATION.
OF COURSE, COLONEL.
SCRICK?
I DON'T KNOW WHERE THEY'RE GOING, BUT I THINK WE'D BETTER FOLLOW THEM AND FIND OUT.
SCREEK!
DON'T WORRY, WE'LL FIND NURI. NONE OF US IS GOING ANYWHERE ANYTIME SOON. COME ON.

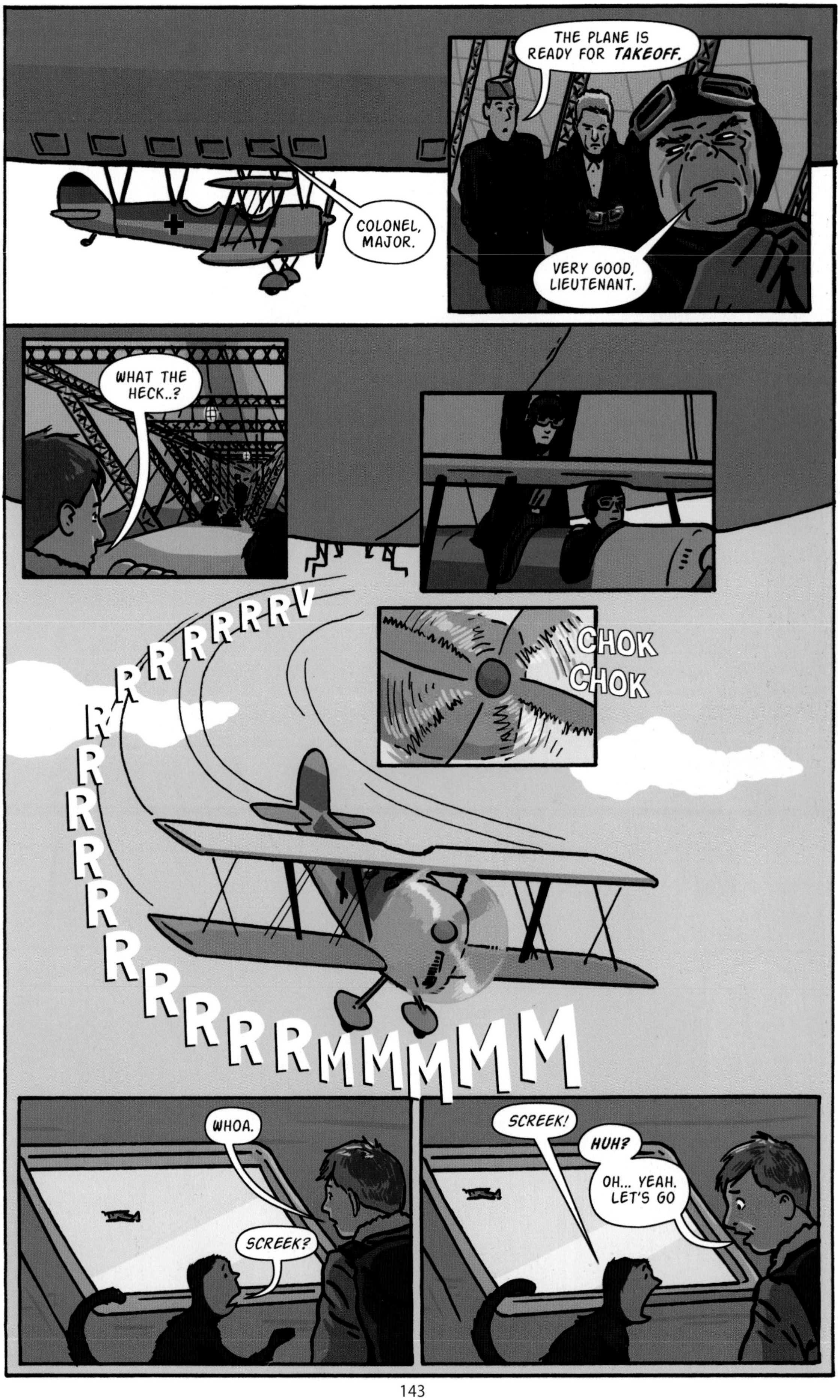
COLONEL, MAJOR.
THE PLANE IS READY FOR TAKEOFF.
VERY GOOD, LIEUTENANT.
WHAT THE HECK..?
RRRRRRRRRRRRRRRRRRRRRRV
CHOK CHOK
RRRRRRRRRRRRRRMMMMMM
WHOA.
SCREEK?
SCREEK!
HUH?
OH... YEAH. LET'S GO

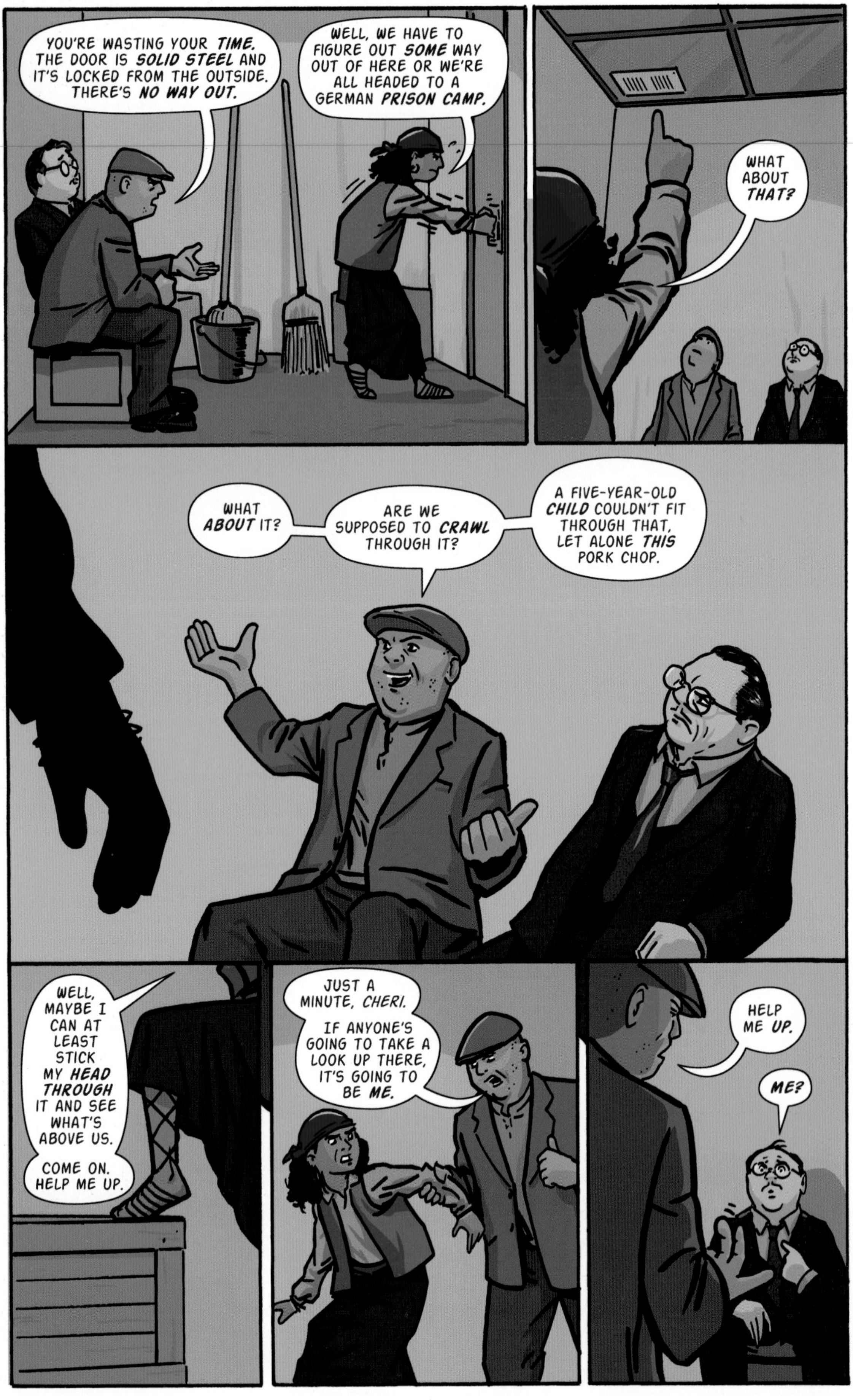

YOU'RE WASTING YOUR TIME. THE DOOR IS SOLID STEEL AND IT'S LOCKED FROM THE OUTSIDE. THERE'S NO WAY OUT.
WELL, WE HAVE TO FIGURE OUT SOME WAY OUT OF HERE OR WE'RE ALL HEADED TO A GERMAN PRISON CAMP.
WHAT ABOUT THAT?
WHAT ABOUT IT?
ARE WE SUPPOSED TO CRAWL THROUGH IT?
A FIVE-YEAR-OLD CHILD COULDN'T FIT THROUGH THAT, LET ALONE THIS PORK CHOP.
WELL, MAYBE I CAN AT LEAST STICK MY HEAD THROUGH IT AND SEE WHAT'S ABOVE US.
COME ON. HELP ME UP.
JUST A MINUTE, CHERI.
IF ANYONE'S GOING TO TAKE A LOOK UP THERE, IT'S GOING TO BE ME.
HELP ME UP.
ME?

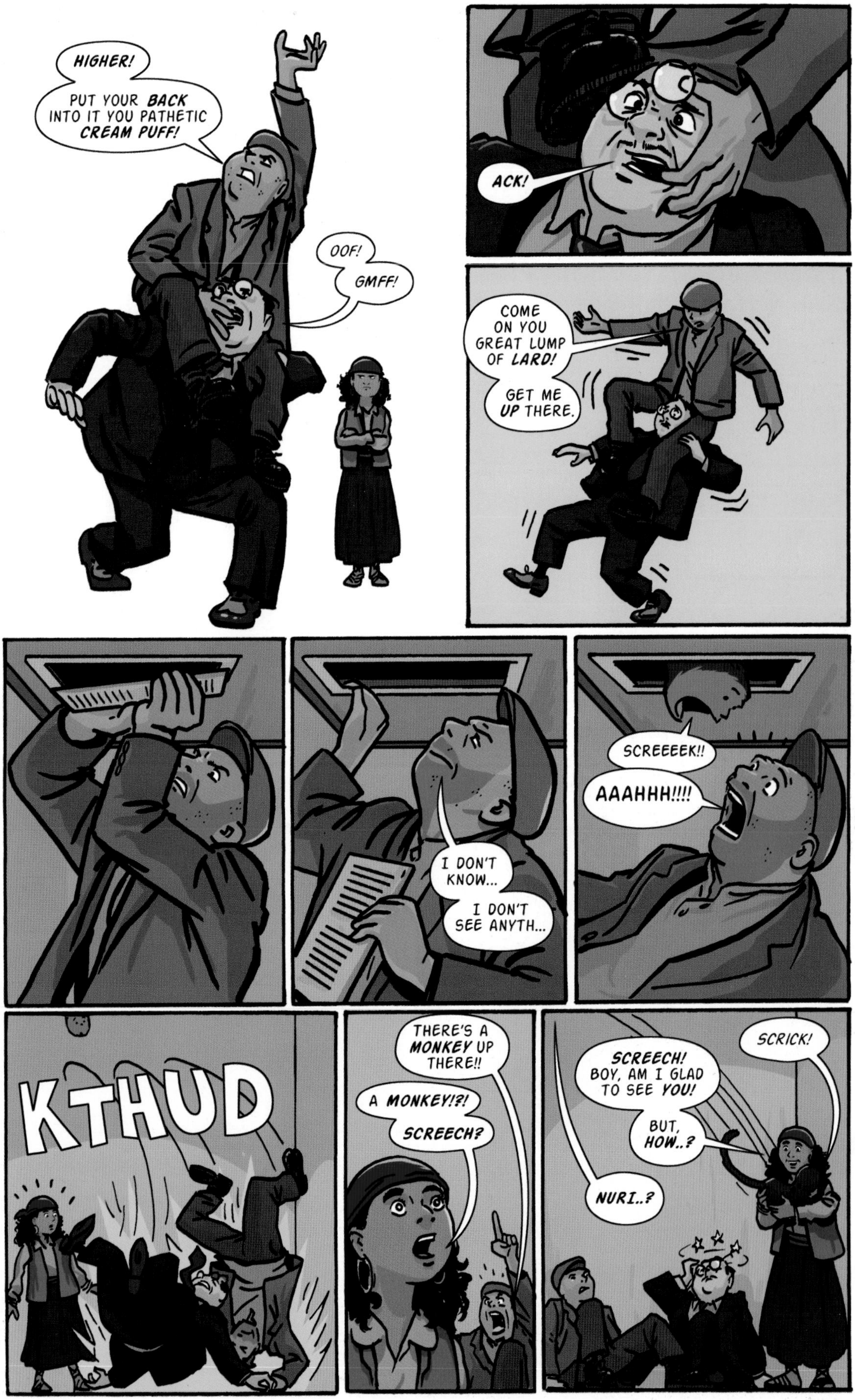
HIGHER!
PUT YOUR BACK INTO IT YOU PATHETIC CREAM PUFF!
OOF!
GMFF!
ACK!
COME ON YOU GREAT LUMP OF LARD!
GET ME UP THERE.
I DON'T KNOW...
I DON'T SEE ANYTH...
SCREEEEK!!
AAAHHH!!!!
KTHUD
THERE'S A MONKEY UP THERE!!
A MONKEY!?!
SCREECH?
SCRICK!
SCREECH! BOY, AM I GLAD TO SEE YOU!
BUT, HOW..?
NURI..?

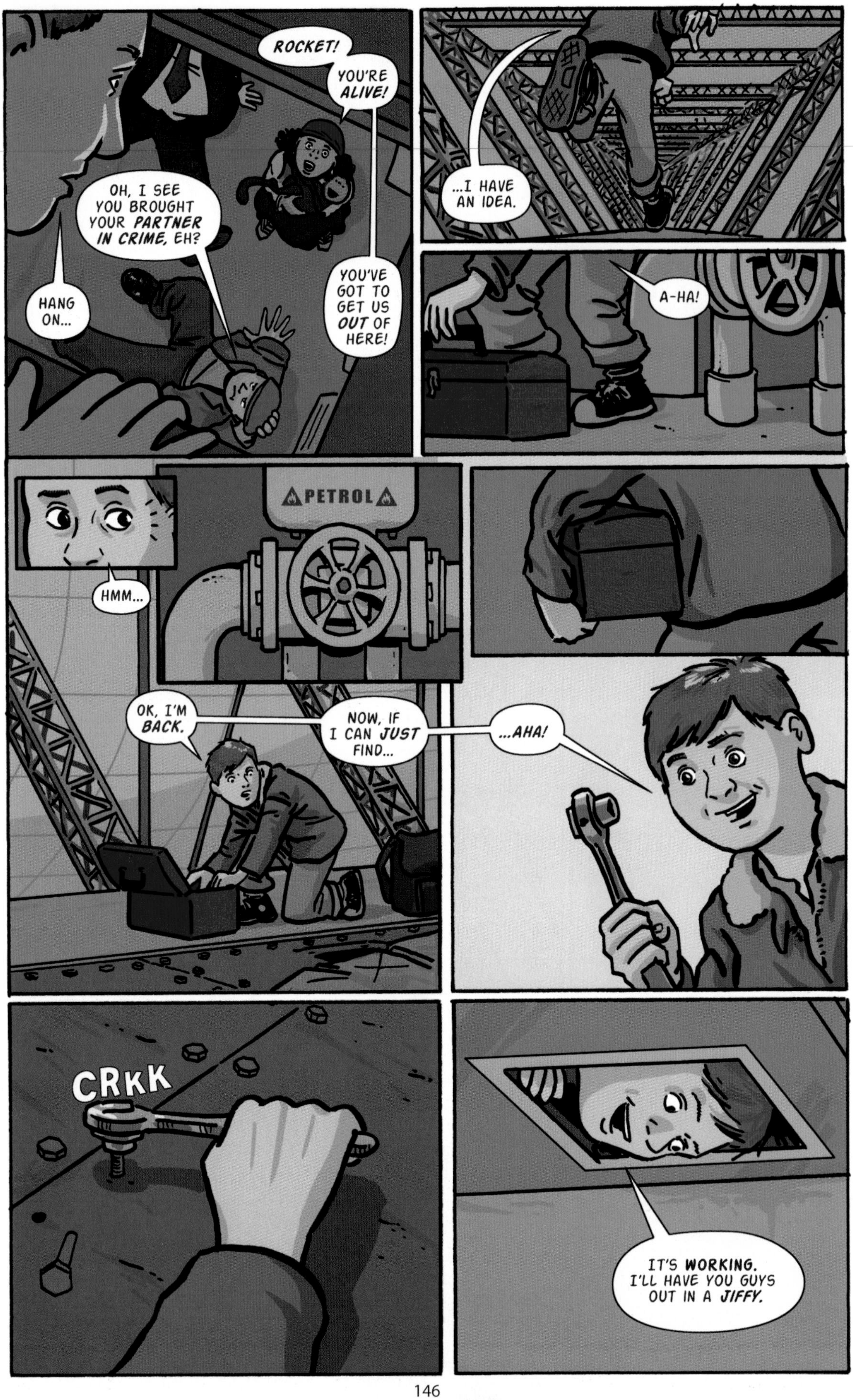
ROCKET!
YOU'RE ALIVE!
OH, I SEE YOU BROUGHT YOUR PARTNER IN CRIME, EH?
HANG ON...
YOU'VE GOT TO GET US OUT OF HERE!
...I HAVE AN IDEA.
A-HA!
HMM...
PETROL
OK, I'M BACK.
NOW, IF I CAN JUST FIND...
...AHA!
CRKK
IT'S WORKING. I'LL HAVE YOU GUYS OUT IN A JIFFY.

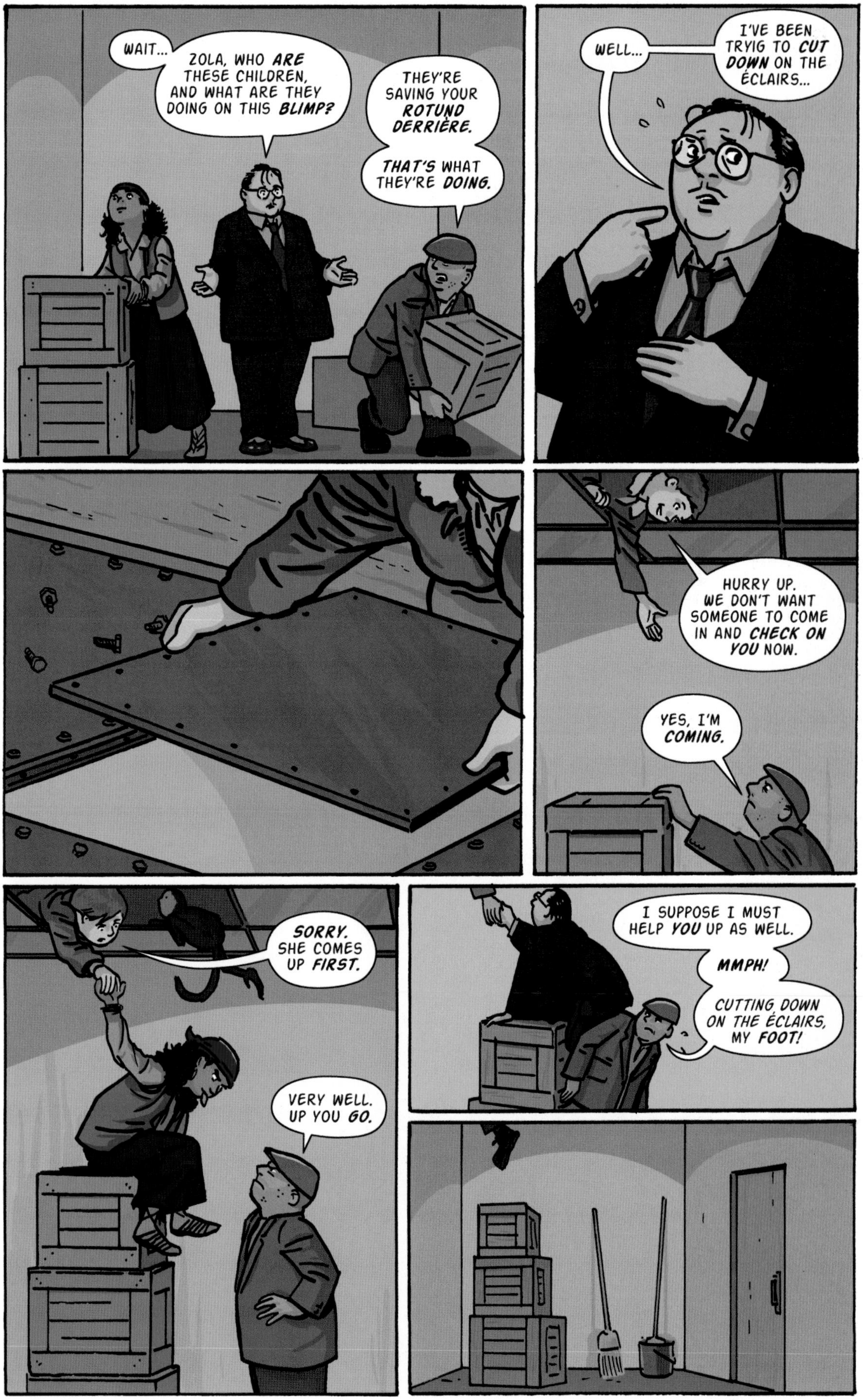
WAIT...
ZOLA, WHO ARE THESE CHILDREN, AND WHAT ARE THEY DOING ON THIS BLIMP?
THEY'RE SAVING YOUR ROTUND DERRIÈRE.
THAT'S WHAT THEY'RE DOING.
WELL...
I'VE BEEN TRYIG TO CUT DOWN ON THE ÉCLAIRS...
HURRY UP. WE DON'T WANT SOMEONE TO COME IN AND CHECK ON YOU NOW.
YES, I'M COMING.
SORRY. SHE COMES UP FIRST.
VERY WELL. UP YOU GO.
I SUPPOSE I MUST HELP YOU UP AS WELL.
MMPH!
CUTTING DOWN ON THE ÉCLAIRS, MY FOOT!

WOW! LOOK AT THIS THING.

I KNOW. *HUGE*, RIGHT?

YOU WON'T *BELIEVE* WHAT SCREECH AND I JUST SAW. THE *BLONDE MAN* AND SOME OTHER GERMAN OFFICER GOT INTO A *BIPLANE* THAT WAS HANGING FROM THE BLIMP AND *TOOK OFF!*

THEY MUST BE ON THEIR WAY TO *LA ROCHELLE*.

WHAT'S *LA ROCHELLE?*

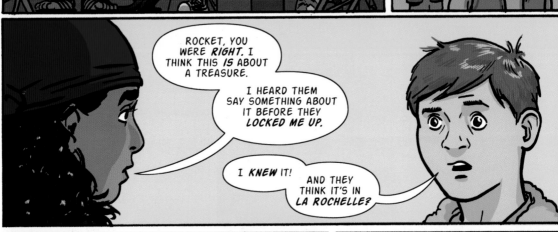

ROCKET, YOU WERE *RIGHT*. I THINK THIS *IS* ABOUT A TREASURE.

I HEARD THEM SAY SOMETHING ABOUT IT BEFORE THEY *LOCKED ME UP*.

I *KNEW* IT!

AND THEY THINK IT'S IN *LA ROCHELLE?*

EXCUSE ME...

WHAT'S THIS ABOUT A *TREASURE?*

OH, HE DIDN'T *TELL* YOU?

TELL ME *WHAT?*

ZOLA!

PAY NO ATTENTION TO *THEM*--THEY ARE *CHILDREN* WITH *WILD* IMAGINATIONS!

AND I SUPPOSE YOU WERE PLANNING ON *TELLING ME* ABOUT THIS TREASURE AT SOME POINT?

ZOLA, AMI! I'VE NEVER *HEARD* OF ANY TREASURE!

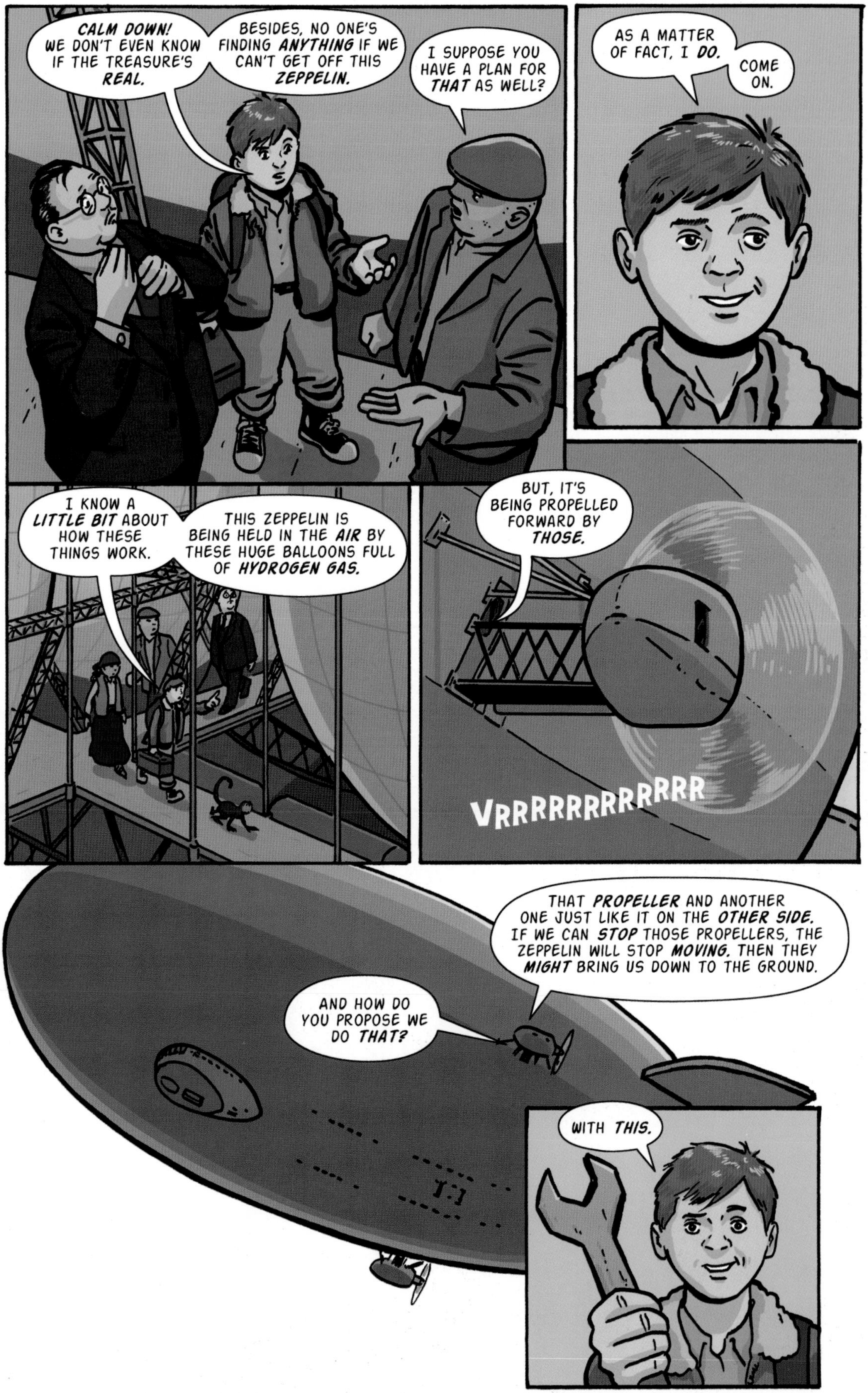
CALM DOWN! WE DON'T EVEN KNOW IF THE TREASURE'S REAL.
BESIDES, NO ONE'S FINDING ANYTHING IF WE CAN'T GET OFF THIS ZEPPELIN.
I SUPPOSE YOU HAVE A PLAN FOR THAT AS WELL?
AS A MATTER OF FACT, I DO.
COME ON.
I KNOW A LITTLE BIT ABOUT HOW THESE THINGS WORK.
THIS ZEPPELIN IS BEING HELD IN THE AIR BY THESE HUGE BALLOONS FULL OF HYDROGEN GAS.
BUT, IT'S BEING PROPELLED FORWARD BY THOSE.
VRRRRRRRRRRR
THAT PROPELLER AND ANOTHER ONE JUST LIKE IT ON THE OTHER SIDE. IF WE CAN STOP THOSE PROPELLERS, THE ZEPPELIN WILL STOP MOVING. THEN THEY MIGHT BRING US DOWN TO THE GROUND.
AND HOW DO YOU PROPOSE WE DO THAT?
WITH THIS.

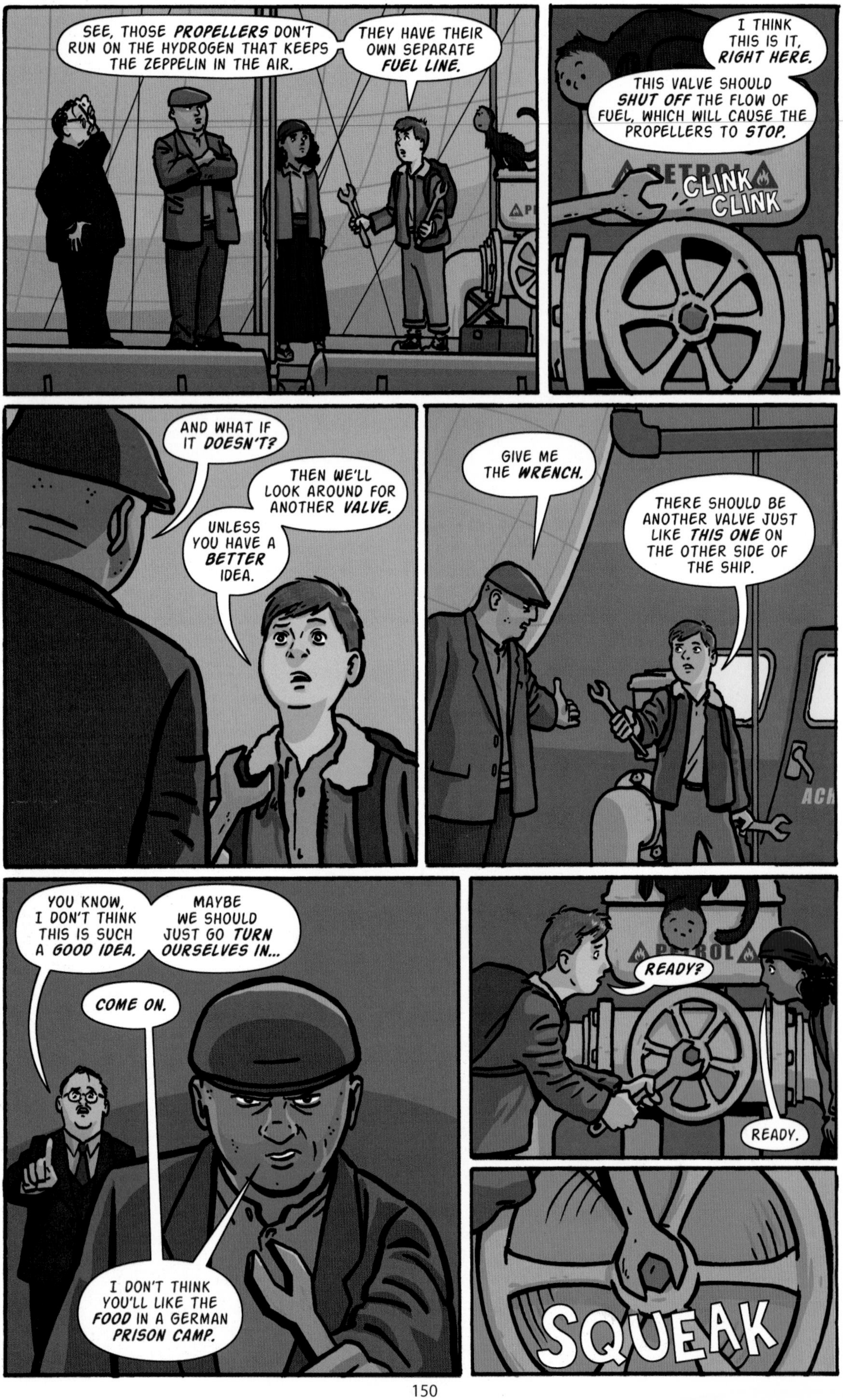
SEE, THOSE PROPELLERS DON'T RUN ON THE HYDROGEN THAT KEEPS THE ZEPPELIN IN THE AIR.
THEY HAVE THEIR OWN SEPARATE FUEL LINE.
I THINK THIS IS IT, RIGHT HERE.
THIS VALVE SHOULD SHUT OFF THE FLOW OF FUEL, WHICH WILL CAUSE THE PROPELLERS TO STOP.
PETROL
CLINK CLINK
AND WHAT IF IT DOESN'T?
THEN WE'LL LOOK AROUND FOR ANOTHER VALVE.
UNLESS YOU HAVE A BETTER IDEA.
GIVE ME THE WRENCH.
THERE SHOULD BE ANOTHER VALVE JUST LIKE THIS ONE ON THE OTHER SIDE OF THE SHIP.
YOU KNOW, I DON'T THINK THIS IS SUCH A GOOD IDEA.
MAYBE WE SHOULD JUST GO TURN OURSELVES IN...
COME ON.
I DON'T THINK YOU'LL LIKE THE FOOD IN A GERMAN PRISON CAMP.
PETROL
READY?
READY.
SQUEAK

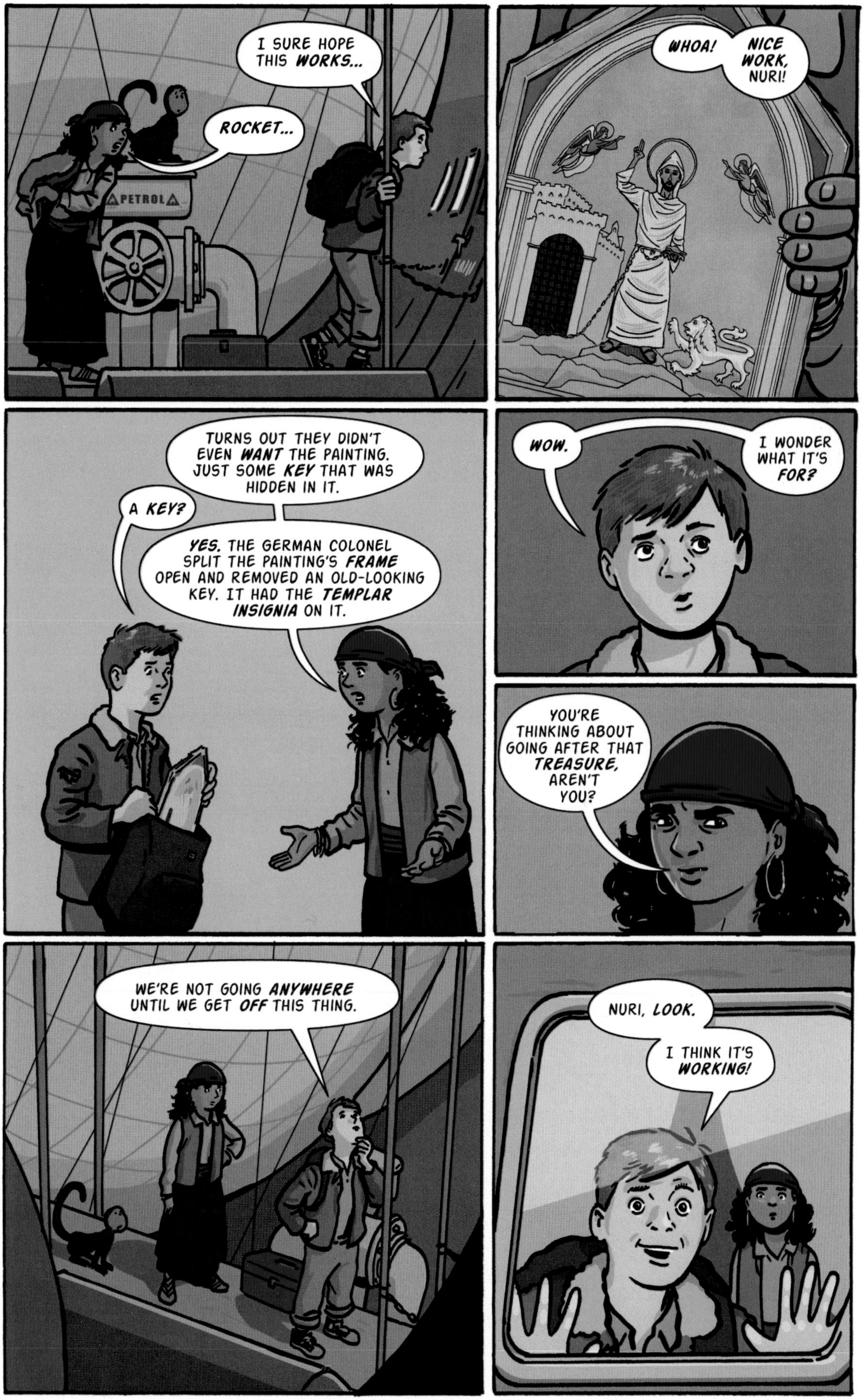
I SURE HOPE THIS WORKS...
ROCKET...
PETROL
WHOA!
NICE WORK, NURI!
TURNS OUT THEY DIDN'T EVEN WANT THE PAINTING. JUST SOME KEY THAT WAS HIDDEN IN IT.
A KEY?
YES. THE GERMAN COLONEL SPLIT THE PAINTING'S FRAME OPEN AND REMOVED AN OLD-LOOKING KEY. IT HAD THE TEMPLAR INSIGNIA ON IT.
WOW.
I WONDER WHAT IT'S FOR?
YOU'RE THINKING ABOUT GOING AFTER THAT TREASURE, AREN'T YOU?
WE'RE NOT GOING ANYWHERE UNTIL WE GET OFF THIS THING.
NURI, LOOK.
I THINK IT'S WORKING!

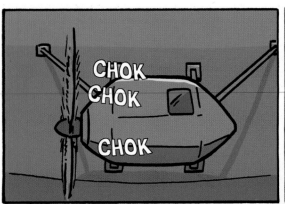
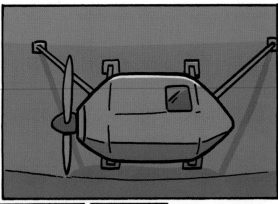

CHOK
CHOK
CHOK

EH?

ENSIGN! THERE APPEARS TO BE SOMETHING WRONG WITH THE *ENGINES.* WE'RE GETTING NO POWER. GO BACK AND *CHECK IT OUT.*

YES, SIR.

UNTIL WE FIGURE OUT WHAT'S *GOING ON* WITH THE ENGINES, WE'D BETTER BRING OUR *ALTITUDE* DOWN.

THEY'RE BRINGING US *DOWN.* COME ON, WE SHOULD GET *OUT OF SIGHT* IN CASE THEY SEND SOMEONE BACK HERE TO *CHECK* ON THIS.

I THINK THERE'S A SMALL COMPARTMENT IN THE *TAIL FIN.*

BUT, SHOULD WE HAVE TOLD *ZOLA AND ROUSSEAU* TO GET OUT OF SIGHT TOO?

THOSE TWO AREN'T TOO *BRIGHT,* BUT I DON'T THINK THEY'RE *DUMB ENOUGH* TO STAND AROUND IN THE OPEN AND WAIT TO GET *CAUGHT.*

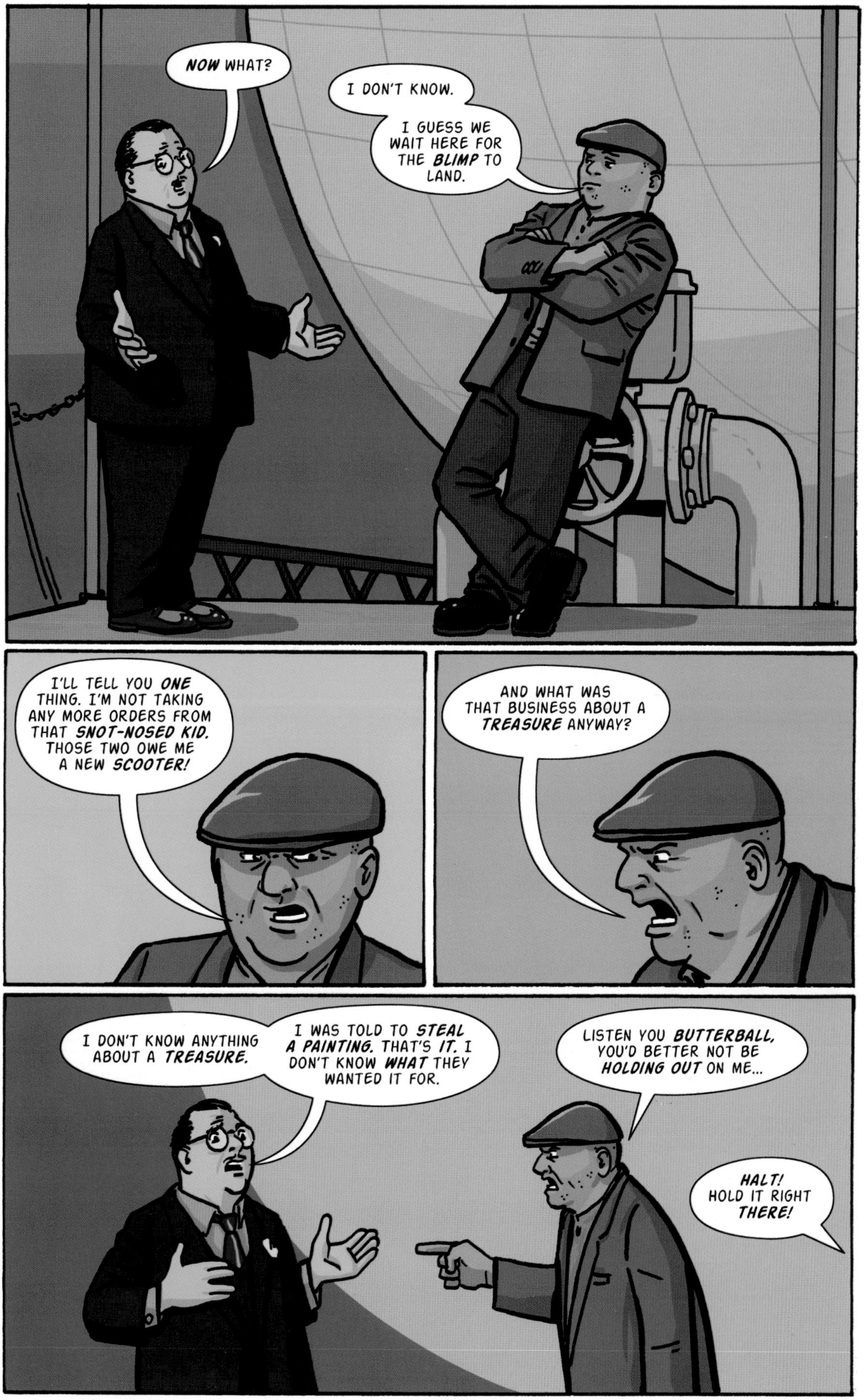
NOW WHAT?
I DON'T KNOW.
I GUESS WE WAIT HERE FOR THE BLIMP TO LAND.
I'LL TELL YOU ONE THING. I'M NOT TAKING ANY MORE ORDERS FROM THAT SNOT-NOSED KID. THOSE TWO OWE ME A NEW SCOOTER!
AND WHAT WAS THAT BUSINESS ABOUT A TREASURE ANYWAY?
I DON'T KNOW ANYTHING ABOUT A TREASURE.
I WAS TOLD TO STEAL A PAINTING. THAT'S IT. I DON'T KNOW WHAT THEY WANTED IT FOR.
LISTEN YOU BUTTERBALL, YOU'D BETTER NOT BE HOLDING OUT ON ME...
HALT! HOLD IT RIGHT THERE!

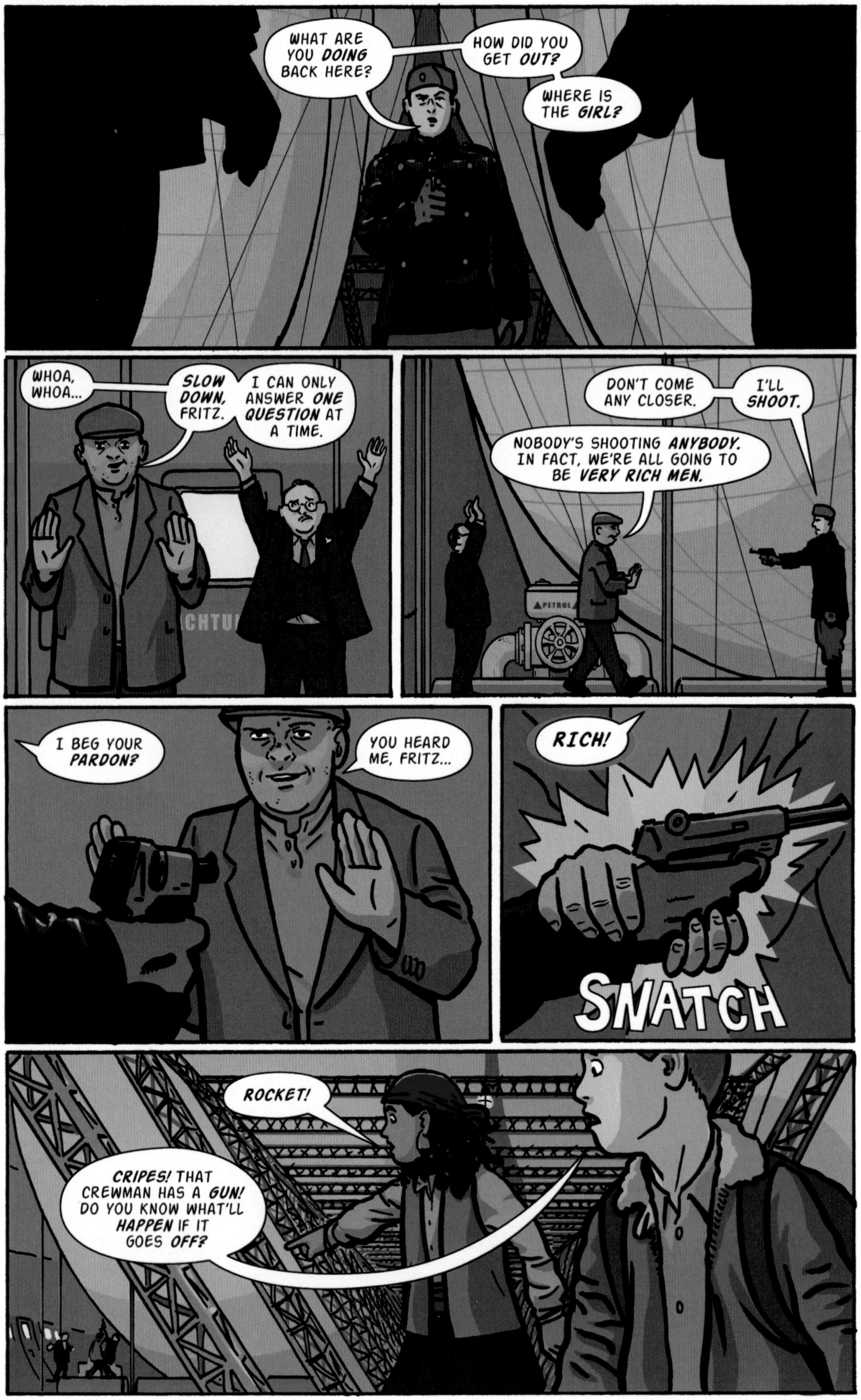
WHAT ARE YOU DOING BACK HERE?
HOW DID YOU GET OUT?
WHERE IS THE GIRL?
WHOA, WHOA...
SLOW DOWN, FRITZ.
I CAN ONLY ANSWER ONE QUESTION AT A TIME.
ACHTUN
DON'T COME ANY CLOSER.
I'LL SHOOT.
NOBODY'S SHOOTING ANYBODY. IN FACT, WE'RE ALL GOING TO BE VERY RICH MEN.
PETROL
I BEG YOUR PARDON?
YOU HEARD ME, FRITZ...
RICH!
SNATCH
ROCKET!
CRIPES! THAT CREWMAN HAS A GUN! DO YOU KNOW WHAT'LL HAPPEN IF IT GOES OFF?

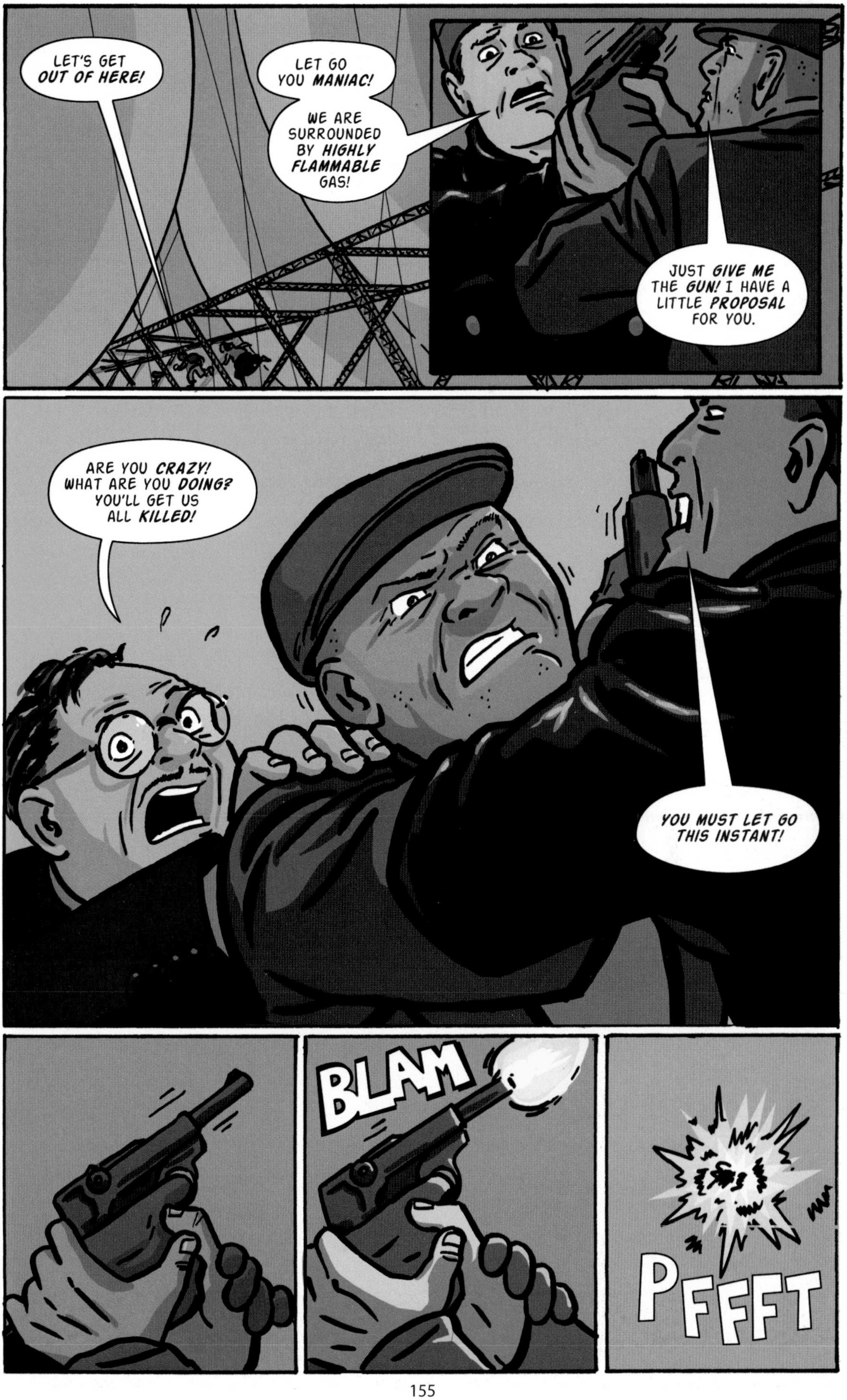
LET'S GET OUT OF HERE!
LET GO YOU MANIAC!
WE ARE SURROUNDED BY HIGHLY FLAMMABLE GAS!
JUST GIVE ME THE GUN! I HAVE A LITTLE PROPOSAL FOR YOU.
ARE YOU CRAZY! WHAT ARE YOU DOING? YOU'LL GET US ALL KILLED!
YOU MUST LET GO THIS INSTANT!
BLAM
PFFFT

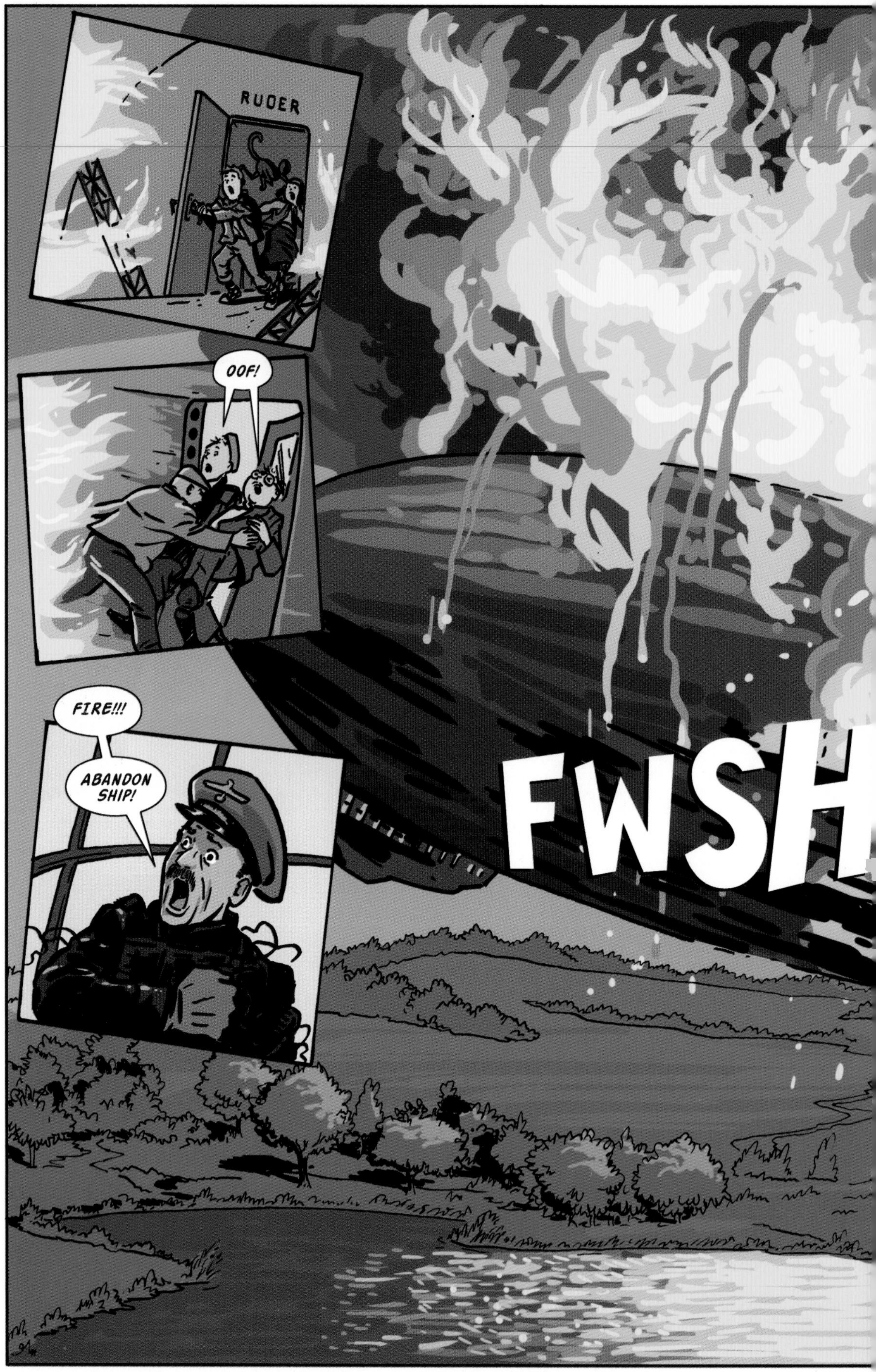
RUDER
OOF!
FIRE!!!
ABANDON SHIP!
FWSH

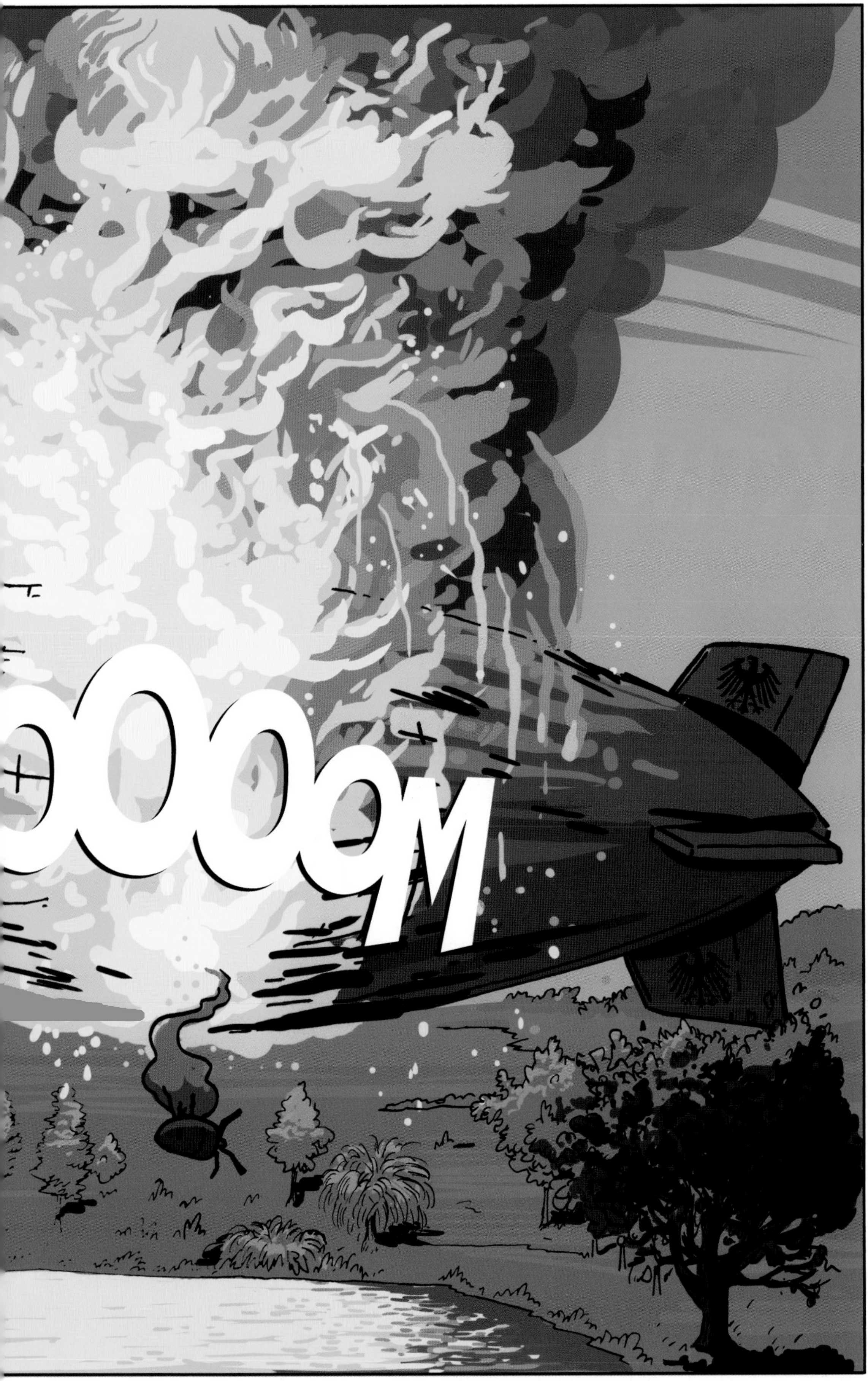
OOOOM

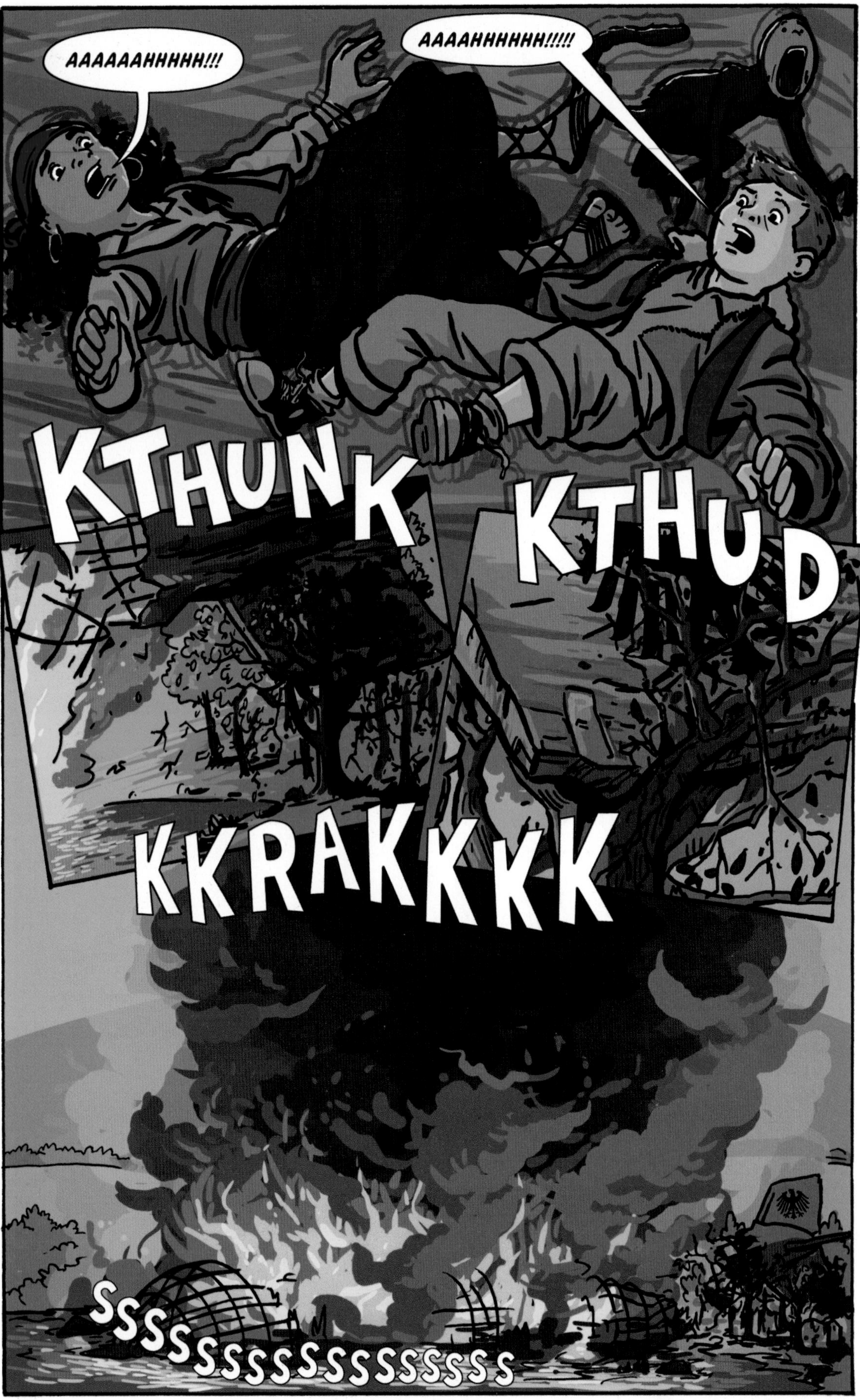
AAAAAAAHHHHH!!!
AAAAAHHHHHH!!!!!
KTHUNK
KTHUD
KKRAKKKK
SSSSSSSSSSSSSSSSS

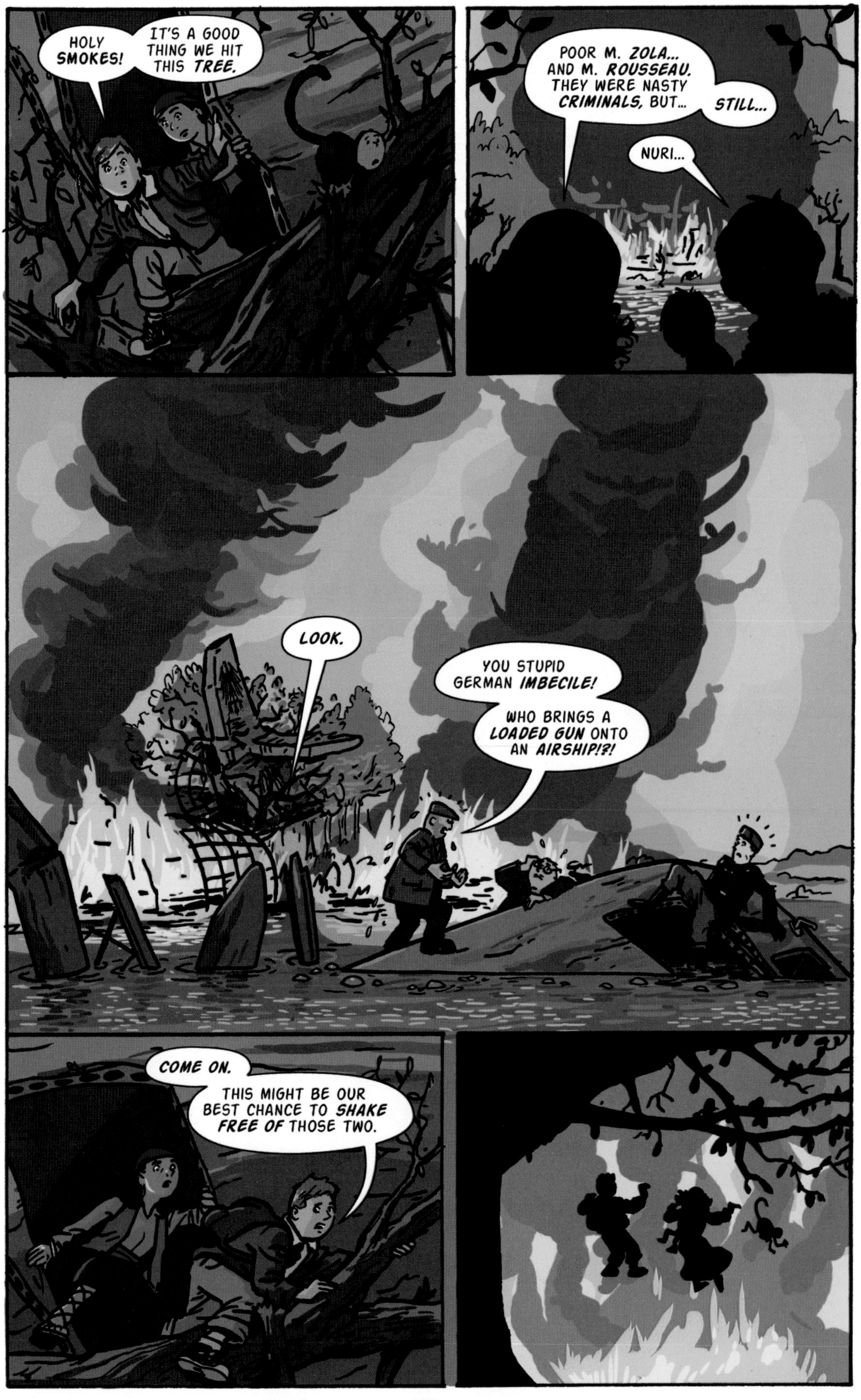
HOLY SMOKES!
IT'S A GOOD THING WE HIT THIS TREE.
POOR M. ZOLA... AND M. ROUSSEAU. THEY WERE NASTY CRIMINALS, BUT...
STILL...
NURI...
LOOK.
YOU STUPID GERMAN IMBECILE!
WHO BRINGS A LOADED GUN ONTO AN AIRSHIP!?!
COME ON.
THIS MIGHT BE OUR BEST CHANCE TO SHAKE FREE OF THOSE TWO.

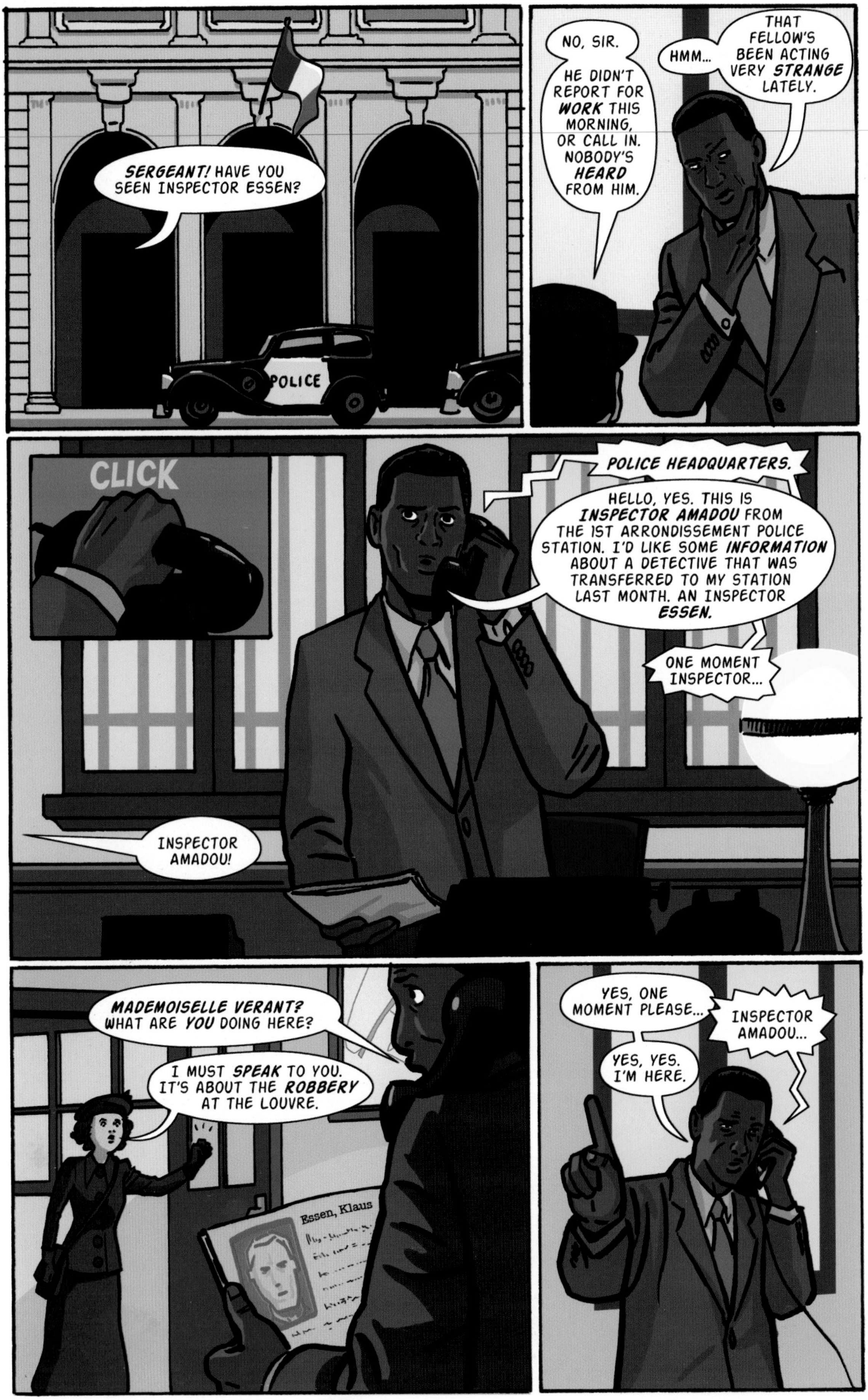
SERGEANT! HAVE YOU SEEN INSPECTOR ESSEN?
POLICE
NO, SIR.
HE DIDN'T REPORT FOR WORK THIS MORNING, OR CALL IN. NOBODY'S HEARD FROM HIM.
HMM...
THAT FELLOW'S BEEN ACTING VERY STRANGE LATELY.
CLICK
POLICE HEADQUARTERS.
HELLO, YES. THIS IS INSPECTOR AMADOU FROM THE 1ST ARRONDISSEMENT POLICE STATION. I'D LIKE SOME INFORMATION ABOUT A DETECTIVE THAT WAS TRANSFERRED TO MY STATION LAST MONTH. AN INSPECTOR ESSEN.
ONE MOMENT INSPECTOR...
INSPECTOR AMADOU!
MADEMOISELLE VERANT? WHAT ARE YOU DOING HERE?
I MUST SPEAK TO YOU. IT'S ABOUT THE ROBBERY AT THE LOUVRE.
Essen, Klaus
YES, ONE MOMENT PLEASE...
INSPECTOR AMADOU...
YES, YES. I'M HERE.

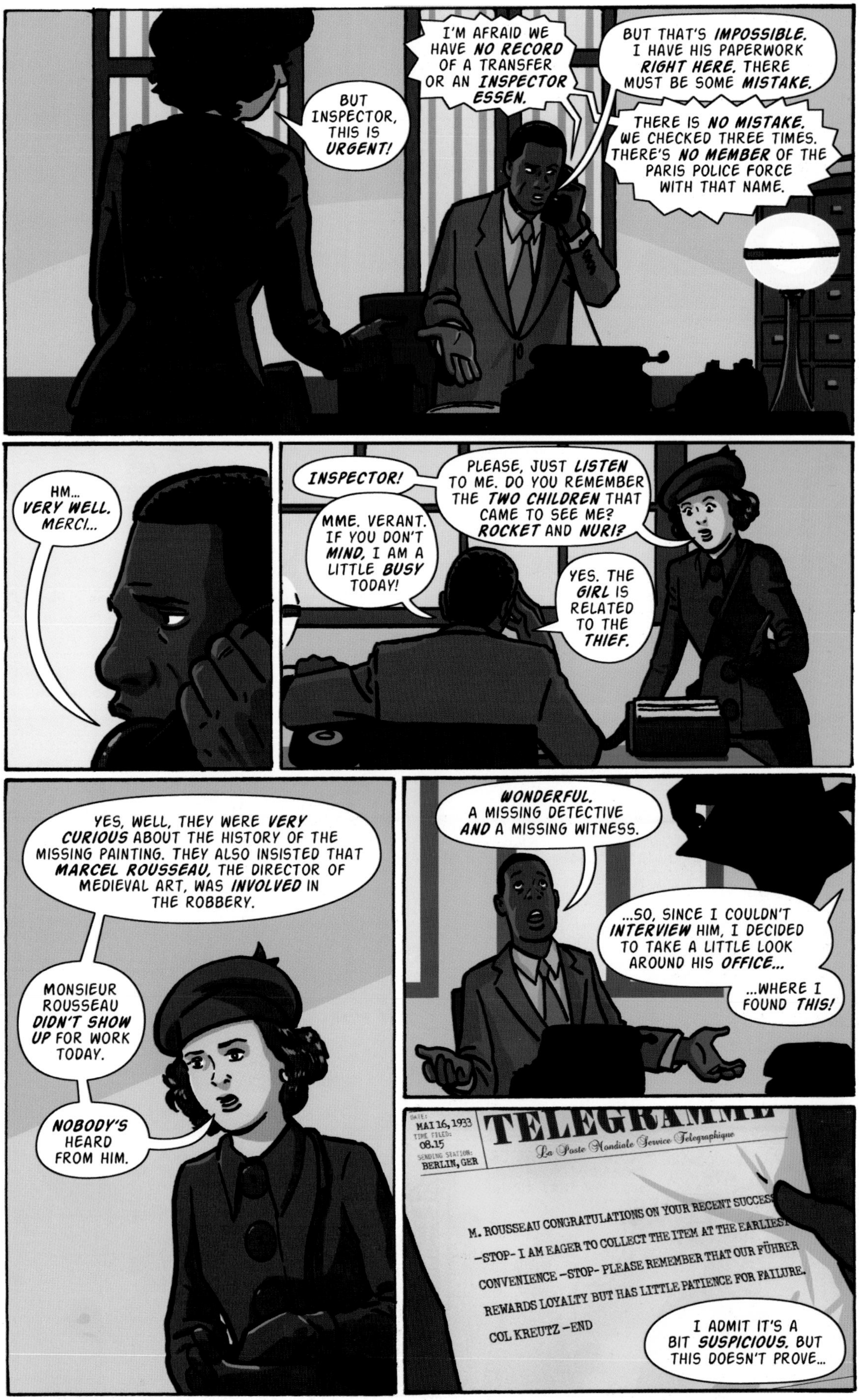
BUT INSPECTOR, THIS IS URGENT!
I'M AFRAID WE HAVE NO RECORD OF A TRANSFER OR AN INSPECTOR ESSEN.
BUT THAT'S IMPOSSIBLE. I HAVE HIS PAPERWORK RIGHT HERE. THERE MUST BE SOME MISTAKE.
THERE IS NO MISTAKE. WE CHECKED THREE TIMES. THERE'S NO MEMBER OF THE PARIS POLICE FORCE WITH THAT NAME.
HM... VERY WELL. MERCI...
INSPECTOR!
MME. VERANT. IF YOU DON'T MIND, I AM A LITTLE BUSY TODAY!
PLEASE, JUST LISTEN TO ME. DO YOU REMEMBER THE TWO CHILDREN THAT CAME TO SEE ME? ROCKET AND NURI?
YES. THE GIRL IS RELATED TO THE THIEF.
YES, WELL, THEY WERE VERY CURIOUS ABOUT THE HISTORY OF THE MISSING PAINTING. THEY ALSO INSISTED THAT MARCEL ROUSSEAU, THE DIRECTOR OF MEDIEVAL ART, WAS INVOLVED IN THE ROBBERY.
MONSIEUR ROUSSEAU DIDN'T SHOW UP FOR WORK TODAY.
NOBODY'S HEARD FROM HIM.
WONDERFUL. A MISSING DETECTIVE AND A MISSING WITNESS.
...SO, SINCE I COULDN'T INTERVIEW HIM, I DECIDED TO TAKE A LITTLE LOOK AROUND HIS OFFICE...
...WHERE I FOUND THIS!
DATE: MAI 16, 1933
TIME FILED: 08.15
SENDING STATION: BERLIN, GER
TELEGRAMME
La Poste Mondiale Service Telegraphique
M. ROUSSEAU CONGRATULATIONS ON YOUR RECENT SUCCESS
-STOP- I AM EAGER TO COLLECT THE ITEM AT THE EARLIEST
CONVENIENCE -STOP- PLEASE REMEMBER THAT OUR FÜHRER
REWARDS LOYALTY BUT HAS LITTLE PATIENCE FOR FAILURE.
COL KREUTZ -END
I ADMIT IT'S A BIT SUSPICIOUS. BUT THIS DOESN'T PROVE...

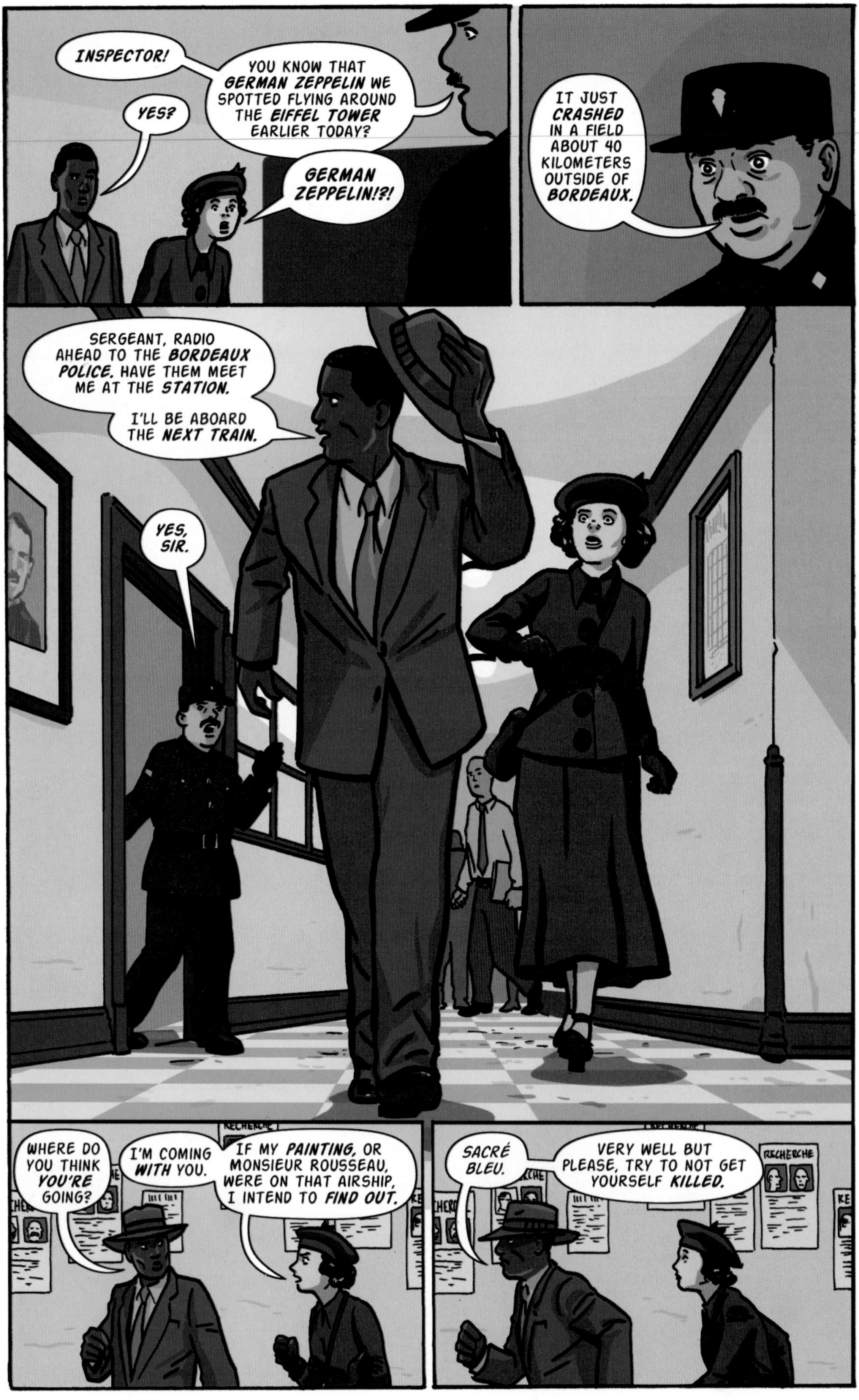
INSPECTOR!
YES?
YOU KNOW THAT GERMAN ZEPPELIN WE SPOTTED FLYING AROUND THE EIFFEL TOWER EARLIER TODAY?
GERMAN ZEPPELIN!?!
IT JUST CRASHED IN A FIELD ABOUT 40 KILOMETERS OUTSIDE OF BORDEAUX.
SERGEANT, RADIO AHEAD TO THE BORDEAUX POLICE. HAVE THEM MEET ME AT THE STATION.
I'LL BE ABOARD THE NEXT TRAIN.
YES, SIR.
WHERE DO YOU THINK YOU'RE GOING?
I'M COMING WITH YOU.
IF MY PAINTING, OR MONSIEUR ROUSSEAU, WERE ON THAT AIRSHIP, I INTEND TO FIND OUT.
SACRÉ BLEU.
VERY WELL BUT PLEASE, TRY TO NOT GET YOURSELF KILLED.
RECHERCHE

CHAPTER NINE

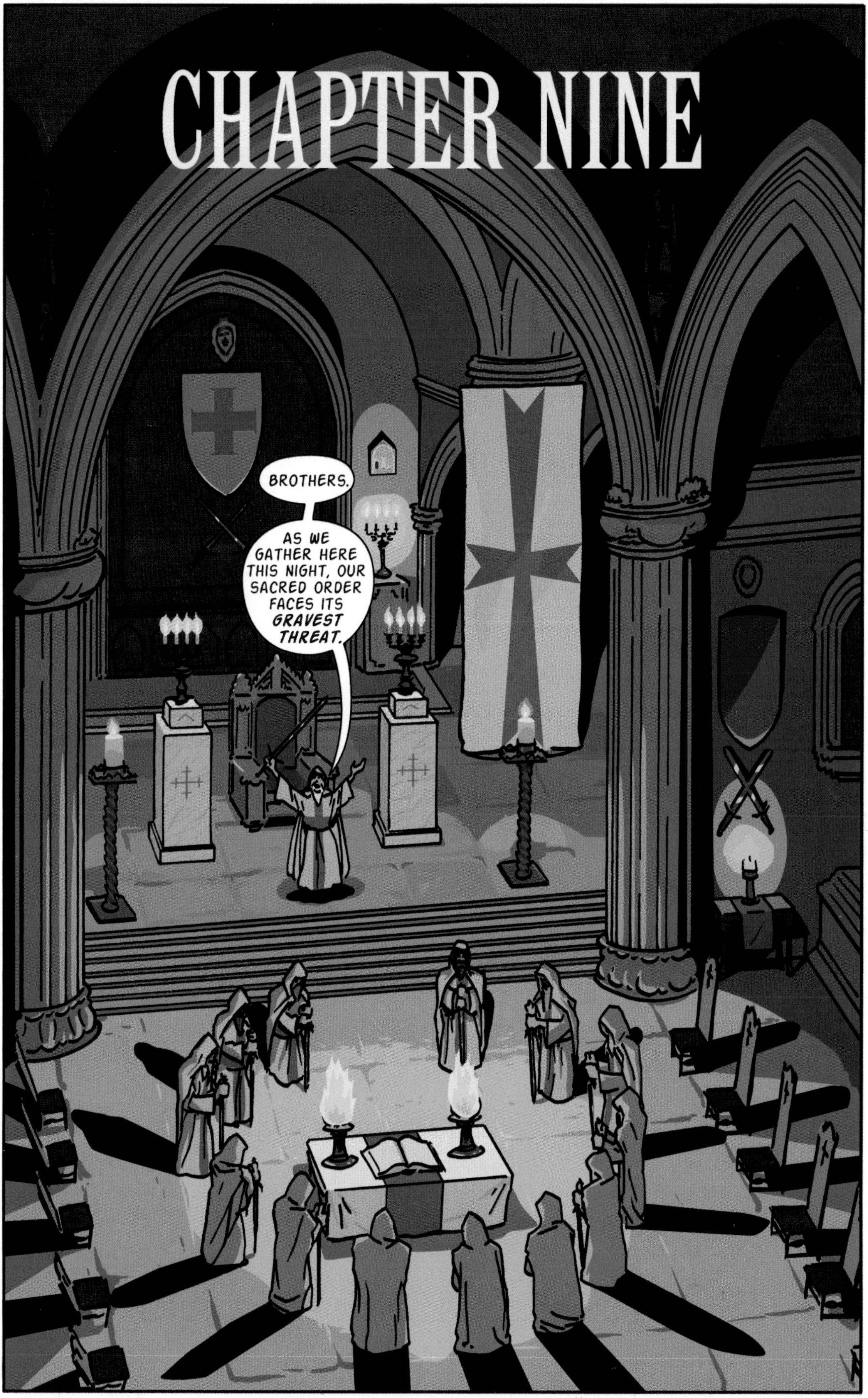
BROTHERS.
AS WE GATHER HERE THIS NIGHT, OUR SACRED ORDER FACES ITS *GRAVEST THREAT.*

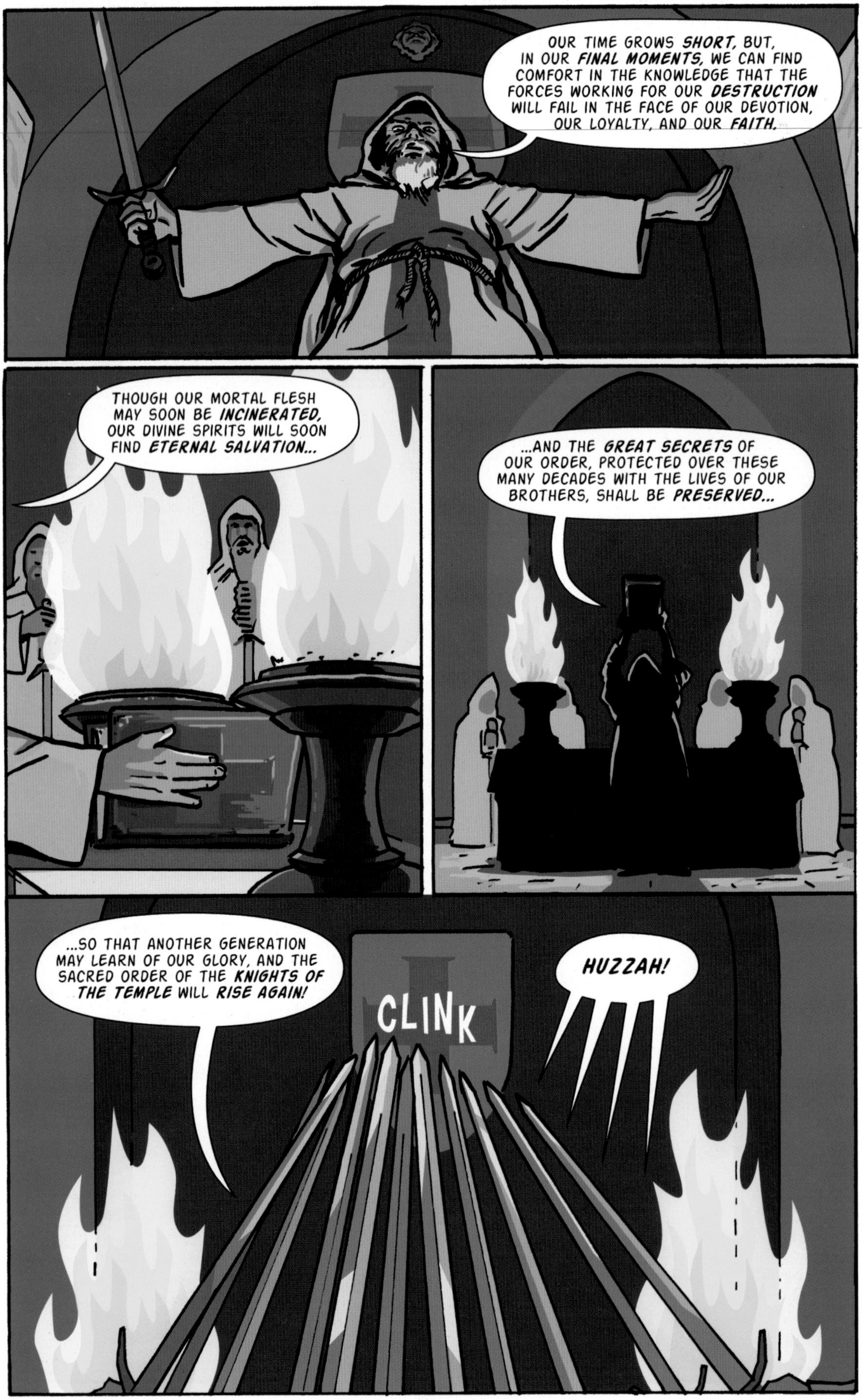
OUR TIME GROWS SHORT, BUT, IN OUR FINAL MOMENTS, WE CAN FIND COMFORT IN THE KNOWLEDGE THAT THE FORCES WORKING FOR OUR DESTRUCTION WILL FAIL IN THE FACE OF OUR DEVOTION, OUR LOYALTY, AND OUR FAITH.
THOUGH OUR MORTAL FLESH MAY SOON BE INCINERATED, OUR DIVINE SPIRITS WILL SOON FIND ETERNAL SALVATION...
...AND THE GREAT SECRETS OF OUR ORDER, PROTECTED OVER THESE MANY DECADES WITH THE LIVES OF OUR BROTHERS, SHALL BE PRESERVED...
...SO THAT ANOTHER GENERATION MAY LEARN OF OUR GLORY, AND THE SACRED ORDER OF THE KNIGHTS OF THE TEMPLE WILL RISE AGAIN!
CLINK
HUZZAH!

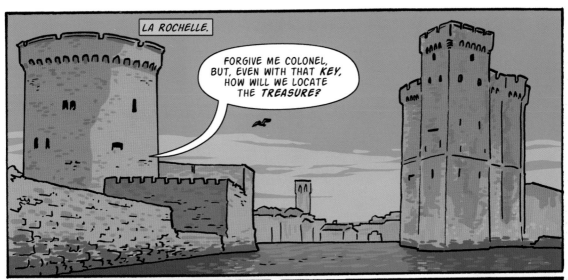

LA ROCHELLE.

FORGIVE ME COLONEL, BUT, EVEN WITH THAT *KEY*, HOW WILL WE LOCATE THE *TREASURE*?

IN THE 1300S, THIS WAS A BUSY *TRADE PORT*, AND IT WAS COMPLETELY RULED BY THE KNIGHTS TEMPLAR FOR THEIR COMMERCIAL INTERESTS, WHICH INCLUDED *SHIPPING*.

THESE CHAMBERS WERE USED TO STORE VARIOUS GOODS ON THEIR WAY INTO AND OUT OF *FRANCE*.

SURELY THE TEMPLARS, AS CUSTODIANS OF THIS PORT, WOULD HAVE KEPT A *SECURE LOCATION* FOR MATERIALS OF A *SENSITIVE* NATURE.

BUT WHY WOULD THEY GO TO ALL OF THE *TROUBLE* OF TRANSPORTING THEIR TREASURE TO THIS PORT, ONLY TO *LEAVE IT* HERE?

THE NIGHT OF THE TEMPLARS' ARREST, THINGS WERE HAPPENING VERY *QUICKLY*. THEY WERE VERY *FORTUNATE* TO GET THE TREASURE OUT OF THE PARIS VAULT, LET ALONE TO *THIS PORT*.

PERHAPS THERE WAS SOME *MISCOMMUNICATION* AND THE SHIPS LEFT WITHOUT THEM.

OR, PERHAPS THE SHIPS WERE A *DECOY*.

MAYBE THEY LEFT THE TREASURE *HERE*, BECAUSE THEY KNEW IT WAS THE ONE PLACE NO ONE WOULD *EVER LOOK*.

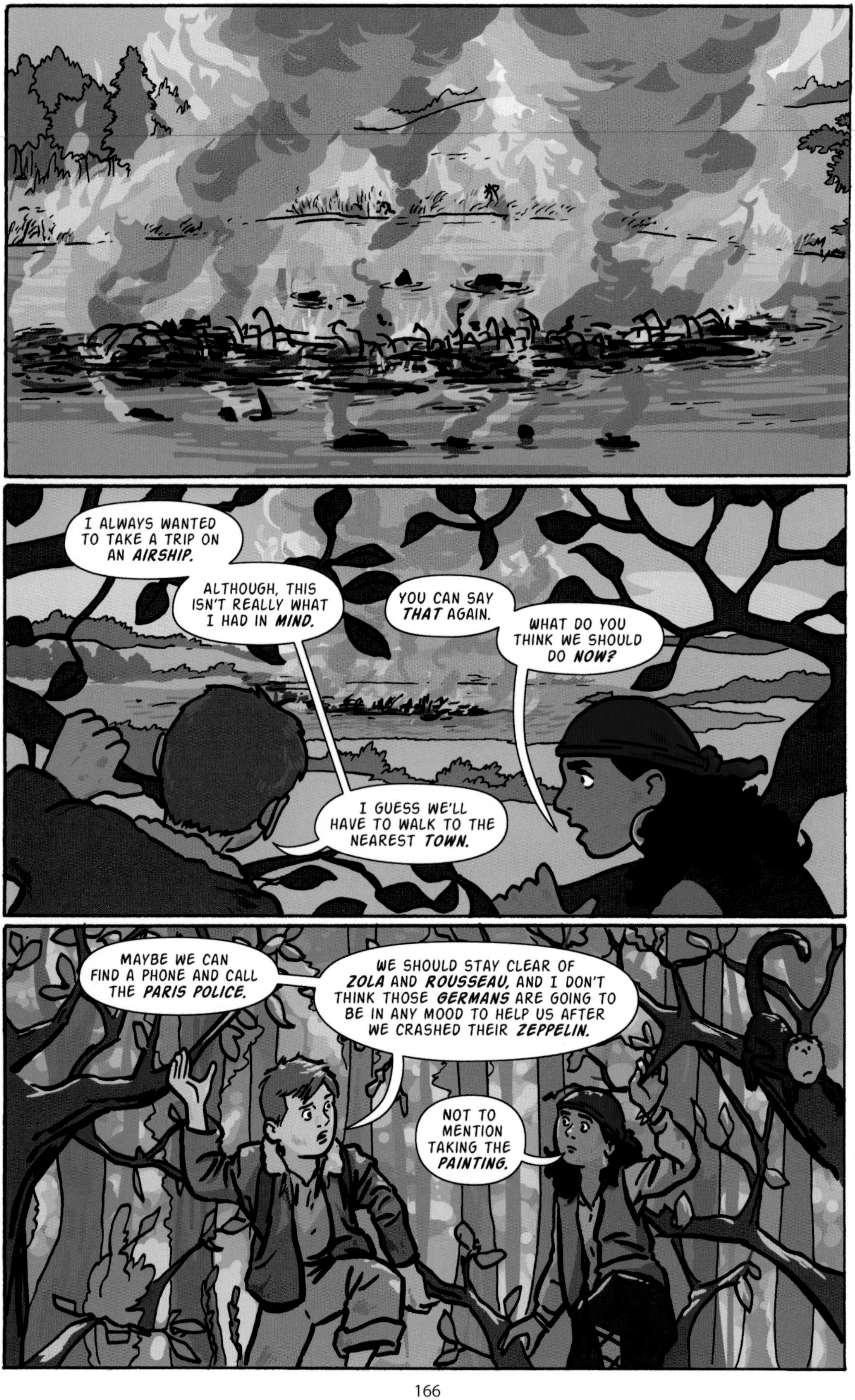
I ALWAYS WANTED TO TAKE A TRIP ON AN AIRSHIP.
ALTHOUGH, THIS ISN'T REALLY WHAT I HAD IN MIND.
YOU CAN SAY THAT AGAIN.
WHAT DO YOU THINK WE SHOULD DO NOW?
I GUESS WE'LL HAVE TO WALK TO THE NEAREST TOWN.
MAYBE WE CAN FIND A PHONE AND CALL THE PARIS POLICE.
WE SHOULD STAY CLEAR OF ZOLA AND ROUSSEAU, AND I DON'T THINK THOSE GERMANS ARE GOING TO BE IN ANY MOOD TO HELP US AFTER WE CRASHED THEIR ZEPPELIN.
NOT TO MENTION TAKING THE PAINTING.

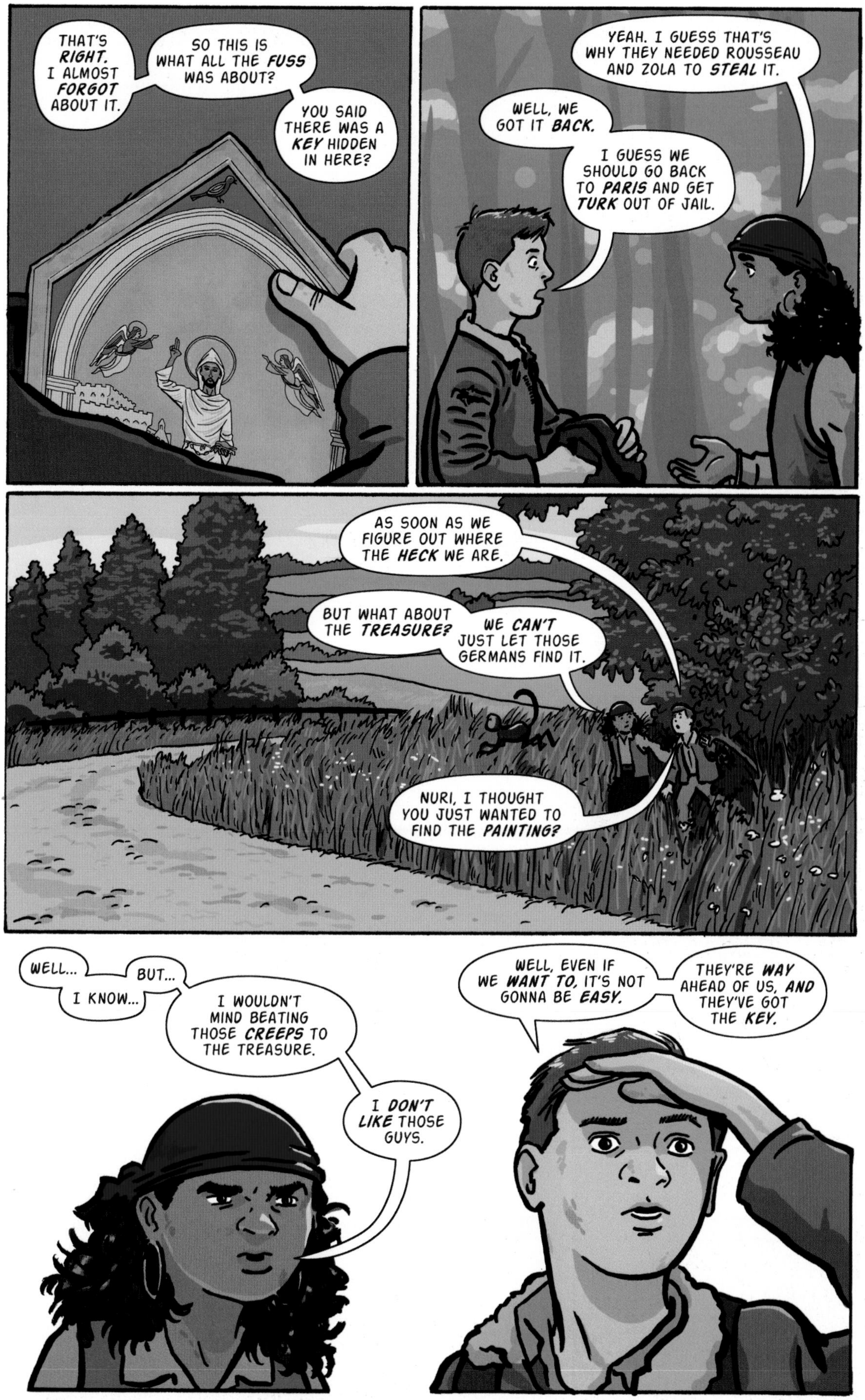
THAT'S RIGHT. I ALMOST FORGOT ABOUT IT.
SO THIS IS WHAT ALL THE FUSS WAS ABOUT?
YOU SAID THERE WAS A KEY HIDDEN IN HERE?
YEAH. I GUESS THAT'S WHY THEY NEEDED ROUSSEAU AND ZOLA TO STEAL IT.
WELL, WE GOT IT BACK.
I GUESS WE SHOULD GO BACK TO PARIS AND GET TURK OUT OF JAIL.
AS SOON AS WE FIGURE OUT WHERE THE HECK WE ARE.
BUT WHAT ABOUT THE TREASURE?
WE CAN'T JUST LET THOSE GERMANS FIND IT.
NURI, I THOUGHT YOU JUST WANTED TO FIND THE PAINTING?
WELL...
I KNOW...
BUT...
I WOULDN'T MIND BEATING THOSE CREEPS TO THE TREASURE.
I DON'T LIKE THOSE GUYS.
WELL, EVEN IF WE WANT TO, IT'S NOT GONNA BE EASY.
THEY'RE WAY AHEAD OF US, AND THEY'VE GOT THE KEY.

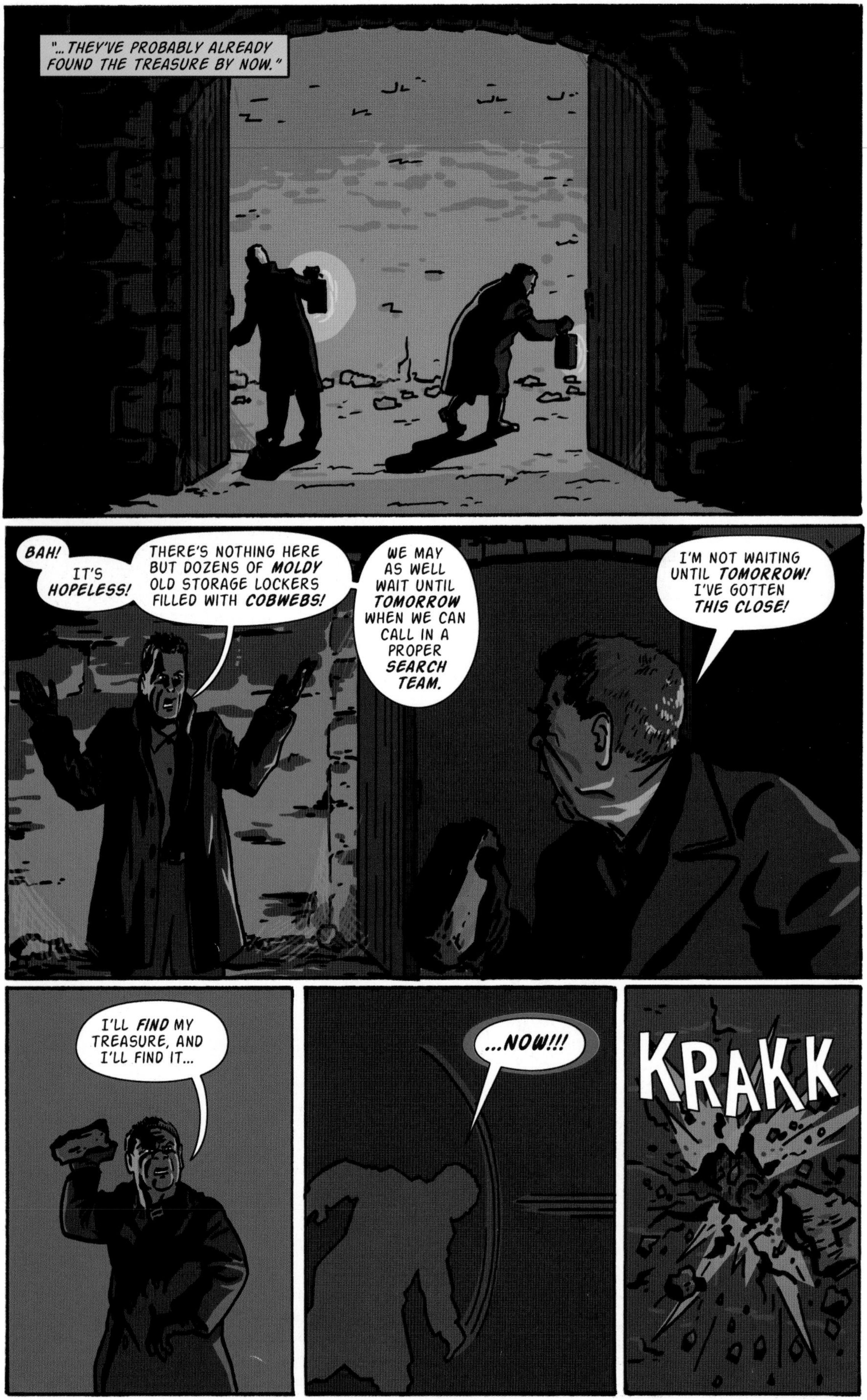
"...THEY'VE PROBABLY ALREADY FOUND THE TREASURE BY NOW."
BAH!
IT'S HOPELESS!
THERE'S NOTHING HERE BUT DOZENS OF MOLDY OLD STORAGE LOCKERS FILLED WITH COBWEBS!
WE MAY AS WELL WAIT UNTIL TOMORROW WHEN WE CAN CALL IN A PROPER SEARCH TEAM.
I'M NOT WAITING UNTIL TOMORROW! I'VE GOTTEN THIS CLOSE!
I'LL FIND MY TREASURE, AND I'LL FIND IT...
...NOW!!!
KRAKK

WHAT IS *THAT?*

THIS IS A *FALSE WALL.* THERE'S AN *IRON DOOR* BEHIND HERE!

QUICK! REMOVE THE *STONES!*

CRUMBLE CRUMBLE

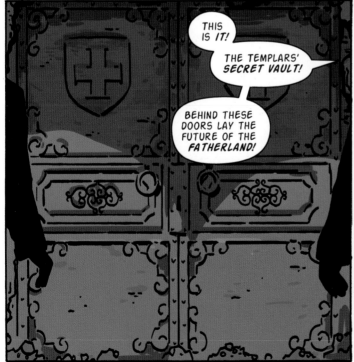

THIS IS *IT!*

THE TEMPLARS' *SECRET VAULT!*

BEHIND THESE DOORS LAY THE FUTURE OF THE *FATHERLAND!*

KCHK

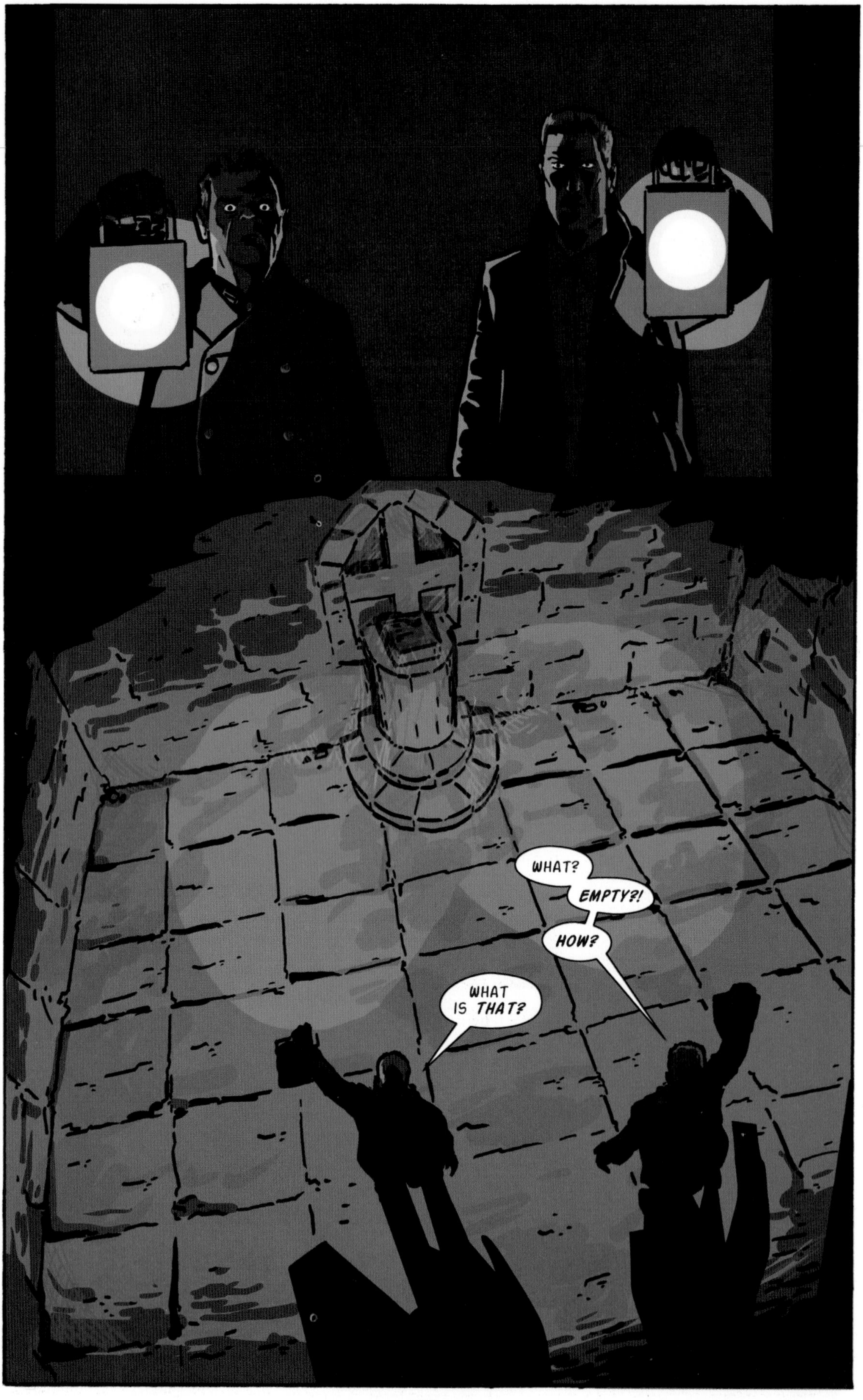
WHAT?
EMPTY?!
HOW?
WHAT IS THAT?

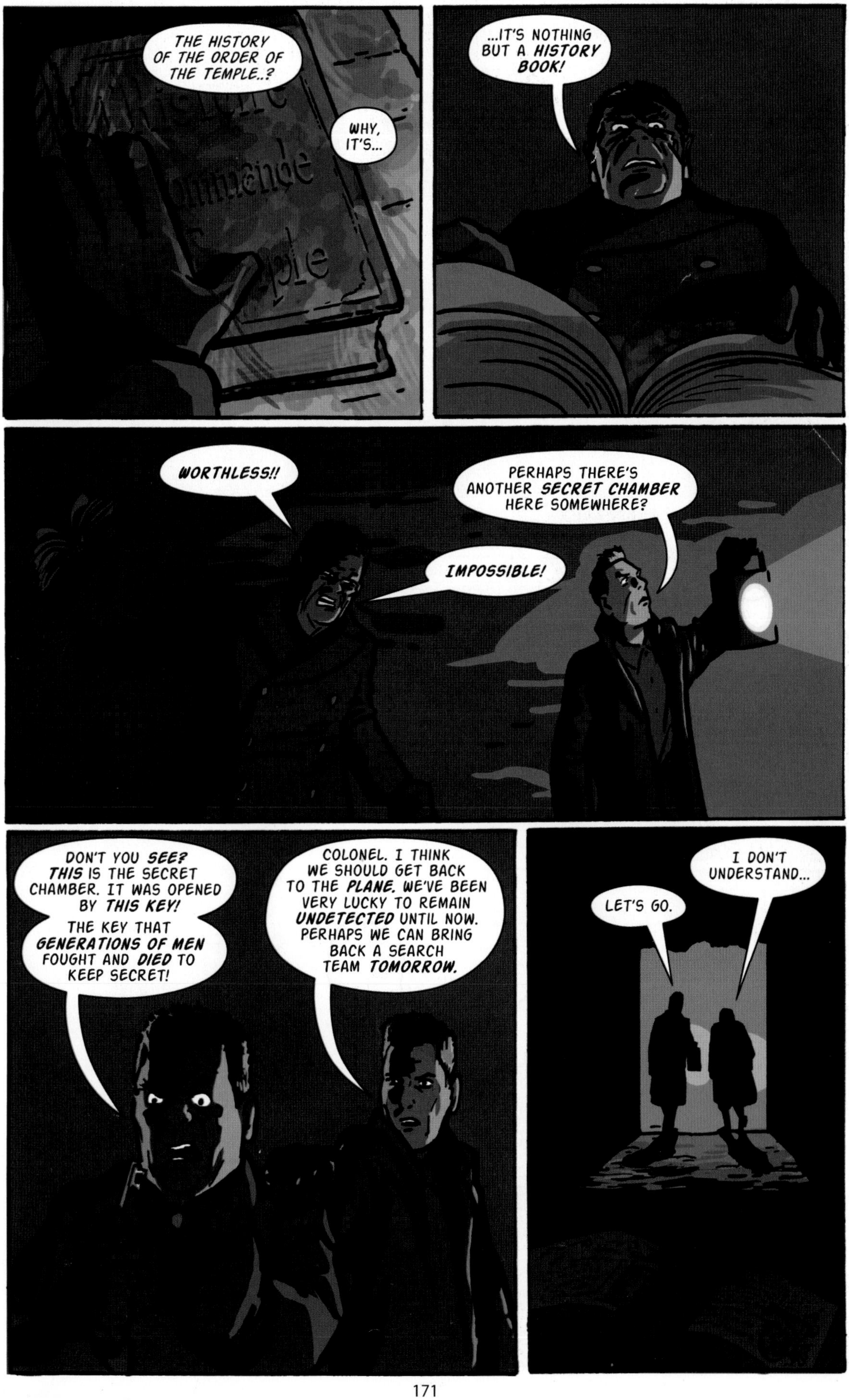
THE HISTORY OF THE ORDER OF THE TEMPLE..?
WHY, IT'S...
...IT'S NOTHING BUT A HISTORY BOOK!
WORTHLESS!!
PERHAPS THERE'S ANOTHER SECRET CHAMBER HERE SOMEWHERE?
IMPOSSIBLE!
DON'T YOU SEE? THIS IS THE SECRET CHAMBER. IT WAS OPENED BY THIS KEY!
THE KEY THAT GENERATIONS OF MEN FOUGHT AND DIED TO KEEP SECRET!
COLONEL. I THINK WE SHOULD GET BACK TO THE PLANE. WE'VE BEEN VERY LUCKY TO REMAIN UNDETECTED UNTIL NOW. PERHAPS WE CAN BRING BACK A SEARCH TEAM TOMORROW.
I DON'T UNDERSTAND...
LET'S GO.

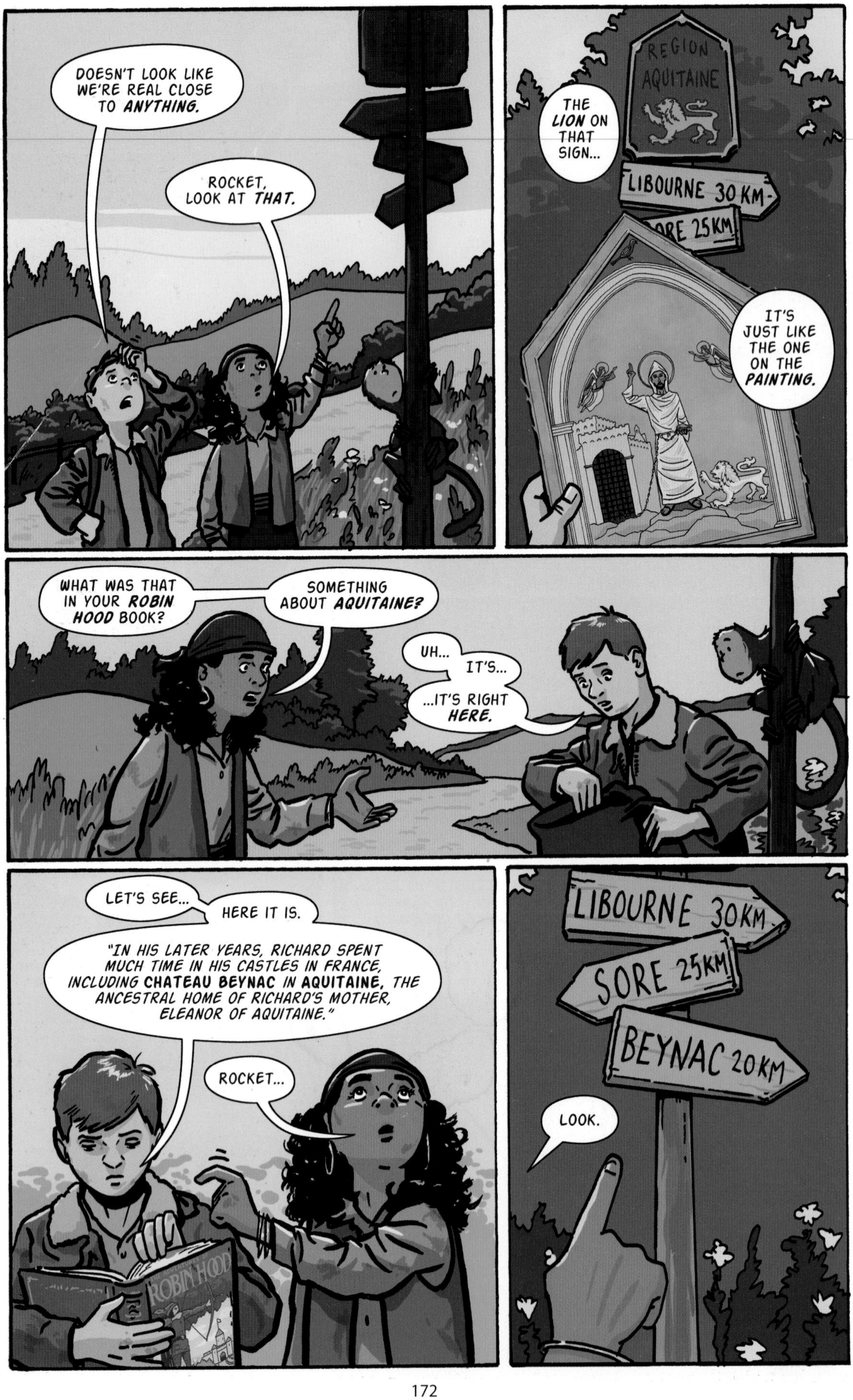

DOESN'T LOOK LIKE WE'RE REAL CLOSE TO ANYTHING.
ROCKET, LOOK AT THAT.
REGION AQUITAINE
THE LION ON THAT SIGN...
LIBOURNE 30 KM
ORE 25 KM
IT'S JUST LIKE THE ONE ON THE PAINTING.
WHAT WAS THAT IN YOUR ROBIN HOOD BOOK?
SOMETHING ABOUT AQUITAINE?
UH...
IT'S...
...IT'S RIGHT HERE.
LET'S SEE...
HERE IT IS.
"IN HIS LATER YEARS, RICHARD SPENT MUCH TIME IN HIS CASTLES IN FRANCE, INCLUDING CHATEAU BEYNAC IN AQUITAINE, THE ANCESTRAL HOME OF RICHARD'S MOTHER, ELEANOR OF AQUITAINE."
ROCKET...
ROBIN HOOD
LIBOURNE 30KM
SORE 25KM
BEYNAC 20KM
LOOK.

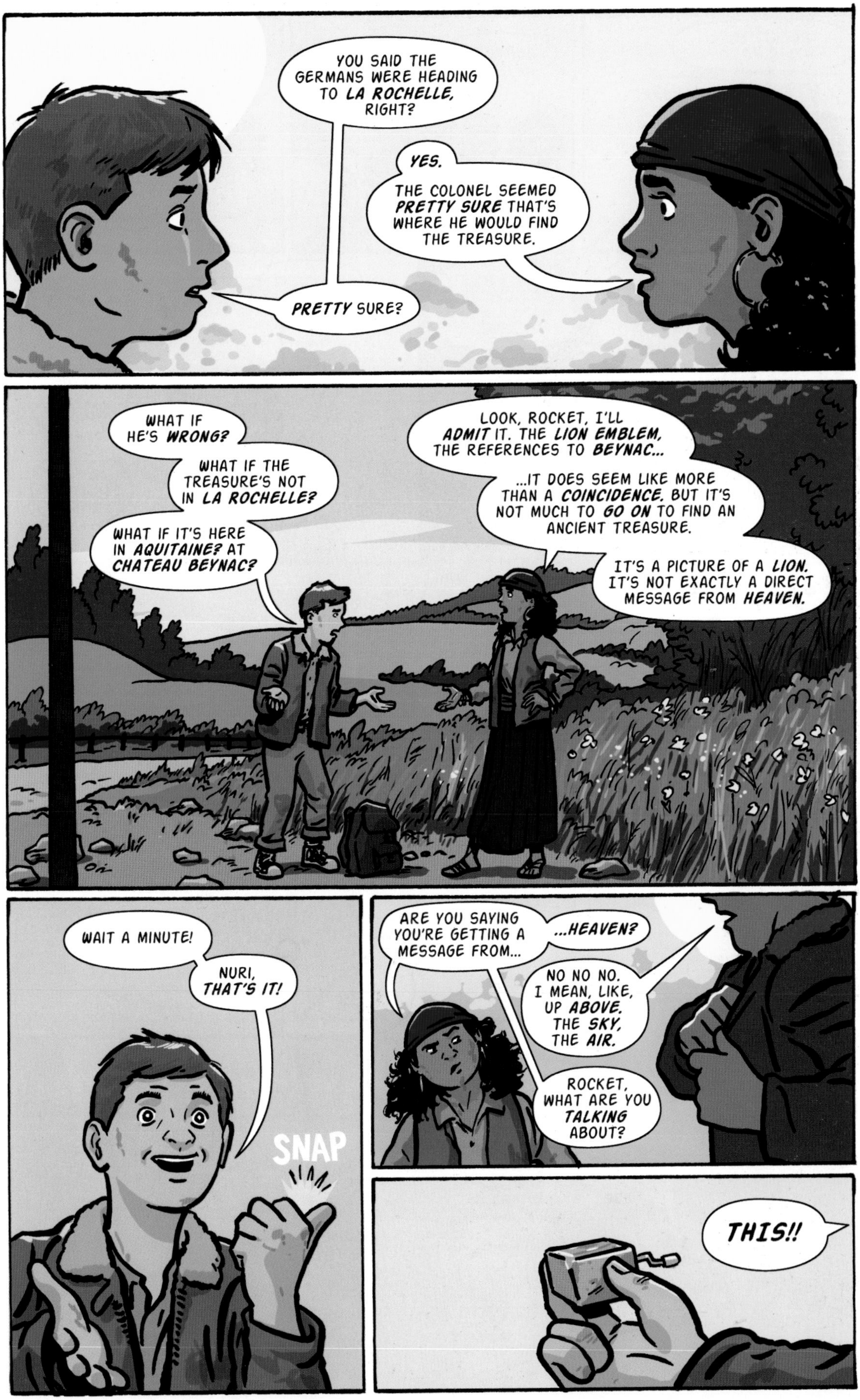
YOU SAID THE GERMANS WERE HEADING TO LA ROCHELLE, RIGHT?
YES.
THE COLONEL SEEMED PRETTY SURE THAT'S WHERE HE WOULD FIND THE TREASURE.
PRETTY SURE?
WHAT IF HE'S WRONG?
WHAT IF THE TREASURE'S NOT IN LA ROCHELLE?
WHAT IF IT'S HERE IN AQUITAINE? AT CHATEAU BEYNAC?
LOOK, ROCKET, I'LL ADMIT IT. THE LION EMBLEM, THE REFERENCES TO BEYNAC...
...IT DOES SEEM LIKE MORE THAN A COINCIDENCE. BUT IT'S NOT MUCH TO GO ON TO FIND AN ANCIENT TREASURE.
IT'S A PICTURE OF A LION. IT'S NOT EXACTLY A DIRECT MESSAGE FROM HEAVEN.
WAIT A MINUTE!
NURI, THAT'S IT!
SNAP
ARE YOU SAYING YOU'RE GETTING A MESSAGE FROM...
...HEAVEN?
NO NO NO. I MEAN, LIKE, UP ABOVE. THE SKY. THE AIR.
ROCKET, WHAT ARE YOU TALKING ABOUT?
THIS!!

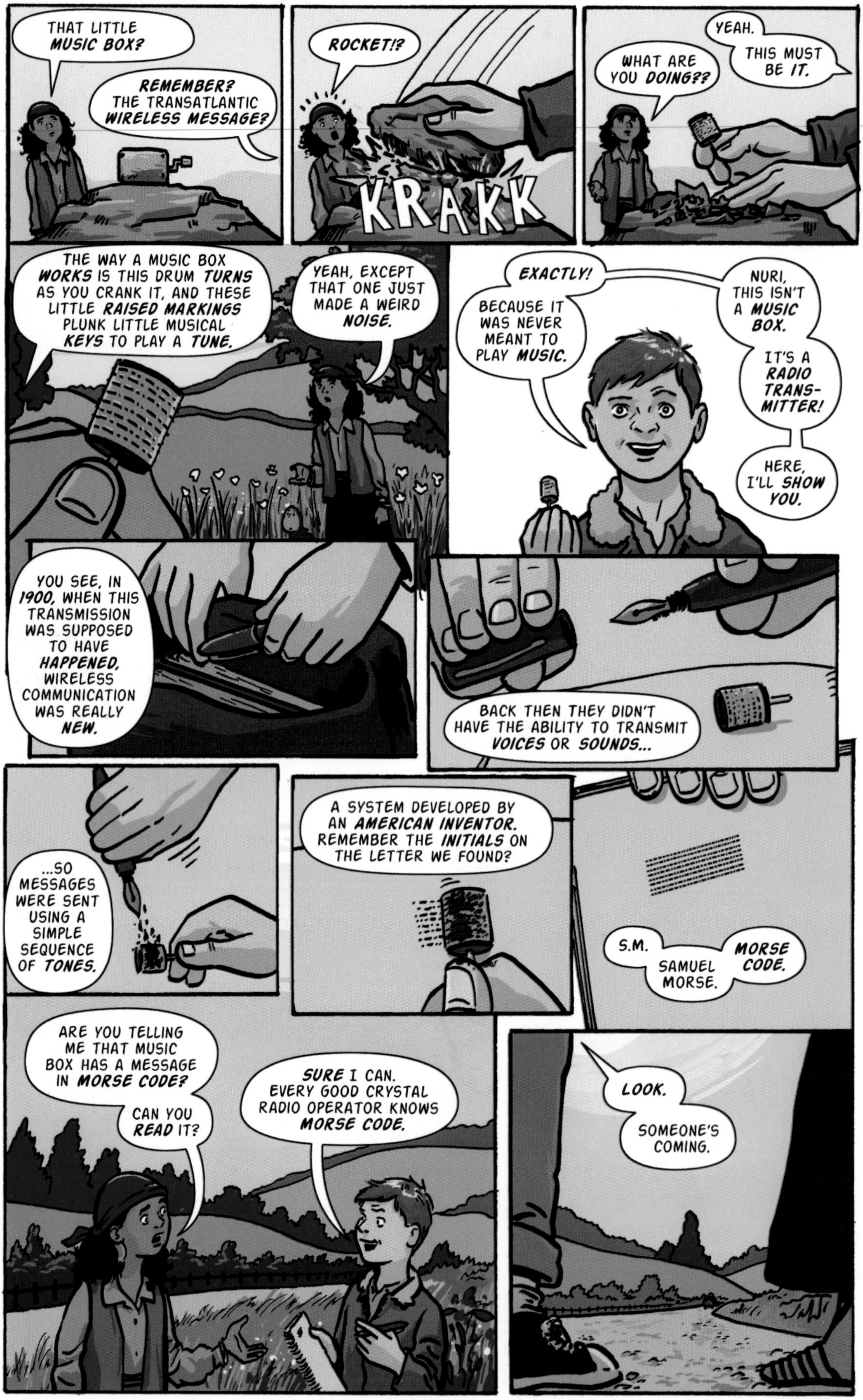
THAT LITTLE MUSIC BOX?
REMEMBER? THE TRANSATLANTIC WIRELESS MESSAGE?
ROCKET!?
KRAKK
WHAT ARE YOU DOING??
YEAH.
THIS MUST BE IT.
THE WAY A MUSIC BOX WORKS IS THIS DRUM TURNS AS YOU CRANK IT, AND THESE LITTLE RAISED MARKINGS PLUNK LITTLE MUSICAL KEYS TO PLAY A TUNE.
YEAH, EXCEPT THAT ONE JUST MADE A WEIRD NOISE.
EXACTLY!
BECAUSE IT WAS NEVER MEANT TO PLAY MUSIC.
NURI, THIS ISN'T A MUSIC BOX.
IT'S A RADIO TRANS-MITTER!
HERE, I'LL SHOW YOU.
YOU SEE, IN 1900, WHEN THIS TRANSMISSION WAS SUPPOSED TO HAVE HAPPENED, WIRELESS COMMUNICATION WAS REALLY NEW.
BACK THEN THEY DIDN'T HAVE THE ABILITY TO TRANSMIT VOICES OR SOUNDS...
...SO MESSAGES WERE SENT USING A SIMPLE SEQUENCE OF TONES.
A SYSTEM DEVELOPED BY AN AMERICAN INVENTOR. REMEMBER THE INITIALS ON THE LETTER WE FOUND?
S.M.
SAMUEL MORSE.
MORSE CODE.
ARE YOU TELLING ME THAT MUSIC BOX HAS A MESSAGE IN MORSE CODE?
CAN YOU READ IT?
SURE I CAN. EVERY GOOD CRYSTAL RADIO OPERATOR KNOWS MORSE CODE.
LOOK.
SOMEONE'S COMING.

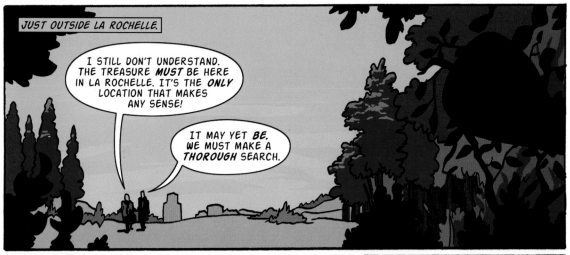

JUST OUTSIDE LA ROCHELLE.

I STILL DON'T UNDERSTAND. THE TREASURE *MUST* BE HERE IN LA ROCHELLE. IT'S THE *ONLY* LOCATION THAT MAKES ANY SENSE!

IT MAY YET *BE*. WE MUST MAKE A *THOROUGH* SEARCH.

COLONEL, YOU SHOULD HAVE LET ME INTERROGATE THE *GIRL*. I THINK SHE *KNOWS* SOMETHING.

MAJOR, I GENERALLY HAVE *GREAT RESPECT* FOR YOUR INSTINCTS, BUT...

IN *THIS* CASE...

A TWELVE-YEAR-OLD *GYPSY GIRL?*

WAIT.

DO YOU *HEAR* THAT?

CRACKLE

CRACKLE

IT'S THE PLANE'S *RADIO!*

COLONEL! COLONEL!

CRACKLE

ARE YOU THERE?

OVER!

CRACKLE

IT IS AN EMERGENCY!

PLEASE REPORT! OVER!

THIS IS *KREUTZ*. WHAT THE DEVIL IS *GOING ON?*

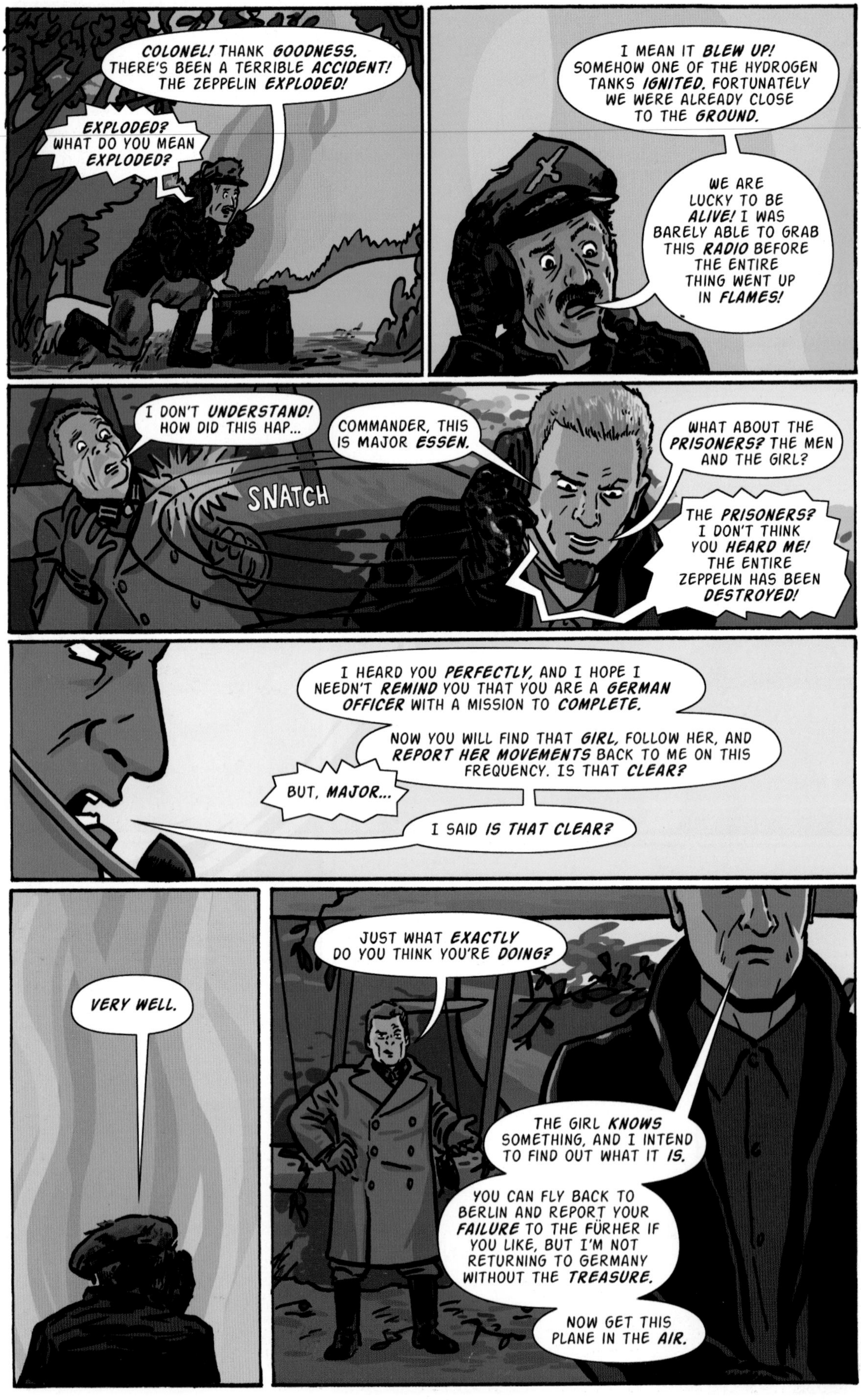
COLONEL! THANK GOODNESS. THERE'S BEEN A TERRIBLE ACCIDENT! THE ZEPPELIN EXPLODED!
EXPLODED? WHAT DO YOU MEAN EXPLODED?
I MEAN IT BLEW UP! SOMEHOW ONE OF THE HYDROGEN TANKS IGNITED. FORTUNATELY WE WERE ALREADY CLOSE TO THE GROUND.
WE ARE LUCKY TO BE ALIVE! I WAS BARELY ABLE TO GRAB THIS RADIO BEFORE THE ENTIRE THING WENT UP IN FLAMES!
I DON'T UNDERSTAND! HOW DID THIS HAP...
SNATCH
COMMANDER, THIS IS MAJOR ESSEN.
WHAT ABOUT THE PRISONERS? THE MEN AND THE GIRL?
THE PRISONERS? I DON'T THINK YOU HEARD ME! THE ENTIRE ZEPPELIN HAS BEEN DESTROYED!
I HEARD YOU PERFECTLY, AND I HOPE I NEEDN'T REMIND YOU THAT YOU ARE A GERMAN OFFICER WITH A MISSION TO COMPLETE.
NOW YOU WILL FIND THAT GIRL, FOLLOW HER, AND REPORT HER MOVEMENTS BACK TO ME ON THIS FREQUENCY. IS THAT CLEAR?
BUT, MAJOR...
I SAID IS THAT CLEAR?
VERY WELL.
JUST WHAT EXACTLY DO YOU THINK YOU'RE DOING?
THE GIRL KNOWS SOMETHING, AND I INTEND TO FIND OUT WHAT IT IS.
YOU CAN FLY BACK TO BERLIN AND REPORT YOUR FAILURE TO THE FÜRHER IF YOU LIKE, BUT I'M NOT RETURNING TO GERMANY WITHOUT THE TREASURE.
NOW GET THIS PLANE IN THE AIR.

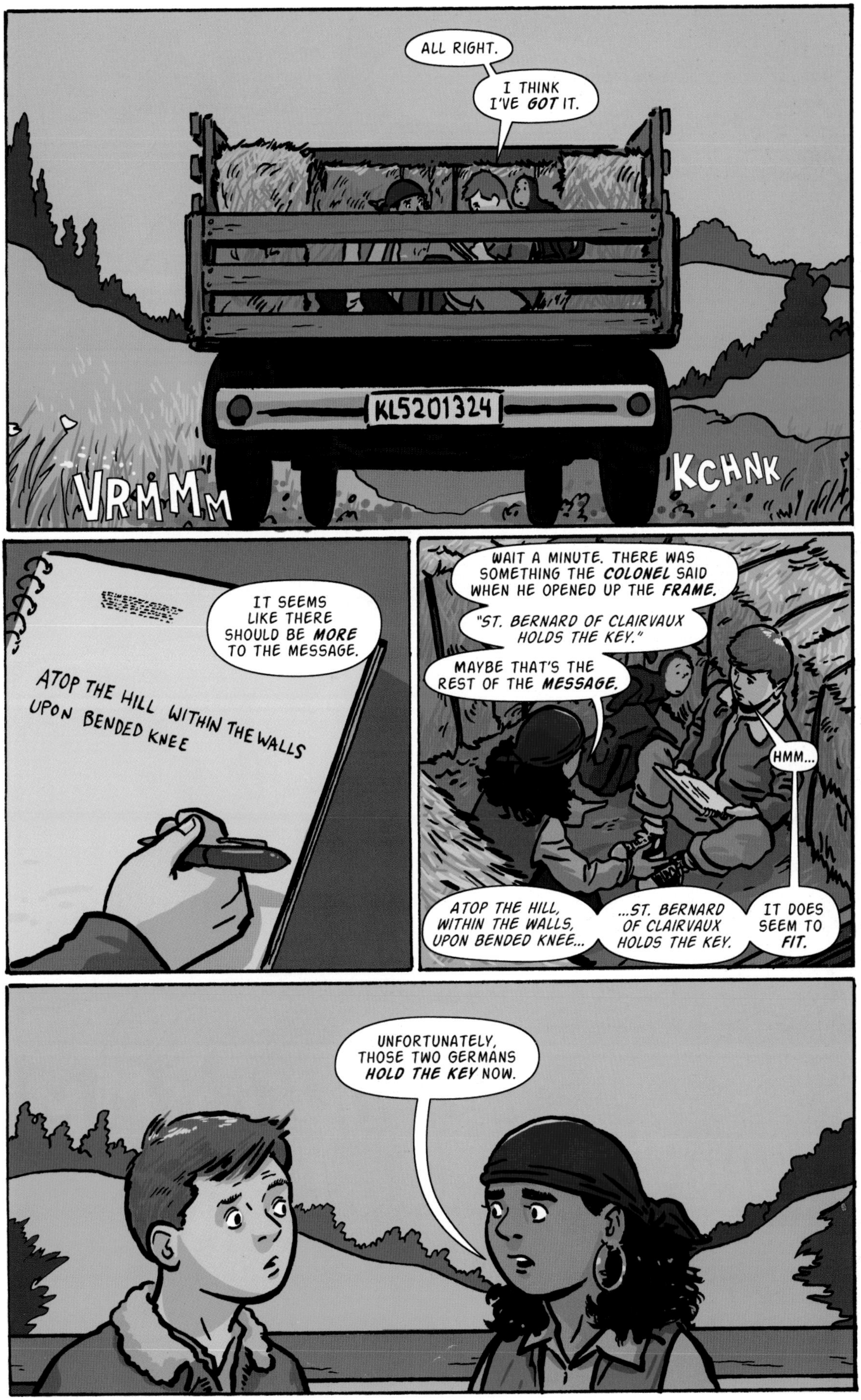
ALL RIGHT.
I THINK I'VE GOT IT.
KL5201324
VRMMMM
KCHNK
IT SEEMS LIKE THERE SHOULD BE MORE TO THE MESSAGE.
ATOP THE HILL WITHIN THE WALLS UPON BENDED KNEE
WAIT A MINUTE. THERE WAS SOMETHING THE COLONEL SAID WHEN HE OPENED UP THE FRAME.
"ST. BERNARD OF CLAIRVAUX HOLDS THE KEY."
MAYBE THAT'S THE REST OF THE MESSAGE.
HMM...
ATOP THE HILL, WITHIN THE WALLS, UPON BENDED KNEE...
...ST. BERNARD OF CLAIRVAUX HOLDS THE KEY.
IT DOES SEEM TO FIT.
UNFORTUNATELY, THOSE TWO GERMANS HOLD THE KEY NOW.

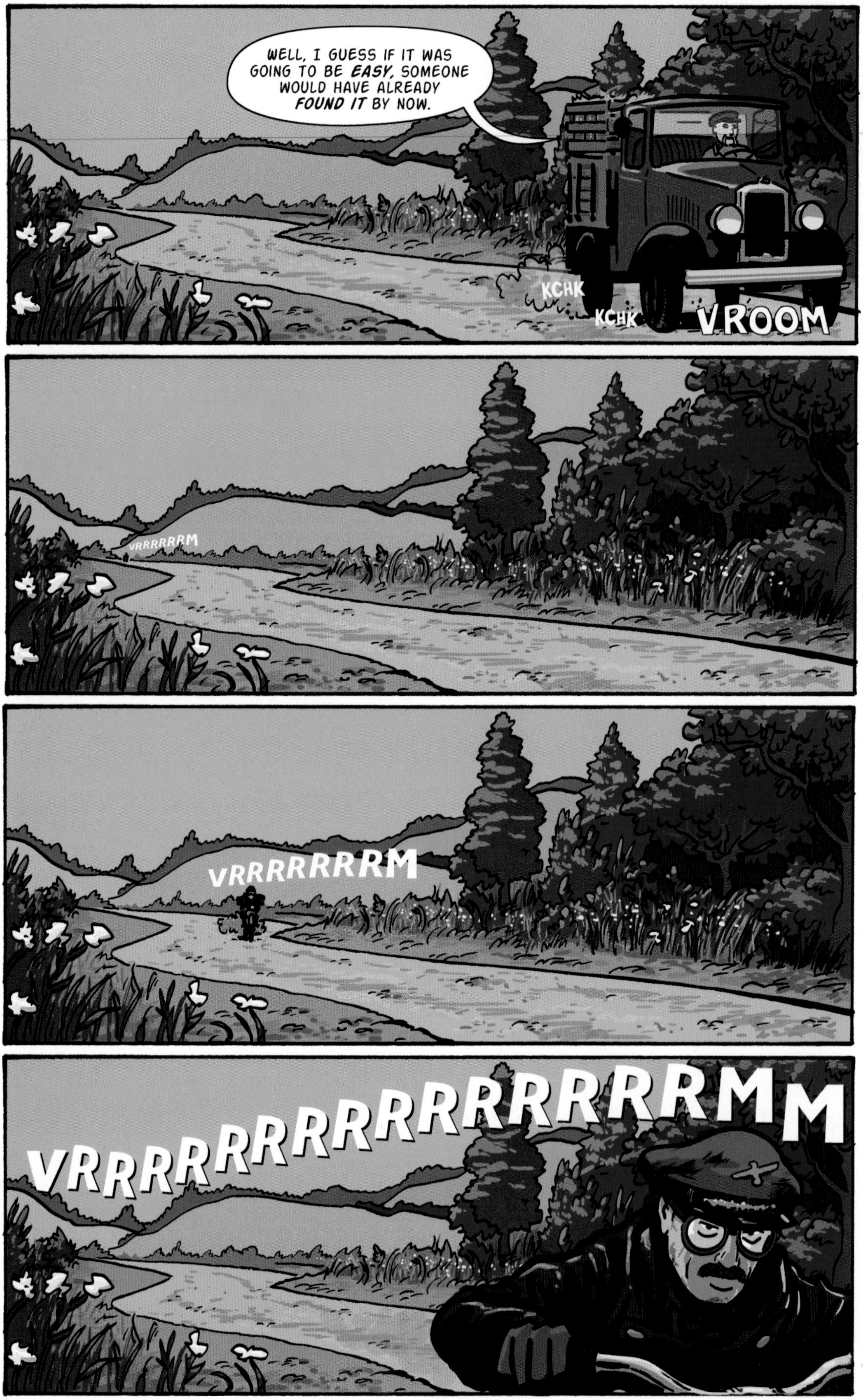
WELL, I GUESS IF IT WAS GOING TO BE *EASY*, SOMEONE WOULD HAVE ALREADY *FOUND IT* BY NOW.
KCHK
KCHK
VROOM
VRRRRRRM
VRRRRRRRM
VRRRRRRRRRRRRRRRMM

CHAPTER TEN

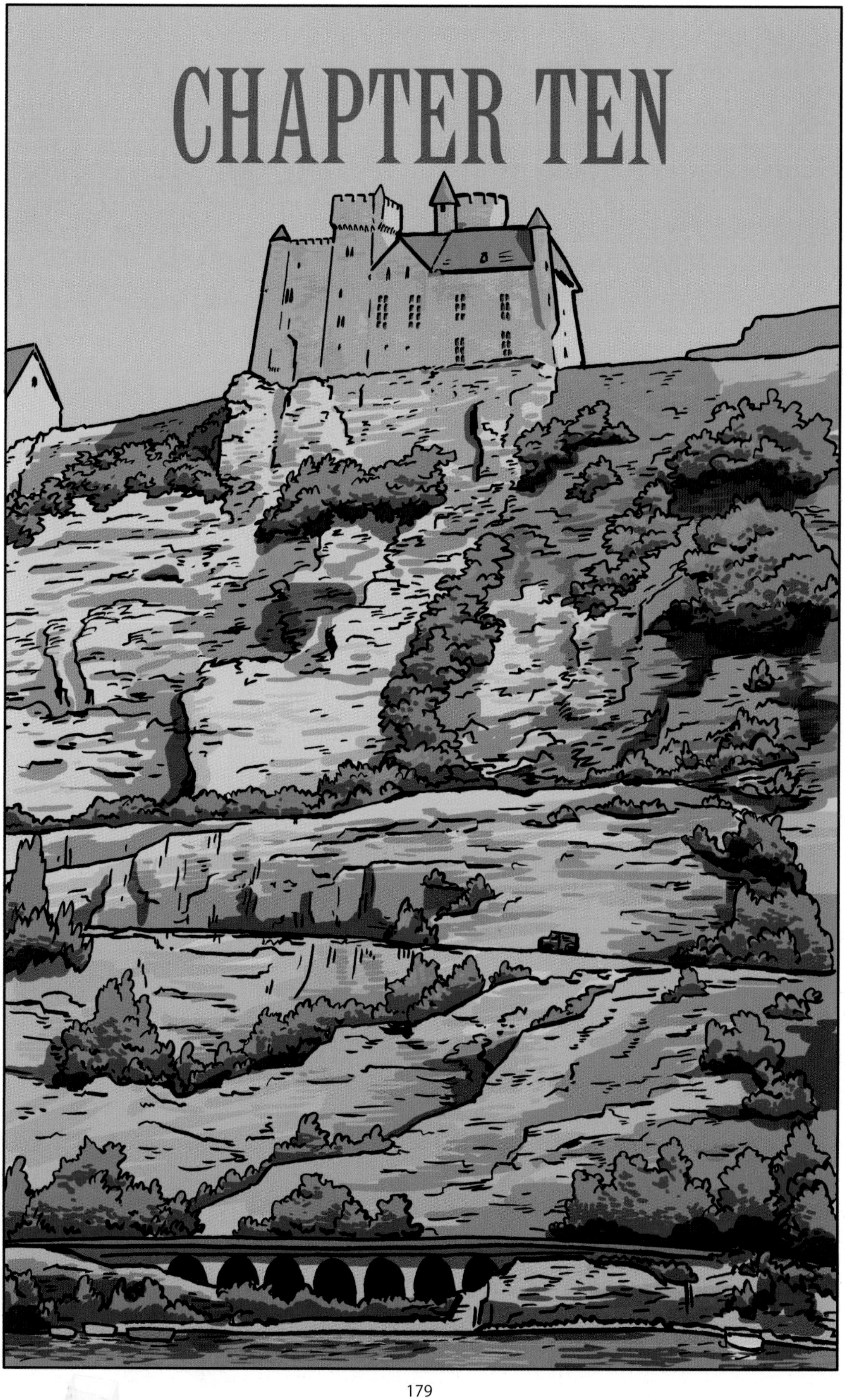

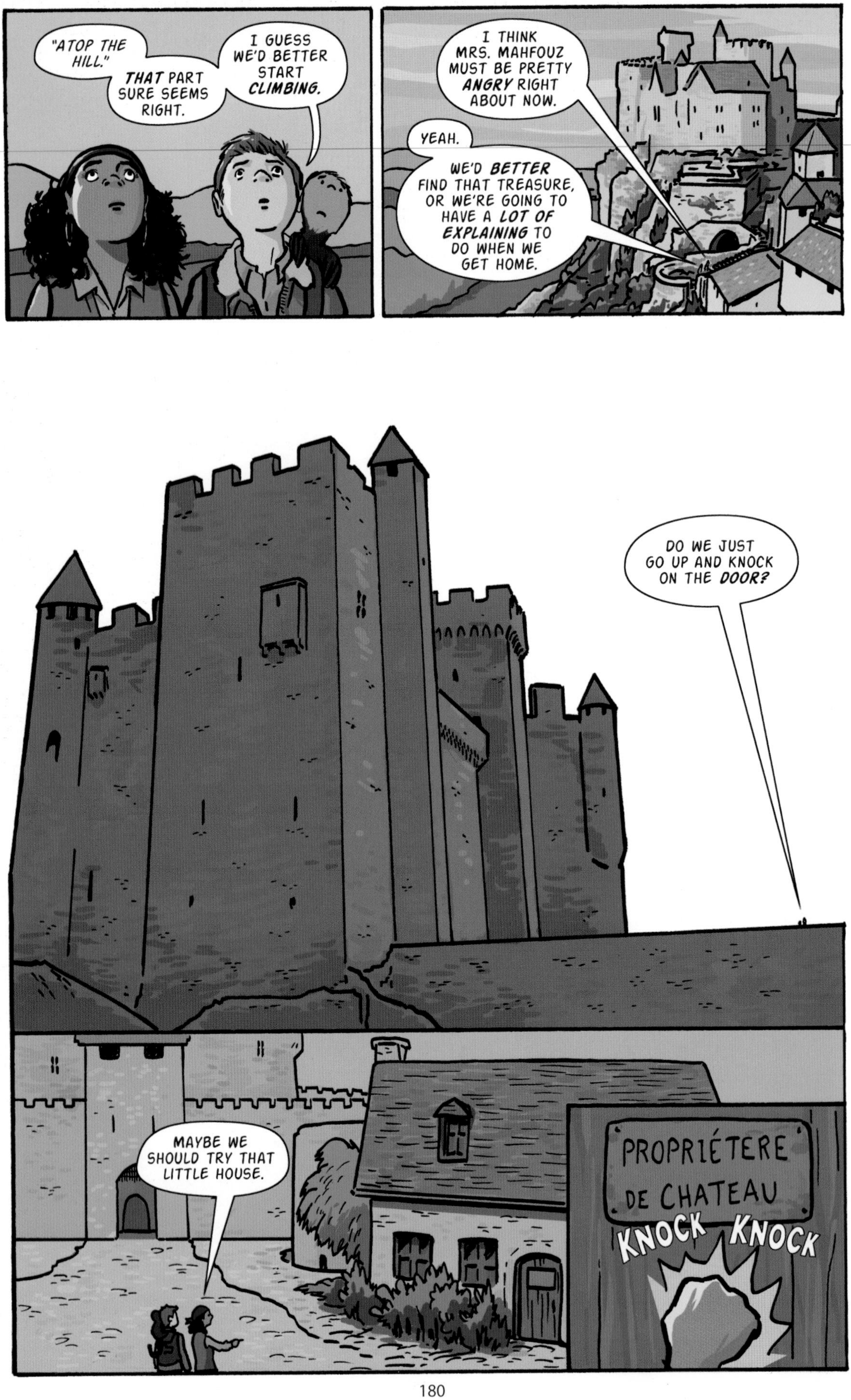
"ATOP THE HILL." THAT PART SURE SEEMS RIGHT.
I GUESS WE'D BETTER START CLIMBING.
I THINK MRS. MAHFOUZ MUST BE PRETTY ANGRY RIGHT ABOUT NOW.
YEAH.
WE'D BETTER FIND THAT TREASURE, OR WE'RE GOING TO HAVE A LOT OF EXPLAINING TO DO WHEN WE GET HOME.
DO WE JUST GO UP AND KNOCK ON THE DOOR?
MAYBE WE SHOULD TRY THAT LITTLE HOUSE.
PROPRIÉTERE DE CHATEAU
KNOCK KNOCK

BON JOUR.

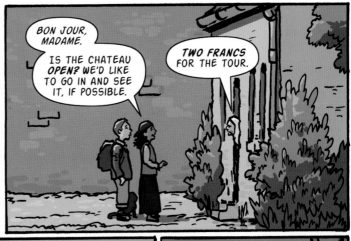

BON JOUR, MADAME.

IS THE CHATEAU *OPEN?* WE'D LIKE TO GO IN AND SEE IT, IF POSSIBLE.

TWO FRANCS FOR THE TOUR.

OH, THAT'S OK, WE DON'T NEED THE *GUIDED TOUR.* WE JUST WANT TO LOOK AROUND.

TWO FRANCS FOR THE TOUR.

UH...

ACTUALLY, WE WERE JUST, KINDA, HOPING TO TAKE A LOOK *AROUND...*

TWO FRANCS FOR THE TOUR.

LOOKS LIKE WE'RE TAKING THE *TOUR.*

MERCI.

HENRI!!!

WHAT *IS* IT, MAMA!?

THE FOUR O'CLOCK *TOUR* IS HERE!

UN MOMENT.

GLUG GLUG GLUG

'ZIS WAY.

AS WE ENTER THE CHATEAU, PLEASE LOOK *UP* TO VIEW THE CHATEAU'S *PORTCULLIS.*

THE PORTCULLIS WAS AN IMPORTANT *SECURITY MEASURE.* IT COULD BE *LOWERED* IN THE EVENT OF AN ATTACK AND *BLOCK ENTRY* TO THE CHATEAU, PROTECTING THE PEOPLE GATHERED *INSIDE.*

WOW. HOW MUCH DOES IT *WEIGH?*

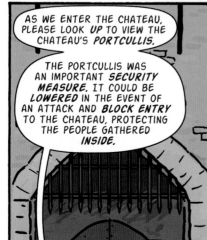

ABOUT *1,000* POUNDS.

HOW DID THEY *RAISE* AND *LOWER* IT?

THIS PORTCULLIS USES A *COUNTER-WEIGHT SYSTEM.*

THERE ARE HEAVY *WEIGHTS* INSIDE THE WALLS THAT ARE ATTACHED TO A SYSTEM OF *PULLEYS.*

LOWERING THE WEIGHTS *COUNTERACTS* THE WEIGHT OF THE *GATE,* MAKING IT EASY TO RAISE AND LOWER.

ONCE LOWERED, IT CAN BE *LOCKED* INTO PLACE.

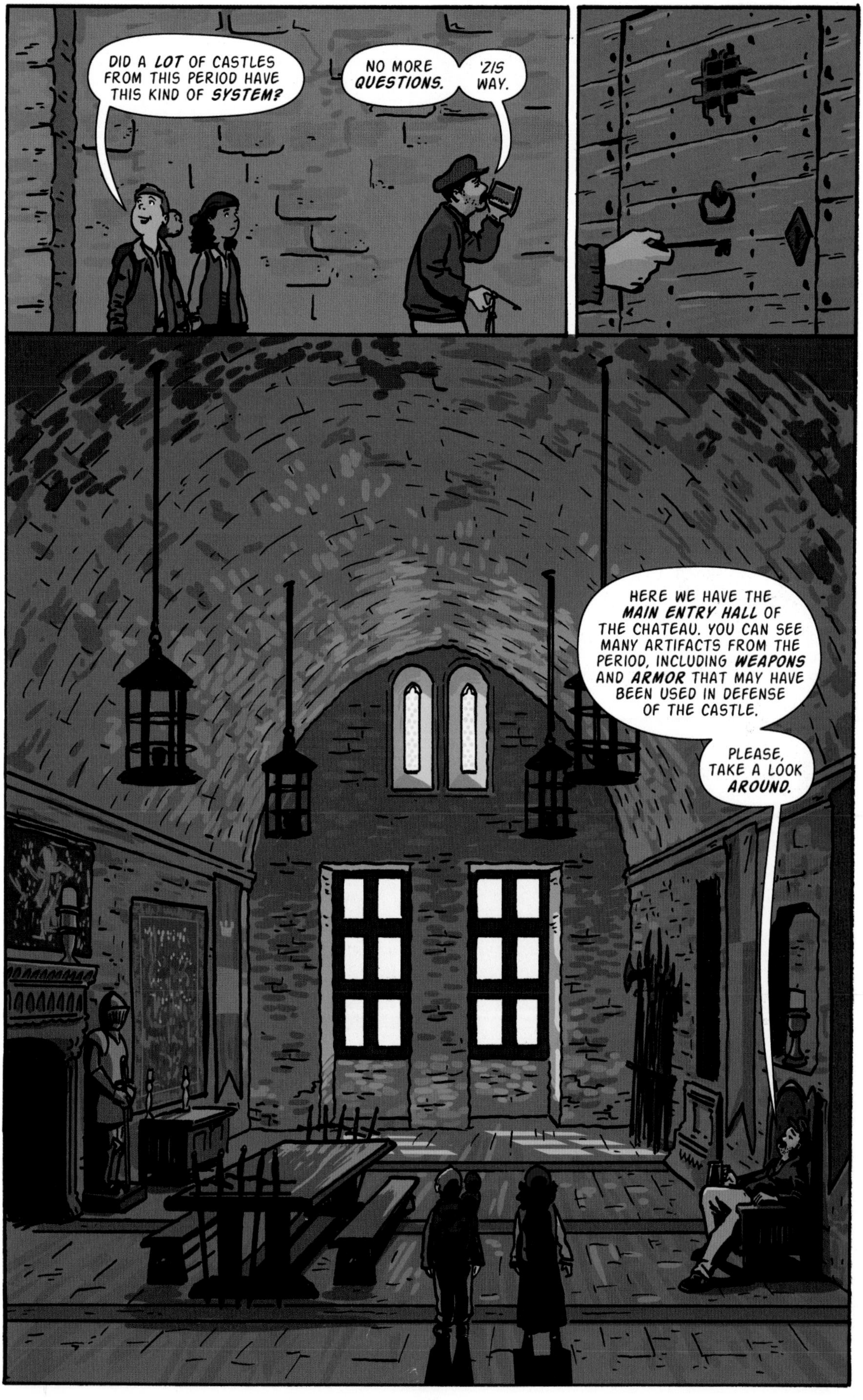
DID A LOT OF CASTLES FROM THIS PERIOD HAVE THIS KIND OF SYSTEM?
NO MORE QUESTIONS.
'ZIS WAY.
HERE WE HAVE THE MAIN ENTRY HALL OF THE CHATEAU. YOU CAN SEE MANY ARTIFACTS FROM THE PERIOD, INCLUDING WEAPONS AND ARMOR THAT MAY HAVE BEEN USED IN DEFENSE OF THE CASTLE.
PLEASE, TAKE A LOOK AROUND.

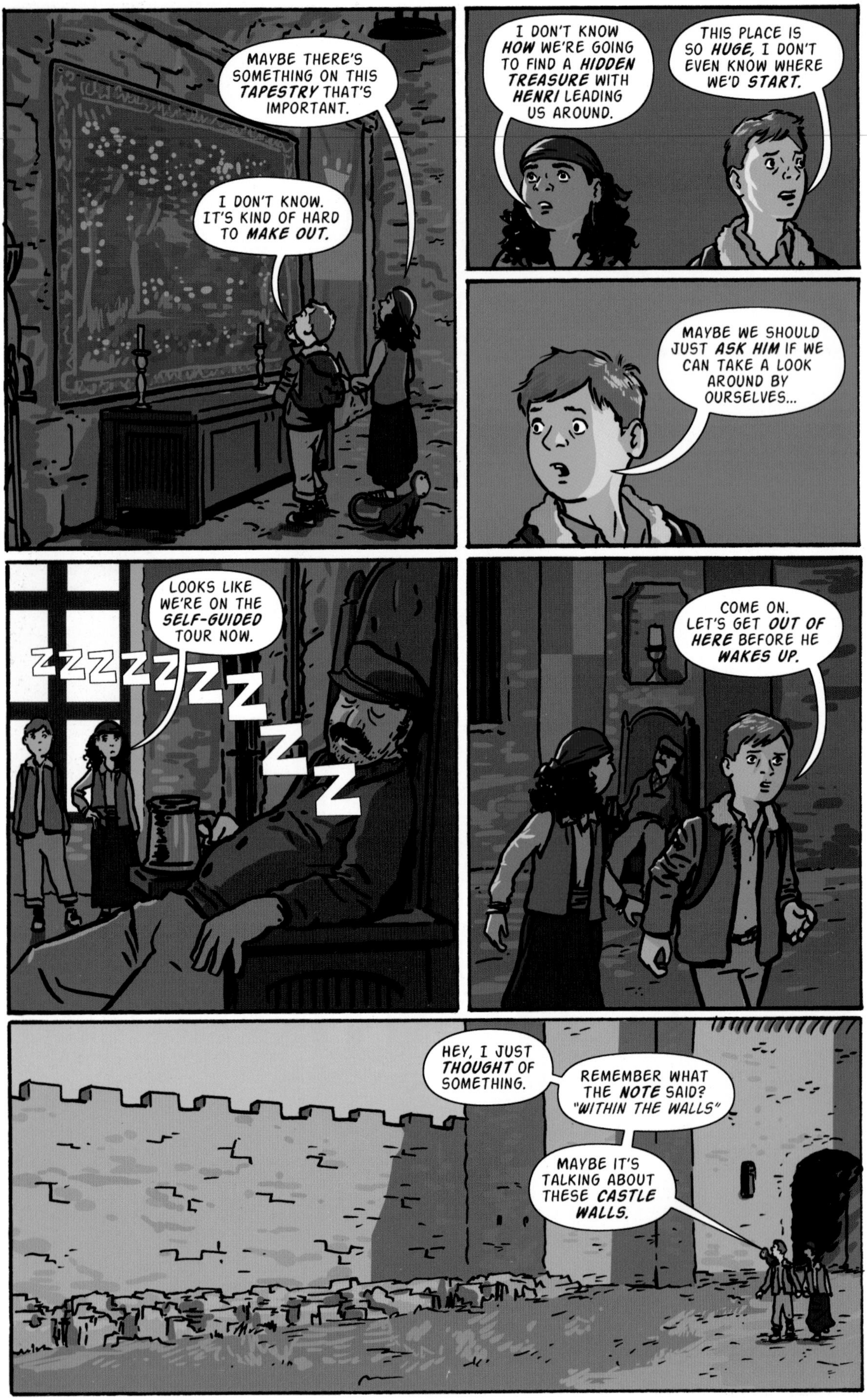
MAYBE THERE'S SOMETHING ON THIS TAPESTRY THAT'S IMPORTANT.
I DON'T KNOW. IT'S KIND OF HARD TO MAKE OUT.
I DON'T KNOW HOW WE'RE GOING TO FIND A HIDDEN TREASURE WITH HENRI LEADING US AROUND.
THIS PLACE IS SO HUGE, I DON'T EVEN KNOW WHERE WE'D START.
MAYBE WE SHOULD JUST ASK HIM IF WE CAN TAKE A LOOK AROUND BY OURSELVES...
LOOKS LIKE WE'RE ON THE SELF-GUIDED TOUR NOW.
ZZZZZZZZZZ
COME ON. LET'S GET OUT OF HERE BEFORE HE WAKES UP.
HEY, I JUST THOUGHT OF SOMETHING.
REMEMBER WHAT THE NOTE SAID? "WITHIN THE WALLS"
MAYBE IT'S TALKING ABOUT THESE CASTLE WALLS.

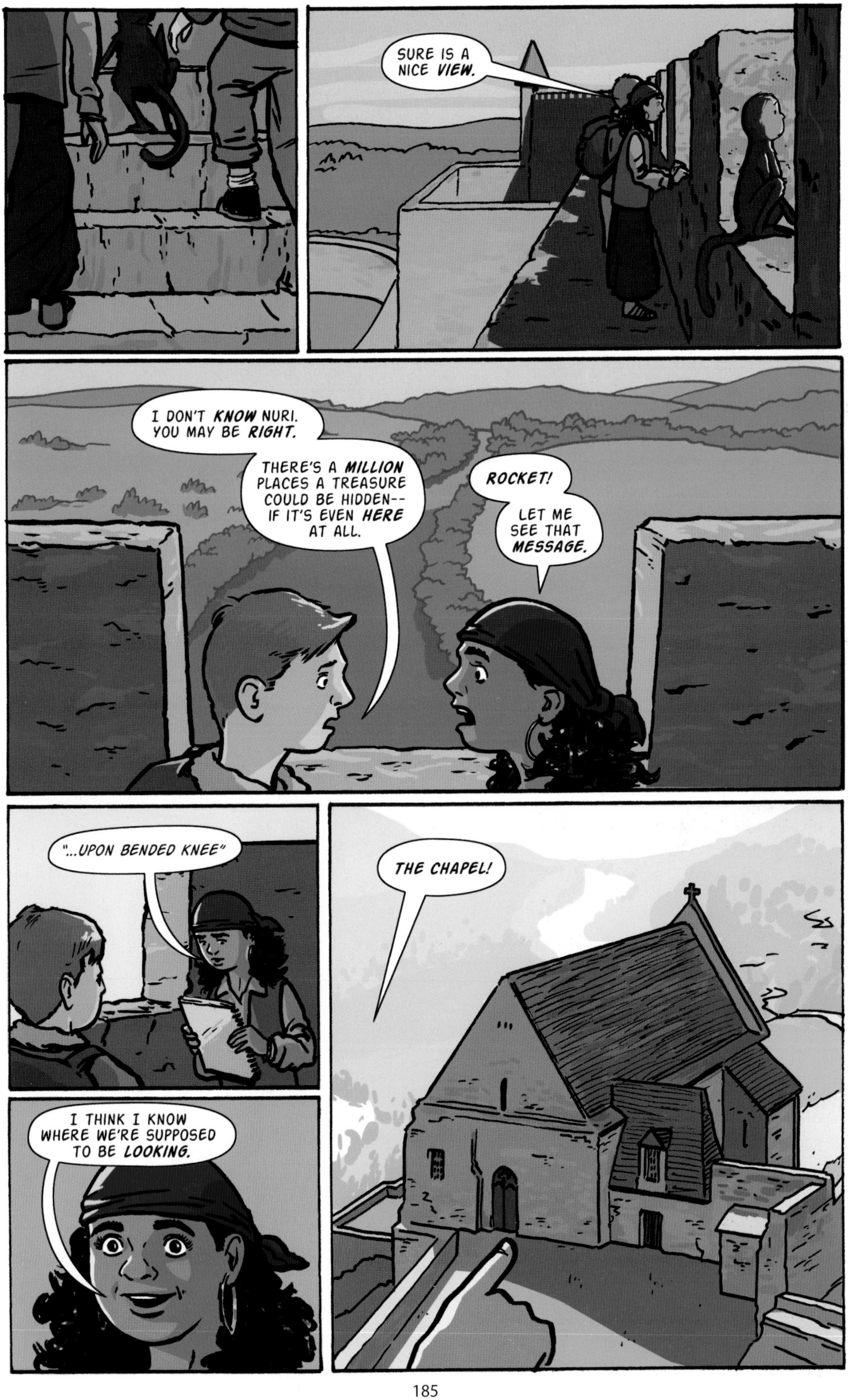
SURE IS A NICE VIEW.
I DON'T KNOW NURI. YOU MAY BE RIGHT.
THERE'S A MILLION PLACES A TREASURE COULD BE HIDDEN-- IF IT'S EVEN HERE AT ALL.
ROCKET!
LET ME SEE THAT MESSAGE.
"...UPON BENDED KNEE"
I THINK I KNOW WHERE WE'RE SUPPOSED TO BE LOOKING.
THE CHAPEL!

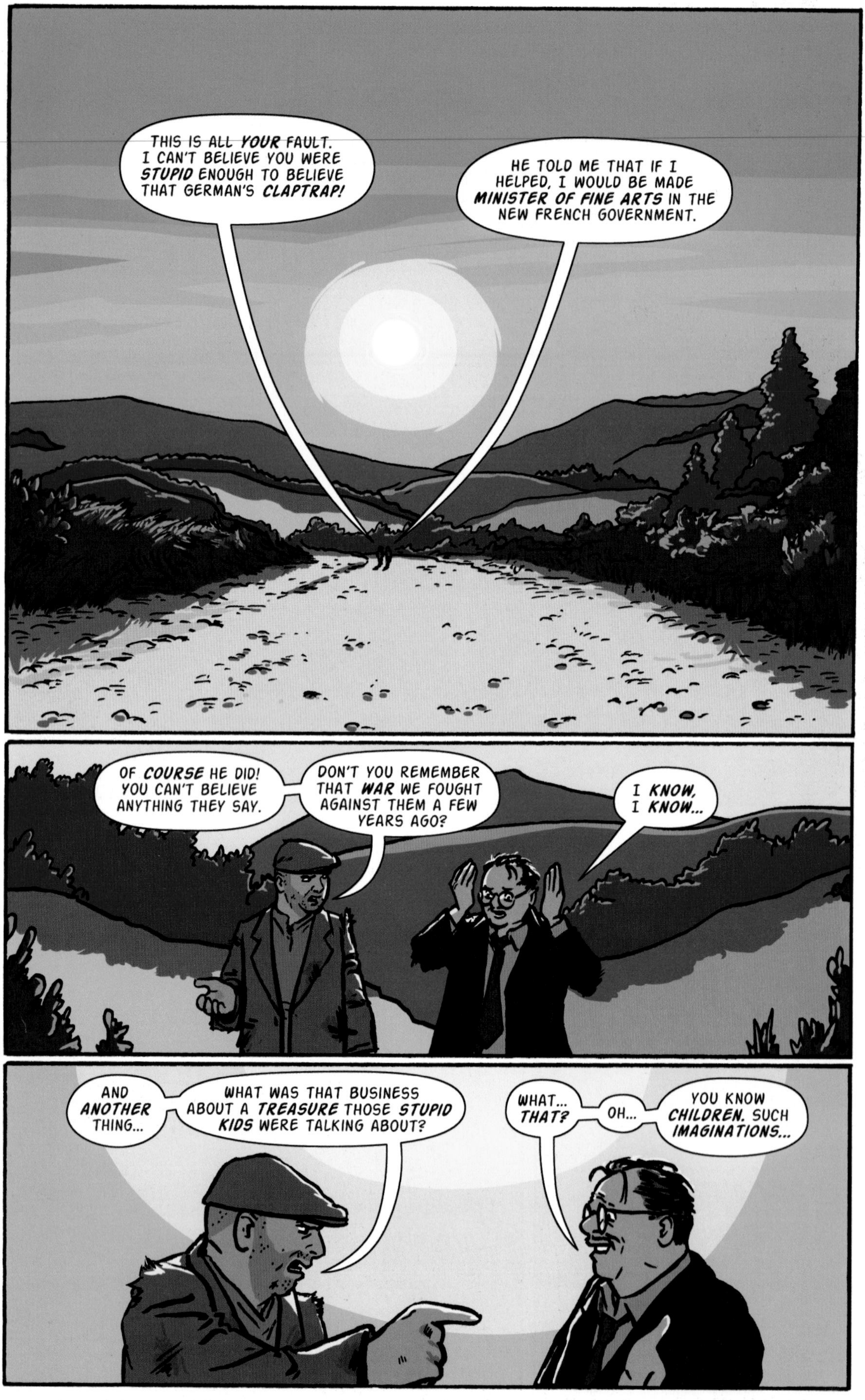
THIS IS ALL YOUR FAULT. I CAN'T BELIEVE YOU WERE STUPID ENOUGH TO BELIEVE THAT GERMAN'S CLAPTRAP!
HE TOLD ME THAT IF I HELPED, I WOULD BE MADE MINISTER OF FINE ARTS IN THE NEW FRENCH GOVERNMENT.
OF COURSE HE DID! YOU CAN'T BELIEVE ANYTHING THEY SAY.
DON'T YOU REMEMBER THAT WAR WE FOUGHT AGAINST THEM A FEW YEARS AGO?
I KNOW, I KNOW...
AND ANOTHER THING...
WHAT WAS THAT BUSINESS ABOUT A TREASURE THOSE STUPID KIDS WERE TALKING ABOUT?
WHAT... THAT?
OH...
YOU KNOW CHILDREN. SUCH IMAGINATIONS...

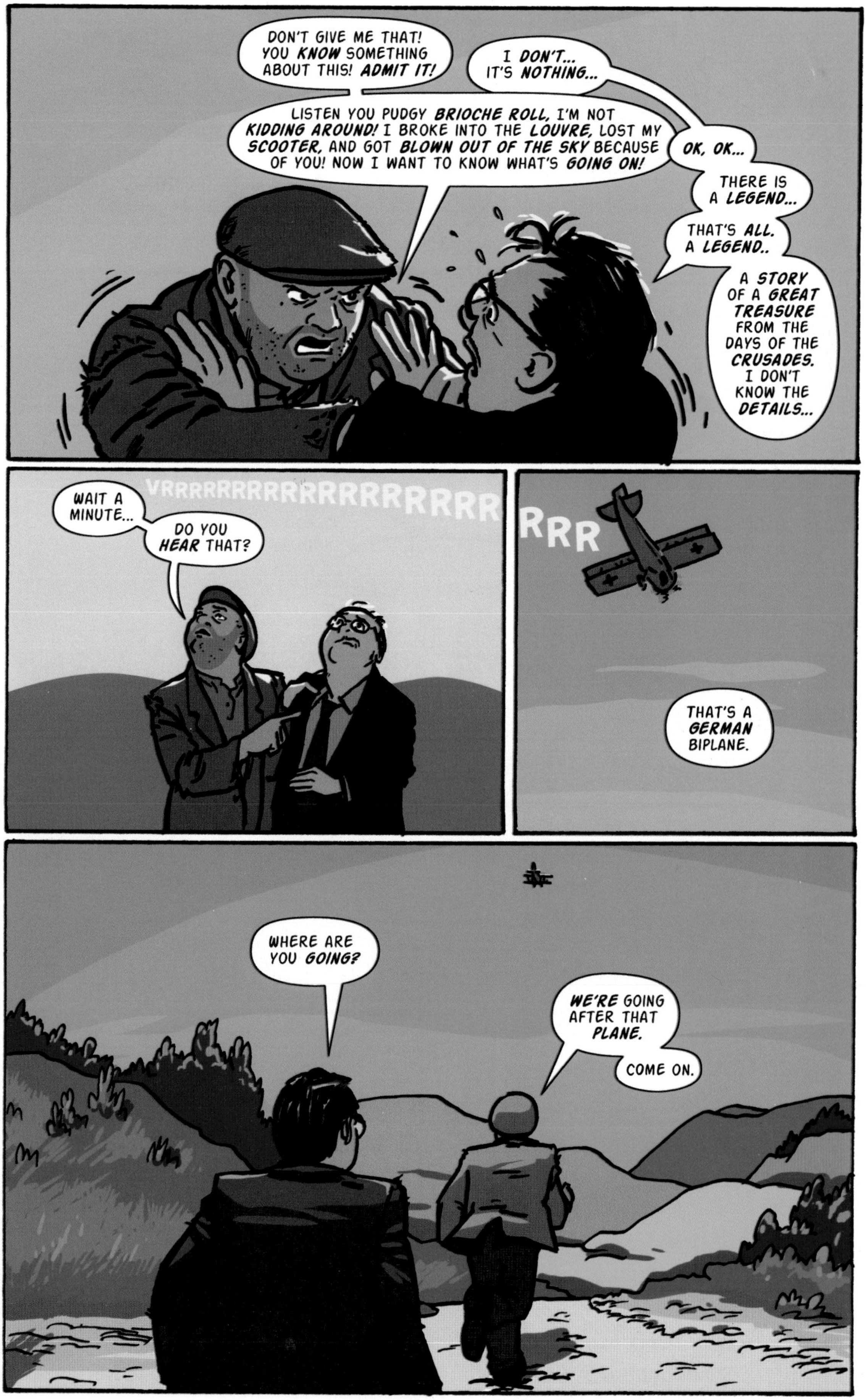
DON'T GIVE ME THAT! YOU KNOW SOMETHING ABOUT THIS! ADMIT IT!
I DON'T... IT'S NOTHING...
LISTEN YOU PUDGY BRIOCHE ROLL, I'M NOT KIDDING AROUND! I BROKE INTO THE LOUVRE, LOST MY SCOOTER, AND GOT BLOWN OUT OF THE SKY BECAUSE OF YOU! NOW I WANT TO KNOW WHAT'S GOING ON!
OK, OK...
THERE IS A LEGEND...
THAT'S ALL. A LEGEND..
A STORY OF A GREAT TREASURE FROM THE DAYS OF THE CRUSADES. I DON'T KNOW THE DETAILS...
WAIT A MINUTE...
VRRRRRRRRRRRRRRRRRRRRR
DO YOU HEAR THAT?
THAT'S A GERMAN BIPLANE.
WHERE ARE YOU GOING?
WE'RE GOING AFTER THAT PLANE.
COME ON.

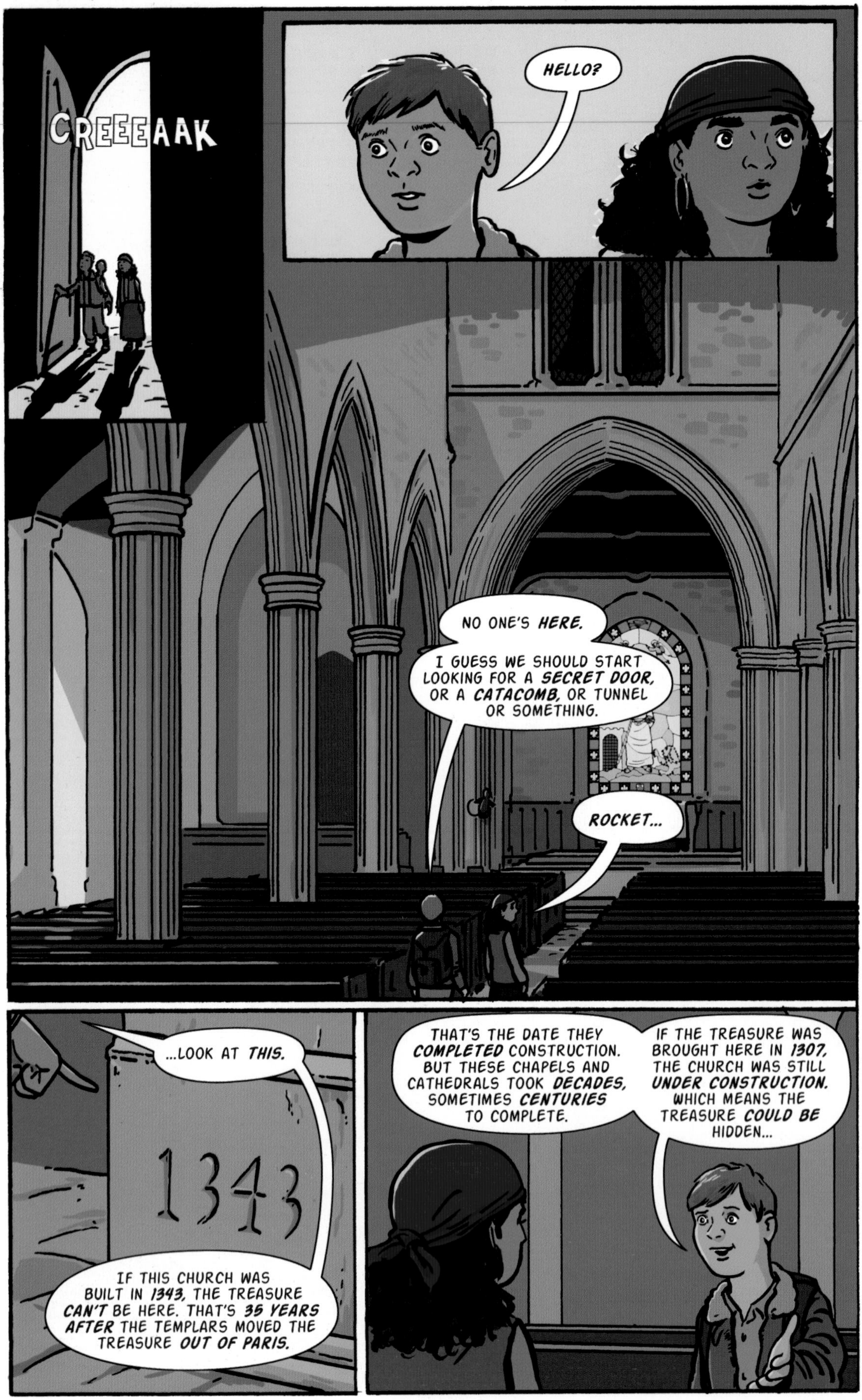
CREEEAAK
HELLO?
NO ONE'S HERE.
I GUESS WE SHOULD START LOOKING FOR A SECRET DOOR, OR A CATACOMB, OR TUNNEL OR SOMETHING.
ROCKET...
...LOOK AT THIS.
1343
IF THIS CHURCH WAS BUILT IN 1343, THE TREASURE CAN'T BE HERE. THAT'S 35 YEARS AFTER THE TEMPLARS MOVED THE TREASURE OUT OF PARIS.
THAT'S THE DATE THEY COMPLETED CONSTRUCTION. BUT THESE CHAPELS AND CATHEDRALS TOOK DECADES, SOMETIMES CENTURIES TO COMPLETE.
IF THE TREASURE WAS BROUGHT HERE IN 1307, THE CHURCH WAS STILL UNDER CONSTRUCTION. WHICH MEANS THE TREASURE COULD BE HIDDEN...

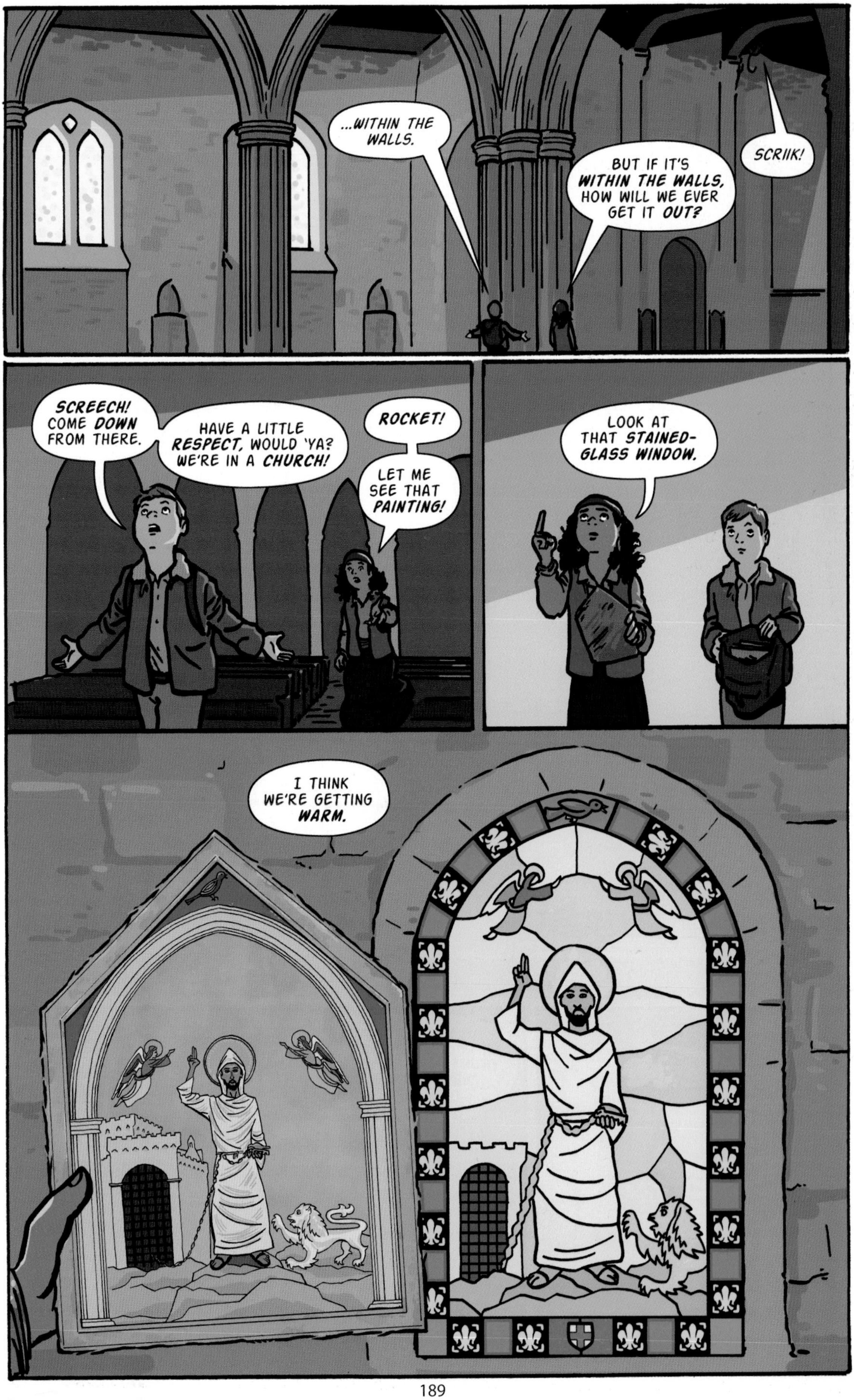
...WITHIN THE WALLS.
BUT IF IT'S WITHIN THE WALLS, HOW WILL WE EVER GET IT OUT?
SCRIIK!
SCREECH! COME DOWN FROM THERE.
HAVE A LITTLE RESPECT, WOULD 'YA? WE'RE IN A CHURCH!
ROCKET!
LET ME SEE THAT PAINTING!
LOOK AT THAT STAINED-GLASS WINDOW.
I THINK WE'RE GETTING WARM.

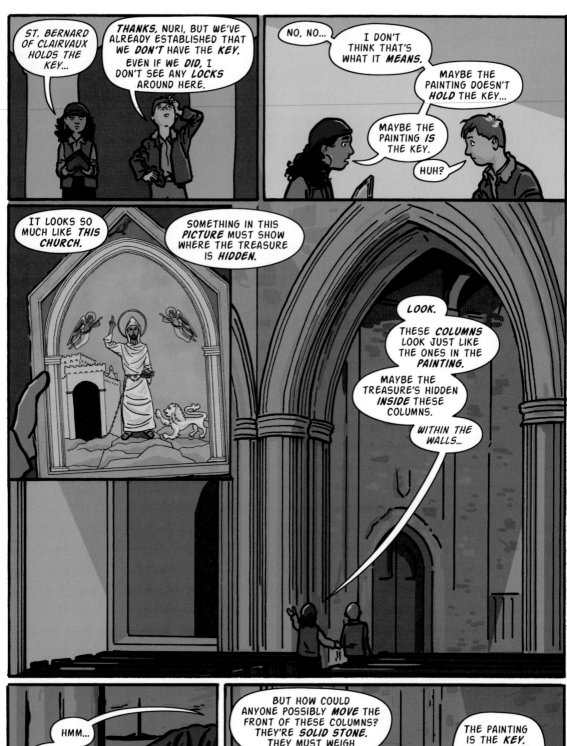

ST. BERNARD OF CLAIRVAUX HOLDS THE KEY...

THANKS, NURI, BUT WE'VE ALREADY ESTABLISHED THAT WE *DON'T* HAVE THE *KEY.* EVEN IF WE *DID,* I DON'T SEE ANY *LOCKS* AROUND HERE.

NO, NO...

I DON'T THINK THAT'S WHAT IT *MEANS.*

MAYBE THE PAINTING DOESN'T *HOLD* THE KEY...

MAYBE THE PAINTING *IS* THE KEY.

HUH?

IT LOOKS SO MUCH LIKE *THIS* CHURCH.

SOMETHING IN THIS *PICTURE* MUST SHOW WHERE THE TREASURE IS *HIDDEN.*

LOOK.

THESE *COLUMNS* LOOK JUST LIKE THE ONES IN THE *PAINTING.*

MAYBE THE TREASURE'S HIDDEN *INSIDE* THESE COLUMNS.

WITHIN THE WALLS...

HMM...

THERE'S NO *MORTAR* CONNECTING THE *FRONT* OF THE COLUMN TO THE *WALL.*

I SUPPOSE THE TREASURE COULD BE *BEHIND* THESE COLUMNS.

BUT HOW COULD ANYONE POSSIBLY *MOVE* THE FRONT OF THESE COLUMNS? THEY'RE *SOLID STONE.* THEY MUST WEIGH OVER A *TON!*

THE PAINTING IS THE *KEY.* THERE'S *GOT* TO BE A CLUE IN HERE.

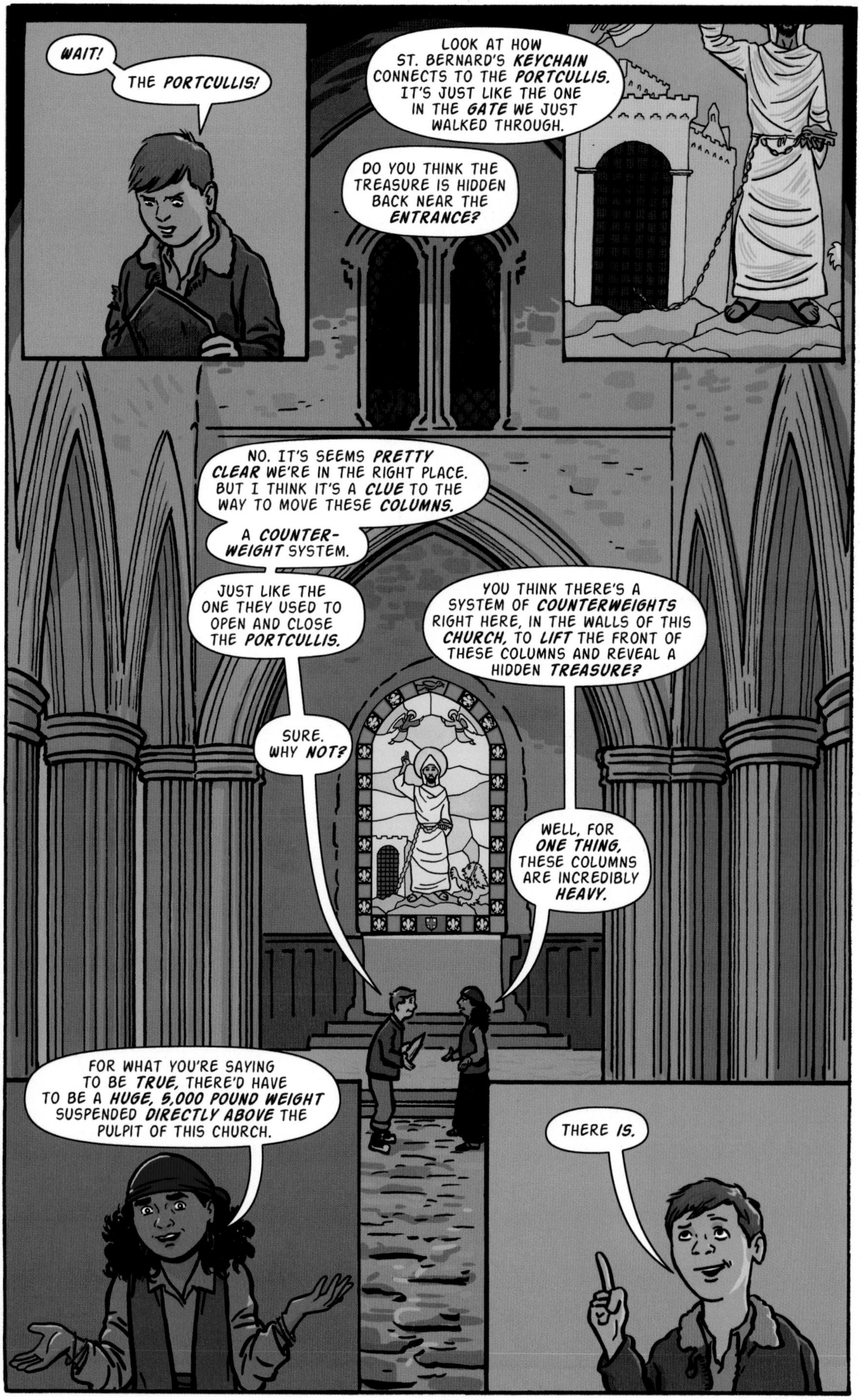
WAIT!
THE PORTCULLIS!
LOOK AT HOW ST. BERNARD'S KEYCHAIN CONNECTS TO THE PORTCULLIS. IT'S JUST LIKE THE ONE IN THE GATE WE JUST WALKED THROUGH.
DO YOU THINK THE TREASURE IS HIDDEN BACK NEAR THE ENTRANCE?
NO. IT'S SEEMS PRETTY CLEAR WE'RE IN THE RIGHT PLACE. BUT I THINK IT'S A CLUE TO THE WAY TO MOVE THESE COLUMNS.
A COUNTER-WEIGHT SYSTEM.
JUST LIKE THE ONE THEY USED TO OPEN AND CLOSE THE PORTCULLIS.
YOU THINK THERE'S A SYSTEM OF COUNTERWEIGHTS RIGHT HERE, IN THE WALLS OF THIS CHURCH, TO LIFT THE FRONT OF THESE COLUMNS AND REVEAL A HIDDEN TREASURE?
SURE. WHY NOT?
WELL, FOR ONE THING, THESE COLUMNS ARE INCREDIBLY HEAVY.
FOR WHAT YOU'RE SAYING TO BE TRUE, THERE'D HAVE TO BE A HUGE, 5,000 POUND WEIGHT SUSPENDED DIRECTLY ABOVE THE PULPIT OF THIS CHURCH.
THERE IS.

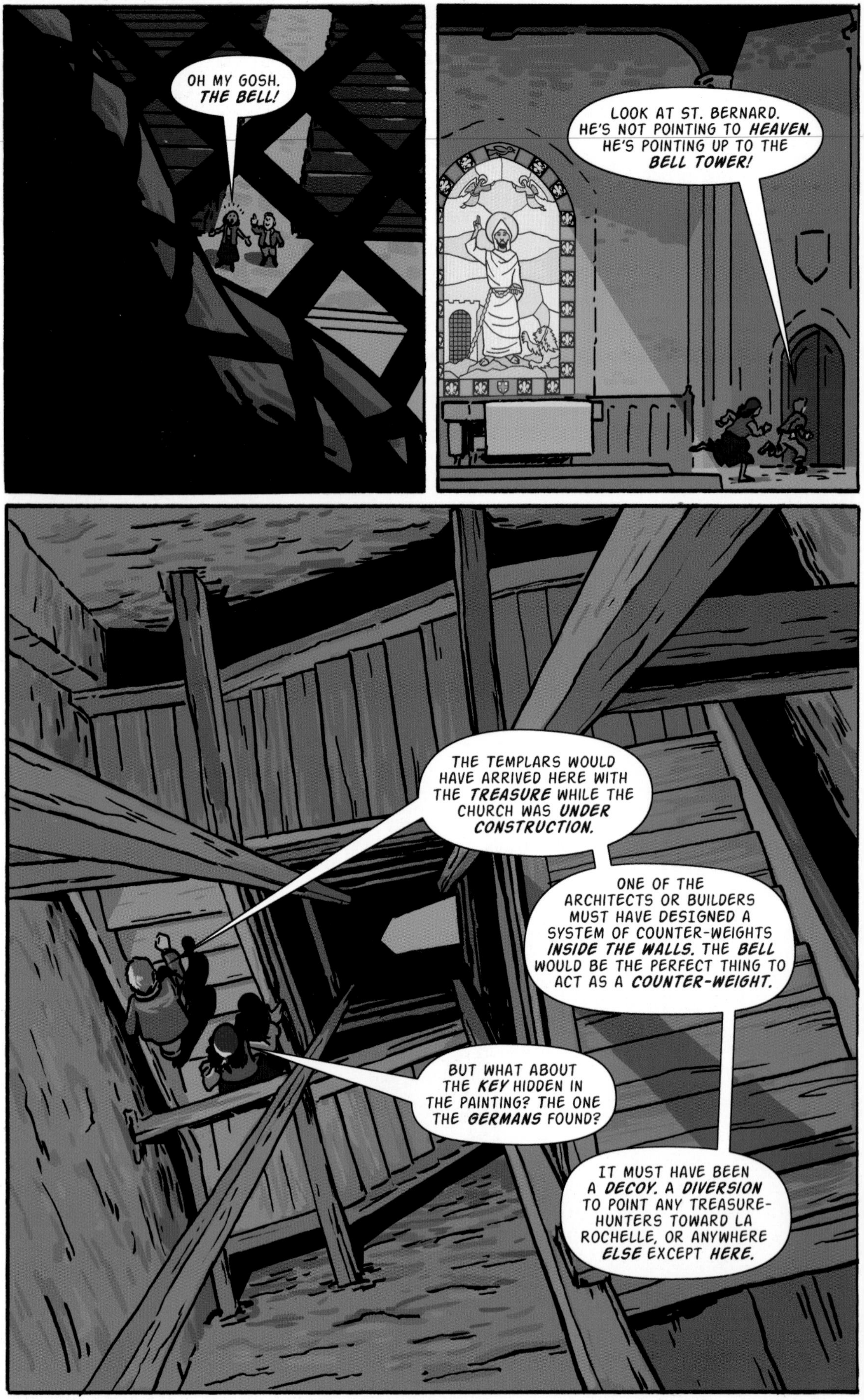
OH MY GOSH. THE BELL!
LOOK AT ST. BERNARD. HE'S NOT POINTING TO HEAVEN. HE'S POINTING UP TO THE BELL TOWER!
THE TEMPLARS WOULD HAVE ARRIVED HERE WITH THE TREASURE WHILE THE CHURCH WAS UNDER CONSTRUCTION.
ONE OF THE ARCHITECTS OR BUILDERS MUST HAVE DESIGNED A SYSTEM OF COUNTER-WEIGHTS INSIDE THE WALLS. THE BELL WOULD BE THE PERFECT THING TO ACT AS A COUNTER-WEIGHT.
BUT WHAT ABOUT THE KEY HIDDEN IN THE PAINTING? THE ONE THE GERMANS FOUND?
IT MUST HAVE BEEN A DECOY. A DIVERSION TO POINT ANY TREASURE-HUNTERS TOWARD LA ROCHELLE, OR ANYWHERE ELSE EXCEPT HERE.

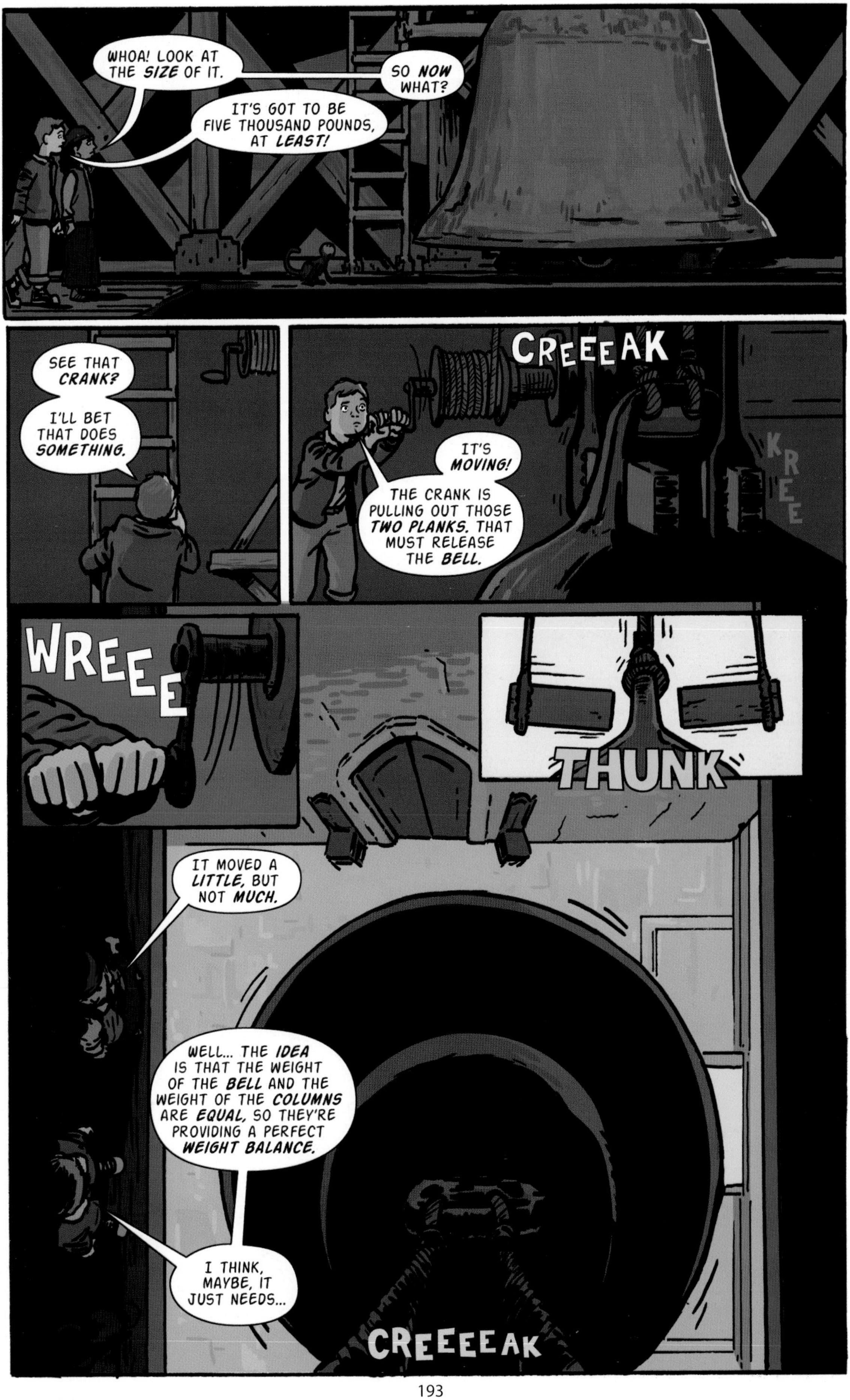

WHOA! LOOK AT THE SIZE OF IT.
SO NOW WHAT?
IT'S GOT TO BE FIVE THOUSAND POUNDS, AT LEAST!
SEE THAT CRANK?
I'LL BET THAT DOES SOMETHING.
CREEEAK
KREE
IT'S MOVING!
THE CRANK IS PULLING OUT THOSE TWO PLANKS. THAT MUST RELEASE THE BELL.
WREEE
THUNK
IT MOVED A LITTLE, BUT NOT MUCH.
WELL... THE IDEA IS THAT THE WEIGHT OF THE BELL AND THE WEIGHT OF THE COLUMNS ARE EQUAL, SO THEY'RE PROVIDING A PERFECT WEIGHT BALANCE.
I THINK, MAYBE, IT JUST NEEDS...
CREEEEAK

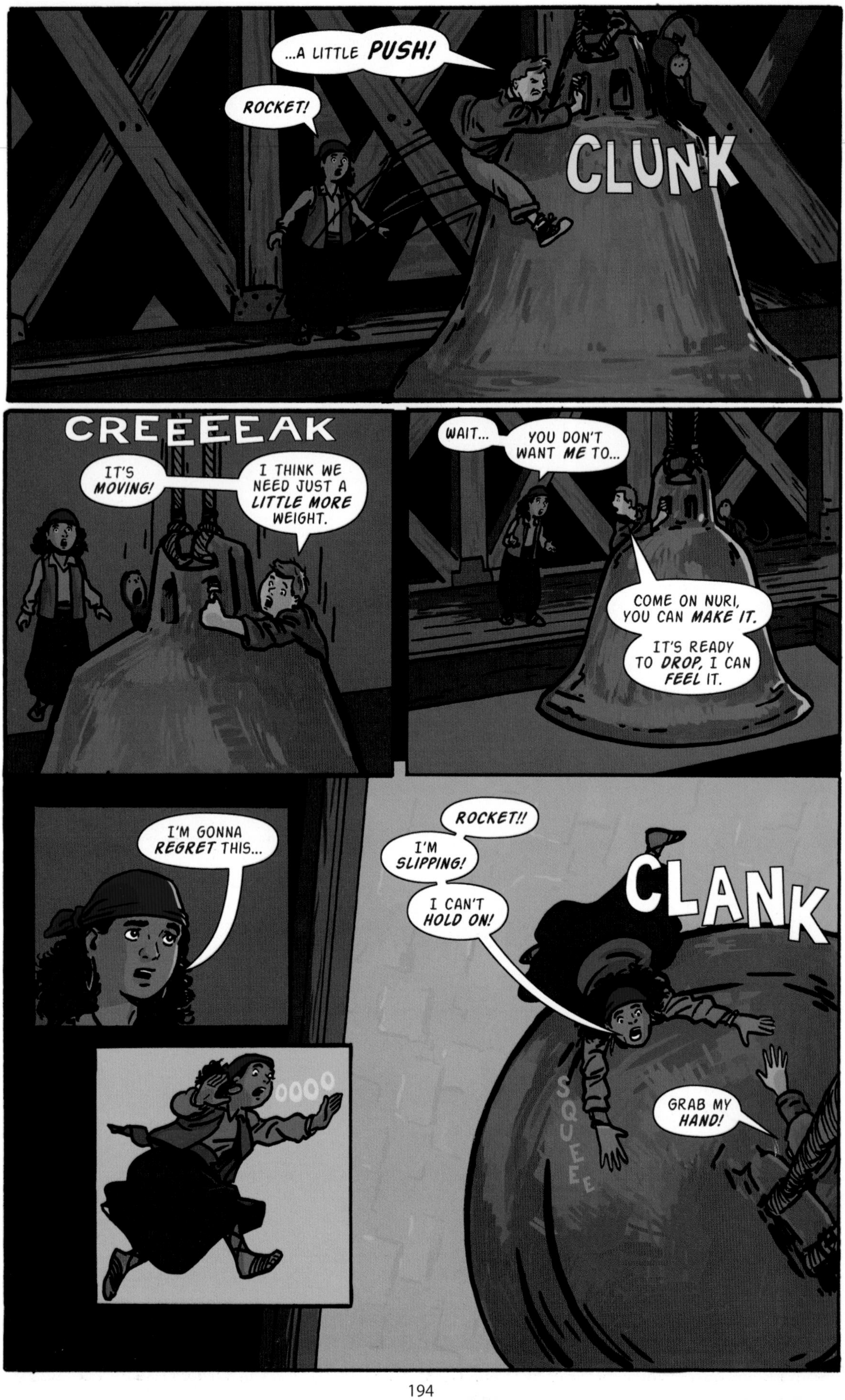
...A LITTLE PUSH!
ROCKET!
CLUNK
CREEEEAK
IT'S MOVING!
I THINK WE NEED JUST A LITTLE MORE WEIGHT.
WAIT...
YOU DON'T WANT ME TO...
COME ON NURI, YOU CAN MAKE IT.
IT'S READY TO DROP, I CAN FEEL IT.
I'M GONNA REGRET THIS...
OOOO
ROCKET!!
I'M SLIPPING!
I CAN'T HOLD ON!
CLANK
SQUEEE
GRAB MY HAND!

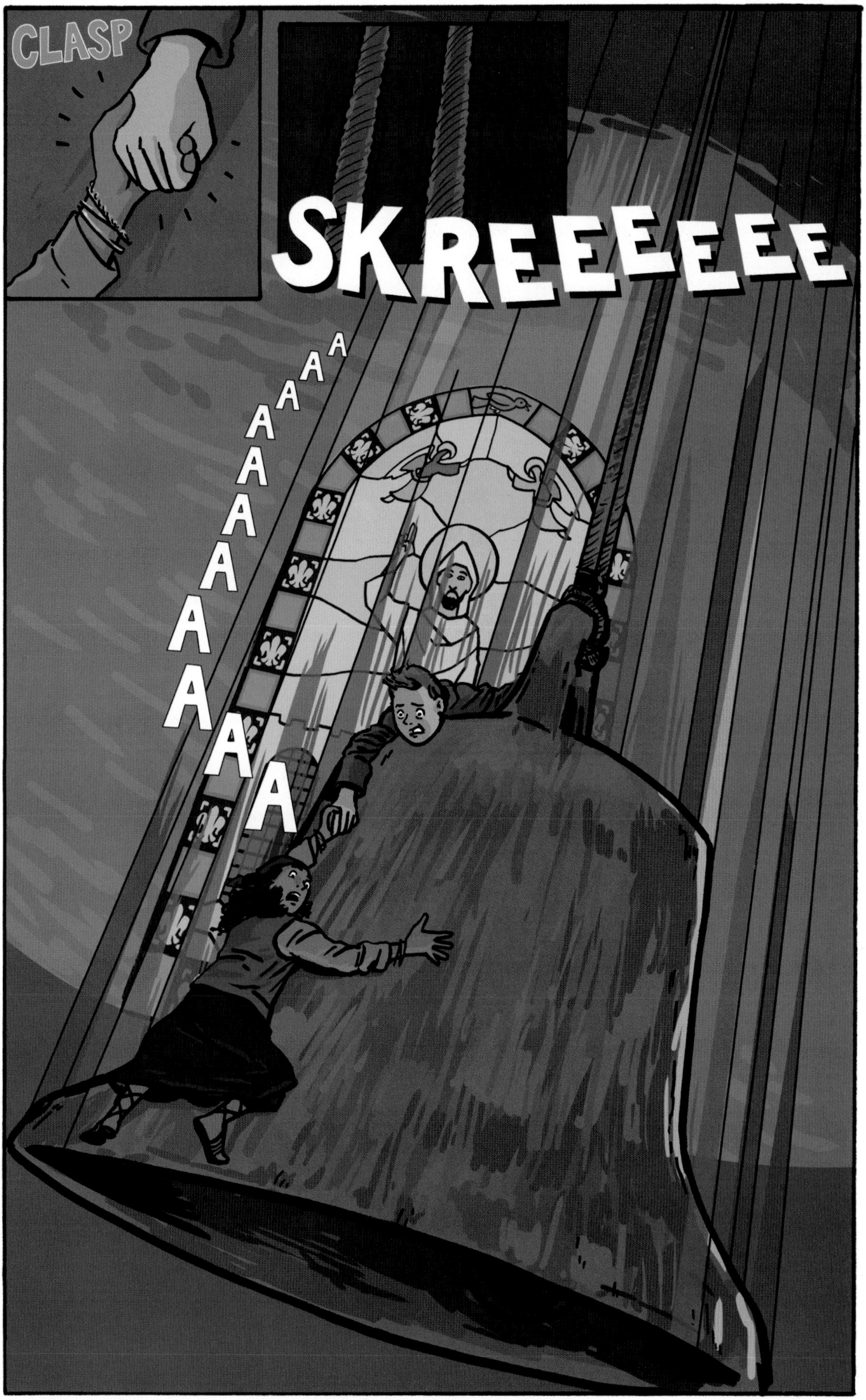
CLASP
SKREEEEEE
AAAAAAAAAAA

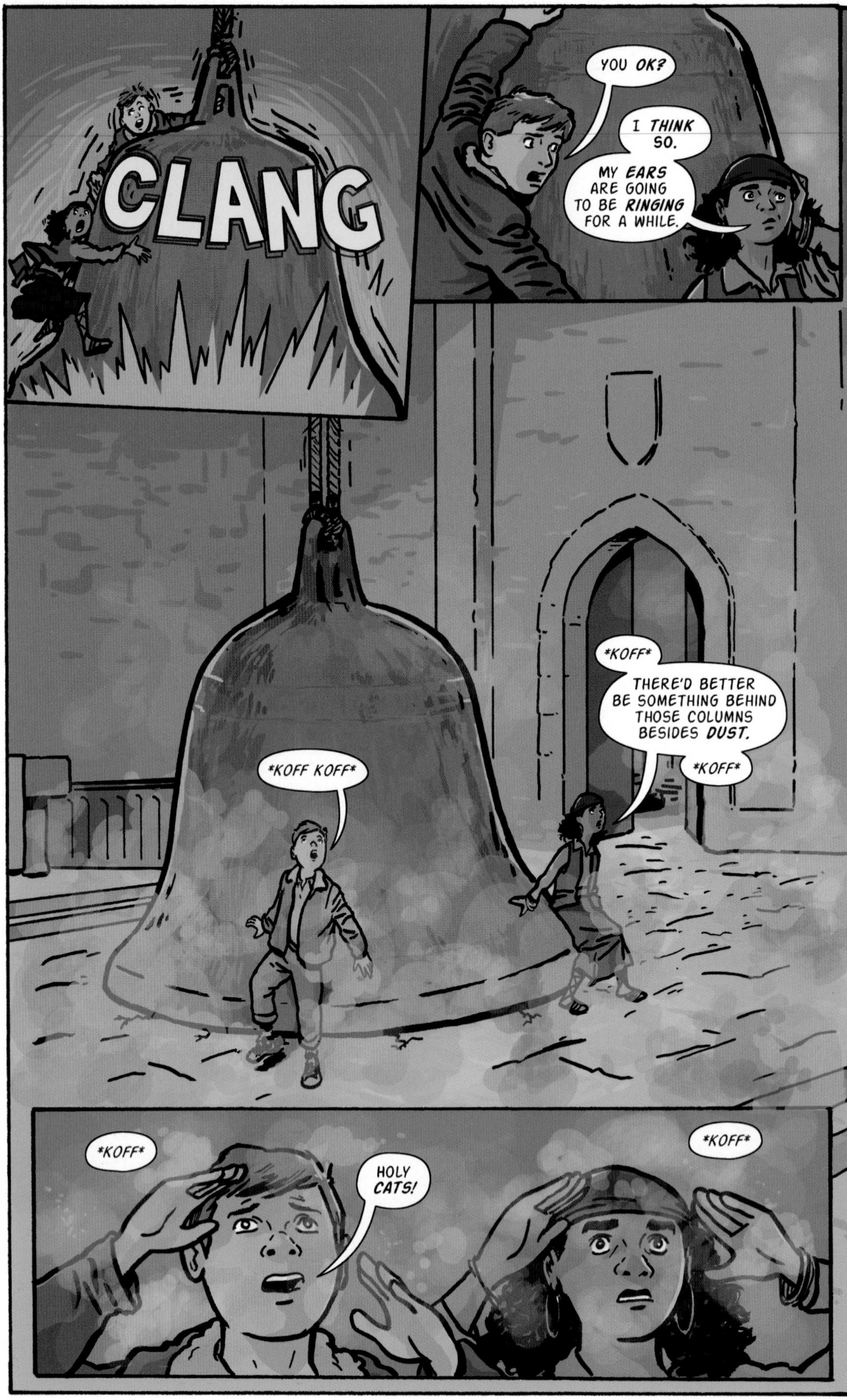
CLANG
YOU OK?
I THINK SO.
MY EARS ARE GOING TO BE RINGING FOR A WHILE.
KOFF KOFF
KOFF
THERE'D BETTER BE SOMETHING BEHIND THOSE COLUMNS BESIDES DUST.
KOFF
KOFF
HOLY CATS!
KOFF

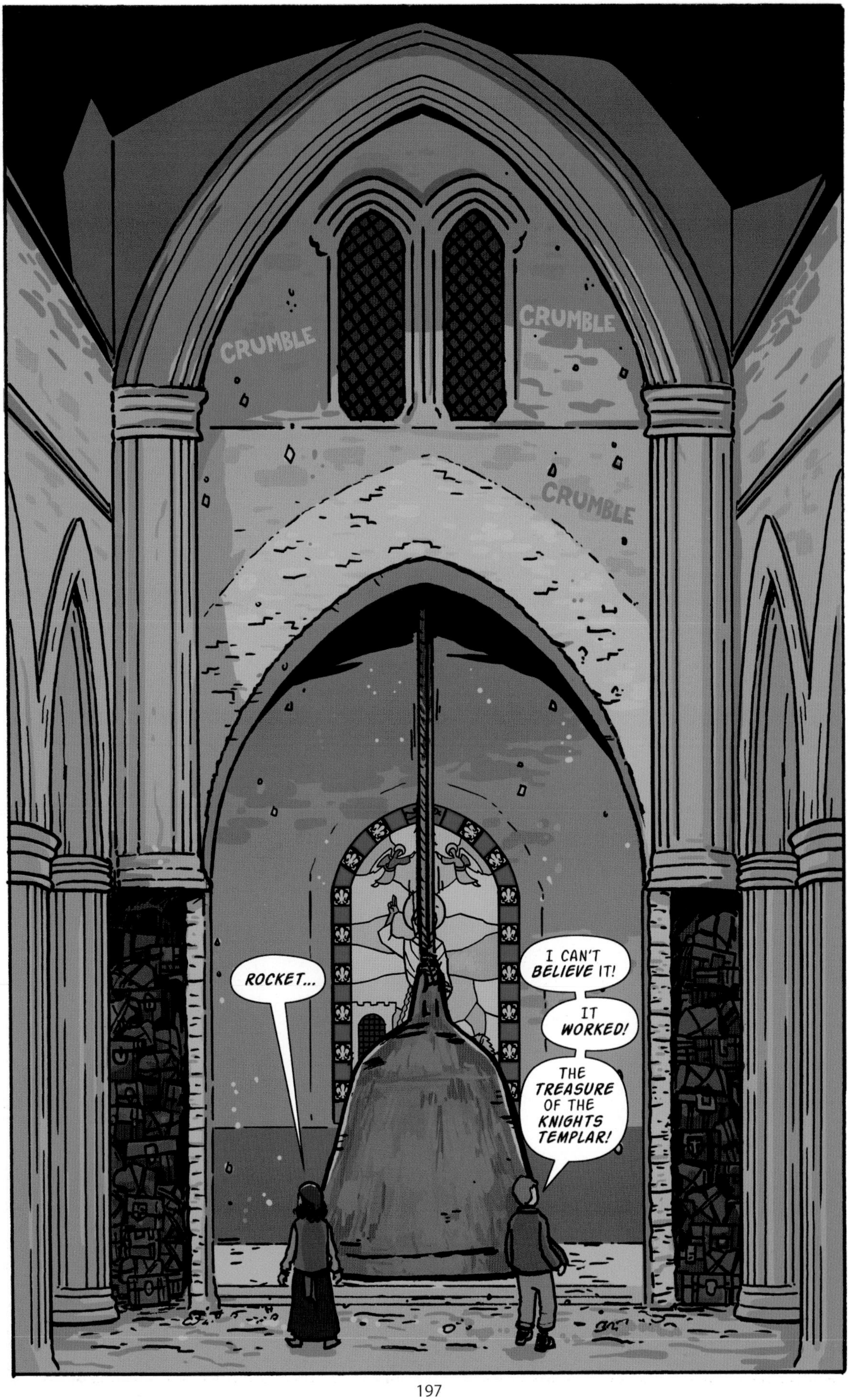

CRUMBLE
CRUMBLE
CRUMBLE
ROCKET...
I CAN'T BELIEVE IT!
IT WORKED!
THE TREASURE OF THE KNIGHTS TEMPLAR!

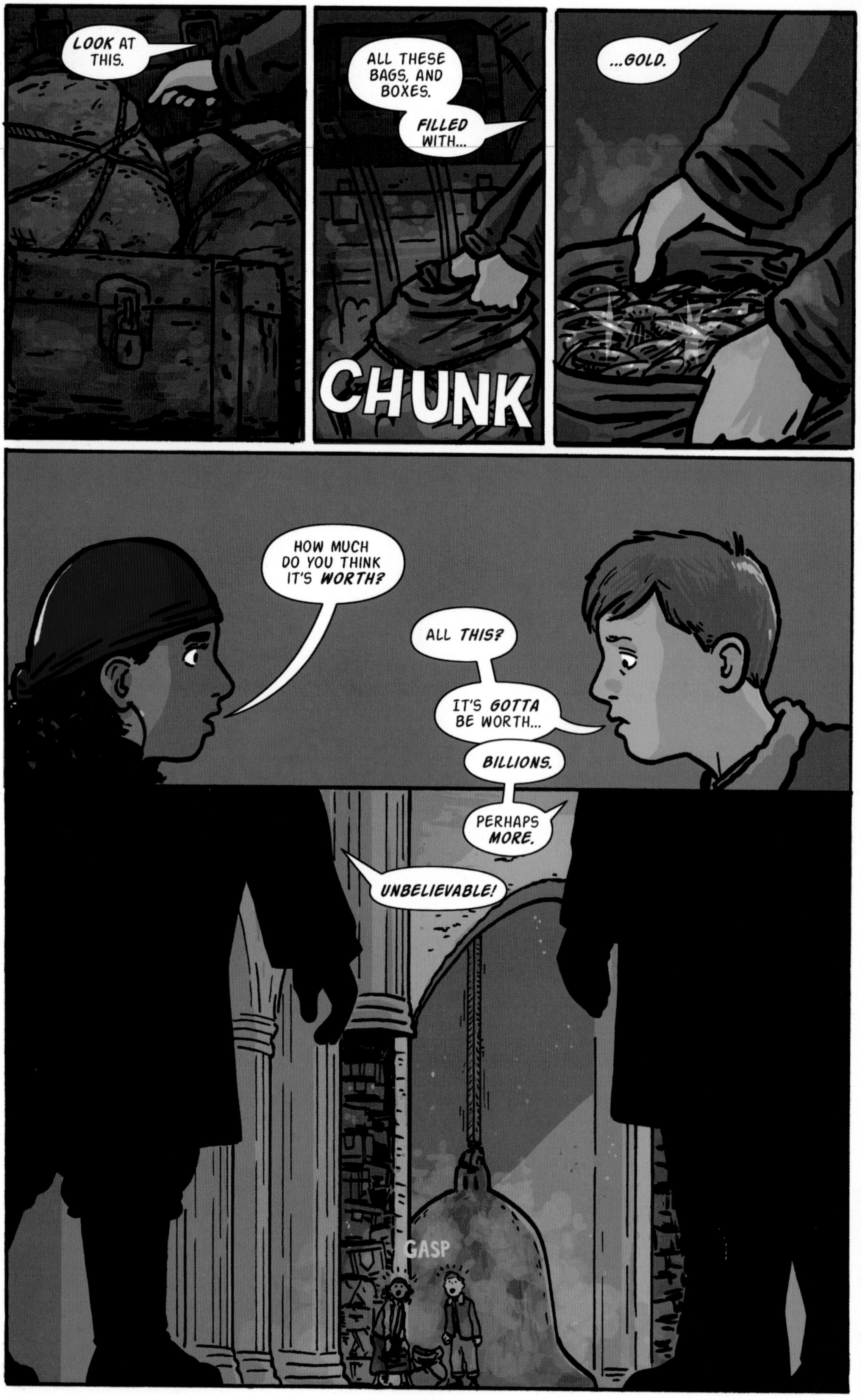
LOOK AT THIS.
ALL THESE BAGS, AND BOXES.
FILLED WITH...
CHUNK
...GOLD.
HOW MUCH DO YOU THINK IT'S WORTH?
ALL THIS?
IT'S GOTTA BE WORTH...
BILLIONS.
PERHAPS MORE.
UNBELIEVABLE!
GASP

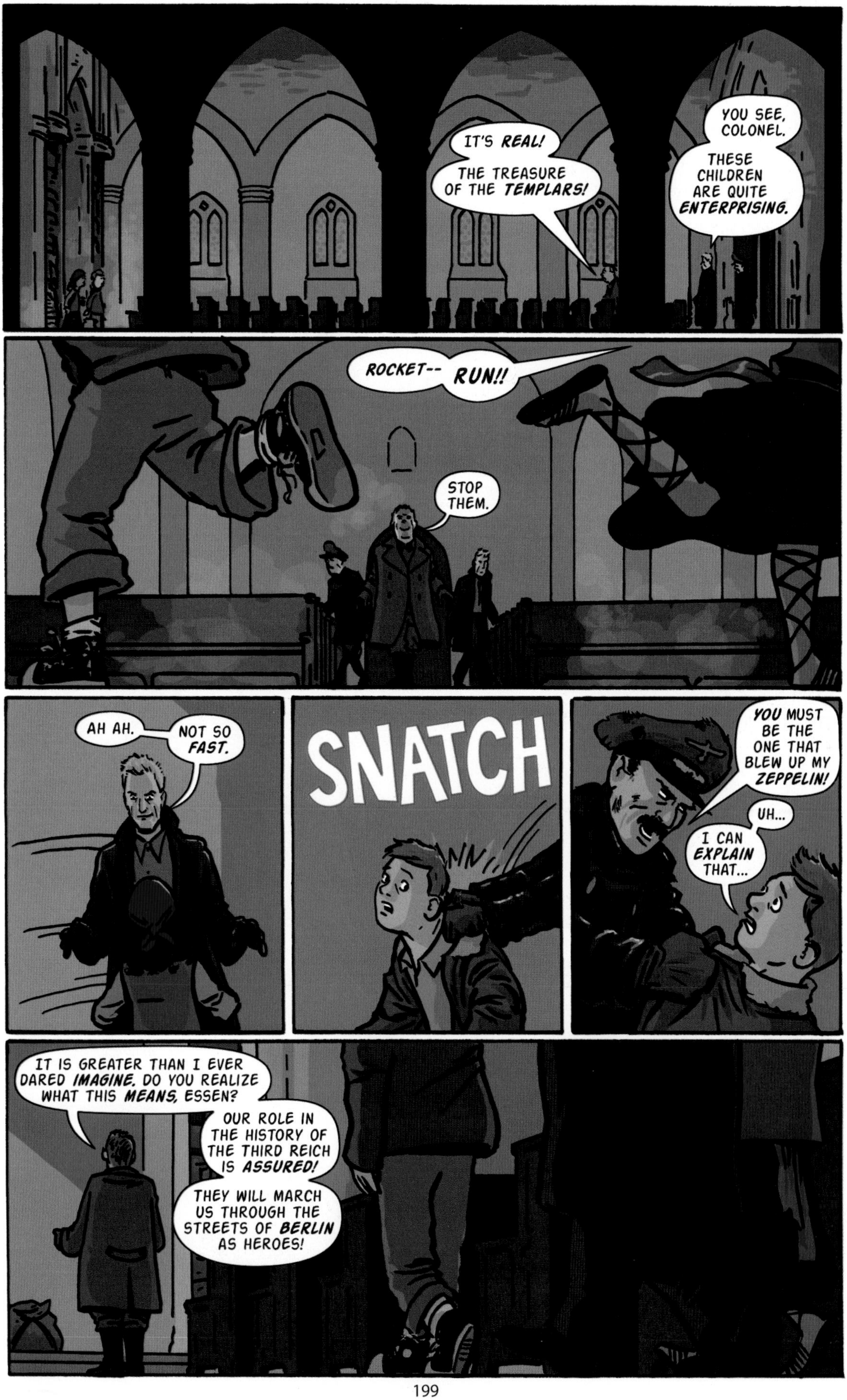
IT'S *REAL!*
THE TREASURE OF THE *TEMPLARS!*
YOU SEE, COLONEL.
THESE CHILDREN ARE QUITE *ENTERPRISING.*
ROCKET-- RUN!!
STOP THEM.
AH AH.
NOT SO *FAST.*
SNATCH
YOU MUST BE THE ONE THAT BLEW UP MY *ZEPPELIN!*
UH...
I CAN *EXPLAIN* THAT...
IT IS GREATER THAN I EVER DARED *IMAGINE.* DO YOU REALIZE WHAT THIS *MEANS,* ESSEN?
OUR ROLE IN THE HISTORY OF THE THIRD REICH IS *ASSURED!*
THEY WILL MARCH US THROUGH THE STREETS OF *BERLIN* AS HEROES!

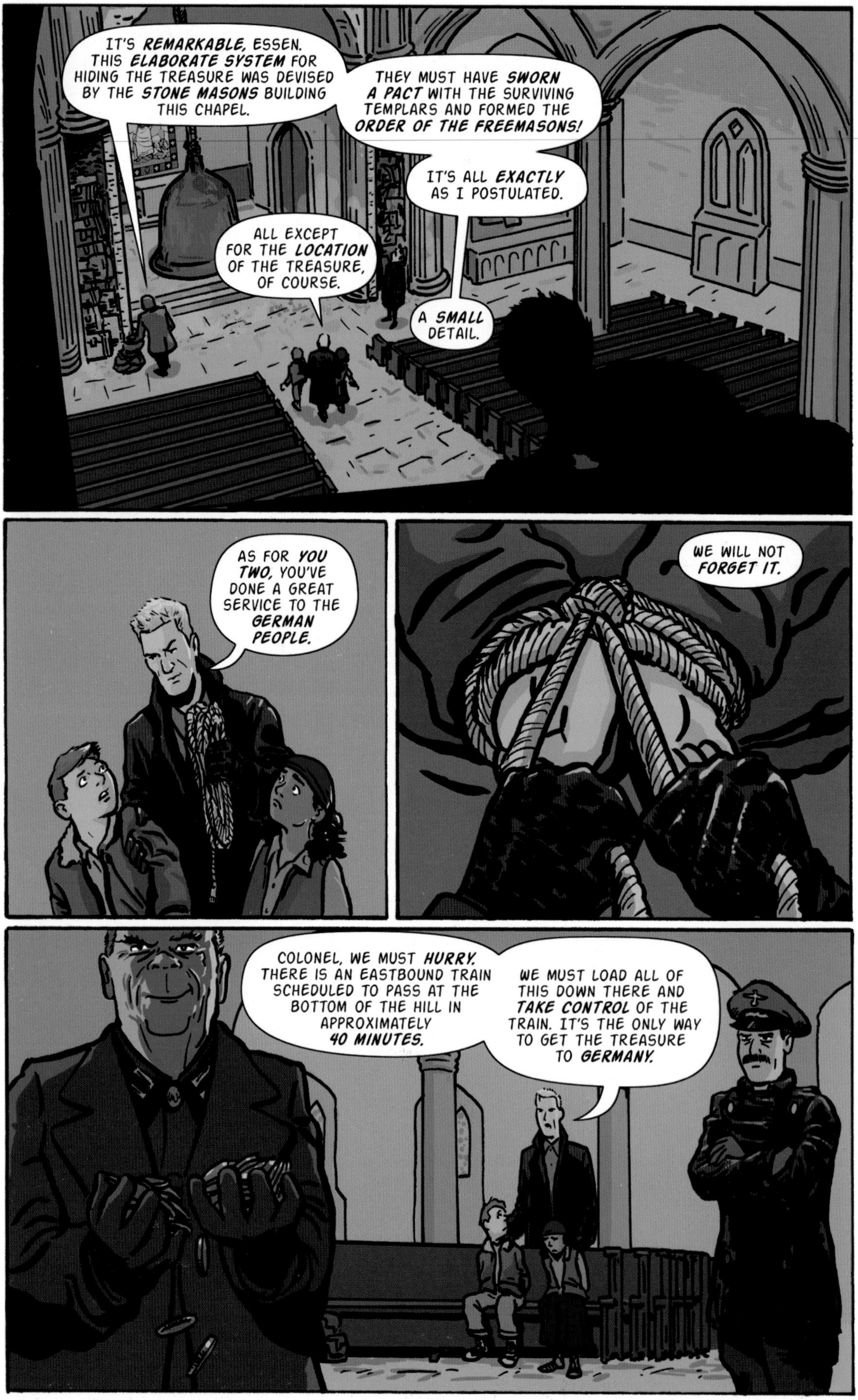
IT'S REMARKABLE, ESSEN. THIS ELABORATE SYSTEM FOR HIDING THE TREASURE WAS DEVISED BY THE STONE MASONS BUILDING THIS CHAPEL.
THEY MUST HAVE SWORN A PACT WITH THE SURVIVING TEMPLARS AND FORMED THE ORDER OF THE FREEMASONS!
IT'S ALL EXACTLY AS I POSTULATED.
ALL EXCEPT FOR THE LOCATION OF THE TREASURE, OF COURSE.
A SMALL DETAIL.
AS FOR YOU TWO, YOU'VE DONE A GREAT SERVICE TO THE GERMAN PEOPLE.
WE WILL NOT FORGET IT.
COLONEL, WE MUST HURRY. THERE IS AN EASTBOUND TRAIN SCHEDULED TO PASS AT THE BOTTOM OF THE HILL IN APPROXIMATELY 40 MINUTES.
WE MUST LOAD ALL OF THIS DOWN THERE AND TAKE CONTROL OF THE TRAIN. IT'S THE ONLY WAY TO GET THE TREASURE TO GERMANY.

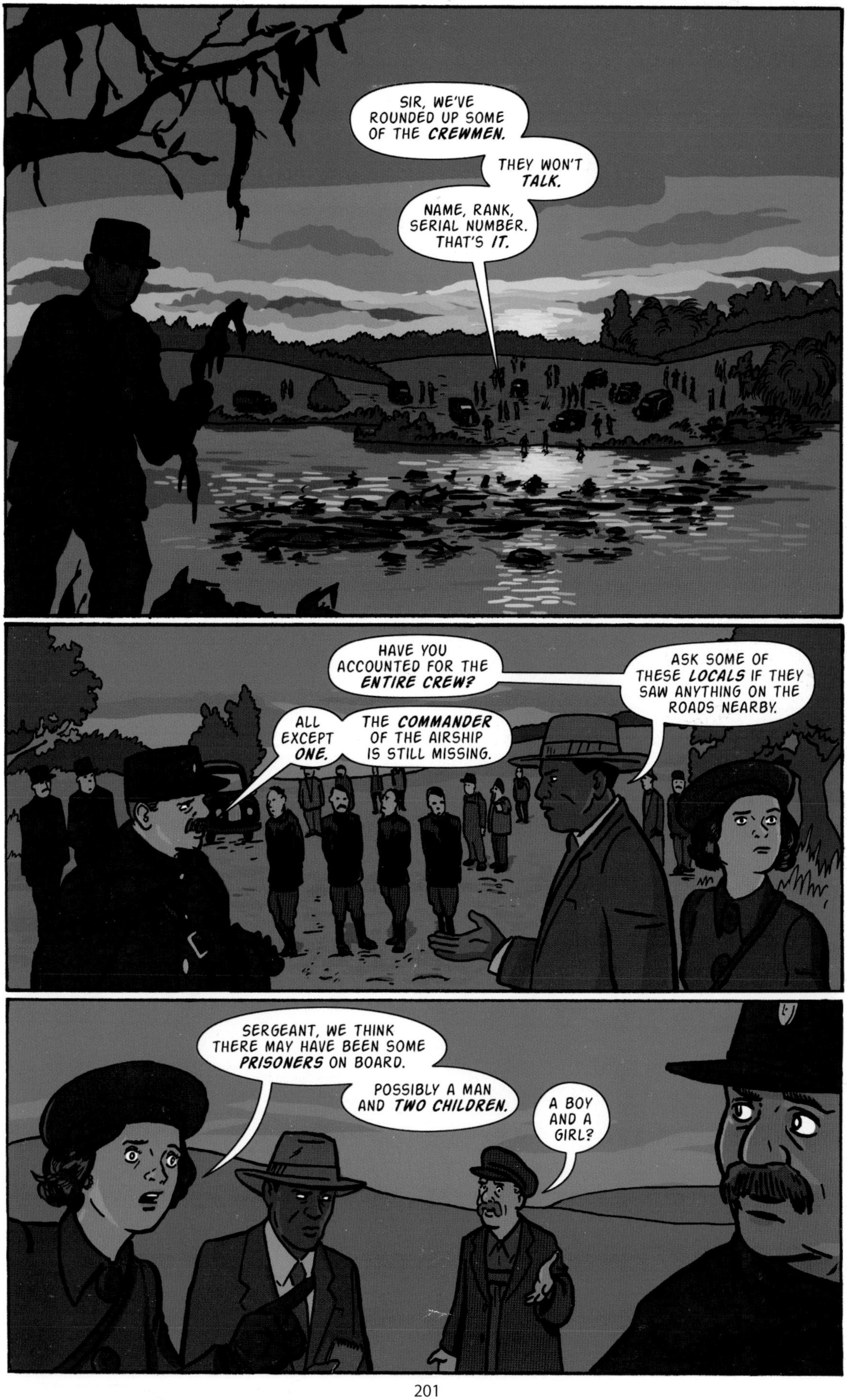
SIR, WE'VE ROUNDED UP SOME OF THE CREWMEN.
THEY WON'T TALK.
NAME, RANK, SERIAL NUMBER. THAT'S IT.
HAVE YOU ACCOUNTED FOR THE ENTIRE CREW?
ALL EXCEPT ONE.
THE COMMANDER OF THE AIRSHIP IS STILL MISSING.
ASK SOME OF THESE LOCALS IF THEY SAW ANYTHING ON THE ROADS NEARBY.
SERGEANT, WE THINK THERE MAY HAVE BEEN SOME PRISONERS ON BOARD.
POSSIBLY A MAN AND TWO CHILDREN.
A BOY AND A GIRL?

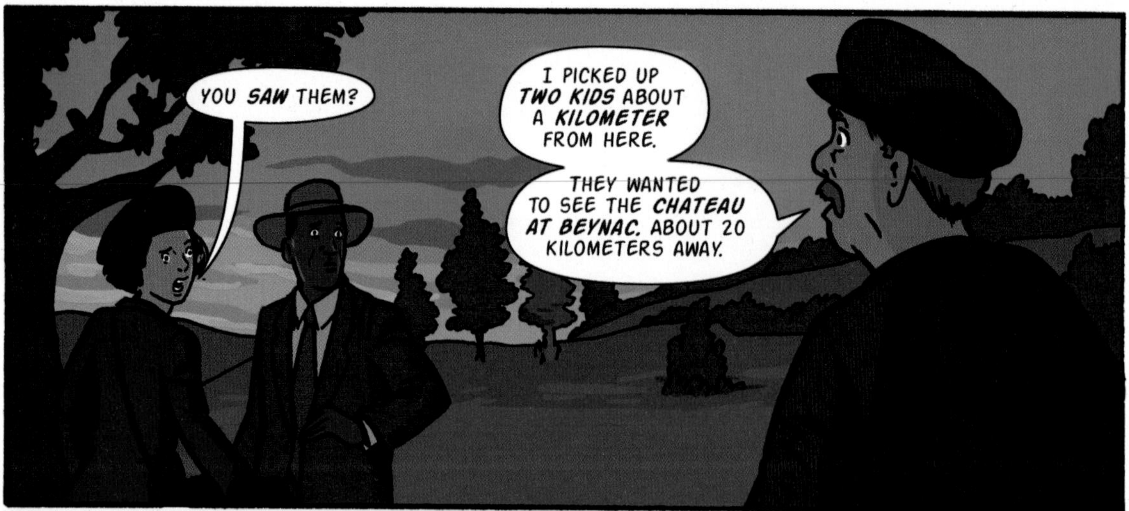
YOU SAW THEM?
I PICKED UP TWO KIDS ABOUT A KILOMETER FROM HERE.
THEY WANTED TO SEE THE CHATEAU AT BEYNAC. ABOUT 20 KILOMETERS AWAY.

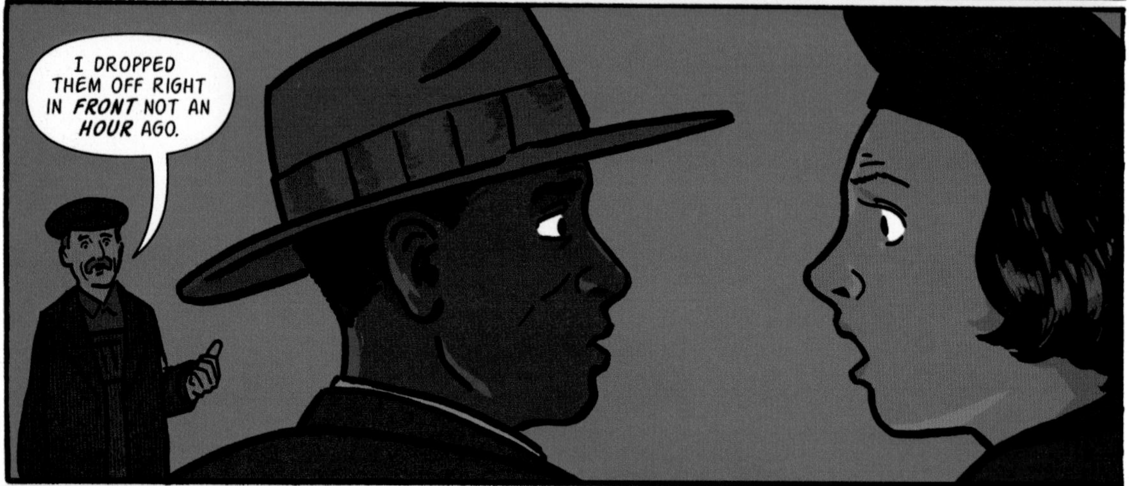
I DROPPED THEM OFF RIGHT IN FRONT NOT AN HOUR AGO.

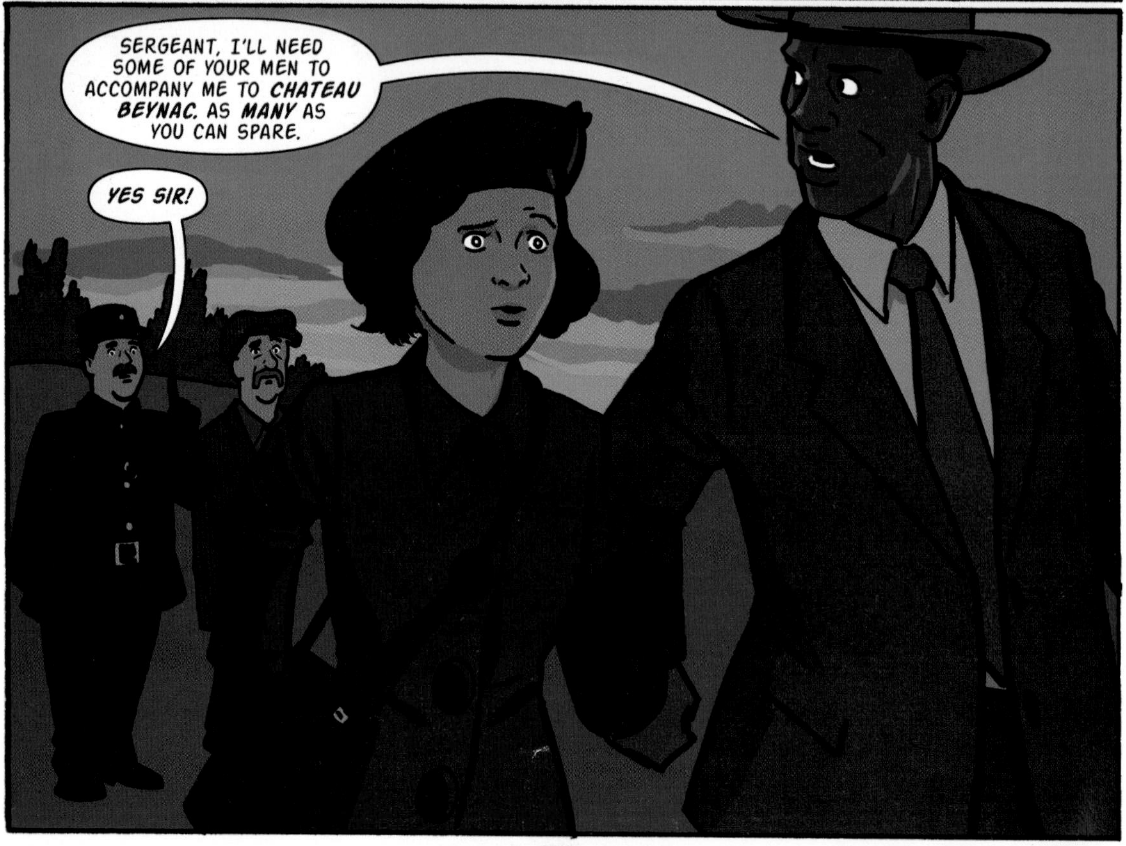
SERGEANT, I'LL NEED SOME OF YOUR MEN TO ACCOMPANY ME TO CHATEAU BEYNAC. AS MANY AS YOU CAN SPARE.
YES SIR!

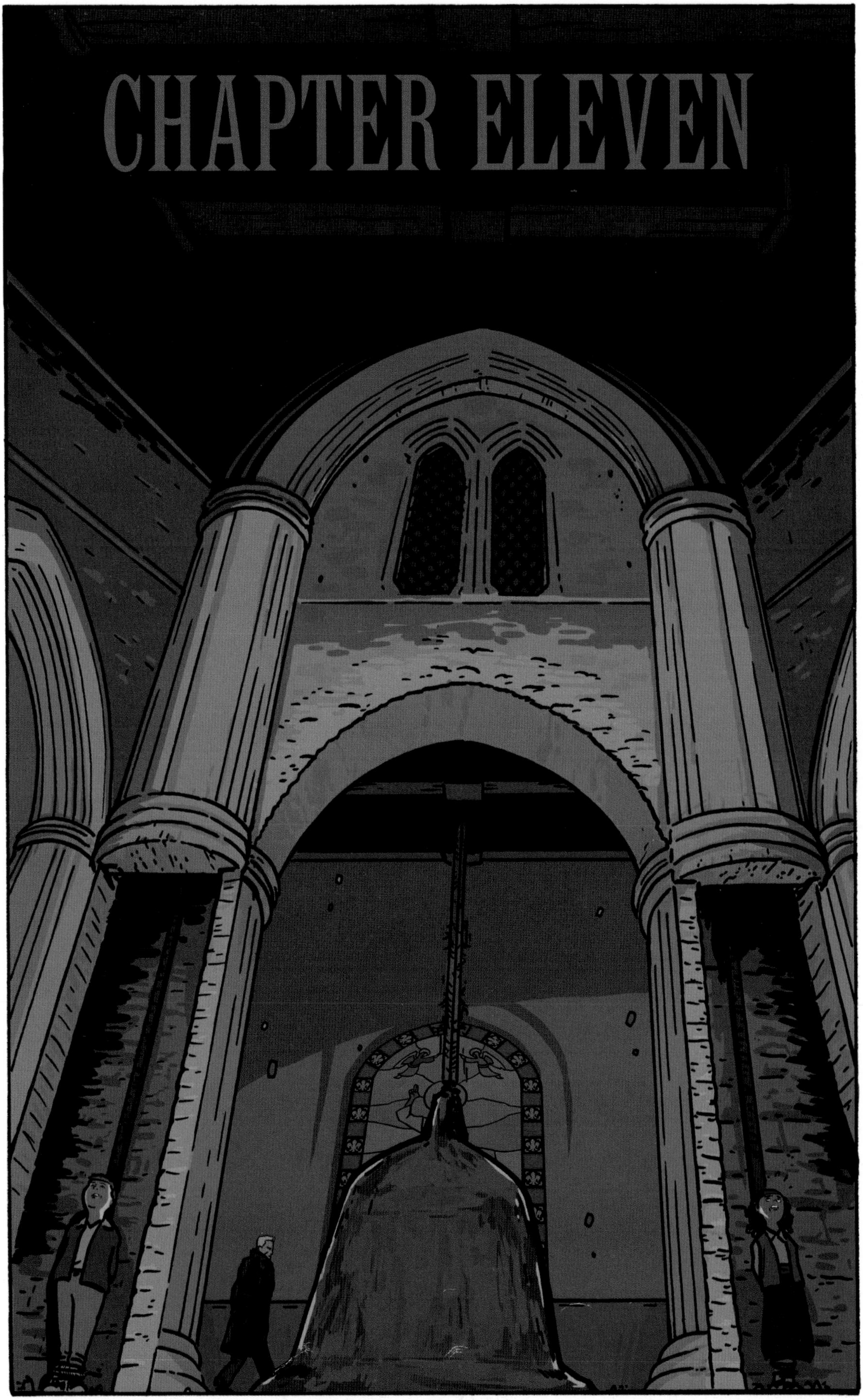
CHAPTER ELEVEN

REMARKABLE.

THESE ROPES MUST HAVE BEEN MADE FROM THE *STRONGEST HEMP* AVAILABLE.

STILL, THEY ARE SHOWING THEIR *AGE*.

I CAN'T IMAGINE THAT THEY'LL BE ABLE TO HOLD THE *WEIGHT* OF THESE *STONE COLUMNS* FOR MUCH LONGER.

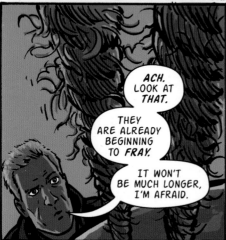

ACH. LOOK AT *THAT*.

THEY ARE ALREADY BEGINNING TO *FRAY*.

IT WON'T BE MUCH LONGER, I'M AFRAID.

Y-YOU DON'T HAVE TO *DO* THIS! YOU *HAVE* THE TREASURE.

WHY NOT JUST LET US *GO?* WE WON'T TELL *ANYONE!*

I APPRECIATE YOUR *DISCRETION*, BUT I'M *AFRAID* I CAN'T TAKE THAT CHANCE.

I DON'T KNOW WHERE YOU TWO *CAME FROM*, BUT YOU ARE CERTAINLY *RESOURCEFUL*.

AND YOU HAVE A REMARKABLE *SKILL* FOR STAYING ALIVE.

WE WILL SEE HOW LONG THAT *LASTS*.

AUF WIEDERSEHEN.

CREAK

CREAK

CLACK CLACK. CLACK

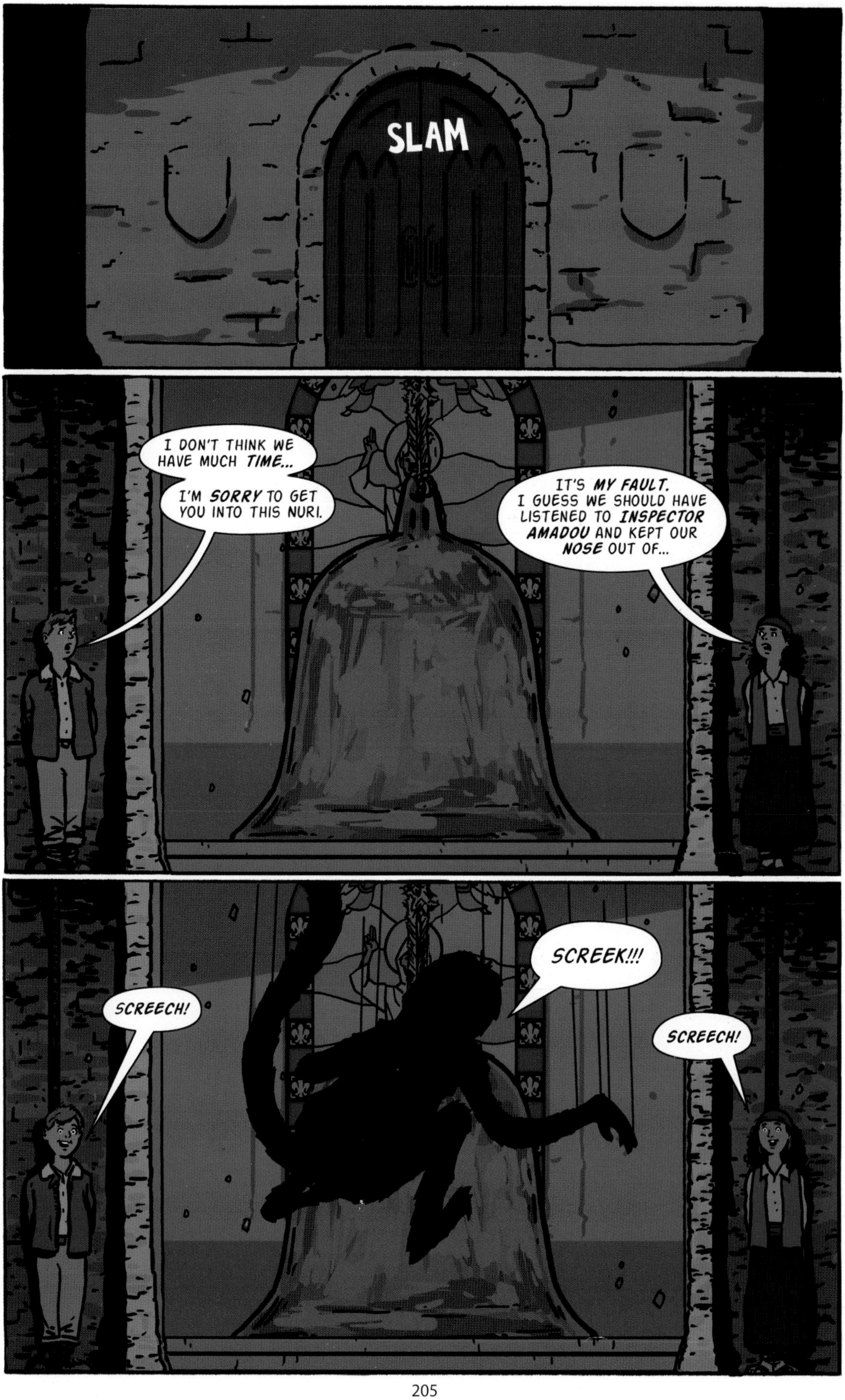
SLAM
I DON'T THINK WE HAVE MUCH TIME...
I'M SORRY TO GET YOU INTO THIS NURI.
IT'S MY FAULT. I GUESS WE SHOULD HAVE LISTENED TO INSPECTOR AMADOU AND KEPT OUR NOSE OUT OF...
SCREECH!
SCREEK!!!
SCREECH!

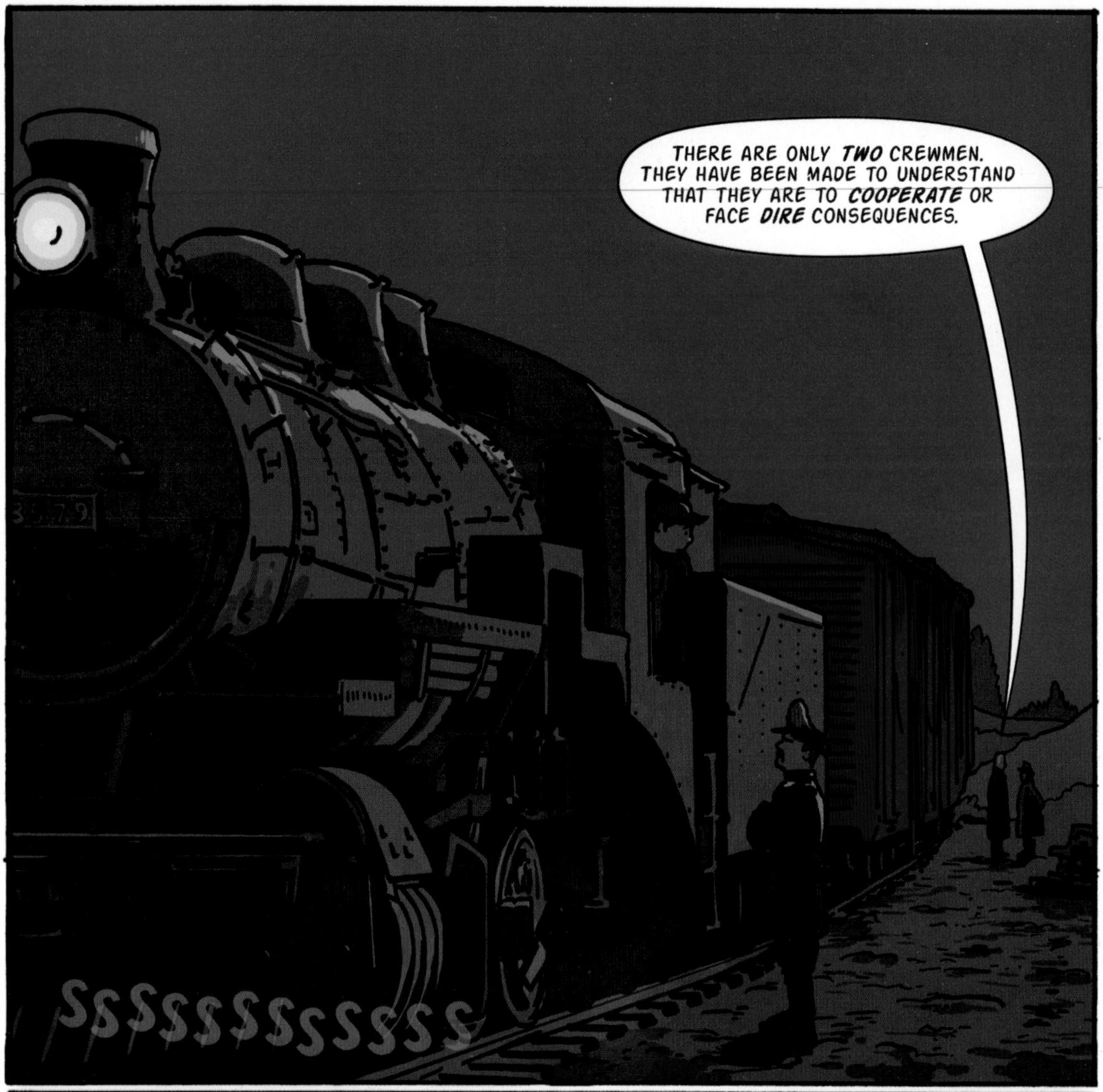
THERE ARE ONLY TWO CREWMEN. THEY HAVE BEEN MADE TO UNDERSTAND THAT THEY ARE TO COOPERATE OR FACE DIRE CONSEQUENCES.
SSSSSSSSSSSSS

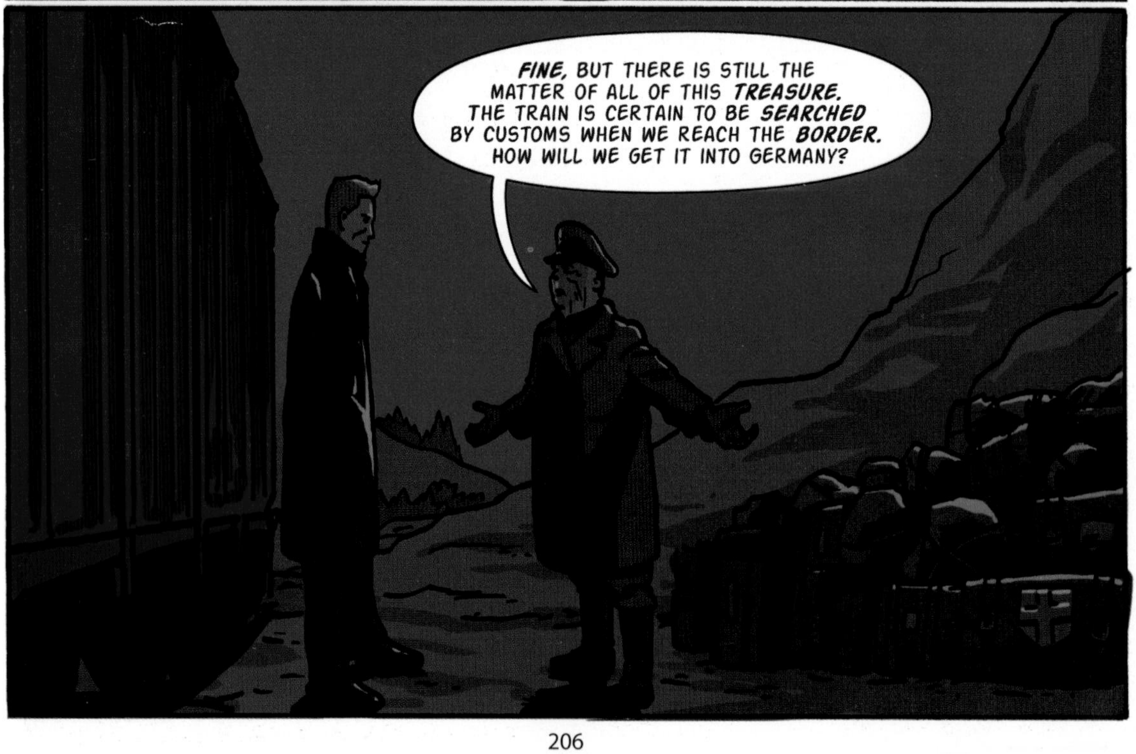
FINE, BUT THERE IS STILL THE MATTER OF ALL OF THIS TREASURE. THE TRAIN IS CERTAIN TO BE SEARCHED BY CUSTOMS WHEN WE REACH THE BORDER. HOW WILL WE GET IT INTO GERMANY?

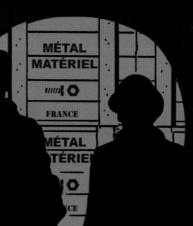

CHK

IT WILL CERTAINLY AROUSE *SUSPICION* AS IT *IS*.

SHCHHHK

BUT *PERHAPS*...

MÉTAL
MATÉRIEL

FRANCE

MÉTAL
TÉRIE

CE

COMMANDER!

COME OVER HERE, AND BRING THE TWO *PRISONERS* WITH YOU.

WE HAVE SOME *PACKING* TO DO!

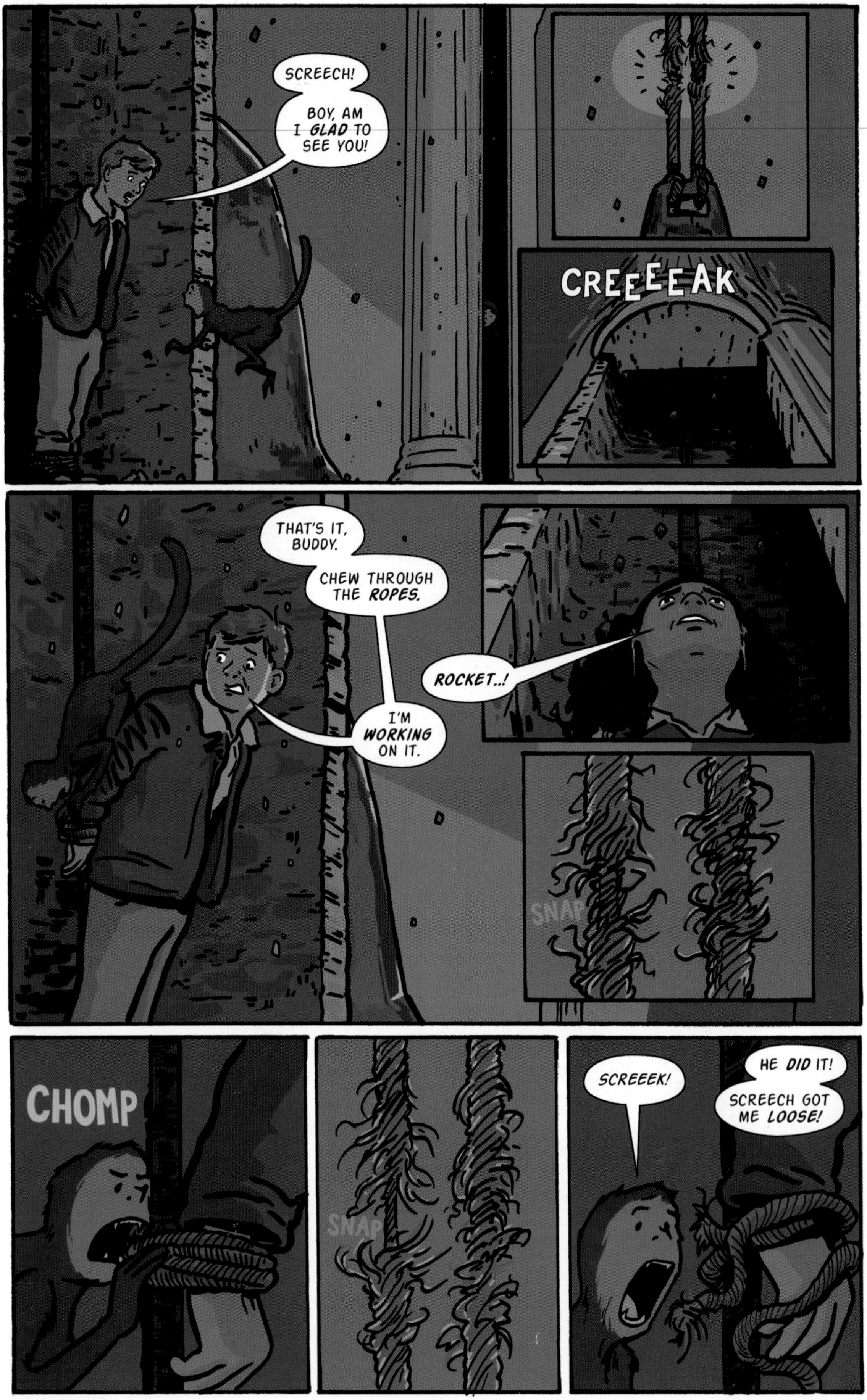
SCREECH!
BOY, AM I GLAD TO SEE YOU!
CREEEEAK
THAT'S IT, BUDDY.
CHEW THROUGH THE ROPES.
I'M WORKING ON IT.
ROCKET..!
SNAP
CHOMP
SNAP
SCREEEK!
HE DID IT!
SCREECH GOT ME LOOSE!

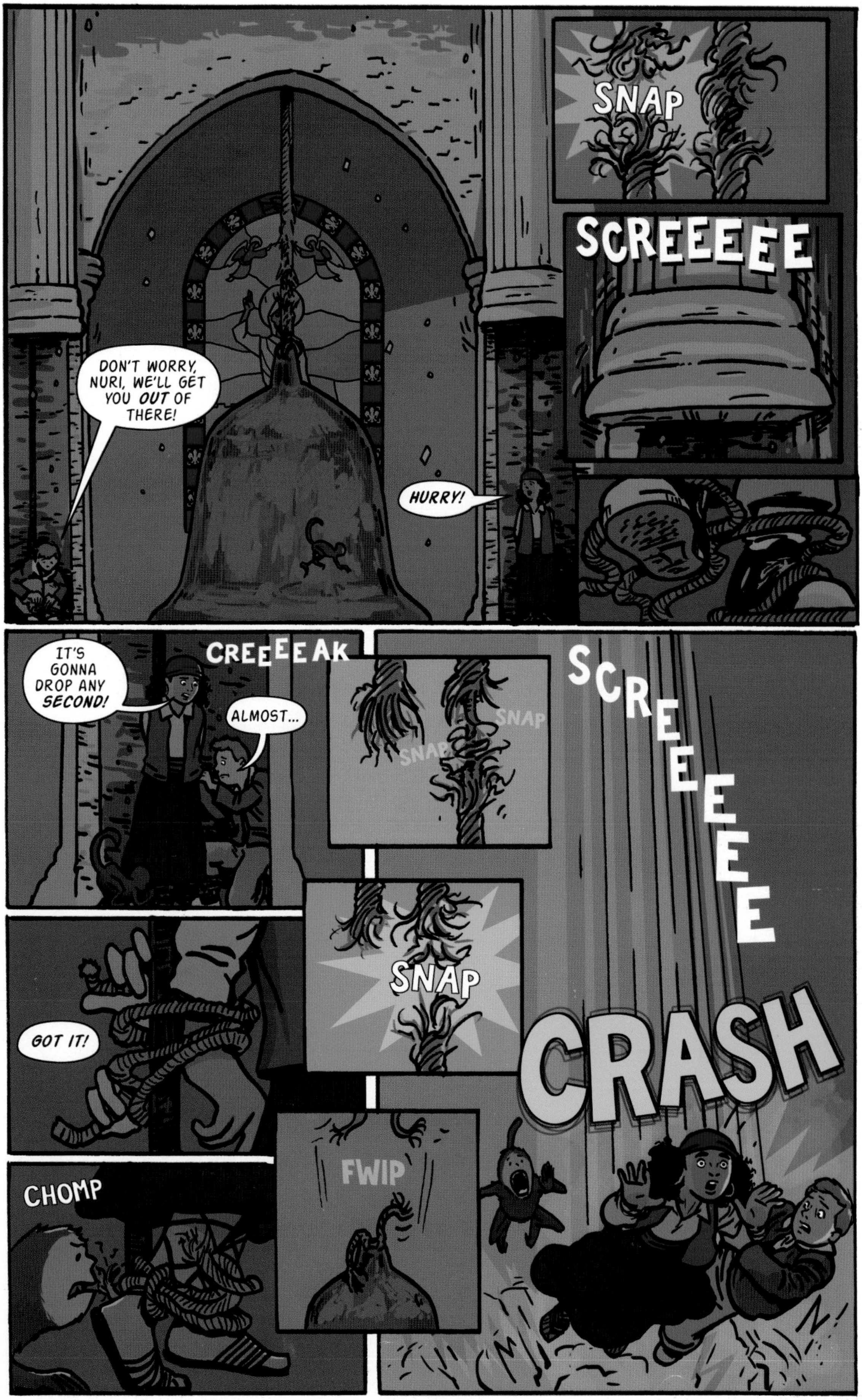
SNAP
SCREEEEEE
DON'T WORRY, NURI, WE'LL GET YOU OUT OF THERE!
HURRY!
IT'S GONNA DROP ANY SECOND!
CREEEEAK
ALMOST...
SNAP
SNAP
GOT IT!
SNAP
CHOMP
FWIP
SCREEEEEE
CRASH

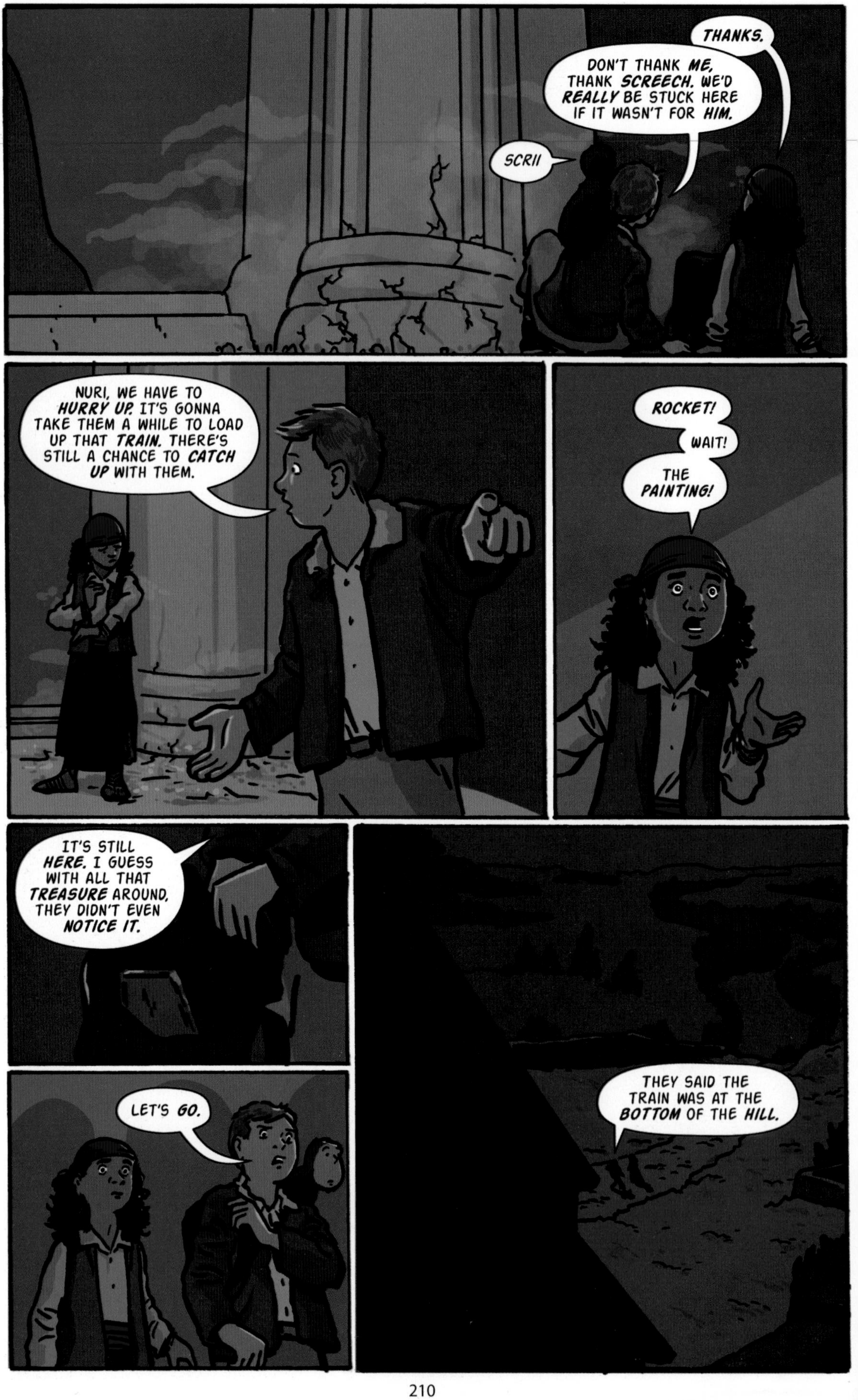
THANKS.
DON'T THANK ME, THANK SCREECH. WE'D REALLY BE STUCK HERE IF IT WASN'T FOR HIM.
SCRII
NURI, WE HAVE TO HURRY UP. IT'S GONNA TAKE THEM A WHILE TO LOAD UP THAT TRAIN. THERE'S STILL A CHANCE TO CATCH UP WITH THEM.
ROCKET!
WAIT!
THE PAINTING!
IT'S STILL HERE. I GUESS WITH ALL THAT TREASURE AROUND, THEY DIDN'T EVEN NOTICE IT.
LET'S GO.
THEY SAID THE TRAIN WAS AT THE BOTTOM OF THE HILL.

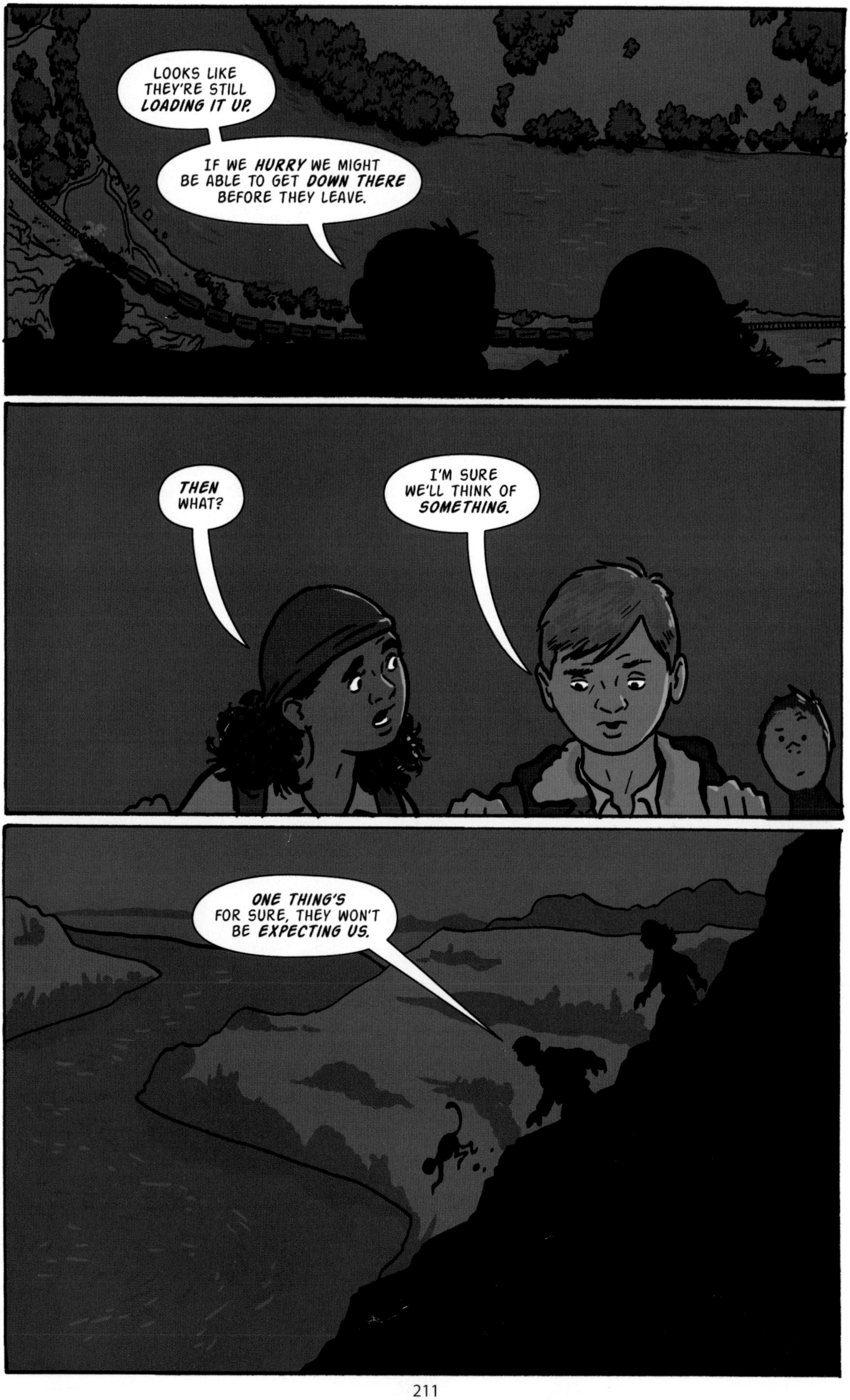
LOOKS LIKE THEY'RE STILL ***LOADING IT UP.***
IF WE ***HURRY*** WE MIGHT BE ABLE TO GET ***DOWN THERE*** BEFORE THEY LEAVE.
THEN WHAT?
I'M SURE WE'LL THINK OF ***SOMETHING.***
ONE THING'S FOR SURE, THEY WON'T BE ***EXPECTING US.***

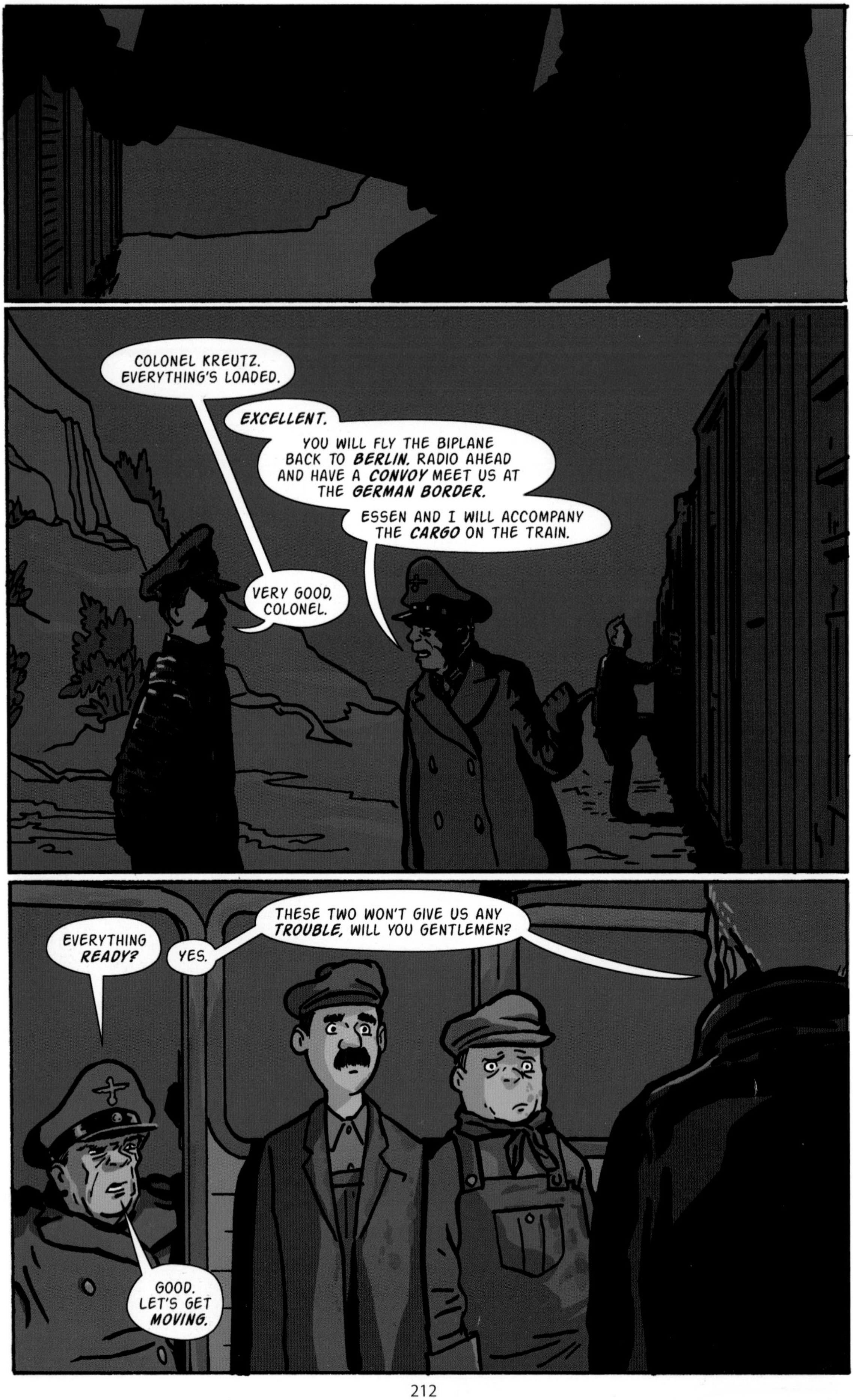
COLONEL KREUTZ. EVERYTHING'S LOADED.
EXCELLENT.
YOU WILL FLY THE BIPLANE BACK TO BERLIN. RADIO AHEAD AND HAVE A CONVOY MEET US AT THE GERMAN BORDER.
ESSEN AND I WILL ACCOMPANY THE CARGO ON THE TRAIN.
VERY GOOD, COLONEL.
EVERYTHING READY?
YES.
THESE TWO WON'T GIVE US ANY TROUBLE, WILL YOU GENTLEMEN?
GOOD. LET'S GET MOVING.

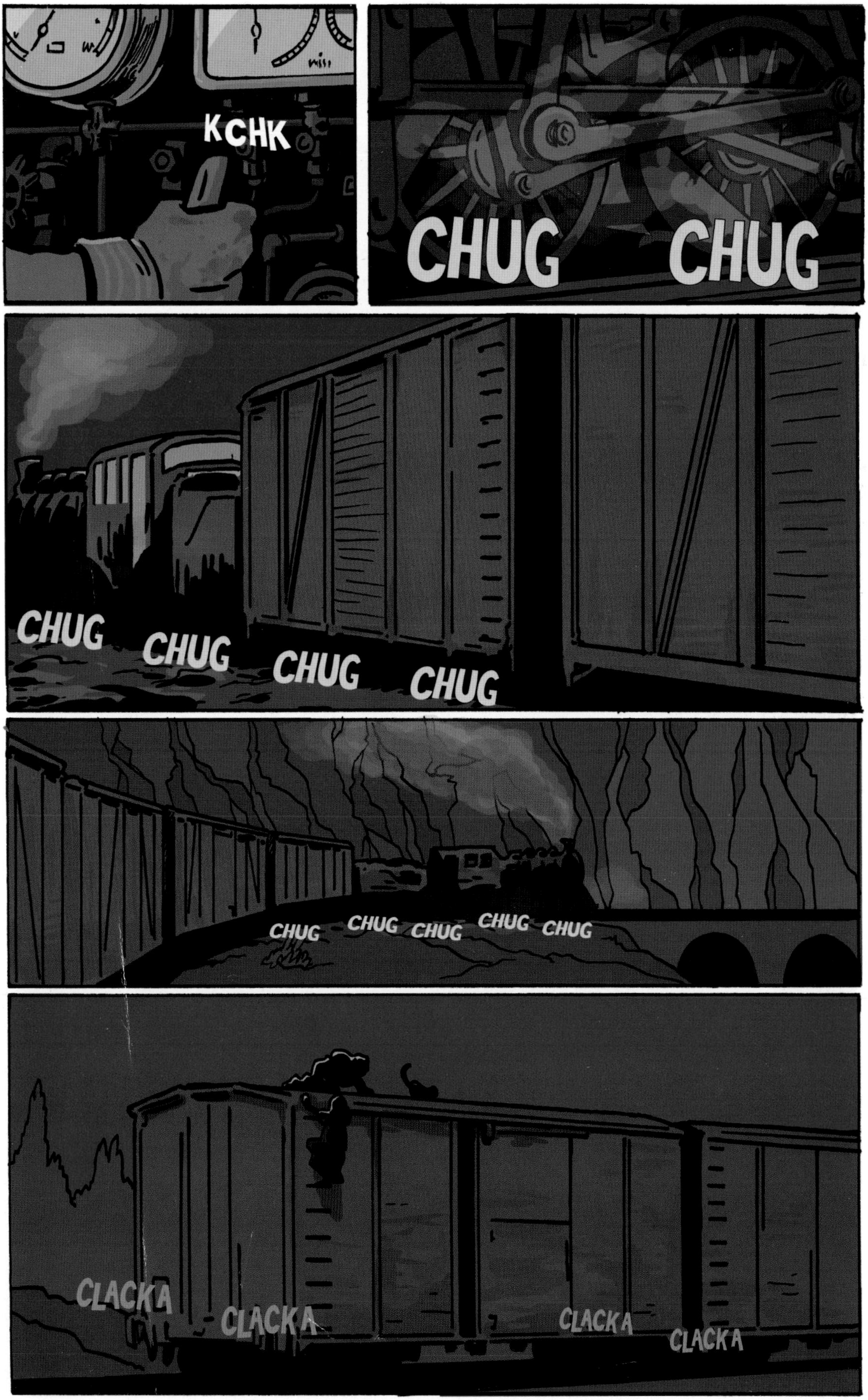
KCHK
CHUG CHUG
CHUG CHUG CHUG CHUG
CHUG CHUG CHUG CHUG CHUG
CLACKA CLACKA CLACKA CLACKA

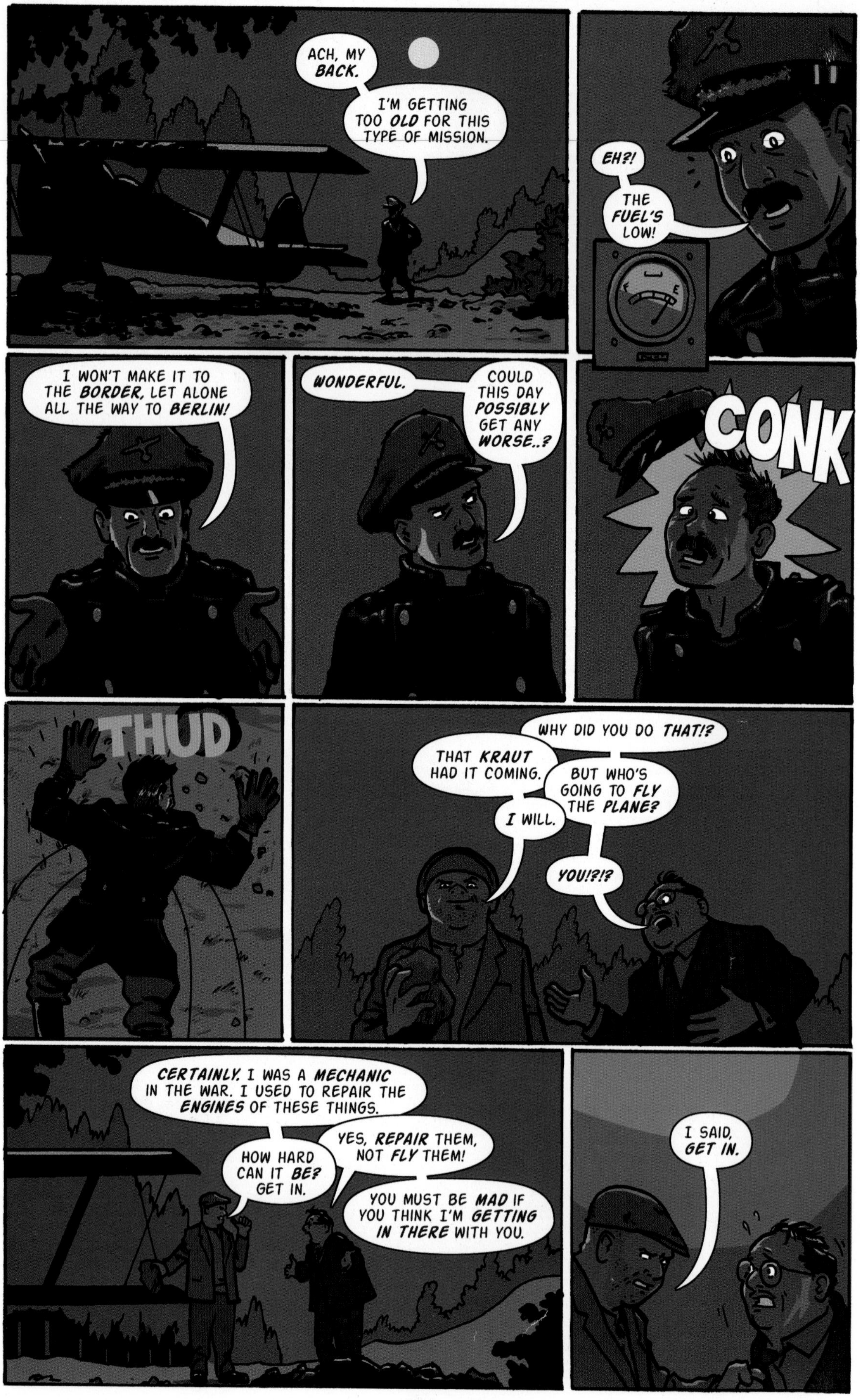
ACH, MY BACK.
I'M GETTING TOO OLD FOR THIS TYPE OF MISSION.
EH?!
THE FUEL'S LOW!
F
E
I WON'T MAKE IT TO THE BORDER, LET ALONE ALL THE WAY TO BERLIN!
WONDERFUL.
COULD THIS DAY POSSIBLY GET ANY WORSE..?
CONK
THUD
WHY DID YOU DO THAT!?
THAT KRAUT HAD IT COMING.
BUT WHO'S GOING TO FLY THE PLANE?
I WILL.
YOU!?!?
CERTAINLY. I WAS A MECHANIC IN THE WAR. I USED TO REPAIR THE ENGINES OF THESE THINGS.
HOW HARD CAN IT BE? GET IN.
YES, REPAIR THEM, NOT FLY THEM!
YOU MUST BE MAD IF YOU THINK I'M GETTING IN THERE WITH YOU.
I SAID, GET IN.

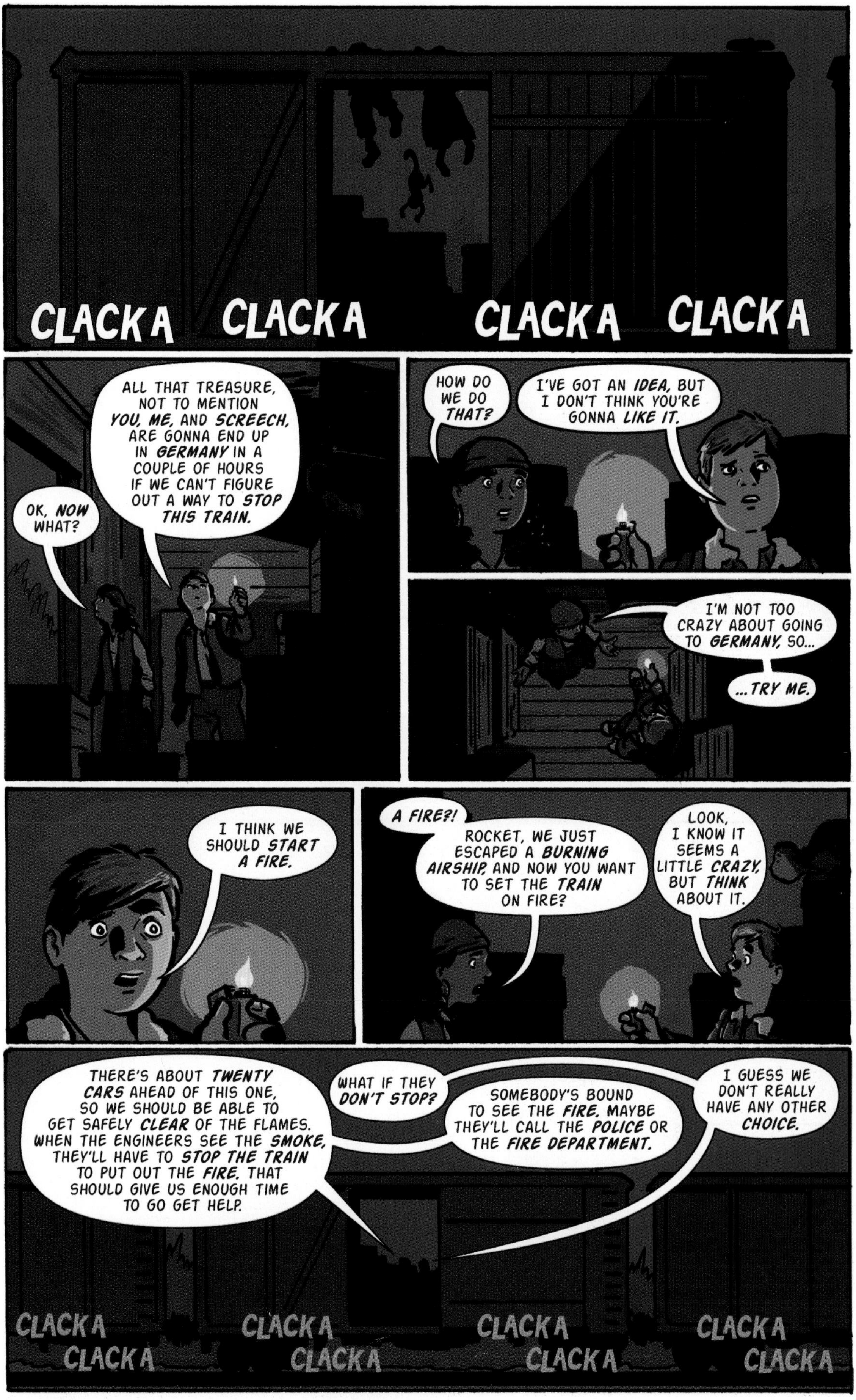
CLACKA CLACKA CLACKA CLACKA
ALL THAT TREASURE, NOT TO MENTION YOU, ME, AND SCREECH, ARE GONNA END UP IN GERMANY IN A COUPLE OF HOURS IF WE CAN'T FIGURE OUT A WAY TO STOP THIS TRAIN.
OK, NOW WHAT?
HOW DO WE DO THAT?
I'VE GOT AN IDEA, BUT I DON'T THINK YOU'RE GONNA LIKE IT.
I'M NOT TOO CRAZY ABOUT GOING TO GERMANY, SO...
...TRY ME.
I THINK WE SHOULD START A FIRE.
A FIRE?!
ROCKET, WE JUST ESCAPED A BURNING AIRSHIP, AND NOW YOU WANT TO SET THE TRAIN ON FIRE?
LOOK, I KNOW IT SEEMS A LITTLE CRAZY, BUT THINK ABOUT IT.
THERE'S ABOUT TWENTY CARS AHEAD OF THIS ONE, SO WE SHOULD BE ABLE TO GET SAFELY CLEAR OF THE FLAMES. WHEN THE ENGINEERS SEE THE SMOKE, THEY'LL HAVE TO STOP THE TRAIN TO PUT OUT THE FIRE. THAT SHOULD GIVE US ENOUGH TIME TO GO GET HELP.
WHAT IF THEY DON'T STOP?
SOMEBODY'S BOUND TO SEE THE FIRE. MAYBE THEY'LL CALL THE POLICE OR THE FIRE DEPARTMENT.
I GUESS WE DON'T REALLY HAVE ANY OTHER CHOICE.
CLACKA CLACKA CLACKA CLACKA CLACKA CLACKA CLACKA CLACKA

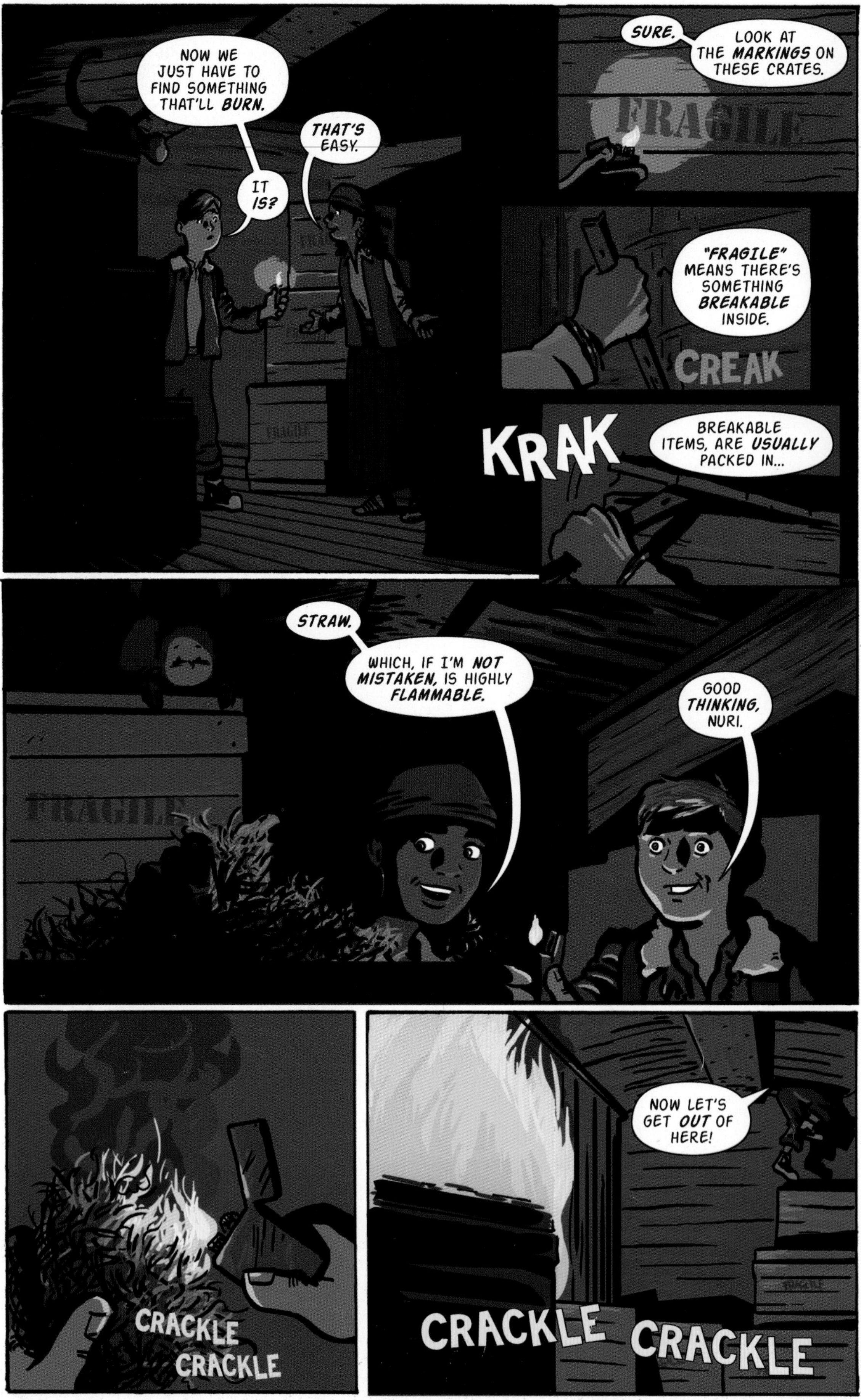
NOW WE JUST HAVE TO FIND SOMETHING THAT'LL BURN.
THAT'S EASY.
IT IS?
SURE.
LOOK AT THE MARKINGS ON THESE CRATES.
FRAGILE
"FRAGILE" MEANS THERE'S SOMETHING BREAKABLE INSIDE.
CREAK
KRAK
BREAKABLE ITEMS, ARE USUALLY PACKED IN...
STRAW.
WHICH, IF I'M NOT MISTAKEN, IS HIGHLY FLAMMABLE.
GOOD THINKING, NURI.
FRAGILE
CRACKLE
CRACKLE
NOW LET'S GET OUT OF HERE!
CRACKLE CRACKLE

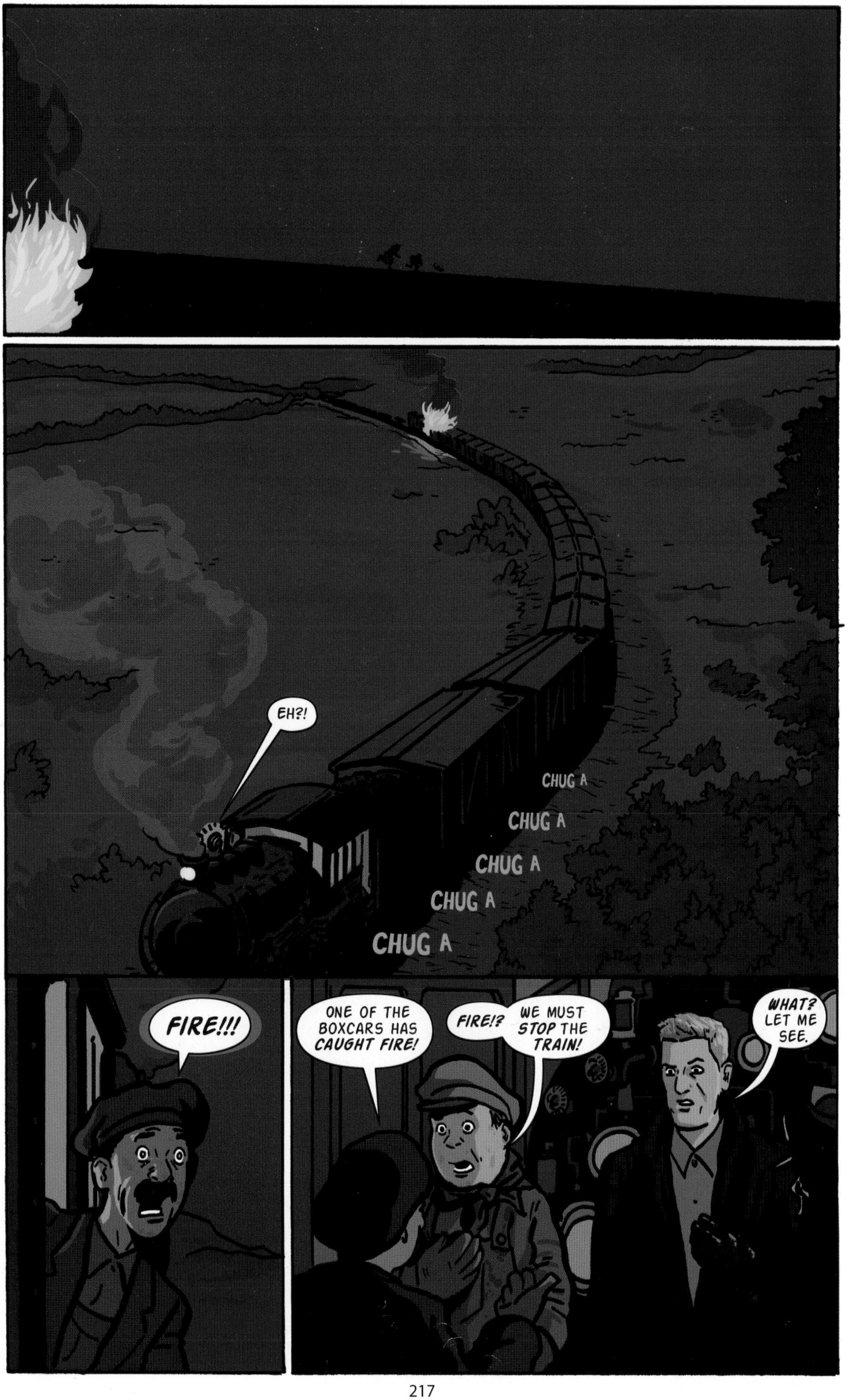
EH?!
CHUG A
CHUG A
CHUG A
CHUG A
CHUG A
FIRE!!!
ONE OF THE BOXCARS HAS CAUGHT FIRE!
FIRE!?
WE MUST STOP THE TRAIN!
WHAT? LET ME SEE.

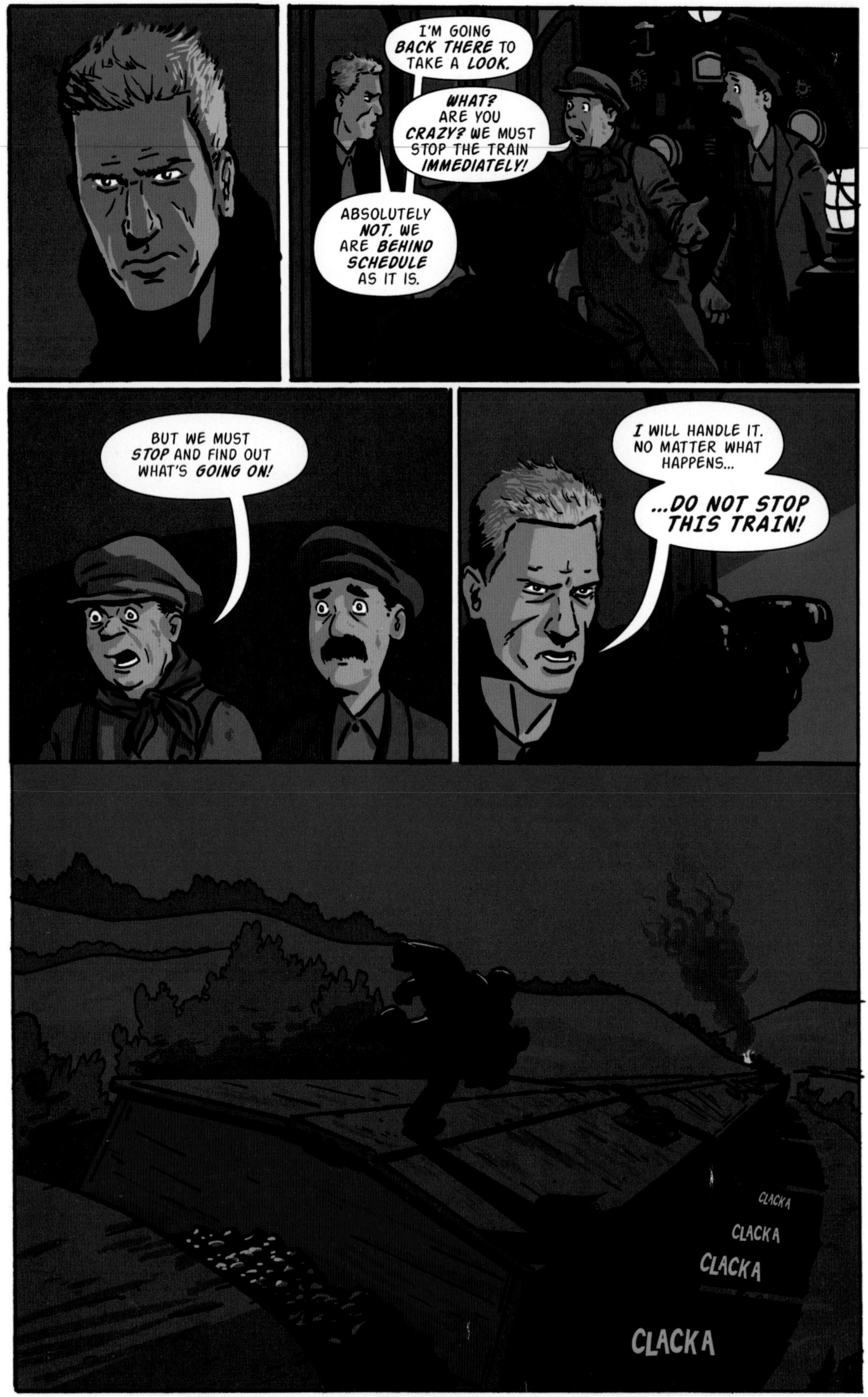
I'M GOING BACK THERE TO TAKE A LOOK.
WHAT? ARE YOU CRAZY? WE MUST STOP THE TRAIN IMMEDIATELY!
ABSOLUTELY NOT. WE ARE BEHIND SCHEDULE AS IT IS.
BUT WE MUST STOP AND FIND OUT WHAT'S GOING ON!
I WILL HANDLE IT. NO MATTER WHAT HAPPENS...
...DO NOT STOP THIS TRAIN!
CLACKA
CLACKA
CLACKA
CLACKA

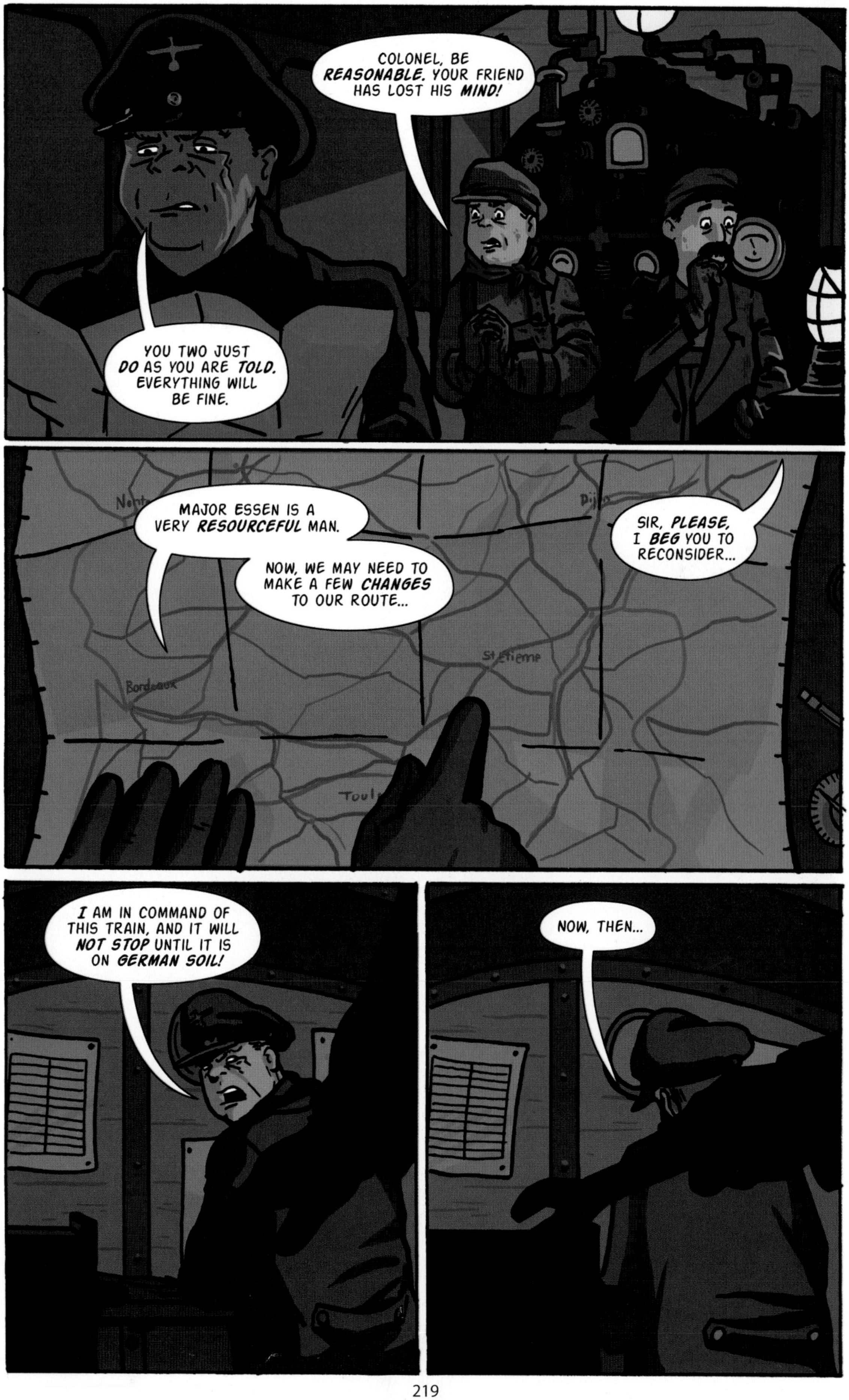
COLONEL, BE REASONABLE. YOUR FRIEND HAS LOST HIS MIND!
YOU TWO JUST DO AS YOU ARE TOLD. EVERYTHING WILL BE FINE.
MAJOR ESSEN IS A VERY RESOURCEFUL MAN.
NOW, WE MAY NEED TO MAKE A FEW CHANGES TO OUR ROUTE...
SIR, PLEASE, I BEG YOU TO RECONSIDER...
St Etienne
Bordeaux
I AM IN COMMAND OF THIS TRAIN, AND IT WILL NOT STOP UNTIL IT IS ON GERMAN SOIL!
NOW, THEN...

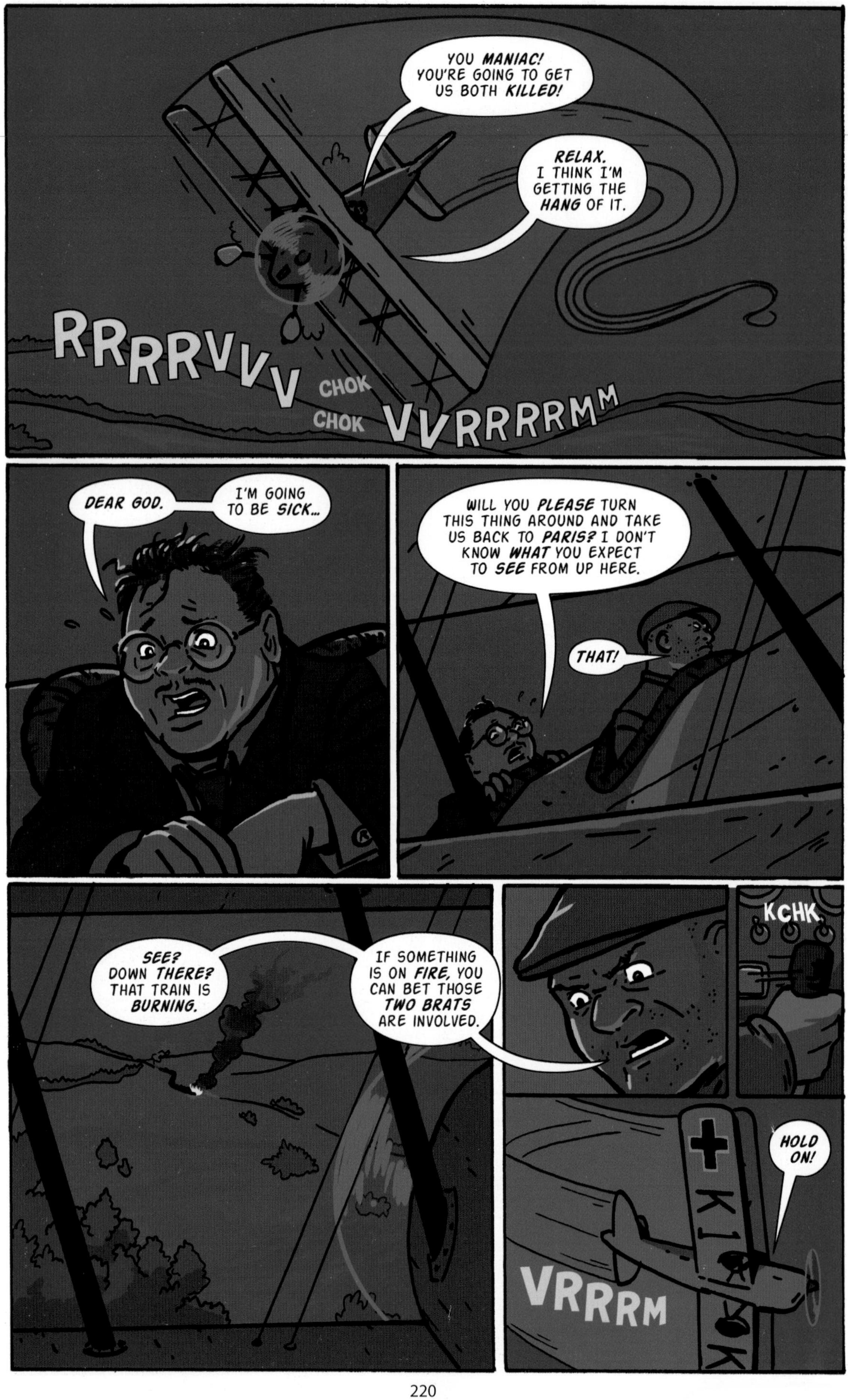

YOU MANIAC! YOU'RE GOING TO GET US BOTH KILLED!
RELAX. I THINK I'M GETTING THE HANG OF IT.
RRRRVVVV
CHOK
CHOK
VVRRRRMM
DEAR GOD.
I'M GOING TO BE SICK...
WILL YOU PLEASE TURN THIS THING AROUND AND TAKE US BACK TO PARIS? I DON'T KNOW WHAT YOU EXPECT TO SEE FROM UP HERE.
THAT!
SEE? DOWN THERE? THAT TRAIN IS BURNING.
IF SOMETHING IS ON FIRE, YOU CAN BET THOSE TWO BRATS ARE INVOLVED.
KCHK
HOLD ON!
VRRRM

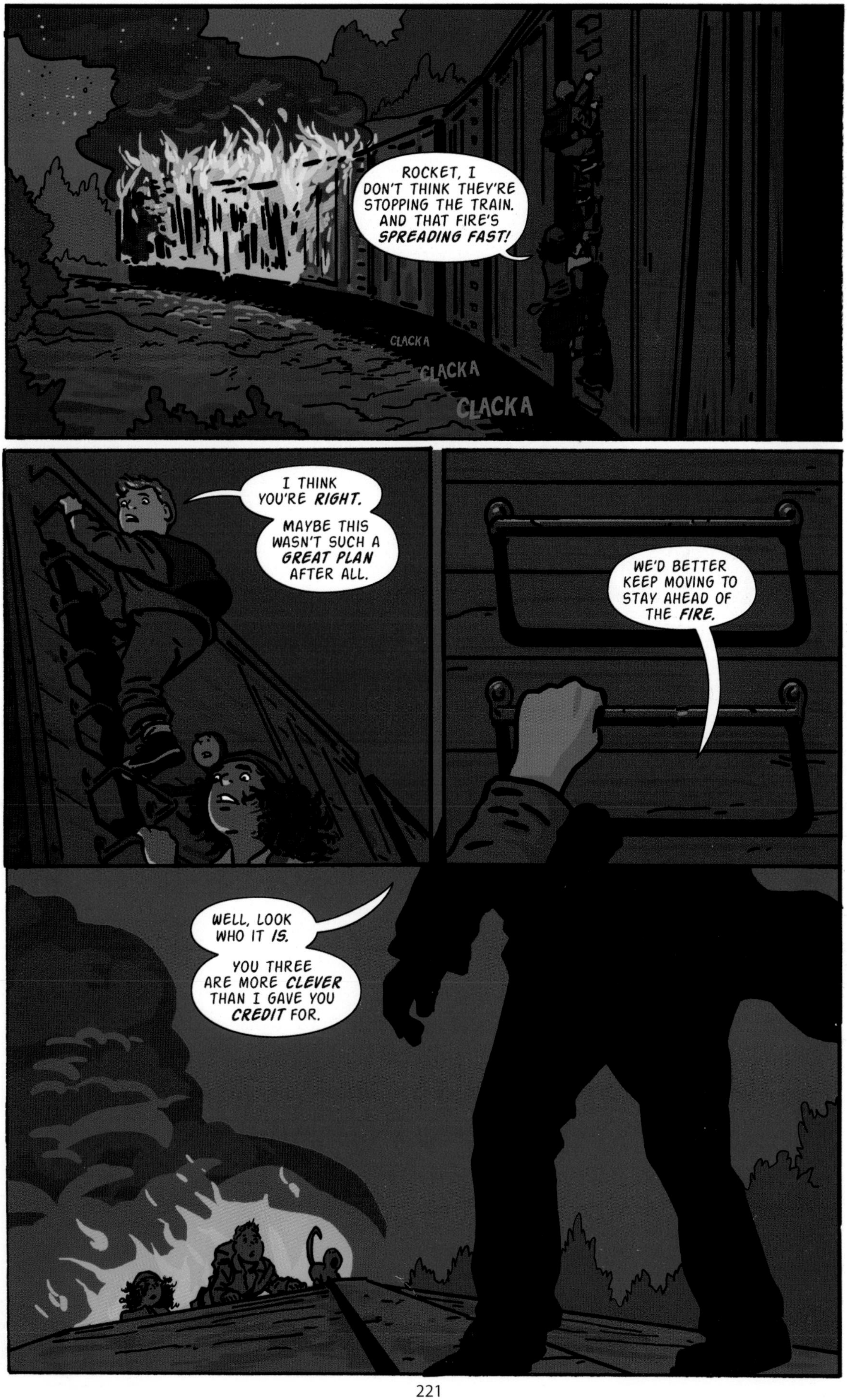
ROCKET, I DON'T THINK THEY'RE STOPPING THE TRAIN. AND THAT FIRE'S SPREADING FAST!
CLACKA
CLACKA
CLACKA
I THINK YOU'RE RIGHT.
MAYBE THIS WASN'T SUCH A GREAT PLAN AFTER ALL.
WE'D BETTER KEEP MOVING TO STAY AHEAD OF THE FIRE.
WELL, LOOK WHO IT IS.
YOU THREE ARE MORE CLEVER THAN I GAVE YOU CREDIT FOR.

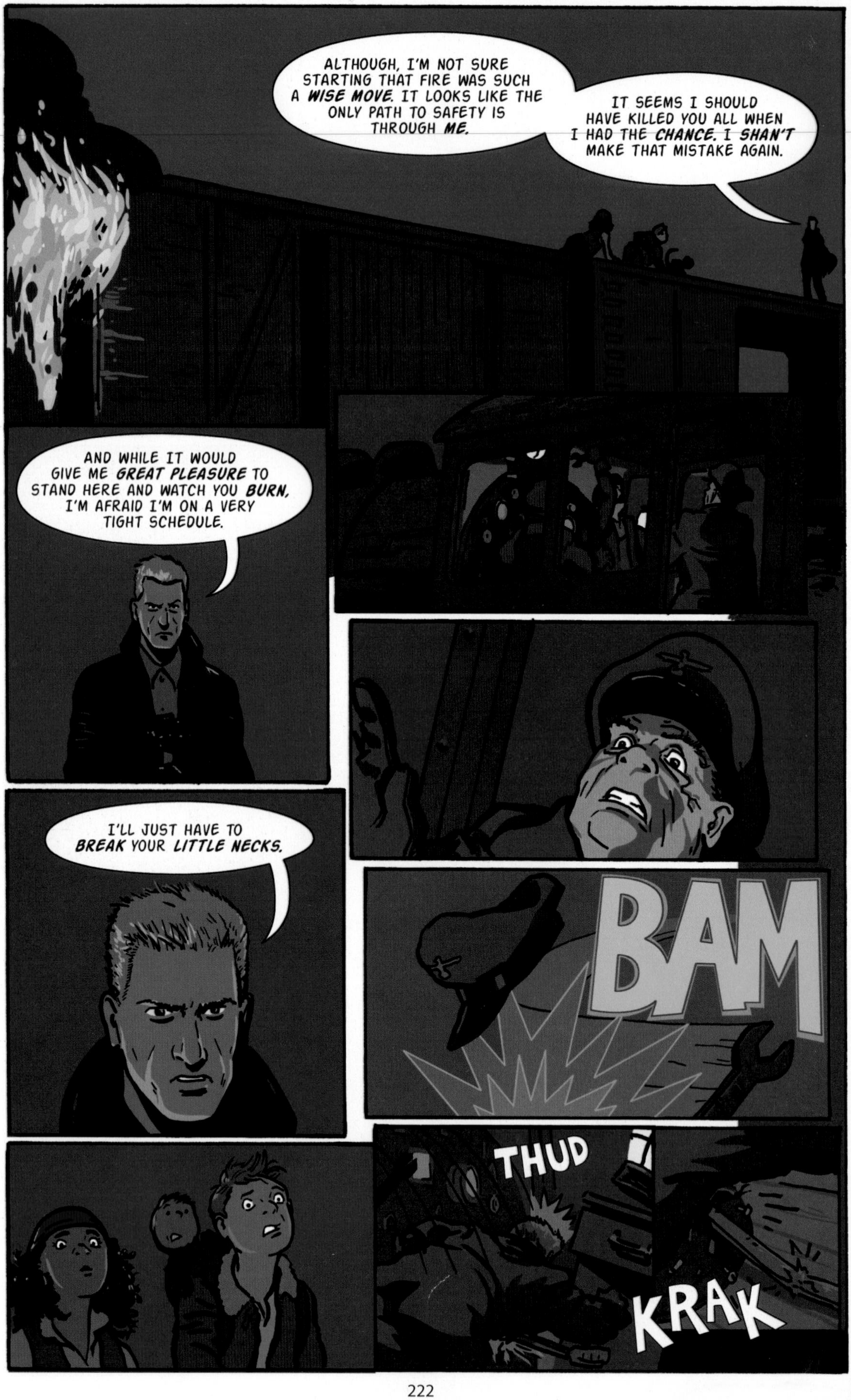
ALTHOUGH, I'M NOT SURE STARTING THAT FIRE WAS SUCH A WISE MOVE. IT LOOKS LIKE THE ONLY PATH TO SAFETY IS THROUGH ME.
IT SEEMS I SHOULD HAVE KILLED YOU ALL WHEN I HAD THE CHANCE. I SHAN'T MAKE THAT MISTAKE AGAIN.
AND WHILE IT WOULD GIVE ME GREAT PLEASURE TO STAND HERE AND WATCH YOU BURN, I'M AFRAID I'M ON A VERY TIGHT SCHEDULE.
I'LL JUST HAVE TO BREAK YOUR LITTLE NECKS.
BAM
THUD
KRAK

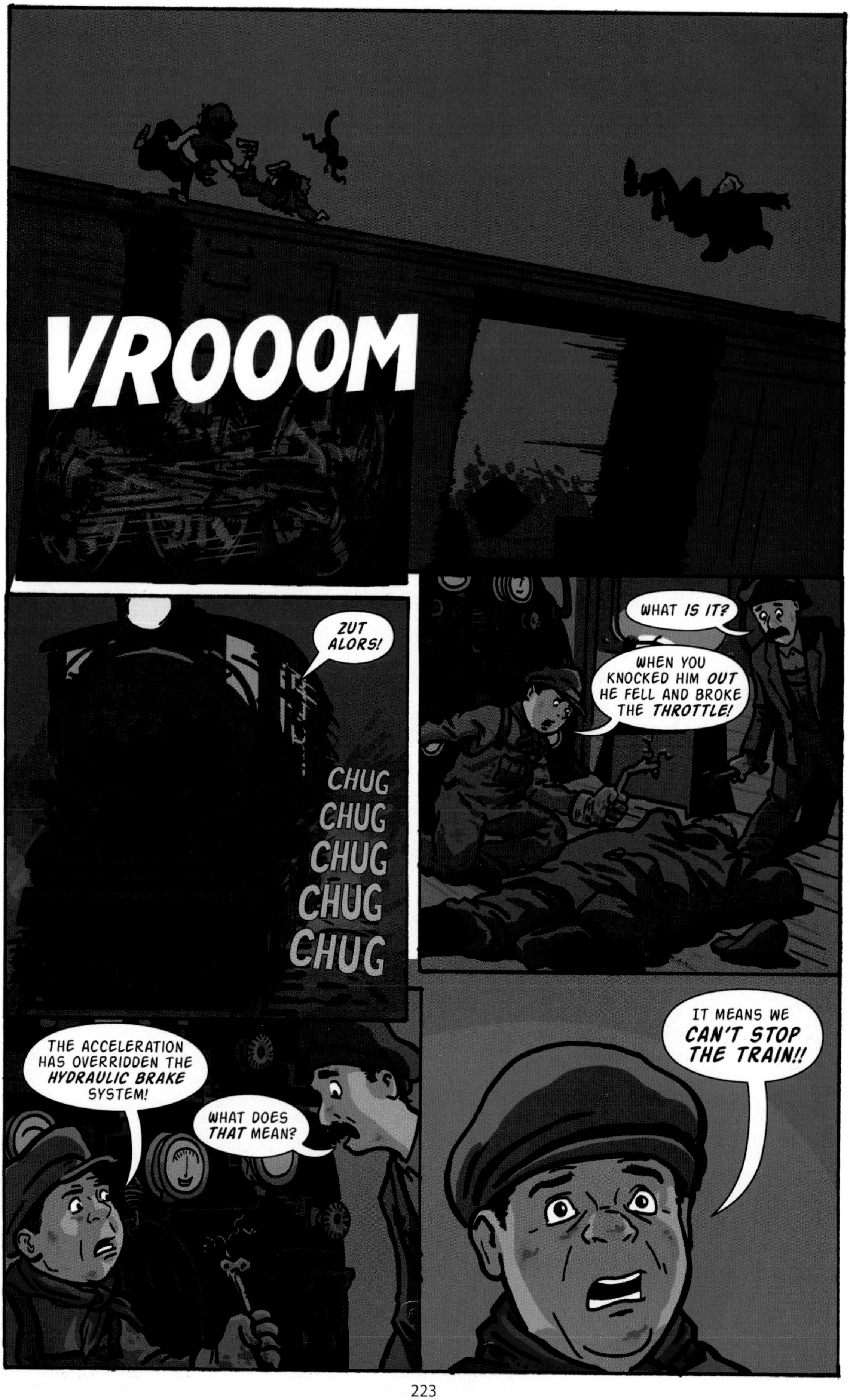
VROOOM
ZUT ALORS!
CHUG CHUG CHUG CHUG CHUG
WHAT IS IT?
WHEN YOU KNOCKED HIM OUT HE FELL AND BROKE THE THROTTLE!
THE ACCELERATION HAS OVERRIDDEN THE HYDRAULIC BRAKE SYSTEM!
WHAT DOES THAT MEAN?
IT MEANS WE CAN'T STOP THE TRAIN!!

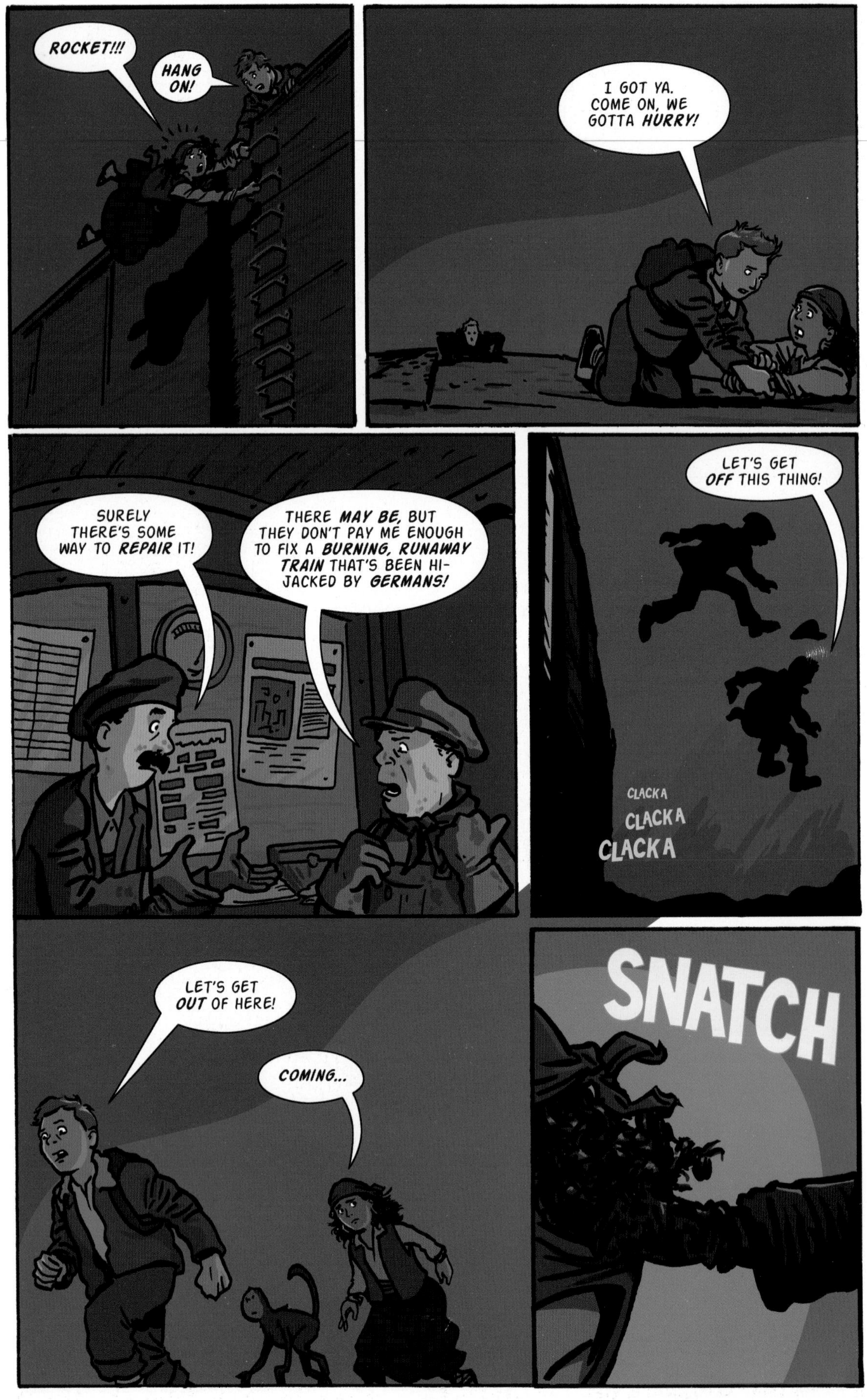
ROCKET!!!
HANG ON!
I GOT YA. COME ON, WE GOTTA HURRY!
SURELY THERE'S SOME WAY TO REPAIR IT!
THERE MAY BE, BUT THEY DON'T PAY ME ENOUGH TO FIX A BURNING, RUNAWAY TRAIN THAT'S BEEN HI-JACKED BY GERMANS!
LET'S GET OFF THIS THING!
CLACKA
CLACKA
CLACKA
LET'S GET OUT OF HERE!
COMING...
SNATCH

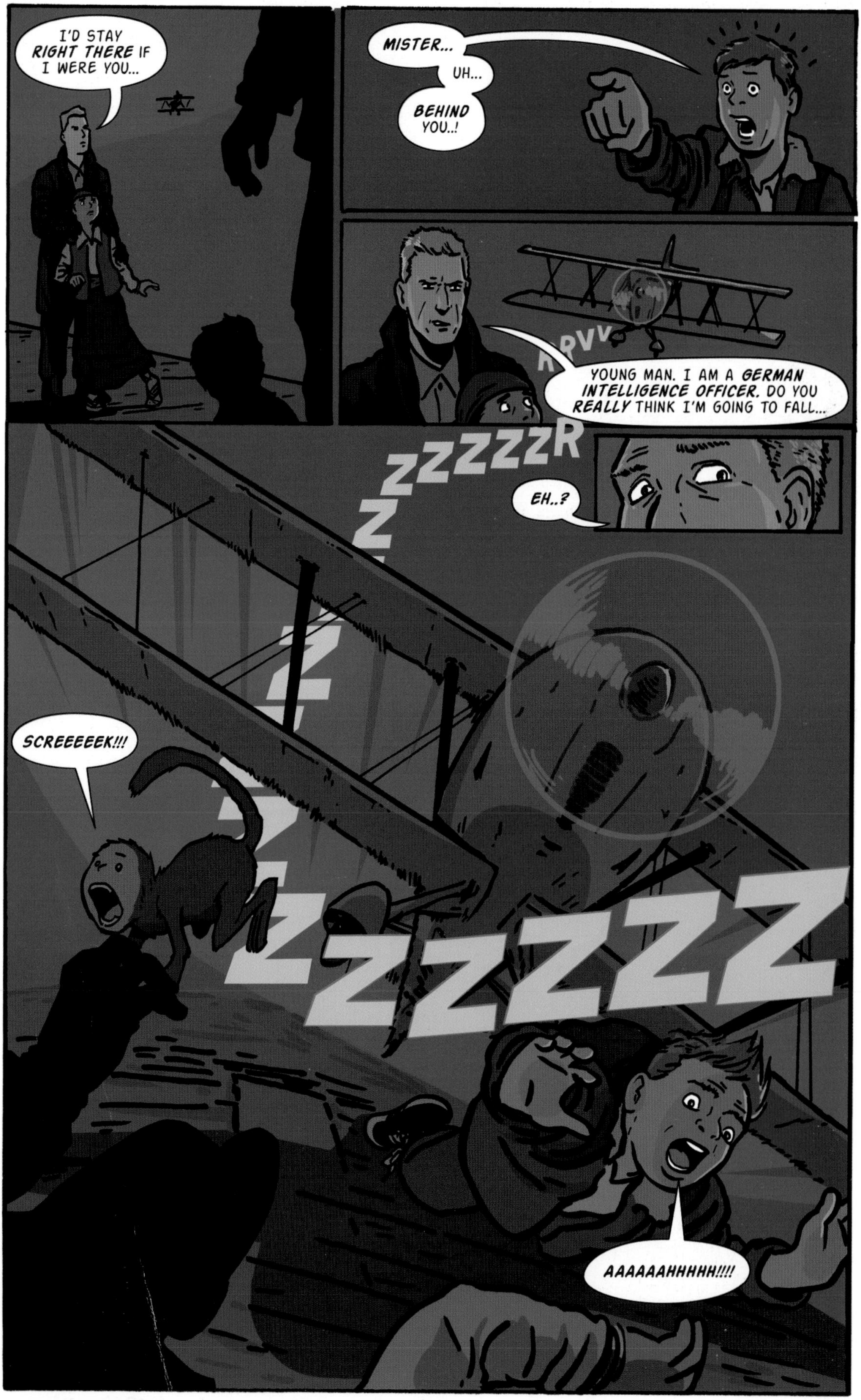

I'D STAY RIGHT THERE IF I WERE YOU...
MISTER... UH... BEHIND YOU..!
RRVV
YOUNG MAN. I AM A GERMAN INTELLIGENCE OFFICER. DO YOU REALLY THINK I'M GOING TO FALL...
ZZZZZZR
EH..?
SCREEEEEK!!!
ZZZZZZ
AAAAAAHHHHH!!!!

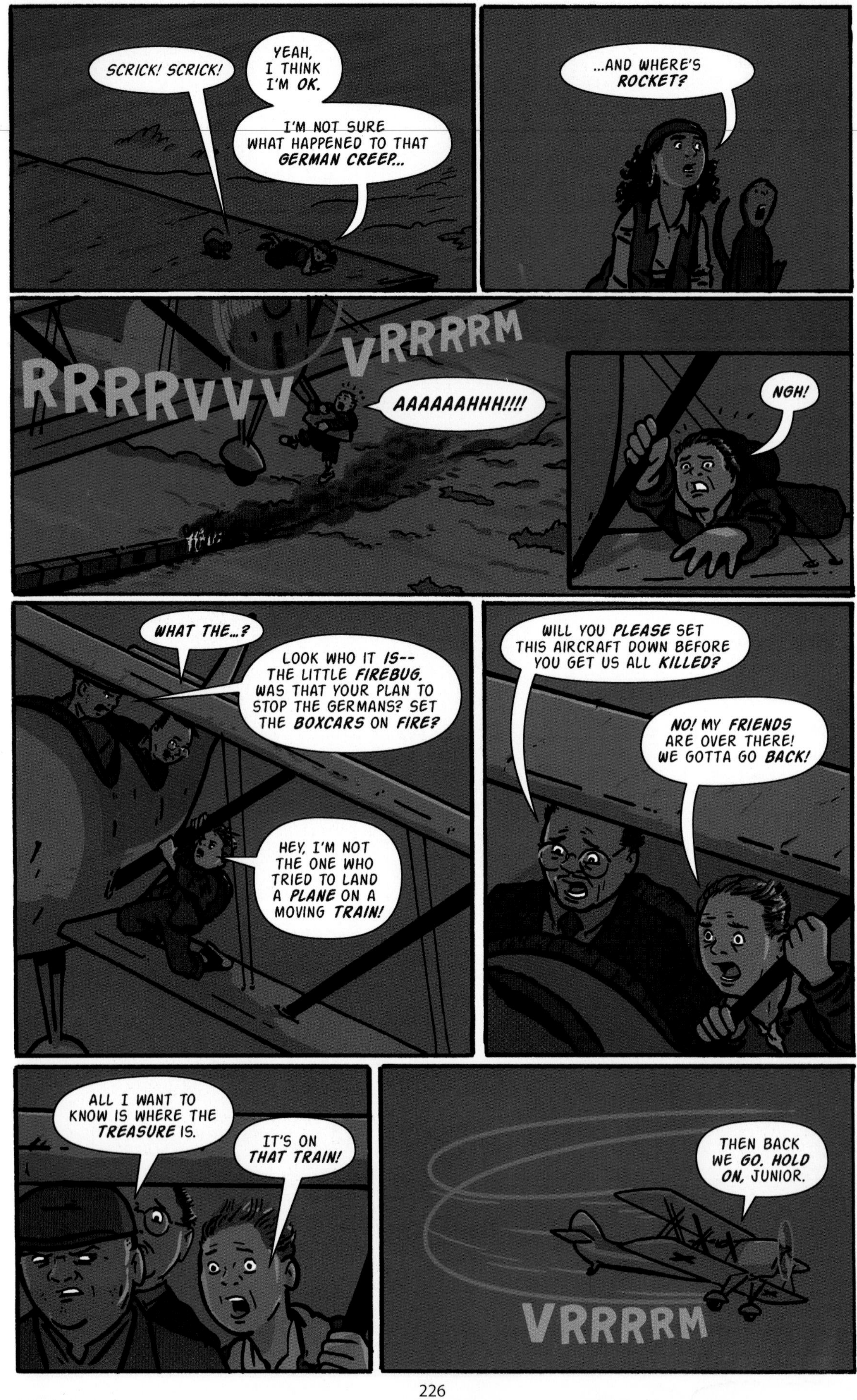
SCRICK! SCRICK!
YEAH, I THINK I'M OK.
I'M NOT SURE WHAT HAPPENED TO THAT GERMAN CREEP...
...AND WHERE'S ROCKET?
RRRRVVVV
VRRRRM
AAAAAAHHH!!!!
NGH!
WHAT THE...?
LOOK WHO IT IS-- THE LITTLE FIREBUG. WAS THAT YOUR PLAN TO STOP THE GERMANS? SET THE BOXCARS ON FIRE?
HEY, I'M NOT THE ONE WHO TRIED TO LAND A PLANE ON A MOVING TRAIN!
WILL YOU PLEASE SET THIS AIRCRAFT DOWN BEFORE YOU GET US ALL KILLED?
NO! MY FRIENDS ARE OVER THERE! WE GOTTA GO BACK!
ALL I WANT TO KNOW IS WHERE THE TREASURE IS.
IT'S ON THAT TRAIN!
THEN BACK WE GO. HOLD ON, JUNIOR.
VRRRRM

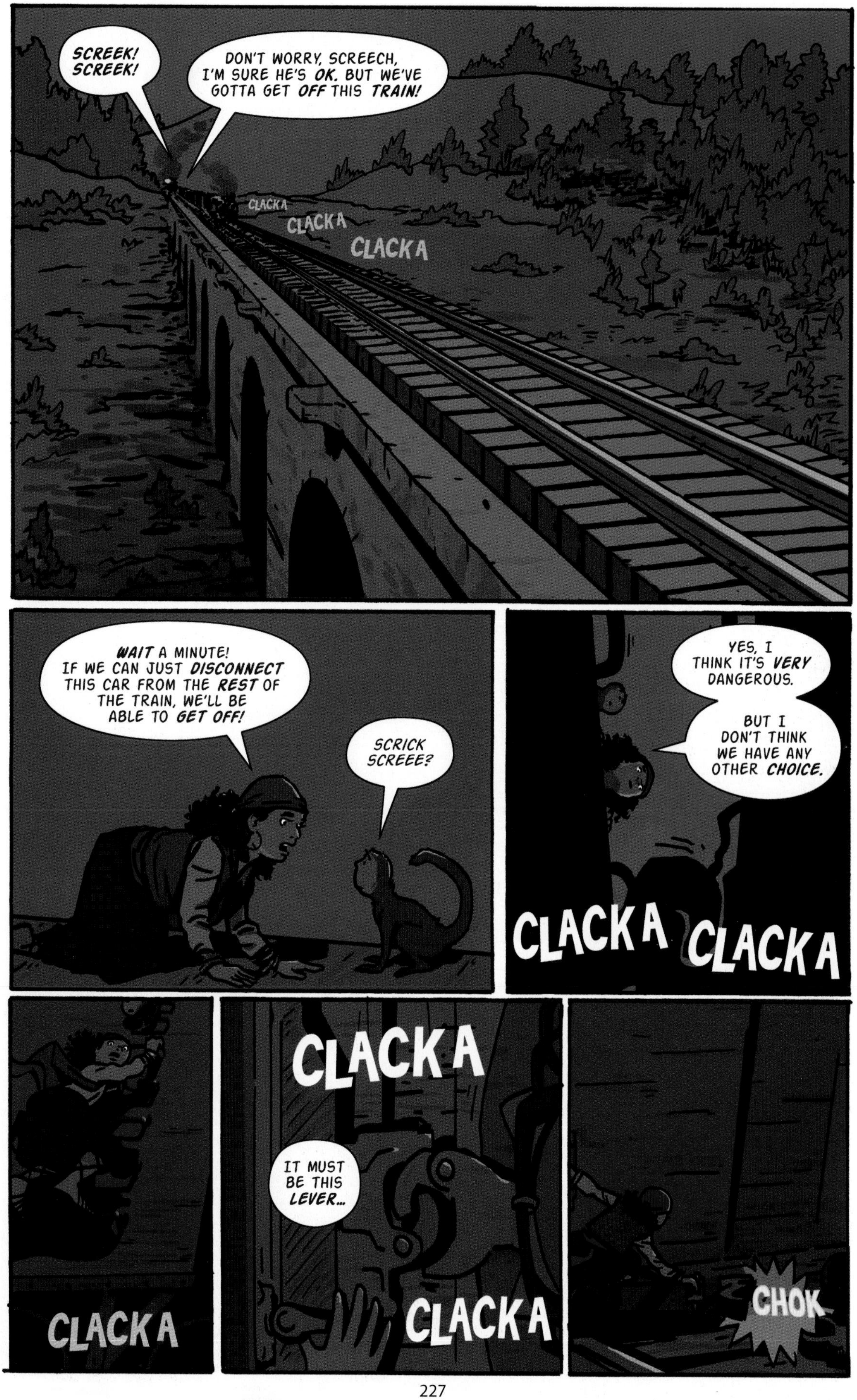
SCREEK! SCREEK!
DON'T WORRY, SCREECH, I'M SURE HE'S OK. BUT WE'VE GOTTA GET OFF THIS TRAIN!
CLACKA
CLACKA
CLACKA
WAIT A MINUTE! IF WE CAN JUST DISCONNECT THIS CAR FROM THE REST OF THE TRAIN, WE'LL BE ABLE TO GET OFF!
SCRICK SCREEE?
YES, I THINK IT'S VERY DANGEROUS.
BUT I DON'T THINK WE HAVE ANY OTHER CHOICE.
CLACKA CLACKA
CLACKA
CLACKA
IT MUST BE THIS LEVER...
CLACKA
CHOK

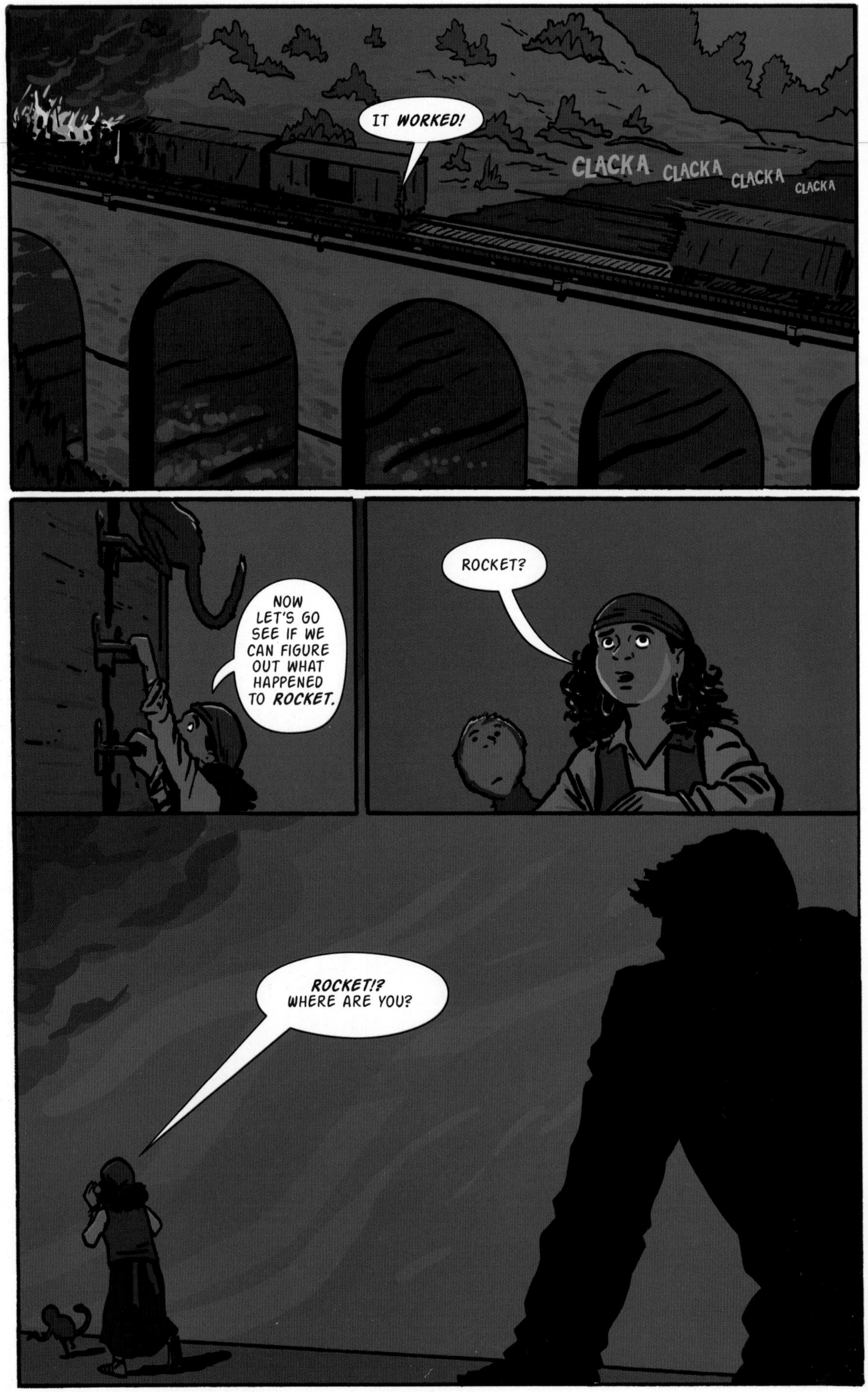
IT WORKED!
CLACKA CLACKA CLACKA CLACKA
NOW LET'S GO SEE IF WE CAN FIGURE OUT WHAT HAPPENED TO ROCKET.
ROCKET?
ROCKET!? WHERE ARE YOU?

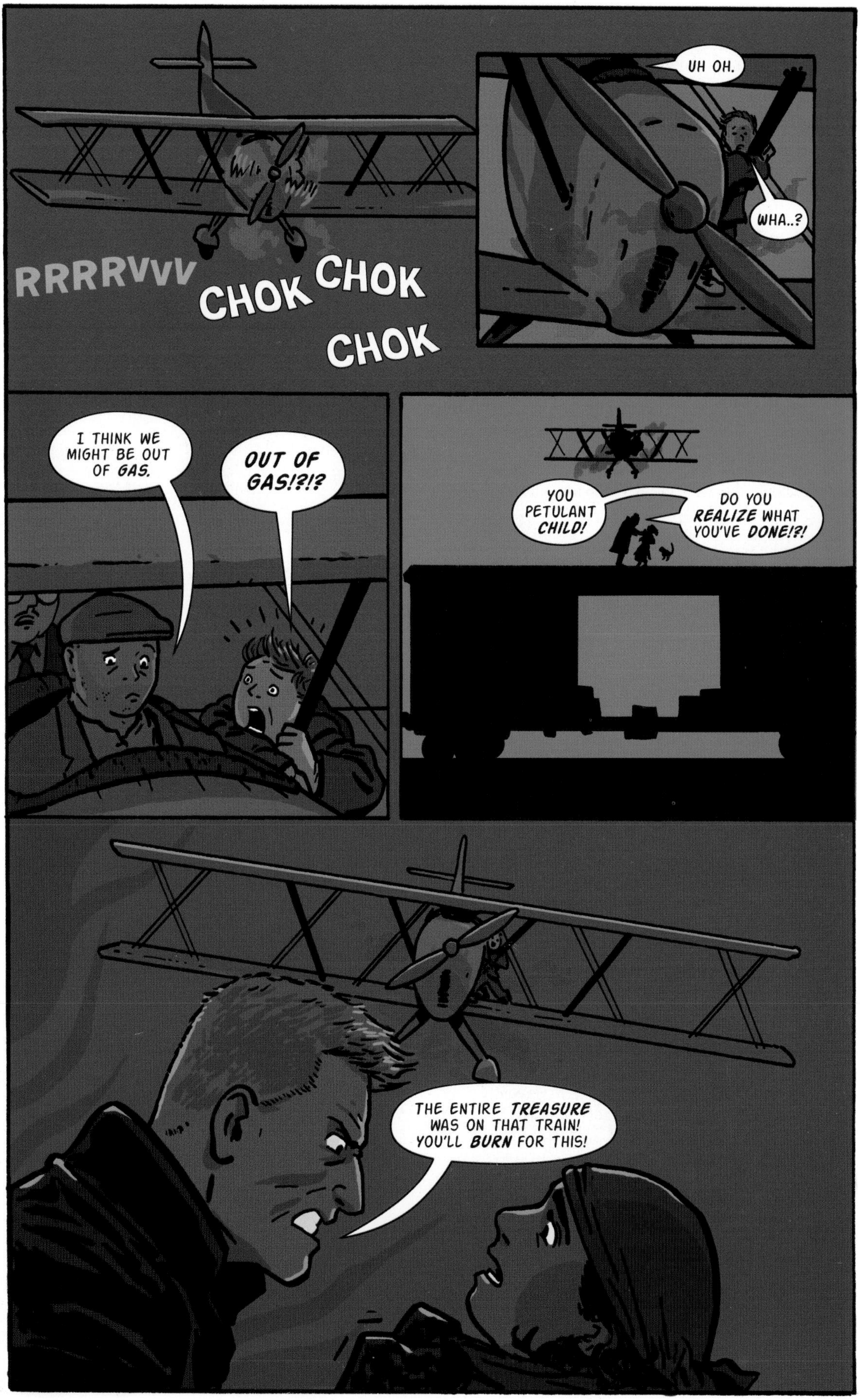
RRRRVVV
CHOK CHOK
CHOK
UH OH.
WHA..?
I THINK WE MIGHT BE OUT OF GAS.
OUT OF GAS!?!?
YOU PETULANT CHILD!
DO YOU REALIZE WHAT YOU'VE DONE!?!
THE ENTIRE TREASURE WAS ON THAT TRAIN! YOU'LL BURN FOR THIS!

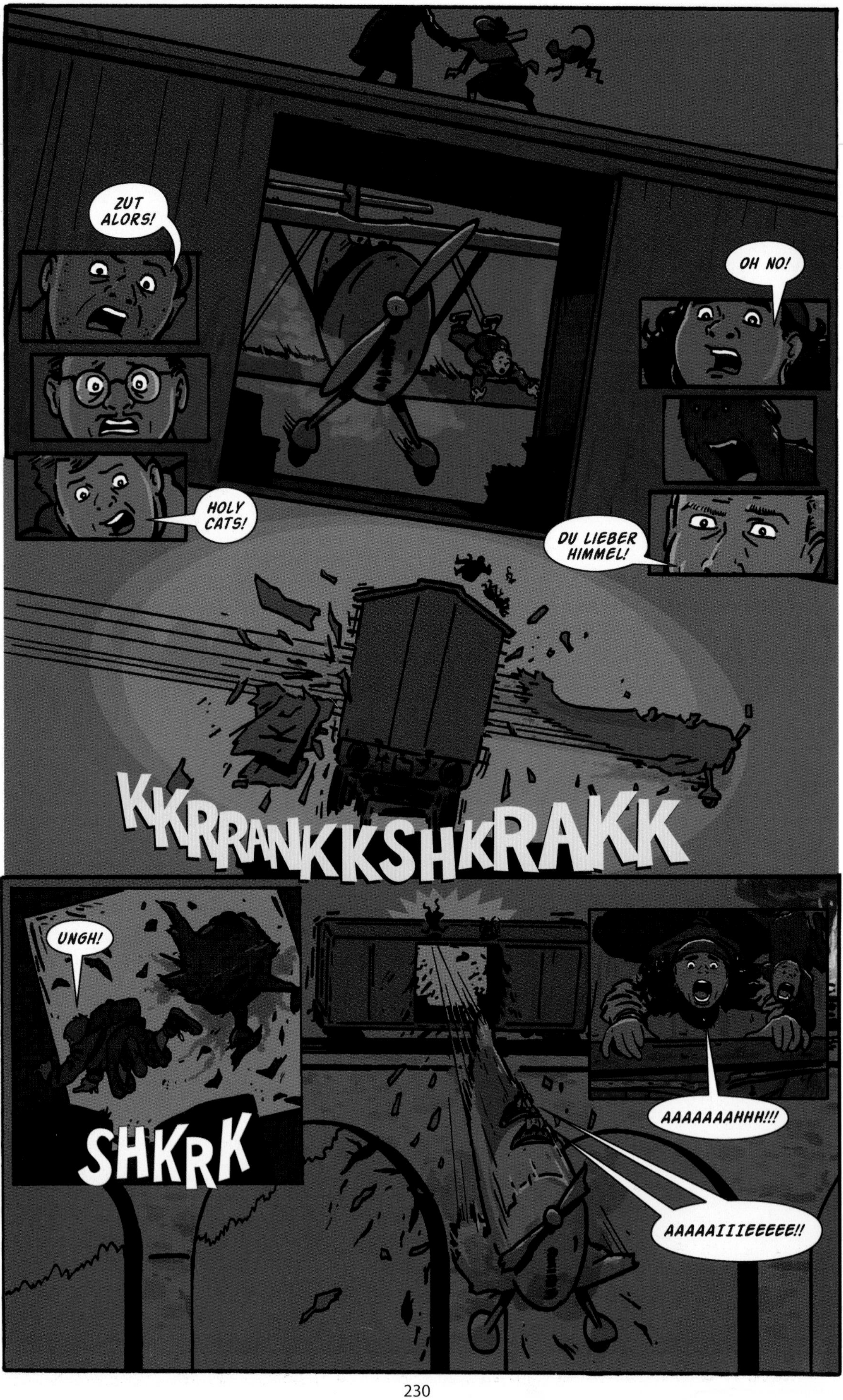
ZUT ALORS!
OH NO!
HOLY CATS!
DU LIEBER HIMMEL!
KKRRANKKSHKRAKK
UNGH!
SHKRK
AAAAAAAHHH!!!
AAAAAIIIEEEEE!!

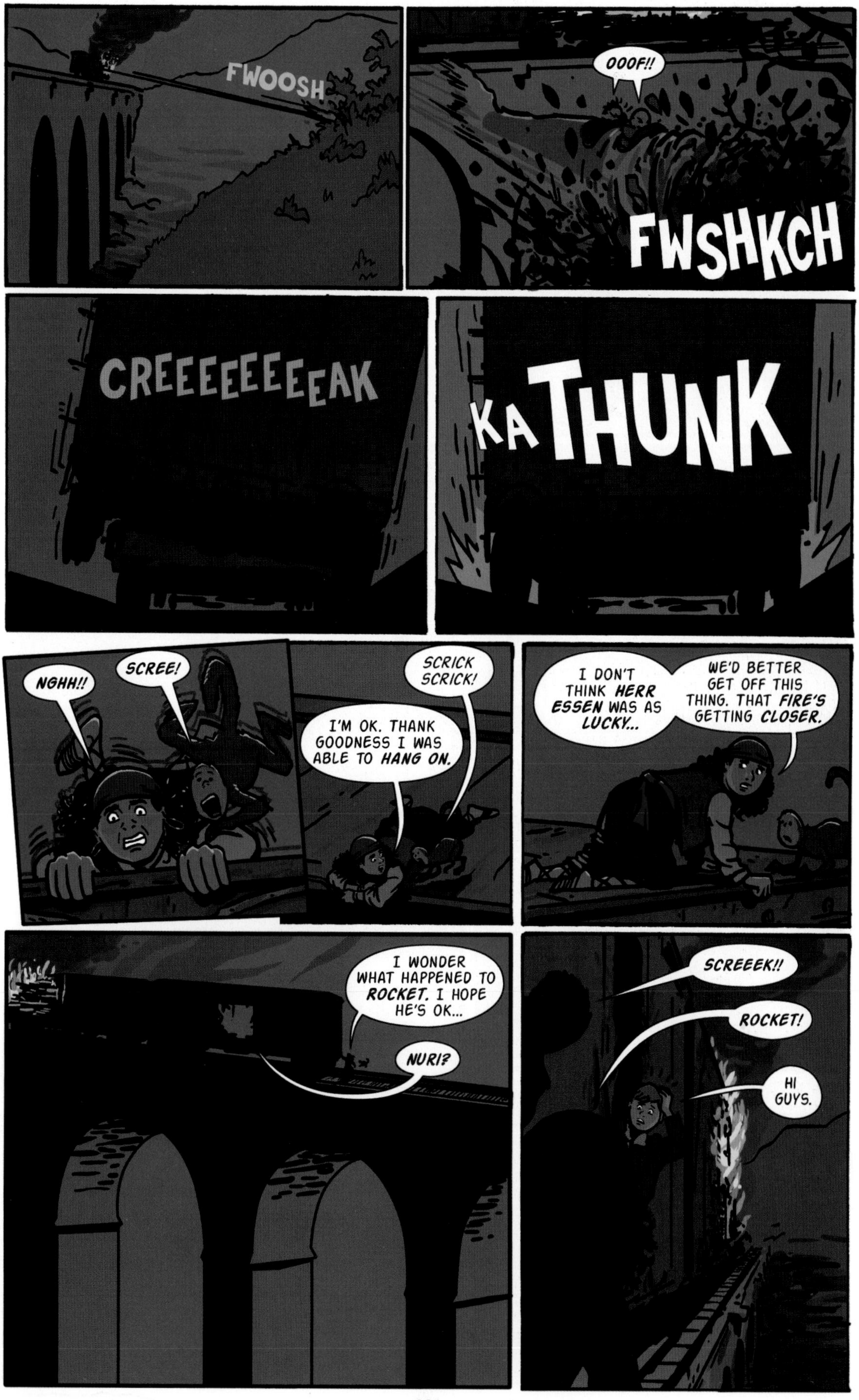
FWOOSH
OOOF!!
FWSHKCH
CREEEEEEEEAK
KA THUNK
NGHH!!
SCREE!
SCRICK SCRICK!
I'M OK. THANK GOODNESS I WAS ABLE TO HANG ON.
I DON'T THINK HERR ESSEN WAS AS LUCKY...
WE'D BETTER GET OFF THIS THING. THAT FIRE'S GETTING CLOSER.
I WONDER WHAT HAPPENED TO ROCKET. I HOPE HE'S OK...
NURI?
SCREEEK!!
ROCKET!
HI GUYS.

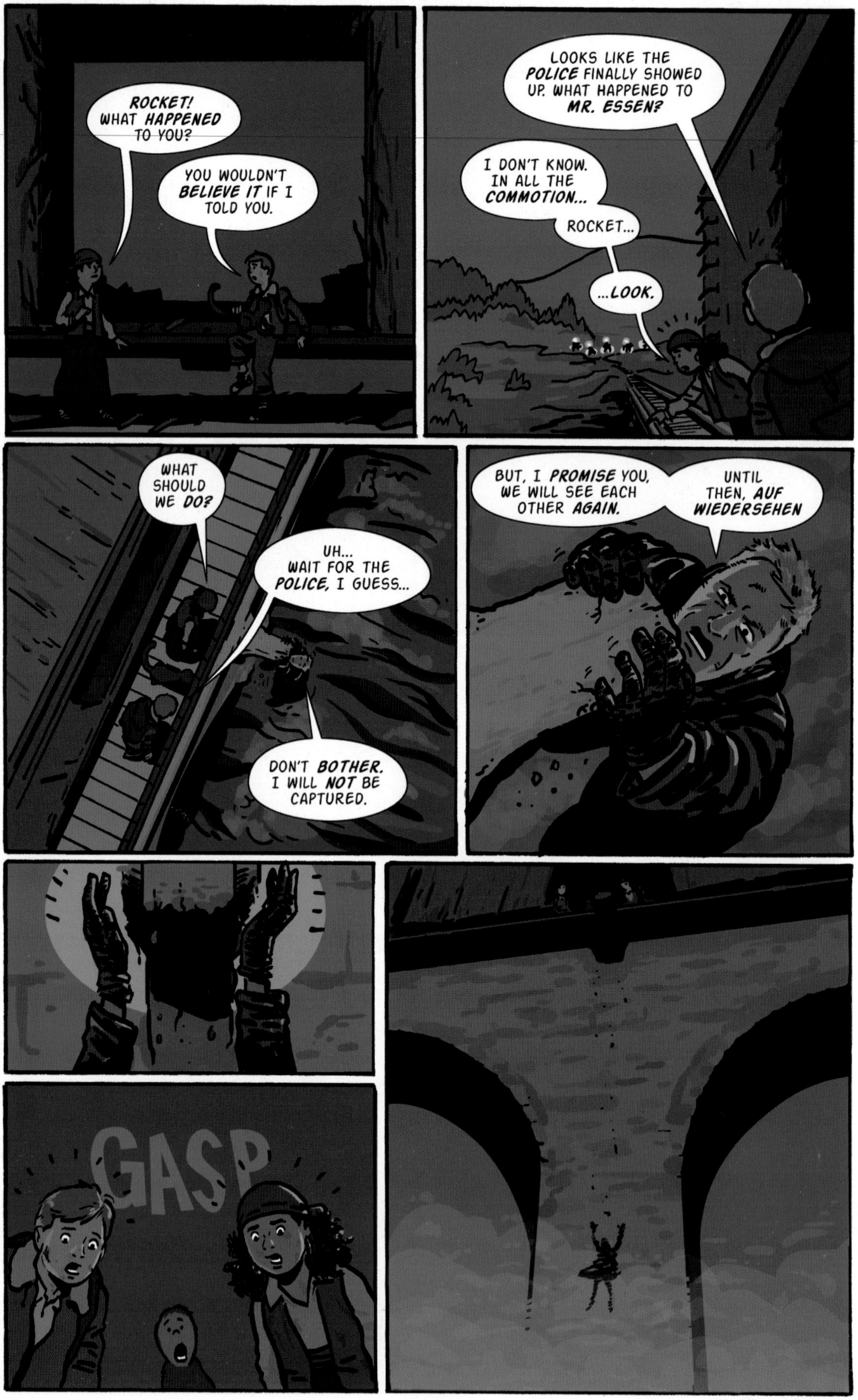
ROCKET! WHAT HAPPENED TO YOU?
YOU WOULDN'T BELIEVE IT IF I TOLD YOU.
LOOKS LIKE THE POLICE FINALLY SHOWED UP. WHAT HAPPENED TO MR. ESSEN?
I DON'T KNOW. IN ALL THE COMMOTION...
ROCKET...
...LOOK.
WHAT SHOULD WE DO?
UH... WAIT FOR THE POLICE, I GUESS...
DON'T BOTHER. I WILL NOT BE CAPTURED.
BUT, I PROMISE YOU, WE WILL SEE EACH OTHER AGAIN.
UNTIL THEN, AUF WIEDERSEHEN
GASP

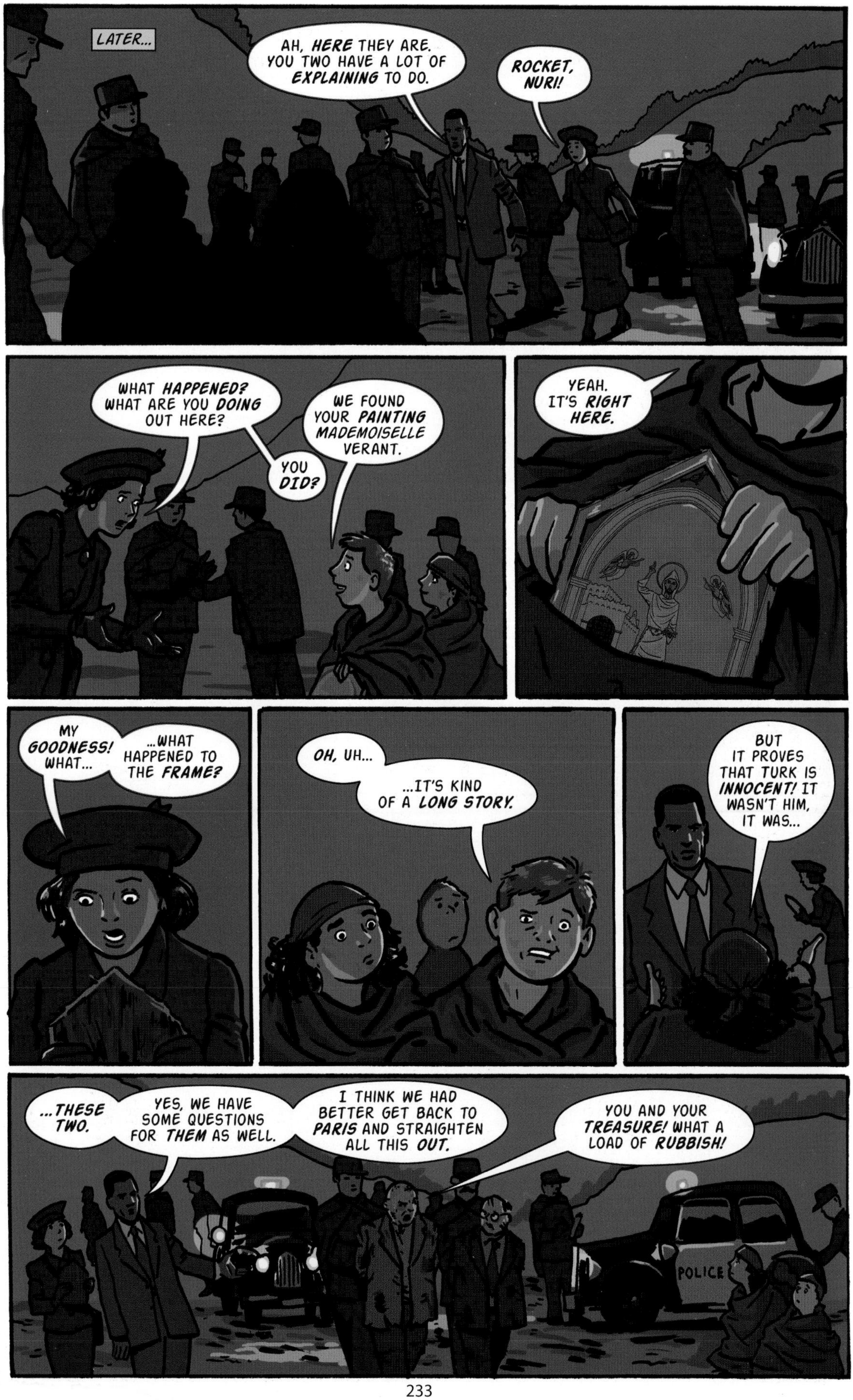
LATER...
AH, HERE THEY ARE. YOU TWO HAVE A LOT OF EXPLAINING TO DO.
ROCKET, NURI!
WHAT HAPPENED? WHAT ARE YOU DOING OUT HERE?
YOU DID?
WE FOUND YOUR PAINTING MADEMOISELLE VERANT.
YEAH. IT'S RIGHT HERE.
MY GOODNESS! WHAT...
...WHAT HAPPENED TO THE FRAME?
OH, UH...
...IT'S KIND OF A LONG STORY.
BUT IT PROVES THAT TURK IS INNOCENT! IT WASN'T HIM, IT WAS...
...THESE TWO.
YES, WE HAVE SOME QUESTIONS FOR THEM AS WELL.
I THINK WE HAD BETTER GET BACK TO PARIS AND STRAIGHTEN ALL THIS OUT.
YOU AND YOUR TREASURE! WHAT A LOAD OF RUBBISH!
POLICE

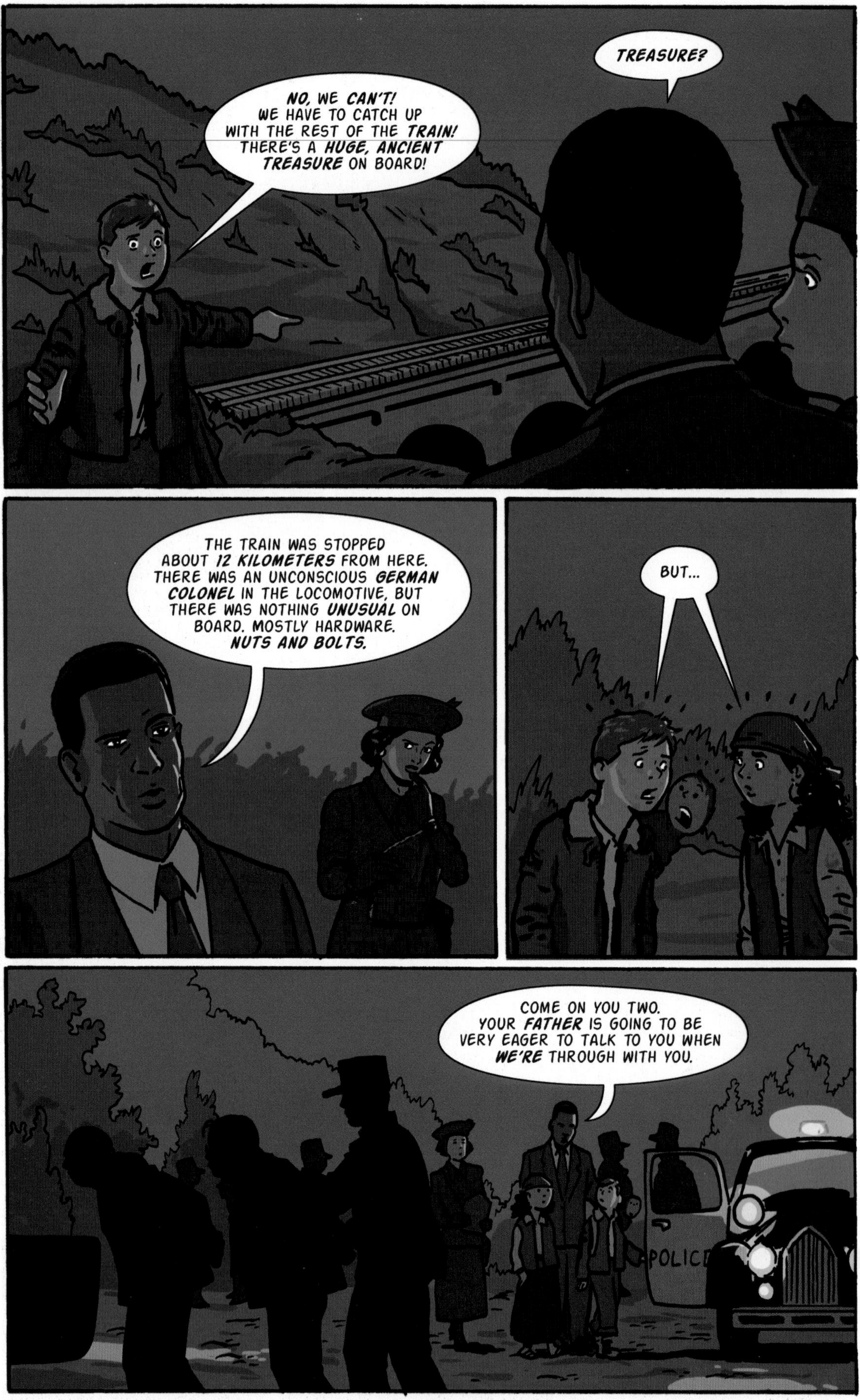
NO, WE CAN'T! WE HAVE TO CATCH UP WITH THE REST OF THE TRAIN! THERE'S A HUGE, ANCIENT TREASURE ON BOARD!
TREASURE?
THE TRAIN WAS STOPPED ABOUT 12 KILOMETERS FROM HERE. THERE WAS AN UNCONSCIOUS GERMAN COLONEL IN THE LOCOMOTIVE, BUT THERE WAS NOTHING UNUSUAL ON BOARD. MOSTLY HARDWARE. NUTS AND BOLTS.
BUT...
COME ON YOU TWO. YOUR FATHER IS GOING TO BE VERY EAGER TO TALK TO YOU WHEN WE'RE THROUGH WITH YOU.
POLIC

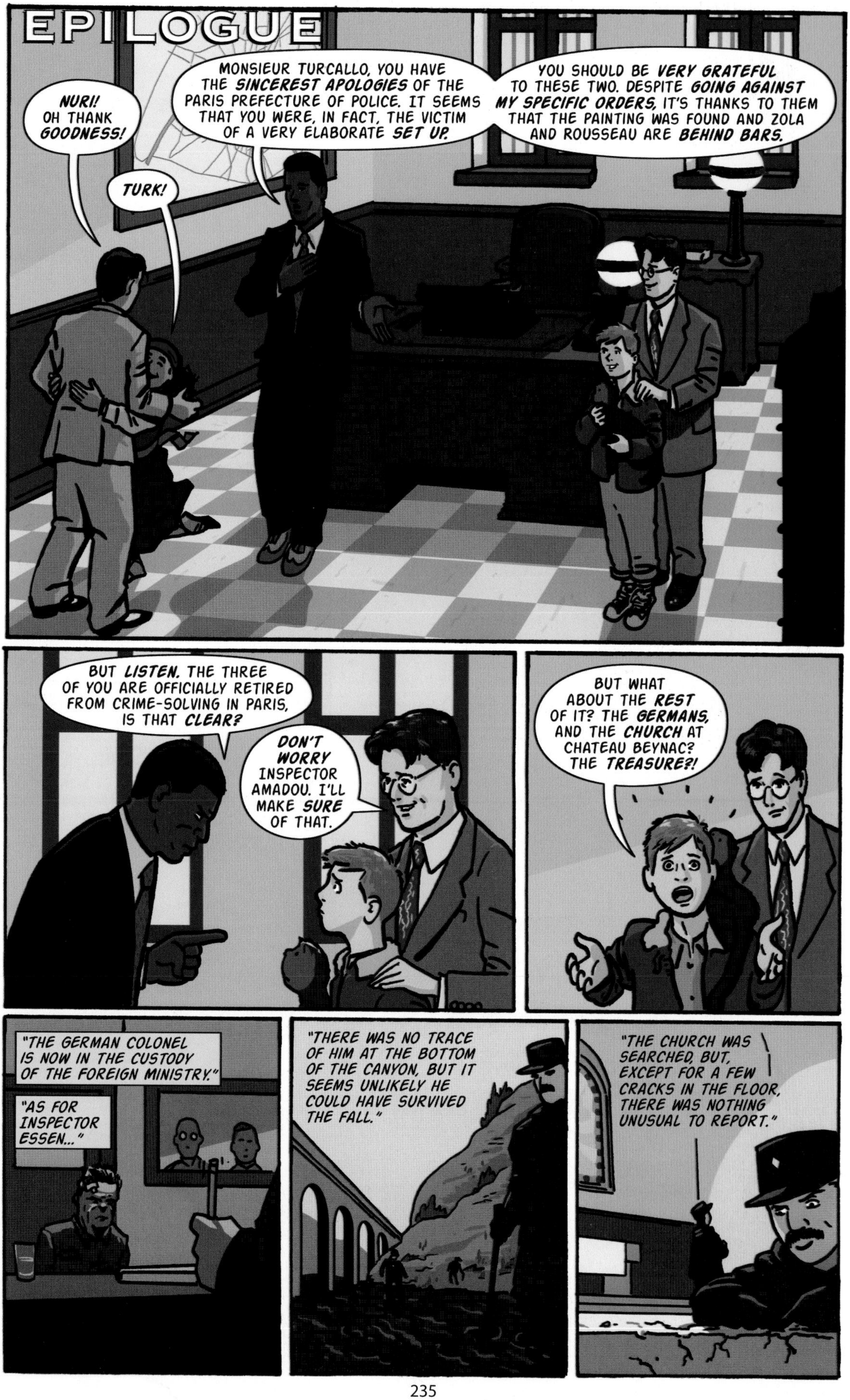
EPILOGUE
NURI! OH THANK GOODNESS!
TURK!
MONSIEUR TURCALLO, YOU HAVE THE SINCEREST APOLOGIES OF THE PARIS PREFECTURE OF POLICE. IT SEEMS THAT YOU WERE, IN FACT, THE VICTIM OF A VERY ELABORATE SET UP.
YOU SHOULD BE VERY GRATEFUL TO THESE TWO. DESPITE GOING AGAINST MY SPECIFIC ORDERS, IT'S THANKS TO THEM THAT THE PAINTING WAS FOUND AND ZOLA AND ROUSSEAU ARE BEHIND BARS.
BUT LISTEN. THE THREE OF YOU ARE OFFICIALLY RETIRED FROM CRIME-SOLVING IN PARIS, IS THAT CLEAR?
DON'T WORRY INSPECTOR AMADOU. I'LL MAKE SURE OF THAT.
BUT WHAT ABOUT THE REST OF IT? THE GERMANS, AND THE CHURCH AT CHATEAU BEYNAC? THE TREASURE?!
"THE GERMAN COLONEL IS NOW IN THE CUSTODY OF THE FOREIGN MINISTRY."
"AS FOR INSPECTOR ESSEN..."
"THERE WAS NO TRACE OF HIM AT THE BOTTOM OF THE CANYON, BUT IT SEEMS UNLIKELY HE COULD HAVE SURVIVED THE FALL."
"THE CHURCH WAS SEARCHED, BUT, EXCEPT FOR A FEW CRACKS IN THE FLOOR, THERE WAS NOTHING UNUSUAL TO REPORT."

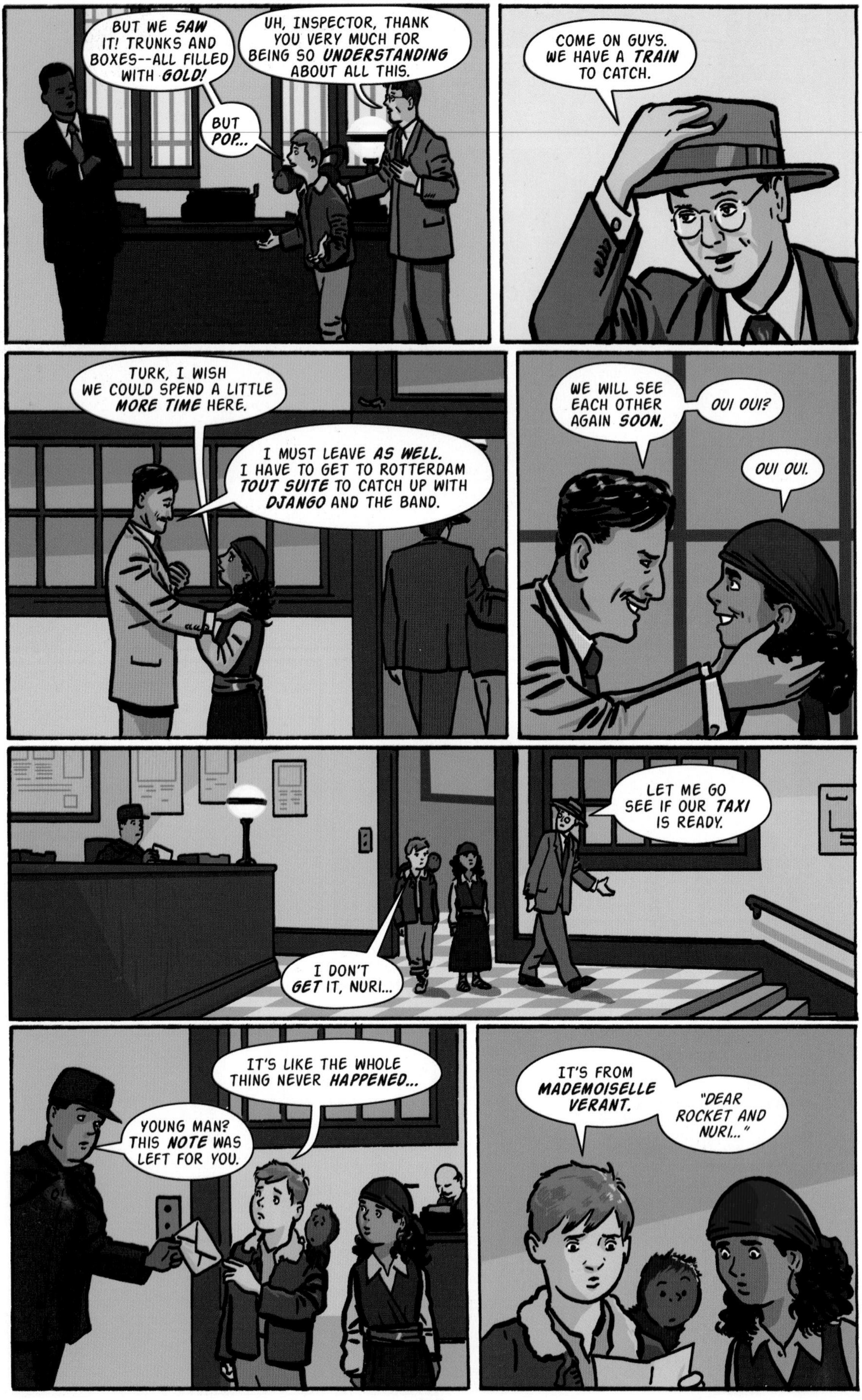
BUT WE SAW IT! TRUNKS AND BOXES--ALL FILLED WITH GOLD!
UH, INSPECTOR, THANK YOU VERY MUCH FOR BEING SO UNDERSTANDING ABOUT ALL THIS.
BUT POP...
COME ON GUYS. WE HAVE A TRAIN TO CATCH.
TURK, I WISH WE COULD SPEND A LITTLE MORE TIME HERE.
I MUST LEAVE AS WELL. I HAVE TO GET TO ROTTERDAM TOUT SUITE TO CATCH UP WITH DJANGO AND THE BAND.
WE WILL SEE EACH OTHER AGAIN SOON.
OUI OUI?
OUI OUI.
LET ME GO SEE IF OUR TAXI IS READY.
I DON'T GET IT, NURI...
IT'S LIKE THE WHOLE THING NEVER HAPPENED...
YOUNG MAN? THIS NOTE WAS LEFT FOR YOU.
IT'S FROM MADEMOISELLE VERANT.
"DEAR ROCKET AND NURI..."

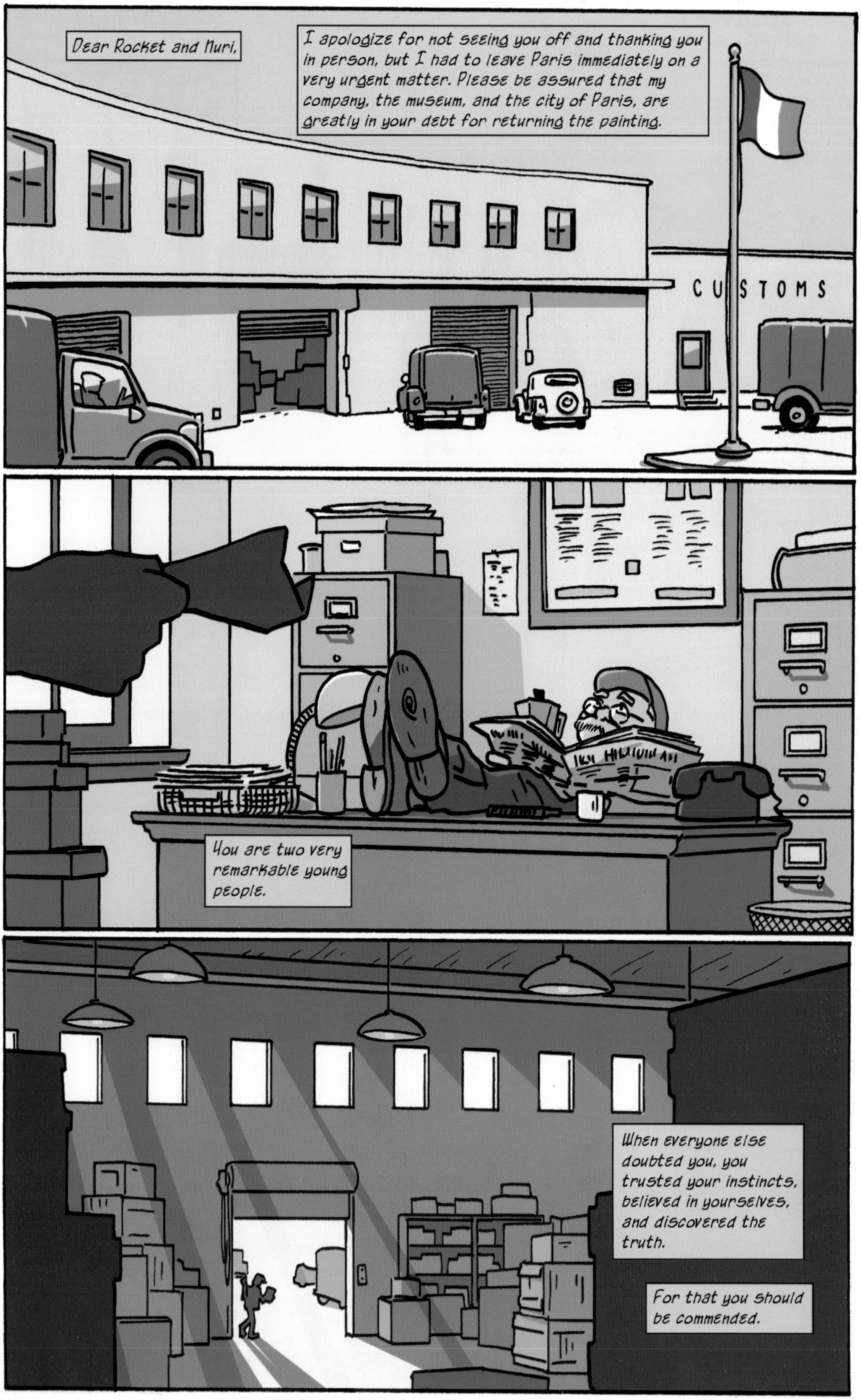
Dear Rocket and Nuri,
I apologize for not seeing you off and thanking you in person, but I had to leave Paris immediately on a very urgent matter. Please be assured that my company, the museum, and the city of Paris, are greatly in your debt for returning the painting.
CUSTOMS
You are two very remarkable young people.
When everyone else doubted you, you trusted your instincts, believed in yourselves, and discovered the truth.
For that you should be commended.

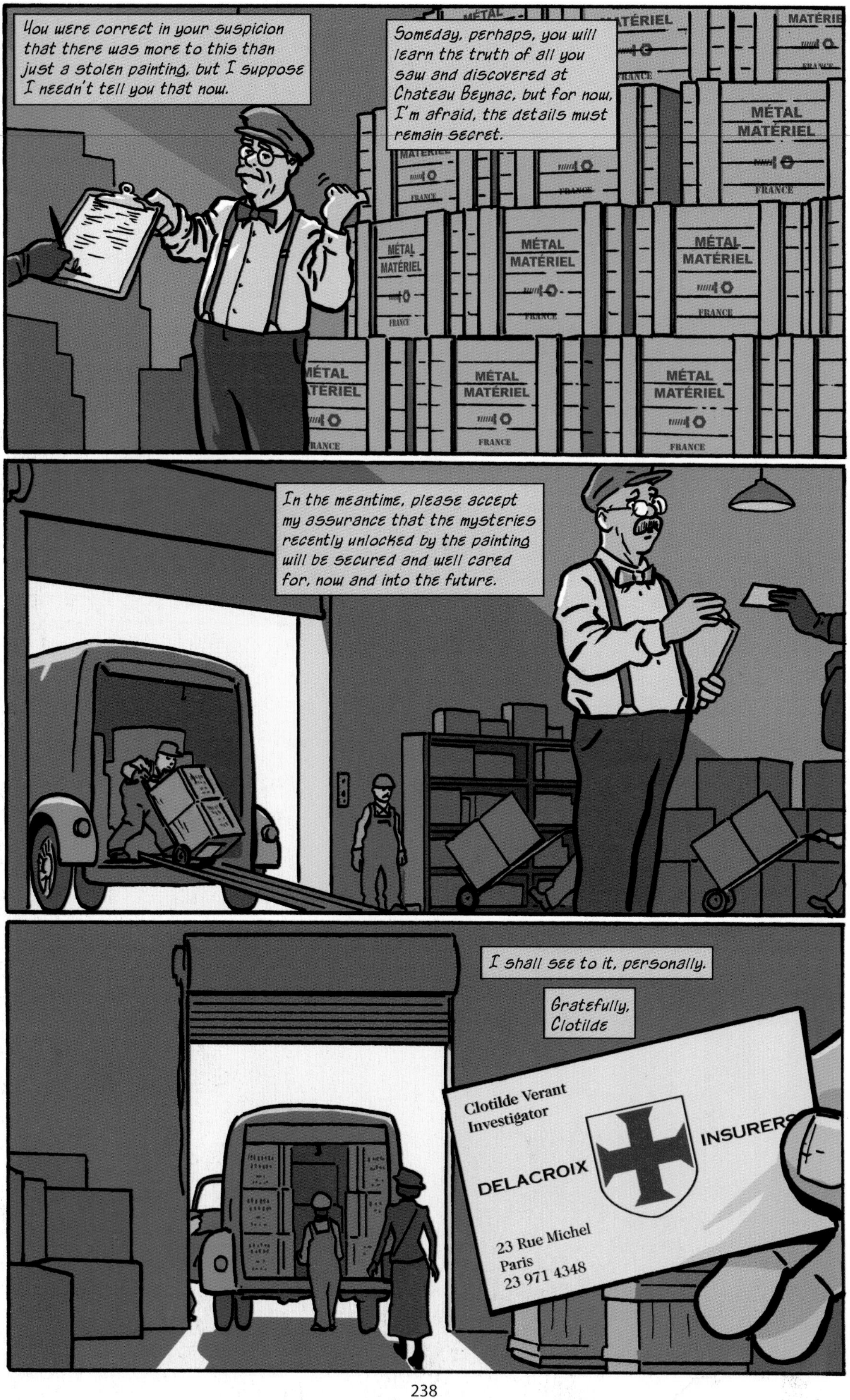
You were correct in your suspicion that there was more to this than just a stolen painting, but I suppose I needn't tell you that now.
Someday, perhaps, you will learn the truth of all you saw and discovered at Chateau Beynac, but for now, I'm afraid, the details must remain secret.
MÉTAL MATÉRIEL
FRANCE
In the meantime, please accept my assurance that the mysteries recently unlocked by the painting will be secured and well cared for, now and into the future.
I shall see to it, personally.
Gratefully,
Clotilde
Clotilde Verant
Investigator
DELACROIX
INSURERS
23 Rue Michel
Paris
23 971 4348

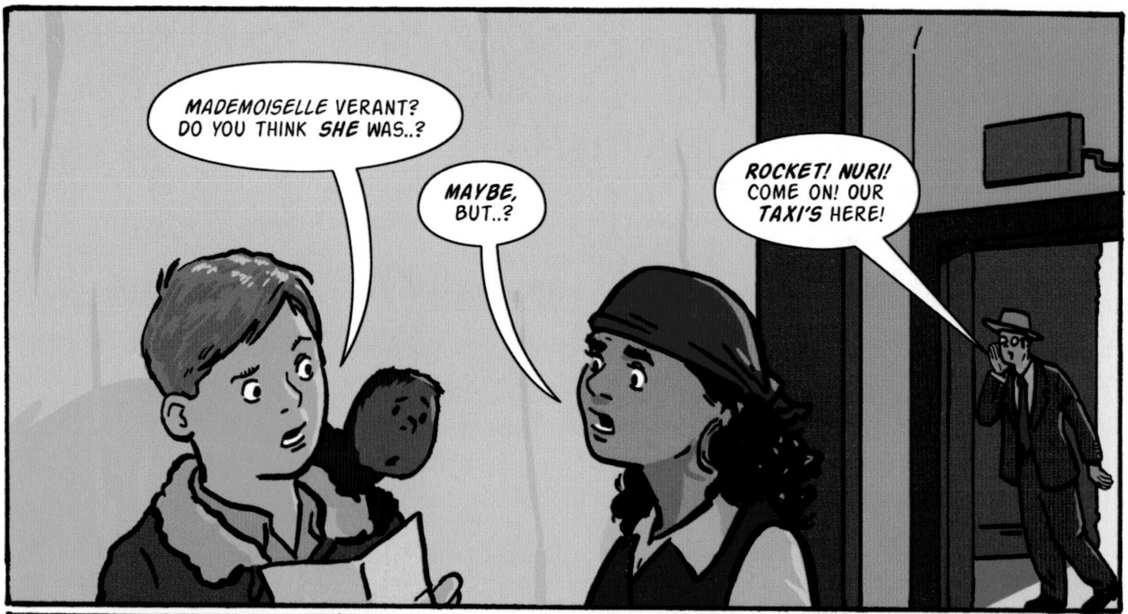
MADEMOISELLE VERANT? DO YOU THINK SHE WAS..?
MAYBE, BUT..?
ROCKET! NURI! COME ON! OUR TAXI'S HERE!

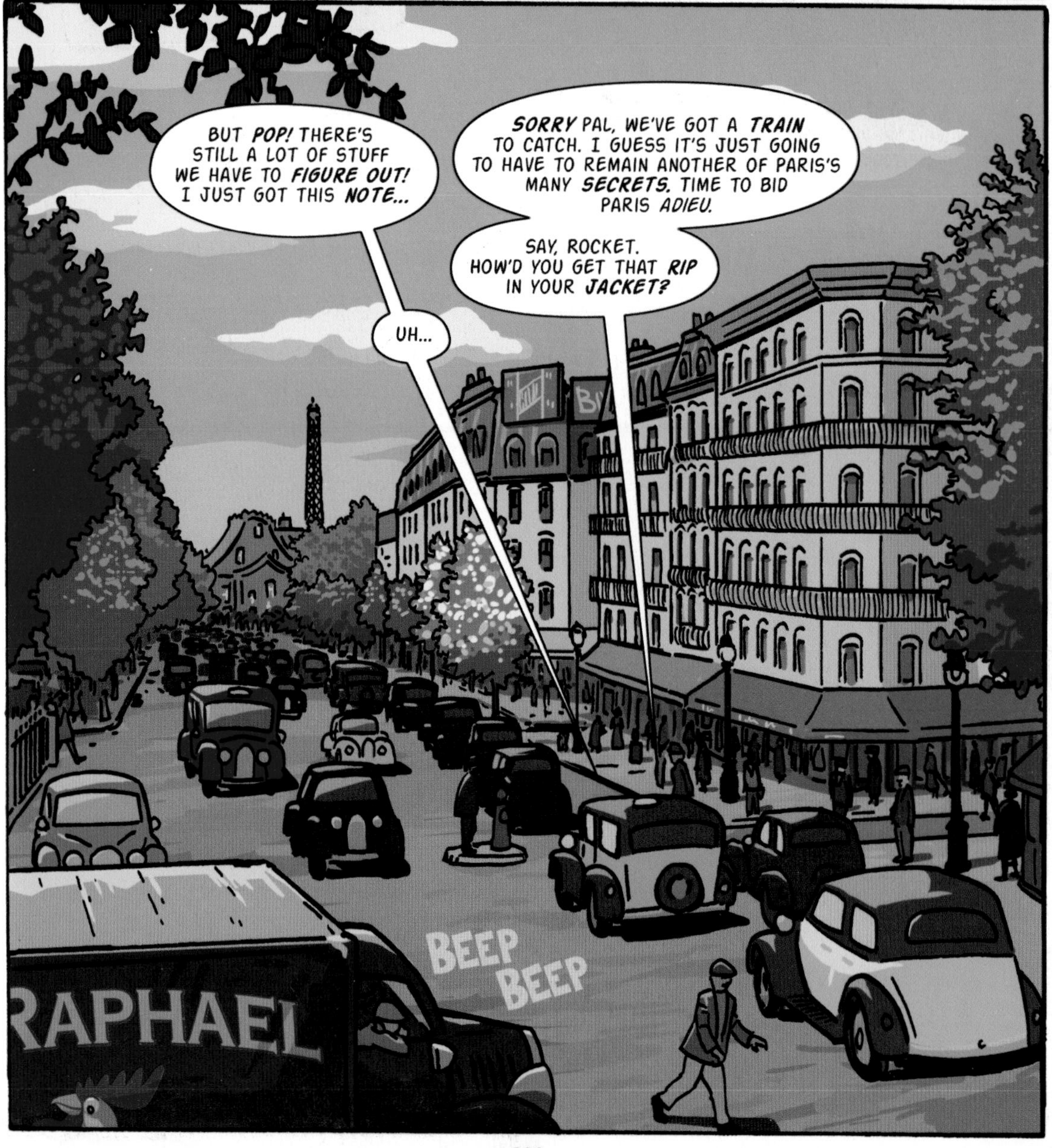
BUT POP! THERE'S STILL A LOT OF STUFF WE HAVE TO FIGURE OUT! I JUST GOT THIS NOTE...
SORRY PAL, WE'VE GOT A TRAIN TO CATCH. I GUESS IT'S JUST GOING TO HAVE TO REMAIN ANOTHER OF PARIS'S MANY SECRETS. TIME TO BID PARIS ADIEU.
SAY, ROCKET. HOW'D YOU GET THAT RIP IN YOUR JACKET?
UH...
BEEP BEEP
RAPHAEL

ACKNOWLEDGEMENTS

I'm very grateful to the many people who have provided so much encouragement and support throughout the process of creating this book. I'm particularly thankful to those of you that read and enjoyed the first *Rocket Robinson* book and asked for a second. Of course, there's no way this project could have been completed without the generosity and support of my many Kickstarter backers. I'm also indebted, once again, to the wonderful Kathy Lynch for her editorial input and content expertise. My biggest thanks are for my loving and supportive family, especially my amazing wife, Jennifer Farrington. Once again, you made it all possible.

Sean O'Neill
Chicago, Illinois

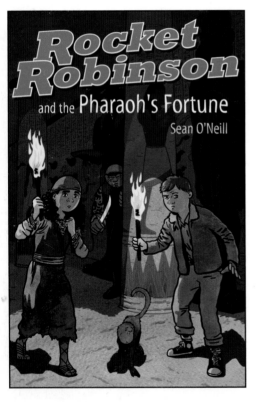